The
Impeachment
of
Abraham Lincoln

ALSO BY STEPHEN L. CARTER

FICTION

Jericho's Fall

Palace Council

New England White

The Emperor of Ocean Park

NONFICTION

The Violence of Peace: America's Wars in the Age of Obama

*God's Name in Vain: The Wrongs and Rights
of Religion in Politics*

*The Dissent of the Governed: A Meditation on
Law, Religion, and Loyalty*

Civility: Manners, Morals, and the Etiquette of Democracy

Integrity

*The Confirmation Mess: Cleaning Up
the Federal Appointments Process*

*The Culture of Disbelief: How American Law and Politics
Trivialize Religious Devotion*

Reflections of an Affirmative Action Baby

The
Impeachment
of
Abraham Lincoln

STEPHEN L.
CARTER

ALFRED A. KNOPF NEW YORK 2012

THIS IS A BORZOI BOOK
PUBLISHED BY ALFRED A. KNOPF

www.aaknopf.com

Knopf, Borzoi Books, and the colophon are registered trademarks of Random House, Inc.

Library of Congress Cataloging-in-Publication Data
Carter, Stephen L., [date]
    The impeachment of Abraham Lincoln / by Stephen L. Carter — 1st ed.
        p. cm.
    "This is a Borzoi book."
    ISBN 978-0-307-27263-8 (alk. paper)
    1. Lincoln, Abraham, 1809–1865—Fiction. I. Title.
PS3603.A78147 2012
813'.6—dc23   2012005890

Jacket design by Kelly + Cardon Webb

Manufactured in the United States of America
First Edition

for Antoinette Wright

This is a work of fiction. I have played games with far more history than even the title suggests; and yet many parts of the story are truer to the historical narrative than, at first blush, the reader might suppose. A compendium of my changes may be found in the author's note at the end of the book.

— S.L.C.

"I conceive that I may in an emergency do things on military grounds which cannot be done constitutionally by Congress."

—*Abraham Lincoln, July 4, 1864, as recorded in the diary of his secretary, John Hay*

"Mr. Lincoln has four long years of strife before him; and as he seems little inclined to change his advisers, his course of action, or his generals, we do not believe that the termination of his second period of government will find him President of the United States."

—London Gazette, *commenting on Lincoln's re-election in 1864*

The
Impeachment
of
Abraham Lincoln

Prologue

April 14–16, 1865

TURMOIL.

The President was dying.

As the grim news spread through Washington City, angry crowds spilled into the cold, muddy night. Abraham Lincoln had been shot at Ford's Theatre, on Tenth Street. The wounds were mortal, people were saying. There was no way he could survive. The war was over, the South utterly vanquished, yet somehow its withered hand had reached up into the nation's capital and extracted this bitter revenge. The crowds became mobs, looking for somebody to hang. Some wanted to burn Ford's to the ground. Others marched toward Old Capitol Prison, where many leaders of the late rebellion were still being held. Rumors passed from mouth to mouth: The Vice-President had been murdered in his rooms at Kirkwood House. The Secretary of State had been stabbed to death in his mansion on Lafayette Square. Confederate troops were advancing on the city. Or Union troops: nobody seemed to know for sure, and a coup d'état had been rumored for years. Outside Ford's Theatre, a man in the blood-spattered uniform of an army major and a doctor carrying a candle fought their way into the street. A group bearing Lincoln's unmoving body followed behind. Mrs. Lincoln, face like chalk, clutched her husband's stiff hand. People leaned in, trying to see or touch. Men groaned. Women wept. A soldier banged on the door of a row house across the way. They carried the President inside and shut the door. People craned to peer in the windows. Minutes later, Secretary of War

Stanton, the most feared man in Washington, arrived in an unguarded carriage and raced inside. Other officials followed. Furious soldiers took up positions on the sidewalk but seemed to have no clear orders. They battered members of the crowd for practice. Other men went in. The people who had been closest to the body passed on the story: the President's head was a mass of blood.

Meanwhile, the hue and cry had been raised. That actor fellow. Wilkes Booth. He had shot the President and leaped to the stage, then escaped on horseback. Somehow the mob was armed now, looking for someone to whom they might do mayhem. Booth would be best, but any Southern sympathizer or paroled Confederate soldier would do, or, in the absence of so obvious a target, any man dressed in gray, or a Catholic, or a darkie. In the confusion, Stanton took command. He ordered the city sealed. Trains were stopped. Guards allowed no one across the bridges. Telegrams were sent to military commanders in Virginia and Maryland, warning them to watch for men on horses fleeing Washington. On the Potomac River, a steamer was prepared as a floating prison should any of the conspirators be apprehended, the better to protect them from the mob: good order required that they be hanged swiftly by soldiers rather than by citizens.

The Union had been struck a hard blow, and wanted revenge.

From Philadelphia to New York to Chicago, newspapers were out with special late editions, their entire front pages devoted to the shooting. Some headlines pronounced the President already dead. Editors who had been Lincoln's sworn foes eulogized him as the nation's savior; others, who had openly despised Mrs. Lincoln, assured the nation that they stood beside the First Lady in her impending widowhood. In the war-ravaged South, where few telegraph lines were intact, the news moved more slowly. Lincoln's longtime bodyguard, Allan Pinkerton, was in New Orleans, and would not learn of the shooting for several days. In the cities of the North, vengeful citizens marched. Church doors were flung open so that people might pray for the President's recovery. But the prayers, like the mobs, seemed fruitless. Everybody knew that it was too late. Little squares of black crepe began to appear in windows, signaling a nation already mourning.

That was Friday. By Saturday, however, the rumors began to change. Perhaps all was not lost. The doctors had cleaned the wound repeatedly and removed the clotting blood. And a miracle was occurring. The President's indomitable will was asserting itself. He was breathing strongly on his own, his eyes were fluttering open, and the damage to his brain appeared less severe than first thought. The telegraph flashed the news across the country: *Lincoln lives!* True, Vice-President Andrew Johnson was dead, and the Secretary of State so badly wounded that he might not see another day, but Abraham Lincoln, savior of the nation, seemed to be improving.

He had been shot on Good Friday. On Easter Sunday, he rose.

By the middle of the week, the President was sitting up, meeting with his staff, once again in charge of the affairs of the nation. Across the country, people cheered. Those who felt otherwise kept their disappointment to themselves, content to bide their time.

November 19, 1866

The night riders were gaining.

Bending low, the black man spurred his tiring horse down the tangled leaf-strewn lane. On either side, fields thick with brightleaf tobacco stretched into the chilly Virginia darkness. Just a few miles ahead loomed the lower slopes of the Shenandoah, with its welcoming forest. If he could only reach the tree belt, he would be safe. A few miles to the north, an entire brigade of Union troops garrisoned the town of Winchester, but with three hooded pursuers only a few hundred yards behind, his chances of reaching either sanctuary were small. He had a pistol in his saddlebag and a knife in his belt, and he knew that if he slowed to draw either, the night riders would have him.

That would be bad.

In a hidden pocket sewn beneath the lining of his right boot was the message. If he was caught and searched, the night riders might find it.

That would be worse.

He rode faster. The autumn drizzle turned to steam on the horse's burning flanks. He heard a low crackle that might have been distant lightning or a nearby gunshot. He rounded a bend, jumped a fallen tree, nearly spilled on the other side. Very soon his mount would collapse.

Pounding hooves and shouting voices carried across the night air. The riders were close behind. He searched for a turnoff but found none. Had he possessed a sense of irony, he might have considered that not far to the south was Appomattox Court House, where, a year and a half earlier, Lee had surrendered the Army of Virginia, ending the Civil War but setting off the more secretive conflict in which he himself was now playing so carefully scripted a part. But there was no time for such musings. The moon had burst from the clouds, and lighted the path to escape.

Up ahead, the road split into two branches. He took the southmost fork, which led, if he remembered correctly, to a shattered plantation and an old church. His pursuers, he reasoned, would break into two groups to make sure that they did not lose him. He could make his stand in the church, or even the plantation house, if he just got there ahead of them. He was not a great shot, but from hiding he could certainly handle one or two men coming up the road toward—

The sudden hard burning in his leg, followed by the horse's shriek, told him that bullets were being fired. He heard the flat clap of the gun as the horse threw him. He hit the frozen earth hard. More shots followed. Just before he passed out, he realized that he had been chased into a trap, forgetting, in his desperation to escape the men behind him, to worry about what might be waiting out front.

HE OPENED HIS eyes, and was aware at once that the burning in his leg was worse. He groaned and tried to shift, only to realize that a boot was pressing into the wound. He was propped against a tree, hands bound behind him. Through the haze of pain, he was able to make out a small group of men, all of them hooded. The man with his foot on the wound was thickset, and wore a blue mask. Beside him was a taller and thinner man, head covered by a burlap sack with eyeholes cut into it.

"He's awake," said the man in blue.

"Course he is," said the man in burlap, "seeing as how you're pretty much breaking his leg."

The heavy man stooped. He was sodden with sweat. "Whatcha doin out here, boy? There's a curfew."

The black man grimaced, and dropped his eyes. "Sorry, suh."

"Say that again."

"Sorry, suh."

The man in the blue mask stood up and walked over to the others. The black man laid his head against the tree, glad to be free of the pain. His eyes were glazed, but his hearing was fine.

"I don't like how he sounds," said the man in blue, who seemed to be the leader. "He's faking. He's not one of ours. He's one of them Northern niggers."

"I've seen this boy," said the man in brown burlap. "He's a Dempsey boy."

The leader's face was invisible inside the blue hood, but, even so, his posture seemed to communicate disappointment. He leaned close to the prisoner. "Is that true, boy? Do you work for Mr. Dempsey?"

"Mrs. Dempsey, suh. Yassuh."

"Mrs. Claire Dempsey up Warrenton way?"

"Suh, I don't know a Missus Claire. I works for Missus Henrietta, at Heddon Hills."

The release of tension was general. Heddon Hills was indeed the Dempsey family plantation: fallen on hard times, to be sure, since the Yankees came through, but still in Dempsey hands. The man in burlap put his hand on the leader's shoulder. "Satisfied?"

"No."

"He's a Dempsey boy, I told you—"

"Maybe he is, maybe he isn't," said the leader. He shook himself free of the other's grip. "I say he's educated."

All five hoods turned his way.

"He's an educated nigger," he continued, eyes fairly glowing through the slits. "He'll 'Yassuh' and 'Nossuh' till Judgment Day, but behind that black face he's laughing at us. He's one of those educated niggers, he's been to some nigger school somewhere, and now he thinks he's better than we are." With a movement of sublime laziness, he tucked the muzzle of his shotgun up against the black man's chin. "Is that right, boy? You've been to some nigger school, haven't you?"

"Nossuh," said the prisoner, eyes wide in the smooth brown face.

"You're a Dempsey boy."

"Yassuh."

"Search him."

Immediately the black man felt his bound hands drawn farther behind him. The pain would have doubled him over but for the shotgun pressing into his neck. One of his captors was going through his pockets, and another through his saddlebags. He heard an exclamation and knew they had found his little supply of greenbacks. Another, and he knew they had found the weapons.

"There's a letter," somebody said, and handed it to the thin man who had tried to protect him. He tore open the envelope. "It's from Mrs. Dempsey all right. It says this here is Royal, and he's been loyal to her since he was a boy. He never ran off with the Yankees. It says he's carrying a message down to a Mr. Toombs in Snickers Gap." He gave the paper to the leader. "That's Mrs. Dempsey's signature. She does some of her banking with me."

The leader sneered. "And now this boy knows who you are."

Silence.

The gun barrel prodded the black man's neck. "What's the message?"

"Suh?"

"What message does Mrs. Dempsey have you sending to Mr. Toombs?"

"Suh, Mrs. Dempsey wants to invite her goddaughter to spend the holidays at Heddon Hills."

"That's the whole message?"

"Yassuh."

"Enough," said the man in burlap. "This ain't who we're looking for. Let him go, Bill."

The leader turned his way. "And now he knows who I am, too." He lowered the shotgun and, without warning, pulled the trigger.

The black man cried out in agony. Wounded now in both thigh and foot, he collapsed against the tree.

Bill crouched beside the prisoner. "Do you think we're stupid, boy? You think we're illiterate crackers? I was with Jubal Early for two years. I was a colonel. My friend Jedediah here—since we're telling names— was a captain. He was with Whiting at Fort Fisher. Now, let me tell you something." The gun caressed the wounded man's thigh. "I know who you are. I know what you're doing. You are a courier for the Yankee secret service." The black man was shaking his head frantically. "You are a courier, and you are carrying a secret message. Tell us the truth, and tell us where the message is hidden, or I'll blow your balls off and let you bleed to death, and meanwhile we'll find the message anyway."

The man called Jedediah tugged at his arm. The others were already inching toward their mounts. "Come on, Bill. Let's get out of here."

"Get him up."

"What?"

"Get him up. I want him on his horse."

"Why?"

"Because we're gonna have us a hanging."

"But—"

"He's a spy, Jedediah. Spies get hanged."

The man in burlap shook his head. "The war's over."

"Not for me."

THE BODY WAS found two days later by a Union patrol. The night riders had left him in a ditch, after stealing his horse, his weapons, and his money. The soldiers made nothing of it. The night riders were killing colored men all over the South, and there was not much to be done about it. There was no way of investigating, even if anybody had wanted to. Nobody talked to the Yankees.

The soldiers took the corpse up to Winchester and turned it over to the colored Benevolent Association, who would bury the remains somewhere. But before the soldiers surrendered the body, they took the boots, because supplies were still short, and if they didn't fit you, you could always trade with somebody they did. And the boots were passed a good way down the line before somebody found the false lining, and the wad of paper hidden inside. He thought it was money, but it turned out to be just a list of names. The private told his sergeant, who said the dead man was probably in the black market. The names were his customers. The sergeant told the private to deliver the paper to the office of the adjutant general, just in case military personnel were involved. The soldier meant to do just that in the morning, but that night he went drinking in town, got into a bar fight, and wound up with his head smashed in. He died the next morning.

The sergeant took his duties seriously. He asked the dead private's tentmates to go through the man's things and bring him the letter with the list of names. When they came back an hour later to say they couldn't find it, the sergeant looked for himself.

The letter was gone.

BOOK I

February–March 1867
Indictment

∽

"The President, Vice President and all civil Officers of the United States, shall be removed from Office on Impeachment for, and Conviction of, Treason, Bribery, or other high Crimes and Misdemeanors."

—*Constitution of the United States,*
Article II, Section 4

"The House of Representatives shall chuse their Speaker and other Officers; and shall have the sole Power of Impeachment."

—*Constitution of the United States,*
Article I, Section 2

CHAPTER 1

Clerk

I

THEY WERE HANGING white folks in Louisiana and shooting black folks in Richmond. Union troops had invaded Mexico, Canada, Cuba, and every brothel in the South. Confederate troops were holed up in the Smoky Mountains, waiting for the signal to attack. The casket of the First Lady, who had drowned last year while visiting relations in Illinois, had been exhumed, and found empty. Meanwhile, Abe Lincoln, facing an impeachment trial, was sneaking off to see a medium in New York, and Jefferson Davis, onetime leader of the rebellion and supposedly locked up in Fort Monroe, was actually in Philadelphia, sipping champagne with his rich friends.

None of this was true, but all of it was in the newspapers.

It was late winter of 1867, nearly two years after the end of the war, and reporters were inventing rumors almost faster than their editors could print them. The nation, everyone agreed, was a mess. If only it had been old Abe who was shot dead that night instead of Andy Johnson, his Vice-President. If Johnson were President now—so moaned the editorial writers—the nation would be in considerably better shape.

All of which helped explain why Abigail Canner had finally given up on reading the papers. She was smarter than any five reporters put together, and perfectly capable of making up her own stories. But she didn't want to be a reporter: she had a brother and a distant cousin in that business already. She wanted to be a lawyer. This was impossible, she was told, given her color and her sex. But she was determined to try, unaware of how her ambition would carry her to the center of great events.

The romance, like the violence, came later.

I I

On the first Monday in February, in the Year of Our Lord one thousand eight hundred sixty-seven—or, in the larger history, one month exactly before the trial of the sixteenth President of the United States was to begin—Abigail set out upon her journey. Ignoring her mad brother's derisive insistence that nothing good would come of the effort, she rode the horse-drawn streetcars through the filthy snow to prove to the world that she was indeed the woman she claimed. She had her college degree and her letter of employment and the stony conviction, learned from her late mother, that, whatever limitations the society might place on ordinary negroes, they would never apply to her.

Abigail boarded the Seventh Street line, which passed near her home, then changed at Pennsylvania Avenue, choosing the second row to avoid a squabble with the white citizens of Washington City, who seemed to consider the rear of the car their own private preserve, but also to avoid the ignominy that came of riding up front with the driver, where nowadays most men and women of her race tucked themselves without a second thought: a discrimination until recently enshrined in city law. The war was over, the slaves were free, and the government of the United States guaranteed the rights of the colored race, but here in the nation's triumphant capital, in the midst of the most frigid winter in years, everybody was at pains to establish who was who.

Abigail was a tall young woman, unfashionably slender, with smooth mahogany skin that bespoke more than one dallying slavemaster in her ancestral tree. The hooded coat she wore against the cold was a product of the finest dressmaker in Boston, a gift from her uncle, a physician. The trim was silver fur. The face that peered out suggested a woman who pondered a great deal over the issues of the day, and very deeply, but frowned on most forms of fun. Her gray eyes were sharp and probing; her dimpled chin seemed confident and disapproving. Men tended to find her reasonably pretty, even if not so vivacious as her older sister, Judith, or so innocently beautiful as her younger sister, Louisa. They also tended to find her too distant, too judgmental, too intelligent altogether, for Abigail would always rather read another book than have another dance. Nanny Pork, who ran the Canner household, preached the evils of dancing and carousing and most forms of enjoyment, and although Abigail was not precisely the sort to do what she was told, she regarded Nanny with the sort of awe usually reserved for less visible agents of divinity.

Abigail was twenty-one years old, and parentless, and black, and expecting, somehow, to affect the course of history.

Maybe even starting today.

The streetcar pulled up at the carriage block on the corner of Fourteenth Street, near the Willard Hotel, where negroes were not welcome except in service. Abigail stepped carefully down onto the broken stone. Neither the driver nor any of the gentlemen passing on the street made any effort to assist her, but she had not expected them to. The newsboy was the only one who paid her any attention, shouting that Senator Wade was predicting that at least forty of the fifty-four members of the Senate would vote to remove the President from office, and forty, she knew, was more than enough. The boy thrust a newspaper at her with one hand and held out the other for a coin. Abigail ignored him. She stood in the swirling snow and checked the address she had written in her commonplace book. Actually, she had the address marked down firmly in her memory, but her late mother had always taught her to make assurance double sure. Abigail folded the book into her handbag and walked north. The tiny flakes were like pinpricks on her bright cheeks. She took care not to slip on the ice, but a wall of wind still almost knocked her from the cobbled sidewalk into the frozen mud of Fourteenth Street. As she regained her footing, two white women, heading the other way, began a very loud conversation about how, since the war, half the negroes in town seemed to be drunk from breakfast on.

Abigail ignored them, too.

She found the address at the corner of G Street. A policeman patrolled out front, resplendent and shivering in blue serge and brass buttons. The policeman was an unexpected obstacle, but Abigail chose to deal with him the way her late mother had taught her to deal with most barriers. She walked straight past him, head held high.

He scarcely gave her a glance.

The narrow lobby was dark after the glare of the snow. She took the creaking stairs to the second floor, where the bronze plaque read DENNARD & MCSHANE, and knocked on the door. Waiting, she was surprised to find herself nervous. She hated uneasiness as she hated most signs of human weakness, most of all in herself. Fear is a test, her late mother used to say. Fear is how God challenges us.

Accepting the challenge, she knocked again.

The door swung open, and there stood a gangly young man in high-collared shirt and black necktie. He was missing the jacket that doubtless completed his working attire. Straw-colored hair was pressed back in fashionable waves against a long, slim head. Even standing still, he displayed an economy of movement that implied a life lived without challenges. He was white, of course, and about her age, and Abigail could tell at once that he was ill at ease around women. Nevertheless, he found an awkward smile somewhere, and glanced, she noted, at her hands. Perhaps he thought she was carrying a delivery.

"May I help you?" the young man said.

"My name is Abigail Canner," she said. "I have an appointment." The man said nothing, so she tried again. "About the job."

"Job?" he repeated doubtfully, as if she were speaking Greek. In his shy earnestness, he gave the impression of a man trying desperately to live up to something terribly difficult.

"The job as a law clerk." She tilted her head toward the plaque. "For Dennard & McShane."

"Ah." Nodding firmly, more sure of his ground. "That would be Mr. Dennard. His clerk left. I'm Hilliman. I'm Mr. McShane's clerk. The partners are out just now, but if you would leave your employer's card, one of the messengers will be round to set up an appointment." When she said nothing, his smile began to fade. He gestured, vaguely. Peering past him, Abigail saw a long, narrow room dominated by a heavy wooden table heaped with papers and books. Shelves lined every wall, and the heavy volumes looked well used. In one corner, numbers were scribbled on a blackboard. In another, an elderly colored man tended a weak coal fire. "I'm afraid we are rather busy right now—"

"I imagine you are, Mr. Hilliman. Preparing for the impeachment trial."

"Well, yes." He looked at her with new respect, or at least growing curiosity, perhaps because she did not speak in the manner of the colored people to whom he was accustomed. Abigail Canner had provoked this reaction in others. She worked at it. "That's right. The trial. I'm sorry," he added, although, as yet, he had done nothing to apologize for.

Almost nothing.

"I find it most intriguing," said Abigail, "that the Congress would attempt such a thing."

"Yes, well, if you would just—"

"The committee has proposed four counts of impeachment, has it not? Half relating to the conduct of the war, and half relating to events since the war ended."

"How do you know that?" His tone suggested that she could not possibly have read a newspaper. He caught her expression, and realized his error. "I mean—well, that is very impressive."

"I try to be prepared," she said, unable to keep the sarcasm from her voice. She had faced silly boys like this at college, too, unable to believe the evidence of their eyes and ears. No colored girl could possibly be their equal. "Do you know yet whether the House will adopt all four counts?"

"There has been no vote as yet—"

"They will vote in two weeks." A prim smile. "I am here," she said, "to help."

"To help what?"

"Help you, Mr. Hilliman. With the impeachment trial."

"I beg your pardon."

"I am the new law clerk." She drew the letter confirming her employment from her commonplace book. "Mr. Dennard hired me."

III

There are in life moments that are irretrievable, and one opportunity fate never grants twice is making a first impression. Jonathan Hilliman, confronted with the least likely of all the possible explanations for this peculiar woman's presence at Dennard & McShane, spoke out of utter confusion, and therefore from the heart:

"That is not possible," he said, jaw agape.

Abigail's eyes went very wide. They were wide enough already, gray and flecked and watchful, eyes that neither overlooked nor forgot. But, as Jonathan would come to learn, when Abigail was angry, those eyes could grow wide enough to swallow a room. Now, as he fumbled for the words to repair his mistake, Abigail, unbidden, stepped past him into the foyer. A long sooty window dominated one wall. Four inner doors were closed, two presumably leading to the partners' offices. The old colored man got to his feet, bowed, touched his cap.

"My name is Little," he said, with an affecting grin. He was nearly toothless. "I'se been with the Dennards going on sixty years now."

"A pleasure to meet you, Mr. Little," she said, extending a hand.

He hesitated, then shook. "Just Little, miss."

"I'm sorry?"

"My name is Little, miss. Just Little."

"Excuse me," said Mr. Hilliman, having recovered his composure. "Perhaps I could see that letter."

The black woman smiled blandly, the way Jonathan's mother smiled at the servants when about to berate them. "Of course, Mr. Hilliman."

He took the page in his hands and read it slowly, then again, mouthing the words as if reading were new to him. At last he raised his eyes. "You are the new clerk."

"I believe I told you that."

"You are Miss Abigail Canner."

"Yes."

"I'm sorry." He glanced around the messy room. It was obvious to them both what he wanted to say and could not. Instead, he retreated into a show of confusion. "I understood that Mr. Dennard was planning to hire a new clerk. I had no idea that he had—I mean, that he—that you were—um, that you were coming today."

"I understand, Mr. Hilliman," said Abigail, standing there with bag in hand. There were, as yet, fewer than a dozen lawyers of African descent practicing in American courts. There were no women of any color. The Supreme Court had admitted the first colored attorney to its bar only a year and a half ago, and he had promptly gone into a wasting decline, from which he was not expected to recover. The wags said the Court's members knew of his illness in advance, and wanted the credit for having admitted him without ever having to allow him to argue before them. "But I assume that there is plenty of work to do."

"Well, yes—"

The door burst open, and in swept Arthur McShane, Jonathan's boss, accompanied by a tough-looking man Jonathan did not recognize.

"We're thirteen votes down," McShane growled, unwrapping himself. He was a diminutive man, small and trim and almost boyish except for the weathered face, all hollows and valleys. He handed his scarf to Little. "Thirteen votes. I don't believe it. If the vote were held today, it would be fourteen for acquittal, twenty-seven for conviction. The rest are undecided so far—"

"That's still short of two-thirds," soothed the stranger. He was paunchy and confident, and sported a magnificent black beard. He had just laid his coat across Little's waiting arms. "They need two-thirds."

McShane ignored him. "One bit of good news"—eyeing Abigail suddenly, obviously not sure who she might be, but, after a moment's hesitation, plunging on—"good news, that is, for our side. They won't vote on admitting Nebraska to the Union until after the trial. You remember what happened with Nevada last year. The price of statehood was sending two anti-Lincoln men to the Senate, bound to vote for conviction. Well, that bit of skulduggery embarrassed the Radicals, so they've agreed not to admit Nebraska just yet. This is Mr. Baker."

"Jonathan Hilliman." He thrust out a hand, which Baker seemed to examine for traps before grabbing. The stranger's shake was perfunctory, an unappealing duty to be gotten over with. "And this"—Jonathan hesitated; names had never been his forte. "This is, um, Mr. Dennard's new clerk—"

"Abigail Canner," she said, lifting a white-gloved hand. Baker barely bowed his head, but McShane took her fingers as he would do for any lady, and lightly kissed her knuckles.

"Welcome, Miss Canner," said the lawyer. He smiled. He was shorter than Abigail, and so was smiling up at her. He said, innocently, what Jonathan had been afraid of saying awkwardly. "Dennard did tell me that he had hired a woman. He made no mention of your race. He says that Dr. Charles Finney wrote him on your behalf. Dr. Finney still running things at Oberlin, is he?"

"He is on in years, sir, but in spirit he is strong."

"I believe Dennard and Finney knew each other in the old days, at the Broadway Tabernacle. Well, never mind. Little, clear a space at the table. Jonathan, I'm afraid there is a bit of a crisis. You will come with me to see the President."

Abigail said, "What should I—"

McShane continued to smile. "You should wait here until Mr. Dennard returns." Jonathan had stepped to the blackboard and was using a cloth to wipe off the numbers inscribed there. He wrote: *14–27–11.* Abigail realized that he was recording the likely votes in the Senate for acquittal and conviction and those undecided. Now, hearing his employer's comment, Jonathan turned and was about to speak, but the lawyer silenced him with a look. "Wait. Let me see your letter."

She handed it over. The lawyer took it in at a glance. "This says you are a clerk. Not a law clerk."

"Is there a difference, Mr. McShane?"

His face remained gentle but his voice hardened. "You have never met Dennard, have you?"

"No, sir. Our interview was entirely via correspondence."

"Did you inform him that you are colored?"

Abigail began to feel as if she had somehow wandered in the wrong door. The way Finney had explained things, it all seemed so simple. "The issue never arose."

"I suspected as much." McShane nodded, evidently in confirmation of a private theory. "A law clerk," he explained, "is a young man who works in an attorney's office while studying the law, in the hope of being called to the bar. A clerk, on the other hand—not a law clerk, just a plain clerk—is a sort of an assistant. A secretary. To take notes, as it were. Do filing. Make deliveries. Copy out documents. Answer correspondence." He could not possibly miss the mortification on her face. Yet his smile actually broadened. "You should be proud of yourself, Miss Canner. I do not believe that there are five female clerks in the entire city working for lawyers. And none of them are colored."

"But it is 1867!"

"Perhaps in 1967 things will be different. What I have told you is the way things are now."

"Mr. McShane," she managed, surprised to find herself fighting tears, "I—I want to read law."

The lawyer was crisp. "That is not the purpose for which you were hired."

"Yes, but—but surely we could arrange—"

"You are of course free to discuss the matter with Mr. Dennard when he returns. You seem a fairly intelligent young woman. I am sure you know how to bargain. Perhaps you and Dennard can reach some arrangement."

The lasciviousness in his voice was impossible to miss; and impossible to prove.

Abigail swallowed. Her brother always said that even the most liberal of white folks gave only when the giving benefitted them. She had lived her young life in the teeth of that dictum, but now, in this room thick with coal smoke, she stood face-to-face with the evidence of its truth. "When will Mr. Dennard be returning?"

"A week from now," said McShane, with satisfaction. Baker looked on in amusement. "He is in California. Until that time, you will work for me. You may start by helping Little with his chores." Nodding toward the old man. "Is that clear?"

"But, sir! I am a graduate of Oberlin!"

"I have told you the way things are. If you wish to work for the firm of Dennard & McShane, you will be a clerk and a copyist. You will not train as a lawyer."

Abigail calculated fast. "Perhaps I can do both—"

"We will keep you busy, I assure you."

"I am willing to work as late as necessary."

McShane was exasperated. "Fine. You want to read law? There are books everywhere." His hand swept the room. "Read as many as you like, as long as you do your chores. You can start with Blackstone. Over there—the brown one, see? *Commentaries on the Laws of England*. Four volumes. Start at page one of volume one, and read all four. When you are through, we can discuss your further ambitions."

Jonathan had found his voice. "Sir, that is nearly three thousand pages."

"So what? The young lady is a graduate of Oberlin. Presumably, she can read. Little, show her where to sit."

Abigail made one final try, even though her voice wavered in a way that she hated. "Sir, if I am to work as a—a secretary—well, then, perhaps I should come to the White House with you. To—to take notes."

McShane was aghast. "Under no circumstances. You are Dennard's clerk, not mine. You will not be working on the impeachment at all." He nodded toward her hand, where she still clutched her commonplace book. "I see you have a diary. So have I. So has Mr. Hilliman. Every lawyer keeps one. But I doubt you shall be needing yours. Little, I told you to show her where to sit. Hilliman, come."

"What about Mr. Baker?" the young man asked.

"He can talk to Miss Canner."

They were out the door.

As they descended the stair, McShane shook his head. "Unbeliev-able," he muttered. "The man is unbelievable. Hiring that woman with-out telling me. I am going to strangle him."

Jonathan said nothing, and was annoyed with himself for this fail-

THE IMPEACHMENT OF ABRAHAM LINCOLN

ure; but a part of him was also amused, because Dennard, although on in years, was a heavy, powerful man, and McShane's tiny hands could not possibly have reached around his neck.

They exited onto Fourteenth Street, and the lawyer let out a purr of pleasure at the sight of his waiting horses. McShane could have had a driver but preferred to hold the reins of his own carriage, a very beautiful rig of dark polished wood with gleaming brass highlights. They climbed up for the short ride to the Executive Mansion, and a porter borrowed from the Willard handed the lawyer the reins.

Jonathan said, suddenly, "Why did we leave Mr. Baker behind?"

McShane called to the horses and gently rippled the reins. They moved off. "In case she is a spy," he said.

"I beg your pardon."

"The letter from Dennard might be a forgery. A colored woman. We would never suspect her. Mr. Lincoln's opponents will stop at nothing."

Jonathan could not quite get his mind around such nonsense. The pending impeachment trial, as he had recently written to his fiancée, Meg, seemed to have driven every man in Washington City mad.

And McShane was not done. "We have received information that a partial record of our deliberations—our strategy, if you will, for the trial—has made its way into unfriendly hands."

Jonathan forgot all about Meg. "Do you mean—you mean the Radicals?"

"Exactly. The Radical Republicans, and some of their associates, seem to have obtained notes of some of our confidential discussions." The hollowed eyes were grave. "That is why Mr. Baker is here."

"And exactly how will Mr. Baker know whether Miss Canner is a spy?"

"You didn't recognize him, did you, Hilliman? That was Lafayette Baker, formerly General Lafayette Baker. The chief of the Union Intelligence Services and the federal police. The man who caught Booth, and saw to it that he did not survive for trial." A curt nod. "He'll get the truth out of her."

CHAPTER 2

Caution

I

"DO YOU THINK he's going to resign? Mary Henry says he is, and she is not nearly so crazy as they say. And of course Horace Greeley says it would be the *best* and most *patriotic* thing for the country. His name would go down in history. Lincoln's, not Greeley's, thank God. But Lucretia Garfield says Mr. Lincoln is going to stand for re-election in 1868. A third term! You know the Garfields, don't you, Mr. Hilliman? They are *fabulously* pro-Lincoln. And, as I am sure you are aware, Lucretia is given to the most *vivid* imaginings. But the *idea*! Even Father Washington only served *twice*! And Mr. Lincoln could be President for the rest of his life. Lucretia Garfield says—well, she asked me to keep her confidence, but telling *you* is not the same as telling the *world*— Lucretia says Mr. Lincoln has not been the same since Mrs. Lincoln passed. He has nothing to go home to. Why *not* live out his days here in the President's House? That's what Lucretia says. I think it is all so fabulously exciting, don't you? That's why I left Madrid. I can't believe that my father left the Senate to be minister to Spain. I had to come back. Spain is hot and wet and boring, and Washington City is so fabulously exciting. And then running into you here, at the Mansion—well, it has to be destiny, don't you think? Delivering the Minister's letter on the very day of your visit. Leaving Mr. Lincoln's office at the very hour of your arrival. Destiny. It can be nothing else. Still. Sometimes life's griefs arrive for a reason. And life's pleasures. Such pleasures as encountering each other here, today, in this hallway. Destiny, Mr. Hilliman. Just as it is destiny that you are staying with the Bannermans, on D Street, and I at the National Hotel. Only two blocks away. We should dine. Yes. We must set a date. But *before* Mr. Lincoln announces his intentions, don't you think? Because after that, I would imagine, you shall be rather busy."

The author of this breathless rumoresque stepped away from him at last, for she had been inching closer with every whispered word. Lucy Lambert Hale, known as Bessie, possessed a trick of dropping her voice toward the end of a sentence, at least when talking to a man, forcing her listener to lean ever nearer her ample chest; or, if he did not lean toward her, she would often lean toward him. As she had been leaning toward Jonathan here in the dank, shadowy corridor outside the President's office, where, as usual, McShane had ordered Jonathan to wait; sometimes he waited for hours without ever entering the sanctum. As soon as the door closed, Bessie's plump body had sprung at him, seizing him in an unsought and unladylike hug right before the bemused eyes of Noah Brooks, the President's private secretary, who sat at a creaky desk behind a hardwood barrier badly in need of varnish.

"Surely you do not believe any of that nonsense," said Jonathan when Bessie finally paused. He had learned to affect a certain sternness with her, in order to keep her at a distance. "Mr. Lincoln is a fine man. He will do what is best for the country."

Bessie was carrying a small fan. It was the middle of winter, but she had the fan nevertheless, an affectation that had become popular among Washington City's more fashionable ladies. Now she fluttered it before her face. "And exactly which part of it is nonsense, Mr. Hilliman? The part where Mr. Lincoln stays or the part where Mr. Lincoln goes? Because both can't be false, you know."

Her logic was so absurd that Jonathan had to smile, as no doubt he was meant to. "I believe that Mr. Lincoln will serve out his term and then retire."

"Now, that is a fascinating notion, Mr. Hilliman." She had the fan going again. "Because I thought you said a moment ago that Mr. Lincoln would do what is best for the country."

"As I am certain he will."

Her smile widened. Bessie Hale was one of the city's great belles. If wagging tongues were to be believed, her charms had snared, over the past few years alone, such men as Oliver Wendell Holmes, Jr., son of the great poet; John Hay, Noah Brooks's predecessor as Lincoln's private secretary; and even Robert Lincoln, the President's eldest son.

There were other stories, too, some of them more sinister, but nobody dared repeat them, because her father, John Parker Hale, American minister to Spain, remained enormously influential in politics at home. It was said that he had stepped down from the Senate and requested the appointment to Madrid in order to remove his headstrong daughter from the moral swamp that all New Englanders believed Washington City to be; but somehow Bessie had managed to escape Madrid; and it had been Jonathan's bad luck to encounter her leaving Lincoln's office just as he and his employer had arrived.

"Then you see my point, Mr. Hilliman. That is what will be so fabulously exciting. Waiting to hear whether Mr. Lincoln has decided that the best interest of the country requires him to remain in this mansion beyond his term." Bessie looked supremely satisfied with herself. She touched his arm. "Now I must be off. I have another engagement. But we shall fix a date for dinner, shan't we?"

"I believe—"

"Shall we say Thursday, at eight? At the National?"

And then she was gone down the hallway, not waiting to hear his response. As usual, Bessie Hale got her way. The commitment was unavoidable, he told himself. He could not risk offending Bessie, whose father still influenced votes in the Senate; votes Mr. Lincoln might need at trial. Yet he shuddered to imagine what his fiancée, Margaret Felix, would say were she to learn that he was to dine with the egregious Miss Hale. When Meg warned him about the wiles of Washington's women, it was Bessie she had in mind.

Jonathan glanced nervously at Noah Brooks, who was busily writing away, pretending to have heard nothing. Although not much more than thirty, Brooks was already balding, and his muttonchop whiskers made him appear older still.

The Executive Mansion, it was said, aged its occupants.

Mr. Lincoln has not been the same since Mrs. Lincoln passed.

The door to the President's office remained firmly shut. Aside from McShane, Edwin Stanton, the Secretary of War, was inside. So was Attorney General James Speed. Jonathan wondered how long he would be waiting. Some days he had remained in the hallway for three or four hours, against the possibility that he might be summoned to record a letter or other document.

Why not *live out his days here in the President's House?*

Jonathan sank onto one of the sagging wooden benches provided for petitioners hoping to see the President. The Executive Mansion was falling apart. Many of the great rooms downstairs had been refurbished beautifully by Mrs. Lincoln, at an expense so fabulous that the Congress had opened an investigation. But the second floor—the puny family apartments, and this rabbit warren of offices for the President and his tiny staff—remained as they had been for most of the century: cramped, dingy, ill lighted.

As recently as a year ago, the shadowed hallway, decrepit or not, would have been full of petitioners, waiting their chance to beg for government jobs, or special exemptions from some law that applied to everyone else, or pardons for nephews who had deserted the army. But those who wanted favors gravitated to power, and nowadays the power was on Capitol Hill. Hardly anyone believed that Lincoln had any favors left to bestow. The newspapers were predicting that Benjamin Wade would be occupying this house in another six weeks. Indeed, rumor had it that even here in the Mansion a goodly number of the staff were already Wade's men.

According to Arthur McShane, someone was giving information about their deliberations to the Radicals. Sitting in the dingy corridor with only Noah Brooks for company, Jonathan found himself wondering who was left at the White House that Lincoln could trust.

II

"So you want to be a lawyer," said General Lafayette Baker. "Well, well."

"I do," said Abigail, fighting to keep her voice steady. Baker had seated himself on the edge of the long conference table that dominated the common room. This forced Abigail to stand. She had chosen the corner nearest one of the two windows. The involute leading in the glass was trimmed with dainty snow.

Baker had his powerful arms folded. His glare had been known to reduce prisoners to babbling incoherence. "Do you know why Mr. McShane left us alone?"

A tight nod. "He wants you to test my . . . bona fides."

"Correct. Do you have any objection to answering a few questions?"

"Would it matter if I did?"

"Not really." He coughed. "I'd like a cup of water."

Abigail never budged. "I am afraid I don't know where they keep the jug."

"Why don't you look for it?"

"Because if I begin to open cabinets and so forth, you will no doubt decide that I am here to snoop."

Baker smiled. His teeth were yellow and uneven, a sharp contrast with so smoothly handsome a countenance. "I've never heard of you," he said amiably. When Abigail, in an abundance of caution, chose not to answer, he continued: "It's bloody odd, isn't it? An alleged law clerk for Dennard shows up while that esteemed gentleman is in California and cannot be reached? And, by coincidence, just as Mr. Lincoln's lawyers are formulating their strategy for trial?" He gave her no opportunity to interrupt. It was clear that he was the sort of man who wanted to be told only what he had already decided was true. She supposed this might make him a successful detective, if the goal was only to obtain a confession, whether or not it was a true one. "There is no way to check your story, you see. You could be anybody. You could be a spy. You could even be another assassin."

Abigail fought a shudder. She could hear Nanny Pork, asking her why she wanted to go off and work with white mens. She could hear her younger sister's teasing lilt, warning that nobody would want to marry a woman who pursued a profession. And she could hear her brother, Michael, whispering that no white man could ever be trusted.

"A spy for whom?" Abigail managed.

"The Radicals. All the colored people love the Radicals, I hear. All of you think the North should keep its boot on the neck of the South. Mr. Lincoln wants to let 'em up easy, as he puts it. The Radicals want to punish them hard. I myself have no position in the matter. But I should imagine that you'd agree with the Radicals."

She had trouble meeting his eyes. At the Oberlin Collegiate Institute she had been the equal of any young man. But this was different. If she put a word wrong, Baker had the power to throw her into Old Capitol Prison, where many an inmate was known to vanish into the dank, lice-ridden cells and never again see the light of day; and the fact that she was a protégée of the great Charles Finney, evangelist and abolitionist, would mean nothing.

"I have no objection to further punishment of the South," she finally said, gaze on the dusty floor and her tightly laced shoes. "But I also do not see its necessity. In any case, Mr. Dennard did not hire me to work on the impeachment trial. He hired me to be his legal secretary." Her head came back up. "Now, if you will excuse me, I have chores."

Baker had no intention of letting her go so easily. "Do you know what the charges against the President are? Suspending habeas corpus, shutting down newspapers, locking up critics? Are you telling me that none of that bothers you?"

From somewhere Abigail found just a bit of the sauciness that had characterized her attitude back at Oberlin. "You sound, General Baker, as if it bothers you."

This won her another baring of yellow teeth. "What about the charge that he means to overthrow the Congress? That he tried to establish a military district—the Department of the Atlantic—to run the government? How does that one strike you?"

"As a patent absurdity."

"Ever met Mr. Lincoln?"

"No."

"Know any member of his family? Any of his friends?"

"No."

"Then how can you know what is in his head? And whether or not the charge is absurd?" Baker sighed, then hopped nimbly to his feet. Without warning, he stepped very close to her, crowding her back against the bookshelves. For a mad moment she thought he meant to kiss her. "We live in difficult times, Miss Canner. No Congress has dared act in this manner against a President. No one is above suspicion. Do you understand?" Once more he did not wait to hear her response. "If you choose to remain at Dennard & McShane, I shall have no choice but to continue to look into your story, finding all the holes. I shall poke and prod until there are only holes, and no longer any story at all. And at that point"—leaning so close that she could smell this morning's garlic on his hot breath—"at that point, Miss Canner, you are mine."

Alone again, Abigail found herself unable to move. She was still on her feet. Her body began to tremble, then to shudder, until her entire being, physical and mental, jerked in uncontrolled spasms. The fear she felt was sharp and raw and red and deep. The hateful tears were but the smallest manifestation of her terror. She leaned over and put her hands on the table. Her late mother always said that God would get you through, and so she tried her best to pray; but in her fear and humiliation had no idea what she was praying for.

She was standing in the same position when Little came in from whatever errand he had been running; although it was also possible that he had just been waiting outside for the general to leave. The old man glanced at her, hastily looked away, went to the cupboard. He took down the water jug, poured some into a glass, handed it to her. She drained it, and with movement came fluency. Her thoughts began to run clearly again. She found a smile, if a shaky one; thanked him; truly meant it.

Little handed her the broom.

"You gots chores, Miss Canner."

III

McShane dropped his clerk at the carriage block twenty yards from the building entrance. He had a meeting, the lawyer said, and had to hurry. Jonathan was exhausted: worn out, like the man in his uncle Brighton's favorite story, from doing nothing all day. He and McShane had arrived at the Mansion at eleven in the morning. Now it was past six in the evening, and nearly full dark. In the months since the firm's retention to represent the President, Jonathan had attended five White House meetings with his employer, and had been invited into Lincoln's office only twice, both times to write out a document that one of the others in the room dictated. Neither time had he stayed for more than a few minutes.

Back at Fourteenth and G, peering up at the second-story windows, Jonathan was surprised to see lanterns burning. Old Little was usually more careful when he closed up. Unlocking the lobby door, Jonathan felt watched. He turned and saw, on the other side of the street, a tethered wagon, the horse resting while the negro driver stroked its flanks and glared at Jonathan with a fury that the young man could not fathom.

Washington City these days.

Upstairs at last, Jonathan stepped into the office, drawing a startled gasp from Abigail Canner, who sat at the long table, a heavy book open before her, flickery lamplight playing across the pages.

"What are you doing here?" he asked, very surprised.

"Reading Blackstone, volume one," she said, calmly. She put down the pencil with which she had been making notes. "I am on page thirty-four."

IV

"Thank you for waiting," said Abigail to her brother, Michael, as the wagon moved slowly through the snow. "I had extra work. There was no way to let you know."

Michael considered this pitiful excuse as he drew the horse around left, turning onto Pennsylvania Avenue. "So, what do you think? Are they going to impeach Old Abe or not?"

"They will impeach him next week."

"Who'll be the President then?"

Abigail shut her eyes, never sure when her brother was baiting her. She spoke as tonelessly as possible, because Michael, when offended, was unpredictable. "To impeach him only means to charge him with high crimes and misdemeanors. There is still a trial in the Senate to decide whether to remove him from office."

"So who'll be President? The Vice-President is dead."

"If Mr. Lincoln is convicted, his successor will be Senator Wade from Ohio. He is what they call the president pro tempore of the Senate, and under the statutes—"

"President pro tempore?"

"He is in charge of the Senate."

A cruel laugh. "White folks."

"I'm sorry?"

They rolled past trees and houses and the occasional hotel or bar. Here and there a federal building stood like a lone sentry.

"Let me understand this," said Michael. "This Wade gets to vote on whether to kick Old Abe out of the White House, and then he also gets to move in and take his place? Who dreamed that up?"

"The gentlemen who wrote the Constitution," she said sleepily.

"The *white* gentlemen."

An ornate carriage passed, traveling much too fast the other way, spattering them both with the freezing Washington mud. The horse shied, but Michael eased it back on course. The trees thickened as they approached the canal. Dozing, Abigail let her hand drift to the seat cushion. She encountered a lump. Delving, she touched a metal cylinder. It felt like—

"Michael, why is there a pistol in the wagon?"

"The city is dangerous at night. Especially for our people."

She digested this. "If the police should stop you—"

"Then I'll protect myself."

CHAPTER 3

Vote

I

"SO I HEAR they'll be impeaching your man in the morning," said Fielding Bannerman, swirling his brandy sourly as he lounged before the grate. "Pity, I suppose." He brightened. "I say. Is that why there are so many soldiers about? On the way back from the club I was all but run over by a troop of cavalry."

Jonathan was toying with the cigar that he would never have touched except that as a man he was expected to. The fire, unreasonably hot, reminded him of the spectacular blazes of his Rhode Island youth, when his dying father complained constantly of cold, and his mother discharged on the spot any servant who let the flames die. It was the late evening of Monday, February 18; or, as Jonathan had come to measure the days, two weeks since the arrival of Abigail Canner at Dennard & McShane.

"Even if the impeachment succeeds," he said woodenly, "the trial is yet ahead of us."

"Where your man is bound to lose."

"I would not say that."

"Then why are there so many soldiers about? Somebody was saying at the club that your man would arrest the Speaker of the House rather than allow himself to be impeached." He shut his eyes. "I say. That would be rather thrilling, wouldn't it?" Fielding chuckled self-importantly. He was grinning and, as usual, drunk. He was a short man, with sloppy black hair and the early paunch of the leisured life. He was, like Jonathan, the heir apparent to his family business; although, to be sure, whereas the Hillimans were decently off, the Bannermans with their banking fortune rivaled the Astors and the Cookes. They were friends because Elise Hilliman expected her children to have wealthy friends; and because Fielding was some sort of distant cousin of Meg Felix, Jonathan's fiancée. Still, he had agreed to take rooms in the Bannerman mansion on Ninth Street only because he was assured that Fielding would be in Europe with his parents, who were trying to marry off the three dreadfully plain Bannerman sisters to minor princelings. Had Jonathan known that Fielding would be in residence, he might have chosen to live somewhere else.

"That is the silliest thing I have ever heard," said Jonathan.

"Is it? Didn't I hear somewhere that one of the articles of the impeachment accuses your man of seeking to overthrow the Congress by force?" He laughed, spilling his brandy. He took no notice. Spills were what servants were for. Ellenborough, the mulatto butler, materialized at once with a napkin and a fresh glass. "But it doesn't matter what Lincoln does," Fielding continued. "Know why? Because the price of gold rose today. Henry Foreman told me at the club. He's with Jay Cooke & Co. If the price of gold is rising, that means the dollar is falling, which means that the bankers believe that Mr. Lincoln will be removed. And you know what my father says. Never bet against the bankers."

Jonathan stirred, perceiving through the haze of spirits and smoke that he was about to be subjected to another of his friend's wild theories about what malevolent forces lay behind the impeachment. "Your father *is* a banker."

But Fielding preferred his own arguments. "I say. When am I going to meet this negress of yours?"

"I beg your pardon."

"The Canner woman. We were talking about the impeachment down at the club, and Tubby Longchamps is sharing a few secrets, and he mentions her. Do you know Tubby at all? No? He was in my year at Harvard, you know, and he's deputy to the sergeant-at-arms now. At the House of Representatives. Good old Tubby. He always did know where there was nice clean graft to be found, didn't he? Goodness me. Why, once, right in the middle of the Yard, he had this idea that we might put one over on old Connie Felton. This was before Felton was made president of the college. In those days he taught freshman Greek. And Tubby, bless him, suggested that we—"

Jonathan was all at once apprehensive. Fielding Bannerman might be a snob, but he and his Harvard friends constituted a web of sources General Baker's Secret Service would envy.

"Fields. The impeachment. What did Tubby say?"

"He said he met the Canner woman last week. Your negress. She was on an errand at the Library of Congress, picking up some books for the lawyers." A frown. "Or was she returning them? Oh dear. I'm not sure Tubby told me which." He took a long swallow of brandy. "The point is, your Miss Canner dropped the books. Of course none of the Washington gentlemen lifted a finger. Not for a negress. But you know Tubby's eye for the ladies. He helped her pick up the books. And he says she's really quite exquisite. Naturally, she thanked him, and you should hear Tubby describe that dulcet voice of hers. How dare you keep her to yourself, Hills. When do I meet her? Say, old man. Why not invite her for dinner? Tell you what. I'll bring Miss Hale. We can make it a foursome. How's that?"

"Fields, please. The impeachment. What secrets did Tubby share?"

"Ah! Well. He says that if Wade becomes President he will make Mr. Ebon Ward Secretary of the Treasury."

"Who on earth is Ebon Ward?"

"Secretary of the Steel Board, old man. I'd have thought you'd know all about it, because of your family."

"My family is in textiles, not steel."

"Yes, well, the textile makers want higher tariffs. So do the steel-makers. High tariffs mean soft money. Wade is a soft-money man, the way most Westerners are. Mr. Lincoln used to be, too, but Tubby says he's about to do a deal with the bankers. If the bankers will support Lincoln, then he'll support a lower tariff."

"Mr. Lincoln would not alter his policies for political support."

"Your man may be President, Hills, but he's still a politician." Fielding sank deeper into his armchair. "Besides, it's just what Tubby says."

Jonathan felt a headache coming on, caused by either the cigar or yet another implausible theory from Fielding's endless supply. "I'm going to bed," he said.

Fielding let his friend get halfway across the room before springing his surprise. "Tubby also said that any day now they will admit Nebraska to the Union."

"We have an agreement!"

"That they will not admit Nebraska until after the trial. I know. But

Tubby says they will go forward next week. And the state legislature in Omaha, in an agony of gratitude, will immediately send to Washington two anti-Lincoln Senators, who will be seated just in time to vote for your man's conviction."

Jonathan was thinking about the blackboard at the office. This afternoon the numbers had read *15–29–8*. If Fielding's information was accurate—and on such matters he was rarely wrong—then by next week there would be fifty-four Senators, not fifty-two, and the count would be fifteen for acquittal, thirty-one for conviction, and eight undecided. And suddenly, rather than winning half of the undecided votes, Lincoln would need a majority of them in order to survive.

"Thank you," said Jonathan, heading for the stairs. "Good night, Fields."

"Hills. Just want you to know. I'm serious."

"About what?"

"Miss Canner. I should very much like to meet her. Sooner the better."

A perfectly proper request, but it bothered Jonathan quite unreasonably for days thereafter.

II

"Well, that was rather exciting," said Dinah Berryhill, who did not sound the least bit ruffled. "I had no idea that observing the House of Representatives could be quite such fun."

"Fun!" cried Abigail. "It was horrible!"

It was Tuesday, February 19, and the House had just voted to impeach the President and send his case to the Senate for trial. Abigail, under the guise of picking up more books at the Library of Congress, had gone with her friend Dinah to watch history being made. She knew by now, the second day of her third week of employment, that Jonathan would cover for her.

Jonathan always covered for her.

With his assistance, at first reluctant but now smilingly conspiratorial, she had been able to slip out of chores to spend more and more time reading. Not often, perhaps, but occasionally. Jonathan treated her with an awkward kindness. The young people of Abigail's set—Dinah foremost among them—were unanimous in their view that the white race meant them no good; whites were kind only when they wanted something. Abigail largely shared these views. And she was no fool. She had spent enough time in the world of men to know what men generally wanted. Therefore, she was at pains to let Jonathan know that she was engaged. As it turned out, so was he.

"Of course he is," said Dinah, the two of them in the midst of the crowd descending the snowy slope from the Capitol following the vote. Her arms were out to her sides for balance, a pose Abigail would not dream of striking in public, even if the cost of her reticence was an occasional fall. Dinah was a stout, saucy woman whose family had arranged for her to be finished—poorly, in Abigail's secret opinion—at a school near Philadelphia. The Berryhills owned tracts of timber in upstate New York and a large shipbuilding firm on Cape Cod. Dinah had traveled all over Europe. One of Abigail's constant frustrations, at Oberlin and in Washington City both, was battling the presumption among her classmates that if you were black you must have been a slave until the Emancipation Proclamation; or, if you had been born free, then your parents surely scrubbed kitchens or waited tables. In either event, you were unlikely to have opened a book until the kind people of the American Missionary Association or the Freedmen's Bureau dragged you off to a dreary one-room schoolhouse in the middle of some benighted Southern swamp. When Abigail told her classmates that her father built houses, they imagined shacks on a plantation; and when she told them that the Berryhills had built frigates for the Royal Navy a century ago, her classmates assumed that they swept out the shipyards after hours.

Dinah, meanwhile, was still talking about Jonathan. "Rich young men," she proclaimed, "are always engaged. They rarely marry, but they are always engaged."

In Hebrew, Dinah's name meant "judgment," and she lived up to it constantly.

"I must say, Mr. Lincoln's opponents seem quite passionate," Dinah continued. "Why, poor Thaddeus Stevens is dying, and he came to the House today to condemn the man."

"Mr. Lincoln has broken no laws," said Abigail, already sounding like the lawyer she hoped to be. Yet she, too, had been saddened by the condition of Stevens, the most senior of the Radicals, and the Abolitionist most beloved by educated negroes. "There is no case."

"Of course there is a case," said Dinah, who, coming from a business family, shied away from abstractions. She laid a saucy hand on her hip. "My father is afraid to commit any important business confidences to either telegram or post for fear that Mr. Lincoln's Secret Service might seize the message. Some who would otherwise speak out against the President choose not to do so, lest they wind up in one of Mr. Stanton's secret military prisons. That is not politics, Abigail. That is tyranny."

"Mr. Lincoln freed the slaves," said Abigail, doggedly. She remembered her grueling interview with General Baker, and wondered at her own certainty—and her motives. Although nobody had mentioned that conversation since, and her standing at the office seemed even to have improved, a part of her worried that some dire consequence still lay ahead.

Dinah's laugh was hard and mannish, the laugh of one who has seen it all and long forgotten how to be impressed. "Abby, darling, he is being impeached by the Radicals of his own party. They would have freed the slaves, too. That is not what this quarrel is about."

"Then what is it about?"

"Goodness, darling. The man tried to put the army over Congress! To establish military government in this city, with himself at the head! He is a petty tyrant, a tyrant running our great Protestant Republic! Really, what else does one expect when we choose an uneducated Westerner to be—Stop! Stop him!"

A small, dark, slim figure had darted from the throng and snatched Dinah's fancy handbag. He ran on—

Only to scream in agony a second later as an absurdly tall man, white and broad and grizzled, stepped out of the crowd and snapped his wrist.

"Sorry, Miss Dinah," said the giant, with a sheepish grin. He had a flaming-red beard, and a bright scar along the side of his neck. His ancient jacket of butternut gray, a relic of the war, was evidence that he had been on the losing side. "I tried not to hurt the fool," he rumbled.

The fool, as it happened, was a negro boy, no more than ten or twelve, and Abigail ached at the image, the brown boy struggling in the painful grip of the white Goliath as the crowd backed away.

"You may release him, Corporal," said Dinah. She bent over, laid a hand on the boy's shoulder, and lectured him in a stern whisper, finger waving in his face. All the time, the boy looked at the ground, and cradled his wounded wrist. He nodded. Dinah slapped him lightly on the side of his head, and he scampered off.

"I imagine," said Dinah, brushing off her bag, "that he will shortly be stealing another." She adjusted her hat. "I do wonder how they live."

She linked her arm through Abigail's and they resumed their stroll, Dinah expostulating on Lincoln's crimes in a voice meant to be overheard, and Abigail barely listening, so sickened was she by the episode with the thief.

The giant had disappeared, but Abigail knew he was nearby. He was never separated from Dinah by more than a dozen paces. His name was Alexander Waverly, late corporal in the Second Corps of the Army of Northern Virginia under "Stonewall" Jackson. He was one of two former Confederates hired by the Berryhills to keep their headstrong daughter out of harm's way: Corporal Waverly guarded Dinah during the day, and a Corporal Cutler by night. Dinah insisted that both men were as gentle as could be, but Abigail found them terrifying.

Why does your father hire only Confederates to protect you? Abigail had once asked her friend.

Dinah's answer was succinct: *Because we won, dear.*

III

McShane spent the afternoon at the White House. The city was dark when he returned. The only illumination in the common room came from a noisy gas chandelier. Jonathan was seated at the table, working his way through an evidence treatise. Little was putting one last shovelful of coal into the stove. Abigail was dusting the shelves. McShane stood silently, but gave her a long look that seemed to Jonathan almost hostile. Then he beckoned the young man to join him in his office. Abigail watched them go.

"Close the door," the lawyer said.

He perched on the edge of his desk. He was a pleasant man, with little use for affectation or formality.

"The President has instructed us," McShane began, "to go to the Hill and get more time to file our response. Never mind. We have more pressing matters to discuss. I am afraid we have a bit of a problem." A heavy pause. "It involves Miss Canner."

"I don't understand."

"What do you think of her?"

A sudden gray rain assaulted the windows. Jonathan fought the instinct to sing Abigail's praises. Instead, he decided to tread carefully, at least until he learned what the "problem" was. "She is intelligent. She is hardworking. Given the proper training, I think she might well succeed in her ambition to become a lawyer."

"Ah," said McShane, but the single syllable somehow registered displeasure.

Jonathan plunged on. "That idea you liked, the one about the disqualification of feudal lords—that idea was Miss Canner's. She found it in Blackstone." He saw no way out. "And she made other suggestions as well."

A prickly pause.

"I see." McShane seemed unhappier than ever. He turned away, as if seeking answers in the storm beyond the window. The rain had grown louder, like gunfire against the panes. "She made suggestions for a memorandum about the legal strategy of the President of the United States." He shook his head. "And how exactly did Miss Canner know what you were working on?"

Jonathan had gone very still. "I told her."

"Never again." The tone was sharp. His employer faced him once more, eyes rock-hard. "Never. She is not to be admitted to the secrets of this office. Am I being clear?"

"Yes, of course, but she might be helpful—"

The little man was suddenly on his feet. Agitated. Pacing. The worry lines in his face seemed to have deepened over the past week. Jonathan remembered that Rufus Dennard, the senior partner, had been dead-set against representing the President, fearing that more lucrative clients might flee to a firm less involved in the nation's nasty politics. "Be quiet and listen. It appears that our difficulties are greater than I suspected. I told you that records of our deliberations are finding their way into the hands of the President's political opponents. That is bad enough. But there are larger forces at play. Powerful men throughout the nation. A conspiracy, if you will, behind the conspiracy." McShane caught something in his clerk's posture. "I know that you have no patience with such theories, Hilliman. But I have sources of my own. One of them tells me that a list of names was lost in Virginia, and the conspirators are frantic to find it. The list, if it exists, very likely would tell us who is plotting against Mr. Lincoln. Not an assassination this time, but his removal through legal means. You don't believe a word, I can see it in your face."

Jonathan had heard the conspiracy theories before. All of Washington seemed infected with the need to blame secret malevolent forces for every misfortune. But McShane had contracted a particularly virulent strain of the disease. In the shadowed office, the wild set of his eyes was actually frightening.

"Please, sir," said Jonathan. "Just tell me what you would like me to do."

The lawyer recovered himself. "Yes. Well. I have just come from Mr. Stanton. We spoke about Miss Canner."

"Yes, sir."

"She has become, in my judgment, a liability." Jonathan started to protest, but the lawyer was still talking. His face was flushed; here, Jonathan realized, was the true source of the man's anger. Whatever he was about to say had him furious at their client. "Not that my judgment matters at the moment. Not where Miss Canner is concerned. Miss Canner is special. Did you know that, Hilliman?" Again he gave Jonathan no time to respond. "Stanton has General Baker looking into her background. She may be connected to the conspiracy." The eyes took on that hunted look again. "And now of course Sumner is involved."

Jonathan was dumbstruck. Senator Charles Sumner of Massachusetts was the most brilliant man in the Senate, and probably the most respected. He had been close to Mrs. Lincoln but somehow had never warmed to the President himself. Officially, Sumner remained neutral on the impeachment, but his fellow Radicals were courting him assiduously. Lincoln, alas, had nothing in his larder that Sumner seemed to want. And because Sumner controlled two or three undecided votes along with his own, any "problem" with him, unless swiftly resolved, would likely spell the end for their client.

"Involved how?" Jonathan finally managed, unable to hide his surprise. "What does Senator Sumner have to do with Miss Canner?"

Again McShane's practical side asserted itself. "Hilliman, look. This thing is going to be close. Any fool can see that. Once upon a time, Mr. Lincoln would have swatted Sumner and his friends like pesky gnats. But he has not been the same man since Mrs. Lincoln's tragic passing, and the Radicals have grown bold. So Mr. Lincoln has sent feelers to Sumner's people. Offers to negotiate. But every attempt has been rebuffed. Now, all of a sudden, it turns out that Sumner wants Miss Canner to work on our client's case."

"Why would he care?"

"Because Sumner is a romantic. Maybe you remember how, just last year, he persuaded the Supreme Court to admit the first negro lawyer to its bar. Well, in Miss Canner, Sumner has found a new cause. His next blow for the colored race. And now it is we who must go along. Stanton has spoken to Sumner directly. He believes that we have no choice. We have decided not to trouble the President." McShane grew wistful. "We may, however, be able to turn her presence to our advantage."

Jonathan nodded eagerly. "I told you, she's very smart—"

"That is not what I was referring to," said the lawyer, tone colder still. "Pay attention, Hilliman. The heart of the Radical case against Mr. Lincoln is that he has been insufficiently supportive of the colored race. If it becomes known that Miss Canner is working for us, we present a powerful symbol to the contrary."

Jonathan chose his words carefully. "I take it, then, that we will be giving Miss Canner real work to do."

"Under no circumstances." The rain strafed the glass in a fresh attack. McShane laughed, mirthlessly. "Oh, we shall have to lead Miss Canner to think that what she is doing is useful, and we'll let the public get the same idea. But she is not involved in any substantive way with our work. She does not learn our secrets, or our client's. Is that clear?"

"Yes, but—"

McShane cut him off. "It shall be your task to supervise Miss Canner. Tell her that she will henceforth have legal work to do. But make sure that none of it carries any significance whatsoever."

"Are you asking me to lie to Miss Canner?"

"No, Hilliman. I am ordering you to lie to her." Jonathan had never known the little man to be so gruff; or so furious. "Now, go on. I have to get ready for a meeting."

"I have nothing on the calendar, sir."

Again McShane spoke with unanticipated sharpness. "Well, my goodness, Hilliman, I did manage to find my way to an appointment or two before you came into my employ."

As Jonathan reached for the doorknob, McShane called his name, held up a single finger. "Hilliman. A word of warning. If you share another of the firm's confidences with that woman, that will be the end of your career at Dennard & McShane."

CHAPTER 4

Unease

I

"A BILL OF impeachment," said the President, "is a remarkable thing." He adjusted his glasses and peered down at the printed pages on his desk. "So many words to express such a simple idea. *We want you gone.* That is what they are saying." He looked up. "The charges don't really matter."

"They matter a great deal," objected James Speed, the attorney general, who was expected shortly to resign his office to assist in preparation for trial. "They are petty and foolish. This is a conspiracy of your enemies. The entire country will see that, sir."

The President's office was crowded: Lincoln, Speed, McShane, and Jonathan, as well as Secretary of War Edwin Stanton. This time Jonathan had sat outside for two hours before being invited in to take a letter—a letter, albeit, that nobody had yet gotten around to dictating. It was Thursday morning, two days after the House vote, and the entire country thought Lincoln was doomed. So did Bessie Hale, whom Jonathan had now met not once but twice for dinner, and who fairly glowed with the untutored excitement of an innocent to whom change is always thrilling. It is time for Lincoln to go, Bessie enthused. Everybody knows he is not the man he was, she said: not since he was shot in the head two years ago! Not since his wife died last year! And McShane, just two days ago, had hinted at the same thought. But Jonathan, who had not met Lincoln during the war years, found the postwar edition enormously impressive: erudite, confident, decisive.

"Are you with us, Hilliman?" said McShane, sotto voce.

Jonathan blinked. "Yes. Of course, sir." He glanced at his notes in the dim, skittering daylight. The weather outside was filthy. The weather in Washington was always filthy: filthy rain in the summer; filthy snow in the winter. "You just said that if the House should indeed vote out a bill of impeachment, the lawyers will seek as much time as possible to file a response in the Senate."

"Try to pay attention," McShane hissed, tapping the paper.

Jonathan colored. His only function was to listen and take notes and keep his own counsel. He commanded himself to look where his employer was pointing. The list of charges against the President was only tentative. The House of Representatives had adopted a bizarre process through which it first voted to impeach, then appointed a committee (known as the Managers) to draft the actual charges, and last of all would vote on whether to endorse the charges and send the case on to the Senate. The paper on Lincoln's desk was the result of the deliberations of the Managers. If, as expected, the full House endorsed the document next week, then the Managers would become the prosecutors in the Senate trial.

Lincoln ignored Speed's foray. "No President in history has been so treated. They tried to do it to poor Tyler, but . . ."

He trailed off.

"Sir," Stanton began. "I think that if we—"

Lincoln spoke right over his Secretary of War. "It makes no difference," he said, morosely, "whether we are the victims of a conspiracy or not. The impeachment will go forward in any case." He seemed no longer to be looking at anything in the room. His heavy gaze was directed, if anywhere, into a misty future he alone could discern, even if it appeared to those present that he was studying the map of Virginia pinned to the wall. "The Radicals never thought I was the man to fight the war, and now they do not think I am the man to make the peace. I long only to re-create the Union, whereas our congressional friends . . ." Again he trailed off; shook his head. His Kentucky accent was especially pronounced today. "It is well that Mrs. Lincoln has been spared this indignity."

"She died a noble death, sir," said Stanton, who could lie better than any man in Washington City. "Providence be thanked."

The President nodded. He was on his feet, and so were the other men. He had kept them standing for over an hour, and his Secretary of

War, better known for his temper than for his endurance, was growing wobbly.

"Providence has a mighty peculiar way of distributing her blessings," said Lincoln. "Sometimes I'm not all that sure she knows which side she's on."

"But we know," Stanton insisted. He coughed into a large handkerchief. His eyes watered. "She is on our side, sir. She has always been on the side of righteousness."

Another silence. Jonathan was wondering what precisely Stanton considered noble about Mrs. Lincoln's passing. She had not died of the assassin's bullet, or even of the Potomac fever. A year ago, while in Illinois on an extended visit, the First Lady had fallen into Lake Springfield and drowned. People said she had entered a long period of mental decline after the attempt on her husband's life at Ford's Theatre, but there were always people.

The President finally spoke. "The victors always think they're righteous, but then they always seem to start a mighty unrighteous squabbling over the spoils." He continued gazing at the map. The war was nearly two years over, but the President's office on the second floor of the Executive Mansion was crowded with evidence of his constant worry that the conflict might at any moment erupt again. On a side table, Northern newspapers screamed rumors of Confederate troops continuing to do battle in the Smoky Mountains. Pigeonholes in the President's desk held dispatches from military governors, warning of dire conspiracies being hatched beneath their feet.

"If I might make a suggestion," McShane began. Stanton, as if by way of comment, coughed harder, and had no time to grab a handkerchief. His bushy beard was a mess.

Mr. Lincoln turned away from the map and waved McShane silent. His gaze passed slowly around the room, then returned to rest on Jonathan. And although, when the President spoke, he was addressing the entire group, Jonathan could not resist the feeling that the words were directed particularly to his own ears.

"The Congress has a constitutional duty," said Lincoln, "but I have a constitutional duty of my own. They want me out of this office, and, believe me, I would willingly yield it if I could. But the work of binding up the Union is not yet completed, and, until it is, I cannot yield." Lincoln's right eyelid began to droop, making him look sleepy, but Jonathan sensed a growing alertness. "They have their duty," the President repeated, "but I have mine, too. I have taken an oath registered in Heaven to see that the laws are faithfully executed. I will rebuild the Union. I will not allow the Congress to break apart what has been so carefully knit back together. And it is your job"—the eyes began to roam again—"to make them accept it. We must not let this thing come down to a contest of wills. But I will do my constitutional duty." A slow smile. "So, now that they've voted out this impeachment bill, you fellows go up to Capitol Hill and make sure they're not in all that big a hurry to hold the trial."

McShane said, "They will probably give us no more than a week to prepare."

The President's nod was amused. "Make them see reason. That's your job."

"If they refuse—"

"They will not refuse," said Stanton, voice thick with unexpected fury. "They *dare* not refuse."

Arthur McShane was a small man, but he stood up to the towering President and his vicious Secretary of War. Jonathan had worked for the lawyer for nearly a year, and had never been prouder of him. "With respect," said McShane, "the Congress is likely to do pretty much as it pleases. The members believe that the President ignores their wishes and their decrees. In a sense, that is what this trouble is about."

Stanton turned toward the President. "Sir, these are difficult times. You have, as you said, a constitutional responsibility. And I think, given the power you wield under the Constitution, that the Senators would have to accept as *fait accompli* whatever you decided."

The President's expression never changed, but those eyelids drooped a little lower. Satisfaction? Anger? Jonathan had no way to guess. Yet he sensed a great sorrow in the man, together with a degree of disappointment in his available advisers of the moment: the sycophantish Speed, the volcanic Stanton. Absent from these counsels was the man on whose advice the President had most relied over the years. Secretary of State William Seward had been attacked on the same night that Lincoln was shot and Vice-President Johnson murdered. Seward had survived, but with injuries so debilitating that in the two years since he had not set foot outside his house, across the avenue from the Mansion. Lincoln still visited his old friend regularly, but those occasional conversations could not substitute for daily meetings in this office. Many a Washington hand insisted that, had Seward been healthy, his peculiar ability to pour balm on troubled political waters might have avoided the impeachment fight altogether.

When, at last, Lincoln spoke, he seemed to be addressing no one at all.

"The cost of a war," said the President, "is impossible to estimate in advance. Later, when a great conflict ends, yes, we look back and engage in our learned arguments on whether the end was worth the great sacrifice. But that comes later. When we are deciding whether to begin, our judgment rests on the principles we believe to be at stake. Somehow, to somebody, they always seem to be worth fighting for. And maybe sometimes they are. But wars continue long after one side surrenders. Every conflict plagues the peace that follows it." Mr. Lincoln's gaze had fixed once more upon the map.

It occurred to Jonathan that the President had not made up his mind; that he was struggling, as he had during the war, between the need to follow the strictures of the Constitution and the need to prevail. That Lincoln wrestled, where most men followed the expedient path, increased Jonathan's admiration for him.

"The god of war," said Lincoln, sadly, "is never satisfied."

II

Neither, as it happened, was Abigail Canner, left alone in the office while the others went over to the Mansion to meet the President. Holding the fort, McShane called it, borrowing from General Sherman, under whom he had served. Here she was, an honors graduate of Oberlin Collegiate Institute, and for two weeks she had been assigned to sweep and dust and, on a good day, collect the unruly files McShane left hither and thither, tying their green ribbons into neat bows, and slipping them into the proper drawers and pigeonholes.

"You're not just holding the fort," Michael had teased her. "You're cleaning it."

Yet Abigail did it all without complaint. She had learned the rules of hard work from Nanny Pork, who yelled at you if you failed to do your chores; if you did them, she yelled at you for failing to do them right. If Abigail spent her days dusting and filing; if she was frustrated daily by her exclusion from important meetings, she nevertheless was here, in this momentous time, near enough to the center of things that she fancied she could feel the throbbing excitement of the nation's leaders as, day by day, the possibilities for Lincoln's survival waxed and waned.

But Abigail did her tidying, then sat down with the same first volume of Blackstone she had been examining in her private hours for the past two weeks. Mr. Little, who seemed to come and go as he pleased, had caught her more than once, but never said anything about it. Since Jonathan did not seem to mind, and even encouraged her, she supposed that the only person from whom she was hiding her secret studies was Mr. McShane, who turned out to be serious in his intention to limit her to chores scarcely removed from those assigned to Mr. Little. She was busily making notes about feudal land tenures when a knock on the door announced a visitor, who walked in without ever quite being invited: David Grafton, a lawyer with offices down on the first floor.

"I gather that you are here alone for the moment," he said. "Good. I have been looking forward to this chance."

He was an elegantly attired but oddly bent man, hips one way, torso the other, shoulders a third. He looked as if he had been twisted into a corkscrew by inhuman hands: the crooked man from the fairy tale. The truth was, he had been run over by a horsecar ten years ago, and should have died from the experience. But David Grafton was a man of indomitable will. Until two years ago, he had been the middle partner in what was then known as Dennard, Grafton & McShane. Jonathan was hazy on what had led to the crooked man's departure, but on one rule he was crystal clear: Abigail was not to speak to him, at any time, for any reason.

"But why not?" she had asked. "He said hello to me the other day in the street."

"Because he is evil come to earth," said Jonathan, by no means a religious man. "Because he has made it his life's work to sow discord, and to see to it that others reap the whirlwind."

III

"Mr. McShane is not in," said Abigail, on her feet, fists tightly clenched. "I shall tell him you were here."

"Tell him what you like," said Grafton lightly; his dark cloak fit perfectly the image Jonathan had sketched. "I am not here to see McShane, Miss Canner. I am here to see you."

"I . . . I am rather busy."

"I see that." Eyeing the volume of Blackstone, then turning toward the wood stove. He stooped, opened the door, peered in. "Quite a fire burning there. Your work, or Mr. Little's?" He slammed the door, then crossed his arms over his chest and rubbed his upper arms. "The others are over at the Mansion, but not you, eh?"

"I am . . . holding the fort."

"Indeed. In my offices, there is a man who keeps the fire burning and there are clerks who work on legal matters. Only on legal matters. They do not hold the fort." He was near the window now. He had pulled a pipe from somewhere in his cloak and made to clean the bowl. "Perhaps you would like to make a change."

He has made it his life's work to sow discord.

"You are very kind, Mr. Grafton, but I am quite happy where I am."

"Pity."

"I am afraid I must—"

"McShane is a good man," said Grafton, as if Dennard was not. The visitor was prodding inside his pipe with a metal reamer. He turned the bowl upside down, rapped it on the side table. Wet dottle fell onto a silk handkerchief he had thoughtfully laid out. "A fine lawyer. Sound in his politics," Grafton continued. He spooned fresh tobacco from a pouch. "Rather a rare thing these days, isn't it?"

"I wouldn't know, Mr. Grafton."

"Sorry Dennard snared you first. Wish I'd had a shot at you."

"Very kind of you, sir."

"Suppose I were to double what Dennard & McShane are paying you." His smile was sudden, and feral, the smile of a hunting cat. "If you were my law clerk, Miss Canner, I would not have you waste your time dusting and running errands. I would spend two years training you, after which you would sit for the bar. No woman in this Republic has ever sat for the bar. You could be the first. How does that sound?"

Abigail wondered whether her hearing was off, or whether she might be dreaming, asleep in the bedroom she shared with her younger sister, Louisa. She stared in determined fascination at Grafton's pipe tool, imported from the look of it: all those shining attachments on a single stem. Nanny Pork smoked a pipe, too, but cleaned the bowl with bits of this and that. Abigail stared at the gleaming tool and concentrated on the great mystery of how one properly cleaned a pipe, because something about this conversation scared her half to death.

"Mr. Grafton—"

"Think of it, Miss Canner. At this very moment, over at the Mansion, they are working out the strategy to defend in the Senate the President who freed the slaves. And you are here. Left behind. Holding the fort. Is that the life you prefer?"

She felt quite breathless, as if she were halfway up a very steep hill. "Mr. Grafton, please. I have duties to attend to."

"Yes, I do believe I noticed a bit of dust in the corner." He wobbled to the closet, took out the broom. "I imagine you'll be needing this."

I V

"Were you out with Miss Hale last night? Henry Foreman says he saw you dining together at Willard's."

"Mr. McShane has encouraged me to spend time with her," said Jonathan, who had hoped, foolishly, that his employer would forbid him instead. He and Fielding were eating a dinner of cold chop in the dining room. Ellenborough and a footman were serving. With the rest of the family in Europe, most of the house staff had been furloughed. "He believes she might provide useful information."

"And should you refuse her, Miss Hale might take offense and complain to her father, eh? And there would go any chance of picking up the vote of one of his New Hampshire friends in the Senate. You would seem to be trapped both ways, wouldn't you, Hills? Still, Henry says the two of you looked rather cozy. I do wonder what my cousin would say."

"Meg would not understand—"

"Oh, I would never tell. Gentlemen do not tell other gentlemen's secrets. Now, Henry, on the other hand, fancies Meg. Did you know that? I believe that he would be delighted were your engagement to fracture. And he is no gentleman." Signaling for more wine. "By the by, you haven't forgotten, I hope, that I wish an introduction to Miss Canner? You really have no right to keep her to yourself, Hills. Not her *and* Miss Hale."

Jonathan, spreading butter on bread, eyed his friend curiously. He longed to share with someone his fears about McShane's increasingly lurid conspiracy theories. But Fielding was not the man. Fielding would only endorse them.

V

Abigail dined that night at the home of the Mellisons, a colored family who had prospered in the dry-goods trade. In the course of the evening, several of the many evil Mellison daughters taunted her about the fact that she had not yet met Mr. Lincoln; and Abigail, with Grafton's taunts ringing in her ears, could hardly leave fast enough. She rode with Dinah, whose coachman, Cutler, kept a shotgun under his seat, for Washington City was thick with criminals, all set to prey on innocent young ladies; or so the Berryhills believed.

The night fog swirled around the carriage, softening the glow from the gas lamps along the avenue. The buildings beyond were hidden by a wall of gray gauze. Here and there they passed a soldier, or a beggar, or a man pushing a cart. The frozen ground was rutted, and the rig bumped and swayed.

"Don't pay any attention to them," said Dinah. "Everybody is proud of you."

"Not everybody."

"You know how the Mellison girls are. They want all the attention, but in that room the conversation was all about you and Mr. Lincoln."

"I know how they are."

"Don't worry," said Dinah, touching her friend's hand. "My parents dined last night at Edgewood, with Senator and Mrs. Sprague." The most sought-after table in Washington City, now that the President no longer entertained. "Senator Sprague assured my father that the President will not be convicted. Even now, negotiations are under way at the highest level. So, you see, all will work out for the best, as it always does."

Abigail refused to be consoled, least of all by a reminder that, in the midst of an impeachment crisis in which the firm that employed her was intimately involved, the Berryhill family had better information about the affairs of Mr. Lincoln than she did. Beneath the blanket, she clenched her fists. She had been made to look a fool, a role she hated at the best of times; but tonight of all nights, when the whole table had been impressed by her employment at the firm that was defending the President that colored America so adored! It had been a deliberate provocation, of course. The Mellison sisters did such things, sometimes out of envy, sometimes for sport, always dripping with malice. She should have known better. She had told Dinah she would rather not attend the dinner, and Dinah had insisted that she go and show off. And now—

"What is that?" said Dinah, suddenly.

"What is what?"

"Behind us."

Abigail craned her neck. Another carriage might have been back there, black and vague in the night fog. "Someone's rig."

"It's following us."

"This is a public street, Dinah. Anybody can use it."

"Nonsense." Even in worry, Dinah was brisk, and in charge. "Nobody would bring so fancy a rig down to this neighborhood." More Washington mythology.

"The Island is no more dangerous than any other part of the city. And, besides, Dinah, your carriage is quite fancy."

"I do not live here. I am dropping you."

"Perhaps he is heading to the ferry."

"At this hour?" Dinah snorted; and said something to the driver, who, touched by the urgency in her voice, picked up the pace. The black carriage fell behind, but whenever Abigail turned to look, she fancied she could discern its wavery lines, and hear the steady clopping of hooves.

CHAPTER 5

Ambition

I

WASHINGTON WAS A modern city, alive with sound: streetcars rattling, horses whinnying, shopkeepers shouting their prices through half-open doors, machinery thudding and pumping in the factories, crowds thronging the avenues in hopes of glimpsing the rich and the powerful in their grand homes, trains rumbling through the middle of town on their way south and then others rumbling north, beggars calling as you passed, builders constructing ever-larger edifices for the government and its departments. At night some parts of the city grew silent, but for the susurration of the gas lamps. In other neighborhoods different sounds were heard, sounds proper to activities that the well-bred avoided: the angry remonstrances of the inebriated, the brassy boister of the illicit clubs, the whispered threats of the gangs, and the softly compelling calls of the streetwalkers. And coiling through it all came the whipping winter wind that rose or fell but never quite faded, winding along the streets, slithering frigidly through cracks into the smallest room of the largest house.

Alive with sound.

The city's separate neighborhoods had their own rhythms. The farms to the north and east awoke to the lowing of cattle and the cries of the roosters. Nearer Capitol Hill, the householders were roused by the sound of wagons brattling to the Eastern and Center Markets for a long day of haggling. Among the shanties of George Town, it was the cries of the junk man and the street peddler; in the retreating forests of Tennally Town, the factory whistles; and in the mansions north of Pennsylvania Avenue, the quiet rapping of a servant at the bedroom door. On the Island, as it was known, the irregular southwest corner of the city, bounded by the Potomac and Anacostia Rivers and the fetid remains of the barge canal to the north, the new day was announced by the bells of the dairy wagon on its rounds, and the clattering of hooves as cabs and horsecars arrived at the Seventh Street Wharf, disgorging passengers and cargo to catch the first ferry of the day over to the Virginia side.

These were the sounds to which Abigail Canner opened her eyes each day, precisely at dawn, unless she had awakened earlier: for it was a peculiarity of her family that the women needed little sleep. Her father, a plumber and bricklayer, had constructed the two-story brick house on Tenth Street, about half a mile south of the towers of the Smithsonian Institution. Several of the better colored families had built nearby, but most of those living on the Island were poor. Now and then the entire house would be jolted from dreams by the thunder of a train rattling off the Long Bridge. Cars moving at that hour almost always carried troops, and Abigail, ever since her return from Oberlin, would lie in her bed, eyes boring into the gray, dreamless dark, hoping against hope that this at last might be the transport bringing Aaron back to her arms.

But it never was.

She would rise from the bed she shared with her younger sister, Louisa, who would groan and snuffle and snatch at the covers. Abigail would sit in the window overlooking the frozen mud of Tenth Street, reading her Bible and saying her morning prayers at the ugly brass tripod table, made in England, of which their late mother had been so proud. Then she would perform her ablutions and dress for work in a satin-and-muslin walking dress. She had several, and never wore anything else to the office, even though Dinah said the outfits made Abigail look like her own grandmother. She would wake Louisa, who did not rise easily, making sure that the child was not late for the carriage that collected her and a few others from the Island for transport to the Quaker Method school near the end of Massachusetts Avenue, just below the Patent Office—which, in some peculiar testament to the changing times, stood on the grand hill set aside, in the original plan of the city, for the federal government's official cathedral.

With Louisa safely launched, Abigail would see to any needs of Nanny Pork, who was likely at the kitchen table, smoking her pipe and glaring disapproval at whatever caught her glance. Thrice a week a silly young thing named Tilly came to clean and cook and lug coal and do the washing, and on those days Abigail would wait until the girl arrived and give her stern instructions, because Nanny liked to take herself off visiting or shopping when Tilly was in the house, leaving her unsupervised. They had already learned to lock up the silver whenever Tilly or any of her predecessors was due. Nanny liked to say that if Tilly stole anything it would serve Abigail right for going off every day to do men's work.

When Nanny finished listing her niece's latest sins and errors, Abigail would leave the house at last, walking three blocks to catch the cars of the Metropolitan Line for the ride to the office. She would march past the familiar houses, now dusted with bright snowy coverlets: there the home of Mr. and Mrs. Amos, who owned a lumberyard down near the wharf; next the dwelling of old Dr. Sandrin, whose credentials to practice medicine were suspect; and finally, at the corner of Seventh Street, the grand mansion of the sisters Quillen, widows of a certain age who nobody believed were actually sisters, or had ever been married— the young ladies of the neighborhood were forbidden to go near them. There were shanties, too, and the dilapidated farmhouses of the penurious, and from these, too, Abigail kept a safe distance, not out of physical fear but out of an ineffable worry that if she did not remain upon the narrow path, she, too, might wind up as an ordinary colored girl.

At Seventh Street, she would queue for the streetcar, along with washerwomen and valets headed to work at the hotels and grand houses north of Pennsylvania Avenue. She sat near the center of the car, and always had a book or two tucked beneath her arm, because, even before Jonathan Hilliman's oddly shamefaced announcement that she would be helping prepare for the impeachment trial, she had grown accustomed to cajoling him into advising her on what she should read. The normal length of an apprenticeship in preparation for the bar was two years, and Abigail supposed it was longer when your reading was surreptitious, and largely unguided by actual lawyers. But her determination never flagged. She had been encouraged by the example of a man named George Vashon, a friend of her mother's family, who was the first negro admitted to the bar of New York, and would have been the first negro admitted in Pennsylvania, too, had the bar of that fine abolitionist state not rewritten its rules to keep negroes out. Vashon spoke half a dozen languages, several of them dead, and in his time he had taught everything from mathematics to literature to philosophy. He had been working with General Oliver O. Howard, known as "the Christian general," at the Freedmen's Bureau, and recently had been appointed as the first professor at the newly opened colored university in Washington, named in Howard's honor. It was Vashon who had suggested to the Canners six years ago that they send their peculiar daughter to Oberlin Collegiate Institute, where he himself had matriculated.

"Do they take girls there?" her father had exclaimed, very surprised: for the great universities of New England did not.

"Sir," said Vashon, with pride, "they are good Christian people. They take everyone."

And so, in 1861, at the age of fifteen, Abigail took the cars for Pittsburgh and then onward to Ohio, a decision taken in equal measure to further her education and to protect her from the war; for in those early days, as defeats mounted, the Union victory was anything but inevitable, and the capital seemed doomed to fall any day. Across America, negroes trembled, and made provisions. They bought guns, they formed protective associations, they tried to erect walls around their families. Children were sent to what the wags called the Deep North. Louisa, ten, went to live with relatives in Boston. Michael was thirteen, apprenticed to a printer and living in Baltimore. Worried that Maryland was not far enough, the Canners found him a position in Syracuse, New York, where George Vashon had briefly practiced law. But Michael, who already had his own way of looking at the world, refused to go.

It was at Oberlin that Abigail met Aaron Yount, who entranced her, and who was himself entranced by Charles Finney's sermons declaring the battle to end slavery a holy war in which every Christian man should enlist. Finney, by that time close to eighty, would raise both fists and shout his righteous fury, looking energetic enough at those moments to join the army himself. And of course he never allowed them to forget that two of John Brown's raiders were Oberlin men. So Aaron went to war, and Abigail returned to Washington to await his return.

And to prepare for the bar: for the head of the Female Department at Oberlin taught her girls that their sex was no barrier to entering the professions.

So now Abigail read. She would sit up at the kitchen table into the late hours, turning the pages in fascination, making notes by the light of the lantern. She read Coke and Blackstone and Chitty and the other great treatise-writers. She had not imagined that there would be so much to take in. At the office each morning, she would slide the borrowed volumes back into their places, then do her sweeping and dusting, all the while waiting for McShane or Jonathan to give her something to do: copy a letter, deliver a package, or visit the Library of Congress to fetch a source not in the firm's collection. While waiting, she would read. If sent on an errand, she would read while bumping along in cab or streetcar. At other times she would sit in the office and listen to the legal arguments, wondering when Dennard would return, and whether she would then be allowed to begin her formal apprenticeship.

Jonathan had made clear that Abigail was expected to continue with her chores, even as she read a bit of law, and did a bit of research. She did not understand why he seemed embarrassed whenever he gave her an assignment. Yesterday she had handed him a short memorandum summarizing the trial of Charles I. She was not entirely sure what relevance might be found in the deposition of an English monarch, but she was sufficiently excited to be part of what was going on that she murmured no dissent. Abigail had never worked so hard in her life. Two nights ago, she had missed dinner at the Berryhills'. Dinah had stopped by the house, thinking her friend must be ill, and had found her bent over her books instead. Angry, Dinah warned Abigail that she was wasting her time with this law nonsense. Whether or not Lincoln was removed from office, Dinah scolded, their lives would go on as before.

"That is not the point," said Abigail.

No, said Dinah. The point was that, if Abigail was not very careful, Octavius Addison would be snatched from under her nose—Octavius being a boring young mortician with a bit of education whose father ran one of Washington City's colored newspapers.

"And?"

"And he will marry one of the Mellison girls rather than you."

"I am betrothed."

But Dinah had already returned to her list of the eligible men of their set who would soon be snatched up, by one of the predatory Mellison girls or some other pretty little shrew: Dinah's term for most of the young colored women they knew, although others might suggest that the term applied best to Dinah herself.

Abigail replied that she had no interest in Octavius or anyone other than her beloved Aaron; that any man who would marry one of the Mellison sisters was hardly worth competing for; and that, in any case, she intended to be a lawyer, and would not be sidetracked by worry over the domestic portion of life. And if a part of her understood that to give too many reasons was often to give no reason at all, another part of her was pleased to mislead even those she loved most, like Dinah or Nanny Pork, resisting any intrusion into the secret shadows of her remarkable mind.

II

On the morning of Friday, February 22, Abigail arrived early as usual, waved cheerily to the policeman guarding the lobby, who knew her by now and waved back, and climbed the stairs to the landing. Since Little was not yet in, she started a fire in the stove, then began sweeping the floor, even though she had already swept it last night. She sang as she worked. She did not particularly enjoy these chores, but they were a good deal easier than those laid upon her strong back by Nanny Pork; and if menial work proved the price of her advancement in the law, she would perform it with joy. For, as Nanny also said, no road worth traveling was smooth.

Abigail had just settled at the table to resume her study of Blackstone when a heavy rapping drew her to the door.

In the hallway stood Mr. Plum, the nervous, middle-aged legal secretary and copyist from Grafton's firm down on the first floor, who sometimes did small tasks for Dennard & McShane. Plum was fluttery and disordered at best, and just now was not at his best.

"Oh dear," he said, eyes smeary behind smudged spectacles. "Oh dear." Wringing his hands. "Oh, there you are!" he cried, as if she had been lost for many months. Then he turned and shouted down the stairs: "She is here! I found her!"

"Who is out there, Mr. Plum?" asked Abigail, quite thrown. "What is the matter?"

"Mr. Hilliman sent me to find you."

"I am where I always am at this hour."

Poor Plum could not meet her gaze. His hands were trembling, and he shuffled his feet like a schoolboy. "You'd better get down to the carriage, Miss Canner," he said. "Something has happened." A nervous pause. "Something bad."

CHAPTER 6

Inspector

I

THE BODIES HAD been found outside a colored brothel operated by one Sophia Harbour, also known as Madame Sophie, at 489 Third Street, in the shadow of the Capitol with its grand new dome. *Bodies*, plural, because Mr. Arthur McShane did not die alone. He was found with a young colored woman. Inspector Varak acquainted Jonathan and Abigail, in perhaps more detail than necessary, with the bloodthirsty nature of the offense. *Sliced up*, he kept saying. *Your friend was sliced up.*

And wanted to know who might have done such a thing.

Jonathan confessed, shivering, that he had no idea. Abigail, sitting beside him, looked gray-faced and stricken. Jonathan had no words of comfort to offer. He had been in battle. He had charged the Confederate works at Petersburg, and watched men beside him blown to bits. He had shivered and wept. He had never known a man, or a woman, to be *sliced up*. He was angry and frightened, and wanted to see the body, but the inspector would not let him go to the morgue: *Not really your job, son. More the sort of thing for family.*

The police were headquartered in a small brick building not far from the prison for high Confederate officials, near the Capitol. The fetid room where Varak asked his questions was in a corner of one of the basements. The murder, as the inspector had already noted, took place just a few short blocks from the Bannerman residence.

"Have any enemies at all, your Mr. McShane?"

"Not to my knowledge."

The inspector turned to Abigail, who murmured a negative.

"A friendly sort of man? Gruff? Describe him for me." Tapping his pen impatiently on his desk. "It's just that I haven't a picture of him at all."

Jonathan pondered how to explain his employer's simple likability, his gregariousness, his way of guessing what you were thinking before you knew it yourself; his encyclopedic knowledge of obscure precedents from the British common law, and his easy familiarity with the Law Latin and the Law French. Jonathan wanted to put this into words, but all he managed was "Mr. McShane was an outstanding lawyer."

"Was he, then?"

"Yes. A great legal mind." Varak was proving difficult to impress. "One of the finest."

"Everyone liked him," blurted Abigail, one of the few sentences she had uttered since entering the room.

"Not everyone," said the inspector, writing hard. Abigail blushed. Varak moistened a sausagy finger, turned a page. He was a broad, bluff man, mighty chest all but popping the brass buttons of his blue jacket. Shaggy brown locks hid a weathered, exhausted face, and Jonathan had the impression, the way one did around certain men, that he had done something heroic in the war. "Tell me again when you saw him last."

"Around six in the evening."

"Yesterday evening. Thursday."

"Yes."

"He was off to a meeting."

"Yes."

"What sort of meeting?"

"I'm not really sure."

Varak stopped writing. His eyes were bulbous, and ready to disbelieve every word out of Jonathan's mouth, or Abigail's. "You are his law clerk."

"Yes."

He turned to Abigail. "And you?"

"I have the honor to be employed as a clerk for Mr. Dennard, his partner."

"Currently out of town."

"Yes."

Varak's podgy eyes moved from one face to the other. "And neither of you knows where Mr. McShane was going?"

"No."

"But you can hazard a guess, can't you?" Addressing himself to Jonathan. "You're an intelligent young man. Been at Yale, or so they tell me. I would imagine you've been considering nothing else since you heard the news."

Water was dripping somewhere. In the hallway a man laughed huskily. Jonathan spread his hands. He wanted out of the airless room. "Mr. McShane is a lawyer. Was. He drafted contracts, tried cases—whatever his clients needed. I have no idea on which client's behalf he was working yesterday."

Those huge eyes held Jonathan's for another second or two, then dropped once more to the page. "But he was working for only one client these days, so they tell me. I very much doubt he would have run off to draft a contract when he had a President to defend." Before either could answer, Varak shifted his attention to Abigail, his look appraising. "Or maybe there wasn't any client. Maybe his only meeting was with, say, this negress"—he peered at his notes—"this Rebecca Deveaux. Negotiating the price of her services, say."

Jonathan could not restrain himself. "You cannot be serious."

"Why? Do you think Miss Deveaux provided services to your friend Mr. McShane for free?"

"No, but—"

"Then I would say we've solved the mystery of where and with whom your Mr. McShane was meeting yesterday evening."

Before Jonathan could come up with a suitable response to this terrible calumny, Abigail interrupted.

"Has it been established that Miss Deveaux was indeed a prostitute?"

Varak's heavy eyes burned. "Are you presuming to tell me my business?"

Abigail's voice was as submissive as Jonathan had ever heard it. "I would never do that, sir. It's just that, if Miss Deveaux was not a prostitute, then it is possible that the meeting had another purpose."

"She was a prostitute," said the inspector, closing the matter. He turned another page. His next question, asked without so much as a lift of the heavy head, took them by surprise. "Benjamin Wade. Benjamin Wade is who, please?"

"Do you mean Senator Wade?" said Jonathan. "Senator Benjamin Wade from Ohio?"

Varak's eyes moved greedily. "I don't mean anyone in particular."

"Senator Wade is leader of the Radicals."

"And the Radicals would be who, then, please?"

Jonathan glanced at Abigail. He kept expecting her to stun Varak with her brilliance, the way she stunned Jonathan himself. But she was looking at the stained floor, her fists balled tightly, her chin tucked against her neck, a pose he had seen from time to time in civilians who survived the battle. He wanted to offer a smile of encouragement, but that was impossible if she never looked his way.

"Who, please?" said the inspector, tapping the paper impatiently. "The Radicals."

"The Radicals," said Jonathan, too didactically, "are a wing of the Republican Party. The President's own party, but they despise him. They're trying to get rid of him. Surely you have read about it in the papers."

"A lot of people despise this President. A couple of them have tried their hand at doing away with him." He scribbled a note, turned another page. "I seem to recall that the late Vice-President might have been involved in one of those plots."

"That was a complete fabrication—"

Inspector Varak was not even interested. "And why would these Radicals of yours hate the President so much?"

"The conduct of the war, for one thing. And his policy—"

"Opposing Mr. Lincoln's war hardly makes a man a radical." An echoing laugh, surprisingly hearty in the dank little room. "Everyone with any sense was against it. Whole thing was completely unnecessary. None of our business what the South does with its negroes." He shook that heavy head, glanced at Abigail, then back at his book. "Half a million or more dead because of Abraham Lincoln's vanity and lies."

Abigail's head came back up, but she said nothing. Jonathan chose to challenge only the inspector's implicit minor premise. "No, no, the Radicals thought the President's war policy insufficiently energetic."

"He crushed the South, slaughtered its young men, burned their homes, and confiscated its slaves." Varak's voice was perfectly calm. "I understand the Union soldiers even melted down the railroad tracks when they weren't busy helping themselves to all the silver and gold they could steal. That wasn't energetic enough for your Mr. Wade and his Radicals?"

Again Jonathan hesitated. The conversation had taken an absurd turn. He wanted to correct the inspector, who had evidently been reading the pro-Southern broadsheets. But Varak, like Lincoln himself, projected an air of competence that made one want to assist him in his inquiries.

"They object to his policy toward the defeated states," Jonathan explained. "The Radicals believe the South should be treated as a conquered territory. Mr. Lincoln considers the Southern states to be our wayward brothers. Inspector, please. I was not being serious. I am sure that the Radicals had nothing to do with—"

Varak waved him silent. "I shouldn't worry, Mr. Hilliman. Your friend Mr. McShane was sliced open with a prostitute at his side. Whoever did the deed took the time to slice her open as well. These are violent times, Mr. Hilliman. I shouldn't think it has anything to do with politics."

But in Washington City during those sullen gray years after the war, everything had to do with politics. And so the newspapers, lately starved for scandal, dutifully exploited the crime. "President's Lawyer Is Stabbed to Death," said an anti-Lincoln sheet. "Lincoln's Ally Dead with Negress," said another. But the Republican press was scarcely better, omitting only the political connection: "Lawyer, Prostitute Murdered." Jonathan wondered how Lincoln and his staff had reacted to the news; and who would now advise the President in the impeachment inquiry.

Certainly his own days on the case, and Abigail's, were likely at an end, given that Dennard had opposed the firm's involvement from the start.

Abigail surprised them both by speaking up. "Inspector, may I ask a question?"

The huge eyes looked interested. Not in the question. In the species: a negress who thought for herself.

"Please," he said.

"You said that Mr. McShane and Miss Deveaux were found on the sidewalk outside the brothel."

"That is correct."

"Do you happen to know whether they were on their way into the building, or on their way out?"

Varak's forehead creased. With irritation. "What possible difference does that make?"

"I was just wondering," said Abigail, meekly.

The inspector gave her a long, searching policeman's stare, the sort of look that was supposed to make you confess on the spot, then turned his attention back to Jonathan. "You asked why I raised the name of Benjamin Wade. Look at this." From his desk he drew a wrinkled envelope, slit open at knife point. A brown stain might have been blood. *Sliced up.* He turned it over. "Happen to recognize the handwriting at all, do we?"

"No," said Jonathan.

"No," said Abigail, after a spooky pause.

"Any idea what might have been *in* the envelope?"

Jonathan shook his head. "I'm afraid I've never seen it before."

"Pity. We found it just like this, beside McShane's body. Bloody odd of them to leave it behind, don't you think?"

Jonathan might have nodded. He might have argued. He might have done a lot of things, had he not been staring at the inscription on the outside, in spiky handwriting he did not recognize:

For Mr. Benjamin Wade
Personal and Confidential

"Bloody odd," Varak repeated, and, with a rough, angry shove, slid the envelope back into his desk.

II

From the police headquarters on Capitol Hill, they rode up to Nineteenth Street to pay a call on Mrs. McShane and express condolences. Abigail seemed shrunken and distracted. She insisted on waiting in the carriage. At the door, the maid told Jonathan that the widow was not receiving at this time, and that he should return tomorrow. Now, heading back to the firm's offices, he turned to Abigail.

"I'm sorry," he said. "You should not have been there."

"It was I who insisted."

"Still."

"You are kind, Jonathan, but you need not worry about me. I know you have your own grieving to which to attend."

They rode along in silence for a bit. The winter sun was bright but cheerless. With Arthur McShane gone, Jonathan was possessed of a sudden longing to quit this sad little city. He should marry Meg and go back to Rhode Island, which was where in any event she wanted to go. She despised Washington society, as did nearly everyone not from Washington. Jonathan had come to the city because his late father and McShane had been good friends, and because Uncle Brighton, who nowadays ran the family business, thought his nephew should learn the law before taking the reins. Meg considered the whole thing a detour, and also suspected that Brighton was robbing the business blind, but Jonathan was not the sort of man who turned easily once his path was chosen.

In that sense, at least, Abigail seemed a kindred spirit.

Finally, he said, "There is no need to go to the office. If you would like, I can take you home."

"No, thank you. I have work to do."

A streetcar passed, horses struggling on the icy cobbles. Unfriendly eyes burned their way. Jonathan wondered whether passersby considered the two of them a couple.

"You do realize that we are unlikely to continue representing the President in this matter."

She lifted her chin. "Until we are discharged, however, we should continue as we began, should we not?"

About to argue, Jonathan decided to let the matter drop. Dennard's views were plain, but if Abigail wanted to postpone accepting that truth until the lawyer returned from the West Coast, he saw no reason to disabuse her.

He said, "Our response is due on Tuesday." When Abigail did not reply, he continued. "Mr. McShane was supposed to go to the Senate today with Mr. Speed to request more time to answer the charges." Still she would not rise. "I imagine that Mr. Speed can do that alone. He is the attorney general of the United States, after all."

"Yes," she said, vaguely.

"Why did you ask that question? You asked Inspector Varak whether they were . . . killed . . . going into the brothel or coming out. Why does that matter?"

Abigail was a while answering. They stopped at Seventh Street while a train passed, bringing passengers and produce from the South to the depot of the Baltimore and Potomac line. Acrid gray smoke made their eyes water. Faces glared from the windows. None looked happy to be arriving in Washington City.

"I was testing a theory," she said.

"And what theory is that?"

"That the inspector is not really investigating the case." She closed her eyes. "His inability to answer my simple question suggests that I am correct."

Jonathan was appalled. "Why wouldn't he be investigating the case?"

But Abigail only shook her head, and then, suddenly, straightened. "I have changed my mind. I shall get out here."

"I beg your pardon."

"I will catch the horsecars. I am going home."

"I can take you—"

"I need to be alone." She touched his hand, briefly, with gloved fingers. "We both do."

III

Jonathan returned to the offices on Fourteenth Street and barricaded himself inside with Mr. Plum, whom he scooped up from Grafton's office on his own authority. He had Little guard the door, because the police officers below—in light of events, there were now two—were letting too many reporters slip past. To Plum, he dictated a telegram to Rufus Dennard, McShane's partner. Dennard had been away in the West this past month, trolling for railroad business, because nowadays no firm could grow without any. Jonathan's telegram urged Dennard's immediate return. Plum wrung slender hands. The wires were down, he said. Jonathan asked how he knew. They were always down, Plum explained, desperately. He had previously worked as a clerk in the War Department, said Plum, and knew sabotage when he saw it. The rebels, no question. They'd been hiding out for the past year and a half in the Shenandoah Valley, and now they were emerging, getting ready to isolate the capital again, the way they did back in '61, and the best thing for all concerned might be to pack our bags and head for—

Jonathan shushed the poor man, reassured him, and sent him on his way to the telegraph office.

Alone again, Jonathan paged through each of the city's half dozen or so daily newspapers, but learned nothing he had not learned the first time. *Sliced up.* The newspapers loved that detail. Full of energy, he roamed the suite. He realized that he should have sent Plum with a note to the White House, too. To Speed. Or perhaps to Stanton. It occurred to him that he did not know precisely who was in charge. The others surely knew that Mr. Lincoln's response was due on Tuesday, but they had been expecting McShane to take the lead. As far as Jonathan knew, there were no files or memoranda for tomorrow. At least, he had not been told to write any. He was not sure precisely what his responsibilities were.

Jonathan stood at the window, looking down at the crowd looking up. He felt alone, and cold, and unhappy, the office alive with neither McShane's air of acerbic dismissal nor Abigail's constant argumentative chatter.

He tried to work out why McShane would have been carrying an envelope addressed to the hated Senator Wade. Perhaps he wanted to meet to discuss the procedures for the trial—but then why make the letter confidential? Why risk carrying it to a brothel? So perhaps matters were the other way around, and McShane had been conveying a secret offer from his client. The Democratic papers had been hinting for a year that Mr. Lincoln planned to resign his office and retire to Illinois. Perhaps he was bargaining to do just that.

But the brothel. The brothel was the strangest part of all. If ever a man adored his wife, it was Arthur McShane. Jonathan was no fool. He could hardly have attended school in New Haven without gaining a proper appreciation for the fleshy side of life and for the variety of places where a variety of men sought their pleasures outside of marriage. Yet he could not imagine—

"Mister Jonathan?"

He started, and turned. Little stood in the doorway.

"Sir, you has a visitor."

Almost before the words were out of the black man's mouth, a woman's form brushed past him.

Jonathan gaped in surprise, but swiftly found a smile.

Margaret Felix. His Meg. His fiancée.

IV

Meg was broad and tough and deliberate. Every movement of her soft body exuded a winning confidence: you knew at first glance that she would accomplish whatever she set her mind to. Margaret Felix took after her father, the famous General Hiram Felix, the Lion of Louisiana, who had taken over the war in the West after Lincoln reassigned

Grant to Virginia. Her alabaster skin glowed with energy. Her eyes were a cool, determined green. She offered a quick hug and a formal, delicate kiss, and he noticed her mammy in the hallway.

"I wish to extend my condolences," Meg announced in her clear, military voice. "Otherwise, I would not disturb your work."

Her father's schedule had changed, so the two of them had taken the cars last night, Meg continued: for she had a way of answering questions not yet asked. They were staying at Aunt Clara's, on Eighth Street, as she had told him they would. She had wanted to surprise him. But now, she said, wanted instead to reassure him.

"Father and I must return to Philadelphia on Sunday. Will you dine with us tomorrow? Pleasant company will surely help you to put all of this unpleasantness out of your mind."

And as Margaret Felix murmured and answered and questioned, it became clear to Jonathan that her principal intention was making sure that the events of last night, as she kept calling them, would not lead somehow to the postponing of the wedding, now set for October.

As for Jonathan, he did what he could to reassure her in turn, but Meg was raising questions he had not yet thought to consider. Contemplating a future without his mentor, Jonathan found himself unable to sit still. Did McShane's partner, Dennard, even plan to keep the practice open? Meg asked, matching her fiancé's stride as he paced through the rooms. Did Jonathan intend to continue in the law? Was there perhaps a chance that he might go back to New England to work in the family business? She was asking, secretly, if they might leave the swampy waste where a young and confusing nation had chosen eighty years previously to establish its capital, and go north, to the swirl of grand houses and colossal entertainments that marked the life that she imagined his family led.

"I don't know," he answered, over and over.

Some women become angry or teary when they fail to gain their ends; as do some men. Margaret Felix, daughter of the celebrated Lion, was of neither sort. She simply grew more adamant. Meg accused her beau, from time to time, of drifting indecisively through life, meaning that he did not reach decisions as rapidly and confidently as she—at least not the right decisions. For a Felix, a bad plan was better than having no plan. Margaret was nineteen years old, and Jonathan was fairly certain that even their coming marriage, although the nervous proposal was entirely his, had been a plan entirely of hers.

"You must decide, Jonathan," she announced now. They were standing in McShane's office, with its view down Fourteenth Street. "New England and business, or Washington City and law. You cannot let this matter linger."

"I have to know what happened," he said, surprising himself with his resolve, although the statement was, in fact, the simple truth. "To Mr. McShane."

Meg pursed her lips, then took him firmly by the upper arm and drew him back to the common room. She lifted the top newspaper from the unruly stack, thrust it into his hand, and pointed to the headline: *Fatal Stabbing Outside Bawdy House. Lincoln's Lawyer Dead.*

"That's what happened," she said.

CHAPTER 7

Visitor

I

ABIGAIL ARRIVED FOR work on Saturday morning an hour earlier than usual, for she still felt guilty about having gone home the afternoon before. A frigid wind came off the Potomac. Outside the building, the policeman was stamping his feet to keep warm. Yesterday, the Senate had grudgingly granted the President's counsel an additional week and a half to answer the charges. Trial would now begin on Monday, March 18, and run for two to three weeks. And Abigail, until formally told otherwise, intended to continue her research.

She hurried upstairs and opened the door. But as soon as she stepped inside, she noticed two oddities. First, the gas lamp was on in the main room. Second, there were heavy sounds emanating from the private office of the late Arthur McShane.

She froze. McShane's door was closed. She could go down to the street and summon the policeman, but then she would likely risk embarrassment before the white race, which she feared above all things. Most likely Jonathan had simply arrived early; or Little was cleaning. She forced herself to move. No miscreant could possibly be inside. The policeman would have stopped him.

She did not ask herself why, as she crossed the anteroom, she stooped to grab the poker from the fireplace, or why she tiptoed over the floor. She shoved the door open. Peering inside, she was stunned to see a stranger, a slender man with clever moustaches, seated at McShane's desk, prying at an open drawer with a knife.

"What are you doing?" she cried. Her fingers tightened on the weapon. "Who are you?"

The stranger glanced up. He looked to be close to fifty. He had a broad, magnetic face and dark, ingenuous eyes. He wore an expensive suit, and was smoking what appeared to be one of Mr. McShane's cigars. He seemed quite unbothered to have been caught. He had evidently dumped the contents of the desk all over the floor. He nodded toward her hand. "Planning a criminal assault? Grievous bodily harm?"

"Who are you?" she repeated.

"Because, if you are planning to strike me with that thing, I would clean up the mess first if I were you." The stranger glanced around the room, bushy eyebrows moving, his distaste evident. His face was narrow and disciplined, a soldier's face, but the luxurious black moustaches softened the hard edges, and an infectious hint of smile danced between pinched cheeks. "Or you could just lend me a hand."

Abigail needed a moment; as, in the future, she would often need a moment around this man.

"You are breaking into Mr. McShane's desk," she said, a bit stupidly. She stepped back. "I am going to summon the police."

The stranger shook a shaggy head.

"I'm not breaking in. Somebody did that already." He was back to his prying. When he saw that Abigail continued to brandish the poker, he sighed, and straightened, and that was when she noticed for the first time his wooden leg. "Put the poker down. I'm not the man who did this."

"That is not precisely as it appears to me," she said, nervousness making her syntax over-perfect.

"And how, precisely, does it appear to you?"

"That you have been searching for something. That I have surprised you. That you have assumed this pose of innocence hoping to fool me."

The stranger puffed on his cigar. "Sorry to disappoint you, Miss Canner, but I'm afraid I arrived and found it this way."

"How do you know my name?" she asked, astonished.

"The President sent me. I am to assist in his defense." With an easy, languid sweep, he swung his stump from atop the chair. He had a long, fancy walking stick, something between a cane and a crutch, the support of a man who was clever and confident, who wanted you to know he could beat anything on two legs in a duel. He had even done it. Before the visitor identified himself, Abigail already knew whom she was facing. "I'm Dan Sickles."

II

Abigail stared. For once, she had no idea what to say. So this was Daniel Sickles, lawyer and rake, the most elegant scoundrel of the age. Dan Sickles, who eight years ago had shot to death his wife's lover in broad daylight, quite close to the White House, in front of innumerable witnesses, and was acquitted. Dan Sickles, who had served the Union with honor as a major general, had lost a leg to a cannonball at Gettysburg, and somehow arrived back in the capital as a hero, although in truth he had disobeyed orders and nearly lost the battle for the North.

Dan Sickles, one of Mr. Lincoln's most trusted friends.

Dan Sickles, the famous villain whom many of the young men of Abigail's circle secretly envied for his daring, and his success. Abigail herself considered the man a murderer, but saw no point in saying so. Indeed, so great was her continuing surprise that the next words out of her mouth sounded, even to her own ear, bizarre.

"You should put the cigar out."

Sickles was standing at the window, looking down into Fourteenth Street. He balanced rather well on the wooden leg; it was the getting to his feet that was difficult. He took the cigar from his mouth, examined it, put it back, puffed. "Why?" he finally asked.

"The cigars belong to Mr. McShane," she said. But she lowered the poker.

The general considered this. He picked up a book from the shelf—a Bible, as it happened. Biblical quotes worked well with the young nation's judges, especially with a man like Salmon P. Chase serving as Chief Justice. Chase quoted Scripture constantly. As Treasury secretary a few years ago, he had placed the motto IN GOD WE TRUST on the coinage. "Will the cigars be buried with him?" asked Sickles.

"I would expect not."

"Does the widow smoke?"

"I don't believe so."

"Then I doubt I'm doing any harm." He took the cigar out of his mouth, examined the broad end, flicked a bit of ash onto the worn blue carpet, then began puffing again. "Unless you plan to preserve the cigars for the monument to be constructed in your employer's honor." Another glance at the window, perhaps indicating the ugly uncompleted obelisk south of the White House, intended as a monument to the nation's first President. "Your employer had very good taste," said Sickles. A pause. "Except in women."

"I'm sure I don't know what you mean," said Abigail, stiffly.

"I most certainly was not referring to you, Miss Canner." His contagious smile was a bright surprise. "That would change my evaluation, I assure you."

While Abigail struggled to work through all the implications of his impertinence, Sickles, not without difficulty, sat down once more. "I suppose you heard that Speed got us more time. With Lincoln's lawyer dead, I don't see that the Senators had much of a choice. Not that they care about whether they're fair or not, but to say no just wouldn't look good back home." He patted his pockets. "Now, Miss Canner. Are you going to help me or not?"

"Help you what?"

"Break into McShane's desk."

She blinked. She felt oddly dull. "You said you didn't do that."

"I lied. You were holding a poker, and I didn't particularly want to get hit." He was pressing his knife into the drawer again. His charm had caused her to forget for a moment that he had killed a man in cold blood. "There's some kind of false bottom. We need to see what's underneath it."

"Mr. Sickles, I hardly think—"

"Ouch," he said, having stubbed his finger.

Abigail managed to rouse herself from her torpor. "Please tell me what you are looking for."

Sickles looked at her. "They say you're the smart one."

"I beg your pardon."

The general twirled his moustache. "I am looking for an item that Mr. Lincoln delivered to his lawyer for safekeeping. I would need Mr. Lincoln's permission to tell you more than that. But that doesn't mean you can't help me find it." He pointed. "I assume you have the combination to that safe."

"Only Jonathan—Mr. Hilliman has it."

"Well, then, I hope you're better at burglary than I am."

"Mr. Sickles!"

"A joke, Miss Canner. A poor one. I apologize." He bent to the desk, motioned her over. "Where I grew up, everybody knew how to burgle."

Abigail hesitated, but only for a moment. Her mind worked with a speed that was sometimes frightening. Sickles she sized up at a glance: never trust him, except to protect his friends. The best sort of friend to have in a fight. Dinah Berryhill was like that, too—she had spent her life lying her way out of one mess, then lying her way into another, but Abigail knew that Dinah would never abandon her. If that was what Sickles was to Lincoln, then, however distasteful she might find the man, she was prepared to help him in any way she could.

"Tell me what to do," she said.

III

After they broke two knife blades trying to pry open the secret compartment, Abigail suggested that they look instead for a knob or toggle. Sickles eyed her. "That's a little obvious, don't you think?"

Nevertheless, they swiftly found the switch, mounted beneath the drawer, and, when they pulled it, the panel snapped back.

Inside was a sheaf of papers and a brown envelope. Sickles glanced at the papers and shoved them aside, then peeked into the envelope, and stuffed it in his breast pocket.

"Excellent," he said.

"What is it?"

"What Mr. Lincoln sent me to find." Again he toyed with the moustache. "Don't give me that look, Miss Canner. We are down to the last few votes, and the trial hasn't even started yet. I assume you heard that Nebraska became a state yesterday? So that's where we are. Not a single piece of evidence has been placed forward, and there are thirty-one Senators ready to convict. They only need three more votes."

"We have been . . . keeping track."

"And do you wish Mr. Lincoln to be convicted?"

"Of course not!"

"Good. Because I understand that you want to be a lawyer. Well, you are going to have to learn that nothing is more important than protecting your clients."

She nodded toward a book on the shelf. Jonathan had recommended it, but Abigail had found time to read only ten or twelve pages. "In the introduction to his treatise on ethics, Mr. Curran De Bruler says that a lawyer's highest duty is not to his client but to the public whom the bar serves."

"Then Mr. Curran De Bruler is a fool. If you decide that a lawyer's highest duty isn't to his clients, pretty soon you'll lose your clients to somebody who decides it is." Heading for the door, he eyed the mess. "As I said, I really think you should clean the place. Tell Dennard I'll be by later."

"Mr. Dennard is in California."

"No, he's here. He arrived in town yesterday. Didn't anybody tell you?" A laugh, low and affectionate. "Well, don't worry about it. Nobody tells anybody anything in this town. If they did, everybody would be in jail."

He was gone.

Abigail looked around the room, then stopped and, as Sickles had suggested, began to clear the papers he had strewn about the floor. She studied them closely, trying not to wonder what was in the envelope he had taken from the drawer. Her admiration of Mr. Lincoln was too great for her to take seriously the possibility that he might be concealing evidence. And it occurred to her, as she fetched the broom to begin sweeping up the chips of wood thrown off by all the prying, that the entire episode was too obvious. Precisely because she did not know what might have been in the envelope, she did not know for sure that it was important. It was peculiar indeed that she should have happened on Dan Sickles at precisely the right moment to catch him in the act of jimmying the drawer. She wondered what he was really looking for, and why he was so interested in the safe. And she reminded herself that Lincoln's own reputation as "Honest Abe" said nothing about the veracity of his friends.

CHAPTER 8

Widow

I

THAT SAME SATURDAY morning, Jonathan Hilliman called again upon Mr. McShane's widow, Virginia—a most unfortunate name with which to be saddled during the conflict. The McShanes lived on K Street near Nineteenth, halfway between the President's House and the outskirts of the city proper. Beyond their house were the canal, several belts of trees, and George Town, with its rows of shanties for the negroes and poor whites. Mrs. McShane was a tiny woman. Seated in the dark parlor of her home, draped in enough black crepe to cover a catafalque, she blended into the shadows. Even squinting Jonathan barely was able to pick her out. She sat very still, a bird seeking cover. Friends and relatives fluttered round her like avian bodyguards. He apologized for the inconvenience, but before he could finish his condolences, Virginia McShane launched upon a discourse. Her husband had been a good man, said Mrs. McShane; a man of kindness and decency. It was his decency that had drawn him to the law. He had studied for the ministry before deciding to read for the bar. He had served as a vestryman at Saint John's Episcopal Church, just north of the Executive Mansion, where Mr. Lincoln occasionally attended services. Her husband would never have consorted with a fallen woman, Mrs. McShane insisted, and had never visited a bawdy house in his life.

Jonathan had not intended to discuss the murder itself, but now that the widow had brought it up, he thought he might proceed, delicately, down that road. And so he began by asking Mrs. McShane whether she had any idea why her husband had been in the neighborhood.

She did not.

He asked whether her husband had received any mysterious messages or strange callers in the days before the attack.

"I would scarcely know," she said.

He asked whether she knew Miss Rebecca Deveaux, the negro woman who had been murdered alongside her Arthur.

Mrs. McShane sniffed.

He asked if she had any idea how her husband might have known Miss Deveaux.

Not for nothing was Virginia McShane a lawyer's wife. "I was not aware," she said, "that it has been established that they knew each other."

Jonathan had not considered this point, and said nothing. But he tied what a professor of his at Yale used to call a knot in the strands of thought, a place to climb back to later, when time allowed.

Furthermore—said Mrs. McShane—until it *was* established by what she called, correctly, competent evidence, she saw no reason to presume that this Miss Deveaux had anything to do with her husband.

"You tell them that," she commanded.

So he did.

Inspector Varak was dismissive. "Wives," he muttered, with the angry certainty of one who had endured long and perhaps bitter experience with the species.

Half the men in the city visited those houses, the inspector said, hardly looking up from his desk, and every wife would swear on a stack of Bibles that her husband was in the other half. Look at Bishop Richmond, the inspector went on, referring to an embarrassing episode involving a prominent preacher, an important political supporter of Mr. Lincoln, who had come to town at the height of the war promising to clean up the bawdy houses, and left in disgrace after exposure of his filthy love letters to a Treasury Department clerk.

"Do you know which half Mr. McShane fell into?" Jonathan inquired, as ingenuously as he knew how, which was not very.

"The res is rather ipsa on the loquitur," said Varak, the mangled Latin proposing that he knew his guest for an educated man. Realizing that he had misfired, the inspector shuffled papers and tried again. "Believe me, Mr. Hilliman, I would be happy to fix this if I could. I don't like troubling the widow any more than you do. But there's nothing I can do. Your Mr. McShane was stabbed on the pavement outside Sophia Harbour's place. He was with one of Madame Sophie's girls. A child could draw the inference."

Jonathan asked how he knew that Rebecca Deveaux was one of Sophia's girls. The inspector said he just knew.

"Did you interview Madame Sophie?"

"Madame Sophie is indisposed."

"Did you interview the other girls?" Receiving no answer, Jonathan pressed. He imagined Abigail at his side, tried to ask what she would ask. "What about Miss Deveaux's friends? She must have some, mustn't she? Or her family? Have you interviewed them?"

The weathered face reddened. His meaty hands formed huge fists atop the cluttered blotter. Jonathan looked at those hands and reminded himself that he was a Hilliman. The inspector would not dare strike him. "Are you telling me how to do my job?"

"No, sir, but—"

"Then be so good as to accept what I am telling you. Good day, Mr. Hilliman."

II

"Dennard didn't care," said Jonathan. "That was the strangest part. He and McShane were not only partners but very close friends, and yet Dennard was all but in frothing furies when he learned I'd been back to see the policeman. As much as ordered me to leave the murder alone and tend to business."

In the opposite chair, Fielding Bannerman swirled his brandy. "But he did say you'll be continuing the representation of the President, I take it?"

Jonathan nodded. He was in evening attire, on his way shortly to the home of Meg's aunt Clara for dinner. "Funny. I thought we were done. Two of the firm's biggest clients sent telegrams, regretting the untimely death and so on, and adding that they assumed that politics would no longer serve as an obstacle to their representation."

"In other words, telling Dennard to drop the case."

"He showed some pluck, I must say." Jonathan took another small sip. He was pacing himself, not wanting to dine with Meg and her father while unfortified, but not wanting his fortification to be too obvious. "He never wanted the firm to take on Mr. Lincoln as a client, and I don't think he wanted to continue. But he went over to the White House this morning, and the President talked him into it." He shut his eyes briefly. "I wish we had more time. The Senate only gave us an extra week and a half."

"So trial starts when? Three weeks? Is that enough time for Dennard to prepare?"

"We don't have a choice. The great Thaddeus Stevens rose from his sickbed to go down to the Capitol and explain why the nation cannot afford another month of the tyrant Lincoln."

"Didn't know that old fossil was still alive. Stevens." Fielding topped up the glasses. "Does he still have that colored wife?"

"She isn't his wife exactly."

"Right. Not *exactly*." A tipsy laugh. "Is that what you are planning to argue about the Department of the Atlantic? That Mr. Lincoln's plan for military government in Washington did not *exactly* comprehend the overthrow of the Congress?"

"There was never any such plan!"

"Makes no difference to me either way." Another long swallow. This was by far the most serious allegation against Lincoln: that he had planned to impose martial law on the nation's capital. The allegations concerning the Department of the Atlantic might have made no difference to Fielding Bannerman, but they mattered enormously to the Congress. "Funny. With McShane gone, the finest trial lawyer in the country is already in the Administration."

"Stanton."

"Precisely. Stanton got Sickles off when he shot Mr. Barton Key in front of twenty witnesses. I'd have thought he'd resign as Secretary of War to defend Lincoln in the Senate. Dennard, I'm sure, is an excellent lawyer. But he's no Stanton. So why isn't Stanton part of the defense team?"

"I assume that the President finds him more valuable where he is."

"Or else . . ." Fielding trailed off. For him, all of life, especially in Washington City, was machination and double-dealing.

"Or else what?" asked Jonathan.

"Well, Stanton controls the army. With Seward out of the picture, he controls both the Secret Service and the federal police."

"So?"

"So . . . I wonder what would happen if Stanton and Lincoln ever had a falling out." And he took a long swallow.

III

"Knew McShane a bit," said the Lion of Louisiana between mouthfuls of roasted beef. He chewed hard and methodically, the way he did everything. "We served together in the war." One reason Hiram Felix's soldiers loved him was his effortless leveling. Most general officers would say of a subordinate, "He served under me"—but not General Felix. "Good man. Full of energy, and loved the Union. Well, we all do, don't we?"

"I'm sure we do, sir," Jonathan answered dutifully. He felt Margaret's attention tauten. Had she caught something in her father's tone that he had missed? Dinner was just the three of them. Aunt Clara had absented herself for the evening.

"My condolences," said the Lion. "Been to see the widow. She's in bad shape. Well, I suppose one would expect that. Husband dead, found with that woman. The negress."

"Rebecca Deveaux."

"That's the one." General Felix's meaty fist pummeled the air in triumph. A servant, misinterpreting the gesture, advanced to pour more wine, and was ordered testily away. The general's glare was murderous, but when he turned back to the table, his expression was calm, or as calm as it ever was. He was broad-shouldered and powerful and had been widely quoted during the war to the effect that he loved the fighting and killing. He had led the attack that captured Port Hudson, Louisiana, the Confederacy's last redoubt on the Mississippi River. After the fall of Louisiana, the outcome of the war was foreordained, as General Felix's acolytes in the press had been reminding the nation ever since. The same acolytes had given him his nickname: Ulysses Grant was the Lion of Vicksburg, so Hiram Felix became the Lion of Louisiana. "Right. Yes. Deveaux. I remember. Wainwright tells me she was a hooker. I beg your pardon, Meg. But a hooker. That right, Hilliman?"

"Actually, sir, I gather the investigation is still in an early—"

"You're not offended, are you, Hilliman? Man to man. By the word, I mean. 'Hooker.' That's what she was, wasn't she? What would you prefer that I call her? What's the polite word, Meg? My little Margaret wants me to be more polite."

"A woman of easy virtue," Margaret murmured, eyes downcast.

"I like 'hooker' better," said General Felix, dipping his head to take a sip of water. " 'Prostitute' is a silly word, 'woman of easy virtue' is worse. Let's call her what she is. Was. Never knew McShane inclined that way."

Jonathan was about to answer, but Margaret kicked him, hard, beneath the table. Arguing with the Lion of Louisiana was like charging an enemy battalion, alone. Meg preferred that her fiancé keep his silence when her father took on one of his moods. Jonathan glanced her way, but she was concentrating on the plate before her. She was an earnest, practical soul, brimming with crisp, unspoilt ideas about roles and obligations. With Kate Chase, daughter of the Chief Justice, safely married, Margaret Felix, on her frequent visits to her aunt, was probably the most sought-after young woman in the city; or had been, until her engagement.

Meanwhile, the Lion was continuing his eulogy. "McShane had a fine record in the war, Hilliman. His colonelcy was well deserved. We fought together in the West—we were with Grant back then. Later, we were with Sherman." Evidently, the egalitarian Hiram Felix never fought "under" another man, either. "Good soldier, your Colonel McShane. In charge of signals. Codes, ciphers. Good leader of men, but unsound in his politics. A Lincoln man from the beginning—I suppose you knew that, Hilliman—but you didn't know the Lincoln we knew back in Illinois. Ambitious man. Bit of the bumpkin, isn't that right, Meg? Not that Meg would remember. But it's true. Didn't know his table manners, not at first. Had that squeaky voice, all high and Western. That atrocious accent. Remember, Meg? She wouldn't really."

Another kick, the hardest of all. Plainly, Margaret Felix had heard the story before, and knew that something was coming that would annoy her fiancé greatly.

"But Lincoln knew what he wanted," the Lion continued. "Heavens, yes. Kicked and clawed, stole clients like everybody else, married above his station. You're offended, Hilliman, I can see it in your face. You look at Lincoln and you see the man who ended slavery and saved the Union and all the rest of that folderol. Let me tell you something about your Mr. Lincoln. The convention that nominated him for the presidency— they held it in Chicago, remember, Meg? She wouldn't, I suppose. Never mind. Point is, I was there. I was a Bates man. Never much cared for your Mr. Lincoln. A schemer, Hilliman. Wanted the purple too much, my opinion. Willing to cross the Rubicon. Didn't care who he trampled. You don't believe me, I can see it in your face. Listen. Tell you a story. Day of the nomination vote, Lincoln's people packed the benches and crowded the doors. The men who wanted Chase, Seward, Bates, all the others—they couldn't get into the hall. If they weren't in the hall, they couldn't vote. That's Lincoln for you. Anything to win."

"But, sir, isn't that what we want in war?" Jonathan interjected, unwisely. "A man of determination?"

General Felix was sopping up sauce with his bread. The food at Aunt Clara's residence was always heavy and tasteless, as if the cook had been instructed to serve no dish unavailable to the troops in the field. Answering the sally, the Lion struck a surprising Delphic note. "What you want in war, yes. But the war's over, Hilliman. We're at peace. Not at all sure your Mr. Lincoln is the right leader for a country trying to bind up the wounds and so forth."

"Some of the Confederates are still fighting," Jonathan pointed out before Meg could kick him again.

"Mostly trying to control the negroes, Hilliman. They're not fighting us. They're simply trying to preserve their accustomed social relations. Don't see why that's our business, to be frank." Pointing with a crust. "A lot of fine men left their lives on the field, Hilliman. Proud to have fought beside them. But we weren't fighting for the negroes. We were fighting for the Union. Some of us who were out there leading them are not altogether comfortable with the direction of policy since then. Your Mr. Lincoln says the Southern states are our wayward brothers. Well, then, let's treat them like our brothers. Nonsense with military districts and so forth, troops in the state houses, setting the negroes over the white man, when your Mr. Lincoln himself said the war had nothing to do with—"

General Felix had worked himself into a state. His cheeks bulged redly. He waved to a servant, who refilled his glass. He gulped at the flaming-red wine like a drowning man tasting water.

"Not your McShane, though," he went on, calm again. "McShane was fighting for the negroes. Last time I saw him—oh, two months ago, it must have been—he was on about how the constitutional amendment to end slavery was the mightiest achievement in the history of the Republic. I suppose Mr. Lincoln feels the same." The Lion's mighty hands demolished a crust of bread. He dipped it in the wine as his daughter looked away. "Doesn't matter. Lincoln is finished, isn't he? Trial starts in a couple of weeks, and he'll be gone in a month."

This time Meg's kick was not fast enough. "I believe, sir," said Jonathan, "that we are going to prevail."

Hiram Felix nodded distractedly; he was not signaling agreement. "I'm not a political man, Hilliman. Don't much care who's in the White House and so forth, as long as our policy is sound. Of course, one has one's friends. Associates. Men of ideas. The thing is, Hilliman, if this impeachment business goes anywhere—you see my point—if Mr. Lincoln has to leave, well, without a Vice-President, it would be Wade, wouldn't it? Wade's an old man, Hilliman. A sort of a caretaker. Besides, it wouldn't look very good, would it, to attack Lincoln from Capitol Hill, take over the office, then run in '68. Not the sort of thing our Protestant Republic could countenance. Too European. France, Italy get up to that sort of thing all the time. Not here. No. The ship of state would need a new captain at the helm. Even if the impeachment fails, the Republican Party is split wide open. The country will be ready for change, Hilliman. Somebody new. Reliable. A hero from the war and so forth. Grant, say, if he's willing. Sherman. Even a man like Garfield has sufficient ambition, from what I hear." Dark eyes sparkling now as he took another sip. "You never know where the country might turn," said the Lion of Louisiana.

CHAPTER 9

Consolation

I

THEY BURIED ARTHUR McShane the following Monday, in a swirling, feathery snow. The President did not attend the funeral. There had been rumors that he might, and the rumors brought the press out in force, but Lincoln stayed in the White House. Except for the occasional ride out to the Soldiers' Home, where a stone cottage waited always upon his pleasure, Lincoln had hardly left the Mansion in the year since his wife died. Newspaper stories often described him nowadays as "stooped" or "shrunken," to say nothing of "moody" or "distracted"—taking care, always, to quote unnamed visitors. According to Dan Sickles, many of the stories were planted by the Radicals, who, faced with the formidable task of reducing the public admiration of the President, had hit upon the strategy of persuading readers that Lincoln had become a pitiful shadow of the man who had won the great war, and no longer possessed the fiber to carry out his duties.

"There is a tradition," said Sickles, as they sat around the common room later that afternoon, "that once a great war has been won, the leader must at once be deposed. The Romans used to do it. The British, too."

"Not General Washington," Abigail pointed out. "He won the war and then served two terms as President."

"A tradition," said Sickles, airily. He was stretched on the settee beneath the long window at the end of the room, giving his leg a rest. "Not a law."

Strained laughter, in which Abigail did not join. She felt, just now, a distance from the others, perhaps because she had been ordered once again to remain behind and hold the fort while the others attended the service and accompanied the remains onward to the Catholic cemetery at Silver Spring. Abigail understood why. Arthur McShane had died in the company of a young black woman. It made perfect sense to spare Mrs. McShane the indignity of burying her husband in the company of another.

The decision rankled nevertheless.

"Speed will be joining us in a day or two," said Dennard. "He has taken offices on Eleventh Street, but his clerk will work mainly at this table." A sour glance at the blackboard, where the numbers now read *15–32–7.* They had lost both the newly elected Nebraskans, as expected—the result of the broken deal—and one additional Senator, whose name for the moment escaped Abigail. In any event, they were under one third again, and needed four of the last seven to prevail. The likelihood of Lincoln's acquittal seemed small, unless they were able to persuade Sumner. But the great man had not budged from his refusal to meet any of the President's emissaries. Impeachment was no matter, he was known to have told friends, for wheeling and dealing.

"I suppose I should get myself a clerk," said Sickles. "Everybody else seems to have one." He glanced at Abigail. "Are you available, my dear?"

She chose to take the question as rhetorical.

"We have a great deal of work, et cetera, ahead of us," said Dennard. He was a more distant man than McShane, with none of the familiarity or teasing. He was a man of considerable girth, yet lacked the bonhomie common to her experience of fat people. Instead, Rufus Dennard was staid, even stiff, and often spoke in a murmur that suggested that anything louder would constitute a breach of professional ethics. "I see no reason to worry about that habeas nonsense and the rest. That is just for the newspapers. The real fight will be over Counts Three and Four." Adjusting his thick glasses as he glanced at the broadsheet. "Failing to protect the freedmen. Defying the authority of the Congress, et cetera."

"In other words," intoned Sickles, from his spot by the window, "they are irritated at Mr. Lincoln for making up his own mind." He grunted, shifting the wooden leg to a more comfortable angle. "Our fine solons will not be satisfied until they can give orders to the President."

Dennard colored slightly but made no response. "The House Managers—that is evidently what the prosecutors are calling themselves—the Managers have promised us a list of their witnesses this week. Under the rules adopted by the Senate, the prosecution is under no obligation to tell us why they are calling particular witnesses, and I believe that the Managers will do their best to confuse us as to their purposes. So among our most important tasks will be—"

A peremptory knock on the door. Before Mr. Little could open it, in strode Edwin Stanton, the Secretary of War, followed by a uniformed soldier with long, luxuriant moustaches and a red patch on his epaulette: the bodyguard who accompanied him everywhere.

Stanton glared around the room. His eyes lingered on Abigail, then swept onward. "Dennard. A word."

The two men stepped into Dennard's office, leaving the door ajar. Abigail, sitting nearest, strained to catch a word. Stanton was obviously angry; from what Jonathan had told her of the man, he usually was. She heard "that woman" and she heard "confidential" and she heard "message" and she heard "President." The choleric and mistrustful Stanton was complaining about her presence. Any moment, Dennard would emerge and command her to the Library of Congress on a trumped-up errand, while the others remained to hear Stanton out.

Then came Dennard's low rumble, clear as crystal and perhaps meant to be so. "Miss Canner is my clerk. I will not send her away."

Abigail was unable to help peering into the room. The taller Stanton stared furiously at pudgy Dennard, and Stanton's anger had been known to reduce the toughest of men to groveling. Even now, two years after the war, those who opposed him too sharply had a way of finding themselves under investigation by War Department auditors, or, in a few sad cases, vanishing into some dank and distant military prison. But pudgy Dennard, leaning against his desk, soft arms folded, was casual in his disdain of Stanton's power: he did not even bother to contest the stare.

"Very well," said Stanton. "Be it on your head."

The two men trooped back into the common room.

Dennard started to speak, but the Secretary of War rode right over him. "Gentlemen," he said, as if Abigail were not present. "The leaders of this conspiracy are traitors. In any other nation they would hang. But Mr. Lincoln is a meek and forgiving man, the soul of charity. We must therefore let events carry us along a bit longer." A wet cough nearly bent him in two. "My sources tell me that the Managers are searching for a document, a letter of some kind that supposedly is some sort of admission of guilt on Count Four." He looked around the room, fingers combing through the rich brown beard. His eyes and nose both watered slightly, and Abigail wondered whether the stories were true, that Stanton used opium. "The letter, supposedly, is in Mr. Lincoln's hand, or the hand of a close adviser, and discusses a plan, under certain contingencies, to impose military government on the District of Columbia. Not a war measure. The letter, supposedly, is dated after the war. Within the past year and a half." He paused to allow them to absorb this. He meant, since Lincoln's troubles with the Radicals began. "I am here to assure you," Stanton concluded, "that no such letter exists."

Abigail resisted the urge to look over at Sickles, but recalled sharply the envelope she had caught him removing from McShane's desk two days after the murder.

Dennard, no fool, filled the silence. "Are you assuring us in your own name or in the name of our client?"

Stanton wiped his mouth on his sleeve. "In this matter, there is no distinction." He smiled savagely. "Of course, you are always welcome to ask Mr. Lincoln yourself. He will tell you the same."

"I will likely do exactly that."

The murderous glare again. "And he will tell you precisely what I said he will tell you." He looked around. "I'll tell you what does exist, at least according to rumor. There is a list out there. A list of the men who are conspiring against the President. We will find the list, and then we will hang the conspirators." With that, Stanton swept up his moustachioed bodyguard by eye, and was gone.

II

As a consolation prize for her exclusion from the funeral that morning, Dennard had given Abigail a motion to draft. *Just for practice, et cetera,* he had explained. *Not to be filed. Just to see how you do.* The motion asked for the exclusion of all testimony in which witnesses would say what others had told them the President said or did. This was covered by the hearsay rule, one of the oldest and most treasured propositions in Anglo-American jurisprudence. In her innocence, Abigail had imagined that she would impress them all by finishing her work by the time the funeral ended; instead, she had barely found time to begin. By the time Stanton left, it was past four in the afternoon. Dennard and Sickles left just after, leaving Abigail and Jonathan alone in the common room.

"I wanted to apologize," he said after a bit.

"Apologize for what?"

"The funeral—"

"Please, do not trouble yourself. I managed to keep myself occupied." She returned to the evidence treatise she had been consulting. She had never imagined that there might be so many exceptions to so seemingly simple a rule. She liked her rules straightforward and clear, like the ones Nanny Pork preached at home, and the pastor reinforced on Sundays. She had imagined, somehow, that law would be the same.

"Do you think it exists?" said Jonathan, suddenly. "The letter Stanton was talking about?"

Again she lifted her head. "I really wouldn't have any idea."

"I saw your face. You were less surprised than the rest of us. Come on, Abigail. Tell me what you think."

Again she saw Sickles prying the drawer; and wondered what had possessed her to assist him; and subsequently to keep silent. The excitement of being invited, however briefly, into the inner circle?

"I think," said Abigail, "that you and I have a great deal of work to do."

But now she was disturbed. One of those simple rules she so cherished forbade false witness. Real life was always harder than the rules made it seem. Maybe that was why people spent so much time looking for ways around them.

She turned a page, not really concentrating. The gas lamps sputtered. One went out with a gasp of surprise. They both looked up sharply; and laughed; and returned to their work.

But Jonathan found his gaze drawn again and again toward Abigail, whom he found, quite simply, remarkable.

He had never spent so much time in the company of a woman of her color. Those with whom he had had conversations had mostly been women he met in service, or perhaps working in some shop. He had known educated negroes, of course. They were not uncommon at the North. Indeed, at the dinner table of his uncle Thrace, the Episcopal bishop in Boston and a director of the Massachusetts Anti-Slavery Society, Jonathan had been held rapt by the rhetorical brilliance of men like Frederick Douglass and Alexander Crummell and a schoolteacher said to be a grand-nephew of the poet Phillis Wheatley, although that claim, Uncle Thrace told him later, was unlikely: there were faux Wheatley relatives everywhere. A year or two before the war, Jonathan had traveled with his uncle on a trip west to raise funds to purchase slaves and free them. In the town of Chatham, near Toronto, they had sat in the parlor of a man named Stanton Hunton, a major property owner and former slave who had been associated with John Brown, and whose children were all being educated in the modern way. Hunton had become prosperous, and owned valuable land in Canada and Michigan. On the train ride back east, Uncle Thrace assured his nephew that the black man, if once offered the opportunity to improve his mind and keep what he earned, could within a generation or two take his place beside the white in the political councils of the nation. But he said nothing about social life, and he said nothing about the black woman.

Until the moment Jonathan met Abigail Canner, he had never had a lengthy conversation with a woman of the colored race. But once she started talking, he very much wanted her not to stop.

III

"You don't need to keep driving all the way up to my office," said Abigail as she climbed up into the trap. "I can perfectly well take the horsecars home."

"I'm your brother," said Michael, snapping the reins. "I want you safe." He laughed, not pleasantly. "Besides. It's not *your* office. It's *their* office. Haven't you figured that out by now?"

Abigail lapsed into a sullen silence. There was no point in arguing. Her brother had always known her fears and weaknesses. In consequence, he had always been able to wound her at will. She wondered whether he practiced this skill on his many women, or whether she was his only target. He never picked on Louisa, the youngest, who adored him, and had rarely dared say a cross word to Judith, the eldest, whose tongue could lash with a fervor to rival Nanny's own. But Judith had vanished: tired of how she carried on with men, Nanny Pork had put her out of the house while Abigail was still away at Oberlin, and nobody had seen her since—

"Where are you going?" said Abigail, looking around. "This is not the way home."

For Michael had turned the wagon to the right at Pennsylvania Avenue, rather than left toward the bridge over the canal, and was approaching the intimidating granite bulk of the Treasury Department. This route would lead past the Executive Mansion and on into the dangerous slums of George Town, where no sane Washingtonian ventured after dark.

"I thought we might ride around for a bit," her brother said. His tone was somber, his face a hidden shadow in the night. "I want to talk to you about Senator Wade."

"Oh?"

"I've been reading up on him, Abby," said Michael. "Wade was for abolition before Lincoln was. He was for arming the slaves before Lincoln was. Wade is for giving the freedmen land and money. He is for keeping troops in all the Southern states, when Lincoln wants to remove them as quickly as possible." An angry chuckle. "Wade says Lincoln's views are what you would expect in a man from a slave state, born to poor white trash. I agree." A sharp nod. "Anyway, I've been thinking that it might not be such a bad thing if Old Abe were removed from office. From what I can tell, Wade might be a better man for our people."

Abigail stared in astonishment. "You cannot seriously be suggesting that you wish the impeachment to succeed!"

"I just don't see why all the colored folks treat Old Abe like he lifted his staff and parted the waters of the Red Sea."

"Mr. Lincoln freed our people, Michael. You cannot deny that simple fact. And he has declared that no Southern state may rejoin the Union until it ratifies the constitutional amendment barring slavery."

"Old Abe was dragged to those positions by better men than— Whoa!" Drawing in the reins; but the horse had already stopped. Up ahead, the grand avenue was blocked by a pair of carriages, halted by a Union soldier. Michael craned his neck; turned to her with a grin. "Well, well. Moses himself, in the flesh."

Even through the rain they could hear the loud huzzahs up ahead. Abigail stood on her seat but still could not see. Suddenly determined to catch a glimpse of the client she had not been permitted to meet, she climbed down, ignoring her brother's shout of warning, and pressed through the throng. She reached the front just in time to see Abraham Lincoln himself, victor in the war and savior of her people, crossing Pennsylvania Avenue toward Lafayette Park, trailed by a lone Bucktail, as members of the Pennsylvania regiment who guarded the President were known. Lincoln was heading for the grim fortress known as the Old Clubhouse, home of Secretary of State Seward, his closest friend and adviser, who had not left the house in the two years since he himself was attacked, Lincoln gravely wounded, and Vice-President Andrew Johnson murdered.

Abigail crept closer.

The President was a tall man, and his stovepipe hat made him seem taller, but he was hunched forward against the wind and rain, clutching the brim comically. His long stride made it difficult for the soldier to keep pace. Then Lincoln vanished into the Clubhouse, and the Bucktail took up station by the door. As the onlookers began to disperse, Abigail noticed, to her surprise, dozens of awestruck dark faces in the street. Washington's colored population usually effaced itself, and the negroes tended to linger toward the back of any crowd. But Lincoln's presence had drawn them forward, as it had drawn Abigail, and now, in the absence of soldiers to restrain them, they formed a loose ring around the Clubhouse.

"For a man who's been shot in the head," said Michael, who had come up silently beside her, "Old Abe doesn't seem to care too much about bodyguards."

"The war is over," said Abigail.

As traffic began moving again, Michael nodded across the way, where several hard-faced white men skulked in the shadows. They had not joined in the cheering. "Not for everybody," he said.

CHAPTER 10

Proposition

I

"THE PRECEDENTS ARE unclear," said Jonathan. He tried and failed to wish away the slight tremor in his voice, and he knew that his pale cheeks were tinged with pink. These same indicia of nervousness had plagued him at Yale, especially when he was called upon to translate Latin or Greek at speed. Eventually, he had managed to hide the jitters from classmates and professors. But now, speaking for only the second time in the presence of the President of the United States, Jonathan Hilliman felt all the old symptoms return.

It was Tuesday afternoon, and windy, the sky low and gray and impending in a way that foretokened snow. Lincoln had assembled what he called his lawyers' coterie to discuss tactics for the trial. Rufus Dennard had instructed Jonathan to apprise the coterie of the fruits of his research on the voting rule in the Senate.

"Two-thirds of the votes," Jonathan continued, "are required to convict. We know that, of course. What we don't know is what counts as two-thirds."

"What do you mean?" demanded Stanton, quite out of turn. "There are fifty-four Senators. Two-thirds of fifty-four is thirty-six. Ergo, they need thirty-six votes. Anything less means we win."

Jonathan colored, but made no response. He did not want to get into a tussle with Stanton.

Lincoln grinned. "I don't reckon that Mr. Hilliman has forgotten how many Senators there are."

At a nod from Dennard, Jonathan resumed, but not before casting a nervous glance toward the imperious Secretary of War. "The legal question is whether, when the Senate sits to try an impeachment, it is still the Senate, run by all the rules of the Senate, or whether, under the Constitution, it becomes a different body, judicial in nature—that is, a court." He checked his notes as heavy wind shook the Mansion. The windows rattled. "In the records," said Jonathan, "you can find references both ways. Evidently, the question has never been formally resolved. All the Constitution tells us for sure is that the Chief Justice presides, and that conviction occurs only if two-thirds of the members concur."

"Meaning that we need nineteen votes our way," said Stanton, still not satisfied.

The President's smile was sardonic. This time they were meeting in the more spacious Cabinet Room, but his chair was once more tottering on its hind legs. "I reckon, if they're a court, they have to follow the rules of evidence. If they're a legislature, they can kind of make the rules up as they go along."

"If the Senate is really a court," said Dennard, "then the Chief Justice might be permitted to vote." His breathing was more labored than ever, perhaps from the hard work of dragging his bulk up and down the stairs.

Sickles adjusted his wooden leg. Another gust of wind struck the windows, and now the first tiny flakes began to fall. "Chase voting might be good for us. Or it might be bad for us."

"Whether there are fifty-four eligible to vote or fifty-five," Stanton objected, "we still need nineteen."

"I don't believe," said Lincoln, voice placid, "that Mr. Dennard is thinking about how many votes *we* need." The drooping left eye seemed to wink. "I believe he's thinking about how many votes *they* need."

"That is correct, sir," said Dennard. "If Chase is permitted to vote, et cetera, then the Managers will need thirty-seven votes, not thirty-six."

Stanton said nothing. Jonathan was impressed. Arthur McShane had the swifter legal mind, but Rufus Dennard's plodding style seemed to be exactly what was needed to keep the raging Secretary of War at bay.

"Chase wants to be President," said Speed suddenly, once more announcing as a great discovery what everybody knew. And not just everybody in the room. Everybody in Washington knew that Chase still hoped to be nominated for President—perhaps in 1868, or at the latest in 1872. Should the Senate organize as a court, and come within a single vote of removal, the Chief Justice might be forced to decide whether the President stayed in office. One school of thought held that Chase would prefer a weakened Lincoln in the White House, and a broken Republican Party, so that he could pursue the Democratic nomination in 1868. Another contended that Chase, by vanquishing his longtime political enemy, could then present himself to either party as the most respected and powerful man in the country. What nobody thought for an instant was that Chase's decision would have anything to do with law or evidence.

"It has always been Chase's way," said Lincoln, "to choose the path of policy that most strengthens himself. When he was my Treasury secretary, that was not such a bad thing, because a strong Treasury meant funds for the war." The President was up now, circling the room. His mood grew meditative. "You know, ambition is like a chin fly. A long time ago, my brother and I were out plowing corn when I noticed a fly on the horse's chin. I shooed it off, but my brother told me to stop. I said that I didn't want the horse to be bitten, but my brother said being bitten by the fly was the only thing that kept that old horse moving."

"I am skeptical," said Dennard. He had this way of drawing everyone's attention through his terseness: now the entire room wanted to know what precisely he was skeptical of. "I hardly think," the lawyer continued, "that we particularly want Chase's political ambitions, et cetera, et cetera, getting in the way of a fair trial."

"That depends," Sickles retorted, "on which way he runs to keep from being bitten."

A moment's general laughter, in which everyone joined but Dennard.

"I spoke with Seward last night," said the President, back at the window, hands linked behind his back. "He thinks Chase wants to vote. He says Chase will not be able to bear the notion that events rest in the hands of others."

As always, the name of the Secretary of State had an almost magical effect on the assembled company. Two years after the attack, Seward remained hidden from public view, in his house across Lafayette Park from the Mansion, tended by his son Frederick and a servant or two, seeing nobody except a few intimates—including Mr. Lincoln. Jonathan had never laid eyes on Seward. The latest Washington rumor had it that the Secretary was long dead, and the household maintained in the Clubhouse was a sort of conjuring trick, to preserve the public's faith in the Administration. Lincoln, on the other hand, consulted Seward constantly. Dead or alive, Seward retained the canniest political mind in the country.

"I think," said Sickles, "that we should give Mr. Chase a little bit more rope."

"And let him hang himself," said the President.

There was more laughter, in which Jonathan uneasily joined. Only Dennard struck a sour note. "Sir," he said, "hanging the Chief Justice politically will not necessarily get you off the hook."

Lincoln remained amicable. "It is not myself I am trying to save," he said, voice scarcely above a murmur. "It is a country."

"In that case—"

The President hated to be interrupted. "The threat to this country, Mr. Dennard, comes not from the Chief Justice. The threat comes from the president pro tempore."

"Senator Wade?" Dennard seemed not to follow. "Wade will surely disqualify himself. It would be unseemly for the man who would succeed you to cast a vote on whether to remove you."

"Being unseemly," drawled Sickles, "has never bothered Mr. Wade."

Lincoln was brisk; and devastating. "Benjamin Wade is an intelligent man. He is old and sick, but his mind is still sharp. He is ambitious. Not for himself. For the triumph of his own holy views. He alone knows what is best for the colored race. Just ask him. Ask his friends."

Jonathan looked up sharply from his notepad. Rarely had he heard this tone from the President, who was so often gentle, even in describing his enemies.

"I am not concerned with whether or not Wade votes," Lincoln continued. "But it is intolerable that such a man should sit in this chair."

Dennard tried to interject: "Sir, with respect, the line of succession is as clear as—"

The President cut him off. "Under no circumstances," he said, hard-eyed, "will I allow that event to occur."

II

"Maybe it's real," said Jonathan. "The letter in Lincoln's hand regarding military government. Maybe it actually exists."

It was the afternoon of the same filthy day. There were three of them now—Jonathan, Abigail, and a truculent redhead called Rellman, a prudish soul whose green eyes and ready scowl punished whomever they happened upon, for sins not yet committed. Rellman, alarmingly fat, was James Speed's clerk. Speed had left the Administration and found offices on Twelfth Street, but Rellman, they were told, would be spending half of his time here, because this was where Dennard would divide up the assignments each day; although, so far—apart from that single memorandum "for practice"—Abigail's assignments continued to consist principally of dusting and deliveries.

"The atmosphere at the Mansion was eerie," Jonathan continued. Abigail sat on one side of the conference table, Jonathan and Rellman on the other. Books were heaped everywhere. Files were strewn across the credenza, each bound with its own brightly colored bow. "They all seem worried about something."

Abigail pointed at the blackboard, and the ominous numbers: _15–32–7._ "Perhaps they are simply counting the votes."

Jonathan shook his head. "It's more than that. And if the letter exists, and the Managers find it, I do not see how Mr. Lincoln could survive."

"Our client says the letter doesn't exist," interjected Rellman. "Ergo, it doesn't exist. The matter is closed." He was pink and pudgy and exuded an air of superiority, no doubt because he had been Speed's clerk for two years and would soon be sitting for his examinations. He spoke with his master's certainty of rightness on matters he knew nothing about. His face had the saggy softness of a man carrying thrice his years. His eyes, tiny and dark, seemed lost in the broad flesh. "We have important tasks," he added. He looked at Abigail, then at Jonathan, as if expecting them to take notes. "We should be about them."

Abigail shut her eyes briefly. The "important tasks" assigned her consisted entirely of copying marked passages from various volumes' onto sheets of paper the lawyers could carry in their files. Dennard had even remarked on the excellence of her copperplate.

The work was suddenly a struggle. She had slept poorly last night. A strange congruence was growing in her mind, a connection between the fate of her missing older sister and the fate of Rebecca Deveaux. She knew nothing about where Rebecca had come from; she had only the vaguest notions about where Judith had gone after Nanny put her out of the house. But both were, evidently, overfamiliar with men; and if one had been found

(_sliced up_)

dead, then why not the other? Unable to bear the tension any longer, Abigail stood abruptly. She stepped toward the door, knowing that both men were watching her. When Rellman went back to his work, she flicked her head to the side, indicating that Jonathan should join her.

Out in the shadowy corridor, he smiled nervously. "If we keep this up, people will talk."

Abigail studied the worried features of this man who, whenever he chose, could leave Washington City, return home to Newport, claim his inheritance, and live as the rich do. "I require your assistance," she said.

"Of course." Still agitated, glancing at the half-open door to the office. "Naturally, I am happy to assist you in any way I—"

Abigail interrupted. "My concern, at the moment, is for Rebecca Deveaux. I see no evidence that her murder is being pursued in a serious manner."

His pale jaw jutted slightly. "The murders"—emphasizing the plural—"took place outside a brothel. There is no real question of what happened."

"Assuming that Miss Deveaux was employed there."

"Do you know for a fact that she was not?"

"No. But I do not believe that Inspector Varak knows, either."

"What do you suggest?"

She put her hands on her hips. "You are a man of means. A successful young man, welcome in every great house in this city. Surely you number, among your many acquaintances, at least one who might be of assistance." His look of surprise was almost comical, and she smiled. In truth, Abigail did not much care for herself in this role—she considered this sort of teasing flattery more Dinah Berryhill's talent than her own—but experience had taught her its effectiveness. "Madame Sophie's establishment, I am given to understand, is at the higher end of the trade. Such establishments would not exist without the patronage of those who are well off."

"I hardly think—"

"Naturally, I am not suggesting that you personally would possess any knowledge, but you surely are on terms with young men who might."

"Do you seriously expect me simply to walk up to one of my friends and ask him whether he happens to know whether Madame Sophie employed a colored girl named Rebecca, now deceased?"

"Why not? Unless, that is, you would rather inquire of Madame Sophie herself." Her smile broadened. "Think of it as another favor for Mrs. McShane."

She went back inside.

III

Jonathan Hilliman had no intention of complying with Abigail's absurd request. He was fond of her—they were friends, confound it—but the temerity of the woman, to think that he would do such a thing merely because she asked! He fumed most of the afternoon, and that evening, too, as he shared the tale with Fielding.

"Can you imagine?" Jonathan kept saying. "Who does she think she is?"

"More to the point, who does she think *you* are?"

Fielding found the whole thing hilarious, but, then, he was quite drunk. He had dined—poorly, he insisted—at the home of Congressman James Blaine, a longtime Lincoln friend and associate, who had inexplicably voted in favor of the impeachment resolution.

"Said he thought Lincoln should have the chance to clear himself at trial." Fielding chuckled, shook his head, took a long pull on his cigar. Trembling fingers fumbled at his collar. He was sweating quite unreasonably. "Said it was only fair."

"How thoughtful," snapped Jonathan, in his dudgeon. Above the fireplace hung a standing portrait, a bad oil of an earlier, landed Bannerman who had fought on the wrong side in the Revolution. The eyes were half lidded, the face was waxy, and it occurred to Jonathan that the man might have been painted after the Continental Army hanged him.

"Simply a matter of trying to have it both ways, old man. A skill you should cultivate if you wish to succeed in this town." He subsided, gazing into the fire. Like Jonathan, Fielding Bannerman was resisting pressure to enter upon the family business. Unlike Jonathan, he was unable to point to another goal he had to pursue first, unless of course one counted dissolution. "Oh, but say. On what your friend the negress asked about."

"She has a name."

"Miss Canner, then. The point is, she's rather clever—isn't that what you're always telling me? An agile mind and so forth?"

"Certainly."

"Well, then, look, Hills. I have the most marvelous idea. Weren't you up at Yale with Wily Whit?"

"Who?"

"Whitford Pesky. He was in your year, wasn't he? I run into him at the club from time to time. Now, I've visited Mrs. Scott's and a few of the finer establishments, but Whit knows the worst of those places inside and out. Keeps an eye on them for the Provost General. He'd be the one to ask."

Jonathan rounded on him. "Have you heard a word I've said? I shall not spend my time blundering about Washington City asking questions about . . . about brothels. Really, Fields. Can you imagine if your cousin Meg heard?"

"You're probably right." Fielding lifted his glass in a mocking toast. "Better to let the police handle the investigation. From what you've told me, they're doing a magnificent job."

IV

In the morning, Dennard sent Jonathan down to the municipal courthouse to file motions of postponement in the firm's other pending cases. Outside, the young man hailed a cab for the ride back to G Street. He felt half asleep. He had dreamed of the dead Bannerman above the fireplace, and awoke worried about being on the wrong side. He shouted a new destination. He had to shout several times before the black driver heard him above the clatter of hooves. He ordered the man to take him to the Provost General's headquarters. At the gate, Jonathan asked for Major Pesky. As Fielding had pointed out just last night, Jonathan and Whitford Pesky had been up at Yale together. Jonathan was Skull and Bones, through two of his uncles. Whit, being new money, could not be considered, and had been tapped for Third Society instead. When the war broke out, both men enlisted. Jonathan went down to Virginia with the Thirty-fourth Massachusetts Volunteers, fought at Petersburg, and helped chase down Lee at the end, but the Peskys arranged for their son to stay behind the lines: thus the post with the Provost General, charged with military governance of Washington City. To his family's dismay, Whit Pesky enjoyed military life, and stayed on. Rumor proposed that the part he enjoyed most was pursuing the opportunities for corruption that his sinecure in the Provost's office presented: in particular, the significant wartime traffic in forged discharge papers. Not that Whitford

Pesky had any need of stained money. Like Jonathan, Whit would succeed to his family business one day. The Peskys were big in copper out
west and enjoyed some loose connection to the Union Pacific. Jonathan
suspected that Whit took bribes because he enjoyed the risk.

Whit was tall, and handsome in that naturally roguish way that
most young men aspire to, some attain, and a chosen few, fated to cause
women to swoon whenever they walk across a room, never outgrow. His
uniform was crisp. Everything glittered. He said he was happy to see
his old friend, but he had guessed that the visit was business, and the
flared orange eyes were already calculating how much whatever Jonathan wanted might be worth. They went to the bar of the Maryland
House hotel, a place Whit proposed when Jonathan said that he wanted
nobody who knew him to overhear. It was illegal to serve alcohol this
time of day, so they drank lemonade.

For ten minutes they kept up a stream of pleasantries.

Then Jonathan explained why he was there. He needed a simple
piece of information. The Provost General kept meticulous records
of the city's bawdy houses. Jonathan wanted to know whether one of
Sophia Harbour's girls was missing.

"Missing?" Whit seemed to doubt his hearing; or his friend's sanity.
"Why would one of them be missing?" Then he got it. "Oh. I see. Of
course."

As it turned out, Whit had the answer at his fingertips. Some clamorous police inspector with a foreign name had been by just yesterday,
he said, and the Provost General had instructed Major Pesky to give
him whatever assistance he might require. So Whit had gone to the
records and determined that, yes, the late Rebecca Deveaux was indeed
one of Sophia Harbour's girls.

"Does that answer your question?"

"Yes. Yes, it does." But he felt oddly disappointed, for Abigail's sake.

"Good." The major had to get back to his post. He had remembered
an important meeting. He downed his lemonade in a gulp, tossed a coin
onto the counter. "Oh, and Hills . . ."

"Yes, Whit?"

"There are people looking over my shoulder on this thing. People
of true influence." He leaned close. "We never had this conversation.
Anybody asks, we were reminiscing about New Haven."

CHAPTER 11

Invitation

I

THE MOST GLAMOROUS salon in Washington was the modest home of Mr. and Mrs. Charles Eames, at the corner of Fourteenth and H, just up the street from the law offices of Dennard & McShane. The Eames home was often open to the great men and women of the Republic, but the main event was generally on Saturday evening, when one would find leaders of both major parties, and usually of a few that were extinct, breaking bread together at that most nonpartisan of venues. Senator Charles Sumner, the most eloquent and famous of the Radicals, was a regular guest, and prominent governors, poets, and generals swept through the Eameses' parlor if they happened to be in town. John Hay, who now lived in Paris but until two years ago had served as one of Lincoln's secretaries, had been heard to describe Mrs. Eames as hostess of the most attractive salon in the capital since the time of Dolley Madison. All over New England, the educated classes spoke with reverence of the salon's charm and wit. So, when, on that same Wednesday, Jonathan returned to the office to find waiting an invitation to a reception on Saturday night at Mrs. Eames's salon in honor of the president of the New Orleans chess club, he accepted with alacrity. True, he knew next to nothing about chess and had never been to New Orleans; and he had buried his employer and friend on Monday. Nevertheless, one did not say no to Fanny Campbell Eames. And so he put aside his other worries and began instead anticipating an enjoyable evening at the Eames salon.

What he did not expect was the note that came back when he sent Little over with his acceptance. At first Jonathan thought himself the victim of some bizarre jest. But the bold, curving handwriting of Mrs. Eames was known all over Washington City:

It will be lovely to see you. And do please bring Miss Canner.

The request should not have struck him as odd. Abigail was as educated and clever as most of the guests at the salon would be. Moreover, the story of the colored clerk working on the President's defense had begun to spread through the city, just as McShane had predicted. People were curious.

Jonathan finally decided that what bothered him was not the thought that Abigail would be at the reception, but the wittily crafted language of the note: *please bring.*

Heavy with implication.

He should, of course, find a witty way to decline. All Washington society knew of his engagement. Ellenborough had handed him a letter from Meg just last night, and, as always, Jonathan had answered at once, assuring his beloved of his affection. It would never do to allow anyone to imagine for a moment that his commitment to his beloved Meg was less than entire. Nevertheless, Jonathan resolved to do exactly as Mrs. Eames instructed, to *bring Miss Canner.* And not only because Meg was safely back in Philadelphia; or because one did not say no to Fanny Eames. The more he thought about it, the more he realized that, engaged or not, he looked forward to spending time with the fascinating Abigail in a social setting.

And so, having overcome his own scruples, he set about overcoming hers.

Early that evening, Jonathan sat across from her at the conference table, watching as she copied out a page of Coke's *Institutes.* He enjoyed watching Abigail at work, long neck curved as she bent over her book, full lips pressed tightly together in concentration. She was writing hard, but now and then, deep in thought, she tapped her finger endearingly against her chin. At last the pencil stopped moving. She had noticed his scrutiny. The gray eyes came up, distracted, inquiring. A couple of hours ago, he had got up the nerve to tell her what Whit Pesky had said about Rebecca Deveaux, and the disappointment in those eyes had stung him. Now he longed to see them alight with energy once more. He made two or three false starts, and in the end simply showed her the note from Fanny Eames.

"So, you see, I have no choice," he said, shyly but proudly.

"I cannot go," Abigail said, staring at the invitation in horror. "It would not be appropriate."

"It would be perfectly appropriate."

"I cannot," she said again, and dropped her eyes. He had not seen her so nervous since McShane's abuse on the day she arrived.

And so Jonathan began extolling the virtues of the Eames salon: the glitter, the wit, the conversation. The great men and women she would meet.

"And what makes you think," she demanded, "that it is my ambition to meet these great men and women?"

"You mistake my intention," he said, smoothly. "I believe that they are the ones who should have the opportunity to meet *you*."

Unable to find an answer to this sally, Abigail fell back on her central argument: she was engaged, and he was engaged, and there were things that were simply not proper. Nanny Pork said so. Jonathan was not sure who Nanny Pork was, and at a fitter time he would ask; for now, however, he kept his focus. They fenced a bit longer, but this time, for once, it was Jonathan who did the conversational cornering. If a gentleman should happen to escort a lady to an event—so he explained to both their uneasy consciences—there was no scandal. That each was engaged to marry another made no difference. The lady and gentleman in question were by no means a couple. They were simply taking pleasure in each other's company. Washington society understood these things. Just last week, he himself had escorted Miss Bessie Hale to the theater, and—

"Fine," Abigail blurted.

"Fine, what?"

"I shall go with you."

"Not *with* me, precisely—"

"In your company, Mr. Hilliman. With your escort. Presumably, in your carriage. Hence, *with* you."

And that was that.

11

Except that it wasn't.

Abigail arrived home around eight: courtesy on this occasion of Mr. Little, who sometimes drove her in his wagon when Michael had failed to show up to collect her. That was his way, Abigail reflected as she climbed down onto the carriage block. There were moments when her brother would never leave her side, and moments when he vanished so completely that she all but forgot he existed.

She thanked Mr. Little for the ride, then hurried up the front walk. Stepping into the house, she was astonished to find Nanny Pork, with her preternatural sense of timing, in the kitchen, smoking her pipe. Usually, she went to bed with the sun, the same way she rose: her body, Nanny often said, would live on the plantation until the day she died.

Abigail asked why she was up so late.

"Because I knowed there was trouble."

What kind of trouble?

"With you, girl. With you."

Arguing with Nanny Pork was like arguing with a bullet: she came straight at you, and if you stood your ground you were going to get shot. So Abigail carefully stepped aside, avoiding the slightest word that might aggravate her aunt. Or thought she did. Abigail made tea for them both, took two sugar biscuits from the bin, and put them on doilies, because sugar biscuits were what Nanny liked best. Nanny called them snickerdoodles.

"I'm not in any trouble, Nanny," said Abigail gently while her great-aunt munched away on a snickerdoodle. "There's no reason for you to sit up worrying."

"I has the second sight," said Nanny Pork, unpersuasively. "I can tell when one of my family is in trouble." She shut her eyes briefly, coughed. "Not tonight. Saturday. What is you up to Saturday night?"

Hesitation would be fatal. So would a lie. All these years with Nanny had taught her that much. "Some people I know have asked me to drop by. They're having a sort of party."

The old woman snorted. "Some people. Some *white* people."

"Yes, Nanny. They're white. But—"

"White folks ain't any better than your own. You knows that, Abby."

"Yes, ma'am."

"War's over. We's free."

"Yes, but—"

"I don't know why you spends all this time with the white folks." She stood, the ancient body seeming to creak as it unfolded. Yet Abigail did not dare offer to help. "You works with them all day. Why would you want to dance with them all night?"

Sometimes Nanny Pork backed you into a conversational corner so absurd that you had no choice but to follow her lead. "It's not a dancing party, Nanny."

"And what kinda party is this?"

"Just people having conversation. That's all."

"A talkin party." Another snort, this one not only derisive but somehow condemnatory. "And who's takin you to this talkin party? Some white man?"

Abigail felt about twelve years old. "Nobody's taking me—"

"Well, you ain't gonna be out there wandering the streets by your own self. You get your brother to take you, Abby, do you hear me? A lady don't wander the streets, and a lady don't show up at no talkin party unattended. Do you hear me?"

"I won't be alone—"

"You said nobody's takin you."

"Not taking me exactly. But I will be in the company of a—a friend."

"A male friend," Nanny Pork pronounced, with malicious satisfaction.

Abigail surrendered. "Yes, Nanny."

"A white man?"

"Yes."

Nanny made a sound somewhere between a snort and a sneer: what Abigail's mother used to call "snupping." "You won't go with any of those nice colored mens who courts you, but you'll go with the first white man who comes along."

"This is not courting—"

"What about that nice Octavius? He's a sweet man. Why won't you go with him?"

Abigail took a moment, because if she spoke too soon she would scream. Like Dinah, Nanny considered Octavius Addison perfectly suited to Abigail. Whenever he visited, Nanny, who considered the young man a catch, made her niece sit with him for hours.

"I am engaged," Abigail said finally. "You know that, Nanny."

"Right. Too engaged to go with a nice colored boy, but you'll go with a white man anyway."

"That is not—"

"Better watch out, child, you're gettin as bad as your big sister."

This was a reference to Judith, whom Nanny had banished. Abigail, although she disapproved of her older sister's style of life, nevertheless admired her pluck. On the other hand, Nanny Pork doted on Louisa, whom she called the baby even though she was sixteen, and had suitors; whereas Abigail saw her younger sister as a charming shirker, always trying to escape her chores.

Abigail stood by the kitchen table. "Good night, Nanny," she said.

"Good night," the old woman said, and dragged herself achingly up the stairs. Watching her go, Abigail remembered when Nanny had come to live with them. Abigail had been a child of perhaps twelve. Her mother had explained gently that Nanny needed a place to die. But it was Abigail's own parents who had died instead, first her mother, then her father. The Canners had tried hard to protect their children from full knowledge of the reality of the life of people of their color, because they did not want them to grow up with a sense of limits. They were a free black family, and made sure their children knew it. Even when the newly emancipated Nanny Pork arrived, bringing with her undeniable evidence of the plantation South, the Canners had insisted that the children let nothing hold them back: they were, said her parents, the best of the race. Now her parents were gone, her older sister was banished, and her brother spent his nights running with men so scary that Abigail did not even want to know their names. It was just her and Nanny Pork and Louisa now. Other than the dormitories of the Female Department at the Oberlin Collegiate Institute, this house in what Washingtonians called the Island was the only home Abigail Canner had ever known.

Until this moment, she had not understood how much of her ambition was fed by a desire to escape it forever.

CHAPTER 12

Preparation

I

ABIGAIL WAS LATE the next morning: the streetcar was delayed by a company of cavalry riding by. Actually, it was illegal for troops to cross the city limits without congressional permission, but some of the bolder commanders were ignoring those rules in what the newspapers interpreted as a calculated reminder to the Senate of the esteem in which the military held Lincoln. The other day, in a bar down near the wharf, a couple of soldiers had beaten a local tobacco merchant half to death after he had ventured an injudicious remark about "Emperor Lincoln the First," as the European essayists had taken to calling him. Those same writers were growing more gleeful by the week, predicting that the American democratic experiment they so despised would continue its tragic but inevitable descent: from revolution to civil war to coup d'état.

When, at last, Abigail arrived at the office, Jonathan greeted her with a smile so engaging that she was tempted to smile warmly back, before she remembered herself; as she hung her coat and scarf on the peg, she wondered whether she was allowing the young man to become overfamiliar, whether she had erred in accepting the invitation to the Eameses'. But of course there was no way to take it back; and, in truth, she did not want to. Surreptitiously, she drew from her bag the volume of Coke's *Institutes* she had removed the night before without ever quite receiving permission. Jonathan alone knew that she was reading on her own; not even he knew that she was taking books home. Abigail slipped the Coke onto the shelf. Then, with a quick glance around the ante-room, she began her chores.

"I have to go over to the Library of Congress," said Jonathan. "Rell-man is carrying memoranda over to Mr. Speed."

"And what is my assignment?" Abigail asked.

"Mr. Dennard asks that you wait."

"Wait for what?"

"I am not exactly sure."

Puzzled, Abigail remained at the table. Rellman was gone. Jonathan was gone. Even Little was gone. Dennard's door remained shut. After a moment, she went to get the feather duster. The longer she dusted, the angrier she got. The embarrassment of the Mellison party began to haunt her, and she wondered whether she should expect further humili-ation tonight at the Eameses'.

The door swung wide. As Abigail turned, Dan Sickles came in, shaking snow from his coat. "Where's Dennard?"

"Mr. Dennard is in his office."

"Have the Managers sent over the witness list?"

"Not yet, Mr. Sickles."

He watched her cleaning the shelves. "Where are the other clerks?"

"They have assignments."

That roguish smile. "And you don't."

"Mr. Dennard has asked me to wait."

"And, meanwhile, you thought you'd dust the books and clean the stove."

Abigail nodded. His eyes ran over her body a bit too freely and hun-grily, but she refused for once to drop her gaze. "Was there anything else, Mr. Sickles?" she asked.

Sickles crossed his arms. He tottered slightly on the wooden leg. "You studied under Finney. Dennard tells me that Finney thinks the world of you."

At the praise, she did indeed turn away. "Dr. Finney is kind—"

Sickles waved her silent, glanced at Dennard's door. "Mr. Lin-coln asked me if he should keep Dennard on. After what happened to McShane, I mean. I said yes. He said good, because McShane admired your brain. Not Dennard's. Not Hilliman's. Yours."

Again Abigail was stunned. Arthur McShane, in the two weeks she had known him, had scarcely exchanged ten words with her. "I—I am sure he meant—um—"

"He meant that you're the smart one. Like I told you the other day." He grinned. "And now I understand that you are becoming quite the society lady."

"I beg your pardon."

"Is my information incorrect, or are you and Mr. Hilliman not going to the Eames salon tonight?"

"Why, yes," she said, and this time could not help blushing. "We are."

· "Well, remember that half the Republicans in town will be there. And most likely not our half." Sickles, as it happened, was a Democrat; specifically, a pro-war Democrat, the kind Lincoln liked best. "So be careful what you say. It's probably best to mainly listen. Then let us know what people are saying. A party means champagne, and, well, you never know who might let slip some remark that turns out to be helpful to us."

"Mr. Sickles, are you asking me to spy at the reception?"

"Why, no, Miss Canner. I would never do such a thing. That is more General Baker's style than mine." That grin again, but she could not tell whether she was being mocked. He grew serious. "Now, listen. Senator Sumner may well be in attendance. He rarely misses an evening at the Eameses'. You remember, of course, that he controls the key votes we need." He waited; and so she nodded. "If Sumner is present, make an effort to talk to him. That is most important. He has little to say these days to those who are on the President's side. We have to know what he is thinking. Do you understand?"

She swallowed, hard. Spying after all. "Yes, Mr. Sickles."

"Sumner doesn't much care for the ladies, but in your case"—again that flicker of his eyes—"well, maybe he'll make an exception."

As Abigail stared, he crossed to Dennard's door. Then a thought seemed to strike him. He hobbled to the shelf and pulled down a book of federal-court decisions. "Somewhere in here is a case about the admissibility of documentary evidence when the person who wrote the document is dead. Find it, and write me a summary memorandum."

No words came.

Sickles gave her that roguish smile. "The work you have done so far has been pointless. Surely you realize that. This work has a purpose. Nobody will duplicate your effort. You have to get the answer right." He extended the volume. "One page, Miss Canner. No more."

In her joy, she probably snatched the book too fast.

"Remember that you still are not a law clerk," he warned her. "That decision belongs to Mr. Dennard."

"Yes, Mr. Sickles."

"You are not reading for the bar. You are simply helping out in a crisis."

"I understand."

Again his eyes flicked over her in a most ungentlemanly way. "Young Hilliman is a lucky man." A wink before she could reply. "I will need that memorandum," said Sickles, "before you leave for the reception." He paused. "Grafton, from downstairs, also frequents the Eameses'. You'll want to stay away from him."

"I understand," she said again.

"Especially now," he added; and, offering no further explanation, went in to see Dennard.

II

Over a hundred thousand people lived in Washington City, and nearly half of them were colored. The negroes had long numbered in the tens of thousands, and only a fraction of them had ever been slaves. Over the years, a significant merchant class had evolved, and lately a small but growing professional class, including some half a dozen lawyers and twice as many doctors. Largely shut out of white society, the better-off among the colored residents of the city had established a society of their own, mimicking, insofar as possible, the habits of the white well-to-do. As a consequence, Abigail needed no instruction on the rules of etiquette for evening receptions. Men, she knew, were expected to wear black dress coats, and women full evening attire. The invitation was for eight o'clock, and so she left the office at four to return home and change, under the watchful eye of Dinah, who tutted and fixed and corrected, while Louisa looked on in awe and Nanny stomped about downstairs, signaling her disapproval by making enough noise to shake the house.

The gown Abigail chose was blue, and daringly cut, one that Dinah had made her order from a dressmaker in Philadelphia, and which she had never worn.

"You will be irresistible," Dinah murmured, fluffing the bunched sleeves.

"That is not my goal," said Abigail, staring, astonished, at the unfamiliar creature in the mirror.

"Whether or not it's your goal, darling, it's what you're going to achieve."

"I simply wish not to embarrass the President." She found herself preening, twisting this way and that, studying her reflection. "Or . . . or the firm." She shook her head. "I should not be wearing this dress. It is . . . sinful."

"It is perfect," said Dinah.

"I should change to something more . . . modest."

"Don't be a ninny," said Louisa, eyes still wide.

"Some of Mr. Lincoln's opponents will be there." Still staring in the mirror. "I should not allow myself to be seen this way."

"Believe me, darling," drawled Dinah, leading the way downstairs. "One look at you in that gown and they'll turn into supporters."

Louisa and Dinah helped Abigail into her wrap, then into her coat. Nanny Pork stood at the kitchen door, smoking her pipe. Her eyes said that this was no way for a lady to behave.

"I won't be late, Nanny."

"Uh-huh."

"Please don't be like this."

"Girl, I'm not bein like nothin."

Jonathan had offered to drive her to the reception, but there Abigail had drawn the line. A colored man in the neighborhood had a cab. Abigail had arranged to have him drop her, with his wife riding along as chaperone.

Dinah would not hear of it.

"I will drop you," she said. "Then Cutler will take me home, and I will send the carriage back to the Eameses' to wait." Cutler being her coachman and nighttime bodyguard.

The Berryhill barouche, with its dark wood inlays and gleaming coach lamps, was among the finest in Washington; certainly it was the finest in black Washington.

"There is no need—"

"That is what we are going to do," said Dinah.

As they stepped out of the house, the coachman pointed to a rider tying his horse to the rail.

"He says he gots to see Miss Abigail."

But Miss Abigail had already recognized the broad, bluff, swaggering figure approaching the house: Varak, the police inspector who either was or was not investigating the murders of Arthur McShane and Rebecca Deveaux.

III

"Perhaps I have come at a bad time," said Varak, no hint of apology in his voice as he eyed the two black women in their finery. "Going out for the evening, are we? And in so fancy a coach." He patted the polished wood. Abigail had not invited him in, so the three of them stood in the cold, watched over by Cutler.

"How may I be of assistance?" asked Abigail coldly.

But Dinah did better, speaking in the practiced tone of one who cannot be bothered to be rude to inferiors. "I'm afraid we're in bit of a hurry, Inspector."

Varak gave her that special policeman's glare, the one that intimidated the biggest crooks in the city. When Dinah refused to flinch, he turned back to Abigail. "Just a couple of questions," he said. "If this is a bad time, I can always come by your offices tomorrow." Not waiting for an answer, he inclined his head toward Dinah. "Private, if it's all the same to you."

"It most certainly is not all the same to her," Dinah snapped. "I am not going anywhere."

Abigail shooed her off. "Get in the carriage. I shall only be a minute." She tried to project Dinah's air of easy condescension. "The inspector only has a couple of questions, after all."

A moment later, they were alone in the front walk, although Dinah watched from one side, and Nanny and Louisa doubtless from the other.

"What can I do for you, Inspector Varak?"

"I was wondering. The dead negress. Rebecca."

This Abigail had to challenge. "Miss Deveaux."

Varak ignored the correction. He had a small notebook in his hand, and turned a page. There was a bit of illumination from the house, and more from the lighted carriage lamps, but still she did not see how he could possibly read what was written there. "Did you know her at all, I wonder?"

"No. Of course not."

"No acquaintance at all? Never met her? You're quite certain?"

"I am."

"Bloody odd." The inspector turned another page. Night mist swirled at their ankles, creating the illusion of a dark, private world.

"Did somebody tell you I knew her?" Abigail ventured.

But Varak did not seem to think he was there to respond to her inquiries. "How did you and Mr. McShane get along?"

"Excellently well," she said, startled.

"Indeed. I am given to understand that he raised some question as to your suitability for a position at his firm."

"That is not so."

He made a note, laboriously, wanting her to watch him do it. "Mind telling me where you were on the night in question?" he asked, not raising his head.

"Surely you don't think—"

"The Thursday. The night of the murder. Where were you, please?"

"I was at a dinner. The Mellisons." She stood straighter. "And if you are implying that I had anything to do with—"

"Just answer my questions, if you would, please." Face still buried in the notebook. "The Mellisons are a colored family, are they not?"

"They are."

"Anybody white present that night, I wonder?" Tapping the page. "Anybody who can corroborate your statement?"

"I beg your pardon."

He wrote a few words, then lifted his head. "And you're sure you never encountered the negress Rebecca? Excuse me, Miss Deveaux?" His bulbous eyes searched her face. "No meetings in out-of-the-way places? Say, the Metzerott Hotel, the weekend prior to her murder?"

"Of course not. Where would you get such an idea?"

Eyes back on the page. A frown. "Oh, but wait. You do know David Grafton, do you not?" Varak looked up again. "Mr. Grafton, from the law office downstairs."

"I do."

"And you would no doubt be astonished to learn that Mr. Grafton, too, was acquainted with your friend Miss Rebecca Deveaux?"

Abigail could think of nothing to say; and so said nothing.

"You will admit that this is all very peculiar, Miss Canner. Mr. Lincoln's lawyer is murdered in the company of a colored prostitute. The prostitute turns out to be acquainted with one of the said lawyer's employees." He silenced her objection with a glance. "She is also acquainted with the said lawyer's former partner, who is said to despise him. But you of course know nothing of any of this. All a series of coincidences, misunderstandings, and lies, is that it?"

"Yes, Inspector. That is it precisely."

"Very well, then. Thank you for your assistance, Miss Canner." He shut the notebook, tucked it away. "Sorry to have detained you. Do enjoy your evening at the Eameses'."

She started to ask Varak how he knew where she was going, but he had already turned away.

CHAPTER 13

Salon

I

IT WAS OBERLIN all over again, but without the innocence. White faces everywhere, all of them comfortable and confident, visible proof of the existence of what her brother, Michael, liked to call *the people who* as in "the people who have money," "the people who run things," "the people who matter." Abigail had long been fascinated by *the people who*. At Oberlin, although she pretended to a disdain for the ways of the people who mattered, everyone knew how desperately she longed to be one of them.

When Dinah's rig pulled up, Jonathan was waiting outside. He helped Abigail down as Dinah smirked. Abigail made the nervous introduction.

"A pleasure," said Jonathan.

Dinah was mischievous. "Abigail has told me simply *everything*, Mr. Hilliman."

The carriage clattered off. Jonathan told Abigail she looked magnificent. She dropped her eyes. She had refused to tell Dinah the details of her conversation with Inspector Varak, and suspected this was not the right moment to share them with Jonathan.

"You are very kind," she said.

A servant admitted them without raising an eyebrow, because Mrs. Eames ran a very modern salon. They stood in the foyer, Jonathan awkward in his tails, Abigail more so in the flowing gown. She considered dressing this way ridiculous, but the attire was what etiquette

now demanded for evening receptions during what Washington society called "the Season"—running, roughly, from New Year's Day to
Lent. There were probably fifty people present. The pianist was playing "Away with the Past," which was presumably Mrs. Eames's way of
being clever, serenading her guests with popular tunes rather than the
chamber music common to the city's salons. Jonathan leaned close to
ask whether she knew the song. Abigail nodded, but said nothing, even
as her mind recited the haunting words: *Away with the past, be it mine to
forget / The hopes, the fond hopes that in darkness have set.* . . . She grimaced.
Inspector Varak's questions had reminded her of a past she was desperate to forget.

Never met her? You're quite certain?

She never had.

No meetings in out-of-the-way places? Say, the Metzerott Hotel?

All at once, she decided to tell Jonathan. But just as she leaned toward
him, he was grabbed by the always grave Senator Fessenden of Maine,
the former Treasury secretary, who was among Lincoln's biggest supporters on Capitol Hill. Before anybody could so much as attempt an
introduction of Abigail, Fessenden had dragged his captive over to a
corner, where he began haranguing him, gesticulating wildly, as if Jonathan were personally to blame for the events of the past few days.

Left alone, Abigail hesitated, not sure what etiquette commanded.
Was she to seek out her hostess? Attach herself to a conversation?
Should she perhaps search for Senator Sumner, as Dan Sickles had
advised? Or enjoy the buffet, which was piled high with more varieties
of meat and fish than Abigail had ever seen on a single table? A moment
later, the choice was snatched from her as Fanny Eames bustled over
and welcomed Abigail enthusiastically, as if she were a long-awaited
arrival from distant shores. Mrs. Eames locked an arm in hers and, as
several prominent Washingtonians looked askance, led her toward the
main group of guests. Mrs. Eames asked her how she liked working as
a clerk, and told her, before she could answer, what a brave and impressive inspiration she was. It was so unjust, Mrs. Eames proclaimed, that
women were barred from so many professions. And, as neatly as that,
the hostess introduced Abigail to the guest of honor, a small, girlishly
handsome man named Morphy, who was said to be the strongest chess
player in the world. Morphy looked unimpressed. Their hands barely
touched. He turned his back on her. An instant later, Mrs. Eames had
deposited a breathless Abigail into the midst of a clutch of large, fluttery

women, augmented by a man or two. They greeted her uncertainly. One of the women was Mary Henry, who was said to be writing a book about growing up inside the Smithsonian Castle, where her father was curator. Another was Lucretia Garfield, known as Crete, a stern-eyed woman whose husband was James Garfield, yet another Civil War officer turned congressman, also said to be interested in higher office. The women treated her with a suspicious amiability, kindly because they were ladies, even if they doubted that Abigail was. A moment later, she was all but smothered by a thickset woman with tight, inky hair and a joyously half-mad half-smile—obviously important, given the way the others deferred. She was two or three years older than Abigail. Her odd silver eyes were bright with excitement as she took Abigail by the forearm and drew her toward the center of the group. "You must tell us the whole story," the newcomer commanded, in a tone that did not admit of contradiction. "Tell us your adventures."

"My adventures?" said Abigail, mystified.

"It's a wonder she doesn't write a book about it," murmured one of the other women, "those books being so popular these days." She turned to her friend. The pianist had switched to "Saint Clare to Little Eva in Heaven," a choice Abigail found ridiculous. "Tell her, Bessie, darling. Tell her she simply *must* write a book."

"If your husband will endorse it," said the silver-eyed woman. Her heavy grin widened. "Are you writing one, dear?"

Abigail realized that the largish woman who still had her by the arm must be Lucy Lambert Hale, known as Bessie, with whom Jonathan was now and then seen around town: he claimed unwillingly.

"I'm not writing a book," said Abigail, bewildered. "I have nothing to write about."

"Nonsense," said Bessie Hale, eyes moist and shining. "Your escape."

"I beg your pardon."

"Your escape," she repeated, slowly this time. "How did you come north? The Underground Railroad? Were you a child still? Or did you leave your plantation and attach yourself to the Union Army during the war?"

"Look at her," said Mrs. Garfield. "So thin. She's been starving. Starved by her master. They used to do that, you know," she confided to Abigail. "Not as a *punishment*. As a *policy*."

"I wonder that the government hasn't fed her better," said someone else.

"When are you going south again?" resumed Miss Hale. "I assume your family will be taking over your forty acres soon?"

Abigail blinked. "My family has been free for three generations," she said, somewhat desperately. "We've been in Washington City all that time."

The women tittered and elbowed each other, as though she had made the funniest joke of the night so far.

"You must forgive them, Miss Canner," said a smooth male voice, very near her ear. Turning, she found herself staring into the brilliant blue eyes of Senator Charles Sumner.

II

Next to the President, General Grant, and perhaps the Secretary of State, Charles Sumner was the most famous man in Washington. He was described, by the newspapers but also himself, as the conscience of the Senate. Tall and straight, powerful through the shoulders, he had smoothly shining blond-gray hair and the confident good looks that marked the hereditary upper classes of a nation that still denied it had any. He was charming and elegant and cultured, a favorite among both the crowned heads and intelligentsia of Europe. Any book of his speeches would become a best seller around the world. He had been perhaps the leading Abolitionist in the country, and was said to despise Lincoln with all the passion of moral superiority.

"You must forgive them," said Sumner again, contriving, without actually touching Abigail, to guide her into a private corner of the drawing room, where two walls of books met. "They know nothing of free black people. They are committed Abolitionists because they hate slavery and because they want to do good, but they have no particular interest in people of your race." A confident smile. "Like so many people of liberal persuasion, they value their own progressive opinions more than they value the people they hold those opinions about." He tilted his head slightly back and away, as if examining a precious but inferior work of art. "I am Charles Sumner."

"Abigail Canner." She lifted her hand. He took it, kissed the air near her fingers in the proper continental manner of the day, returned it dry.

"It is a great pleasure," he declared, "to meet you at last."

Abigail was, for a moment, speechless. "At last?" she managed.

Sumner nodded comfortably. "Professor Finney has naturally corresponded with me. He considers you his finest student. Perhaps you were not aware of his opinion?"

"You know Professor Finney?" she said, feeling a bit stupid. "He said that about me?"

"Of course. And yet I imagine he is somewhat disappointed," Sumner continued, with no change in tone, "to find you laboring on behalf of Mr. Lincoln." Before she could reply, he added, "Finney has never been an admirer of Mr. Lincoln, as I am sure you are aware."

"He taught us to think for ourselves," she managed, as the air in the crowded, noisy room began to feel constricted. Being criticized by the great Charles Sumner was nearly more than she was able to bear. Over near the piano, Jonathan was listening carefully to Fessenden, as Bessie Hale hovered.

"So defending Mr. Lincoln is your own choice?"

"I—yes, Mr. Sumner. It is."

"Why? Doesn't it matter to you that he suspended habeas corpus and jailed political opponents? Or that he doesn't seem to care what happens to the freedmen? Or that the Congress has twice adopted legislation concerning the manner in which the defeated South is to be reconstituted, and Mr. Lincoln has twice thanked us for our advice and told us that the question is military, and therefore none of our business?"

Abigail composed her answer carefully. Sickles had told her only to try to feel Sumner out; he had never for an instant suggested that she try to persuade the great orator. And a side of her, faced with Sumner's browbeating, understood that the greater part of valor would be laughing his question off. But at this moment the other side of her was dominant, the side that would not back down in the face of any white man's presumption of intellectual superiority.

"Whatever wrongs Mr. Lincoln may or may not have committed," she said, "he has also committed the two greatest and most important acts any President has done, or is likely to do. He won the war to restore the Union. In the process, he forced an end to slavery."

Sumner was unimpressed. "Lincoln freed the slaves as a military necessity. He has said that over and over. It was not a moral crusade for him, any more than the war was. All was forced upon him."

Abigail noticed the guests moving toward the drawing room, where the great chess champion was about to give some sort of exhibition. Sumner did not budge. He seemed genuinely interested in her answer.

"Senator," she said, eyes glittering, "I cannot deny any of what you say. But why should the one whose yoke is broken care whether it was broken out of the proper motive? It would be far worse to wait another generation for a President whose motives are pure."

She spotted David Grafton across the room, in animated conversation with a young woman she did not recognize. For the briefest of instants she wondered again about the whispers of conspiracy: *You do know David Grafton, do you not?*

"I would think," said Sumner, "that the answer would depend on what happened to the man after the yoke was broken. A committed Abolitionist would take measures to ensure that the yoke would not, in some other guise, be restored. I am not persuaded that the President has done that. Indeed, I know that he has not." She was about to respond, but he had tired of repartee. "Three times now, the Congress has presented a bill that would keep from ever holding office again all those who rebelled against the Union, or fought for the rebel side, or worked for the rebel government. Three times, Mr. Lincoln has refused to sign it. He is perfectly content to allow the same Southerners who rebelled to be mayors and governors and even Senators, so long as they swear they will not do it again, and that they are against slavery. Well, of course they will swear they are against slavery, since the Thirteenth Amendment abolished it a year and a half ago!"

Grafton had noticed her. He flashed a friendly smile, and began to wend his way through the throng. Not wanting to speak to him, she tried to excuse herself. But Charles Sumner, by common consent the most eloquent man in the nation, had turned upon her the full force of his eloquence, and was not about to allow her to escape.

"And there is another reason, Miss Canner, a problem of which Mr. Lincoln himself is aware. Never in the history of our Protestant Republic has one man gathered to himself as much power as the current occupant of the Executive Mansion. He has nearly sunk the other branches into irrelevance. In a parliamentary system, which I would prefer, such a thing would never happen. His own party would turn a prime minister out of office before allowing him to usurp the legislative function—"

He stopped, and bowed. "I apologize, Miss Canner. At times I forget that I am not on the floor of the Senate."

She nodded, nervously. Grafton was nearly upon them. "I was under the impression that you had not made up your mind how to vote."

"And I have not. I have a great deal of thinking to do. I shall weigh the case with enormous care. Certainly the argument you have just offered will weigh heavily upon my judgment. Good evening, Mr. Grafton. As you well know, I have nothing to say to you." Perfectly calm, Sumner turned his back: Abigail was impressed by the aggressive smoothness of this grave insult, and wished for a silly instant that she were a gentleman, so that she might try it.

For the moment, however, having talked to the one man she had been ordered to talk to, Abigail faced the challenge of avoiding the one man she had been ordered to avoid.

III

David Grafton appeared not in the least offended by Sumner's rudeness. The smile on the pale, crooked face projected the same feral air she remembered from their first meeting. "A pleasure to see you again, Miss Canner. I trust that you are enjoying yourself."

"I am indeed," she said, backing away.

Like a hunting cat, the crooked man followed her. He crowded her into a corner, where a bookshelf ended and a small corridor began. She smelled the cloying sweetness of breath freshened with the latest European import.

"A pleasure," he repeated, and then, to her surprise, he slipped past her, and into the hallway. She turned to see his crooked form wobbling its way along until, without breaking stride, he sidestepped through a door. The water closet, she told herself, except that she was fairly certain that while she was talking to Sumner, a young woman had slipped into that very room; and not emerged. Abigail had caught only a glimpse of the young woman and had not seen her face; but wanted very badly to know who she was.

Later, Abigail would not be able to say quite what drove her forward. Curiosity, yes, certainly, but she was not one for great risk. The need to prove herself, perhaps by unraveling the great hidden conspiracy of which others whispered. The simple desire to get to the heart of the mystery that was David Grafton. And the conviction, perhaps fanciful, that even if Grafton was indeed the corrupt schemer others supposed, it was odd that he would risk, in the middle of a crowded reception, sneaking off to meet a woman half his age: for much of her understanding of the interaction between the sexes was still colored by lessons drawn from the pages of *Peterson's* and *McClure's* and the other magazines aimed at women of the rising middle classes.

The drawing room was now nearly deserted, because the guests had moved into the parlor to watch the chess exhibition. Abigail gathered from the cheers that the great champion was winning. Satisfied that she was not observed, she crept into the short corridor. Two doors on the right, one on the left. Grafton, and the young woman before him, had entered the farther door on the right.

Abigail crept down the hall until she was outside the room. The door was tightly shut. After a glance over her shoulder, she leaned in and pressed her ear to the dark polished wood. She could hear only a low murmur: no clear words.

Frustration.

She stepped back. Perhaps it would be best to re-join the party.

Suddenly the door jerked open, and Abigail leaped away. She dashed into the room across the way—as it happened, the library. She closed the library door and peered through the crack. The unknown woman stood in the threshold of the opposite room, her back to Abigail. Grafton's voice was as clear as a bell.

"Then we are in agreement? Your doubts are assuaged?"

The young woman whispered something Abigail did not catch.

"You might imagine, my dear, that, because of who your father is, you cannot be reached. That would be a grave error."

Wiping tears from rosy cheeks, the young woman turned toward the light.

"You are a monster," said Bessie Hale, and swept off down the hall.

IV

"Please tell me it went well," said Jonathan as a servant helped Abigail into her coat. "Your conversation with Sumner. You had half the room watching."

"He said he has not made up his mind. He said he will give the matter careful consideration."

"So much we knew already."

"Then we are no worse off," she said, more coldly than either expected, but the evening's events had left her nervy and fraught.

The line of guests awaiting their rigs created a delay at the door. With the crowd now close around them, Jonathan changed the subject, talking airily, as though the event of greatest importance tonight had been meeting the guest of honor. "In any event, Miss Canner, you missed a most fascinating exhibition. Mr. Morphy, the chess champion, played three of us without sight of the board. He won all the games, and it took him only fifteen minutes! Afterward there was a bit of a scene. Mrs. Sprague—do you know Kate Sprague?

"I believe that Mrs. Sprague and I were briefly introduced earlier this evening."

"Ah. Good, then. A useful woman to know. Mrs. Sprague is the daughter of the Chief Justice and the wife of the junior senator from Rhode Island. She is but twenty-seven, and already the most eminent woman in the city. Well. Mrs. Sprague took one of the boards against him. She lost, of course, but that was hardly the end of the matter. Mr. Eames proposed a toast to Mr. Morphy, followed by three huzzahs. Afterward, Mrs. Sprague walked right up to Mr. Morphy and accused him of having fought in the rebel army. She said he was attached to General Beauregard's staff at Bull Run." They were out on the front portico, where he signaled to Abigail's carriage man. "She also said that his family fortune came from slaves. Not using them in the fields but selling them. That his grandfather was a slave importer and auctioneer in New Orleans. The very lowest of human activities, she said." He shook his head ruefully. "I am afraid Mrs. Sprague showed little tact. She disrupted the evening. Hence, the present crush."

"I think she did the right thing," murmured Abigail, impressed.

The group ahead of them climbed aboard their rig. The Berryhill barouche was next in line. With nobody in earshot, Jonathan leaned close to her. "Abigail, listen. Forget all that. Fessenden says there is an offer on the table."

"Oh?"

"He says that the Radicals are willing to make a deal with Mr. Lincoln. Perhaps they are not as confident as everyone thinks. We must go to Mr. Dennard's house."

Abigail considered. "You go," she said. "I am exhausted." Her breath curled whitely in the frigid night air. A gray mist softened the streetlamps to distant gauzy globes. "It is well that tomorrow is the Sabbath."

Handing her up into the carriage, Jonathan asked, "By the way, where did you vanish to? Mr. Sumner was present for the champion's exhibition. You were not."

Abigail looked down, eyes unreadable. She seemed about to explain herself, then thought better of it. "Good night, Mr. Hilliman."

The driver closed the door, and the barouche headed off. As soon as they were out of the driveway, Abigail moved to the opposite seat, up behind the driver. "I have changed my plans, Mr. Cutler. Rather than taking me home directly, I wonder whether you would mind making a stop along the way."

V

The Metzerott Hotel was located on Pennsylvania Avenue between Ninth and Tenth Streets West, just four blocks from the offices of Dennard & McShane. It stood two stories, with a fancy balustrade along the second level, and was one of the few leading hotels in Washington City where it was possible—not easy, but possible—for a negro to find a room. Even at ten-thirty in the evening, the porter answered the door, because it was not unusual for a train to run late, and guests to need to register. The porter roused the night clerk, a softly rounded man, bald and egglike, who pursed thick lips in disappointment upon learning that she was not planning to stay.

"The kitchen is closed," he whispered, tone funereal, eyes downcast. "As is the bar. And I would not like to disturb our guests at this hour."

"I am not looking for refreshment," said Abigail. "I am not looking for a guest."

"Oh?"

She had never quite played the deceiver, and was not sure how precisely it was done. But she could think of only one way Inspector Varak could possibly have been led to believe that she and Rebecca Deveaux had been in this hotel at the same time, and was determined to check her arithmetic. "In truth, I myself was a guest here, oh, two weeks ago. And I am afraid that I lost the receipt for my stay." She cast her eyes demurely downward. "Without the receipt, I fear I shall not be able to obtain reimbursement from my employer."

The night clerk was a friendly man. He had a daughter her age, he said, and she, too, had unfortunately been required to earn for a short period, until a suitable husband had been found. He opened the hotel register happily, but when Abigail told him her name, his round face grew distressed. He started to speak, hesitated.

"Yes, well, there is a bit of a problem." He eyed her fancy clothes, glanced through the shadowed lobby at the expensive carriage waiting outside.

She understood.

"I shall be right back," she said.

Her handbag was in the barouche. She did not carry much money—she did not possess much—but she found a couple of coins. Back inside, she dropped them into the night clerk's sweaty palm.

The money vanished; the ledger appeared; and as the clerk wrote out her receipt by the wavery glow of a single gas lamp, Abigail read upside-down. Her name, as a guest, for one night: Saturday, the sixteenth, five days before the murder of Arthur McShane.

Even though she had never been inside the hotel in her life.

Abigail inquired about Rebecca Deveaux. The answer cost her another half-dollar: Rebecca's name, too, was in the ledger, and on the same date.

"You've been right popular," said the clerk, leering. "A couple of men have been in, asking the same. Maybe one of them from your employer."

"Perhaps," Abigail said, unable to keep from blushing. But at least now she understood the clerk's reticence upon hearing her name. Perhaps Inspector Varak, discovering these entries, had sworn him to secrecy.

In her head echoed Varak's words from a seeming lifetime ago, but really just a few hours: *You do know David Grafton, do you not? . . . I do. . . . And you would no doubt be astonished to learn that he, too, knew your friend Miss Rebecca Deveaux?*

No, Inspector. I am not astonished at all.

Riding home in the fine Berryhill carriage, Abigail pondered. Inspector Varak was trying to solve one mystery. Now Abigail was confronted by another. Someone had taken a great deal of trouble to make it appear that she was acquainted with the murdered Rebecca Deveaux. She had to find out who; more important, she had to find out why.

CHAPTER 14

Emissary

I

"THAT IS NO deal at all," said Stanton. He glanced around the room as if daring the other members of the lawyers' coterie to contradict him. His eyes were wet and swollen from his seemingly perpetual cold. "No deal at all. The Senate dare not dictate to the President of the United States who will and will not be allowed in his Cabinet!"

Lincoln stood at the window, looking down on the park. It was early Sunday afternoon, and rainy, and the President was still dressed for church. He had attended services more often since his wife died— usually at Saint John's, right across Lafayette Square. "Well, now, Mars, let's not be too hasty. I am quite sure our Radical friends would like *you* to remain in office. They just want to subtract everybody else."

Stanton remained unmollified. "If it were up to me, I would have them all in shackles."

A moment of embarrassed silence in the room, the freezing rain like gunshots against the window.

"This might be an argument against interest," said Speed, "but I think, if we are being offered a deal, we are duty-bound to explore it."

"I agree," said Dennard, cautiously.

"Duty," said the President. "Duty. *Duty*," he repeated, playing with the word in a way that Jonathan, head down, scribbling notes, thought conveyed a growing distaste, perhaps even disgust: a man tired of explaining himself. The deal was a simple one. If Lincoln would allow the congressional leadership to decide who would serve in his Cabinet, they would "consider" dropping the impeachment effort. "They want to control me," said the President, now visibly angry. "They want to dictate to the Executive. But my *duty* is not to the Congress. My *duty* is to the nation. To the Constitution, which I took an oath to preserve, protect, and defend. An oath registered in Heaven!"

In the face of this presidential fury, the other men in the room traded uneasy glances. To Jonathan's untutored eye, the look that passed between the Secretary of War and the attorney general seemed one of exasperation. Then, as perhaps they expected all along, the anger faded, and the old Lincoln returned.

"You know, this situation reminds me of a story I heard someone tell in Iowa. He was trying to enforce upon his hearers the truth of the old adage that 'three removes are worse than a fire.' As an illustration, he gave an account of a family who started from western Pennsylvania, pretty well off in this world's goods. But they moved and moved, having less and less every time they moved, till after a while they could carry everything in one wagon. He said that the chickens of the family got so used to being moved, that whenever they saw the wagon sheets brought they laid themselves on their backs and crossed their legs, ready to be tied. Now, gentlemen, if I were to be guided by every committee that comes in at that door, I might just as well cross my hands and let them tie my legs together."

He laughed, as did the entire meeting, all except Rufus Dennard, who looked not so much unamused as disapproving. He was a man of few words, and had difficulty with a client who was much the other way.

Lincoln was not done. "You know, a friend of mine was here visiting not long ago, and he told me that poor McShane getting killed like that probably lost me half a million votes, just through guilt by association. I told him about this old woman I knew back in Kentucky who had a house by the riverbank. There was a terrible storm, and the river overflowed its banks, and the water came in through the door. The old woman picked up her broom and started sweeping the water out. But the flood just kept rising and rising. And she kept sweeping and sweeping. When the water was up to her neck, she shrugged, still sweeping, and said to herself, 'Let's see which lasts longer, the flood or the broom.'"

More laughter. Lincoln had crossed the room to retrieve a paper from his desk. "I have here a communication from Horace Greeley, who is, as usual, being helpful. He advises me that if I leave office now, and avoid the bitter battle to come, I will depart with the thanks of a grateful nation." He adjusted his glasses. "Mr. Greeley says I will have won the war and freed the slaves, and that will be my epitaph. If I stay on, however, history will write of me that I allowed my own ambitions to tear the Union asunder once more. Now, it seems to me it's a mite early to worry about what they might carve on my tombstone, but I suppose Mr. Greeley can see the future more clearly than I can." He put the paper down, looked hard at the others. "Still, even if we cannot see the future, we will do our best to influence it."

He took a moment to consider. Everyone in the room understood when the President's silence meant that he was plotting. "We will respond to our friends on the Hill via the same means they used to send us the message. Jonathan here can go see Fessenden and tell him we aren't much interested in anything but having the Radicals respect the proper separation of powers in the federal government. It is up to me and not up to them who my advisers are. That is the constitutional system, and we could not change it if we wanted to. Which we don't." His face softened. "On the other hand, I am not saying that we would turn down a more reasonable proposition."

Jonathan was alarmed to be thrust so suddenly into the middle of things. Unlike Arthur McShane, Rufus Dennard brought him into nearly every White House meeting; until now, Jonathan had been grateful. "Mr. President, I don't really know if I am the right person—"

He stopped, aware that Lincoln was smiling at him. Dennard touched his elbow gently. "Don't worry, Hilliman. I shall go."

Speed had a concern. "Fessenden is a friend of this Administration. He served you and the nation very ably as Secretary of the Treasury. Perhaps we should not be so indirect as to communicate via an attorney."

"Oh, I think that's exactly the way to do it," Lincoln assured him. "If Fessenden wanted you or me or Mars here to come calling, he'd have brought the offer to the Mansion in the first place. But he didn't. That means he wants to open negotiations, but he can't afford to see one of us at his door. And it can't be you, either, Rufus. I'm afraid it has to be Jonathan. Sickles feels the same."

Stanton nodded his agreement. "Anyone else would be recognized."

Speed said, "Going to see Fessenden, even young Hilliman would probably be recognized. We need an envoy who will be invisible."

Again all eyes were on Jonathan. And, very suddenly, he knew what they wanted him to do—what they had planned all along.

II

Abigail Canner lived in a two-story brick house overlooking one of the city's remaining farms, near where Tenth Street crossed Virginia Avenue and continued on a southward course to the Potomac River. The Island was bordered by the two rivers and two canals. Dwellings and businesses and factories. The air was heavy and wet, as befitted the marshland where the nation had built its capital city. The smells were atrocious, made worse by the scraggly remnants of the canal to the northwest. Jonathan all but held his nose as he climbed down onto a muddy boulder on the west side of Tenth Street. Across the road, a gaggle of negro boys in knickers paused their ball game to watch. Jonathan smiled tentatively. The boys stared. Probably they wondered why some white stranger was smiling at them.

Jonathan wondered, too.

The house was surrounded by a low wooden fence. As he pushed the gate, he noticed that his palms were sweaty, despite the chill. He was more nervous visiting Abigail's home than he was meeting the President of the United States.

He hesitated, feeling watched. He looked around. The boys had returned to their match. To the north, the vista was dominated by the brooding redbrick spire of the Smithsonian Castle on B Street, where mad Mary Henry sat and watched the world. To the south, the river was a gray smear. Beyond lay Virginia: to most Yankees, still enemy territory.

Certainly the negroes must feel that way.

A trio of scrawny chickens hopped about the muddy yard. Half-sunken stones made an uneven path to the porch. The door flew open at his knock. Standing there was a woman he nearly but not quite recognized: a younger version of Abigail, in flowing dress severely buttoned.

Jonathan removed his hat. "You would be Miss Louisa," he murmured.

Louisa Canner had most of her older sister's willowy beauty, and all of her charm, and added to it a mature flirtatiousness all her own. Her skin was perhaps a shade lighter than Abigail's, more café au lait than cacao, and she glowed with an energy both delicate and dangerous.

"And you would be Mr. Hilliman," she said. "The white man my sister has been keeping company with."

One minute behind the gate and already Jonathan was unsure of himself. What, he wondered, would Meg say? Or her father, the Lion of Louisiana? "That is not precisely as I would put it."

"Everybody else puts it that way, Mr. Hilliman." Those huge eyes, larger even than her sister's, took his measure. "And may I take it that you have come to call on her now?"

Jonathan chose his words with care. "I have come to see your sister in the course of business."

Louisa inclined her head toward the boys playing ball across the street. "I am not sure the neighborhood will look at it exactly that way, Mr. Hilliman."

Before he could respond, a heavy growl erupted from within: the voice of authority lumbering angrily toward death.

"Leave him be, Lou. Let him in."

"He shouldn't be here," she said, not turning.

"I said let him in." A cough, wet and rattling, and the sound of something heavy dragging along the floor. "Might as well find out what kinda white man he is."

"The usual kind," said Louisa with a toothsome grin.

"Courtin?"

"Maybe."

"Well, let's have a look at him, then."

And a sharper voice, Abigail's: "Lou, you have chores. Go. Now." She materialized from the darkness to stand beside Jonathan on the porch, watching her sister scurry down the walk and out the gate. Louisa crossed the street and threaded past the clutch of boys. "Why, Jonathan Hilliman," said Abigail, as prettily as any belle. "How good of you to call."

Following her inside, he suspected that she would shortly be a good deal less happy to see him.

III

Nanny Pork turned out to be a broad, dark woman, with hair tightly braided and a way of looking at you that said she could see into your head. She walked poorly, but kept circling Jonathan anyway as he stood in the parlor, unwilling to sit, despite having been bidden, until his hostess did. But his hostess was not even in the room: she had gone to make tea.

"You're kinda scrawny," Nanny said at last.

"I suppose I am," he conceded, actually lifting an arm to look.

"You a lawyer, Mr. Jonathan?"

Mr. Jonathan. What the servants called him at Newport. His skin prickled with unexpected embarrassment.

"A law clerk. I—I am studying to be a lawyer."

She was behind him now, and he half turned. Her palms were on the wide hips, rubbing them as if they ached. "Abby says you're rich."

Abby. *Abby.* He had never heard Abigail mention a nickname, or dreamed that she might answer to one. He had swiveled completely now, and was facing the old woman. "My family owns a couple of mills."

The clever yellow eyes tracked him. "I knowed a man in Clarendon County who owned a mill. A colored man. Free. This was before the war. But they burned it down anyway. When he complained about it, they locked him up."

"Then it is well," he said carefully, "that the Union won the war."

She made a spitting sound. "The war ain't over. For you, maybe. Not for us."

Nanny Pork cut her gaze to the side. Following, he noticed first a piano, and then a shotgun resting beneath the window beside it: an odd place to leave a firearm. And he wondered, for a mad moment, whether this old woman, or even young Louisa, had kept a bead on him all the way up the walk. As a white man, he was uneasy in colored neighborhoods; it had not occurred to him until now that a white stranger might worry the colored folk even more than they worried him, or that they lived in a world in which a knock at the door might portend cruel, swift violence.

His eyes met Nanny Pork's again, and he knew that she knew where he had been looking. The shapeless dress was wrinkled and dark.

"I just wants you to understand," she said, "that my Abby is gonna be married. She's waitin on her fiancé to come back from the war. And no girl livin under my roof is gonna mess around like a lowlife. Is that clear?"

Jonathan had expected this, and even had a little speech ready. He did not expect to botch it quite so badly. "I assure you, my intentions are entirely—Ah, what I mean is, we have only a—a professional relationship."

"Yeah, well, a lot of mens has professional relationships with a lot of girls, and that better not be the kind of business you means."

"No, of course not. Of course not. I am sorry if I—"

"Leave him alone, Nanny," said Abigail from the doorway. She was carrying a tray, and resting on it were, pointedly, two teacups, not three.

Nanny Pork crossed her arms. She grinned suddenly, showing yellowy but even teeth. "We's just gettin to know each other, isn't that right, Mr. Jonathan?"

"Yes, ma'am."

"Don't you *ma'am* me, boy. I'se been Nanny Pork since before your mama was borned. You just call me Nanny."

"Yes, Nanny."

Her eyes darted toward Abigail. "You behave yourselfs," she said, and dragged from the room.

"You must forgive her," said Abigail, gesturing him toward the sofa, draped with an obviously expensive but very worn golden fabric. All of the furniture was a little too big, a little too fancy, and a little too old. Jonathan had seen similar efforts during his childhood, gleefully pointed out by his mother: families that struggled from generation to generation to keep up the appearance of prosperity after the money was gone.

"There is nothing to forgive," he said, sitting uneasily beside her. "She is rather . . . fascinating."

"She is rather irritating."

"She strikes me as a wise woman."

"I suppose." Abigail's tone was skeptical. She had placed the tea set on a small wooden table. As she poured out, Jonathan felt more than ever like a gentleman caller. Music sheets lay across the piano: Schubert's Sonata in B-flat; the overture from *Der Freischütz*. Jonathan wondered whether Abigail had been to see Jenny Lind when she performed in the city. He had never before wondered such a thing about a negro, but with Abigail Canner everything seemed possible.

"So," she said, eyes aglow, "what brings you to my home on this lovely winter afternoon?"

"I have just come from the Executive Mansion."

"I see." Her brow furrowed, and he wondered whether she was thinking, as he was, that, although Jonathan now attended nearly every meeting of the President and his lawyers, Abigail had yet to be invited. "Then perhaps we should get to the point. I fear that I am expecting another caller shortly."

Puzzled by her sudden coldness, Jonathan complied. "You will remember that last night I told you that Senator Fessenden had conveyed the outlines of a deal to end the impeachment proceedings."

"I do."

"The President," Jonathan continued, "is not inclined to accept the deal in its current form. He would, however, be willing to consider alternatives." Those huge eyes were so full and trusting that he found it difficult to say the rest. "The trouble is, he cannot be seen to negotiate openly, any more than the Radicals can."

Abigail caught the theme. "He requires an emissary to negotiate."

Jonathan nodded. "The emissary will not be negotiating. The emissary will be carrying messages."

For the first time in their acquaintance, she seemed uneasy—fearing, perhaps, where the conversation was headed. "And the President, I take it, has chosen you." Even her smile was tentative. "That is a great honor, Mr. Hilliman. You will be carrying the messages that may save Mr. Lincoln's presidency. I congratulate you." She laughed. Harshly. "I imagine that you and Miss Hale will be celebrating."

So that was it. Jonathan wondered what Abigail thought she knew; and scarcely dared wonder why she would care. He longed to explain himself, to drive that look of severe disappointment from the smooth brown face; but duty was duty, and this was not the moment to discuss the matter.

"I fear that I am not the chosen emissary. It is you, not I, who shall save Mr. Lincoln's presidency."

And Abigail's eyes grew wide indeed.

CHAPTER 15

Deputation

I

ON MONDAY MORNING, a windswept winter rain froze the capital. Abigail was delayed when the horsecars jumped the icy track near Tenth Street. The events of the past few days and nights had left her on edge, and by the time she reached the office, she was shivering, only partly from cold. She sat in McShane's office with Dan Sickles, who rehearsed her carefully on the mission she was to undertake. She had never known him to be so serious. Fessenden liked things tidy, Sickles told her. As Treasury secretary, he had cleaned up the mess left behind by his predecessor, who had pretty much bankrupted the federal government trying to pay for the war. Fessenden hadn't fixed things out of loyalty to Lincoln or even to country; he had fixed things because he hated untidiness.

"What are you trying to tell me, Mr. Sickles?"

"Don't add to the message. Don't subtract from it. You are there as an emissary from whom?"

"This office. Not the President."

"And are you bringing a response to the proposal?"

"Only a request for more details."

"And if he asks you which details in particular need to be clarified?"

Abigail had her hands in her lap. She had to fight the urge to squeeze them nervously together. Yesterday, after services at the Baptist church on the wharf, she had been embarrassed to find herself the center of fluttery female attention, everyone wanting to know what Lincoln was really like; and Abigail had wished desperately to wake up and find herself truly a member of the inner circle. Now, on the verge of becoming exactly that, she found her hands were shaking.

"That is not for me to say," she said. "But I believe that our client might be open to alternatives."

"Good." He laid a hand on her shoulder. "Try to relax, Miss Canner. You'll be surprised at how well things will go."

"Thank you, Mr. Sickles."

"Call me Dan. And remember. Fessenden is a stern man, and he has that prim look of disapproval all the time. But he isn't actually unkind. If you have any trouble getting in to see him, give his man the note from Speed. Otherwise, keep it in your bag. And one other thing." At last, a tiny smile. "I'm afraid we cannot let you have a driver. If you are to be unnoticed, you will have to take the horsecars."

Abigail hesitated. Among the President's men, Sickles was the rogue. She had told nobody of the madness of the past two days: how Varak thought she knew Rebecca, how somebody had forged her name alongside Rebecca's in the register of the Metzerott Hotel. If anyone would understand, and offer practical advice, it would be this . . . scoundrel.

And yet she could not imagine sharing a confidence with such a man as Dan Sickles, and so she only nodded, and left.

II

Jonathan walked Abigail down to the street. Last night, Fielding had repeated his request for an introduction. Jonathan had promised, but considered this hardly the moment to raise the question.

"I shall be here when you return," he said. "And I shall be with you in spirit."

Abigail smiled, but without the usual hint of mischief. He had never seen her so uneasy. She nodded, said nothing. Jonathan stood on the sidewalk, watching, until she vanished around the corner.

Back upstairs, more work awaited. Dennard had left a note on the table instructing Jonathan to copy out several motions the lawyer had prepared. An hour later, Jonathan was still writing hard when Inspector Varak walked in without knocking.

"I hoped to see Mr. Dennard," said the officer, his helmet beneath his arm in ironic deference to the surroundings. He brushed a bit of sleet from his tunic. "Perhaps I ought to wait."

"I have no way of estimating when he might return."

"I see," said Varak, the puffy eyes roaming the lines of books. His round face was still pink with cold. "Read all of this, have you?"

"No, sir. The books are there for reference."

"This is how you spend your day, is it, Mr. Hilliman? Using the books, looking up cases, and so forth? I shouldn't think that a particularly fulfilling task for a grown man." As Jonathan digested this insult, the inspector, who up to now had remained near the door, stepped farther into the room. "Tell me about your employer."

"I believe I have already told you all I know about Mr. McShane."

"Not your former employer. Your current employer. Dennard. What's he like?"

"Surely you can't believe he had anything to do with the murder!"

"Don't believe I said I thought anything of the sort. Peculiar turn of mind you have." He paged through one of the books lying on the table. *"The Trial of Charles I,"* he read aloud. "By Sir Thomas Herbert and John Rushworth. Read this one, have you?"

"Miss Canner is using that one."

"Is she indeed? That Dennard's idea, was it?" He lifted another. *"Precedents of Equity.* This Miss Canner's, too?"

"Yes." Jonathan's burgeoning irritation made the *sir* difficult.

"Only there are those who claim that the colored girl isn't doing any of the work. But I suppose she is, isn't she?"

"She is."

"And Dennard. He's happy with this arrangement, is he?"

"Why wouldn't he be?"

"Because my sources tell me there is some tension between Dennard and the President. It's my understanding that there might have been some pressure to include Miss Canner as part of the defense."

"That's ridiculous," said Jonathan, his unease growing. "And I fail to see how any such rumor could be related to the murder of Mr. McShane."

"Don't you?" He was at the window, tugging the broken handle, producing a terrible growl even though the pane did not budge. "People tell me Dennard didn't want to take this case. Thought it might be bad for business. Thought McShane was being a bit of a romantic, even." He left the window, began perusing the shelves. "You do see the pattern, don't you, Mr. Hilliman? McShane brings in a case that Dennard thinks will wreck the firm, and then McShane conveniently dies."

"You cannot be serious." He recovered himself. "And Mr. Dennard has taken the case."

"But under pressure from the President, you see. That is my point. Maybe he didn't foresee the pressure."

Jonathan stared, remembering Dennard's sudden reversal, on the very day a telegram arrived from two of their railroad clients urging the firm to stand down. "You cannot possibly be serious," he repeated. "Mr. Dennard is the kindest of men."

"Not my impression. People tell me Dennard is rude and rather overbearing. Quite a difficult man, actually." He drew a book out, shoved it back. "Now, tell me, Mr. Hilliman. Why did your employer need fifty dollars?"

"Mr. Dennard? Why not ask him?"

"Not Dennard. McShane." The policeman had managed, in his traverse of the room, to wind up directly in front of Jonathan. His hands were behind his back, his broad chest thrust aggressively forward. "The morning of the day he was killed, your former employer went to Cooke's bank, at Pennsylvania and Fifteenth Street, and withdrew fifty dollars from his account. Any idea why?"

"No."

"Rather expensive for a colored prostitute, I would think. Not my world, you understand, but those with more experience than I assure me that the going rate at Madame Sophie's establishment is closer to a dollar or two, depending on the girl one chooses. Still, I suppose he might have had it in mind to leave a gratuity."

"I have no idea what Mr. McShane would need fifty dollars for," said Jonathan, ignoring the gibe. But he was thinking that no man would be so big a fool as to carry so much money on his person, especially into Hooker's Division. "Perhaps you should ask Mrs. McShane."

"She says she has no idea." The inspector pursed his heavy lips, as if in disapproval of the opposite sex. "The difficulty is that the fifty dollars was not found on the person of either decedent."

"Then perhaps the crime was a robbery."

"That is what my commander believes. He tells me that the time has come to turn to more pressing matters. Perhaps he is correct." He examined the shiny helmet. "But on the off chance that my commander is wrong, and this terrible crime was not after all about the fifty dollars, then the degree of violence proposes a quite different motive."

"What motive would that be? Anger? Jealousy?"

Varak was at the door. "Panic," he said; and went out.

III

Senator William Pitt Fessenden lived in a modest house on B Street South, in the shadow of the Capitol. Abigail had to change lines on the horsecars three times to get there, and still wound up walking the last block and a half, so that when she arrived she was half frozen.

Shivering on the cobbled walk, she immediately confronted a dilemma.

At the decent houses of Washington City, as in most of the nation, negroes were expected to go around to the kitchen door. But Abigail had been raised to challenge such strictures by ignoring them: she sat where she liked on the horsecars, and walked past policemen without asking permission. Moreover, she was visiting Fessenden as a more or less official emissary: she had every reason in the world to enter through the front door. Yet there was the danger that such a choice might give away her role: neighbors would wonder why a colored girl showed such effrontery. On the other hand, were she arriving at the house as Abigail Canner, citizen, unconnected to politics or the impeachment trial, she would without question have proceeded to knock at—

The front door opened. A slim redhead beckoned her close, and Abigail, happy to have the weight of decision lifted, hurried forward—to greet, she imagined, Mrs. Fessenden.

"What do you want?" demanded the redhead suspiciously, and Abigail realized that the woman was a good deal younger than she: no more than fifteen. And although she had drawn a shawl around her shoulders before opening the door, it was obvious now that she wore a uniform.

A housemaid.

"I have come to see the Senator." When the maid looked skeptical, Abigail handed over the note from James Speed. "Please give him this."

The redhead hesitated, and for a bad instant Abigail wondered whether this child intended to leave her standing on the porch in the icy wind. "You wait in the kitchen," the maid finally said, and led the way. And Abigail, even in the midst of her considerable relief at getting out of the cold, found herself irritated at not having been invited to sit in the parlor.

I V

"I was under the impression that the matter had been settled," said Dennard when Jonathan was finished. The lawyer was out of breath as usual, sprawling more than sitting behind the wide desk as Jonathan remained on his feet. "I have been assured by General Baker that the investigation is closed."

"Evidently, the inspector disagrees."

"Yes. Yes." Dennard's soft hands were pawing through a file that lay open on his desk, his eyes drifting over the words, a trick he often used to gain time to ponder. "And the man actually implied that *I* might have—Well, never mind. I shall take care of the matter." His pouchy gaze rose. "Was there something else, Hilliman?"

Jonathan hesitated. He was wondering whether Varak might be right. Not his innuendos about Dennard, but on the larger matter, that the motive for the murder was not robbery but panic. He met his employer's scrutiny. He dared not raise the matter: Dennard has already told him to forget McShane and concentrate on representing their client.

"No, sir."

"Good. Any word from Miss Canner?"

"She has not yet returned, sir."

The aged eyes narrowed. The news seemed to bother Dennard a good deal more than the inspector's visit.

"Well, that is most unfortunate," the lawyer finally said.

"Surely her absence means that progress is being made."

"No, Hilliman. I rather suspect that it augurs the opposite."

V

"He refused to see me," said Abigail.

Jonathan was hanging her hooded coat in the cabinet. A sullen Washington rain pattered the windows without enthusiasm. "I don't understand."

"I went to Senator Fessenden's home, just as you told me. The maid admitted me. The housemaid told me that the Senator was in. I waited for three hours, but he wouldn't see me."

"Did you give him the card? The one from Speed?"

"No, Jonathan. I am the village idiot."

He faced the full fury of those wide gray eyes. Most women, in Jonathan's experience, grew uglier when angry; as did most men. Abigail was as much an exception to that rule as she was to so many others: the rising color in her sandy cheeks simply made her more beautiful. And yet the pain in her expression was undeniable. It occurred to him that she had been humiliated by Fessenden, and did not much care for it. "I apologize. I just wanted to be sure—"

"Three hours!"

"Yes, I—"

"In the kitchen, Jonathan. He kept me waiting in the kitchen, like a servant!" Abigail regained her control. "Never mind. It makes no difference. What matters is that he would not see me. He has changed his mind." She nodded toward the door to Dennard's office. "You will have to tell your employer."

"He is your employer as well. We shall both tell him."

"No. There is a chain of command. The President and his men talked to you, you talked to me. The commands made their way down the chain. The bad news must make its way back up." She went to the side table, picked up a broom. "I have chores."

Jonathan watched as she turned her back. Then he straightened his tie and knocked on Dennard's door. There was a protocol for these meetings. Jonathan remained standing while the lawyer sat. Usually, Dennard was giving instructions. Now and then he would assign reading and test his clerk on various fine points of the law, as preparation for Jonathan's coming examinations for the bar. Today, however, Jonathan did the talking, relating everything Abigail had told him, and then, on a nod from Dennard, going over it again.

The lawyer heard him out, then nodded. "About what I expected."

"Would you like to speak to Miss Canner?"

"There's no need."

"Maybe we should send her back to Fessenden."

"To what end?"

"I thought we were expecting to negotiate."

The lawyer stood. His office was smaller than McShane's but nearly filled by the huge mahogany desk, with its twin kneeholes—known in the parlance as a partners desk—with room to sit on either side, and a plentitude of slots and drawers and cubbyholes to help keep things sorted. Bundled files lay neatly atop a cabinet, each tied with green or blue string, the records of lawsuits Dennard had put aside to handle the impeachment. Now he turned to the window and folded his arms.

"You are an intelligent young man," said Dennard, "and I am sure you will be a fine lawyer. But you have a good deal to learn about the ways of Washington. This was never a negotiation, Hilliman. Never. It was a test of wills."

"I don't understand."

"Consider. Fessenden is an ally of the President's. That much you know. Wade and his people hate the President, et cetera. You know that, too. The Radicals think they have the battle won. They do not think Mr. Lincoln can escape. Now, I'm not sure they're right. Trial has yet to begin. The most brilliant evidence, once challenged, often loses its luster. My point is, they sent a message through Fessenden for one reason only: to find out whether the President is as confident as they are. If he was confident, he would reject their overture. If he was worried, he would accept it."

Jonathan tried to work this out. "We sent Abigail—Miss Canner—with the intention of negotiating further."

"Remember your elementary contract law, Hilliman. If I offer to purchase your house for five hundred dollars, and you make me a counteroffer of six, your counteroffer serves as a rejection of my original offer. We sent Miss Canner with a counteroffer. Her very presence made plain that we were rejecting what the Radicals had proposed. If we meant to accept, I would have gone, or Stanton, or Speed. Even you. Sending Miss Canner, however, was a slap in the face."

"What!"

"She is nobody, Hilliman. Oh, don't give me that look. One doesn't mean literally. She is smart. She will be a fine lawyer, et cetera. Finney adores her. Sumner. Everybody. But she holds no official rank. She is not in the Cabinet, et cetera. She is not a lawyer. She is a clerk. She is also a woman, and she is colored. She could not possibly be carrying a secret message from the President, because nobody would believe she was in the President's confidence. That is why Fessenden refused to see her. He knew as soon as Miss Canner arrived at his home that Mr. Lincoln had rejected the offer. By making her wait, he is telling us he knows—and that the opportunity for negotiation is over. We're going to have ourselves a trial, Hilliman."

"But you used her!"

"No, Jonathan." A rare use of his Christian name. "We used you. *You* used her. That is the way of Washington, my boy. You'd better get used to it."

CHAPTER 16

Nocturne

I

NIGHT.

Abigail decided to treat herself to a bath. She would have to heat the water in the kitchen and carry it down the hall to the back of the house, but that was a chore she had performed hundreds of times. She turned the knob and water came gushing out, first brown-tinged, then gray. When the water cleared, she put a big kettle under the tap and waited. Her late father had installed the attic tank, which was kept full by a combination of rainwater and regular purchases from the water sellers who drove their wagons through the neighborhood twice a week. The tank was just one way in which the Canner house differed from its neighbors. Her father had considered himself an inventor. They even had a bathing-tub, fashioned by her father from wood and stone and copper. The bathing-room had a stone sink fed by pipes leading to the attic tank. The room also featured what Abigail suspected was the only flush toilet south of the Smithsonian and west of the Navy Yard. Edolphus Canner had improved, he claimed, on the toilets of the rich, which he in his trade as a plumber had helped construct. The one in the Canner bathing-room used the siphoning action of three water pipes, all controlled by a single lever, and the system made a terrible racket, shaking the entire house and frightening the dogs, but no one in Washington City—insisted her father—could claim its like.

When the kettle was full, she hung it in the hearth and, by the light of the fire, sat down to study. She was still frustrated—well, furious—about being made to wait in Senator Fessenden's kitchen for three hours and then coming away with nothing, and hoped that reading law would calm her. And so opened her notebook and began to review what she had copied out from Blackstone's *Commentaries* today on the forms of trespass. If you poisoned a man's dogs or shot his cattle, wrote Blackstone (in England, it seemed, things were always happening to dogs and cattle, or so one would gather from reading Blackstone), then you were guilty of trespass *vi et armis*, but only if the act was "immediately injurious" and involved force. If, on the other hand, your action involved no force and caused only indirect injury to a man or his property—never a woman in Blackstone and certainly never a woman's property—then you were guilty only of trespass on the case. She did not yet know what either term meant, because she had been sent off to deliver some papers before she had the opportunity to copy the next page. But already she was wondering what possible difference it made to the man injured whether the injury arose directly or indirectly from the act of another—

A sharp knock at the front door drew her from her legal meditations. She glanced around in surprise, although the door was not visible from the kitchen. A thrill of fear danced through her tired body.

No sane black family opened the door after dark—not these days. Not with the White Camellia and the Ku Klux and the Southern Cross on the rampage. Hundreds of freedmen had been killed over the past two years; some said thousands. The Union troops seemed helpless. Northern newspapers insisted that the night riders were a Southern phenomenon, but Abigail remembered what most Washingtonians had schooled themselves to forget: Maryland was a Southern state, a slave-holding state, kept from joining the rebellion only because Lincoln had sent troops to occupy Annapolis.

Besides, Virginia was right across the river.

The knock came a second time.

Varak, she told herself. The inspector was back for a further interrogation. Her brother, Michael, come to hector her. Or Jonathan, wishing once more to apologize. Perhaps wishing for more: she knew how he looked at her. But if he imagined for an instant that she—

A third knock.

Abigail left the kettle and crept into the parlor, staying beneath the window. She glanced toward the stairs. No movement. A fourth knock.

She reached beneath the sofa until her fingers touched metal. She pulled out the shotgun, and, sitting on the floor, broke it to be sure it was loaded. She scampered into the hallway and crouched beside the door.

She waited.

Another knock.

"Who is it?" she called, voice trembling.

"It's me, honey," said a woman's voice, the tone mildly amused. "Don't shoot, okay?"

Judith.

II

"I am surprised to see you," said Abigail, feeling a bit stupid and a bit superior, the way she always did around Judith. Abigail's tone was frosty. She tended to see the moral world through Nanny Pork's eyes, and although she had missed her sister, she was unable quite to approve of her.

Judith was amused. "Aren't you going to ask where I have been keeping myself?"

"I understood that you had moved south."

"Well, I am back."

Abigail could not help herself. Every word out of her sister's mouth left her angrier. "It is the middle of the night. Who comes calling at this hour?"

"We must talk," said her sister, ignoring Abigail's remark.

"What can there possibly be for us to talk about?"

"A great deal." Judith had moved to the stove. "Bathing yourself, I see. You always were a great one for decadence."

Abigail's face flared.

"How dare you come here to insult me—"

Again Judith spoke right over her. "Silly girl. I'm not here to insult you. I'm here to help you."

"I am in no trouble. And if I were, it is not you I would approach for assistance."

Judith spun toward her. Abigail was surprised to see tears in her older sister's eyes. "Is that what they taught you at your little Christian college out west? To slap the sinner on the other cheek?"

Abigail felt her face burn. Her mouth moved, but for a few seconds, no sound emerged. "I am sorry," she said finally. "I should not have spoken harshly."

Her older sister's gaze rejected this confession. "I don't suppose you will ever change. You're Nanny Pork all over again, aren't you? There is no forgiveness in your soul. No love for anything less than perfection."

"That is untrue!"

"It has been two years since we have laid eyes on each other. In all of that time, did you once try to find me?"

"Did you once write me?"

Judith, about to respond in kind, sighed instead. "It doesn't matter. I'll be gone in five minutes, and you'll never see me again. Your life can go back to whatever it was five minutes before I arrived." She straightened her shawl. "But first I have something to tell you. It concerns your work."

"I don't understand. What does my work—"

"For once in your life, Abby, don't say anything. Please. Just listen." Judith had moved quite close. She smelled of orange blossoms, and a hint of rosemary, and Abigail could not help wondering which of her sister's men had gifted her with scented water. "What I am going to say will sound unpleasant. But you have to hear it." She waited, but this time her younger sister did not interrupt. "The man you were working with—the white man—the lawyer—"

"Jonathan?"

Again her older sister was amused. "No, darling. Not your precious Jonathan. The lawyer. The one who died. McShane. I knew the woman who died with him."

"I am not surprised," said Abigail, before she could catch herself. Judith's eyes flashed. Abigail regretted her words at once, but knew that no apology would suffice. Judith was right. She was just like Nanny Pork, firing off her ammunition before checking to see whether the approaching stranger was friend or foe. "I did not mean that," she began.

Judith waved her to silence. "Never mind. Just listen. I knew Rebecca. She was a . . . a friend."

Catching the pain in her sister's tone, Abigail struggled for the proper response. "I am sorry about your friend," she said.

"Thank you." She wiped her eyes. "Rebecca was a decent woman, Abigail. She wasn't like me. She was more like . . . like you." A hard swallow. "She was not a prostitute."

"But the Provost General said—"

"The military will say whatever General Lafayette Baker commands them to say. I am telling you the truth. Rebecca was not a prostitute. Nor did she give herself to men."

Abigail had joined her at the stove and began heating the smaller kettle, to make tea. "Then why was she meeting Mr. McShane outside a brothel?"

Judith took two cups from the shelf. "I don't know. I do know that she had met him before."

"Then perhaps the two of them—"

"No, Abby. I told you. Rebecca wasn't like that. She had regular work. She was employed as a domestic. She worked in one of the great houses. And, besides." Hesitating. Weighing a final truth. "Besides. Rebecca was helping Mr. Lincoln. That was why she was meeting Mr. McShane." She held up a hand. "I do not know the details. But I had the impression, from things that she said, that she was giving Mr. McShane information."

"What sort of information?"

"Again, I am not sure. She said there was something Mr. McShane needed, and she was helping him to find it. I do not know what he was looking for, but, whatever it was, Rebecca thought it important." The hard jaw trembled. "And whatever it was, she died for it." Judith was on her feet. "I must go."

"You have not had your tea."

"I dare not tarry. Please do not tell Nanny I was here."

Abigail felt an unaccountable panic. "Let me wake her."

"No."

"You could come back home. The two of you could reconcile—"

"Not possible."

"What if—"

Judith laid a hand on her younger sister's shoulder. "Remember when we were little? When Mother would read to us from Shakespeare?"

"Of course."

"Then you'll remember *Twelfth Night:* 'My stars shine darkly over me; the malignancy of my fate might, perhaps, distemper yours . . .'" She leaned over, kissed Abigail on the cheek. "It's best that I bear my evils alone." And then, as if in afterthought, she delved in the folds of her shawl. Abigail tensed, but her sister pulled out only an envelope.

"What is this?"

"Rebecca asked me to hold on to it. If anything happened to her, I was to deliver it to Mr. McShane." Her voice trembled. "She said he would know what to do with it. She did not anticipate that they might die together, and—well—"

Tears rolling down her long cheeks, Judith thrust the envelope into her sister's hands. A last clumsy hug, and she was gone into the night. Abigail stood in the window, watching her sister's trap until it vanished.

Back in the kitchen, she opened the envelope. Inside was a single piece of paper, which she spread on the kitchen counter. There were no words, but only a string of numbers:

13163222232121244

Abigail frowned and puzzled, but could connect the peculiar note with nothing in her experience. Though she was no expert, the numbers looked to her like a code. In this city of conspiracies and fears, of plots and unknown sources, the President's lawyer had been receiving coded messages from a colored woman; and now both were dead.

And everything everybody thought they knew about the murder was wrong.

CHAPTER 17

Obsession

I

"SO WHAT?"

Abigail stared at Rufus Dennard, unable to believe that he had offered so cavalier a response to her sister's information. She was standing in his office. Dennard himself was seated, his bulk overflowing the chair. The brass fittings gleamed against the polished dark wood. A partners desk was designed so that two could sit, facing each other. But nobody would take the chair opposite without being invited, and Abigail had not been invited.

"What I am saying," she resumed, picking her words carefully, in case her first attempt had been unclear, "is that if the woman who died with Mr. McShane was not a prostitute, what happened might after all be connected to the trial."

"It isn't," Dennard snapped.

"But what if—"

He leaned toward her, steepling his hands. "Listen to me, Miss Canner. I took you into my employ because Dr. Finney speaks well of you. He told me that you possess one of the finest brains he has ever encountered. Maybe so. We'll find out whether the evaluation is true. So far, you're just fine." His eyes steamed at her, and the praise that should have made her heart sing struck her like a cudgel. "Nevertheless, there is such a thing as being too intelligent for one's own good. Your mind is leading you into flights of imagination. This conspiracy business is just the thing McShane would have liked, because he had that devious sort of mind. I like to keep my eye on the work—nothing but the work. McShane is dead, and I'm sorry about that. He was an exemplary partner and a dear friend. But his murder is a matter for the city police. Our task is to defend Mr. Lincoln. We face the most important trial in the history of this nation. God willing, these United States shall never again see its like. That trial shall demand every bit of our energy. If we get involved in spinning the sort of wild theories that fascinated McShane, that will make our job harder rather than easier. Do I make myself clear?"

With an effort, she restrained the urge to argue further. "Yes, Mr. Dennard. Perfectly clear."

"May I see the note?"

Reluctantly, she handed over the envelope. Dennard did not even open it. Instead, he slipped it into his pocket. "If this was intended for Mr. McShane, then it is the property of the firm."

"I suppose that you will be sharing it with the police?"

The pouchy eyes darkened. "That is not your judgment to make."

Abigail struggled for calm. "Yes, sir," she managed. "Only Inspector Varak seems to think—"

"Inspector Varak seems to be making a rare nuisance of himself. Bothering you, bothering Hilliman—I don't know what could be driving the man. My understanding is that the case is closed."

"But possibly in error."

He pointed to a calendar on the wall. "Trial begins in less than two weeks. Haven't forgotten, have you?"

"No, sir."

"You are a clerk in this firm, Miss Canner. I am glad to have you. But try to focus on your responsibilities. You are here to help acquit the President of these outrageous charges, not to hunt for conspiracies or solve murders the police have closed. If this Varak shows up again, do not say a word. You send him straight to me. Is that clear?"

"Yes, sir."

"I believe you have work to do."

"Yes, sir."

"Then perhaps you would be so kind as to get about it. And pull the door behind you, please."

Back in the main room, watched curiously by Jonathan and Rellman, Abigail stood for a moment, hand still gripping the knob. She watched Mr. Little sweeping, and watched the others ignore him. Her face burned. Rejection, exclusion, condescension—these were the price the nation daily exacted from the colored race, like a special tax on darkness. When one was shoved aside, there was nobody to complain to. In Abigail's lifetime, there never had been, except at Oberlin, where Dr. Finney had solved the problem of white students' not wanting negro students to sit at their tables by inviting black students to sit at the faculty tables, where everybody wanted a place. This plan was in keeping with Finney's preference for inspiration over regulation; and, just like that, the attempted segregation had collapsed. Still, the first time the white students had refused to let her sit down had stung her, and the pain was never far from memory. That had been the first occasion in Abigail's life when she had been tempted to utter a blasphemy.

This was the second.

Her sole consolation was that she had copied the numerical message into her diary; nevertheless, as she slid into her accustomed place at the table, Abigail promised herself never again to share her secret suspicions with anyone in authority. If she had to solve the mystery herself, then she would.

For Judith's sake.

She wondered if Rufus Dennard was aware of how large a clue he had given her—even if she was not yet sure how to pursue it.

The sort of wild theories that fascinated McShane, he had said.

I I

In the afternoon, the lawyers went to the White House, but not before Dennard instructed her to deliver a package to the copyists, and afterward to go downstairs to Grafton's office to return the books she had picked up last week. Abigail was mortified—Grafton's office was the last place on earth she wanted to go—but she could hardly tell her employer that she wanted to avoid his former law partner because he had made Bessie Hale cry; or because he had offered Abigail herself a position.

To her relief, only nervous Plum was present. He scooped the pile of books from her arms in a surprising show of speed and grace, and had them reshelved, in proper order, by the time she finished thanking him for the loan.

Abigail retreated toward the door, but Mr. Plum stopped her. "I almost forgot," he said, grinning sheepishly. He opened a drawer, drew out an envelope. "Mr. Grafton said to give this to you if you happened by."

She did not want to accept anything from David Grafton, but saw no polite way to decline. In the hallway, she considered tossing the envelope into a dustbin, but curiosity got the better of her. The letter was short and to the point. Grafton hoped she would reconsider her decision to reject his offer. And he wanted her to know—just in case it might affect her decision—that Dennard, like McShane, had lost three relatives in the war.

The difference was that Dennard's family had fought on the rebel side.

III

Back in the common room, a package had arrived. There was nothing unusual about that, and at first she ignored it. The package was addressed to Arthur McShane, who had been dead now nearly two weeks. Following his standing instructions from Dennard, Jonathan was slitting the package open. He had been McShane's clerk, and in theory was best positioned to know which of the late attorney's cases the package might pertain to, and what should be done with the contents.

Jonathan said to the others, "Come look at this."

The contents were bizarre.

First there was a handwritten letter, undated, brief and to the point. The paper was an expensive vellum, the style dramatically curlicued and decorated:

Also, see enclosed. Burgess's for Sept to come
Chanticleer

That was the entire text. The three clerks puzzled together over possible meanings.

"I suspect that 'Sept' is September," said Rellman, importantly.

Abigail hid a smile, and put in her own contribution. "The 'Also' implies the existence of an earlier letter."

Jonathan spread his hands. "So Mr. McShane is advised that he will soon hear about Burgess's, whatever that is, for September. That is not terribly illuminating. And I know of no case or correspondent called Chanticleer."

They laid the letter aside and dug into the box. A sheaf of notes appeared to be the proceedings of an investigation into a battle between two railroads in South Carolina. The handwriting was different—cramped and quick—and the paper was of a much cheaper variety, well lined. They found a couple of newspaper articles about the city-council election in Columbia, the state capital: evidently, the city had chosen the first colored councilman in its history.

"This isn't about the impeachment," Rellman announced.

"Wait," said Abigail.

They had reached the bottom of the package. More handwritten notes, this time a list of shareholders in one of the two railroads that were at war.

"It's one of Mr. McShane's cases," said Rellman, losing interest. "Has to be."

Jonathan was leafing through the pages. "I don't believe we have any clients in South Carolina. Had." *Sliced up.* He kept the thought at bay, pointed to the original note. "And, again, I don't believe that we have a client called Chanticleer."

Rellman was defiant. "You can't possibly have every client committed to memory."

"I believe that I would recall that name."

"Well, then, what's it all about?"

"Nothing," said Dennard, who, despite his bulk, had managed somehow to creep up on them. "Another one of McShane's crazy ideas." He nodded. "Hilliman. Put everything back in the box. We'll send it on to the widow."

"But if it involves a client—"

"It doesn't."

"How can we be sure?"

The lawyer glowered at him; but answered. "See the letter? Chanticleer? Some friend of his from one of those clubs he was in, most likely. I never had time for all of that foolishness, but McShane loved every bit of it, bless him. Fancy names. Funny hats. All that Latin nonsense. It's nothing. Pack it up and send it on."

"Yes, sir," Jonathan said.

Dennard glanced around. "Where's Rellman? Ah, good. Speed is over at the Mansion. You and I will join him. Hilliman, Miss Canner, you have your assignments."

I V

"Why do you call her Nanny Pork?"

Abigail had her nose in the volume about the trial and beheading of Charles I. She had made copious notes. Without lifting her head from the book, she said, "Because that is her name."

Jonathan was at the other end of the table, paging through volumes of speeches of some of the leaders of the anti-Lincoln cabal, searching for language that might be turned against them. "Surely Nanny Pork isn't her real name."

"Her *real* name?" said Abigail, glancing up, and the mischief in those eyes told him that one of her games was afoot. "What on earth does that mean?"

"What name would she use in signing a legal document?"

"Nanny would sign with an 'X.' She is illiterate."

"What name appears on her birth certificate?"

"I have never seen her birth certificate, Mr. Hilliman. I am not sure whether the laws of South Carolina provided for birth certificates for slaves."

"So she was a slave," said Jonathan, relieved to have at least one fact.

"She was. Until recently, as you may recall, a few of my people were." She laid the book aside. "And she is not my grandmother. My mother said Nanny Pork is my great-aunt, and she calls us her nieces, but I suspect that the actual family relation is somewhat more distant. One branch of our family—on my mother's side—purchased its freedom before the Revolution. Nanny Pork is from another branch."

Jonathan found himself fascinated by this glimpse, however small, into the life of the free negroes, an insular and even secretive society about which almost nothing was known.

By white people, anyway.

"How did she come to live with you?"

Abigail placed a leather marker at her page and closed the book. "Why are you so interested in my aunt? We have a great deal of work to do."

"Please," said Jonathan, spreading his hands. He could not tell whether she was teasing. Nevertheless, he felt, suddenly, an urgent need to hear the story. And Abigail put the volume aside and told him.

"Nanny was freed eight or nine years ago. She was old even then, and she was sick, and her master had no use for her any more. Had she remained his property, he would have had to provide a roof over her head and food for her to eat, to say nothing of a burial plot, and he was not about to do all of that for a slave who couldn't work. So, in his Christian magnanimity, he set her free instead. She was taken into a mission home outside of Charleston, and the missionaries wrote to all the living relatives she could think of, trying to find somewhere for her to go; and die. I don't know how many of my relatives wrote back, but I imagine that they made excuses: Not enough money. Too busy to care for her. The house too small. What-have-you. But my mother was not like that. My mother would never leave a stranger out on the street: we always had people with nowhere to go living in the barn or the stable behind the house. Naturally, she could not abandon a relative to the fates. So she wrote back and even sent the train fare. Nanny Pork arrived a month later. My mother was never secretive with us. She told us that Nanny had come to the house to die. She was given a bed in my older sister, Judith's room. I already shared with Louisa. My mother said it would probably be only a few months."

Abigail had turned away now, face toward the dying fire. One of her hands was in her lap, the other lay carelessly on the table. Both fists were clenched.

"But the Lord had other plans, Mr. Hilliman. He often does. By a miracle, Nanny was healed of whatever disease was killing her. Instead, my mother died of the varioloid a few months after Nanny moved in. The varioloid is not supposed to kill people who have already had smallpox, but it killed my mother. After that, my father just wasted away. He was dead in a year. And Nanny Pork—well, she had come to the house to die but wound up more or less running it." She laughed. "She even put Judith out. Not just out of the room. Out of the house, because she did not like her behavior with men." A shadow crossed Abigail's face. When she spoke again, there was a tremor in a voice. "And here is the irony, Mr. Hilliman. Here is the irony. It is not Nanny's house. My father left it in equal shares to the children. So the four of us own it, but we do what Nanny tells us."

"You respect her."

"We are scared of her." A rough laugh, painful to hear. "Jonathan, I must ask you directly. Do you believe this business about the Department of the Atlantic? The plot to overthrow the Congress?"

Jonathan hesitated. Among men of his class, direct questions were simply not asked. He had been taught to prevaricate and hedge, to use words only as a means of gaining your ends. "The Managers do not have a shred of evidence to support their claim," he said. He waved toward the boxes of files. "We have here all of Mr. Lincoln's correspondence with the War Department. You and I have been through every page. There is nothing."

Abigail digested this. He sensed that his evasion had disappointed her. "Very well," she finally said. "And this business about a conspiracy behind the impeachment. Finishing what Booth began, but by legal means. What Mr. Dennard forbids us to pursue. Do you believe a word? Or is it all a bizarre fantasy, created by Stanton or perhaps Seward to distract the public from the issues at stake?"

"Remember when Stanton was here in this office?" he asked. "Railing about the missing list of conspirators, and how he would hang everyone on the list should it come into his possession? I do not believe that his fury was an invention."

"That tells me only that you believe that Stanton believes in the conspiracy. I asked what *you* believe, Jonathan."

He tried to make a joke of it. "Well, if a conspiracy exists, I am sure that the Hillimans are at the center of it. We may not have much money any more, but just about everyone in the family hates Mr. Lincoln."

V

Two hours later, Dennard and Speed clomped in, shaking snow from their coats. Dennard was furious about something, and Speed was trying to placate him. Rellman came smirking behind them like a bad conscience.

"The President does have other duties," Speed was saying.

"Not as important as winning at trial and staying in office, et cetera."

"We can resume tomorrow."

"We have a schedule."

The lawyers shucked off their coats. In Little's absence, Abigail knew her role; hated it, but duty was duty. She leaped to her feet, but Jonathan was faster. He had both men's coats over his arm and was halfway to the closet before she could get halfway around the table. She fought down a rising gratitude that nearly made her smile.

"Hilliman," snapped Dennard. "Miss Canner. We have just come from the President." He had his hands linked behind his back. His great bulk swayed a bit. "He has decided to undertake further negotiations with the Radicals."

"He is *considering* further negotiations," Speed murmured.

"The President is acting in this matter against my advice," Dennard resumed, glaring at Speed. "I do not believe that we have anything to offer that the Radicals would find of interest."

Again Speed interjected softly. "There is, however, the suggestion of a *slightly* different approach to the matter of reconstructing the defeated South."

"Not enough. They are confident. *Too* confident." He took a step toward his office. "Go over every piece of evidence we are expecting. Speed and I will go to the Hill tomorrow and try to get them to give us more. They have something. I am sure of it. They will not negotiate." He pointed at Jonathan. "Study the rules they have adopted for the trial. The Managers are not required to give us an advance look at their case, but there might be some rule we can twist against them." He turned to Rellman. "Dig out those precedents from when they tried to impeach Tyler." And he eyed Abigail. "Miss Canner, we will see you tomorrow."

She was stunned; and Jonathan, upset on her behalf, forgot entirely to mention that he had found additional Chanticleer letters in McShane's files.

It would be some days before anyone realized how large an error he had just made.

CHAPTER 18

Audience

I

THE FOLLOWING AFTERNOON, just as dusk began to gray the city, a military runner arrived at the law office to deliver an official note—not to Dennard or Speed, but to Jonathan. Abigail and Rellman could not conceal their surprise. Jonathan fumbled with the envelope. The officer waited patiently, eyes on the middle distance. The missive, in the handwriting of Noah Brooks, asked Jonathan to come to the Executive Mansion at once to see the President.

"Just you?" said Rellman doubtfully when Jonathan read the note aloud.

"Evidently."

"Does he say why?" the fat man persisted.

Jonathan ignored him. He told the officer that he naturally was prepared to serve at the President's pleasure and would be along directly, then watched through the window as the man mounted his horse. If Mr. Lincoln was using soldiers to run his errands, matters had turned decidedly worse. Too many of the civilians around the Mansion, from stewards to doorkeepers to clerks, were Ben Wade's men now.

"You have to tell us something," Rellman said while Little was helping Jonathan into his coat. "The President doesn't just send for people."

Abigail shushed him. "If Mr. Lincoln doesn't want Jonathan to tell, then he must not tell." But her eyes, too, were curious.

Jonathan said, "I have no idea what this is about."

The other clerks' faces said they did not believe him.

Stepping into the street, Jonathan at once jumped aside to avoid a spray of mud kicked up by a passing carriage. Washingmud, some of the Southern papers had taken to calling the place. There were streets where the muck was waist-deep. He wondered whether the Congress would ever get around to properly grading the avenues. Mr. Lincoln had been elected to the Congress back in the forties on the promise of internal improvements. Every state wanted its share of the nation's revenues to build bridges and canals and roads. Odd how none of the money ever seemed to be spent here in Washington City—unless, of course, one counted the fabulous marble palace the Congress had built for itself, as though the first duty of the legislature was to the comfort of its own members.

At the Mansion, a pair of sentries gave Jonathan a scare. Or perhaps he gave them a scare, because, even in the midst of impeachment, assassination plots were rumored on every hand. Jonathan showed them the note. One of the guards went to find his lieutenant, who got one of the stewards to bring Noah Brooks, the President's secretary, who vouched for Jonathan's bona fides.

Nobody apologized.

II

"Why would Mr. Lincoln ask for Jonathan?" said Rellman, very cross. "He isn't a lawyer. He's a clerk. What would the President want with him?"

"I have no idea," said Abigail.

"He tells you everything." A heavy pause. "Even things he shouldn't."

She tried to make her tone as arch as Dinah Berryhill would be at this moment. "And what things are those exactly, Mr. Rellman?"

"When Mr. Dennard gets here, he'll want to know why his clerk has a private meeting with our client. He'll ask you same question."

"And I'll give him the same answer: I have no idea."

"Just as you have no idea what happened to Mr. McShane."

She put down her pencil. "I beg your pardon."

"Inspector Varak seems to think you know more than you are saying."

"Have you been talking to the inspector? What did he tell you?"

But Rellman preferred asking questions to answering them; he seemed immune to charm, reason, or simple offers of friendship. Now, suspicions kindled, the dark, unfriendly gaze promised a reckoning for crimes she did not know she had committed.

"He's in that much better a mood today," said Noah, leading the way up the rickety stairs.

Better than what? Jonathan wondered, but did not say.

"Wait, please," said Noah, and went ahead into the office. Through the opened door, Jonathan glimpsed Stanton's furious profile. Noah returned, shut the door, said the President would not be long.

But it was another hour, and Stanton was long gone, before Jonathan was summoned.

The President was sitting on the edge of his desk, one bony leg rattling. He was wearing half-glasses, and scarcely looked up when Jonathan walked in. "Young Mr. Hilliman," he murmured, offering that crooked smile as he read. Noah stood by, holding a sheaf of papers. He was obviously waiting for Mr. Lincoln to hand him the letter he was reading, so that it could be returned to the appropriate file. "Sit," the President ordered.

Still not sure why he had been invited to visit the President alone, and still nervous in his presence, Jonathan, swiftly, sat.

The President turned to Noah, who had a blank sheet of paper at ready. Mr. Lincoln signed his name, with a large flourish, the way he did when relaxed. He blotted it, then frowned. "The longer this struggle goes on," he said, "the sloppier my signature seems to get."

"It looks wonderful," said Brooks. "Mr. Kinney will be delighted."

Lincoln nodded. His secretary collected the page, and, smirking at Jonathan, vanished from the room. "It is a most peculiar thing," said the President, mostly to the air, "that the autograph of a man as unpopular as I should be thought to have value." He continued to swing the long leg. "The gentleman who asked for my autograph—I have never met him. His name is Ezra Kinney. He is a man of the cloth, up at the North, in Connecticut. His son was graduated at Yale—not your year, a year or two later—and then enlisted. When his three years were up, he re-enlisted. He was wounded twice in battle. He fought in New Orleans, in Pennsylvania, all over. All in the name of the Union. Kinney's son risked his life for his native land, and all his father asks in return is the autograph of the man who sent him and lots of others like him out to be blown to bits!" He shook his head. "All these young men. So many killed, so many maimed forever, so many just vanished from the face of the earth. Had I known the cost when we began this great enterprise—"

The President stopped, and stood up, and seemed aware of Jonathan for the first time. Or perhaps he was aware that his visitor had heard this speech before. Mr. Lincoln's countrymen saw him, according to their several prejudices, as a monster or a giant, the tyrant who had crushed the Southern way of life or the demigod who had saved the Union. But, the more time Jonathan spent in his company, the more he saw a deeply conflicted man, certain that his course was right, uncertain that the means required to achieve it were honorable.

"You have done what needed to be done," Jonathan said, "both morally and legally." The President's eyebrows went up, in what Jonathan had not yet come to realize was a sign of irritation. He floundered on. "Dr. Woolsey often says, sir, that you are as wise as good." In repeating praise, Jonathan knew he must sound sycophantish. Yet, having taken the first step on the road, he saw no turning point. "Your Emancipation Proclamation, according to Dr. Woolsey, was a masterpiece, written neither too soon nor too late—"

Lincoln waved the young man silent. "When the president of Yale lauds a backwoods lawyer without formal education," he said, "it's time to lock up the silver." The words entirely lacked the President's usual jocular tone. His voice was frigid. Jonathan remembered too late how much Lincoln hated flattery. "Thank you for coming, Mr. Hilliman."

"It is my pleasure, sir."

"Well, I imagine that it is your duty. I could even believe that doing your duty might give you some pleasure. But if you are like the other young men of my experience, doing your duty at this time of evening is not terribly high on your list of pleasures." His stony expression did not invite response. "Let me explain exactly why you are here. I assume that Dennard told you that I am inclined to do a little more horse-trading."

"He did, sir."

"Good." Sometimes Lincoln's eyes could be so sleepy you thought you had lost him; other times, they hunted like a predator's. This evening he looked predatory. "I want to ask you a favor, Mr. Hilliman. A presidential favor."

"Of course, sir."

"I assume that you know who August Belmont is."

"The head of the Democratic Party in the North," Jonathan said promptly. Then, seeing from Lincoln's face that more was expected, he added, "He is very rich."

"Among other things." A thin-lipped smile, somewhere between mocking and disapproving. On a side table was a plate with an apple, the President's dinner. He had taken only a single bite. "I would have assumed that the Hillimans and the Belmonts traveled in much the same circles."

"Not really, sir. I mean—that is—well, we've never actually met," Jonathan concluded, feeling silly.

"Well, you're going to meet him soon," said the President, mysteriously. "Mr. Belmont doesn't think much of me. He doesn't think much of the Republican Party. He supported the war, which naturally endears him to me, but not so much that I am unaware of the sort of comments he makes about me every time he opens his mouth. And he opens his mouth a lot." The hard face softened suddenly, and the President gave a small chuckle. "Matter of fact, he sort of reminds me of the two brothers who went hunting one day. The younger brother started firing, over and over again, and the older brother asked what he was shooting at. The younger boy said he was sure he saw a squirrel, and pulled the trigger again. His brother knew there was nothing there, so he took a look at the younger brother's eye. Sure enough, there was a big louse in there, crawling around. He imagined he saw squirrels everywhere, when he had nothing but lice." Lincoln sighed. "That is our Mr. Belmont. He sees squirrels every time he looks my way, and he fires off a round or two."

Jonathan this time had the wit to stay silent.

"I have never understood the ways of the rich," said the President. A sudden smile. "But I'll tell you. Early on in the war, a group of wealthy New Yorkers came down to see me. They were introduced as being worth, together, more than one hundred millions of dollars. I myself cannot conceive of such a sum, although I am told the war cost the nation that very sum every month—and that was just the share of the North! What the South, with its smaller resources, must have gone through, and all to defend a system of production that was doomed in any case!" With a shake of his head, Lincoln returned to his tale. "Anyway, these rich men came to see me. They were worried that a rebel gunboat might steam into New York Harbor and sink all the ships that carry the goods that make rich men rich. And so they asked me to assign a Union gunboat to protect New York. I explained to them that I had no boats to spare. But I also pointed out that, if they were really worth one hundred millions, and they were so worried about protecting the city, they could easily arrange to buy a gunboat, and give it to the government, and I would be more than happy to send the sailors to man it and guard the harbor!"

By this time the President was gasping with laughter at his own story; and so was Jonathan, not out of politeness, but because Lincoln had a talent for delivering even the blandest of his tales in a way that drew you in so completely that laughter was your only way out.

"They left, of course," said the President, still smiling. "They never bought a gunboat, and they never again complained about their undefended harbor. The ways of the rich." He shook his head. "A very strange breed."

"Yes, sir," said Jonathan when it became plain that Lincoln was waiting for a response.

"And Mr. Belmont, they say, is pretty nearly the richest of them all."

"So I understand, sir."

"That should make him, I suppose, very nearly the strangest of them all."

"Yes, sir," said Jonathan, aware that the syllogism did not quite work, but unwilling to say so.

"Anyway," the President resumed, "Mr. Belmont, through a mutual friend, has made clear that, under the right circumstances, he might come over to our side in the current difficulty. He has asked me to send an intermediary to hear what he has to say, and I am inclined to send you."

"Me?"

"To tell you the truth," said Lincoln, locking his hands behind his neck and tilting his chair back, "he sort of asked for you." The sleepy eyes settled on Jonathan's face. For a moment, the tension of true mistrust hung in the still air. "And I guess I sort of wondered why."

"I have no idea, sir," said the young man awkwardly. "As I said, I have never met Mr. Belmont—"

"Does your family have dealings with him?"

"I don't know, Mr. President. I have heard of none." A pause as Jonathan considered how to put the next point. "I'm afraid I have little connection with the family business."

Lincoln nodded, as if confirming a private theory. "Well, it doesn't matter. You'll go."

"Yes, sir."

"A number of these rich gentlemen were for the war. Belmont. Aspinwall. Astor. Even Commodore Vanderbilt himself. They all told me the important thing was to get it over with as quick as possible, because war is bad for business. The commodore even gave us his yacht, to turn into a gunboat, all to help get the war over with. Well, now it's over, and it wasn't quick, and these same gentlemen are having trouble deciding which side they're on." The strange watchful gaze studied him. "So you can see why this is important."

"Yes, sir."

"Men like that can swing a lot of votes in the Senate."

"Yes, sir," said Jonathan, who had already grasped the point.

The President handed him a slip of paper. On it were scribbled an address and a time: Monday evening next. The handwriting was not Lincoln's.

The mood lightened again. Lincoln asked about a couple of common acquaintances and told a few more stories, including a rather complicated one about a boy trying to let go of a pig that was dragging him in circles as he held its tail and it tried to bite him. Lincoln seemed to think that the tale described his presidency. Then, all at once, they were both on their feet and Noah Brooks was back in the room.

Jonathan was at the door when Lincoln called him back. "One more thing, Mr. Hilliman."

"Yes, sir."

The President's gaze had hardened once more. "My lawyers have a great deal on their minds just now. I don't think there's any reason to burden them with what we talked about."

In his innocence, and despite Noah's presence, Jonathan needed clarification. "Mr. President, are you asking me to conceal the purpose of this trip from my employer?"

The dark eyes widened in faux innocence. "Mr. Hilliman, I am not asking you to hide a thing. I would imagine that the purpose of the trip is to visit General Felix and his lovely daughter in Philadelphia." He shrugged. "If you should happen to continue on to New York City, well, that's nobody's business but your own."

Jonathan swallowed. "Yes, sir."

Lincoln's tone was light. "You know, Mr. Hilliman, we were talking a moment ago about Commodore Vanderbilt. That reminds me of one more story. Back in the 1850s, when I was busy practicing law out in

Illinois, Mr. Vanderbilt sent a couple of men down to Nicaragua to see about running a stagecoach across the country. Much to his surprise, they started a revolution instead. Mr. Vanderbilt sent them a letter: 'Gentlemen: You have undertaken to cheat me. I won't sue you, for the law is too slow. I'll ruin you. Yours truly, Cornelius Vanderbilt.' Lovely prose. I especially like the 'Yours truly.' Don't you?"

The President laughed, but the chill in his eyes made Jonathan's blood run cold.

CHAPTER 19

Luncheon

I

ON FRIDAY MORNING, Jonathan took the cars for Philadelphia, off on his mysterious presidential errand. The lawyers were on Capitol Hill, negotiating further details of the trial. So only Abigail and Rellman were in the office when the messenger arrived with an invitation for Abigail to attend the Eames salon again on Saturday night.

"You must be very important," said Rellman, not bothering to disguise his envy. "Going everywhere, meeting everybody."

"I haven't met the President yet."

"That's right."

"And I don't know that there is time for . . . this." Indicating the card from Fanny Eames. "We have a great deal of work to do."

Rellman sneered. He was looking unusually fat today. It was an odd thing. Dennard was immense, yet his corpulence seemed appropriate to his decades of experience in the profession and the gravitas of his mien. But in Rellman, just a few years older than she, the extra pounds he carried lent an immature aura, like the fat on a baby, something he should have outgrown.

"Of course you will go," he said. "It is what you do, isn't it? The rest of us may be buried in work, but you have time to be belle of the ball, haven't you?"

Abigail did not know what she had done to anger him so; all the same, she resolved to spend as little time alone with him as possible.

"I have books to gather," she said, and departed.

II

It was nearly midday, so she stopped at the Willard Hotel to leave the lunch order for the firm, one of her occasional duties. The waiter promised delivery within the hour. When she stepped from the kitchen back into the lobby, Dan Sickles was waiting, leaning on his cane.

"I was just going to lunch," he said. "Join me."

She blinked. "I beg your pardon."

He waved toward the most famous dining room in the city. "Let us lunch together, Miss Canner. This is perfect. Exactly what's needed."

"I—I hardly think—I mean, it would not be appropriate—"

That mocking laugh. "We are business colleagues, Miss Canner. If you insist on becoming a lawyer, you will have to manage to overcome your discomfort in the company of gentlemen."

Abigail bristled, as perhaps he meant her to. "I am not in the least uncomfortable around gentlemen, Mr. Sickles."

"Just around rogues like me, right?" He grinned. "Come. We have things to discuss." He was already limping toward the dining room, but she still hung back. "What's the matter, Miss Canner? Don't you eat meals, or do you just argue all day along?"

"The Willard does not serve negroes," she said, miserably. Her mother had raised her to avoid above all things humiliation before the white race; and here she was, breaking that rule with this unmannerly acquitted murderer.

Sickles took her by the arm. "It does now," he said, and marched the unwilling Abigail through the door.

III

Dan Sickles was a rogue, no question. A rogue, a bit of a crook, a bit of a scamp. He was a lowborn rascal, and unashamed of it. One of the city's favorite stories involved the time that Sickles, then at the American legation in London, brought a prostitute to the palace to meet Queen Victoria, introducing her as a Philadelphia socialite. The entire royal court was fooled. Abigail Canner had been raised to avoid gossip, but she was perfectly willing to believe that this particular tale was true. According to Nanny Pork, the white folks preached a lot more morality than they acted, and nothing Abigail had seen in her twenty-one years persuaded her of anything else. There were exceptions, of course—Mr. Finney, for one—but the white race, as far as Abigail was concerned, had no business preaching anything to anybody.

As they ate and talked, she began to realize that Sickles never preached; indeed, this was a part of his charm. Whatever you might have done in life, no matter how shameful, he suggested, through his posture and his expression, that he had done far worse, and managed to remain on his feet.

Or on his foot, as he liked to put it.

Dan Sickles asked her lively questions about Oberlin, about her interest in the law, about Judith. Abigail had just started to wonder whether his entire purpose was to gather information on her sister, or whether he planned to join Dennard in lecturing her about the importance of avoiding scandal, when, all at once, he glanced toward the door and rubbed his hands together.

"Excellent," he said. "This is it. Be ready."

"Be ready for what?" She turned, and saw the headwaiter leading a primly disapproving man in high collar and black topcoat. He put her in mind of the sort of pastor who could spot a sin before you thought of it.

He looked familiar, but she could not place him.

"Who is it?" she whispered. "What are we doing?"

"Just sit there and look skeptical."

"I beg your pardon."

But Sickles was up on his feet—his foot—smiling and beckoning. The stranger murmured to the headwaiter, changed direction, crossed to their table.

"Mr. Sickles," he said.

"Congressman Blaine, may I present Miss Abigail Canner."

"Oh," said the newcomer. Abigail remained seated, as befitted a lady. "Yes. Well. I have heard of you."

He did not indicate whether he liked what he had heard.

"A pleasure, Congressman," she said.

Sickles put a confiding hand on Blaine's shoulder. "I was hoping that we might continue our conversation."

Alarm in those disapproving eyes. "What? Here? You cannot be serious."

"Miss Canner has my entire trust," said Sickles. "And the President's, of course."

"Not here."

"Where, then?"

Blaine hesitated. Abigail's presence had unsettled him, which was doubtless what Sickles had intended. "I'll send my man around to make an appointment," the congressman finally said.

"I shall expect him no later than tomorrow."

They said their farewells, and the hovering headwaiter seated Blaine over by the window. Sickles, seated once more, chuckled. "You did just fine."

"What exactly did I do?"

"You don't know who that was, do you?"

Her chance to show off. "James Blaine. Congressman from Maine. He voted for the impeachment."

Sickles nodded, impressed. "He's a friend of Mr. Lincoln's. Or he was. He's a very smart man. Very pious. Thinks Washington City is a cesspool. He's a sort of lay elder in his church. Preaches against the brothels and so forth. Quite popular on Capitol Hill." He speared a slice of rare roast beef with his fork, gestured with it. "The House will probably elect him Speaker in a couple of years."

Abigail nodded, said nothing. She took a small bite of salmon. Once more she had that sense of being very near the inner circle, but not quite near enough to enter.

"Blaine didn't vote against Mr. Lincoln because of some high principle," said Sickles. "He was paid."

"You know that for certain?"

"He's as corrupt as they come, Miss Canner. That's what I know. The rest I believe. I've been pressing him. He seems scared half to death—whether of our side or the other side, I'm not sure. I've implied that the President is prepared to forgive and forget if he will just give us a little information. Such as, say, who paid him. He's been avoiding me, but he has lunch every day right at that table. I came here to intercept him. Finding you was bonus." He was talking and chewing at once, an unattractive spectacle. "If he was scared before, he'll be terrified now. In a day or two, he'll send his messenger, just like he said. We'll set up a time to meet."

"I still don't understand my role."

"Neither do I, to tell you the truth. But your name seems to have a magical effect on Mr. Lincoln's enemies. I'm not sure why." He took a long swallow of water. "Maybe you're what Blaine's afraid of."

"Now you are making fun of me."

That rogue's smile. "Not at all, Miss Canner. I gambled that your presence would upset Blaine, and it did. I don't know why, and I'm not disposed to worry about it just now. So—tell me about your Aaron."

The change of subject startled her. "He is my fiancé."

"I know."

"He is with the Union Army. We are to be wed when he returns," said Abigail, studying the damask tablecloth. "We met at Oberlin."

"When is he due back?" asked Sickles, softly.

"Soon." She felt uneasy under the intensity of his clever eyes, and, for the briefest of moments, her hold on her story weakened.

Then it was all over. Sickles pulled a gold watch from his waistcoat pocket, squawked in surprise, told her he was sorry, and lunch had been lovely, but he was late. Two waiters materialized to help him to his feet.

"I have to see the President," Sickles explained as he handed her up into the wagon. "And then I'm going north to see General Grant."

"On business?" she asked, mainly out of curiosity.

Sickles twirled his moustache. "Let me put it this way. Grant is staying neutral. That is what he keeps saying. But nobody is really neutral in this thing. It is time for people who matter to take sides."

Stunned that he would share such a thing, Abigail tried her luck. "Do I take it, Mr. Sickles, that you now trust me?"

"Miss Canner," he said, grinning, "if I did not trust you, I would never have asked you to lunch with me so that we might pleasantly discuss the affairs of the nation. I would have asked General Baker to toss you into prison."

IV

That same night, up in Philadelphia, Jonathan dined with Margaret and her father. The Lion now was singing a different tune: he had decided that the Radicals were all traitors and should be hanged. He did not know why the President had not yet closed down the Congress, but he wanted it clear that the army stood ready to do its duty. There was, however, the small matter of the many loyal Union soldiers who had been unable to find work since being discharged and were now destitute. Just a few months ago, a convention of former military men had demanded payment of a bounty in gratitude for their service. Mr. Lincoln had promised to look into finding the funds, but nothing else had been heard. Surely there must be some way Jonathan could mention the problem the next time he and the President—

Yes, yes, of course, and yes again.

Afterward, he stood with Margaret on the sweeping porch. The air off the Delaware River was frigid, but she had always liked the cold. Dark gray clouds scudded across inky sky.

"And what was that about?" Margaret asked, brown eyes steady and accusing, because demureness was an attitude she assumed only around the General. "You and Father. You weren't arguing about money for veterans. There's something else. Something the two of you know and I don't."

Jonathan smiled and touched a knuckle gently to her cheek. She blushed, as always, at the contact, for he was breaking one of her rules, and she was letting him do it.

"It's nothing," he lied.

Meg stepped away and turned her back. She stood straight and determined. She was clad in blue, her favorite color. In the skittering light of the gas lamps, she might have been wearing the uniform of a soldier.

"Father is proud of you." Her voice was flat. A tired horse whinnied somewhere. Otherwise, the estate had the sudden quiet that sometimes comes just before a battle. A part of him waited for the cannonade. "Father says you are doing your duty, and nobody can ask for anything more."

Jonathan was surprised. It had never occurred to him that the Lion was capable of pride in someone else, least of all his prospective son-in-law. "Your father is kind," he finally said.

"No," Margaret said. "He isn't kind at all. He is one of the unkindest men I have ever known. But he is still proud of you. He believes that a special integrity is required to do one's duty when one is facing certain defeat."

"We don't believe defeat is certain at all—"

"*We.*" She picked up on the word, played with it. She seemed very angry. "We. We? *We.* We."

"Meg—"

"The word means you and another. You are telling me what you and another believe. Why don't you ever tell me what Jonathan Hilliman the Third believes? Why do you always hide behind the opinion of others?" She glanced at him, then gave him her back once more. "Tell me, Jonathan. Tell me whether you, you yourself, believe that Abraham Lincoln deserves to remain in the Executive Mansion."

"Of course I believe it," he said, much too quickly. In truth, he was not sure of his motives. He was defending Lincoln because McShane had decided to take the matter on, and then Dennard had decided to continue. Had he spent his two-year apprenticeship in Washington doing corporation law, he would likely have had no strong feeling one way or the other about the trial.

And the others? Sickles and Speed were representing Lincoln with great fervor, but each was a longtime friend; their willingness to fight hard for him was entirely independent of any question of guilt or innocence. If Dennard had a cause at all, it was lost in his affection for legal abstraction. Perhaps the best word to describe his motive was *fascination*—but with the issues raised, not with the personalities or the politics. The only one of them who was acting out of a belief in Lincoln was Abigail.

About whom he dared not think just now.

"Of course I believe it," he repeated, putting passion into his voice.

A mirthless laugh. "Well, I shan't tell Father. He believes that the highest form of duty is carrying out your assigned tasks when you think your commander is a madman."

This time Jonathan had the wit to wait. He knew that Margaret was working around to her point.

"I don't think I care much for Washington City," she said. "It is a cheerless place. A place of ambition. And dreary, Jonathan. So dreary."

She was hugging herself, rubbing her upper arms in a way that reminded him, unfortunately, of Abigail, who had struck the same pose the other night, while making a similar complaint.

"Washington has its pleasures," he said, trying to lighten the mood.

"Pleasures," she echoed, and a knifelike quality in her voice made something deep inside him twist painfully. "Yes. I suppose so."

He was suddenly out of his depth. "What's wrong?" he said, stupidly.

Margaret would not face him. She had a strong fist at her mouth. He would have thought she was crying, had she been a crier. "I understand, Jonathan. I do." She seemed to be resuming a conversation he did not remember. "But, please, whatever else you do—please don't embarrass Father." A pause. "Or me. And don't pretend you have no idea what I'm talking about."

He spread his hands, even though she could not see them. "I'm sorry, Meg. Please. Tell me what's upset you."

She continued showing him her back. The shoulders might have drooped a smidgen. Margaret had to say the words twice before he heard. "Bessie Hale," she whispered, to Jonathan's astonishment. Precisely the rumor he had most feared had evidently made its way northward.

"Meg, I assure you—"

"And then, of course"—a small pause—"the colored woman."

Jonathan went very still. Probably Margaret felt it. "All that's going on—"

"I have no need of the details. Men are what men are. I understand that, Jonathan. And, goodness knows, I have been my father's daughter long enough to understand what marriage is. There is a public role a woman plays, and a . . . a private role a man plays. I accept that entirely." In the half-light she half turned. The Lion's heavy, furious glare burned in her eyes. "But, Jonathan, my goodness. You could be more discreet. If not for my sake, then for Father's."

She went into the house.

CHAPTER 20

Expertise

I

OCTAVIUS ADDISON HAD come courting again. They sat together in the parlor as he read aloud from Shakespeare's sonnets, because he knew that Abigail appreciated them. It was Saturday afternoon, and Nanny Pork was out for once, shopping at Center Market with Old Ellie, another former slave, who lived on the farm across the way. The two young people were not of course alone in the house; that would have been improper. Louisa was in the kitchen, learning from her sister how to be a hostess. As a practical matter, she was hovering in the wings, hoping for a glimpse of something untoward.

But nothing untoward occurred. Abigail, hands folded, perched at one end of the sofa; Octavius sat at the other, the heavy green volume of Shakespeare open on his lap. He wore a suit of the finest wool. He had spent two and a half years being tutored at the College of New Jersey, studying mathematics and biology, but mainly reading theology, in preparation for his work as a Presbyterian minister. The war had changed his mind, and he had left school to begin a mortuary business. The bodies, Octavius had explained to Abigail once, were just lying on the battlefields. Picking them up, identifying them, and writing to their families for shipping instructions had proved lucrative. She had nodded politely, listening to his proudly morbid tale without commenting. Octavius was brilliant and earnest and sweet, as well as painfully shy, and the last thing Abigail wanted was to wound him. She would rather not be spending this time with him, but as he was here, she saw no reason to be rude. Besides, the smallest argument would have infuriated Nanny Pork, who considered Octavius a catch. The young man's father edited one of the capital's colored newspapers. His grandfather was supposed to have been one of the slaves Thomas Jefferson freed on his deathbed, but half the colored families in Washington City claimed that their ancestors had been owned by one of the nation's Founders, and, the way Abigail saw it, at least a few had to be lying.

Meanwhile, Octavius was still reading:

> *"Fair, kind, and true, have often lived alone,*
> *"Which three till now, never kept seat in one."*

"Very lovely indeed, Mr. Addison," said Abigail, relieved that her suitor had finished yet another sonnet, and hoping earnestly that he would soon stop.

Octavius beamed. "I am not sure I have told you, Miss Abigail, how much I admire the work you are doing."

"Oh?"

"For Mr. Lincoln," he explained. "You may not be aware of this, Miss Abigail, but all our people are proud of you."

Embarrassed by the praise, not sure how to respond, she made to rise. "Let me refresh your lemonade."

"Let *me*," said Louisa, who had been listening in the doorway. She scurried in and removed the tray before Abigail could stop her. "You just sit."

So sit Abigail did, exchanging pleasantries, even listening to another two sonnets, all the while seething deep inside that Nanny was forcing her through this exercise again. For although Abigail herself kept alive in her heart the hope that her Aaron would return, no one else in the household believed it for an instant; and, at sour moments, even Abigail accepted that she might indeed have to make a different choice, because, with each passing month, the odds of her fiancé's safe return were declining.

She went still.

The odds—

"Is something wrong, Miss Abigail?" said Octavius softly, squinting behind his glasses. "Have I said something to offend? I apologize if—"

"No, Mr. Addison. Not at all." She actually smiled, and put a hand on his arm. "You studied mathematics at college, didn't you?"

A confused nod. "Mathematics is pure and beautiful, God's creation in pristine unsullied form. I had a mathematics tutor, of course, but I also traveled to England to hear Professor Cayley's lectures on pure mathematics on the occasion of his ascension to the Sadlerian Chair at Cambridge—"

Abigail was not listening. She was on her feet, suddenly excited, bidding her guest wait while she flew with unladylike haste up the stairs. In the room she shared with Louisa, she opened the cabinet and pulled out one of her notebooks. Ignoring the clear signs that her younger sister's fingers had been on every page, she flipped past quotations painstakingly copied out from Coke and Blackstone, until she found what she was looking for. She hurried back down to the parlor, where Octavius stood near the window, and Louisa was seated in an armchair, laughing at a joke, leaning forward daringly, even as she hid her face behind an entirely inappropriate fan.

Abigail's face reddened. There was a hard tone she could assume when she wanted to, inherited in equal measures from her mother and Nanny Pork—a tone even the mischievous Louisa dared not disobey.

She put it on now. "Go upstairs, young lady. Now." Her sister shot to her feet and, inclining her head toward their guest, drifted from the room. "Stay up there until I call you," Abigail snapped.

Louisa's answering mumble was inaudible.

"I apologize for my sister, Mr. Addison."

Octavius smiled nervously. "I am not offended, Miss Abigail."

Abigail crossed to the sofa. "Please. Sit with me. I should like to show you something."

He sat, round face expectant and alive. She opened the notebook. "Can you tell me what this might be?"

13163222232121244

"It is simply a number, Miss Abigail," said Octavius, puzzled. "Surely you know that. Thirteen quadrillion, one hundred and sixty-three trillion—"

He stopped. She had intended to explain, but knew at once she would not have to.

"Ah. I see. I see." Nodding, muttering to himself. "The highest digit is six. Did you notice that? And no other numbers above four."

"I noticed," she said, but Octavius was in his own world.

"No numbers above four. That's not very clever of them." He glanced up at her. "A cipher. It's a cipher, isn't it?"

II

"I believe so," said Abigail.

"A cipher," Octavius repeated. He frowned. "Yes. Yes. One would have to know where the groups begin and end. Either the recipient already knows where to break the lines, or part of the message tells him. Seventeen figures. Well, that could mean anything, or nothing at all. The numbers are low, so the method does not involve either displacement or substitution." His face seemed mesmerized, eyes flicking back and forth as he studied the page. "Do you know what it says?"

"I am afraid not, Mr. Addison. I was hoping you might be able to help."

"Possibly. Possibly. My tutor showed us some of the ciphers used over the years to protect military and diplomatic secrets." His fingers ran lightly along the figures. "That's what this is. Not a code. A cipher. Not a very sophisticated one. There is pagination in here. That much must be obvious to you. Pagination, lines, and so forth. Still, you cannot break it without the code book."

Abigail could not help herself. "Can you explain that, please?"

And so he did. The key was that the digits were so low, other than the six. His tutor had explained that low numbers were generally a sign that the cipher was based on a book. Books rarely had more than two or three hundred pages, so a high proportion of low numbers—especially ones and twos—was evidence that pages were meant.

"Generally, the cipher is keyed to the words on a page. One number gives the page, another the line, another the word. Put the words together, and you will have the message." He frowned. "It is unusual, however, to have only a single six, and nothing higher. I suppose that whoever enciphered the message needed to use only the first few lines on each page to find the words he needed. That likely means either a very simple message or a very sophisticated book. Usually, the book is one that is readily available. The Bible, for example. Or a volume of Shakespeare. It would not appear that the message contains more than five or six words. Seven, perhaps. I wonder if—"

He was on his feet again. Abigail stood with him. "With your permission, Miss Abigail, I would like to look this over for a few days.

There is something odd about the cipher. I believe that it is designed to deceive. It may not be a book code at all, even if intended to look like one. I should like to see whether I can work out where the deceit occurs."

"By all means, Mr. Addison. Let me copy it out for you—"

"No need," he said, and without looking at the page, recited: "One-three-one-six-three-two-two-two-two-three-two-one-two-one-two-four-four." He inclined his head. "May I have your leave?"

She had to smile. And not only because he was so gallantly determined to help. His archaic formality, no doubt gleaned from his lonely readings of Shakespeare, she had always found off-putting, but now it was somehow endearing. And what charmed Abigail most about the episode was also what she had secretly counted on: that Octavius Addison was too much the gentleman to ask why she need to know what the cipher represented, or how it had come into her possession. Best of all, she would soon know what great secret Rebecca Deveaux had died to protect.

"Of course," Abigail said. She considered asking him to keep the project to himself, but decided that cloaking the cipher in mystery might draw unwanted attention. Besides, Octavius was a gentleman, and would keep a lady's secrets. "I shall look forward to hearing from you soon."

At the door, Octavius took her hand shyly and, with a sudden surge of excitement, said, "I know that the trial begins in nine days. If you are not too busy preparing, I wonder whether you might do me the honor of going riding with me next weekend."

"It would be my pleasure," she murmured.

"Shall we say Sunday?"

"Sunday would be lovely."

When the young man had gone, Abigail said, not turning, "Come out, Louisa, dear." After a moment, her sister emerged grudgingly from her hiding place behind the stairs. "Did you enjoy your eavesdropping?"

"What's a cipher?"

"Nothing!"

"Is it a love note?"

"Forget what you heard, Louisa."

Her sister giggled. "He is a very sweet man."

"Indeed."

"Still. You know what Nanny always says."

Abigail drew herself up. "No. What does Nanny say?"

"If you ask a man for a favor, he's going to want one, too." A giggle. "And I don't mean riding."

III

That night was her second reception at the Eameses'. Nanny considered it unladylike to attend any social event unescorted. When Abigail explained that the young ladies of Washington City often did, Nanny laughed. Unpleasantly. "Child, all that proves is that they ain't no ladies." She chomped on her pipe while Abigail fought the urge to roll her eyes. "You should get that nice white gentleman to escort you."

"He is in Philadelphia."

"Then find another white gentleman. I knows you don't like the colored ones to take you to your talkin parties."

"That is untrue!"

"Then get that nice Octavius."

"Nanny, I am a professional of this city. I am employed by the firm that is defending the President of the United States. I believe that I can manage a single reception."

But this objection led only to a further peroration from Nanny on the subject of the corrupting aspects of employment, and why a true lady avoided it like the plague. In the end, they compromised. Abigail refused to be escorted, but she agreed to allow her brother, who was back in town, to carry her to the party and back in his wagon. Along the way, Michael told her he had been down in Virginia, helping some of the farmers organize groups to protect their property from the night riders.

"Armed groups?" she asked.

"There wouldn't be much point to any other kind, now, would there?"

"Are you in danger?"

"Every negro in this country is in danger, every minute."

"Thank you for the ride," she said as the wagon drew up at the Eameses'. "I shall be ready to depart at ten."

"Yes, ma'am," he said, and touched his forehead, as some of the other negro drivers did. Michael had told her once that this common salute was actually a secret signal of mocking disrespect, but the white folks were too dumb to realize it.

She went in.

IV

Ash Wednesday had fallen in the middle of the week just past, and with the start of Lent, the Season had ended in Washington City; but Fanny Eames was not bound by convention. In deference to Christian sensibilities, she teased her guests by withholding alcohol. But there was food enough to feed an army; given rumors that a legion of destitute veterans was marching south from New York, provender on this order might prove necessary.

There was no Sumner this time, and no Grafton either, and little talk of politics, but shortly after Abigail stepped through the door the same clutch of Washington ladies who last time had demanded to know when she was writing her book descended upon her. "Miss Canner!" burbled Crete Garfield, grabbing Abigail's hand, looking her up and down. "You simply must tell us where you get those marvelous clothes, dear."

"Oh, yes," burbled Bessie Hale. "Why, they look right out of the pages of *Peterson's Magazine*."

Abigail smiled. It was difficult to believe that just a week ago she had found these women intimidating. She knew that they were putting her down, because *Peterson's* was aimed at women of the working classes who wanted to look and behave as though they were members of the upper class. "Indeed they are," she gushed. "And yours!" she exclaimed, happily. "So beautiful and expensive! Why, they are right out of the *Peterson's* story on fashions of the eighteenth century."

A fresh round of tittering; but this time, if only for a lovely instant, the great ladies of Washington were on Abigail's side; and if she did indeed in private hours read *Peterson's* and *Godey's* and the other magazines for social pretenders, well, that was nobody's business but her own.

Then Lucy Lambert Hale linked a plump arm through hers and led her away from the group. The last time Abigail had laid eyes on Bessie, the young woman had been in tears following her argument with David Grafton. Tonight she was bright and alert.

"It's such a tragedy, isn't it?" she gushed. "That Mr. Hilliman has gone north? Really, I wonder what the young ladies of this city are going to do without him. Do you have any idea when he will be returning? Or where he has gone?"

"I believe he is visiting Miss Felix."

"With the start of Mr. Lincoln's trial a week away? I don't believe that silly story, and neither do you. Where has he gone, Abigail? He wouldn't tell me, the lamb. I begged him and flattered and teased and he simply wouldn't say a word. Do tell me if you know. For my own private ear. What *is* that silly boy up to that he refuses to talk about?" Bessie leaned close. "Crete Garfield says Mr. Hilliman is on a secret mission for the President. Now, that would be a feather in his cap, wouldn't it? If he's the man who saves Mr. Lincoln, why, he would have his pick of the young ladies of this city, wouldn't he? Only where would that leave you and me?" She squeezed Abigail's upper arm. "He hasn't told you, dear? He hasn't let anything slip?"

"No," said Abigail, head spinning. "Not at all."

"Pity," said Bessie, and was gone.

A few minutes later, as Abigail stood recovering near the piano, listening while an amiable British journalist expostulated on America's many flaws, a cultured male voice cried, "Oh, say! There you are! You're the one Hills is on about, aren't you?"

Which was her introduction to Fielding Bannerman.

V

He was beautiful, in that peculiar way that only the very rich and very careless ever quite attained. Dinah Berryhill possessed the same graceful certainty that the world cared greatly for her opinions on all subjects but dared offer none of its own; Fielding Bannerman managed it better, and less disdainfully. He was about her height, with the fleshy, pampered softness of a man too busy to be bothered, a little wild about the hair, a little sloppy in his absurdly expensive dinner jacket. The dark, moist eyes were frank and appraising, the eyes of a man who neither asked permission nor offered apologies. Jonathan said that the Bannermans owned banks—"lots of banks"—as well as bits of railroads, bits of shipping, bits of everything.

Fielding steered her away from the crowd, never questioning that she would go with him. He admired a piece of sculpture, dismissed an oil as fourth-rate, and asked her opinion. When she sounded knowledgeable, he offered to show her his father's collection of Renaissance art.

"That would be very kind of you," she said.

"I am at your service," he said, with a little bow. "Let's set a date, shall we? We live mostly in Philadelphia, but the main part of the collection is in New York. We have a place in the city and a place up on one of the lakes. We could take the cars. What do you say?"

Abigail had trouble suppressing a giggle.

"I suppose you're busy right now. This silly trial and so forth. Perhaps in the summer. Nobody stays in Washington City in the summer. Didn't Hills tell me that you summer in Ohio?"

"No, no, I went to school in Ohio."

"I have a cousin in Ohio. Wants to be governor, imagine. Or Senator. I don't recall." Fielding studied her. "Hills is right for once."

"About what?"

"You are an absolutely fascinating creature."

"Why do you call him Hills?" she asked by way of diversion as she tried not to blush. She could not remember when she had met a man so charming; or one, at least, who focused all of that charm on her.

"Goes back to when we were in rompers. He was Hills, I was Fields." He flapped a hand dismissively. "Never mind. Private thing. Between friends and all that." He looked her up and down, not bothering to hide his scrutiny. "I can see why he's taken with you."

"Mr. Bannerman, please."

"He says you're engaged, though. Pity." He brightened. "Say. He's not in the city, is he? Your fiancé?"

"Ah, no." The hectic leaps from subject to subject were dizzying. "No, he isn't."

"Then you could perfectly well go to the theater with me."

"I beg your pardon."

"Well, Miss Hale goes with Hills, and he's engaged." He seemed not to notice her sudden unease; or was too much the gentleman to mention it. "And then we shall go to the lake in the summer. You can look at my father's collection, and I shall introduce you to New York society. How does that sound?"

"Sir, I am not . . . I mean . . ."

"Say. What do you think of Bessie Hale, anyway?"

"I . . . I don't really know her."

"I thought I saw you talking to her a moment ago. Didn't I rescue you from her clutches? Well, you must return the favor. Not for me. For Hills. She is after him, and we have to protect him, you and I. We are his friends, and that woman is a monster."

"I beg your pardon."

"Every time Hills has been out with her, he tells me some fantastic story she came up with. Some piece of evidence the House Managers have in their possession. Some rumor. I think Bessie is most likely lying through her teeth to snare young Hilliman, the way she snared Robert Lincoln. He would have married her, you know, but Mrs. Lincoln would not permit it. Mrs. Lincoln considered the young lady a trollop." His eyes brightened, as though the whole matter was hilarious. "And it's true that Miss Hale has had a number of beaux. Came after me, as a matter of fact, but I'm rather impervious. And then, of course, there was Booth. Poor Bessie. He broke her heart."

"Who is Booth?" Abigail asked shakily. Her head was spinning. Octavius this afternoon, Fielding Bannerman tonight, Jonathan mooning every day. She had never been popular with men, the way Dinah was, or even Judith: why this sudden embarrassment of beaux?

"You know. Booth. The actor. The one who shot Mr. Lincoln in the head."

"Wilkes Booth? Is that who you mean?" She stared. "Are you telling me that John Wilkes Booth and Bessie Hale were . . . were . . ."

"Involved," said Fielding. A chuckle. "One story even claims they were engaged. They say that Booth was carrying a photograph of Bessie when he was caught, but nobody has ever produced it, and I am inclined to think the story isn't true. Still, she has had quite a life, has our Miss Hale." He saw the look on her face, and laughed. "Oh, it's a lot worse than that. The reason her father took her to Spain in the first place, the whole reason he left the Senate, was to get his daughter out of this city and away from rumor. But she couldn't stay away. This is her city, Miss Canner. Bessie Hale knows everybody and hears everything. Washington is like a giant web to her, and she loves nothing more than catching men in it. Spinning those tales is part of how she snares them."

Abigail found her voice. "So her stories . . . those things she tells Jonathan . . . Mr. Hilliman . . . are you saying she makes them up?"

"No idea. But that would be her style." He shook his head. "She can't stand Mr. Lincoln, you know. Her father used to be an enemy, too. Now I'm not so sure. Lincoln gave him the appointment to Spain." That throbbing chuckle again. "I will say this for him. He is a man of integrity."

"I have not had the honor of meeting Mr. Lincoln, but I would be inclined to agree."

"Not Lincoln. Hills." He had a hand on her elbow, steering her away from the crowd once more. "The pressure he's under, I mean. Standing up to his family, all that."

"I don't understand."

"Nobody's told you? Oh dear. I'm not sure it's my place." A cautious look over his shoulder. "Mother owns the business: Elise Hilliman. Heard of her? She's a harridan. Uncle runs it; he's a thief. But they know how to get what they want. They want Hills to quit and come back home to Rhode Island. Know why?" He did not wait. "They've switched sides, that's why. They were for Lincoln in '60 and '64, and now they're against him. Thrown in with the soft-money crowd. The family business is deeply in debt. Easier to pay back with soft money than hard. They are worried that Lincoln is listening to the hard-money people, low-tariff types—the bankers, say—people like my dad—and so they want him out of office. Wade is more a soft-money type. High tariffs. The family likes that. Their business is textiles, and they only sell in the States, so the tariff protects them. They hate that Hills is in there defending Lincoln. Most likely he'll be disinherited."

"You are jesting."

But the look in his eyes, for the first time that evening, was entirely serious. "That's why Meg is on him to go home. Doesn't want him to lose the business, you see. Always wanted to marry rich, my cousin did. Like Bessie. And Hills—well, this is what he always does. He keeps his mouth shut and does what he thinks is right." Fielding brightened. "But, say. On a happier subject. When can you go to the theater? Let's fix a date, shall we?"

VI

As for Jonathan Hilliman, he spent Saturday in Philadelphia, attending to minor affairs for two of the firm's clients. Dennard, although skeptical of the young man's purposes in making the trip, had assigned him the work. On Sunday morning Jonathan attended Presbyterian services with Margaret Felix and her father, and joined them afterward for breakfast. That evening he escorted Meg to the theater. On Monday morning he took the cars for New York, uneasy at the multiple deceits he found himself practicing. Meg thought he was returning to Washington today, and Dennard and Abigail and the rest thought he was staying another night in Philadelphia. Only Lincoln and Noah Brooks knew where Jonathan was really going.

As the train pulled out, Jonathan told himself that all would be well. He had already selected a quiet rooming house on Sixth Avenue, far from the places frequented by people who might know him. He watched the sooty towers of the city slip past and reviewed his plans. He would remain secluded until evening, when he would walk to Belmont's mansion for the meeting. In the morning he would board the cars for Washington City with nobody the wiser—

"Mr. Hilliman? Is that you? It is!"

At the sound of his name, Jonathan looked up in astonishment; and dismay. Beside him in the aisle stood nervous Plum, David Grafton's clerk.

"Such a pleasant surprise to see a friend," said Plum, seating himself in the row just behind. He patted a heavy valise. "I'm on my way to Manhattan to deliver papers to a client, and of course the earlier train never arrived. No explanation, as usual. Sabotage. I'm sure it's sabotage. I keep telling people that the rebels are massing in the mountains, preparing a strike at the capital, but does anyone listen?" Plum ranted on, never bothering to ask why Jonathan was headed to New York, and so sparing the young man the necessity of a lie. But Jonathan was shaken all the same, and wondered what might go wrong next.

CHAPTER 21

Financier

I

AUGUST BELMONT LIVED in a stately four-story mansion at 109 Fifth Avenue, at the corner of Eighteenth Street. On Monday evening, Jonathan sat with the great financier in his study, the two of them in facing chairs set near the bay window. The night sounds of the city drifted faintly through the thick glass. The room was sweltering from the enormous fire in the grate, and smoky as well, although a lot of the smoke was from the cigars. Jonathan was not a smoker but considered it unwise to do anything but indulge his host. Including his host's penchant for quick judgments, and his dislike of being disagreed with.

"You're a peculiar young man," Belmont said. He was a stout, broad-chested man who favored waistcoats and fashionable burnsides, although his chin was nearly clean-shaven. "You come from a fine family, but you're with Lincoln. Why?"

Jonathan squirmed. "I'm not sure what you mean, sir." When Belmont just kept staring, the young man tried another tack. "I'm reading law. My uncle arranged for me to read in Mr. McShane's office, and Mr. McShane took on Mr. Lincoln as a client."

"He's dead," said Belmont, meaning McShane, Jonathan supposed, although, on the other hand, the financier might have been commenting on the trial.

"Yes, sir. But Mr. Dennard took me over, and took over representing Lincoln, and—"

"Dennard's a Democrat." Belmont waited to be contradicted. "He's what they called a War Democrat. So was I. We didn't support the Republicans, but we supported the Union. We supported the war. Well, you know that."

"Yes, sir."

Belmont was studying his cigar. His nostrils flared with distaste. Although he made no obvious signal, a servant at once slipped into the room, replacing the offensive cigar with a fresh one. Jonathan tried to form a conception of the mountain of money on which a man like Belmont must sit, and the much larger mountain that he influenced and controlled—tried, and failed.

"Mr. Belmont, if I might—"

"What do I want? That is what you are trying to find a way to ask. Very well, Mr. Hilliman. I will tell you what I want. I want the Radicals not to win. I want a President strong enough to keep them under control." Making a fist to illustrate the point. "We won the war. The Union won, through the sacrifice of its people. Slavery has been vanquished. Now is the moment to bury the past. But that isn't what the Radicals want. Instead of restoring the Southern states to their constitutional rights, instead of trying to wipe out the miseries of the past by a magnanimous policy, dictated by humanity and sound statesmanship, the Radicals have placed upon the South the iron heel of the conqueror." Belmont was gaining energy as he pressed his point. Jonathan had the sense that the great man was trying out language for a speech. "Military satraps instead of civilian courts. A race just released from servitude is placed in authority. And, meanwhile, the national legislature seeks to trample executive and judicial alike under its feet. The impeachment trial shows the lengths to which these men will go. What the Radicals really want is to usurp all the functions of government, and enforce their edicts by the bayonets of a military despotism. No," he said, forcefully, as if Jonathan had contradicted him. "That cannot be permitted. A free and intelligent people will never stand by while such measures are taken. And I will be for any man who is against them."

Jonathan was not sure what answer was expected of him. His instructions were to feel Belmont out. The great financier was thought to be working behind the scenes for Chase. It seemed unlikely that a lowly law clerk could win him to Lincoln's side. Jonathan did not understand why the task had been entrusted to him.

"When I say that I will be for that man," Belmont murmured, "do bear in mind that the resources I command are in essence limitless."

So that was it. He was offering to throw the Belmont interests behind Lincoln. That meant the *New York World* and its huge readership, along with any number of interlocking firms. A man like Belmont could send a single telegram, and a factory in the home state of a politician who opposed his will would shut down, constituents out of work and angry: it had happened before. Such power boggled the imagination. Jonathan's family was decently off, and Fielding Bannerman's rich beyond belief, but beside August Belmont they were paupers. Yet there must, he knew, be a quid pro quo. Jonathan had been around Washington long enough to learn that no offer was ever exactly what it seemed. A hidden motive always lurked behind the stated one, and a secret motive beneath the hidden one. Beyond all that was the true motive, almost never discovered.

Belmont, moreover, was a Democrat, and a fiery one. A decision on his part to support Lincoln might push wavering Republican moderates into the Radical camp. Indeed, Belmont was known to despise Lincoln: not merely to oppose him or dislike him but actually to despise him. In a speech just three years ago, the financier had referred to Lincoln and his advisers as "the fanatical disorganizers"—a reference to the Administration's supposed incompetence—and had insisted that Lincoln's election had been procured "in an evil hour" by "the madness of sectional fanaticism."

On the other hand, this was politics, where men changed conviction as often as convenient.

Belmont wanted something. They both understood that. And now he told Jonathan what it was.

"You are familiar of course with the Morrill Tariff." Belmont swirled his brandy but did not sip, so neither did Jonathan. "Our blockade of the Southern ports during the war nearly caused the states of Europe to recognize the Confederacy. I had it from Lord Palmerston himself. Do you want to know what Palmerston said to me? 'We do not like slavery, but we want cotton.' And it was not merely the cotton. The unfortunate Morrill Tariff was also part of the reason the Europeans grew restless. As simple as that, Hilliman. I myself wrote to Secretary Seward to warn him of this risk, and to Baron Rothschild, among others, to express my concern. The Europeans hate our tariffs, obviously, because the tariff makes it harder for them to sell us their goods. The tariff originally passed under Mr. Buchanan, of course, not Mr. Lincoln. But Mr. Lincoln has retained the tariff, and even increased it. I know, I know"—

again answering an objection Jonathan had not raised—"the tariff was increased because of the war. But now the war has ended, and the tariff can be repealed, can it not?"

Jonathan advanced cautiously, sniffing for traps. "I should explain that I have no influence in these matters."

"Don't be absurd, Hilliman. I know exactly who you are." A wave of the famous cigar. "I knew your father well. We did business together. He was a fine man."

Solving at least one mystery: how Jonathan became the emissary.

"Very kind of you, sir."

"During the war," Belmont resumed, "many of the great European syndicates considered loaning money to the Confederacy. You are aware of this, of course."

"Yes, sir."

"You may also be aware that my advice, if I may say so, was instrumental in persuading them to do otherwise. The rebels might have been much better financed had I, and other like-minded men of business, not taken a strong stand in Europe against buying their bonds. They call us 'silk-stocking,' I know, but there must be someone, Hilliman, someone who has the common sense to limit the extent to which politics is able to upset commerce. It is commerce that will build the better future, Hilliman. Not politics." He paused as if waiting for Jonathan to write this down. "It is commerce that saved the Union. It is commerce that won the war. I do not trust many people, Hilliman, but I trusted your father, and I have generally found that if you can trust a father you can trust a son. There are exceptions, to be sure. The rule, however, is a sensible one, much proved by experience. You tell me that you wield little influence. Frankly, I don't care. I trust you to be honest. With me and with Mr. Lincoln both. Therefore, I ask again: can the tariff be repealed or not?"

Jonathan chose his words with care. He knew full well—and assumed that Belmont did, too—that his own family, along with other textile makers, was fighting furiously behind the scenes to keep the tariff in place. "I would suppose that such a thing might be possible."

"Correct," said Belmont, and Jonathan had the uneasy sense of having made a commitment without meaning to. "Few things are impossible, I have found. And those few, someone will tomorrow invent a means to accomplish."

"Yes, sir."

"Then there is the matter of the money itself."

"Sir?"

"Consider, Hilliman. During the war, the Europeans bought our bonds. Now we sell them here at home. The savings of the rich and poor, the widow and the orphan, are confided to the safekeeping and custody of the United States at the low rate of four percent. It would be the most disgraceful breach of public faith if these bonds or their interest were to be paid in anything but gold."

The currency again. First Fielding Bannerman, now August Belmont. They shared a common understanding of the battle between President and Congress. From their point of view, the struggle had nothing to do with the freedmen or the Reconstruction or the proper allocation of power between the executive and legislative branches. For the great men of business, impeachment was simply another investment opportunity. They had to decide whether buying or selling Lincoln shares would deliver the higher profit.

"I see," said Jonathan finally. The permutations were dizzying. He found himself wishing that he could talk to Abigail. She had a way of explaining things.

"Excellent," said Belmont. "Then we have an understanding?"

"I will do my best to convey your views, sir."

"One can ask no more."

II

Jonathan assumed that the séance was over. Forgetting protocol, he even made to rise. His mind was foggy from the smoke, and he was starting to worry that, should he stay any longer, he would say the wrong thing. He did not imagine for a moment that Lincoln would accept Belmont's offer, and not only because it was obvious and stupid. Lincoln was simply not that kind of man.

And yet all of this was so clear that Jonathan could not understand what he was doing here, why Belmont had sent for him. Surely the financier was smarter than he, and could easily work out the unlikelihood that his offer would be accepted. And it was this realization—that Belmont was by no means finished with him—that planted Jonathan firmly back in his seat.

The banker looked amused, as if he had read the struggle on Jonathan's face. "How is your father?" Belmont said, suddenly.

Jonathan was, for an instant, thrown. "He died, sir. Nine years ago."

"Did he?" Belmont seemed lost in thought. The cigar smoke drifted around his smoothly shaven chin like a soft gray beard. Jonathan wondered whether he had even heard. "Is it difficult for you? Day after day, sitting in Washington City, watching Mr. Lincoln's presidency crumble? I should have thought by now you would have resigned your position and returned to Newport to run the family firm. I know that was your father's wish." So he had heard after all. "You may not know this, Hilliman, but Belmont & Co. own a certain interest in the Hilliman firm. Were you aware of this?"

"No," said Jonathan, wondering if here at last was the explanation for his family's miraculous escape from debt ten years ago.

"A small share. Forty percent. Brighton never told you?"

"No, sir. He did not." *Forty!*

A bob of the small head, as if in confirmation of secret knowledge. "Well, I suppose you would have found out sooner or later. Presumably, when you take the reins, you will in due course inspect the books."

"Yes," said Jonathan, faintly.

"Never delegate that responsibility. The head of the firm must know to the penny how much is spent on printer's ink."

"Yes, sir."

Belmont regarded him with something like disappointment. "That is your ambition, is it not? To marry Miss Felix and run the firm?"

"I suppose so."

"Do not suppose, Hilliman. The man who runs a great company must be decisive and ambitious and daring. Do you have those qualities?"

"I—I hope so, sir."

"Well, let us find out. I need some advice of a business nature. Perhaps you can be of assistance." He did not wait for an answer. "You will recall what I said a moment ago, that Belmont & Co. own forty percent of the shares of your family's firm. This holding is, as you doubtless realize, sufficient to give us, if not practical control, certainly a veto over the firm's major decisions." He waited a moment for his message to sink in: neither Brighton Hilliman, who ran the firm, nor Jonathan's mother, Elise, who in theory owned it, could make a move without this man's approval. "Now, here is the difficulty. We obtained the shares when we extended credit to Hilliman & Sons a decade ago. In addition to the shares, Belmont & Co. obtained certain warrants that, if exercised by the end of this calendar year, would allow us to purchase an additional twenty percent."

Jonathan stared. He could think of, literally, nothing to say. The firm had always been there, vast and untouchable. That the family had suffered in the great Panic of 1857 he accepted. That was the year they had let all but two of the servants go, and the year his father's health had entered the decline from which it never recovered. But that year of terrible agony was like a brief instant in the family's storied past. Hilliman & Sons, to outward appearances, was as potent as ever. The factories were fully staffed. The profits, to hear Uncle Brighton tell it, were rolling in. Jonathan had always assumed that at some point, when he had completed his entirely appropriate young-man's meanderings, he would return to run the company, and thus secure his financial position. It had never entered his imagination that the reason for the firm's survival might be the existence of a silent partner; or that the silent partner might, with the stroke of a pen, cause the firm to disappear.

"Belmont & Co.," the financier continued, "have not yet decided whether to exercise the warrants."

With impeccable timing, the butler knocked and entered, informing Mr. Belmont that the carriage was waiting to depart for the theater.

"Thank you for your time, sir," said Jonathan, rising.

"I shall look forward to your prompt response," said Belmont. "And to your advice."

"My advice, sir?"

"About the warrants."

The butler showed Jonathan out. The message was clear. If the President would agree to dump the tariff and strengthen the currency, he would have Belmont's support. Otherwise, Lincoln would be convicted, and Hilliman & Sons would cease to exist.

CHAPTER 22

Respects

I

ON TUESDAY MORNING, Abigail rode into town in Patsy Quillen's wagon. She enjoyed the Quillen sisters, despite the unspoken rule around the neighborhood that younger colored girls were not to speak to them. Patsy had an appointment with her banker. On the way, she gossiped about their mutual neighbors for a bit, then talked airily of electrical power: that was the future, Patsy insisted; that was where Abigail should be putting her money.

"I don't have any money."

"When you get some, dear."

The office was alive with excitement. The Radicals, it seemed, wanted to reopen negotiations. Dennard and Speed were on their way over to Congressman Garfield's house, which had been chosen as a neutral ground: Garfield, who hoped to be President one day, had to keep both camps happy. So he had voted against the impeachment motion, but had criticized in the harshest terms Lincoln's defiance of Congress.

Jonathan was not yet back from the North; Sickles was still off visiting Grant, or whatever other errands Lincoln had sent him on.

Before departing, Dennard instructed Abigail and Rellman to go into McShane's office and pack up "all that Chanticleer silliness" for delivery to the widow.

"I want it in her hands today," he said.

The "silliness" turned out to comprise not only the newly arrived package but four thick folders besides. Abigail wanted to look inside, but Rellman said that to do so would constitute a serious breach of confidentiality. His tone of voice suggested to her that he had invented this principle on the spot, but already in her short apprenticeship she had learned to admire the lawyerly skill of stating utter nonsense while displaying so sober a mien that everybody assumed you were right.

Wrapping all of this into a single parcel took no more than fifteen minutes.

"I wonder why Mr. Dennard wanted us both to do it," mused Rellman, obviously miffed to have been handed so menial an assignment.

Abigail shrugged. But she thought she knew. Dennard wanted each to keep an eye on the other. Whatever was in the Chanticleer materials, he wanted the firm to have no part of it.

"Little is supposed to take it," said Rellman, looking around. They were back in the anteroom, with the parcel on the table. "He should be back any minute."

"One of us should go with him."

"Why?"

"As a sign of respect." She smiled. "Don't worry. I'll do it."

Although Rellman gave her a suspicious look—wondering, perhaps, whether she might peek inside after all—he raised no objection. She had not expected him to. Deliveries were beneath his station, but he would not for a moment consider them beneath Abigail's.

And, for once, the prejudice attaching to her color and sex suited her just fine.

II

She asked Mr. Little to wait in the wagon. Carrying the parcel herself was awkward, but she considered the symbol important. She went to the front door, not the back, because she was a clerk from the firm, here on official business. Though she was haunted still by the experience of waiting in Senator Fessenden's kitchen for hours, her mother had taught her that, if you once allow your nightmares to hold you back, you will never get moving again. She was determined, therefore, not to let a maid dismiss her. But the dark-haired and elegant woman who answered the door was nobody's maid, and wore the pearls to prove it.

"Mrs. McShane? I'm Abigail Canner. From the firm."

The woman looked fifty, and pinched, and skeptical. "I am not Mrs. McShane," she announced to the air above Abigail's head. Her accent had its origin well up in New England. "I am her sister, Mrs. Huntley."

"I apologize for the intrusion. But I have a package from the firm. Items of her husband's." Mrs. Huntley only stared. Her dark eyes were small and close together, the eyes of a rodent. "And I wanted to . . . to pay my respects."

"My sister is not receiving."

"I understand. Might I leave a note?"

The tiny eyes narrowed, and the tiny mouth made a moue of disapproval, as if a note were an unwanted modern invention. "You are the clerk," she finally said.

"Yes. Yes, I am. Abigail Canner."

"My sister says that Mr. McShane made quite a fuss over you." The lips twisted. "And of course the ladies of Washington can speak of nothing else."

Abigail dropped her eyes. She was learning when silence and discretion were called for.

"I believe my sister might wish to speak to you after all," said Mrs. Huntley.

III

It was evident that Mrs. McShane had never entertained a colored woman, but she was making a brave show, for her husband's sake. She had the maid serve tea in the solarium, because she liked to feel the sun on her skin. She was as tiny and birdlike as Jonathan had described her, and wearing widow's black. She seemed to have nothing to say, so it was left to Abigail to offer condolences, to apologize for having missed the funeral, and to explain that she had brought a package from the office at the instruction of Mr. Dennard.

"I see," said Mrs. McShane, and sipped.

Abigail sipped, too, wondering at the air of expectancy in the room. There were slices of toast and jars of marmalade and jam.

"Your husband was very kind to me," she said, and saw Mrs. Huntley, sitting beside her sister, close her eyes briefly. Abigail hastened to correct her error. "I arrived at the office unexpectedly—Mr. Dennard was still in California. But Mr. McShane was kind enough to supervise my work until . . ."

She trailed off. The atmosphere confused her. Mrs. Huntley did not want her here, but Mrs. McShane seemed almost to have expected her to call.

"Until he died," said Mrs. McShane.

Abigail swallowed. Despite the season, the room was warm. Pallid sunlight spilled through the wide southern windows. "Yes, ma'am."

"And you are here to thank me."

"Yes, ma'am."

"And to bring me this parcel."

"Yes, ma'am."

Mrs. Huntley was on her feet. "Thank you, Miss Canner. Now, I am afraid we have a good deal to do, preparing for our return to New Hampshire—"

Abigail made to rise, too, but something in Mrs. McShane's face . . .

"Ma'am, I wanted to tell you . . . I have been looking into the circumstances of . . . of your husband's death."

"That will be enough, Miss Canner," said the sister.

"Wait," said the widow. She sipped. "And?"

"And I . . . I do not think that what the police believe is accurate." Knowing that she was only minutes or seconds from being thrown out of the house, Abigail rushed on, words tumbling over each other. "Ma'am, I do not believe that Miss Deveaux was a prostitute, and I also—"

"Leave now," hissed Mrs. Huntley, "or I shall summon the servants."

Mrs. McShane ignored her. "And?"

"And I . . . I think his death was related to . . . to the work he was doing. . . ."

Mrs. Huntley had the door open. "Beth. Please ask Marvin to come at once. We have a bit of a problem."

"Leave us," said Mrs. McShane.

"She obviously won't. I'll have Marvin—"

"You, Susan," said Mrs. McShane, eyes still on Abigail. "Leave us. I wish to speak to this child alone."

IV

"Now, tell me," said Virginia McShane when her sister had gone. "Tell me, please, what you think happened to my husband."

Abigail took a breath. This was what she had rehearsed. This was the point toward which she had been working ever since the day Dennard told her to stop her investigation. "I believe that your husband suspected the existence of a conspiracy against Mr. Lincoln. Miss Deveaux was relaying information to him."

"I see." Mrs. McShane sipped, made a face: the tea had gone cold. She reached for the little gold bell to summon the maid, then let her hand fall. "Mr. Lincoln was here to pay his respects. Did you know that?"

"No, ma'am. But I am not surprised. I understand that he is a most gracious gentleman—"

"He is not a gentleman at all. He is an unlettered Westerner." Her voice was perfectly composed, but a single tear trailed along her pale cheek. "I never cared for him. But Arthur believed in Mr. Lincoln. He believed in the great cause. He always said that the constitutional amendment to abolish slavery was the single greatest act of state in his lifetime. Possibly so. But I lost two nephews to Mr. Lincoln's war, Miss Canner. Now you are here telling me that I lost my husband to the peace. Isn't that what you are saying? You believe my Arthur died because of the work he was doing on Mr. Lincoln's behalf. If that is true, then my tragedy is complete."

Again Abigail dropped her gaze. "Mrs. McShane, I apologize. I am not here to add to your pain—"

"Then tell me why you are here, Miss Canner."

"Ma'am?"

"You didn't come to bring the parcel." Slapping it. "Any messenger could have done that. And although I appreciate your condolences, I don't think the desire to pay your respects was quite enough. No. You want something, Miss Canner. Now, suppose you tell me what it is."

In another age, Abigail decided, it was Virginia McShane who would likely have been the lawyer in her family; and, given her gift for reading people, probably quite a good one.

"Ma'am, I did come to pay my respects. And I am truly sorry that I was not able to attend the funeral—"

"That was just Rufus Dennard worrying too much." She laughed; and drained the cup. "He believes women to be fragile."

"Yes, ma'am. But Mr. Dennard is also the reason I am here. He has mentioned, twice now, that your husband was pursuing an unusual idea about what is going on." She straightened. "Ma'am, you were not in the least surprised when I spoke of a conspiracy. I think your husband suspected one. I would like to know, if I could, just what he thought was going on."

"And you think I would know?"

"I do."

She waited.

"Yes," Mrs. McShane finally said. "Yes, Arthur did have a few silly ideas. He didn't share many of them with me. He knew that I was not enamored of Mr. Lincoln, and that I had doubts about whether the firm should be involved in the impeachment at all." She was gazing out at the bare winter trees. "Perhaps I wanted the impeachment to succeed. Perhaps I still do." Her attention shifted back to Abigail. "Arthur did indeed believe that there was a conspiracy. Not to assassinate him, but to put him out of the way by legal means. That was Arthur's phrase. 'Put him out of the way by legal means.' He did not know who it involved, but he doubted that the Radicals were part of it. Do you know what he used to say? 'Good men and evil men often have different motives for the same mischief.'" She took up the teacup again, forgetting that it was no longer warm. "He thought that the conspiracy reached the heights of the President's closest friends and advisers. I told him that was silly, that Mr. Lincoln, whatever his failings, was far too shrewd. But that was what Arthur said. And one more thing." She gave Abigail a long look. "He said he wished Mrs. Lincoln had not died. If she were here to explain herself, he said, the worst would be behind us."

"I don't understand."

"Neither do I. But that was what he said."

"Did he say whether—"

"He said nothing more." Mrs. McShane nibbled on a slice of toast, then rang the bell. The maid appeared at once, followed by Mrs. Huntley. Abigail and Virginia McShane both stood. "Miss Canner is leaving. I do not believe she will visit us again, will she?"

"No, ma'am," said Abigail after a moment.

"Good." She handed the Chanticleer parcel back. "You may take this."

"I couldn't, ma'am. It's yours."

"I have no need of it, dear. But I fear you do."

She would say no more.

V

Heading back to the office with Mr. Little, Abigail reviewed the little she knew about the last years of Mrs. Lincoln's life. After the assassination attempt on her husband, she had quit Washington, returning to Springfield with Tad, the youngest Lincoln son. She had been ill, Abigail remembered. There were stories that she was in and out of hospital. Her husband had visited often, and some had expected him to resign his office to care for her. Then she drowned—

If she were here to explain herself, the worst would be behind us.

One of McShane's silly notions, as Dennard thought? Or the key to the conspiracy he had died believing in?

That night, Abigail took the Chanticleer parcel home with her, opened all the folders, and began to read.

CHAPTER 23

Interruption

I

"YOU ARE LATE," said Abigail, and it was true: usually Jonathan was at the office by eight-thirty, but on Wednesday morning, five days before the trial, he arrived closer to ten, looking haggard. Pudgy Rellman sat across from her, and followed him with those froggy eyes, Rellman, who never said a word himself, but doubtless repeated to James Speed every word spoken in his presence.

Little took Jonathan's coat and scarf. The young man yawned as he moved toward the table. "Where is Mr. Sickles?" he asked, without preamble.

Abigail was surprised. No banter. No teasing. He was as serious as she had ever seen him. He had arrived from the North yesterday morning, gone at once to the White House, then returned to the office and spent the rest of the day closeted with Dennard. She knew he had been out with Bessie Hale last night, and refused absolutely to speculate on what relationship that fact might have to his exhaustion. Abigail herself had been at the office since eight, trying to complete her research on leaders all through history who had been threatened with overthrow by their legislatures: Dennard said their arguments were rather abstract and needed a bit of color. It was a fair day at last, the sparkling sunshine bringing brightness if not warmth.

"I do not believe that Mr. Sickles has returned."

"Returned from where?"

"He said he was going to visit Grant. I suspect that he may be making other stops as well." The blankness in Jonathan's eyes worried her: what had happened in Philadelphia? "Mr. Speed and Mr. Dennard are on Capitol Hill." She waited a beat, then gave him the rest. "You were supposed to go with them, Mr. Hilliman. They waited as long as they could. Mr. Dennard was quite cross. They are working out the final rules of procedure for the trial."

"If there is a trial," said Jonathan. "I believe that matters may follow an unexpected path."

"What do you mean?" asked Abigail. "Why are you being so cryptic?"

He glanced at Rellman, whose flabby face said he had known all along that Jonathan was unreliable. "I am not being cryptic at all." He went to the peg, took down the coat that Little had just hung. "I had better get up to the Hill," he said, and went out.

Abigail could not help herself. If Rellman was going to tell stories, then he would tell stories. She hurried into the hall, calling Jonathan's name, and caught him at the top of the stair.

"What is it?" she demanded. "What happened?"

The shadows beneath his eyes told her that he had slept poorly, if at all. When he spoke, his voice was toneless. "Remember what Stanton said? About the letter that supposedly doesn't exist? The one that will convict Mr. Lincoln? Well, Miss Hale says they have one. She says it was given them by one of the President's close associates. A written order instructing a general to ignore congressional statutes."

"Do you know who the general is?" she asked, not unreasonably. "Will he be testifying in person?"

"I don't know. Bessie—Miss Hale—doesn't know."

"What is her source?"

"She is not in a position to say."

Abigail tapped a long finger against her chin. "That means her father, I suspect. Mr. Bannerman says his loyalties are unclear."

"Mr. Bannerman? Do you mean Fielding?"

"We met at the Eameses'."

Jonathan was hardly listening. "I wish Sickles were here. Dennard thinks only of legal argument, and Speed is a fool." He was inching toward the stair. "And both of them would dismiss the tale as rumor. Dan Sickles understands politics. More important, he understands Washington. He will know what to do."

What Abigail said next, she said kindly. "You know, Jonathan, we have to consider the possibility that there is no letter." He stopped in mid-stride. "Miss Hale may be scattering these breadcrumbs to keep you, as it were, on her trail."

Jonathan opened his mouth, shut it again. "I suppose that is possible. Still, when she speaks of it, she is very persuasive." He realized how he must sound. "Perhaps you are right. But we cannot afford to assume that the letter is chimerical. We must plan for the possibility that it has turned up."

II

Dan Sickles arrived late in the afternoon. Rellman had disappeared, so Abigail was holding the fort. Sickles listened to her repetition of Jonathan's tale, and told her not to worry about it.

"But if there is a letter—"

"If there is, there is. No point in worrying about what you can't change."

He lounged on the settee with his bad leg up and hummed a couple of popular tunes, beating time with his walking stick. He seemed quite pleased with himself.

"Mr. Sickles," she finally said, "I am trying to work."

He nodded. "The sheer power of my presence is often distracting." He sat straighter. "I saw Grant. I saw a few more people, too. I think everything is going to work out."

"And by everything, you mean . . . ?"

"Never mind. Let's just say we have a few surprises of our own now." He turned toward McShane's office. "The materials from Chanticleer still in there?"

Abigail swallowed. "No."

"Dennard sent everything on to Mrs. McShane, right?"

"Yes. Only Mrs. McShane would not accept the package. She gave it back. She said that we needed it."

"If she gave it back, and it's not in the office, then I assume you took it home with you." She nodded. "Good," said Sickles. He rubbed his hands together. "Have you been through it?"

"Please don't tell Mr. Dennard," she said, coloring. "But, yes. I have been through the package. There were four other folders of materials from Chanticleer. I have been through those, too. I'm still not sure what it all means."

"What's in the folders?"

"Nothing that seems important," Abigail confessed. "A statement of ownership of a steelworks in Pennsylvania. Additional papers concerning the railroad dispute in South Carolina. A contract for shipping cotton. A few other matters. I fear that Mr. Dennard may be right. These materials may be unrelated to the trial."

"I am quite sure Dennard is wrong. Go back and study those papers. There is something there." He shut his eyes briefly. "I won't tell Dennard you kept the package. You won't tell him, either." He shut his eyes briefly. "Speed is going to stay up at the Capitol negotiating the rules of the trial. Dennard and I are going over to Congressman Garfield's to see if we can't work out a compromise. Hilliman will take notes. You get the night off." Even with his eyes closed, Sickles sensed her stiffening. "Fine. It's not fair. But our only goal in this thing is to help our client." He laughed. "It's all a waste of time anyway. We'll negotiate into the night, but it will never come to anything. Mr. Lincoln can't back down. Neither can the other side." His voice grew fainter. "Know something? That's how the Civil War started."

III

That night, Abigail attended the theater with the persistent Fielding Bannerman, who not only refused to consider allowing her to find her own transport, but brought along a lovely bouquet for Nanny Pork. He was charming and courteous, and regaled Abigail with stories of his many absurd relatives, including a particularly eccentric uncle who had decided to invest his entire fortune to try to find a method of transmitting telegraph signals through the air without wires, which every scientist knew to be impossible.

Said Fielding.

The show was a comedy revue. Parts were satirical; parts were risqué, and Fielding's whispered asides were even more so. At the intermission, she was spotted by Crete Garfield, who bustled over, pretending to be delighted, and dropped broad hints about the vital negotiations going on even now at her home: she had been sent out for the evening while the men did the work.

"I suppose you are suffering the same tragic fate, Miss Canner."

"I beg your pardon."

"Your fellow clerk, Mr. Hilliman, is even now closeted with the others, working on the details of a compromise. Whereas you"—eyeing Fielding—"have plenty of time for fun."

Abigail was word-struck. A bell signaled the second act, and Fielding took her by the arm, but by that time General Lafayette Baker was at her side, wondering whether he might have a word.

IV

"I understand you dropped in on the widow McShane the other day," said the head of the federal Secret Service. "I understand you upset her tremendously."

They were in a small, airless room, stuffed full of programs and props, the chamber of the theater manager. Abigail had told Fielding to go back in, that she would join him presently, but he was waiting loyally in the lobby.

"I went to pay my respects," said Abigail.

"But that wasn't the only reason, was it?"

"Wasn't it?"

"Don't fence with me, Miss Canner. We haven't the time. Mrs. McShane says that you suspect a conspiracy, and that you think the police have the facts of Mr. McShane's murder all wrong."

"That is what I told her."

The little office was very hot, and Abigail found herself perspiring. Out in the theater proper, the audience was laughing hard, so Abigail supposed the second act must be a good deal funnier than the first.

"Mrs. McShane says she told you that she has accepted the conclusions of the police, and that you should, too. She said you refused. She said you made insinuations that the conspiracy included some of the most powerful people in Washington City. Is this correct?"

Abigail considered. Either General Baker was lying about what Virginia McShane had told him, or, more likely, Virginia McShane had lied to General Baker: for some reason, Mrs. McShane did not want the head of the federal Secret Service to know about her husband's suspicions. And that meant—

"Is this correct, Miss Canner?"

"We had a disagreement, General. Let the matter end at that."

Baker had his hands on his wide hips. He towered over her. She was reminded forcefully that this was the man who had seen to it that none of the major conspirators in the plot to assassinate Lincoln two years ago had lived to tell their stories.

"You have been told to leave this matter alone, Miss Canner. Now I am telling you again, for the last time. The murder of Arthur McShane is solved. The case is closed. There will be no further questions about it. Not by you. Not by anybody. Is that clear?"

"Yes, General. It is clear."

"Good. Because, if I have to tell you again, I'm locking you up." Grinning savagely. "And believe me, Miss Canner, all those tales you've heard of what happens to prisoners in Elmira and Point Lookout? They're all true."

One of Baker's men ushered her back to the lobby. Fielding took one look at her face and offered to drive her home. Abigail shook her head. She insisted on seeing the rest of the revue. After the show, they shared cracked crabs at the late buffet at the National Hotel. Fielding gossiped and made jokes, and a grateful Abigail tried not to think about Baker's threats. She was pondering instead Mrs. McShane's lie to him about their conversation. Lafayette Baker spoke for Stanton; and Stanton was these days Lincoln's closest adviser. If the widow was willing to hide from General Baker what she shared so readily with Abigail, that could only mean—

"I need to speak to Jonathan," she finally said.

"Oh, absolutely. Absolutely. Hills is a delight. When one is down, his sense of humor will fill—Oh." He saw her expression. "You mean *now*."

V

For Jonathan Hilliman, the events after his arrival at the Bannerman manse that night would always remain a blur.

The negotiations at the Garfield residence had been long and dispiriting, with Jonathan himself frequently exiled to the kitchen. Dennard, on behalf of the President, had offered several compromises. Stevens and Butler, on behalf of the House Managers, were adamant. Lincoln's Cabinet had to resign, with the exception of Stanton, to be replaced with a Cabinet more consonant with congressional policy. Lincoln had to agree, in writing, that no major decisions regarding either the disposition of troops in the Southern states or the question of eligibility of Southerners for office would be made without the approval of the

Congressional Joint Committee on Reconstruction. When Dennard finally agreed to take all of this back to his client, Butler added a third condition: the President had to admit, publicly and in writing, that he was guilty of the charges against him.

Dennard said such a course was impossible: Lincoln would lose all ability to govern. Butler refused to back down; and, just like that, the negotiations collapsed.

It was nearly eleven before Jonathan arrived home. He expected to find Fielding drinking in the library as usual, but Ellenborough told him that "young Mr. Bannerman" had not yet returned from the theater. Jonathan poured himself a drink and settled down to wait. Ellenborough freshened the fire. Jonathan tried to get him to go to bed, but the butler explained that his duties did not permit him to turn in just yet. Not until young Mr. Bannerman was home. Surprised to find his glass empty, Jonathan poured himself a refill. The clock on the mantelpiece ticked on toward midnight. Only now did Jonathan admit to himself that he had been brooding, all through the negotiations, on the fact that Fielding and Abigail were out together.

Again.

Absurd, of course. He had no claim on either of them. They were adults and could do as they liked. Another glass. He continued to brood, then had a sudden, brilliant notion to pen a note. He was not sure to whom he was writing, and after a while not sure what he was writing, either, so he tossed the pages into the grate. That would teach her. At some point he decided to shut his eyes for a minute, and in his dream Abigail crouched in front of him, softly calling his name as she pressed a wet cloth to his forehead, and then Fielding and Ellenborough were lifting him by the armpits and dragging him to the stairs. Jonathan found the dream hilarious. Fielding could not possibly be helping him to his room and onto the bed, because Fielding was out with Abigail, who was every bit as engaged as Jonathan himself was. Somebody pulled off his shoes and tugged blankets over him. In the dream he heard Fielding whisper, "You are an idiot, Hills," and then Abigail's worried voice on the landing, as though she would ever be upstairs at the Bannerman residence. True, Fielding occasionally brought women home. But Abigail Canner was not that kind of woman. Abigail was—she was—was his—

He slept.

CHAPTER 24

Mollification

I

"I HAVE SPOKEN to Stanton," said Rufus Dennard. "General Baker will not trouble you again. I am outraged that he bothered you last night. You should have informed me at once."

"Thank you," said Abigail, and meant it. She was standing in front of her employer's desk. Jonathan was in his accustomed place at the table, but the two of them had scarcely exchanged a word. It was Thursday morning, four days until trial, and there was a great deal of work to be done.

"There is something else," said Dennard. His jowly face was unusually pink today. "The only reason General Baker tracked you down at the theater is that you upset Mrs. McShane. I cannot imagine what possessed you, et cetera. My instructions were perfectly clear. You are not to pursue the question of what happened to Mr. McShane."

Abigail stood very still. Big soft snowflakes drifted from the darkness to stick briefly against the windowpane before swirling onward.

"Sir, I think—"

Dennard held up a restraining hand. "I know what you think, and I told you to abandon your inquiries. My rules. My firm, my rules." He had balled soft fists on the desktop. "My goodness, Miss Canner. Do you believe yourself to be the only person in Washington City who cares about the crime? Don't you think I wish I could press the police to act with more alacrity? *You* are searching for the killer of a stranger. *I* lost a dear friend. But I cannot spare the effort just now. The risk to our client is too great. If you are going to be a member of the bar, you must learn to temper emotion with duty, et cetera. Is that clear, Miss Canner?"

"Yes, sir."

"You are to drop this matter. Once and for all. I do not want to hear again that you are taking an interest in this terrible crime. Otherwise, I shall dismiss you, no matter what the political consequences. Do you understand, Miss Canner?"

Abigail frowned. "Not entirely. Why would there be political consequences to my being dismissed?"

"You do not know? No one has told you?"

"Told me what?"

The countenance softened. The anger was gone. "Well, never mind. I don't suppose it is important just now." He considered. "When I took you on, I was simply doing a favor for Charles Finney, who is a dear friend, and to whom I owe a great deal. I had no particular expectations. I frankly assumed that Finney was simply trying to make a very public statement in that way that he has. Something to do with equality, et cetera. Well, I see that I was wrong. You are indeed going to be a lawyer, Miss Canner. Oh, you will have problems. As I am sure you are aware, there are yet a fair number of states that, by rule, do not admit negroes to the bar, and many that maintain rules, either formal or informal, against the admission of women. How you deal with that is your own concern." He pulled a letter from his desk. "When the trial is over, you shall begin to study formally, assignments and so forth. The work will be difficult. You will have two years to master all of the law of the Anglo-Saxon people. I have engaged Judge Davis as your tutor. You will have to make some sort of financial arrangement with him. That is your business. I assume that you can afford it."

"Yes," she said, because any other answer would be embarrassing. She would work it out somehow.

"Good. Now. Second. Third, I suppose. You are my apprentice, but you remain the junior clerk. We are going to the Mansion this afternoon, Hilliman and Speed and myself, to discuss what happened last night. No, Miss Canner. Nothing to do with General Baker. Last night, I fear, the settlement negotiations collapsed, just as Sickles predicted. So we must meet the President and take a view. You will remain here and hold the fort. If this arrangement discommodes you in any way, I assume you will keep it to yourself. We haven't the time for more distraction. We have a client to defend and a trial to win, and the time for personal pique is behind us." The pouchy eyes seemed to bore into hers. "Do you understand me, Miss Canner?"

"I do, sir."

"Do you have any complaint?"

"No, sir."

"Good. Now, go away and send in young Mr. Hilliman."

II

"I warned you," thundered Stanton. His eyes were red-rimmed and watery, either from anger or from illness, although there were those who said that he took opium. "They were never serious about these negotiations. They were testing us for weaknesses, and we stepped into their trap. We showed them how weak we believe our own case to be!"

They were at the Executive Mansion once more, in the Cabinet Room, Stanton on his feet, Dennard and Speed and Lincoln seated, Sickles on the divan. Jonathan was in the corner, taking notes. Abigail and Rellman were back at the firm, watching the office. Perhaps by leaving Rellman behind Dennard intended to soften Abigail's exclusion.

But Jonathan turned his thoughts away from her, certain that the whole room was aware of his embarrassed flush. This morning over breakfast, Fielding had called Jonathan several varieties of fool. *Just tell her*, Fielding kept saying. But when Jonathan asked what precisely he should be telling her, Fielding cited the question as more evidence that he was a fool.

"Well, now, Mars," the President was saying, chair tilted back as usual. "I'm not all that sure we showed we were any weaker than they were. Maybe their effort to negotiate was just a feint, but, for all they know, maybe ours was, too."

Stanton, a man of action, did not believe in bluffing, any more than he believed in negotiating or apologizing. He shook his head, but sat down, his face fierce.

Lincoln, meanwhile, was telling a story. "You know, back when I lived in Kentucky, there was a family where every member fell ill after a meal. When the doctor came, he attributed the sickness to the greens that had been served. Now, it happened that the family had a son named Jake, a ne'er-do-well whom nobody particularly liked. And so, the next time the mother announced greens for dinner, the father decided nobody would eat until the greens had been tasted by Jake." He laughed hard, his chair rocking back so that it now balanced precariously on rickety hind legs. "That's why we tried negotiating, Mars. We had to test the greens on the Managers before we feed them to the Senate."

"Very prudent," said Speed, ever the sycophant.

Dennard looked up from his notebook. "Mr. President, I think we should now assume that there will be no further negotiations, whether here or in New York." A hard look at Jonathan. "It is time that we discussed strategy for the trial."

Lincoln had a way of letting his left eyelid droop lower than his right, making him seem sleepy and alert at once. "I am wondering," he said, "about Greeley."

"He is sticking to his story," said Dan Sickles. He was hunched at one end of the divan, the bad leg stretched across the faded cushions. From the way Sickles was rubbing his thigh, Jonathan decided that the pain must be terrible today.

The President nodded. His eyes were shut. His head was resting against the bookshelf. "Mr. Greeley," he said, "possesses that peculiar consistency granted to the man who is always wrong."

Horace Greeley was the well-known editor of the *New York Tribune*, the most widely read newspaper in the country. He had been in his day an early Abolitionist and a great supporter of the war, but by 1864, when the conflict seemed destined for a bloody stalemate, he had called urgently for peace. When Lincoln chose instead to press for victory, Greeley told the Administration that he had made contact with a representative of the rebels, who wanted to find a compromise. Lincoln had sent his secretary, John Hay, to Niagara to meet with Greeley and the rebel commissioners. Nothing had come of the meeting, and Greeley insisted that Lincoln himself had sabotaged the meeting, missing the chance to end the war and save thousands of lives. Lincoln's supporters considered this nonsense. The negotiations failed because the commissioners had no real authority to compromise, and in any case would never have agreed to Lincoln's terms. But Greeley stuck to his story, and was sticking to it still.

"Will they call him to testify?" asked Dennard, anxiously.

"They would not dare," said Stanton, who had found his voice again.

"They might," said Sickles. "Maybe they'll try to argue that the war would have been over a lot sooner if the President had been willing to negotiate seriously with the rebels."

"Then they will look ridiculous," snapped Stanton. "The Radicals can hardly argue, in the same breath, that the President was insufficiently energetic in punishing the South, and that he should have treated them more gently!"

"I am not sure they will mind looking ridiculous," said Lincoln, eyes still lidded. His voice was exhausted. "But they will not call Greeley. Forced to take an oath, a man might say anything at all. The oath changes how people see the world. It's supposed to focus their attention, but it makes some folks giddy. So they won't call him." The chair moved farther back, and was now defying gravity. "You know, back in Salem, I was called as a character witness for a man named Pete Lukins. His lawyer asked me, under oath, what I could tell the court about Mr. Lukins's character and veracity. I told the court that Mr. Lukins's nickname was 'Lying Pete.' Believe me, they won't call Greeley." He began to chuckle, chair still rocking. The laughter calmed him; it relieved his stress. Abraham Lincoln laughed the way lesser men drank.

"Besides," Lincoln was saying, wiping at his eyes. "They are better off with Greeley publishing his lies in the *Tribune* instead of telling them from the witness stand. Bigger audience. So let's not give Horace Greeley another thought." The chair came down with an alarming crash. Everyone but Sickles jumped. "Now, before the negotiations fell apart, Speed here was up on the Hill working on the schedule. He says the Managers want two weeks to present their case."

"That's two trial weeks," Speed clarified, once more stating the obvious. He looked around with satisfaction. "A trial week is four days."

From the divan, Sickles groaned. "They won't limit themselves to two weeks. They'll take as much time as they want. And"—this to Speed—"they might *say* a trial week is four days, but if they want to meet on a Friday, they'll meet on a Friday."

Dennard said, "We should negotiate a more precise time limit."

"There is no point," said Sickles. "The rules the Senate adopted place few limits on the Managers. They need not disclose their evidence to us. They need not limit themselves to what would be admissible in a court of law—"

"They have promised us a witness list," said Speed.

"Which we have yet to see, and trial four days away."

Stanton roused himself from his torpor. "We should not be negotiating with those traitors at all." He coughed hard, wiped his beard, turned to Lincoln. "Mr. President, I will say again, cooperating with these people is a mistake."

"The Constitution leaves us no choice," said Dennard, heavily.

Stanton's glare could freeze an army in place. "The Constitution leaves us a broad range of choices."

Silence. The President's eyes were shut. There was a half-smile on his face, as if he was in the midst of a moderately enjoyable dream.

It was James Speed who finally tried to haul the discussion back to the agenda. "After the Managers have completed their evidence," he said nervously, "we will have two weeks to present ours."

"We won't need it," said Lincoln, suddenly.

Speed looked at him in surprise. Sickles shook his head sadly. Dennard rumbled, "Sir, we do have to put on a case, exhibits, witnesses, et cetera. We might not require the entire time. One never knows. But we might."

"We won't," said the President, crisply. "I've given this a lot of thought. You want to line up military officers to testify, one, that I am not unsympathetic to the freedmen at the South, and, two, that I have never issued any sort of order that would undermine the position of the Congress. Is that about right?"

Dennard was succinct. "Sir, the military is the most respected institution in the country. If people see—"

"No officers," said Lincoln.

Even Sickles was startled. "Mr. President—"

"No," said Lincoln, slashing the air with his hand. "No military officers. They have a hard enough time, doing their duty to their country, risking their lives, and keeping their heads down so the Congress won't get after them for this or that. I will not compound that by having them risk being punished by the Radicals for testifying on my behalf."

Sickles said, "They would testify truthfully—"

"I know they would. That's the problem. That's what they'll be punished for. The Radicals would prefer that they lie."

Dennard tried again. "Mr. President, we have to meet their proof. The Managers will contend that you have been conspiring with military officers to overthrow the constitutional forms of government. The testimony of a few highly decorated officers would rebut that claim."

Lincoln's eyes hardened. "You know as well as I do, Mr. Dennard, that a tale like that is impossible to disprove by witnesses. By this time, my character is well established in the public mind. If people believe me capable of such a thing, then the testimony of a hundred generals will make no difference. If people believe I am not a man of that persuasion, then nothing the Managers say will change their minds."

Noah Brooks, the President's secretary, stepped in. "Pardon me, Mr. President. It is time for your luncheon with Mr. Wells."

Everyone rose. Lincoln said, "Keep working. We will meet this evening if necessary."

III

They stood on the portico waiting for their carriages to be drawn up. To the west, the late afternoon sun was pale and shrunken in the chilly haze. Dennard was plainly irritated.

"Do you know who Wells is?" the lawyer fumed. "He's the commissioner of revenue! We're trying to plan for an impeachment trial, and the President throws us out of his office because he has to meet with the commissioner of revenue!"

"Lincoln does still have to perform the duties of his office, Rufus," said Sickles. He laughed. "And the country does need revenue. Now more than ever."

Dennard was unsatisfied. "He isn't going to have an office much longer if he won't spend more time with his counsel." He had another thought. "Besides, he shouldn't be having meetings with anybody without one of us present. Who knows what he'll let slip? Who knows whom the Managers will subpoena next?"

"Lincoln isn't the kind," said Sickles, putting a hand on the larger man's shoulder, "who lets things slip. Not unless he wants to. He is the shrewdest man I've ever known. If he'd rather meet with Wells than with us, I am sure he has good reason."

Dennard refused to be mollified. Even after his carriage departed, the others could hear him, arguing to the air about his unreliable client who threw his lawyers out to meet with Wells. And all at once Jonathan remembered Belmont's offer to support Lincoln in return for a lowered tariff; and that Wells, as commissioner of revenue, had responsibility for such matters, and had recently visited Europe, and returned, so salon gossip had it, as a committed anti-tariff man, with many new friends on the Democratic side.

Lincoln was still negotiating; he simply was not telling his lawyers.

IV

At about the time that Noah Brooks was reminding the President of his meeting with Mr. Wells, sparking off Dennard's rant, Abigail was descending the slippery west lawn of the Capitol. She had been sent off to the Library of Congress in search of several volumes, and the fruits of her labors were in the heavy book-sack she was cradling with difficulty. One of the clerks had offered superciliously to help, but Abigail was too proud.

Mr. Little was waiting with the carriage. Approaching, Abigail was surprised to see him in conversation with a tall, stooped gentleman in overly fancy dress.

"There she is now," said Mr. Little, moving toward her and relieving her of the sack.

Even before the other man turned her way, she recognized from the twisted waist and bent shoulders the familiar crooked figure of David Grafton.

"Ah, Miss Canner. Excellent. As we are both headed in the same direction, I wonder whether I might trouble you for a ride."

Abigail was trapped: the courtesy was one that all Washingtonians of a certain class provided to one another.

"Of course, Mr. Grafton."

As the carriage started off, he nodded toward her book-sack. "I see that Dennard is keeping you busy with tasks of great significance."

She was stung, but kept her gaze calm and her voice resolute. "Really, Mr. Grafton, I cannot imagine what you would think you and I have to talk about."

The crooked man seemed amused. He sat with his back to the driver, one hand clutching the strap as they rocked and bumped along. "I take it, then, that you have not reconsidered my offer of employment."

"Certainly not."

"Pity." He reached inside his coat, withdrew an envelope, handed it to her. "Recognize this?"

She did, of course; and returned it almost untouched. But not before she spotted the same bloodstains, the same spiky writing:

For Mr. Benjamin Wade
Personal and Confidential

"Where did you get this?" she demanded.

"A friend."

"It was found . . . it was found with"—her voice stumbled—"with the bodies."

Grafton had already tucked it away. "So I am given to understand."

"Shouldn't it be in the police files?"

He ignored this. "Tell me, Miss Canner. Do you have any idea what might have been in the envelope?"

"A letter to Mr. Wade, obviously."

"Obviously. Any notion of the subject?"

"No."

"Miss Deveaux never told you?"

She blinked. "I have already told the police that I never met her. Now I am telling you."

Grafton nodded. "I gather that Inspector Varak has chosen to believe you. I haven't made up my mind." The clever eyes measured her. "The letter that was in this envelope, Miss Canner, concerned the President's defiance of congressional mandates on Reconstruction, on the ground that they are too harsh on the Southern states. As it happens, Dennard believes the President to be right in pursuing a gentler policy. Perhaps you knew that?"

Abigail refused to wilt. "I would be grateful, sir, if you would be so good as to cease your efforts to persuade me to leave Mr. Dennard's employ."

Grafton smiled blandly; and changed the subject. Still holding on, he contrived to bend his twisted body toward her. "The letter that was in this envelope is the property of a client of mine. The contents are confidential. And my client wants it back." A pause. "Obviously."

"Why are you telling me this?"

"In case you should happen to come across it." Another, longer pause. "My client would be prepared to pay handsomely for the return of the letter. Especially if he could receive assurances that its contents have not been disclosed to, let us say, an adverse party."

"Mr. Grafton—"

"My dear Miss Canner. Everyone in Washington City knows that you continue to look into what happened that unfortunate night. I have no objection to your doing so. But I see no reason why you should not profit from whatever information you happen to uncover." A thin smile.

"You would be able to give your great-aunt the comfort she deserves in her late age."

They were held up by a police officer to let crossing traffic pass. Grafton chose that moment to wish her good afternoon and, with a nimbleness that was a surprise in a man so wounded, hopped to the ground. Watching him go, waiting for her heart to return to its normal rhythm, Abigail reflected that at least now she knew the identity of the second man who been taken in by the fake registration at the Metzerott Hotel.

V

Evening. Gentle snowflakes brushed lightly across the gray city. The lawyers departed, followed swiftly by lazy Rellman. Little fed the stove one last time, then excused himself until tomorrow.

"I must apologize," said Jonathan the instant they were alone, "for my condition last night."

"You were exhausted."

He seemed not to hear. "I would be distressed were you to judge me harshly on the basis of a single episode—"

"I don't judge you harshly, Jonathan. I don't judge you at all. Please, let us speak of it no more." Abigail hoped this would be enough. She returned to Chitty, then looked up. "I must tell you what transpired this afternoon as I left the Library of Congress—"

But Jonathan Hilliman, as Fielding had told her at the Eameses', could be terribly stubborn. "It is no business of mine what you do. I want to be very clear. I am delighted that the two of you are friends."

"The two of us."

"You and Fielding. He is a fine young man. You are a fine young woman—"

"Stop it, Jonathan. Please. Just stop. We have more important matters to discuss. Now, will you please listen to me?"

He did. She told him what had happened with Grafton today; and with Mrs. McShane on Tuesday.

"Grafton had the evidence from Varak," Jonathan mused when she was through. "Or from another contact in the police. What you are telling me is that Grafton is indeed a conspirator."

"As we both have suspected all along. And there is more." She told him about Mrs. McShane's confirmation that her husband, too, believed in the conspiracy. "And at the end she said something passing strange. She said that Mr. McShane thought that this entire trouble could have been avoided if Mrs. Lincoln were alive to explain herself."

"Explain *herself*? But what could there be for Mrs. Lincoln to explain?"

Abigail barely glanced up. "Perhaps this is why the Managers are calling Mrs. Orne. To testify to some offhand comment by Mrs. Lincoln that they will twist into something sinister."

Jonathan put down his pencil. "Speed has been trying to talk to Mrs. Orne, to find out what she plans to say. So far she has refused to see him."

Abigail's gaze had shifted to the middle distance as she worked the permutations. "We are missing something, Jonathan. Not about Mrs. Orne. About the motivation of whoever is manipulating events." She closed her book with a snap. "We need more information."

"About what?"

"About who is truly manipulating events. Mr. Dennard refuses to consider the possibility of a conspiracy. I gather that Inspector Varak suspects more, but he is not inclined to share what he knows. General Baker is acting from motives I am unable to fathom. Therefore, it is left to the two of us." She was on her feet. "Will you accompany me?"

Jonathan hesitated. "I am supposed to deliver these pages to the copyist tonight."

"We can do that on the way."

"Very well." Scrambling to the closet. "But where are we going?"

"To the source."

CHAPTER 25

Alley

I

HOOKER'S DIVISION WAS the derisive name given to the triangle south of Pennsylvania Avenue, north of Ohio Avenue, and east of the President's Park, which housed the rougher end of the brothel trade. According to the original plan of Washington City, drawn up at the end of the previous century by the Frenchman L'Enfant, this land was supposed to be set aside for the vast buildings the national government would someday need. Perhaps the day would one day come, although nobody believed it.

For now, Hooker's Division was one of the most dangerous parts of the city; and for those in certain trades, one of the most profitable.

They might have walked the few blocks from the office, but instead they rode together in Jonathan's rig: one of the few occasions when Abigail had consented to have him drive her.

"Are you certain that this is the right place?" he asked, only once.

"The directions are from my brother, who is always certain."

Jonathan was worried about the carriage, so he left it with the porter at the Maryland House hotel, although, to be sure, the clientele looked only a few steps removed from the ruffians spilling from alleys and saloons. He had been here before, to meet Whit Pesky, but that had been daytime. He had never imagined that he might find himself in the heart of Hooker's Division by night.

"How do we find Silver Place?" he whispered.

Abigail nodded toward the colored man tying the reins. "We ask."

"If we ask directions, they will know we are strangers."

She slipped her arm through his. "They will know that in any case."

Nevertheless, they did not ask. They walked. Hooker's Division, according to the gleefully disapproving accounts in the newspapers, contained fifty saloons and a hundred brothels, all squeezed improbably into thirteen square blocks. Jonathan had always considered the tales absurd exaggerations; but now, as they made their way along the muddy walks, watching drunken louts tumble out of one door after another, he decided that the numbers might be accurate after all. There were neighborhoods of the teeming city where the same trades were carried on beneath a veneer of genteelness—the southern end of the Island, for example, and even a small knot of houses of ill repute not far from the Bannerman mansion—but Hooker's Division was special.

Michael had told his sister that Silver Place was off D Street, but D Street ran for six blocks through the heart of the Division, and each block seemed more shocking to the senses than the one before. The night air was frigid, but women in scanty attire leaned from windows and balconies, calling down to passersby. In the saloons, men shouted and cursed and fought. The smells were of cheap alcohol, and sickness, and human waste. Groups on street corners stared sullenly. A few called out lascivious remarks toward Abigail, but when Jonathan bristled she refused to let him turn, and hissed at him to keep walking. This part of Washington City was ruled by criminal gangs, most of them violent. Abigail pressed closer to Jonathan, who wished that he had taken Sickles's advice to go armed in the city. Just now, Jonathan especially wished for a firearm, because they were being followed.

Three toughs, maybe four, men who had made some of the more objectionable comments as Abigail passed, were trailing them at a distance of perhaps two dozen paces.

"Keep walking," whispered Abigail, who knew as well as Jonathan did what was happening.

"Turn here," he answered, tugging her into an alley between a saloon and a shuttered feed store. "And here," he added, emerging on C Street and cutting back the other way.

Yes. The men were definitely following them. No matter which alley Jonathan selected, no matter how many times he and Abigail circled the same apartment block, the boisterous gang made the same turnings, and even grew closer. There were more now, five or six, calling out increasingly lascivious comments, no doubt hoping to provoke a response.

Jonathan said, "Stay in front of me."

Abigail looked at him. "That is hardly gentlemanly, to allow the lady to go first into danger."

"It's the danger behind us that has me worried."

"Oh, *that*," she said.

Closer now. Jonathan, a bit stupidly, looked around for a policeman. And a way out: for he realized, far too late, that the last alley into which he had dragged Abigail, seeking escape, had no outlet.

They were trapped.

II

The toughs stood in a semicircle, hooting and laughing. Jonathan and Abigail were backed against the wall of a saloon, but on this side were neither windows nor doors. The only choice was to stand and fight. Jonathan did not see how he could prevail, but he was determined to do his best.

"Get behind me."

"I thought you wanted me to walk in front of you."

"No. Here. By the wall."

Abigail followed his glance toward the approaching gang. "Excellent suggestion," she said, and stepped to the indicated spot.

Jonathan looked around for a weapon, saw a discarded wooden board about a foot long. The men were close enough now to touch, and their hoots and calls were increasingly vulgar. He decided to make a quick grab for the makeshift weapon, but before he could, Abigail slipped her arms around him and drew him into a tight embrace.

"Abigail—"

"Shush," she said.

And pressed into him.

They did not kiss. Not quite. But her face was rubbing against his neck, and her body was warm and springy in his arms. She squirmed deliciously as Jonathan hugged her tightly to him. He was confused and delighted, and for a lovely moment quite lost; then he heard the toughs laughing, and he understood.

"I'm next," one of them said.

"How much for both of us?" said another.

And then, like magic, the moment passed, and the gang moved on, seeking fresher prey than a whore.

As soon as they vanished around the corner, Abigail straightened, cool and collected, entirely herself again. She was wearing a half-smile, and seemed, on the whole, unruffled.

Jonathan trembled. "What," he began. "What—"

Abigail put a hand over his mouth. "I believe," she said, turning away, "that they will now leave us alone." She gestured in the direction the men had gone. "I believe that our little ruse persuaded them that I . . . that *we* . . . belong here." Her half-smile made the words a joke, but the blush at the back of her neck told a different story.

III

After several more wrong turns, they found Silver Place, a snowy dead-end path between a warehouse and a copse of barren trees, mostly hacked down for wood. There was no sign marking the entrance to the alley. Their only clue was a fading splash of silver paint on the brick-work. There was barely room for the two of them to pass side by side. To imagine the horse plow ever discovering this dying alley was impossible. At the end of the road—if indeed it was a road—they found the rear entrances to a pair of tenement buildings. There was garbage all over the snow, because people threw it out of their windows. The buildings were wood, and four stories tall. Neither looked likely to survive a stiff wind, or a spilled candle flame. A door swung open, and two very large and very drunken colored men reeled out. Jonathan instinctively stepped in front of Abigail, and this time she let him. The men ignored them. When they were alone again, Jonathan tugged at the door, but it was bolted from within. Abigail tried the other building, and the creaking door, in its hasty compliance, nearly fell off its hinges.

Inside were mountainous shadows, and the babble of angry, hopeless humanity, and the smells of hot grease and a thousand cats.

"Are you sure this is the right place?" asked Jonathan.

"No," she said.

"Do you want to turn back?"

"No."

They were in a hallway. A faint flicker of light told them that a lamp was somewhere around a corner up ahead, and they made their way through the darkness, Jonathan leading, Abigail clutching his arm. Twice she stumbled, but she never lost her grip. Once, a door snapped open, and a colored girl stared at them. She was about ten, with her hair disheveled and her dress badly stained. She was breathing very hard. Her eyes were dark and devoid of hope, and for an awful moment Abigail was inside the girl's head, staring out uncomprehendingly on a world that made no place for her. She shared the girl's desperation to escape whatever else was in the flat, and, but for Jonathan pulling her along, would have knelt and taken the child into her arms.

The door slammed.

"I can't do this," Abigail said, suddenly envying Dinah, whose giant bodyguard, Corporal Waverly, followed her everywhere.

"It was your idea."

"Now and then I am mistaken."

Jonathan smiled. "I do not believe that I have ever heard those words pass your lips."

They had reached a small lobby, with tiny tiles on the floor. A heavy door led outside, and a sagging stair led upward.

"Third floor," said Abigail, her heart back with the frightened little girl.

"The stairway is unlighted."

"You may remain here and wait for me if you wish."

They climbed the stairs and, not without adventures, reached the third floor. There were four doors, one with an *8* painted beside it, one with a metallic *4* hanging from a nail, the other two unmarked. They heard a baby crying, but could not tell where. The air was still and cloying.

"Which one?" Jonathan whispered.

Abigail shook her head, picked the first unmarked one, knocked. No answer. She tried the next. They heard movement, and the oldest man in the world opened the door, grinning crazily, hands scratching his chest through his ancient robe. "Well, look who's here!" he cried as if he knew them, which he did not.

"Please excuse us, sir," said Jonathan. "Wrong door."

"It's *my* door."

"Yes, sir. Sorry, sir."

The old man laughed as they moved on.

"Try another," said Jonathan, unnecessarily.

Abigail rapped on number *8*, and the crying grew louder. A mother's voice shouted, and the door opened a tiny crack. A woman's angry voice said, "What?"

Then the door opened the rest of the way, very fast. The woman who stood there was haggard and red-eyed, wearing a dressing gown and holding a puling infant against her shoulder.

"What are you doing here?" Judith demanded, no less angry than before.

IV

Jonathan waited in the fetid hall. Abigail, studying the single room, could not comprehend her sister's circumstances. There was a worn-out divan that might also serve as a worn-out bed, and a storage closet that held food and clothing alike. One aging table, one dying chair. There was no plumbing. There was no place to prepare meals.

There was, however, the baby, tiny and brown and squalling.

"You're my sister," Abigail said.

"And that's why you're here, is it? To see how your sister is doing? Just fine, thank you." She was perched on the bed, holding the child distractedly. Abigail remained standing. "Lydia and I are both fine." Judith laid the baby atop the bedspread, conjured a biscuit from somewhere. "You may leave now."

"Wait—"

"I don't want you here, Abby. This is my world, not yours. I am living life as I choose. Not for Nanny. Not for Mother. For me. And you—you're training to be a lawyer, visiting all the best salons, carrying secret messages for Presidents. Good for you." A laugh, sour as curdled cream. "And running around at night with rich white men. Let's not forget that part."

Abigail stiffened. "I see that Michael keeps you fully informed."

"I am glad that you see. Please leave."

"I just need—"

"You need to get out of here, Abby. How much plainer can I make it? I don't want to talk to you."

"But I don't understand," cried Abigail. "How did this happen?"

"How did what happen, dear?"

"This!" Pointing in exasperation. "And the child!"

"It's not all that difficult," said Judith, languidly. "Having a baby. Anybody can do it." A twitter. "All you need is a willing man, a fertile womb, and a bit of carelessness."

"Yes, but—but you're not married!"

Judith smoothed the robe over her legs. "The equipment works just the same whether a girl is married or not."

Abigail turned toward the child, who sat on the blanket, sucking tearfully on the biscuit. Her niece. Huge eyes, aware of everything. Lydia. A lovely name, she decided.

"And don't you be asking me who the father is," Judith scolded.

"I won't." But she wondered whether her sister even knew.

"Abby. Look at me."

And so she did. Judith was sitting on the divan, looking exhausted and twenty years older than her age. She should have been married to a young man of their set. She should have had a brick house with a maid and three or four children. How exactly Judith had missed the life Abigail expected for herself, her younger sister could not figure out. There had been an arc of life to which all three girls had been raised, first by their mother, then by Nanny Pork. Abigail and Louisa were more or less following the curve, but Judith had gone off on a tangent, the line of her life straight and true, the most rapid distance from the expectations of her family. Something had gone wrong, Abigail told herself, wishing there were a way to repair the damage. It never occurred to her that her sister might have left the path by choice.

"Why are you still here?" said Judith, her voice as exhausted as her posture. She folded her arms on the edge of the settee, laid her head down. "What do you want? And don't pretend you are here out of a concern for my welfare."

"I do care about your welfare."

"Until I interrupted your bath, you had not laid eyes on me in more than two years. And you hadn't come looking, either." She squirmed angrily, as if her body could find no comfort. "No more fairy tales, Abby. Tell me what you want."

A long breath. "I want to know more about Rebecca Deveaux."

"I thought you might."

"Do you mind talking about her?"

A derisive squawk. "Do you care if I mind? I can't get rid of you, can I?"

"Not really," said Abigail, gently. She moved to the divan, sat, and took her sister's feet on her lap. The baby had sprawled, snoring, on the blanket. "Anything you can remember."

"Why is it so important?"

"I am not sure. But she is the key somehow. I do not believe that Mr. McShane was necessarily even the target of the murder. I believe Rebecca was."

Judith snorted. "Impossible."

"They found an envelope with the bodies. Addressed to Senator Wade." She began rubbing her sister's feet, trying to drive the tension away, even though she herself was the cause. "You told me that Rebecca was giving information to Mr. McShane. It seems obvious that she planned to give him the contents of the envelope. No doubt she delivered other documents as well. Mr. McShane withdrew fifty dollars from the bank the day of the murders. I believe the money was to pay Rebecca for the documents, not her services. A sum that large means that she was taking a significant risk. I suspect that the documents were stolen. She must have met Mr. McShane outside brothels to provide the obvious explanation if anyone ever saw them together. What I don't know is where Rebecca was stealing the documents from."

"How would I know?"

"She might have told you."

"She didn't." A yawn. "Sorry."

"She was your friend," Abigail persisted. "That's what you said, Judith. Not just an acquaintance. A friend. She may not have told you where she was getting the documents, but I am sure she supplied some clues, whether she intended to or not. If you tell me what you know about Rebecca, perhaps I can figure it out. And then, by re-establishing the conduit, I can honor her memory."

"So that's why you're here? To honor Rebecca?"

"No. No. I'm here because somebody gave her my name. Her name and mine are in the register at the Metzerott Hotel. In the same handwriting, Judith. I asked myself why anybody would do that. It doesn't make any sense. There is no reason to hide behind my name when she could meet with anybody in the city, anywhere in the city, and not need any name at all. That means, if Rebecca used my name, it was because she wanted someone to find it. She was leaving a clue behind. I think she wanted me to hear about it if anything happened to her. I think she was trying to lead me to you. Now I'd like to know why."

For a moment Abigail thought she had lost. Judith let her eyelids drift shut, yawned again, said nothing. Abigail had the sense that she had offended her sister somehow, had pressed too hard, or guessed too much. She prepared herself for the possibility that Judith would throw her out. Abigail kept massaging. She glanced at the baby, who was still asleep on the blanket. The candles were flickering; the apartment was growing dimmer, and more drafty. Judith gave a sudden snore. Abigail began to compose in her mind an appropriate apology. But in the end, her sister gave her the story, and Abigail knew it to be a parting gift.

V

"Rebecca was born on a tobacco plantation in northern Virginia. When the war broke out, the land up that way was pretty well trampled, and a lot of the slaves ran off. Rebecca lost track of her parents. She made her way to Washington somehow, and got work as a domestic. She'd worked in the house instead of the fields on the plantation, so she had the training. She worked her way up to one of the great houses, then moved on to another. I am not sure exactly why she left the first one. She was about twelve or thirteen, so . . ."

Judith's voice trailed off, and her long face took on a pinched look, as if she were battling pain. There was no need to exchange any words. The availability of young colored women for the pleasure of their masters had survived, fully intact, the demise of the slave system that had given it birth.

"She must have worked in four or five houses. She was working in one of them when she . . . when she died." Judith looked oddly abashed. "I met her a year and a half ago. We met . . . well, through church. I started . . . when I found out I was pregnant. . . . I thought it would be better for the baby if . . . Never mind." Locking treacherous thoughts away. "Well. Rebecca and I met at George Town AME. We got to be friends. She's about your age. A year or two younger, I guess. Or she was. And I . . . well . . . we talked about things. She told me her story. I told her my story. We didn't pry. We just talked. And she told me about the house where she worked, how the master never touched her or even looked at her. That's what she still said. Master."

Judith had her arms over her face, but her shoulders were shaking, and Abigail supposed she was crying.

"The master was a good man. But there had been some sort of tragedy in the house. She never told me what it was. I had the idea that someone had died. And now the master was . . . well, he was distant. No. Not distant. Obsessed. Rebecca wasn't sure about what, but she said she knew an obsession when she saw one. He was an important man, he had a lot of meetings with powerful people, but he also had meetings at his house. Some of those meetings were strange. Rebecca overheard. . . . You know how it is, Abby. Or maybe you don't. I've worked in service; you haven't. Nobody guards his tongue around the servants, especially the colored servants. You hear a great deal. And Rebecca told me . . . she told me that this man . . . the man she was working for . . . she said he hated Mr. Lincoln. I said a lot of people hated him. Rebecca said yes, but the master was plotting against him. There were others who came to the house, and she heard them together. Mostly men, but one of them was a young woman. Well bred. A woman who seemed on easy terms with many of the great figures of the city. Still, Rebecca was surprised. Men of her master's station did not see young women alone. Not at their homes. But this young woman came by a lot. She was giving the master messages. Some of the messages the young woman told him, and some of the messages she handed to him in envelopes. Now and then he gave the young woman messages to take back. Rebecca didn't know who the messages were coming from. They never called him anything but the crooked man."

"The crooked man?" Abigail echoed, speaking for the first time in a while.

A brisk nod. "Just like in the fairy tale."

"What about the young woman who came by? What was her name?"

"Rebecca never said. I didn't . . . I tried not to press her. She told me this toward . . . toward the end. She was frightened. She said her mistress had caught her in the master's study, going through his things. She wanted to see what was in the messages, you see. She wanted to find out who was trying to hurt Mr. Lincoln, and why. The mistress had caught her and thought she was stealing. She said she was just cleaning, but the mistress didn't believe her. She thought she was going to be discharged yet again. That was when she came to me. She turned out to have taken a few of the documents."

"The documents outlining the plot," said Abigail excitedly.

Judith looked away. "I didn't ask her what exactly the documents showed. She said she wasn't sure what to do with them, and I . . . I sent her to Mr. McShane."

"Why?"

Judith's smooth face split in a surprisingly gentle smile. Her eyes were half closed in reminiscence. "He was the President's lawyer. That was perhaps the most obvious reason. And, of course, I had heard good things about him." A pause. "Once my sister began her employ."

Michael again, Abigail realized. Judith might have given Nanny Pork a wide berth, and avoided Abigail and Louisa, too, but she had evidently stayed in close touch with Michael. Michael made a point of staying in touch with everyone.

"What happened then?"

"I am not sure. Rebecca did not confide the details to me." Again that hesitation, as a look very near guilt passed over Judith's countenance. "But I formed the impression that she met Mr. McShane a number of times."

"And gave him documents."

"Yes."

"Documents she . . . removed . . . from the house where she was in service."

"Yes."

"Why didn't you go to the police?"

Judith had an awesome way with sarcasm. "They do love our people so, don't they?"

Abigail considered. It all seemed to fit, and yet she sensed an omission. She could not quite work out where it was. Her sister's presentation was too fluent. She was too eager to divulge confidences, the eagerness suggesting that there was more, withheld. At the same time, Abigail knew from the set of her sister's mouth that this was all she was going to get for now, that Judith already worried that she had said too much. And so, just to wind the conversation down, she asked: "And you have no idea what family she was working for? Who her master was?"

Judith shook her head.

"I told you. I don't know who the family was. Rebecca never stayed with one family too long. She was studying in littles, saving what she could, going to school between jobs."

"She must have given you a clue."

"Must she?" For a moment Judith wore her old mocking smile, and her eyes were bright and young and flirtatious. Then she sagged, and the light went out of her face. She shook her head. The baby had awakened and was screaming again. "I think she might have called the lady of the house 'Mrs. Ellen.' But I'm not sure about that."

They were standing now. Judith, robe flapping loosely, was moving her sister toward the door. The baby was on her shoulder.

"Mrs. Ellen," Abigail repeated.

"Yes."

"And you don't remember anything else?"

"Not about Rebecca. But . . ."

"Please tell me."

Judith caressed her cheek. "I don't want you to get in trouble, Abby."

"I am not in trouble."

"Aren't you? Because it is my understanding that a number of power-ful men are worried about you. The fear seems to be that, unchecked, you will be the cause of considerable mischief." The hand was on Abi-gail's shoulder now. Lydia's squeal had subsided to a whimper. "There is no need to give me that look, Abby. I am only telling you what I have heard. And I heard it, let us say, under circumstances in which a man is unlikely to lie." A tired laugh. "Even a gentleman."

Somehow the door was open. Jonathan was in the hallway, alert, but at a respectful distance.

"I don't think you should come back," said Judith.

"Of course I will."

"No, dear. You have your career to think about. And . . . well, there are other reasons. Shush. I have told you as much as I can. For us to meet again would be dangerous." She leaned forward suddenly, took Abigail's head between her palms, kissed her on the forehead. "Goodbye, dear. God go with you."

"And with you," said Abigail, very shaken.

They never spoke again.

CHAPTER 26

Betrayal

I

"I SUPPOSE WE have to believe it," said Dan Sickles, toying with his moustache. The usual glimmer in his eye seemed dull in the gray morning light. They stood alone in the common room. It was Friday, March 15, and the trial would begin in three days, but Dennard and Speed were up at the Capitol, still negotiating the rules of procedure. Rellman was along to take notes. Little was at Woodward's Hardware, buying supplies; Abigail, to the surprise of everyone but Jonathan, had decided to join him.

You should talk to Sickles alone, she had said the night before. *He doesn't like me, and he isn't the sort of man who wants to hear bad news from a woman.*

"We have to believe it," said Sickles a second time. "It makes sense." He paused. "And because I don't think Judith Canner would lie about something like this."

Jonathan's eyes widened. "You know Judith?"

"Never met. But I know *of* her."

"How?"

"By reputation." That roguish smile. "But a gentleman can say no more."

Jonathan wondered, briefly, what sort of reputation Judith Canner must have, given her circumstances, but he walled off further speculation. What mattered was that Sickles had not, as Jonathan had worried he would, dismissed the entire conversation as fantasy. It was Abigail who had insisted that Sickles, and only Sickles, be told. Once more, her judgment had been vindicated.

"You do see the larger significance, don't you?" mused Sickles. "A wheel in the middle of a wheel. Isn't that what Ezekiel says? A wheel in the middle of a wheel, getting ready to lift us up to the sky. We don't know how many wheels are out there spinning, but at last we get to take a good look at one of them and see where it leads." Dragging himself to his feet. "Speed, Dennard, men like that. They don't see the wheel of conspiracy when it's spinning right in front of their noses. To them the world is clear rules, amenable to sweet reason. Whereas Stanton—McShane, even—well, they see the conspiracy everywhere."

"And Mr. Lincoln?"

Sickles chuckled. "I have never known a man more perceptive. He will see a conspiracy only where one actually exists. And he will never fail to detect one if it is there."

"Then he has known all along!"

"Presumably." A wink. "But don't worry. Mr. Lincoln also conspires better than any man I have ever known. If he has known about the conspiracy and done so little to smash it to bits, we should assume that he has his reasons."

Or that he no longer had the necessary power, because the conspirators had already triumphed: but Jonathan chose not to mention this possibility.

"You said we have a good look at the conspiracy," he said.

"Indeed."

"We only know that it exists. We still do not know the names of a single conspirator."

"But we do. There is only one senior Administration official whose wife is named Ellen, and whose family not long ago suffered a major loss." He went to the desk, began to write.

"What's that?"

"A note. You're to take it to the White House. Give it to Noah Brooks personally. Nobody else. Understand?"

"Yes."

"Give the note to Brooks, and wait for an answer." He sealed the paper in an envelope. "We're going to see the President, Jonathan. Just the two of us."

II

"The Russians want to sell us their little corner of America," Lincoln said. He was standing beside his desk, holding a sheaf of telegrams. "They have that big empty colony up there next to Canada, and it seems they're running out of money because of all those wars they're fighting with the British." He smiled as if he had put one over on the world. He was in a remarkably good mood for a man generally thought to have no more than a couple of weeks before he was turned out of office. "As it happens," the President went on, "we're running out of money, too, but I reckon Baron Stoeckl doesn't know that. Russia wants seven millions, which I am told works out to about two cents an acre. That sounds like a pretty fair price, as the blind man said to the farmer. Unfortunately, we don't happen to have that kind of money lying around. And even if we did, Congress isn't in a particularly generous mood just now. So it looks like Alaska will have to remain Russian for a while. Maybe they'll strike a better deal with Mr. Wade."

The President made a note on the page, and handed it to Noah Brooks, who left the room. Jonathan stood with Sickles, waiting to be acknowledged. He had come to understand during these past weeks that this slow-burning recitation of the events of the day was Lincoln's way of giving himself time to think. Outside an ashen sun was sinking, but this was the soonest Lincoln could clear his schedule to receive them. It occurred to Jonathan that it would be a very easy thing for a country enthralled by the coming impeachment trial to assume that the President had no other work to do. "Mr. Seward thinks we should buy the place. If we do, I have a hunch that future generations will call it 'Lincoln's Folly.' At least, that's what Mr. Stanton says." He took off his glasses. "Now, why don't you fellows sit down and tell me what I can do for you?"

"As a matter of fact," said Sickles amiably, as he adjusted his wooden leg, "it's about Mr. Stanton."

Lincoln seemed not to hear. "I have another dispatch that tells me they're having trouble selling shares in that new canal they're digging in Egypt. From what I've seen, if the big investors don't want a piece of it, we should start buying."

Sickles, catching his friend's mood, said, "I understand they're digging the canal with slave labor."

"The British are upset, as usual," said the President, laying aside another paper. "They're against slavery everywhere on the face of the earth except when they need it, like when they built their railroad in North Africa. I have been trying to remember, as a matter of fact, the last time a British soldier—or a soldier from anywhere in Europe—gave his life to *end* slavery rather than to *protect* it."

"I can't seem to think of one," said Sickles, smiling.

"Neither can I," Lincoln said, chuckling as he shook his head. "The powers of Old Europe are great hypocrites, denouncing as evil the world they made. Are you here to tell me that Stanton is conspiring against me?"

Jonathan was too surprised to speak. Sickles said calmly, "Yes, Mr. President."

Lincoln turned away, bent his long body to peer out the window. The heavy gray clouds blanketed the grand buildings in a kind of sadness. "There is a kind of fish," he said, "that swims with the sharks, and feeds on what they leave behind. A pilot fish, I believe it is called. And what is interesting about the pilot fish, so I am told, is that the sharks don't eat them." He sighed, and straightened. "I suppose politics attracts that kind of man, doesn't it? A man who only chooses sides once he knows who the sharks are."

"I'm sorry, Mr. President," said Sickles after a moment.

Lincoln's sleepy eyes shifted to Jonathan. "And I reckon you are the one who uncovered Stanton's role?"

"Um, yes, sir." Jonathan felt like the tongue-tied Yale freshman he had once been, pronounced by his professors a dunderhead. "I mean, no, sir. It was actually Miss Canner." He hesitated. "She has a . . . a source."

The President glanced at Sickles. "Do you know anything about this?"

"I just heard this morning."

The hunter's eyes swung back toward Jonathan, who knew what was expected of him.

"The source is her sister," said Jonathan, seeing no reason to hide from Lincoln what he had already told Sickles.

"Does this sister of hers know Stanton?"

"No, sir. And I don't believe that her sister is even aware that Stanton was the source." He summarized Rebecca Deveaux's story.

"So McShane was aware of all this and said nothing."

This set Jonathan back. "I suppose not, sir."

Lincoln shook his head. "I am willing to believe that Stanton has gone over to the Radicals. Ever since his son died, Stanton has been growing closer and closer to Chase. They pray together, go to church together. Close to Chase means close to the Radicals." A silence. Jonathan knew that the President was thinking of his own lost sons; and of his wife. "But I refuse to accept that Stanton would be a part of the larger conspiracy you describe. He is not a bad man. I can't see him allied with people who would do murder. Especially because he and McShane were friends of long standing. Stanton may have switched sides, but your murderer is still on the loose." He perched on the edge of his desk. "The police could still be right. The murder doesn't have to be related to this thing."

Jonathan was about to argue, but Sickles gave him a look: the President was not finished.

"Still. Stanton." Lincoln sighed. "I can think of no man we can less afford to lose."

"Yes, sir," said Sickles, while Jonathan looked at the carpet.

"The trial is three days away." Thinking aloud now. "Three days. I wonder how long Stanton has been passing along information." One of his long legs was swinging as he mused. "I reckon this is why the Radicals seem to know so much about our meetings. And I suppose they have full access to the files of the War Department." The second seemed to distress him more than the first. "But that is not even the worst of it. When Seward was active, he controlled the Secret Service. During his . . . convalescence . . . the reins have sort of slipped into Stanton's hands."

Jonathan blanched. Sickles was quicker. "So General Lafayette Baker has been working pretty much full-time for the Radicals."

Lincoln's smile was rueful. "Looks like it."

"Sir," said Jonathan, surprising himself, "you must dismiss Mr. Stanton from your Cabinet."

The bushy eyebrows went up. "Why would I do that?"

"Because he has betrayed you. Because he is no better than a spy."

"Well, a spy can be useful, as long as the side he's spying on knows that he's a spy and the side he's spying for doesn't know they know." Just like that, his good humor returned. He turned to Sickles. "Maybe it's poetic justice, Dan. Stanton defended you when you shot Mr. Barton Key in front of the White House. He took the side everybody thought was going to lose, and he won. Now he's taking the side everybody thinks is going to win, so maybe he'll lose, just to balance things out. Fate will take care of everything, so I reckon I should just leave Stanton where he is." Smiling now. Amazing how he could switch moods so suddenly. "Actually, it reminds me of the story about the farmer who built himself a shed where he raised chickens. Trouble was, the skunks got in after the chickens. So, every night, the farmer sat outside with his shotgun. He'd see a skunk and fire off a round, and he'd see another skunk and fire off another round, but he always missed. Finally, one night, he saw a dozen skunks at once over by the shed. He fired one round after another, but when he went over to see, he'd only killed a single skunk. After that, he hung up his gun. His friends asked why he didn't sit out at night any more, shooting at the skunks. The farmer said it took him weeks just to kill the first one, and he was too busy to waste his time trying to kill a second." Lincoln was laughing now, and his visitors with him. "I reckon sometimes you're better off letting the skunk get at the hens a little bit instead of firing off all your ammunition hoping to hit him."

Jonathan's head was spinning. He did not understand how Stanton could possibly stay in the Administration—sitting at meetings, running the military. Yet Sickles seemed to be going along.

The President, meanwhile, was at the door, calling for Noah Brooks. The secretary appeared so swiftly, he might have been listening at the door. "Get Speed down here."

"Yes, sir."

"No, wait. He's up at the Capitol. Get him down here first thing tomorrow." He turned to his guests. "Dan, I want you and Stanton here, too. Say, eight."

"In the morning?" Sickles groaned.

"We have work to do, Dan. We have to get ready for trial."

"I suppose we do."

"But we're going to prepare some surprises for our friends on the Hill."

Sickles smiled. "That sounds like a good idea."

"As for Stanton . . ." Lincoln paused, seemed to exchange a significant look with Sickles, then laid a strong hand on Jonathan's shoulder. The good humor had faded again, along with the Western accent that Sickles claimed the President only put on for company. "Young man, what you have heard tonight is more or less a secret of state. You were a soldier. You were decorated at Cold Harbor. You understand how important it is to keep secrets."

"Yes, sir," said Jonathan, stomach churning.

"If you violate this confidence, you could find yourself locked up in one of those terrible secret prisons the newspapers are always going on and on about. The secret prisons don't exist, but you could wind up there anyway. Do you understand me, Mr. Hilliman?"

The dingy, cavernous White House, with its vast rooms and leaky walls, was all but impossible to heat. The smoldering coals in the grate offered little real warmth. Even so, the temperature in the room seemed to drop precipitously.

"Yes, Mr. President," said Jonathan.

"Good. You did well." Noah was there, showing him out. "Dan, stay a minute," Lincoln said.

The door closed. Jonathan settled on the bench to wait.

III

For fifteen minutes or so, Jonathan brooded. He tried to reason like Abigail, who had a way of treating the mystery like a hand and the facts like gloves, to see which ones fit.

What were the facts? Rebecca Deveaux was stealing documents from Stanton. Stanton had gone over to the other side. That meant that the Secret Service was with the Radicals. The files of the War Department were open to the Radicals. But Lincoln remained confident. Too confident. Sitting there in the drafty hallway, Jonathan tried to puzzle out what seemed so incongruous. Not the impeachment. The murder, then. Something about the murder. Maybe, as the President suggested, the murder was just what it looked like; in any case, the killer was still at large. But Inspector Varak still believed that Rebecca Deveaux had been a prostitute. Jonathan and Abigail had both tried to disabuse him of this notion, and failed. Varak was certain of his ground because—

Abruptly, Jonathan stood.

"Where are you going?" said Noah. "Facilities are the other way."

"Please tell Mr. Sickles I had to run an errand."

"I am sure he will be done any minute."

"Sorry. Can't wait."

Jonathan hurried down the stairs. He asked the doorkeeper to hail him a cab from the rank out on the street, and told the driver to take him to the Provost General's headquarters. They bumped along the rutted streets, headed west. The answer would be there. After all, it was the Provost General who had assured Varak that Rebecca Deveaux was a hooker; and it was Jonathan's classmate Whitford Pesky who had checked the files.

Jonathan had to make Whit tell who gave him the order to lie.

At the gate, just as before, Jonathan asked for Major Pesky. This time the wait was a lot longer, and the man who came out was shorter and broader than Whit. His name, he boomed, was Lieutenant Fisch. How might he be of service?

"I need to see the major," said Jonathan.

"May I ask about what?"

"It's a confidential matter."

Fisch was overweight, and had to hitch up his pants constantly. He did it now, and thrust out his chest, as if to emphasize his own importance.

"Hilliman," he said. "You're one of the lawyers, aren't you? Representing Mr. Lincoln?"

"I am a law clerk—"

"Well, I hope you win. The Radicals are traitors. They should all be arrested."

Fisch was grinning. Savagely. As if he would like to hang Butler and Stevens himself. Jonathan had forgotten the almost mystical reverence in which the military held Abraham Lincoln, an emotion, surely, left over from the war itself, the love of an army for its confident and triumphant commander-in-chief. And yet Fisch was a couple of years younger than Jonathan, and had almost certainly missed the war.

Jonathan said, "Please, Lieutenant. If I could just see Major Pesky."

The grin widened. So did the girth. "Anything you would say to him, you can say to me. I'm handling his duties for the moment. I'm a brevet captain now, as a matter of fact."

"Why is it necessary for Major Pesky's duties to be handled, whether by you or anybody else?" A horrible thought: "Has something happened to him?"

"Oh, no, not at all. It's just that the major was transferred to the Department of the Cumberland. The orders came through three days ago, and he took the cars the next morning. I'd guess he's well west of the Mississippi by now."

CHAPTER 27

Theories

I

"THREE DAYS AGO," mused Abigail. "As yesterday was Friday, that would mean Tuesday."

"Tuesday is correct," muttered Jonathan, who had already thought this all through. They were in the corridor outside the offices, and would have to go back in momentarily, because Dennard had summoned everyone for a quick review. It was Saturday morning, and there were final tasks to be parceled out before the trial began on Monday. "Right after I returned from New York."

Abigail nodded. "The trouble is, you were supposed to be in Philadelphia." Because by now Jonathan had told her, in confidence, about the mission to Belmont; as he seemed to tell her everything. "So whoever sent Major Pesky out west both knew where you really were and, for some reason, was worried about it."

"There is no point in speculating. It had to be Stanton. He is the Secretary of War. He gives orders to the soldiers."

"But that makes no sense. Not if you believe Mr. Lincoln. He denied that Stanton could be involved in Rebecca's murder. The only role that Major Pesky has played in this tragedy is to help disguise her true background, to send the police looking in the wrong direction. Therefore, if it was Stanton, then he was trying to protect whoever told the major to lie to the police."

Jonathan shook his head, striding away from her, trying to give himself space to think. It had to have been Stanton. Yet it could not possibly have been Stanton—not unless Lincoln had lost his fabled ability to judge character at a glance. But of course he had misjudged Stanton once—his most trusted aide—by not noticing that he had thrown in his lot with Benjamin Wade and his friends.

The answer was close. So close. A clever knot he could not quite undo.

Abigail, meanwhile, was brimming with suggestions, as always. "Suppose it wasn't Stanton. You said you encountered Mr. Plum on the train. Perhaps Mr. Plum told Mr. Grafton—" She stopped, struck by another thought. "Of course, Major Pesky was well connected. If he wanted to resist the transfer order, I suppose his family would raise a howl, and even a Stanton would have to back down."

"From which you conclude?"

Inside, they heard Dennard's roar, demanding to know where everybody might be hiding.

"From which I conclude," she said, as they headed for the office once more, "that Major Pesky might have *requested* the transfer." She put a hand on his arm. "Oh, and one more thing."

He looked at her quizzically.

"My sister also told me that Rebecca mentioned a well-connected young woman carrying messages for the conspirators." A wink. "And, if you recall, I did see your Miss Hale talking to Mr. Grafton at the Eameses'."

"You don't mean to suggest—"

"Why don't you find out?"

II

Dennard told the group that Stanton was, as he delicately put it, no longer with the President, but the expressions around the room made plain that they already knew.

"Nothing has changed," the lawyer rumbled. "Our legal strategy remains precisely what it was. Our arguments, our evidence—everything is the same."

Speed spoke up. He seemed more shaken than anyone around the table. Outside the window, the crowd seemed thinner than usual. "Surely Stanton has betrayed our entire strategy to the House Managers."

Dennard's eyes were rimmed with exhaustion. "So what? We selected our arguments because they are good arguments, well supported, sensible, et cetera. They aren't any worse just because the Managers are likely to be ready for them. We shall just have to be readier still."

From the sofa, Sickles murmured, "I wouldn't worry about it."

Dennard, clearly annoyed, barely turned his head. "And why is that, sir?"

"Because we have a few surprises of our own."

Speed said, "But that is the point. Our surprises will not surprise them. Stanton will disclose them all."

Sickles laughed. "He can only disclose what he knows about."

This, at last, got Dennard's full attention; and the attention of the clerks as well, each of whom, in a different way, had been sitting steeped in despair.

"I have charge of this defense," said Dennard.

Sickles nodded, said nothing, let his head rest on the back of the sofa. For a moment the two men glared at each other. Heat seemed to crackle in the room. Abigail read enmity, rivalry, a dozen other emotions. She wondered what surprises the rogue had in mind.

It was Speed who dragged them back to the matter at hand. "I advised the President this morning to arrest Mr. Stanton. He declined."

"Such measures are impossible," said Dennard.

"Why?" asked Rellman—a rare word.

"Because we have been outplayed," said Sickles. "If the President were to start arresting conspirators now, the public would think it was a sham to avoid removal from office. He would never survive."

"The people love Mr. Lincoln," Speed insisted.

"Maybe they do, maybe they don't. But they won't love him so much if he starts behaving like one of those European monarchs who send out the troops whenever their crowns are threatened."

A fresh silence greeted Sickles's analysis, but Abigail sensed that he was entirely correct. The Managers were charging Lincoln with censoring and locking up his political opponents, and the Radical newspapers were speculating on the possibility of a coup d'état. Were he to arrest Stanton, the President would show himself to be precisely what his enemies wanted people to believe that he was. Sickles was right. The Radicals had gambled and won; Lincoln had indeed been outplayed. Of course, Dennard was also right. They had no choice but to proceed to trial, present their evidence, and offer their arguments. Whatever the shape of the anti-Lincoln cabal, it was unlikely to include any but a tiny number of the Senators. The rest, therefore, would presumably listen, and possibly be persuaded.

Speed had another thought. "Maybe that list of conspirators will still turn up. The President said the Secret Service has tracked it as far as Virginia. It seems that one conspirator was trying to deliver it to another."

Again it was Sickles who had the last word. "The Secret Service," he said dryly, "is in the hands of General Baker. And I'm willing to bet that he, too"—lightly mocking Dennard—"is no longer with the President." Sickles sat up straight, swinging his stump out in front. "Besides. The Radicals and Stanton might be conspiring together, but I don't think they're the folks who slaughtered poor McShane. That's somebody else."

Dennard waved the matter away. "I will have no more talk of conspiracy, et cetera. We have a trial to win. All that matters now is what happens in the courtroom."

As the meeting broke up and final assignments were parceled out, she glanced at the numbers on the blackboard:

15–33–6

No change over the past week. Six Senators remained undecided. The President needed nineteen votes for acquittal, meaning that four of the six must break their way. She hoped fervently that Senator Sumner would be among those willing to listen, not among those already conspiring to elevate Benjamin Wade.

As she stood up and began gathering her papers, Sickles touched her on the shoulder.

"Get your coat," he whispered. "We are going to the White House." He followed her gaze. "No. Just you and I. Mr. Lincoln wants to see you."

III

"I am sure they will not be much longer," murmured Noah Brooks.

Abigail thanked him for perhaps the fifth time, perhaps the tenth. She was seated on a hard wooden bench on the second floor of the Executive

Mansion, doing her best to conceal her growing anxiety. The corridor was poorly lighted, and poorly maintained. And even though a breath of spring was in the air, here she felt cold, as if winter had taken up permanent residence in the drafty halls. A couple of others waiting for the President sat on equally uncomfortable benches across from hers, sneaking looks her way, trying to figure out what she was doing there.

Somebody's servant, they no doubt told themselves.

She and Sickles had arrived an hour and a half ago. He had introduced her to Noah, who had actually kissed her hand. Sickles had then gone in to see Lincoln, telling her to have a seat, only to emerge ten minutes later and head off down the hall. Abigail had rushed after him, but he had told her to go back and sit, that the President would see her soon, but was busy meeting with the commissioner of revenue, Mr. Wells.

With that, Sickles was gone, leaving her alone in this awful place.

Noah Brooks smiled at her. He was a tall, sad faced man, going bald although not yet thirty, with bushy black burnsides that made him look older still: she could imagine him as a druggist or surgeon.

"He shouldn't be much longer," Brooks had said, for the first of several times. And smiled again, like a man not sure whether he will be believed.

It was strange that all of her friends seemed to assume that she saw Mr. Lincoln all the time. Just the other day, Agatha Mellison had flat-out accused her of lying when she insisted that she and the President had never met. Like most negroes, the Mellison girls clung to a view of Lincoln as mythic hero, Father Abraham, kindly and beloved savior of the race: or, as Octavius like to call it, the darker nation. Perhaps Abigail might have shared the view if not for the twin influences of her brother and Dr. Finney, each of whom, in different ways, despised the man; and of Jonathan, from whose stories she had constructed a very different Lincoln, a clever and subtle politician who rarely if ever—

"The President will see you now," said Noah Brooks, and although the two white men sitting across from her rose hopefully, it was Abigail to whom the private secretary gestured.

On shaky legs, she followed him around the wooden barrier, past the Bucktail sentry, and into the office of Abraham Lincoln.

IV

In later years, what Abigail would always remember was how tall the President was; how, in his long-legged, long-armed skinniness, hair awry, tie askew, he managed to convey awkwardness and vigor at once, like a man who might keel over with the next stiff wind if not for the fact that the wind was under his control. He did not, of course, see her alone. Noah Brooks was in the room, and so was a military aide, a Major Clancy. Lincoln greeted her effusively, if a bit awkwardly, and she recalled a story she had heard from Patsy Quillen, that Sojourner Truth, following her only meeting with the President, had told her friends that the man was uncomfortable around women. The men were all standing, but Lincoln offered her a chair, then sat behind his desk. He thanked her for her hard work, complimented her on the apprenticeship with Dennard, then immediately launched into a story about how the trouble with the world today could be summed up in the dilemma of a father who had three sons but only two walnuts, and each wanted a walnut of his own. And what struck her later about the tale, despite the humorous manner of the telling, was how much it taught her about Lincoln. He was the one holding the walnut; he was the one facing the dilemma of how to dole it out.

That others might seek to share in the decision never seemed to cross Mr. Lincoln's mind.

He seemed to sense that his tale had misfired, and as he gave her a measuring glance, she remembered what Jonathan had said about those eyes, the eyes of a sleepy but cunning predator, a man saving his energy yet ready to spring.

"You have been crucial to our efforts," he said. "This is not the moment to go into detail, but I want to assure you that when this unpleasantness is all done with, you will have my gratitude, and the gratitude of the nation."

The interview was plainly over. Abigail rose, still having no idea why she had been summoned. Lincoln was already in conversation with Major Clancy. Noah showed her out.

V

On that same Saturday evening, Jonathan attended the Eameses' salon—this time alone, intending to track down Bessie Hale. The crowd was the largest he had seen in some time, a tribute no doubt to the fact that the impeachment trial would begin on Monday at noon. Half of Washington's upper crust seemed to have squeezed into the parlor and drawing room. Jonathan spotted congressmen and Senators galore, and newspapermen were a penny a pound, but he wisely kept his distance. He saw lawyers and judges, a general and a Cabinet secretary. He saw ladies attired in the latest fashions. He was waylaid by a British diplomat who wanted him to explain the range of available penalties in the event that the President was convicted; and by a poet of some esteem who, mistaking him for John Hay, Mr. Lincoln's former private secretary, now in Paris, said how much he admired his published verses.

Alas, he saw no sign of Lucy Lambert Hale, and he was wary of asking, lest he seem too eager. Escorting a woman other than his fiancée to the occasional social event was perfectly permissible; inquiring after her, however, would suggest an entirely separate register of relationship.

Making his way from room to room, Jonathan was stopped by Charles Eames, his host, who was journalist, lawyer, inventor, and much else besides. There was a rumor, it seemed, that Stanton was going to testify against the President.

"Ridiculous," said Jonathan, with all the conviction he could muster.

"You're certain?"

"Yes."

"But there is some sort of fissure, isn't there, between Mr. Lincoln and his Secretary of War? Serious differences over Reconstruction?"

Scarcely able to believe that the story had spread that fast, Jonathan nevertheless found a smile somewhere. "Yes, of course. I believe that they plan to arrest each other just as soon as they settle on neutral ground." Eames laughed dutifully. Jonathan, more worried still, resumed his fruitless search for Bessie.

At last he spotted Mary Henry and Lucretia Garfield, two of Bessie's closest companions. He charmed his way into the little circle of which they formed a part, and set himself to listen.

He did not have to listen long.

"You must be terribly unhappy, Mr. Hilliman," said Crete Garfield, eyeing him in that sideways manner so in fashion among ladies who, like Mrs. Garfield herself, expected to become First Lady.

Jonathan gave a small bow. "And why would that be, Mrs. Garfield?"

Mary and Crete exchanged a look. It was Mary who spoke. She was a long-waisted woman, awkward and somehow wobbly, who had grown up in the Smithsonian tower, and lived there still. "Poor lamb," she said, a sepulchral grin on her pallid face. "Nobody's told you, have they? Senator Hale arrived yesterday. He's packing up his Bessie and moving her back to Spain."

CHAPTER 28

Urgency

I

WITH THE TRIAL set to begin on Monday, the experienced Dennard had decreed that the Sabbath would be a day of rest. Nobody was to go near Fourteenth and G. "Spend the day with your families," he commanded. And so on Sunday morning, Abigail enjoyed a surprisingly tranquil breakfast with Nanny and Louisa and Michael, who had shown up unexpectedly last night and stayed over in his old room. Nanny Pork made a huge fuss over him, and Abigail fought the urge to jealousy by reminding herself of the story of the prodigal son.

When, over breakfast, Nanny pointed out that Abby was spending all of her time with white mens, Michael came to her defense: The white man, he said gently, held all of the money and all of the power. If their race did not learn to be comfortable around the people who mattered, they would never move forward.

Louisa offered enthusiastic agreement. Nanny sighed and shook her head. Abigail wondered what her brother was up to and why he was suddenly so solicitous. But, being Michael, he could never remain at peace. He began to rail against President Lincoln, who would be remembered, he declared, as the savior of a people perfectly capable of saving itself. "All he did was give white folks a reason to feel proud," Michael declared. "And now we're supposed to be grateful."

Rather than be drawn into an argument, Abigail excused herself from the breakfast table, and decided to take a walk. At Oberlin she had found the beauty of nature a tonic for her unsettled soul.

"Let your brother drive you," said Nanny, for whom the only purpose of walking was to get from one place to another.

"It's just a walk," said Abigail, and braced for a lecture about the highwaymen lurking behind every tree.

"No, no, it's fine," said Michael, catching his sister's mood. "I have errands to run anyway."

She was careful to make sure that her brother departed first, because she did not want him chasing her down. Finally, she set off, strolling up Tenth Street, free to wander through her own mind. Soon her own home was out of sight. The sky displayed that perfect eggshell clarity that heralds spring. Abigail felt her spirit calming. She waved to old Dr. Sandrin, who was climbing into his trap. As she came abreast of the mansion of the sisters Quillen, she saw Patsy, the older Quillen, on the porch, rocking. Abigail liked the Quillens. Her mother, of course, had never let her daughters go near them, worried, she said, that the girls would become what the sisters Quillen were: that is, not married, and also not sisters. As a child, Abigail had no idea what her mother was talking about. Now she did, and although Nanny maintained the same prohibition, Abigail had come to like them.

And so she stopped for a moment to chat.

Patsy said she was proud of Abigail. Lately, everybody seemed to be on her side. It helped.

"Say," said Patsy, as Abigail stood to take her leave. "That was some fire last night, wasn't it?"

"I'm afraid I missed it."

"Working late again."

"I think I'll be working late for the next month."

"That's the way," said Patsy, and resumed her rocking. "Too bad about Sophia, though. I always liked her."

Abigail, who was halfway down the steps, turned back. "Sophia?"

Patsy Quillen nodded. "Sophia Harbour. Madame Sophie. Her establishment burned to the ground last night, with Sophia in it."

II

Abigail ran. Ladies never exerted themselves, least of all in public, and her mother would have been scandalized, but she ran anyway, all the way back home, where she told Nanny she was very sorry but she had to take the wagon. Of course, Nanny pointed out that if she wanted to drive she should have gone with her brother, and Abigail said, *Yes, Nanny,* and *I know, Nanny,* and *I'm sorry, Nanny,* and took the wagon anyway.

"Please, God," she kept saying as she drove the horse much too hard. "God, please, don't let it be, don't let it be!"

With Whit Pesky gone from the city, there were only two people left to testify of their own knowledge that Rebecca Deveaux was not a prostitute, and one of them had burned to death last night.

Abigail charged around fancy carriages, and, pressing, even beat a railroad train to a crossing. She turned left and sped along B Street.

"Please, God. Please, God. Please, God."

She stopped outside a dying hotel, tied up the horse, jumped down, tossing a coin to the valet. Then she was running again, around the corner and down the same alleys. Silver Place looked little different from three days ago. The thaw had snatched most of the snow, but nothing else had changed. The same garbage lying in the same heaps, the same angry eyes staring from the same windows. Abigail expected any moment that someone would accost her, but nobody did. She made her way into the rear lobby of Judith's building, crept through the darkness toward the same swinging lamp, and climbed the same treacherous stairs to the third floor.

She knocked on her sister's door . . . and everything was different.

The door was not locked, and the apartment was empty. No crying baby. No Judith. And nothing intact. Pictures, books, even furniture had been smashed to pieces.

Backing into the hall, Abigail nearly crashed into the same ancient man she had encountered on the night she came up here with Jonathan.

"They's gone," he said, grinning madly. Once more, his aged fingers were scrabbling everywhere.

"Where? Where did they go?"

"They's gone." He took a shaky step toward her. His aroma was, if anything, more pungent than before. "Mama and baby both."

"When? Do you know when they left?"

His grizzled face was already so wrinkled that it was difficult to tell whether he was frowning, but, certainly, he paused in his constant scratching, and his eyes fixed on a point in the middle distance. "Yesterday," he finally said. "Maybe the day before. A man comes to see her, and a minute later she takes the baby and flies the coop. Doesn't even close the door behind." He peered past Abigail into the devastation. "I reckon some of the folks who live hereabouts has needs," he explained. "They finds what they needs where they can."

Or someone was looking for something; and Judith, praise God, was already gone.

Because she was warned?

And it happened within the past two days: not long after Whit Pesky received his transfer orders.

"This man who called just before Judith left," said Abigail. "Can you describe him for me?"

Again the old man fell into thought: *fell* because he seemed to lapse into an entirely different existence, where he could sift, at leisure, through the memories of what was no doubt a fascinating life. He smiled a bit as he pondered, even laughed, then shook his head as if in pain, and shut his eyes briefly, shuddering.

"Thin," he finally said.

Abigail was growing exasperated. She had been taught to revere old age, and to respect those who reached it, but just now could hardly stand still. "Is that all?"

"White," he murmured, after an aeon.

"Please, sir. Can you recall anything else? Was he tall? Short?"

A slow nod. "Yes. Yes." He began to scratch again. "Well spoken, like. Not from around here. A real nervous kind of fella. Like, maybe he didn't wanna be here."

"Nervous?" An idea struck her. She made a washing motion. "Did he rub his hands like this?"

"Nothing like that, no."

Not Plum, then. "Is there anything else you can tell me?"

Again the old man drifted into his netherworld. And again, after a bit of reflection, he returned. "He had those big whiskers." Brushing his fingers along his cheeks. "But he was all bald and shiny up top. Sounded educated. Young fella. Thirty, I reckon. Not too much more, anyway."

Descending the stairs, Abigail strove to calm herself. There had to be a hundred men in Washington who fit that description. A thousand. Even so, she would at that moment have given a great deal to know where exactly Noah Brooks, private secretary to the President of the United States, might have been on the night Judith Canner disappeared.

BOOK II

March–April 1867
Trial

～

"The Senate shall have the sole Power to try all Impeach-
ments. When sitting for that Purpose, they shall be on Oath
or Affirmation. When the President of the United States is
tried, the Chief Justice shall preside: And no Person shall
be convicted without the Concurrence of two thirds of the
Members present. . . .

Judgment in Cases of Impeachment shall not extend further than to removal from Office, and disqualification to
hold and enjoy any Office of honor, Trust or Profit under
the United States: but the Party convicted shall nevertheless be liable and subject to Indictment, Trial, Judgment and
Punishment, according to Law."

—Constitution of the United States,
Article I, Section 3

CHAPTER 29

Managers

I

"GENTLEMEN," SAID CHIEF Justice Salmon P. Chase, "the Senate is now sitting for the trial of articles of impeachment. The President of the United States appears by counsel." A learned frown in their direction. "The Court will now hear you."

Chase sat upon the high dais usually occupied by the Senate's presiding officer. Between him and the Senators, two long tables had been set. The prosecution sat to Chase's right—the left of the audience—and the defense counsel opposite. Now the Chief Justice rapped his gavel. The tittering in the audience ceased.

Abigail watched from the crowded gallery. There were few vacant seats, but two of them bookended hers. It was just past noon on Monday, March 18, and the faint sunlight of late winter lazed through the clerestory windows high in the walls. The gallery ran like a mezzanine around three sides of the chamber. *This is where they debate the future of my race*, she kept thinking. *This is where they vote.* She craned her neck, trying to take in the opulence. She had lived in Washington City all her life but had never been inside the legislative chambers of the Capitol. Even after the frenzy of recent weeks, an unexpected excitement seized her. Although she allowed nothing to show on her face, Abigail fancied that others could hear the swift, unladylike pounding of her heart. *This is where.* The Senate Chamber was a great oval, several stories high, all marble and polished wood. In Washington most things were filthy, but here even the spittoons gleamed. The Capitol building, with its granite and marble and sparkling new dome, was beautiful and vast, designed to intimidate even European dignitaries, who had vast, beautiful buildings of their own. But, for all its outward glory, the Capitol was really a glorified men's club, purchased at enormous expense by the people of the United States for the benefit of those who ruled them without ever quite representing them. The part of Abigail that had learned under the tutelage of Professor Charles Finney to adore the republican principle was repelled by the presumption of aristocracy that the building presented. Professor Finney used to say that the Congress could as well meet in a theater or an auditorium, dispensing with the ostentation.

And yet she could not deny the chamber's breathtaking beauty.

Around her, the ladies of Washington leaned toward each other, whispering. Nobody leaned toward Abigail. Nobody whispered to her. Nobody was sure what she was doing there. The struggle to get a colored woman admitted had been protracted. Down the hall from the chamber was a suite of rooms set aside for the President's use whenever he might come up to Capitol Hill. During the course of the trial, Lincoln's lawyers would use the suite as an office, but they had learned early that Abigail would not be allowed inside. The exclusion was not because of her color but because of her sex: the rules of the men's club. So they obtained for Abigail a ticket entitling her to a seat in the reserved gallery. The ticket had her name on it, but when she presented it at the Capitol this morning, the usher had seemed to lose the ability to read; or else he thought she had stolen it from some whiter Abigail Canner. He told her to leave. She stood her ground. She might have sent a note to the conference room, but just now she did not want some white man straightening out the question of her rights. The great of Washington City flowed by, giving the contretemps a wide berth. Perplexed by her persistence, the usher called over a guard. The guard spoke in the slow, measured tones appropriate to instructing an imbecile. His brass buttons sparkled. His moustache was damp with this morning's bracer. The colored, he said, were not allowed in the reserved gallery. That was how he put it, *the colored*, as if naming a clan. The colored had to sit with the rest of the public in the place set aside for them, he said. The stair was around the back. And I would hurry, he added: the seats are pretty much taken. Abigail had learned long ago that most of life's barriers were surmountable through a combination of intelligence, charm, and obstinacy. She tried the first, asking if the guard had a rule book handy, and whether he could perhaps point to the relevant rule. She tried the second, offering a cute smile and an all-but-giggling assurance that she would behave herself. And she tried the third, informing him that she planned to enter the gallery in any event. If he stopped her, or sought to place her under arrest, he could explain his action to Senator Sumner, who was a personal friend. This was not entirely true, but neither, Abigail told herself, was the guard's fantasy of the rule barring her entrance. She had never caviled at the occasional exaggeration for the sake of navigating the system of injustice under which she lived. Nanny Pork said men lied all the time but a lady never should, unless she was a trollop, or a wife, or both. Yet Nanny would lie to every farmer at the Center Market to save half a penny on a chicken.

Sumner's was a magical name in the city; evidently, neither the guard nor the usher could imagine anybody, least of all a negress, taking it in vain. Marveling at the state of the world, they stepped aside and allowed her to pass.

When she reached the sweeping marble stair to the gallery, the ladies of Washington stepped aside, too. This obstreperous colored woman, well spoken yet devious in the manner they had thought peculiarly their own, was an entirely new species to most of them, but they knew already that they didn't care for her.

II

Abigail was in a better mood than she would have expected. Upon arriving at the office early this morning, she had told Dennard about Judith's disappearance. The lawyer listened impassively, but was unimpressed. If she hoped to be a lawyer, he said, shaking his jowly head, she would have to learn how to honor her commitments notwithstanding whatever private griefs might occur. He told her how, on the eve of a major trial four years ago, he had received word that his brother-in-law, a dear friend, had been killed in action. The body was on its way back to Kentucky for burial.

"I sought no postponement. I let my sister stand at the funeral without my support. And do you know why?" His glare dared Abigail to attempt an answer, but she was remembering how Grafton had told her that Dennard family members died fighting on the Confederate side. "Because life is rich with tragedy. If you are willing to be delayed by the inevitable pains and horrors that will befall, you have no business pursuing a profession."

Chastened, she returned to her work. Sickles had letters for her to deliver to the post office. She drove herself across town in the wagon. A light snow was falling. Gentle flakes fluttered like insects across her eyes. Or maybe it was her own tears that made it hard to see. Either way, she ran the wagon into a ditch, just in front of a quartet of stout mansions on Ninth Street, but although pale faces appeared at the windows, no one emerged to help.

One of the mansions belonged to the Bannermans.

Abigail hesitated, then marched up the walk and pulled the bell. Ellenborough, the mulatto butler, somehow contrived to look down on her, although in actual fact they were the same height. She explained what had happened. Ellenborough explained that she should run along. He closed the door. It opened again an instant later, and Fielding Bannerman invited her in.

She had not laid eyes on Fielding since the night they had walked in to find Jonathan drunk in the library, but he was all smiles. A footman was sent to hitch horses to Abigail's wagon and pull it out of the ditch. Fielding apologized for the "smallness" of the staff: two maids, a cook, two footmen, and Ellenborough. The rest were on furlough until the bulk of the family returned.

"Of course, we have a lot more at the lake house," he added, perhaps worried about what she would think. They were in the front parlor, sipping lemonade.

"Of course," she said.

"Hills will be sorry he missed you."

"He is at the office. I shall see him shortly."

"Repairs could take some time. Let me drive you."

On the way, Abigail found herself telling Fielding about her sister's disappearance. She had his sympathy, he said, and if there was any way in which his humble talents or resources might be of service, she had only to ask—

"You are very kind," she said, and squeezed his hand briefly.

She arrived at Dennard & McShane just as the group was leaving for Capitol Hill. She could tell from his face that Jonathan had been worrying. Probably he knew by now about Judith: Dennard would have told Sickles, and Sickles was too mischievous to restrain himself. Had Jonathan made a consoling remark, or even an overly friendly one, she would have turned on him. But he seemed to sense that, and contented himself with handing her a sealed brown envelope.

"This came for you while you were away." An awkward look. "A messenger brought it."

"From where?" she asked, very surprised, because she recognized the handwriting. "From whom?"

"I fear he didn't say."

The flaps were still sealed—Abigail checked. She tore them open. Judith's note was short, and simple. She was safe, but she had to go away for a while. She warned Abigail not to ask after her or come looking for her. "And please take care of Nanny."

For the first time in hours, Abigail smiled.

III

The gallery quieted. The occasion had begun with great dignity: the Senators had entered, then the Chief Justice. One of the Associate Justices of the Supreme Court had sworn in the Chief Justice as presiding officer, and he in turn swore in the Senators. Representative Bingham, on behalf of the Managers, read aloud the four Articles of Impeachment. The Sergeant-at-Arms then shouted for the President of the United States to come forward, although everybody knew he was nowhere in the vicinity. The body formally took notice of the fact that the President would instead be represented by counsel, who were then summoned. The members of the House marched in, and were assigned seats in the back and along the wings. The counsel for the President presented their credentials. It was all done with splendid pomp and decorum.

And then the shouting started, the battle over the tricky matter of Wade's status. Lincoln's supporters hoped to make him an issue. Their argument was carried on by Senators, not by counsel, who sat with their eyes to the front and their mouths shut, for the vote was expected to be close, and neither side could afford new enemies. Wade, as president pro tempore of the Senate, would of course succeed to the Presidency should Lincoln be removed. Some of the very few pro-Lincoln newspapers considered Wade's not-quite-secret ambition the driving force behind the impeachment. The Radicals answered that Wade was in fading health, and taking on the office would be a burden, a sacrifice on behalf of a shattered nation, no more. On the floor of the Senate, the Lincoln faction contended that Wade, as the potential beneficiary of Senate action, should not be entitled to a vote. The Radicals argued that depriving Wade of a vote would deprive his Ohio constituents of their suffrage, adding that no one had ever challenged Wade's integrity. . . .

In the end, the Senate went into closed conference, and emerged with the conclusion that Wade would be entitled to the same vote as anyone else. But Abigail suspected that the senior Senator from Ohio, who hated Lincoln with the same passion he had once brought to hating slavery, would have little if anything to say.

I V

The preliminaries at last concluded. The Chief Justice adjusted his spectacles and let his heavy gaze move across the chamber. He was a fleshy, fussy man, said to be vain about the dignity due his position. He was vain on other subjects, too, and tended to see himself as surrounded by intellectual and moral pygmies. That, at least, was how Dan Sickles described him, and although Abigail had never warmed to Sickles, she had met no one wiser in the ways, and weaknesses, of Washington's worthies.

"Gentlemen, Managers of the House of Representatives," Chase rumbled, "you will now proceed in support of the articles of impeachment." Another tap of the gavel, for the members proved harder to quell than the spectators. "Senators will please give their attention."

This was it, then. The formal presentation of the case against the President of the United States: in effect, the opening statement of the trial.

Benjamin Butler arose: the same Butler whom Lincoln had tried to recruit as vice-presidential candidate in 1864, and who had rebuffed the overture so rudely. Butler was a rotund, jowly man, now balding; a few years ago, while serving as a general during the war, he had been trim and tall and handsome. He had in common with Lincoln that both had been hated by the Southerners.

To Abigail Canner, men like Benjamin Butler and Thaddeus Stevens were heroes, far larger than this poor mortal life, the great figures of the battle to eradicate slavery. Each was a fierce Radical. Butler, while serving as military governor of New Orleans, had hanged a man for tearing down the Union flag, and ordered that any woman who was impolite to the Union troops should be treated as a prostitute. He had also armed the slaves. As for Stevens, the Pennsylvania congressman had been one of the earliest and most vehement supporters not only of emancipation but of full equality of the races. He shared his house with a colored woman, whom most people considered to be his common-law wife. Unlike Butler, Stevens was small and fierce-eyed, with a full head of hair. As everyone knew, he was dying, and had already picked out a burial plot in one of the rare cemeteries that interred whites and blacks in the same section; but he was determined to live long enough to see Lincoln, whom he hated, overthrown.

"Mr. President and gentlemen of the Senate," Butler began. "The onerous duty has fallen to my fortune to present to you, imperfectly as I must, the several propositions of fact and law upon which the House of Representatives will endeavor to sustain the cause of the people against the President of the United States, now pending at your bar."

The people. Abigail had not thought about the charges that way. Mr. Lincoln and his lawyers talked about the Radicals; as a formal matter, the charges were brought by the House of Representatives; it had not occurred to her that the Managers would proceed as in a criminal trial, asserting that they acted in the name of *the people.* And she wondered whether the late Arthur McShane, who so revered the Constitution in its perfection, would agree.

Butler meanwhile was explaining why, due to "the novelty of the proceeding," he would likely speak for some while. Dennard had estimated ninety minutes. Abigail listened closely as the balding Butler laid out the same charges, in very much the same language, as in the bill of impeachment itself. There were four counts: the first related to the suspension of habeas corpus, the second to the censorship of newspapers and the seizure of private telegrams, the third to the supposed inattention to the protection of the freedmen, and the fourth to his desire to overthrow the authority of the Congress. She had brought her commonplace book and was making notes. The trial would meet four days each week, Monday through Thursday, from noon until five in the afternoon, with Friday sessions as needed. Abigail expected to spend most of those days right here, although she and Rellman were available for other assignments as well. Jonathan would sit at the counsel table with Dennard, Speed, and Sickles. Abigail felt the yearning. To be a lawyer in so important a litigation. Her pencil flew across the page. She would, she knew, grow accustomed in time to the surroundings, to the occasion, even to the fluttering determination of the great ladies of the city to ignore her.

"Excuse me."

A whisper at her ear, breathy and confident at once. Abigail looked up. There stood a slim, pale woman whom Abigail recognized from sketches in the newspapers before she opened her delicate mouth.

"I'm Katherine Sprague," said the newcomer, extending a gloved hand. Beneath her fancy hat, unfashionably blond hair was piled high on her head. "We have not been formally introduced, but we attended the same reception at the Eameses' two weeks ago. Is this seat available?"

Abigail was not often struck wordless, but just now, for a moment, she could conjure nothing to say. Katherine Sprague. The daughter of the Chief Justice, who even now was fussily presiding over the trial. Katherine Sprague, just a few years older than Abigail herself, married to the wealthiest man in the Senate; the same Katherine Sprague who was said to be puzzling constantly over how to manipulate her ambitious father into the White House. When Michael spoke of *the people who*, Kate Sprague would be foremost among them.

No doubt, buried in the texts on professional ethics she had yet to read, she would find rules limiting contact between lawyers and the judges presiding over their cases; but Kate was no judge, and Abigail no lawyer, not after her constant exclusion from the heart of things. And, besides, the ambition that beat like a second heart within her chest would not allow her to consider rebuffing an overture from the foremost of *the people who*.

In truth, the moment only seemed to stretch eternally: all of this flashed through Abigail's mind in no more than a second. And by that time, she was already offering a formal hand to meet the one offered.

"Of course I remember, Mrs. Sprague. You played chess against that Southern gentleman. I fear that I missed the exhibition, but I was impressed by your confidence."

"Thank you, dear. But it took him all of five minutes to defeat me, so, whatever you thought of my confidence, my performance, I fear, was not terribly impressive." A broad smile, seemingly genuine. "And, please, call me Kate."

Abigail smiled back.

As the great ladies of Washington stared in dismayed astonishment, and made lists in their minds of whom to tell first, Kate Sprague, the city's most prominent hostess, settled into the seat beside the obstreperous negress.

V

Meanwhile, a few feet from the counsel table, Congressman Butler was growing angrier; and louder. He railed against the President for not being present in person to answer the charges. "Mr. Lincoln should be here," said Butler, more than once, in what seemed a departure from his text. He nodded toward the defense table, although his argument was with his own colleagues. "The prosecution has been weak in the knees. We should have demanded his presence. He should have been required to stand before this body and listen to the charges against him." As Butler's anger rose, his voice grew more hoarse and throaty.

"Pardon me," said Butler. He sipped his water, resumed his assault. "We face a circumstance unique in history. In other times and in other lands it has been found that despotism could only be tempered by assassination"—a sigh went through the gallery, and Butler, seeing that he had misfired, hurried on—"and nations living under constitutional governments even have found no mode by which to rid themselves of a tyrannical ruler, except by overturning the very foundation and framework of the government itself."

Butler continued in that vein, fulminating about Lincoln's supposed tyranny in the high-sounding language that was the fashion of the day among public men; and it occurred to Jonathan, sitting stoically beside Sickles at the brightly polished counsel table, that Lincoln never talked that way. The President's language was clear and straightforward, without pretension or pomposity. Lincoln's homespun humility provided another reason for his opponents to despise him. Most of the Radicals had matriculated at the finest schools in the land; Lincoln had nary a degree to his name.

When the Radicals looked at the President, they saw not just a moral but an intellectual inferior.

Certainly Ben Butler considered Lincoln a lesser man than himself. One might never know, as his peroration wound down, that just three years ago Butler had seriously considered Lincoln's invitation to join him as vice-presidential candidate.

"You are a law among yourselves," Butler concluded, meaning that it was entirely up to the Senators to decide what constituted an impeachable offense. No crime was necessary, said Butler, having cast his notes aside. "You may remove the President for any act that is either subversive of some fundamental principle of government or highly prejudicial to the public interest." The censorious eyes roamed along the senatorial ranks. "Mr. Lincoln's entire tenure in office easily meets these tests."

Butler sat. He had spoken for an hour and a half.

The Chief Justice declared a thirty-minute recess, after which Thaddeus Stevens would complete the opening statement on the part of the Managers.

As the Senate rose, Jonathan turned to Sickles. "Butler as much as said that they can remove the President because they disagree with him politically!"

Sickles grinned. "This is Washington, son. Down here, no matter what they say, politics is the only reason anybody does anything."

VI

"Have the police made any progress?"

The question took Abigail by surprise. She felt the hollow guilt of one who is caught at sin, for she had been studying the fine dresses and hats of the great Washington ladies, wondering whether they looked down on her simpler costume. She noticed that the ladies, Kate included, had all brought little fans, and were fluttering them furiously. Odd choice in winter: she wondered why.

"My understanding," she admitted, "is that they have very few clues."

"That is very strange," mused Mrs. Sprague, fan working. "Mr. McShane was a man of some prominence in this city." Down below, the Senate was coming back. "And a close friend of Father as well. I wonder that more pressure has not been brought to bear."

Abigail, as it happened, wondered the same thing. In time she would grow accustomed to Kate Sprague's eerie ability to guess what she was thinking, but just now she felt a little frightened; and, in consequence, let slip more than she probably should have.

"It seems to me," Abigail said, "that if there has been pressure, it has been the other way around."

Kate's fan did not quite mask her tiny smile of triumph.

VII

The other House Managers were Representatives Bingham and Stevens. They were, along with Butler, among the purest of the Radicals.

Actually, Butler was in only his first term in the Congress, and the assignment as Manager should by rights have gone to a more senior man. But Butler was popular with the voters; when he demanded a place for himself, the leadership dared not refuse.

Now Thaddeus Stevens rose. He was shaky, and it seemed unlikely that he would be able to remain on his feet, as protocol required, for the hour or so that his remarks were expected to require. Indeed, given his poor health, Abigail wondered if he would even survive the trial. But when he spoke, his voice was almost biblical in its rolling and thunderous power. There was no quaver. There was no doubt. He was speaking what his conscience told him was rock-bottom truth; and he would admit no differences of opinion.

"Mr. Lincoln," he began, "is the greatest tyrant this nation has ever known. And given that he now commands the most formidable army on the face of the planet, and uses it for his own purposes without regard for law or morality, he may be, at this instant, the greatest tyrant in the world."

No quarter, then; no compromise.

"Mr. Stevens is a true hero of the nation," Kate whispered.

"Indeed," said Abigail. She coughed. She had discovered the point of the fluttering fans. Despite the wintry weather outside, here in the upper reaches of the Senate Chamber cigar smoke from below gathered thickly. After two hours, it was like being on a battlefield.

"He may not last the trial," said Kate.

"His voice is as powerful as ever," said Abigail. But she, like all the nation, knew that Stevens was dying. He had been born, she reminded herself, marveling, while George Washington was President. At Oberlin, she had been spellbound by Professor Finney's encomiums to the great orator.

Down in the well, the old man's body began to sag, but he grabbed the edge of the table and pressed on, carried by his own righteous fury. He described the President's offenses in great detail, and with magnificent plumage, his eloquence easily outdoing the practical Butler. He announced, with evident glee, that the chamber would be provided with evidence of a letter "of unchallengeable provenance" that set forth clearly his intention to continue and even expand his tyranny.

A flurry in the chamber.

Stevens never paused. It was not enough, he said, that Lincoln had violated the Constitution and the liberties of the American people. It was not enough that he had shown himself timid and unreliable in protecting the colored race so recently rescued from the most vicious bondage. He was a conspirator, sneered Stevens—a deceiver who made plans in the darkness for that which he would not dare to defend in the bright light of the day. Abigail tensed, guessing what would come next. Stevens looked around the chamber. A deceiver, he said, must be cast out—he was borrowing from Revelation—and his whole wicked Administration with him, as the deceiver's angels were cast out of the Heavenly Firmament.

This brought a gasp, and more catcalls.

Stevens continued to outline the evidence the Managers would present, none of it surprising, except for one detail.

Stanton.

He announced that the Secretary of War would be called—involuntarily, said Stevens—to testify to the President's constant interference with the conducting of military campaigns, the demoralizing effect of his repeated removals of general officers for following the will of Congress, and his insistence on ignoring the pleas of his own martial governors across the South, who warned of the harms suffered by the freedmen, and the growing political power of the former slaveholders.

"How is that possible?" Jonathan whispered.

Sickles told him to hush.

"I thought there was an arrangement," the young man persisted. "Stanton keeps his office but will not testify."

"Never act surprised in a courtroom," said Sickles, his eyes not leaving Stevens's smug face. "As far as anybody knows, everything that happens is exactly what you expected to happen."

The gavel came down. "Silence in the chamber," hissed Chase, his eyes on Sickles, whom the entire Congress seemed unanimously, if mysteriously, to despise.

Stevens resumed. Stanton, he said, would testify with enormous reluctance and under the compulsion of subpoena. He would tell of the President's hostility to the Reconstruction Acts, and to the Congress itself; and how, on more than one occasion, he heard the President propose closing the Congress down, if necessary by force.

"None of that is true," Jonathan murmured.

This time Sickles ignored him.

Stevens was describing Stanton now as a man of rare probity, admired by all sides, a true leader who would never allow mere politics . . .

Jonathan was hardly listening. Once again, Lincoln and his men had been outplayed. Matters were as simple as that. The Secretary of War had broken his solemn word that he would not testify. Perhaps the Managers were exaggerating. Nevertheless, if Stanton endorsed under oath half of what Thaddeus Stevens had just assured the chamber that he would, there was no way for the President's lawyers to meet his proof.

VIII

Chase gaveled the session to a close. The defense would present its opening argument tomorrow. Standing in the grand foyer, Daniel Grafton watched the great of Washington come sweeping down the staircase, tittering madly. He suspected that they were whispering not of the trial they were witnessing but of what they would wear to tonight's parties. He knew that men like Congressman Blaine thought him decadent, but he was nothing compared to the city's true rich, for whom even the war had played out as a sideshow to their otherwise unbothered lives, occasionally forcing them to grab their heirlooms and flee to the battlements of the capital from their mansions in the surrounding countryside, but, for the most part, affecting neither their social season nor their wealth. It occurred to him that it was possible to be rich enough that it actually made no difference who sat in the White House or ruled the Congress. His clients were men like that, and did not even realize it. Their hoards of gold shielded them from everyday concerns, and yet they responded to every change in the price of iron ore as if the barbarians were massing outside the gate. He supposed that there must be people like that in every age, people wielding more power than mere governments but not truly understanding their own capabilities. That was why men like Grafton himself had to exist: to wield the power his clients possessed but did not comprehend.

That was also why men like Benjamin Butler had to exist: men who were, in their own minds, beacons of goodness and light, but whose ambitions were easily twisted in the direction of political mayhem. Grafton liked the men of grand reputation and perfect integrity best: men so beloved that their constituents happily overlooked the destruction they wreaked in the climb toward the top. And they were willing to serve, with perfectly self-interested integrity, the interests of those who stood in the background, twisting democracy to their advantage. Daniel Grafton was among the best of the manipulators.

Based on events so far, he had every reason to be proud of his work.

CHAPTER 30

Consolation

I

"NOT A BAD first day," said Dan Sickles. "Not bad at all."

"We had to sit there and let them say those terrible things—"

"I know, Miss Canner, I know." He was back on the settee, fingers working hard on the thigh muscles, heedless of what others might think. Sitting motionless on the chair for the better part of five hours must have been a considerable chore. "But nothing they said was any worse than we expected."

"What about Mr. Stanton?"

Sickles shut his eyes briefly, perhaps in response to the pain; or perhaps in worry. Jonathan and Nathan Rellman were at the other end of the room, double-checking the catalogue of exhibits. Speed and Dennard were at Fessenden's house, closeted with a group of pro-Lincoln Senators, working out some details for tomorrow, when the defense would present its opening statement. "I do not believe," said Sickles after a moment, "that Stanton will testify."

"Do you think Mr. Stevens was lying?"

"Not at all. But I reckon Stanton will change his mind, once he sees how things are going." He looked at her again. "Things will go our way, Miss Canner. And when they do, Stanton will hop back aboard the ship as nimbly as he hopped off."

"Mr. Stevens said the same thing that Miss Hale did, that the Managers have a letter from the President—"

"Well, no, Miss Canner. That's not exactly what he said. He said they have *evidence* of a letter. That could mean somebody's just going to testify to what the letter said. And if that's all there is—if there's no actual letter—why, then, we have a shot at keeping the evidence from being admitted. That means hunting through the cases, I reckon. More work for you and Hilliman." He grimaced, and shifted the bad leg. "I admit I was a little surprised by Stevens. He's an honest man, and I'm sure he has the evidence he says he has. But I've known Mr. Lincoln a long time. He would never commit to paper anything incriminating. Even if there were a letter, it would be, at best, ambiguous."

Abigail hid her surprise. She would have expected Sickles to insist that there could be no incriminating letter because the President had done no wrong.

He saw her face, but for once misread her concern. "Don't worry, Miss Canner. Mr. Lincoln's not worried; therefore, I'm not worried; therefore, you should not be worried. The Managers were eloquent, but they offered no surprises. They swung no votes." He nodded at the blackboard. "We are where we were days ago, with six undecided votes, of which we must win four."

"Meaning, we must still persuade Senator Sumner."

"Afraid so." He smiled and teased his moustache. "And I am sorry, Miss Canner, that you had to stay up in the gallery. Looks like you made a friend, though."

Abigail returned the smile uneasily. "Mrs. Sprague seems the very soul of kindness."

"And so she is." Sickles winked. "Until she turns into the Princess of Darkness and steals your soul."

"You should not joke about such matters, Mr. Sickles."

Sickles looked at her with renewed interest as he took hold of the chair arm and, with difficulty, arose. He dropped his voice. "And, Miss Canner. For your own private ear—I have made progress with Blaine. I think he is prepared to tell us who bought him. But I will need your help." He leaned closer. "He wants two things. He wants a note from the President, promising to support him for Speaker—"

"Why, he is still selling himself!"

"Can't change his spots, even when he's trying to be honest." That wild, piratical grin flickered, then faded. "The other thing Blaine insists on, Miss Canner, is that you be there when he tells his story. Wouldn't say why. Will you do it?"

"Of course I will," she whispered, feeling herself crossing the boundary at last. They needed her. Not just for show.

"It will be soon, probably with little warning. I will let you know. But you mustn't tell a soul." The other clerks were on their way back over. "Well, let's get to work."

The work was evaluating the witness list, finally turned over by the Managers today. There would be no witnesses on the first two counts of the impeachment resolution. The President's coterie was conceding that Lincoln had suspended habeas corpus, seized telegrams, and shuttered newspapers. Under the agreement worked out with the Managers and approved by the Senate, on these two counts the lawyers would present only argument.

That left Counts Three and Four.

Under Count Three, the supposed refusal of the President to protect the freedmen, there were two witnesses listed—a Corbin Yardley and an Eliza Caffey, neither of whom anybody could identify. Ordinarily, a request would have gone out to the federal police or the Secret Service, but these were both under the control of Baker, meaning Stanton, meaning the Radicals, and therefore not to be trusted. They would have to dig; very fast.

Under Count Four, the President's secret plan to establish the Department of the Atlantic and put Washington City—including the Congress—under martial law, three witnesses were listed. All were known: Major Clancy, who was at the moment the President's military aide; James K. Moorhead, a Republican congressman from Pittsburgh; and Mrs. Sally Orne, a close friend of the late Mrs. Lincoln.

Clancy they could interview at their leisure. Sickles said he and Speed would find ways to talk to Moorhead and Mrs. Orne.

The others they would have to track down.

II

"I have seen those names before," said Abigail. "I cannot remember where, but I have seen them."

"Some of them are pretty well known," said Jonathan.

"But I have seen them together. Not all of them, but at least three. Yardley. Caffey. Moorhead. Together somewhere."

They were in the Bannerman carriage. Jonathan had offered, pro forma, to drive her home. Almost always, Abigail declined, usually on the grounds that her brother would be meeting her. Tonight, however, Michael was evidently busy, because she said yes at once.

"It will come to you," Jonathan said, with perfect confidence.

Abigail scowled. She disliked being unable to live up to her own legend. Jonathan drove the horses cautiously. Yesterday's snow was packed hard and, with nightfall, had started to freeze. To hurry would be to court disaster.

Near the shadowy bulk of the Smithsonian Castle, Jonathan drew in the reins, then slewed to the side to let a column of mounted cavalry pass. They rode in good order, and not hastily, and so he assumed they were not answering an emergency. It was odd to see so many of them at this time of night, but for weeks there had been rumors throughout the city of strange military movements.

"Do you miss Miss Hale?" she said suddenly.

Jonathan was surprised. "That was only—I was asked—"

"I know. It was your grim duty to spend time in her company." She laughed shortly, covering her confusion. She had no idea why she had brought the matter up. "You must be pleased," she said, a little desperately, "that her return to Spain has put an end to unfortunate necessity."

Jonathan fell silent. Abigail sensed that for once her teasing had gone too far, that she had wounded him. It had not previously occurred to her that she might possess the power to do so. She would have apologized, but her mother's years of stern instructions on the behavior of a lady prevented her: she dared not even acknowledge that the gentleman sitting beside her was capable of an emotional pain.

Gliding through the snow, wrapped securely in the blanket as Jonathan drove the horses, Abigail found herself remembering a story in *Peterson's Magazine* about a young woman and her suitor, whom she despised, traveling in a sleigh that became caught in a blizzard. She was not really permitted to read such material, but she had snuck a glance anyway, at her older sister's diabolical urging, and then read it again, and a third time, and perhaps a fourth. The tale had lingered in her mind ever since. Once the sleigh was stuck, the two young people wrapped themselves in the single available blanket. Previously feuding, they began to talk, then to nestle close, after which the editors coyly declined to "follow them through all the hours of that long night." The editors added: "Suffice it to say that time sped swiftly, when on the wings of love." In the morning, the storm abated and the young woman's uncle came searching for them. He discovered them both underneath the blanket—an image that Abigail refused to envision, yet could not help wondering about—"enjoying themselves finely." Perhaps the editors had meant only that they were wrapped up and watching the clean winter morning after the storm. Or perhaps they had meant to imply—

But there Abigail's imagination stopped, walled off by the stiff, proud morality of her raising. She saw Nanny Pork's dark face, stern and censorious, and she realized that she felt eerily if warmly alive, and that the carriage was bouncing beneath her because—

"Hold on!" Jonathan cried, as her eyes snapped open.

"What is it?" she gasped. She looked around. They were in deeper snow, strewn here and there with boulders, and she realized that they were streaking across a meadow. At first she thought Jonathan had lost the reins, but he was holding them tighter than ever, working the whip with a vengeance to which she was unaccustomed. "What's wrong?"

"Don't look back!" he shouted.

And so she did.

The crisp shiny snow was moon-dappled and bright. Lonely, leafless trees swayed gently with the night breeze. The scene was beautiful, like a clipping from one of her magazines. There was absolutely no one in sight, except for the trio of masked men on horseback, chasing the carriage and getting closer.

III

There were no night riders within Washington City. This well-known fact was presented by the newspapers with a certain disdainful pride. Whatever might be happening at the South, up here—so the editorials proclaimed—the white citizens knew how to treat the negroes.

A sentiment to which the negroes generally responded *Amen*—even if they took it in a somewhat different spirit.

The capital had its share of brigands, of course, but the ordinary class of ruffian did not present the principal danger. The larger challenge was the roaming bands of soldiers in tatters of uniform, some Union, some Confederate, some both, all hungry, and angry, and certain that they had been betrayed.

But there were no night riders.

Everybody knew it.

Which was why, when Jonathan saw that the horsemen had covered their faces with bandannas, he assumed that they must be highwaymen.

Indeed, even as he sensed Abigail stiffening beside him, he wanted to turn and reassure her that the three masked men, whoever they might be, were not the White Camellia or the Ku Klux. He might have said it, too, but he was by then too busy using the whip, which he had hardly raised in his life. The carriage careened across the meadow toward Ninth Street, rocking and bucking along the slippery frozen mud, the horses protesting as he drove them mercilessly. Abigail was shouting something beside him, and he was shouting at her to get down, and remembering how Dan Sickles had told him once that any man who wandered Washington City without a pistol was a fool. Remembering the tales of the Ku Klux and their various companions in terror, Jonathan knew in his bones that he would never ignore Sickles again.

They clattered across the canal. The houses were thinner now, and shuttered against the frigid night. Here and there a lamp burned in an upper window, but Jonathan was not about to chance his luck by stopping. Abigail was screaming at him to slow down. Instead, he gave the team its head, urging more speed. But horses pulling a rig will rarely outrun horses carrying men, and the riders drew alongside. One tugged at the bridle of the horse on the right, and another got his hand on the edge of the seat. Jonathan smacked the gloved fingers with his whip, and the rider reeled away. Another man had pulled a derringer, and Jonathan swung the rig toward him, a trick he had learned in the army, knocking the gun from his hand and almost knocking the man from his horse. Another hand grabbed at him. Jonathan jerked the horses the other way, and as the attacker flailed, his glove came off.

Jonathan realized that something wasn't right.

The wrist was dark brown.

The attackers were negroes.

An instant later, the horsemen released the bridles and sped off into the darkness, their laughter carrying back to the carriage on the night air.

Jonathan slowed the rig to a trot. He turned to Abigail, asked if she was all right.

"I am perfectly fine," she said, and sounded as if she meant it.

"I don't know why they left us alone—"

"Because I was with you." Abigail pinched her forehead and shut her eyes. "That was my brother, Michael, and his friends," she said.

"Your brother is a highwayman?" he asked, incredulous.

"He is much more than that, Mr. Hilliman. He is a killer."

IV

The horses were cooling down. They sat in the rig not far from the house where she lived with Louisa and Nanny Pork. The fog had lifted, unveiling a sky of brilliant violet. Tiny unseen animals skittered through the underbrush.

"You told me he worked in Baltimore," Jonathan said. He had stopped to pick up the derringer, and was turning it over and over in his hands. "You told me he was a printer's devil."

"He was. At least for a time."

"And now he's a criminal?"

Her face hardened and she turned away, as if searching for the answer out toward the fetid river. "My brother is not a criminal."

"You said he is a killer."

"But not a criminal."

Jonathan leaned forward, felt the horse's flank, decided to wait a bit longer. "He's a killer but not a criminal. Is he a soldier?"

Again he sensed her hesitation, less a desire to deceive him than a duty to avoid an admission against interest. "Not by your lights," she finally said. "He has never worn a uniform."

In the middle distance, the wind swayed dark trees against darker sky. "I am not asking out of idle curiosity. Your brother's occupation may affect the trial of our client."

Abigail was a long time answering, but finally nodded as if to say he had left her no choice. "You have heard of the Ku Klux."

"Of course."

"They began in Tennessee, but they have branches everywhere at the South now. I am told that they are in parts of the North as well. They ride by night, seeking to intimidate those among my people who assert the most basic civil rights. Going to school, owning property or firearms. Voting." A husky sigh as if the truth was too weighty. "There is no defense against the Ku Klux, Jonathan. In this the Managers are entirely correct. The federal authorities rarely intervene. When they do, there is little to be done. And so we must do it ourselves."

"Are you saying—"

"Some of my people have organized riders of our own. Their purpose is to protect us against the Ku Klux and the White Camellia and the other marauders who terrorize us. My brother is a member of one of those groups." She turned to him with an assumed boldness, but he heard the tremolo in her voice. "Are you going to inform Mr. Dennard now? Do you wish me to leave the firm?"

The intensity in those eyes was too much. Jonathan turned away. The night wind had picked up. This afternoon's light snow swirled in the faint glow of the coach lamps. He gazed at the Smithsonian tower to the north: the direction in which Michael and his gang had vanished.

He thought of Meg; and of the family business; and wondered whether he still wanted any part of the future he had imagined. He thought of Abigail beside him, of her stolid certainties about right and wrong; about her intellect, and her Aaron, and her dreams.

"No," he said at last. He stole a glance at her shadowed face, but she was turned away from him. "No, I am not going to inform Mr. Dennard."

"Thank you." She looked up; pointed. "I will need to return my brother's derringer."

Jonathan handed it over. "Tell me one thing. When you say that your brother is a killer . . ."

"I have no knowledge of the details of Michael's activities," she said, with legalistic precision. The gun had vanished into her bag. "But I know what he is capable of." She shuddered with memory. "Do you know what Michael told me recently? Through friends of his, he actually had advance warning of John Brown's murderous raid at Harper's Ferry eight years ago. Michael wanted to go. They refused to take him, as, at eleven, he was too young. But he wanted to go. That is my brother."

To this there was no response to be made. Jonathan called to the horses and snapped the reins. They headed off at a slow trot.

CHAPTER 31

Ruse

I

THE NEXT DAY, Abigail nearly missed the proceedings. When Dennard arrived at the offices at nine-thirty, he immediately handed her a list of books that were needed at once, not only from the Library of Congress but from a number of libraries around the city that had promised to lend. Many were on topics she could not relate, even abstractly, to the trial: a treatise on trusts and estates, a compilation of pharmaceutical remedies from the seventeenth century.

"That will take her the better part of the day," Jonathan objected.

"Then the better part of the day is what it will take," said Dennard, sourly. When he turned toward Abigail once more, his tone softened. "Take all the time you like, my dear. Little will drive you. Should you finish your rounds in time to come to the Capitol, so much the better. Or you may wait here, or even leave early today if you like. Entirely up to you."

"Yes, Mr. Dennard," said Abigail, bewildered.

The lawyer went into his office to gather his notes. The group would be leaving for trial as soon as Speed and Sickles arrived.

"I have no idea what this is about," said Jonathan when she looked his way.

"Isn't it obvious? They are getting rid of me."

"You cannot think they mean to dismiss you!"

"Dismiss me?" Her laugh was brittle. "No, Jonathan, no. For today. They do not want me there today."

Jonathan glanced at the tightly closed door to Dennard's room. "I cannot see why that would be."

"Nevertheless, that is what is happening."

II

Abigail Canner had been a peculiar child. Everybody said so. At home, and also at her Quaker school. She read everything, and remembered what she read. She could do arithmetic in her head and learn music with ease. Her parents, to her chagrin, used to show her off at parties. People would give little Abby arithmetic problems to solve, or play pieces on the piano that she would mimic by ear. When she erred, everyone would laugh, and she had learned from those earliest days that being laughed at was what she hated most in the world.

Today, as she made her rounds with Mr. Little, she felt laughed at.

The weather was warmer, but the air was sooty. Carriages charged through filthy puddles, drenching passersby.

Abigail fumed.

Everyone was at Capitol Hill, except her. Just as everyone met with Mr. Lincoln regularly, except her.

She looked at her list. The next library they were visiting was up Seventeenth Street, north of the White House. She urged Mr. Little to hurry. She was determined to finish her chores and reach the Capitol before the trial day was over, if only to show them that she could. That was how she had spent her life. Showing them all. She supposed that Nanny would say she had succumbed to the sin of pride. Her mother might have said the same: the very mother who, by showing her daughter off all through childhood, had trained into her the instinct to defeat the expectations of others.

"Hurry, please," Abigail said.

"I'se goin as fast as I can."

"Please," she repeated. But the horses were old and the wagon older. The fancier and swifter carriage the firm used for official business belonged to Mr. Dennard. Now and then Abigail had been permitted to use it for running errands, but today the rig was in use, conveying the others to Capitol Hill.

Without her.

They passed the Old Clubhouse, the grim granite mansion of Secretary of State William Seward, who had not left it in two years. A guard stood nonchalantly outside. Seward was said to be a smooth and persuasive politician, easily able to reach deals in smoky back rooms, and she wondered whether Mr. Lincoln would be in so much trouble had his Secretary of State been available to negotiate with those ranged against him. Everyone knew that Seward and Lincoln, working together, had repeatedly outflanked and humiliated the Radicals during the war, further increasing the bad blood.

From Seventeenth Street, they crossed to Connecticut Avenue, then proceeded down a winding trail to a private library on an estate overlooking Rock Creek. The morning rain had left the roads muddy and slow, and every mile or so they had to rein in the horses and inch their way around somebody's trap stuck in the mire, but in the end Mr. Little managed the miracle, and they were back at the offices by a quarter to four.

"Take the wagon," he said.

"I must carry the parcels upstairs—"

"I can take the parcels. You go."

She flew. She reached the Capitol by four-fifteen, and handed the reins to a surprised valet, the unfortunate fellow not sure which was worse, the parlous state of the rig he was being asked to handle, or the color and sex of the driver who was asking. She hurried up the steps, then paused beneath the Rotunda to compose herself. She used her handkerchief to mat the perspiration from her face. She could not use the facilities here, and so had to adjust her hat by touch. Then she walked calmly to the reserved stair, and showed her pass to the same guard as yesterday, who grunted his disapproval but waved her through.

Upstairs, the crowd was smaller. Many of the ladies of the city had departed, to dress for the round of evening parties. In the nearly empty front row, Kate Sprague was seated exactly as before, alongside the same seat Abigail had used yesterday. Nobody was sitting there, perhaps fearing contamination. For a moment Abigail hesitated. To walk past these ladies and claim the same seat, when there were plenty up here in the back—

And then, with that preternatural sense of courtesy, Kate looked up and, smiling, indicated the seat beside hers.

Abigail excused her way along the row, ignoring the outraged whispers of the great ladies, and, gathering her skirts, sat.

"I thought you were not coming," said Kate.

"I had . . . business."

Mrs. Sprague nodded toward the well of the Senate. Speed held the floor. "You have missed very little. Mr. Dennard required two hours to tell the Senators that the charges are baseless and politically motivated and an embarrassment to the nation. Mr. Speed has been addressing the body for a good forty-five minutes now, answering each charge of the indictment."

Abigail nodded. That had been the decision: Dennard and Speed would open the case for Lincoln. Dennard was a well-known lawyer in Washington City, and had many admirers on Capitol Hill. As for Speed, he had been confirmed by this very Senate as attorney general two years ago. Sickles, on the other hand, was viewed with hostility by many people in this room, not least because he was openly contemptuous of social convention, and of the Radicals; there was no need to press him upon the group until necessary. With McShane gone, there was not a finer trial lawyer in the city; but wisdom dictated that Sickles's voice should be reserved for the presentation of evidence and the examination of witnesses.

Meanwhile, heedless of the glares of those seeking to shush her, Kate continued her dissection of the arguments by the President's counsel. "Mr. Speed has already annoyed a few of the Senators, I suspect, because he has said that Mr. Lincoln's suspension of habeas corpus and his shuttering of certain newspapers were subsequently endorsed by the very Congress that now cites them as grounds for impeachment."

"But that is true!"

"Yes. However, congressmen who are embarrassed by past votes always claim later that they were misled. I am sure that the Managers will say that the Congress would never have given the President what he wanted had he not lied. It seems true in every age: legislators seem to be the most gullible creatures on the planet. They are constantly complaining that they have been made fools of." She smiled, showed tiny, perfect teeth. "I believe he is winding up. Certainly I hope he is."

Down below, Speed was saying that counsel for respondent was planning to call as witnesses several leaders of the colored race, who would testify, contrary to the Managers' assertion, that Abraham Lincoln was viewed as a great friend of their people.

Abigail cringed.

Then it got worse; and she knew why Dennard had wanted her to stay away from the trial today.

"Indeed," said Speed, with the hopeless grandiloquence of the man unable to believe that another view than his own exists, "if Mr. Lincoln harbors the sort of prejudice against the freedmen that the Managers suggest, why would he now have in his employ, working hard on his own defense, a colored woman, a graduate of Oberlin College, one of the best of her race?"

Speed asked his rhetorical question grandly, as though expecting applause, and up in the gallery, Abigail covered her face. She knew people were watching her, some of them, no doubt, surprised that she had reached the Capitol in time. She knew she should be sitting stoically; but could not.

"And why," Speed railed on, still unaware of Abigail's presence in the gallery, "would the President have consulted with this young woman in person, at the Executive Mansion, just days ago, if he did not genuinely value her counsel?"

Speed went on to the final charge—conspiring to usurp the Congress—and lectured the body about how furious he was to have been forced to resign his commission as attorney general in order to come to this venue and defend a personal friend against so ridiculous an allegation.

Abigail scarcely listened. The room wobbled a bit, and she knew why Lincoln had asked her to come to the White House for their five-minute conversation. She began to feel dizzy, and shut her eyes. A sudden breeze was Mrs. Sprague's fan, directed now at Abigail's face.

"They might have warned you," said Kate.

"Indeed they might," Abigail whispered, humiliation making her careless.

III

Speed was not quite through. He had finally noticed Abigail, and embarrassment had made him lose his place briefly. In his agitation, he actually stared at her, accentuating his error. Chairs scraped. The Senators whispered to each other.

Chase rapped the gavel lightly. "Does counsel wish to continue?"

Counsel did. Speed wound up quickly. The President's commitment to the security and support of the freedmen was absolute, he said. The Managers were taking honest differences in policy among people who shared the same goal, and transforming them into crimes. That was the standard, said Speed, hammering upon the point in that imperial tone of his that regarded disagreement as enemy action. Criminality. If the Senate failed to find Mr. Lincoln guilty of a crime, then it must acquit him. The Constitution said so. He quoted: "Treason, Bribery, or other high Crimes and Misdemeanors."

The Managers, said Speed, alleged none.

The notion that the President sought to overthrow the authority of the Congress was a fantasy, he said. Certainly the President had made remarks critical of the Congress, at times quite vehemently so. But his words no more represented a challenge to the constitutional structure than did the far more vehement remarks made by members of Congress about the President.

"The wisdom of our forefathers is being challenged today," said Speed, "not by any action of the President but by this effort to shape mere differences over policy into high crimes and misdemeanors. This is not the constitutional system."

Abruptly Speed was done. He made no effort to summarize. He seemed to believe that indignation was a sufficient argument.

"Now, that," said Kate, chuckling, "was unhelpful."

Not for the first time, Abigail told herself that Lincoln's decision to have Speed share the counsel duties was a terrible mistake. She hoped the consequences would not be too grave.

IV

Back at the office, once the others had left, Jonathan tried to apologize for what had happened, insisting that he had not known what Speed was going to say.

"I would never hold one man accountable for another's statements," Abigail assured him. He was behind her, helping her into her coat. Now she turned cool gray eyes his way. "In any event, you owe me no apology."

He hesitated. "Abigail, we should talk—"

"I have an engagement."

Fielding again, he suspected. An awkward silence. Were he to comment in any way, he would sound a fool. "I only need a moment," he said. "It is about Miss Hale."

Her brown face softened in that mysterious smile that so enchanted him. "I was under the impression that she had embarked with her father for Spain."

"They went to Boston, and they should be departing within the week."

"You keep excellent track of her travels." But the teasing was by habit, carrying none of the gamine lilt that made conversation with Abigail such fun.

"Your sister Judith—didn't she say that Miss Deveaux told her that a young lady often carried messages on behalf of the conspirators? A woman of the upper classes, who seemed wise in the ways of Washington?"

"There are many such women in this city, Jonathan. Perhaps Miss Hale merely enjoys politics, as does everyone else in this dreadful place. You can hardly charge her with conspiracy merely because she has a brain."

"It is just that her departure seems convenient."

"Perhaps." She had finished buttoning her coat and was adjusting her scarf. "You are free to speculate as you please, Jonathan. I am afraid I have other matters on my mind. Good night."

V

Jonathan, as it happened, had a dinner engagement of his own. His uncle Brighton was in town, on business he coyly declined to specify. "Look at it this way," said Brighton as he tucked into his veal at the Willard. "You work for the lawyers. I work for the company. If I go sharing information with you, all kinds of conflicts might arise." Brighton was a voracious eater, and, as Margaret liked to say, a voracious dresser as well. He was always attired in the latest European fashions, and, in Jonathan's judgment, usually looked like the fool he never quite was. He had also somehow acquired spacious lands north of Boston and was building a manor house, at a time when Hilliman & Sons was struggling to stay afloat. "Don't you worry, boy," said Brighton. "Once you're ready to come back and take the reins, why, the books are yours to inspect."

"I am certainly looking forward to that," said Jonathan coldly.

Brighton asked after Margaret and certain other mutual acquaintances, and then, as he liked to put it, got down to the meat.

"I've been talking to your mother," he said. "And she agrees. We think this might just be the right moment for you to leave Washington City." He saw Jonathan's face. "No, no, don't worry. Nobody is thinking about bringing you into the company. Not just yet. No, boy. Your time would be your own. Europe. Now, that's a place. Paris. Berlin. Rome. Top up your culture, attend the lectures. Take a year. More if you like. The family would sponsor you, naturally."

Jonathan's voice was icier than ever. "That is very kind of you and Mother, Uncle, but, as you may have noticed, we are in the middle of trial."

"Yes, well, I wanted to talk to you about that, boy. The trial. This whole Lincoln business. There are rumors that he's done a deal with the bankers. If he'll agree to lower the tariff, they'll call off the dogs." Brighton chewed noisily. "You see what would happen, don't you? The tariff goes down, we have to cut our prices because of those British imports. Profits fall. The company might even go under." Hunching forward. "And even if we survived—well, you see the problem, don't you, boy? If Lincoln really has done a deal, and it becomes known that the Hilliman heir was part of it, the other companies might turn on us. You see how that could be, don't you?" Nodding as if in confirmation of his own thesis. He wiped greasy fingers on the soiled napkin at his neck. "Better if you're not part of it. Better to leave now."

"Good night, Uncle," said Jonathan, rising.

Brighton put a hand on his arm. The fun had died in his eyes. "If you decide to stay with Lincoln," he said, "I am not sure how much longer we can afford to protect you."

"I can protect myself."

Only after he had arrived back at the Bannerman manor and found, to his inestimable relief, that Fielding was at home, and had been home all evening, did it occur to Jonathan that the protection of which his uncle spoke might have nothing to do with business.

VI

She sat with Dan Sickles in his grand barouche at the entrance to the Center Market, which was shuttered for the night. The stalls were empty shadows. Today's buyers and sellers had trampled the day's snow into Washingmud. As recently as two weeks ago, sitting beside a man in the inky darkness—especially a man like Sickles—would have scandalized her, but by now these nocturnal peregrinations were as natural as breathing. Blaine was supposed to arrive at nine, so he was already late. Sickles was entertaining her with unlikely stories of his adventures: how his disobedience to orders would have won the Battle of Gettysburg that much sooner had the cannonball not taken off his leg for him, and how, on his trip to New Granada two years ago, he and his staff wound up in the middle of a pitched battle between two Indian tribes, who left off fighting each other because it was more interesting to join forces against the hideous white invaders in their midst. "I've never known such ferocity on the field. If they had fought the Spanish that way, no European would have dared set foot on this continent."

Abigail listened, half dozing in the cold, and pulled the two plush blankets he had provided more tightly around her shoulders. She reminded herself that this was work, and important; and that she had to stay awake.

He had just started on the history of the carriage in which they were sitting—a gift from his army, said Sickles, in gratitude for his leadership, meaning that, whatever propriety might demand, he could not insult his men by turning it down—when a second carriage drew up.

Sickles tensed. The rig was black, with fancy running lights, and pulled by a beautiful quartet of white horses.

"That isn't Blaine," he said, and reached for something out of sight.

From inside, two pale faces turned their way as the carriage kept going past them, vanishing into the fog until they heard only the clatter of hooves on frozen mud.

Abigail wondered sleepily whether it was the same coach she had spotted behind her the night she was out with Dinah Berryhill.

Now Sickles was detailing his crucial role in Lincoln's re-election victory in 1864. "I was one of the organizers of Democrats for Lincoln," he said. "You should have heard my speech at the Cooper Institute rally, just before Election Day. That was where I uttered my famous line that no man, not even the candidate, had the courage to stand on the Democratic platform. The crowd was huge. They were cheering wildly, of course—"

"Look," she said.

She had been watching the figure for some time now, a tall man approaching through the mist, on foot. He had been waiting inside the Center Market itself, a place where no gentleman of quality would ever be found. Crossing the muddy field, he kept pausing to peer into the night. He had a hand in his jacket pocket, and either was clutching a gun or wanted to be thought to be.

Then James Blaine was beside the carriage, looking every bit as stern and censorious as when Abigail had met him at the restaurant in the Willard Hotel.

"Did you bring it?" he said.

Sickles nodded.

"And you have brought Miss Canner."

"I have upheld my side of the bargain, Blaine." His voice was hostile. "Now suppose you uphold yours."

"May I see the letter?"

"See. Not keep." He drew a slim package from his jacket, still keeping his free hand between the seats. He had not offered to climb down; Blaine had not tried to climb up.

The congressman ran his fingers lightly over the envelope. "Speaker of the House," he said wonderingly.

Sickles was impatient. "You have your letter. Now, let's hear the story."

"They can't know we spoke."

"They won't."

Blaine glanced at Sickles, then looked over at Abigail. "I had an intriguing conversation, my dear Miss Canner. With an Inspector Varak. Your name was mentioned."

"The story," said Sickles, before Abigail could speak.

"This Varak seems to believe that his trail leads to high places. I wonder how long he will be permitted to continue." Abruptly, he handed the envelope back, unopened. "I have changed my mind," he said. Again he paused and squinted into the mist. "There is no conspiracy. There have been no bribes paid that I know of." He was watching Abigail, not Sickles, as he spoke, measuring the effect of his words. "Any allegations of a conspiracy are the fruit of Mr. Lincoln's desperate efforts to escape just punishment for his crimes."

Not waiting for any reply, Blaine backed away, then broke into a run, and was lost in the night fog.

CHAPTER 32

Motivation

I

LINCOLN HAD CONCEDED the facts of Counts One and Two, which covered the suspension of habeas corpus, the shuttering of a handful of newspapers, and the seizure of copies of all telegrams sent within the United States. In consequence, the Senate had decided to spend a single trial day allowing both sides to argue the significance of the President's actions. The Managers would argue Count One for an hour, followed by counsel for the respondent; then the same on Count Two. The great Thaddeus Stevens, sick as he was, would be presenting argument. Although her client's interests were opposed to his, Abigail looked forward to hearing him speak. She had a weakness for oratory, and hoped that the great man's words would be a tonic for the tiny waves of anxiety that rippled through her whenever she thought of last night's adventure, and saw poor James Blaine, who hoped to be Speaker of the House in a couple of years, running terrified into the night.

Shortly after Abigail reached the office, however, Dennard called her in and told her that she would once again miss most of the trial day—this time for a very different reason.

Sickles had discovered who Corbin Yardley was, and even where he was boarding during the trial. It was Abigail's task to try to obtain from Mr. Yardley a preview of his testimony.

"You understand why you're getting this assignment?" asked Dennard, wise old eyes probing. A file was open on his desk.

"Yes."

"Why?"

"Because he is a colored man."

"He is indeed." The lawyer waited for a response; heard none. "Mr. Sickles tells me that the gentleman is currently residing at the Metzerott Hotel."

Abigail, standing before the desk, shifted slightly. "I know the Metzerott."

Dennard nodded. "So I am given to understand." He closed the folder, and began tying the green ribbon with his arthritic fingers. But he had trouble, and she took over automatically. "I am well aware that a part of you feels underused, Miss Canner. You wish to be more involved in matters. So let me be clear. What I am asking is of enormous importance. We have to know what Yardley will say in order to prepare cross-examination." He was already turning away. "Please file that before you go."

II

Corbin Yardley was moon-faced and sad: on his shining dark countenance she could read all the woes of his life. He was about forty, a former slave who owned a feed business in Columbia, South Carolina. His broad shoulders sagged in a suit several sizes too small, and he was ready at every moment to share tales of how badly he had been treated. He rarely made eye contact. Mostly he watched his own hands as they lay, palm upmost, on the table, the long fingers wiggling and twitching. She had sent a note up from the Metzerott lobby. In response, his sister Constance had come clumping down the stairs to inform Abigail that her brother was willing to meet, but only with her along as chaperone.

And so they sat in the lounge and talked; or tried to.

"I don't know what you want of us," Constance kept saying. She was wide and stolid and entirely intimidating. "We're hardworking people trying to hold body and soul together. All we ask is to be left alone to earn a little bit of a living until the Lord in His wisdom decides to take us. That's all."

Abigail tried again, addressing herself to the brother. "What I would like to know, Mr. Yardley, is what you intend to say in your testimony."

"He'll tell the truth," snapped Constance, with an accusing glare.

"Yes, ma'am."

"Tell her, Corbin."

He addressed his hands. "Miss, ise gonna tell the truth. Nothin else."

Abigail consulted her notes. "I understand, Mr. Yardley, that your testimony will be in support of the proposition that the President has not done enough to protect the freedmen—"

"He hasn't," said Constance. "You wouldn't know. You're a Northern negro. You're pampered. Come look at the South. Come see how we live, and you'll understand why Lincoln has to go. Isn't that right?"

"Lincoln has to go," Corbin echoed.

Abigail's brief was to observe and report, nothing more. In particular, she was not supposed to argue or challenge, or in any way imply that she wished to change the witness's mind about his testimony. But the issue between them had become too large to ignore. And so Abigail, having the rhythm of the conversation at last, addressed herself entirely to the sister.

"Isn't Mr. Lincoln the reason you are free?"

Constance made a spitting sound. "The Union Army is the reason we're free." She was becoming seriously riled. "All the other colored folk down there—they all worship him. They call him Uncle Linkum. They name their babies Abraham. Why, my cousin just named hers Abrahamina. They don't see what's going on. We do." She had laid her very large hands on the table, and now she clenched them into very large fists. "We have big troubles in South Carolina, but you wouldn't know about that, would you? Or care. We've heard of you, Miss Canner. Every colored person in this town is talking about you. Did you know that? My brother can't read, but I can." Tossing the morning's newspaper onto the table. "There you are. Uncle Linkum is showing you off! Are you proud of yourself?"

Canner women were known throughout the Island for their tempers. Abigail's control at that moment was almost unnatural.

"I am working on Mr. Lincoln's behalf because I believe that he is in the right." Her voice was calm but firm. "I am sorry that you disagree. Still. I am not trying to change your minds. I am only asking what testimony your brother will be giving before the Senate."

"He will tell the truth." Constance Yardley flung the words. "He will tell the world how, thanks to Uncle Linkum, our feed business was almost destroyed. All we ask is to be left alone. But the troops who are protecting us are on their way home, and the men who once enslaved us are running for office. Come." Addressing her brother now, as she stood: "We've said all we have to say. Tell her."

"I'se got nothin more to say."

Little was waiting outside in the trap. Abigail was miserable. Not only was she missing the trial, but she had failed completely. Dennard had trusted her with a mission of great import, and she had been carried away by the need to defend herself: for Constance Yardley's cutting words had laid bare the confusion in her own soul.

And then she remembered. Big troubles in South Carolina, Constance had said.

"Mr. Little."

"Yes, miss?"

"Before we go to the Capitol, I need to stop home."

Perhaps the day was not a waste after all.

III

At the house on Tenth Street, she hurried up the stairs, ignoring Nanny Pork's demands to know why she was home in the middle of the day and what she called herself up to, making all that racket. She pulled the Chanticleer folders from their place in the closet. Then she bounded back down, kissed her aunt's wrinkled cheek, promised to explain later.

"But right now I have to go. It's important, Nanny."

"Then go, child."

As Mr. Little raced across the city, Abigail sat in the carriage studying the materials the mysterious Chanticleer had sent. She did not know who he was; but at last she understood why Mrs. McShane had made her keep the package.

She had been right; she had not failed; Dennard and Sickles would sing her praises.

Jonathan, too.

IV

Abigail slid into her seat beside Kate Sprague just as Speed was winding up his argument on habeas corpus.

"It is easy, I suppose, to forget the painful process through which that decision was reached." Speed had a thick, dark beard, not unlike his friend Lincoln's. His younger brother Joshua had once been Lincoln's law partner, but had declined the offer of a government position on the ground that Washington was a hopeless cesspool. Speed's fury as he spoke suggested that he believed the same. "How many now remember the clever rebel attack on the fort at Key West, where each soldier was brought out of the fort because a rebel judge issued a writ of habeas corpus? Then, having been brought out, he was set free by the judge, and in this way the fort was emptied of its soldiers. What should Mr. Lincoln have done? Allowed the rebellion to empty every Union fort in the South in this manner, or determine to resist, even if that resistance meant suspending the writ?"

Speed was making no effort to hide his growing fury. "And then, when the troops of the Union moved through Maryland to defend the capital of the country—this capital, gentlemen, where we now sit!—the railroad lines to Washington were severed by the secessionist traitors, and our troops—our good Union troops, volunteers all—were set upon by mobs. Many were killed. Naturally, the President ordered the arrests of those who engaged in violence, and those who incited it, but the rebel judges issued writs of habeas corpus and set them free to attack our troops once more. Gentlemen, the nation was under attack by rebels from within. Would you really have had Mr. Lincoln stand idly by? Should the right of habeas corpus be elevated to so transcendent a status that we must allow it to be used to destroy the country? No plausible reading of the Constitution requires the President to allow our forts to be taken and our troops assaulted while traitorous judges issue orders that encourage and even assist the rebellion."

A smattering of applause greeted these words, and Abigail, still catching her breath from the rush across the city, remembered how Dennard had said that the Managers never expected a conviction on either of the first two counts. They had been included in the resolution in order to excite the press, which would publish stories stressing not the necessity that drove Lincoln but the outrage at his policies. That the country would otherwise have been lost would be forgotten in that peculiar mist that drifts into the public mind once a war is over: people seem to remember the sacrifices they made more than they remember what the sacrifices were for.

"I notice that some of Mr. Lincoln's opponents seem happy with Mr. Speed's speech." Kate Sprague, reading her mind. "But wherever have you been, dear? I had about given up hope that you would be here today."

"I . . . I had business." Following Kate's bemused gaze, Abigail saw mud splattered along the hem of her dress. "I was splashed by the horsecars," she said, lying poorly. Actually, she had stepped in a puddle running out of the house, and decided not to take the time to change.

But perhaps Kate was not looking after all, because her mind was already back to its favorite subject: politics.

"Alas, I doubt that Mr. Speed has swayed any more votes today than he did yesterday," she said. "Do you have a count?"

Abigail, for an instant, did not even realize that her new friend was talking about the trial. "A count?"

"A head count. On the resolution."

The impeachment resolution, she meant. In her mind's eye, Abigail saw the blackboard, with its six undecided votes, of which the President needed four. "I am not sure where the count stands at the moment," she said, uneasily.

Kate chuckled. "You mean, your count is confidential."

"Yes," said Abigail, wondering why she had not just said that in the first place.

"Mine isn't. I am perfectly happy to share it with you."

The boldness of the offer made Abigail dizzy. Kate Chase Sprague possessed one of the sharpest political minds in the capital, to say nothing of contacts in every faction. There was nobody whose estimates would constitute more valuable political intelligence. And yet it was plain that she expected Abigail, in return, to divulge her side's own numbers.

Down below, Speed took a drink from his water glass. "Gentlemen," he said softly. "Some of you here present, sitting in judgment, endorsed the President's actions at that time. That is to your credit, and the nation owes you a debt of thanksgiving. There were others, however, who thought Mr. Lincoln's action unjustified, even illegal. And Mr. Lincoln, mindful of this criticism, submitted his orders suspending habeas corpus to the judgment of the Congress of the United States for ratification, lest there be any question of illegality. It is right there on pages twelve and thirteen of the *Senate Journal*, first session, Thirty-seventh Congress." A thoughtful nod. "And the Congress assented."

A hush. Kate tensed beside her.

"Now, once the President and the Congress agreed to the suspension of habeas corpus, everyone concedes that the suspension was legal. The only question, then, that the Second Article can raise is whether the suspension was legal before the Congress acted. The Constitution allows the suspension of habeas corpus in the case of rebellion. It is silent on who has the power to suspend it. Is it really the position of the House Managers that, when faced with a rebellion that began in April, the President should have waited to take action until Congress convened in July? Had he done nothing, this capital, and perhaps the entire war, would have been lost. Surely it cannot be an impeachable offense to do what is necessary to defend the capital when this Congress subsequently agreed to his act."

Speed sat. No applause.

Argument was over for today. Chase asked counsel for both parties to approach. They whispered about procedural matters as the gallery began to empty. Kate said, suddenly, "Your side is losing, Abigail."

"No evidence has been presented—"

"The evidence makes no difference. As matters stand today, the President will be convicted and removed."

"That is not our count!" Abigail cried, also rising.

"Then count again." Kate pointed to the emptying chamber, the Senators moving toward the exits almost languidly, as if the decision were already behind them. Abigail felt a chill. "As of this morning, the tally is forty for conviction, fourteen for acquittal." Again the easy confidence left no room for doubt. When Katherine Sprague spoke of politics, she spoke *ex cathedra*. "You need to pry five votes away from Mr. Wade's side. I am not sure there is time."

V

Abigail lay in the bathing tub at last. The opportunity presented itself rarely; on most nights, she was too tired or too busy, or the water supply was too weak, or the pipes themselves were too noisy. But tonight she was determined to have the treat.

Kate was counting Sumner. That much was obvious. Only if Sumner and the votes he controlled were cast against the President could the count reach forty for removal. Abigail and Sickles and Jonathan had spent an hour at the office discussing the count, long after Dennard and Speed had left for the day. It was obvious, said Jonathan, that Kate had the numbers from her father. If Chase was talking to Sumner about the trial—a gross breach of ethics—their case was in serious jeopardy.

Sickles was less certain.

Kate could be baiting you, he said. She trades in information. She might be giving you false numbers in the hope that you will disclose the true ones.

He said he would nose around.

Be careful around her, Sickles had said. Stay close—pay attention to every word out of her mouth—but be careful. She isn't your friend. She's her father's presidential campaign manager.

Now, in the tub, Abigail let her eyes drift closed. Numbers. Elections. Arguments. For Sickles, certainly for Dennard and Speed, perhaps even for Jonathan, the votes were numbers on a blackboard. Votes. The case was just a case. Win or lose, their lives would continue as they had before. But for Abigail, the numbers measured off years of her young life. It mattered what the Senators thought of what Lincoln had done, and she resented the way that public and press alike were forgetting.

She remembered the day in 1861 when her parents had put her on the train for Ohio. She had not wanted to go. She was fifteen years old, and, certainly, understood the way that the war everyone had expected to be so short was encroaching upon the capital. The Canners wanted their children out of the way of the Confederate onslaught expected any day. Louisa had already left for Boston. Michael, still in Baltimore, was resisting the plan to send him north. As for Judith, she was working as a nurse at the colored clinic in Washington City—Freedmen's, the negro hospital, had yet to be opened—and had already declared that she would stay until the end.

That was how she had put it, at dinner two nights before Abigail's departure: *the end.*

Judith at that time had been seeing a colored man who worked as an assistant to Charles B. Purvis, the most prominent black physician in the nation; but her beau, too, had fled.

Washington City was in a panic.

After the war began with the attack on Fort Sumter, the view in the city, among highborn and low, had been that the Union troops Lincoln had called for would soon arrive, and, when they did, they would invade Virginia, capture Richmond, and end the war within a month or two.

But the days dragged on, and there were no troops. The city was unprotected from the evil empire across the Potomac River. Stories filtered into the city. The Confederates were massing for an invasion. They had put together an army of twenty thousand men. Forty. A hundred thousand men at the other end of the Long Bridge, awaiting the command to invade. Meanwhile, the untrained Union soldiers trying to march across Maryland were being savaged by secessionist mobs. Others hoped to come to the capital by water, but the rebels had successfully blockaded the heights at the mouth of the Potomac, and would fire on any ship attempting to pass.

The panic grew. The city emptied. Everyone hated Lincoln in those days: the rebels and their supporters because of his determination to hold the Union together by force, the Northerners for what they saw as his incompetence and indecisiveness. He was not, in those days, the Father Abraham he would become. He was the unlettered Westerner, the poorly educated bumbler with the funny accent and the ridiculous stories, the worst possible man to have in the Mansion at a time of crisis. The general view was summed up by an unsigned letter to a loyal Republican newspaper—widely believed but never proved to be the work of Salmon P. Chase—that Lincoln would have made an excellent farmer, a fair mayor, and a poor governor.

That was the atmosphere in the city Abigail had left.

The city to which she returned on holiday a year and eight months later was a military encampment, troops in bright-blue uniforms drilling everywhere, the federal buildings garrisoned, and Lincoln the absolute master of Washington, cheered on every side.

Abigail had no idea how many of the Senators who held Lincoln's fate in their hands remembered the horrible certainty of defeat that had by itself all but conquered Washington City in the first year of the war; they seemed to begin their tale with Lincoln already triumphant. They criticized his decisions at a distance of six years, refusing to remember, or to imagine afresh, the helplessness of the city he was trying to defend.

Abigail climbed from the tub. Dressing for bed, she tried to understand the swirling complexities of her own passions. A part of her loved the Radicals for their purity, their brilliance, and their devotion to the progress of her people. This was the part that Constance Yardley, only this afternoon, had unwittingly stirred. Another part of her resented the Radicals for their self-satisfied cynical manipulation, and understood why some of those closest to Lincoln wanted them lined up and shot.

CHAPTER 33

Errand

I

"CHIEF JUSTICE AND Senators," said Benjamin Butler, "at this time, on behalf of the Managers, I would like to introduce into evidence certain documents." He nodded toward the defense table. "Counsel for the respondent has already been given a list."

Chase commanded the secretary to read the list, and told Dennard, who was already on his feet, to hold his objections until the list had been read. It was Thursday, March 21, the fourth afternoon of trial. The list of documents included various telegrams and official copies of presidential orders. None of that bothered the defense in the slightest. They had discussed this scenario for two nights running. Documents that were public or military records, they would not resist. All could be explained away, and, in any case, even if suppressed, would find their way into the newspapers. Only one category might cause trouble.

When the secretary had completed his recital, Dennard stood.

"Your Honor, on behalf of the respondent, we object to the introduction of correspondence to and from the President."

Butler spoke up. "Your Honor, we are introducing about fifteen letters to Mr. Lincoln from military authorities in the South, all complaining about the growing power of the former slave owners, who were reasserting themselves."

"To what purpose?" asked Chase, squinting at the papers on his desk. His glasses were very thick, because his eyesight was notoriously poor, although vanity often caused him to pretend otherwise.

"Your Honor, as we have made clear, Mr. Lincoln has done little to resist the growing threat as the aristocracy of onetime slave owners reconstitutes itself. He has vetoed or failed to implement congressional legislation intended to protect the freedmen and keep the slave holders from positions of authority. We are introducing the letters to show that the President was at all times aware of the threat."

"Mr. Dennard?"

In the gallery, Abigail experienced a moment of satisfaction. This research had been hers. She had spent three nights and part of a weekend immersing herself in the rules governing admission of documents. She had written a memorandum for Dennard: a memorandum he had evidently memorized, for now he was quoting, almost verbatim, what she had written. He would never acknowledge her in any way, she knew—that was not who he was—but she was proud all the same.

"Your Honor," said Dennard, "the letters to the President do not, in and of themselves, constitute proper evidence. If the Managers wish to introduce them, they must first lay a proper foundation. They must, through the testimony of live witnesses, demonstrate their provenance. They must, also through the testimony of live witnesses, demonstrate that they have not been altered. These principles are too well established to require citation. Until the Managers have laid a proper foundation, the evidence is inadmissible."

Down below, Chase was ruling the document inadmissible, delighting Abigail in both her professional and her political selves.

Senator Hickman, a leading Radical, was already on his feet. "I ask that the Senate be polled on the admissibility of the documents."

"The Senator will be in order," said Chase, rapping his gavel. "All motions must be in writing."

"The page is carrying my motion to the chair," said Hickman.

Under the rules the body had adopted, the only appeal from a ruling of the Chief Justice was to the Senate as a whole; moreover, only a Senator, not one of the lawyers, could request a vote.

"That is a very absurd request," said Abigail.

"Why?" asked Kate.

"Because he has no ground. It is perfectly clear that the letters are not admissible. They must bring the writers of the letters here to testify."

"No military man will testify against Mr. Lincoln."

"That is why the letters are not admissible."

Kate showed that prim, superior smile. "Do not," she said gently, "confuse law with politics."

Once more, Mrs. Sprague proved herself the superior judge of matters electoral: after a delay, the Senators voted, by a slim margin, to admit the documents.

"This is unjust," said Abigail, not for the first time. "They are not even required to give reasons!"

"The reason," said Kate, with finality, "is that they want to see the documents."

Her one solace was that Senator Sumner had voted against admitting the documents. This might mean that he remained undecided; but it might also mean that his legalistic side was asserting itself, for he would never waive a principle of law to satisfy an idle curiosity.

Butler was back at the evidence cart. The Chief Justice, who had spent the past few minutes scribbling notes, explained what he took to be the rule. "The Senate has voted to allow the Managers to introduce the documents in question. The matter of their provenance may be argued at a later time. It is not part of the vote." He nodded to Butler. "On that basis, the objection is overruled. Counsel, you may proceed."

"Your Honor," said Sickles, rising, "if I may be heard a moment."

Grumbling from the assembled Senators, and a few eyebrows elevated in surprise: was not Dennard arguing this point?

The Chief Justice was polishing his spectacles. "Be brief, Mr. Sickles."

"Your Honor, do I understand that the ruling only applies to whether the documents may be read into the record? Not to their authenticity?"

"Correct, counsel."

"So the fact of their admission is not to be construed as a judgment on whether they are accurate?"

"That is what I said, counsel. Mr. Butler, proceed."

Kate nodded briskly; and Abigail, too, saw the point. By drawing out his objection, Sickles had emphasized—not only for the record, but for the reporters present—that some question existed as to the genuineness of the letters.

Butler began to read into the record a letter from a military governor in Georgia to the President, complaining that he lacked adequate forces to put a stop to the raids of the night riders—

"Objection," said Sickles.

Chase's gaze was baleful. "On what ground?"

"Lack of foundation. We have no background—"

"Provenance may be argued later, counsel. I have already told you that. You may argue it as part of your case."

"Your Honor must realize that it is not possible for us to cross-examine a document."

Laughter from the gallery; but Chase hated affronts to his dignity.

"The objection has been overruled, Mr. Sickles. Take your seat." He turned as far toward the right as he could, giving the President's lawyers an excellent view of the soft, thinning hair on the back of his head. "Proceed, Mr. Butler."

"What is he doing?" Kate whispered. "He is deliberately antagonizing the Chief Justice," Kate persisted, continuing her habit, when under this majestic roof, of referring to her father only by his title.

"Perhaps not *deliberately*," Abigail suggested.

Kate swung toward her, surprised by the delicacy of this thrust. For an instant the sky-blue eyes blazed. Then her face softened. "I take your point," she said, and smiled generously—yet dangerously. "Lawyers, being men, are perhaps April when they begin the trial, and December when the verdict arrives."

Abigail recognized that she was being baited and tested once more, and although she knew she was not Mrs. Sprague's equal, she had to do her best. Fortunately, this time she recognized the quotation from *Cymbeline*. "And the vows of the witnesses," she said, "are our traitors."

Kate gave her a searching look but seemed not to find whatever she was seeking.

Abigail turned away, and, looking down, saw Sickles trying to catch her eye. She said, softly, "I must go," then rose and, lifting her skirts and determinedly ignoring the glares of the other ladies, headed for the exit.

She hurried down the stairs and out the door. She had a task to perform; a task that made her feel dirty, but had to be done.

II

Down below, meanwhile, Representative Butler, after conferring with his colleagues, had stepped once more to the evidence cart. A clerk handed him the file he sought.

"Mr. Chief Justice and Senators," Butler intoned, "on behalf of the Managers, I should like to introduce into evidence a letter from General C. C. Andrews, dated 1864, warning the President that numerous wealthy planters in the vicinity of Little Rock—"

Sickles was on his feet. "Mr. Chief Justice, we renew our objection."

Chase ignored him.

"—took the loyalty oath prescribed under the Amnesty Act and nevertheless continued to treat their slaves as property—"

This time, risking Chase's wrath, Sickles moved away from the counsel table. "Mr. Chief Justice, if I may. The rule against hearsay evidence is as solidly established as any in Anglo-American jurisprudence. If Mr. Butler wishes to introduce the advice the good general gave to the President, let him produce General Andrews, and—"

Chase's gavel cracked like a shotgun. "Mr. Sickles, you are out of order. First, I have previously ruled on your objection. The documents in question are *res gestae*. They are not being introduced to show the truth of the matter therein, but to establish that the President was warned and took no action. This the prosecution is free to do." He took off his spectacles, a sure sign of growing fury. "Do you understand me?"

"Yes, Your Honor."

"Good." Pointing with the gavel. "Now, go back to your place and be quiet. You'll have your chance, Mr. Sickles." He turned to Butler. "Sir, proceed."

"May it please the Court," Sickles continued.

Chase's eyes were heavy with menace. "What is it now, counsel?"

Sickles's tone was meek. He made no effort to meet the Chief Justice's glare. "May it please the Court, we would respectfully raise the question posed yesterday by the senior Senator from Illinois, and inquire of Mr. Butler how the prosecution came into possession of the President's private correspondence. If the letter is genuine, it would have been kept either within the Executive Mansion or at the War Department. To my knowledge, the letter has not been the subject of a subpoena."

A titter ran through the gallery. The Chief Justice was nearly apoplectic. He took a moment to compose himself, and spoke one word. "Sit."

Sickles sat.

Only to spring to his feet again three minutes later. Butler had read aloud a second letter from a military governor to the President, again alleging mistreatment of the former slaves by their former masters, and pleading for strong action.

Objection.

Overruled.

For the next hour, then hour and a half, Butler attempted to read the letters into the record, and Sickles objected. All the objections were overruled. True, through this strategy Sickles prevented the Managers from developing the rhythmic adducing of evidence so useful to making out a case. And Sickles was certainly within his rights under the rules to object separately to the introduction of each letter. Yet it was plain that the Chief Justice had grown heartily sick of him.

Very likely the Senators were, too.

Another letter.

"Your Honor, for the record, we renew our objection, on the ground of hearsay."

"For the record," thundered the Chief, not even glancing his way, "your objection is overruled."

"Your Honor, we would also point out that the prosecution has not put into the record the President's response to these letters."

Behind the thick glasses, Chase's eyes were haughty. "That is part of your case, counsel, not theirs. Wait your turn."

At the counsel table, Jonathan leaned toward Sickles. "It's a fix. Chase isn't even pretending to be unbiased."

Sickles covered his face. He seemed to be hiding a smile. "We're doing just fine," he said. "And our esteemed Chief Justice is correct. The letters are perfectly admissible."

"Then why are you objecting?"

"Because everything is moving too fast. Dennard and I sort of worked this up. They hate me anyway, so there is no particular loss."

"Too fast?"

Sickles nodded. "It is just three. I am trying to prevent the Managers from calling their first witness until tomorrow." He made a note on the page in front of him. "Is Miss Canner back yet?"

Jonathan turned in surprise, eyes raking the gallery. The seat beside Kate Sprague was empty. "I didn't realize she had left."

"She's running an errand for me."

"What kind of errand?"

Sickles winked. "I was not under the impression that she was your personal employee. I thought she worked for Dennard & McShane."

"Well, no, but—"

"I expect her back within the hour." Sickles picked up a pen. "Now pay attention to the proceedings, Hilliman, or the Chief Justice will be after you next."

The prosecution read more documents, Sickles made more objections, and Chase displayed less and less patience. Finally, he declared a recess.

"Fifteen minutes," he said. "Not a second more."

Jonathan looked up at the gallery. Abigail was back in her seat.

III

Jonathan adjourned to the conference room with the lawyers, aching inside at the thought that Abigail, as fully as he a member of the team, was trapped outside by the interlocking rules and traditions of the Capitol, and of the nation its solons governed. He marveled at the distance between the men who presided in this building, and the larger America beyond the boundaries of Washington City, and wondered whether, with the passage of time, that distance would grow greater or smaller. Then, with the discipline familiar to him, he forced these thoughts away and focused on the more practical problem of making sure that the cards marked with the various precedents Mr. Dennard might require were properly sorted and properly marked, so that Jonathan could put the needed card into the lawyer's plump hand without any need for him to ask.

Rellman was holding a package for Sickles, and Jonathan knew at once that it was what Abigail had been sent to obtain.

Then he looked again. It was the parcel sent by the mysterious Chanticleer, the one containing scraps of newspaper and the records of some investigation into the doings of South Carolina's railroads.

Jonathan was about to ask why on earth the papers were suddenly so important when a voice spoke beside him: "Excuse me."

Jonathan looked up to see one of the Senate pages, bending low to whisper. He was an Irishman of some years, prim and disapproving. "There is a young lady who wishes to see you. She is in the foyer." A judgmental pause. "I told her you were not to be interrupted, but she was quite adamant."

Jonathan rose, glancing around, but the other members of the team were busy at their notes. It was typical that Abigail would choose this moment to make her stand, to demand entrance precisely when embarrassment to the President and his counsel was likely to be highest: not because she wished Mr. Lincoln ill, but because her sense of justice possesed no patience. Now Jonathan would no doubt have to go and calm matters, and do it in such a way that the incident, whatever it was, would not redound to the detriment of the case.

The corridor, as usual, was busy. Jonathan turned right and approached the barrier, where a sleepy Capitol guard stood theoretical watch. He searched the throng in the foyer beyond but picked out no brown faces. Then he saw, standing near the chicane, Kate Sprague, talking to a stout woman whose hat hid her face. Even before the stranger looked up, Jonathan knew from the set of long neck and strong shoulders that this was a soldier's daughter; and he even knew which soldier.

"What are you doing here?" he cried, inevitably, hurrying forward.

Margaret Felix held both his hands in hers in a great show of gaiety. Even through the gloves he could feel the animal warmth that always so enticed him. She was winter-pale, the green eyes appraising, her prim face oddly distant, despite the intimacy of her touch. She was directly in front of him and yet out of reach, as though they stood on separate floes, passing close in icy waters even as the current carried them in opposite directions.

"I told Father I wanted to see the trial. He was unable to make the trip, but I came anyway. I am staying with Aunt Clara for at least a fortnight, possibly more." Touching his cheek. "Isn't it wonderful, darling? We can spend more time together."

"Wonderful," he echoed, smiling more weakly than either of them expected.

Margaret winked rather prettily and re-joined her rival. The two of them strolled across the foyer and into the crowd of the great and neargreat of Washington, all gathered to watch the most powerful President in the history of the young nation deposed from office by a wholly constitutional coup d'état.

IV

"So Meg is here," said Fielding, the two of them sitting before the fire with their usual brandies. "That makes things nice for you, doesn't it?"

It makes things even nicer for you, Jonathan almost said, thinking of Abigail, but he steered his thoughts away from those paths, reminding himself that he loved Margaret Felix, and would be marrying her in the fall.

"Very nice," said Jonathan, touching the glass to his lips.

"Tubby Longchamps tells me I should start attending the trial. He says the next few days are going to be rather good fun." Fielding freshened both glasses. "He says the Managers will be putting on some rather nice witnesses."

"Did he say who they are?"

"Only that their testimony will devastate your man. That was Tubby's very word. 'Devastate.'"

"We're ready for them." But he could not muster the confidence he needed.

"Glad to hear it, Hills. Oh, say. You'll never guess who dropped by today."

"Who?"

"That police fellow. The inspector. What's his name?"

"Varak."

"Right." Fielding stood up, walked across the Persian rug, prodded the fire with the poker. "Quite a clamorous little man, I must say."

"It was my understanding that the investigation is closed."

"He wasn't asking about McShane, old man. He was asking about you. If you're the trustworthy sort, tell the truth, keep confidences, all that." He straightened up, slashing the poker through the air like an épée. "I suppose he was asking if you are a gentleman."

Jonathan roused himself. "Did he say why he wanted to know?"

"I rather had the impression that he thought he had misjudged you. Owed you an apology and so forth." Fielding sounded more bored than ever. "He did mention some hogwash about matters being other than as they appeared."

"An apology," Jonathan repeated. "Did you ask why?"

"Goodness no, old man. No business of mine. I promised to convey the man's message, and he went on his way."

Later, Jonathan stood in the window of his bedroom on the fourth story. Streetlamps glowed softly in the gray night fog. So Varak wanted to apologize. For dismissing the conspiracy theories Jonathan and Abigail had presented? Or for closing his investigation, and leaving them to press on alone?

CHAPTER 34

Entrepreneur

I

"THE HOUSE MANAGERS will proceed with their evidence," said the Chief Justice, after the reading of the previous day's proceedings. It was Friday, the fifth official day of the trial, and the first witness was about to be called.

"The view is very fine from here," said Meg. Addressing Kate, she said, "I see that you can see your husband."

"And you your husband-to-be," said Mrs. Sprague.

There were three of them now, in the front row of the gallery—Abigail seated in the center with Kate Sprague on her left and Margaret Felix on her right. The Lion's daughter could hardly allow the Chief Justice's daughter to win this minor battle for the public perception: after all, the two fathers might well be rivals next year, or four years after, for the presidency. Today Abigail had remembered her fan, and found herself waving it in time to the movements of the other women, an entire row of feminine hands ticking like metronomes, even if hers was the only dark one.

Fielding Bannerman sat a couple of rows behind. Abigail had been astonished to see him, and he had greeted her with a little bow and explained that he was here to watch the fun.

The Managers, as expected, called Corbin Yardley. As far as the defense knew, he would be the sole colored witness at the trial. They also knew, in general terms, that he would support the claim of the prosecution that Lincoln was not protecting the freedmen as he should. Abigail's interview with him had obtained no more.

Butler led Yardley gently through his story. After freedom, Yardley had founded a feed business, he said. The business had grown, but the white folks were jealous. Eventually, the Ku Klux had burned his barn, and all his feed with it.

A chill passed through the room.

"What happened as a result of the fire?" asked Butler.

Yardley was a wiry man, too long in the arms and legs for his shiny black suit. His unhappy brown face was chipped and pitted, as if he had battled his way through a series of illnesses, to emerge wounded but whole. Abigail felt a warm surge of camaraderie, as if they had fought a war together, and she cringed at the thought of what was going to happen.

"Well, sir," he said, "my stocks of feed was pretty much destroyed."

"And your business?"

"Yes, sir. That was pretty much destroyed, too."

After the fire, said Yardley, he had visited the local sheriff, who had laughed him out of the room, and then the Freedmen's Bureau, which offered a few token supplies but no more. The bureau suggested he get himself a lawyer, but that would have done no good, because Yardley had no idea who the men were who had burned his barn, and the Klan, he told the Senators, don't exist. Not officially. And a jury, Abigail was thinking as her guilt and fury grew, would not in any case have made him whole, even in the unlikely event that a South Carolina court would allow his suit. She harbored no illusions about the strictures of the man's predicament. Corbin Yardley had placed his faith in the government, and for all that he knew, the sheriff, or the judge, or the foreman of the jury might have been one of the Kluxers who burned the barn.

"What did you do next?" asked Butler.

Yardley's voice dropped. He had been speaking softly from the beginning, perhaps out of awe at his surroundings, and now practically whispered. First Butler, then the Chief Justice had to tell him to speak up.

Well, finally—said Yardley—finally, he had gone to see the military governor of South Carolina. Like all the military governors, the man was a Lincoln appointee, confirmed by the Senate.

"When did you see the governor?" asked Butler.

"Sir, it was early September. I remember because it was the day we had that terrible hurricane. People said it was the judgment of God on the South."

He told the governor his story, said Yardley, and waited for some word of hope or encouragement. Instead, said Yardley, the governor had spent a lot of time beating around the bush, and had finally said that he would have somebody look into it, but that Yardley should not expect too much.

Why not? the freedman had asked.

Because—said Yardley—Mr. Lincoln had ordered—

Dennard was on his feet, objecting. "This is hearsay. This is in fact hearsay twice over. The witness is testifying to what another individual said that respondent said."

Chase looked at Butler.

"Your Honor, it is the theory of the Managers that respondent created within the military governments a general sense that the complaints of the freedmen were less important than good relations with white Southerners. We are not introducing this testimony to show what orders Mr. Lincoln may actually have given but to show the general sentiment that he created."

Abigail had not yet studied the hearsay rule, but she could spot an absurdity when she heard one. To her astonishment, Chase announced that the testimony would be admissible. Beside her, Kate put a hand over her face and whispered what sounded like "Oh, Father." Abigail hesitated, then touched her new friend's hand. Kate stiffened, looked at her, then smiled slowly; and sadly. And because the only things that ever saddened Kate Sprague were those that made her father's ascension to the presidency less likely, Abigail assumed that Chase had made not a legal blunder but a political one.

Meg, watching the byplay, did not want to be left out. "I am sure the Chief Justice will not be overruled," she murmured, missing the point.

The fans kept fluttering.

Down below, meanwhile, a Lincoln supporter in the Senate had asked that the chamber be polled on the admissibility of the testimony. A recess was demanded in order that the members might retire to their conference room.

"You are very sweet," said Kate, giving the black woman's fingers a brief squeeze. "I can understand why"—a sly glance at Meg—"so many men adore you."

"Oh?" said Meg, pretending nonchalance. "Which men are those?"

Kate was having fun. She hooked a thumb over her shoulder. "Young Mr. Bannerman, for one," she said, to Abigail's chagrin. The three women turned as one, but Fielding was in the aisle, chatting amiably with a sour-looking fellow whom he addressed as Tubby.

"Are there others?" asked Meg.

"Her fiancé is at the South," said Kate, answering, as was her habit, a slightly different question. "And our Abigail, in the midst of so many admirers, remains true to him. I find that terribly romantic. Don't you?"

Abigail had not told Mrs. Sprague anything about Aaron.

"Terribly," said Meg.

"He must be a remarkable man," said Kate.

Abigail said nothing. At this very moment, if he was alive, her remarkable Aaron was suffering in some dank Southern prison, if he had not actually been returned to slavery, a fate that the rebels had decreed randomly, not even according to their own laws but according instead to the need for labor. There were moments when she was nearly able to let go of the image, to accept what everyone told her. Whether sternly, like Nanny, or gently, like Dinah, everyone told Abigail that her husband-to-be was dead. She shivered. The temptation was strong. But then she would imagine him fully, the confidence of his smile, the warmth of his strong arms and thick body, the delight she felt in being near him, in stretching and squirming against him in ways most unladylike, the aching physical need for him to hold her once more, even if it was the final clasp before death. Judith used to tease her relentlessly—*He is going to war, you need to let him do what men do!*—but Abigail, although it frustrated both her and her beau, had remained true to her mother's teachings. Another time, Judith, smiling maliciously, had told Abigail that their mother, had she lived, would have advised her to yield, in order to ensure the marriage, but that was not true. Hortense Canner had craved not marriage as such but the family's upward progress. She would have counseled Abigail to give in only to a man of a higher class, and lighter hue, and Aaron was neither.

Her mother, Abigail realized with a start, would even have preferred a white man to Aaron; and a rich white man would have been better still.

"She had better remain true to her fiancé," Margaret was saying. "Because rather horrible things can happen to people who don't."

11

The Senators decided to hear the testimony, and Corbin Yardley finished his story. He had visited the military governor, and been turned away empty-handed. The governor had told him that there was nothing to be done. The President—according to the governor—wanted the Union troops to interfere as little as possible. He thought it was time that the South took charge of its own destiny.

"Repeat that, please," said Butler.

Yardley's voice grew reedier than ever. "Sir, he said the President thought it was time the South took charge of its own destiny."

"And by the President, you took him to mean Mr. Lincoln?"

Dennard objected, but Yardley had already answered—"Yes, sir"—and Chase merely shook his head.

"Did the governor say anything else about Mr. Lincoln?"

"Sir, he said that Mr. Lincoln wanted South Carolina to send folks to Congress as soon as possible."

Angry mutters throughout the Senate Chamber. Hearsay or not, the testimony suggested that the President proposed to trespass on the Congress's own sacred right to decide whether to seat new members.

"How would that be possible," asked Butler, "given that South Carolina remains under martial law?"

Chase sustained Dennard's objection: the matter was outside the competence of the witness.

Butler, having made his point, moved on. "Did you ever get full recompense for your feed business?"

"No, sir."

"Were any of the men who burned your barn ever identified?"

"No, sir."

Butler put a hand on the rail. "Mr. Yardley, you served in the Union Army, did you not?"

"Yes, sir. Second Colored Light Artillery."

"Did see action?"

"Sir, I was at Fort Pillow."

Butler let the dread name hang in the air: the infamous massacre of colored troops by Confederates under the command of Nathan Bedford Forrest, who later led the Ku Klux.

"On behalf of the Congress of the United States," Butler said at last, "may I offer you the apologies of this nation, and the assurance that those who did these terrible things will receive their just punishment, whether now or in the world to come."

With that, he tendered the witness.

"Another difficult day for Mr. Lincoln," murmured Margaret Felix, scarcely able to conceal her delight.

"I think not," said Kate, before Abigail could speak.

"Oh?"

"They have something. I can see it in her face."

Both women were staring at Abigail, who knew that she should feel a sense of triumph: what was about to happen to Corbin Yardley was largely her doing.

Instead, she felt only the empty, painful throb of guilt.

III

"Cross-examination," said Chase.

Dennard was a moment rising. He seemed to struggle. From behind the effect was comic, as though his bulk was too weighty for his legs. But his face, Abigail knew, would be thundery, and from the point of view of the witness, Dennard would appear a broad and powerful avenger. She understood this effect in part because her late father had used a version of the same trick when scolding his children, but mostly because Dennard, at his most pedantic, had explained his methods to her, proposing that she file the knowledge away until, in his words, she grew fat enough to use it.

"Good afternoon, Mr. Yardley," said Dennard.

"Good afternoon, sir," said the witness, warily.

"I want to thank you for coming all this way to share your testimony with us today." Yet his tone was anything but kindly. "And I would like to congratulate you on your freedom."

"Thank you, sir."

"That my country admitted and sustained the wicked institution of slavery is a blot on our history, and always will be. The bloody war we fought to extinguish the institution was our just punishment for our sin." He hitched up his pants, as if to say that the trial, sadly, nevertheless had to proceed. "Now, sir. You live where?"

"South Carolina, sir. Columbia."

"And you were previously enslaved nearby?"

"Yes, sir. Out in Lexington County."

"You were a slave until when?"

"Until the Proclamation, sir. Until about 1863."

Dennard's large head moved, as if to suggest surprise, but really to draw attention. "You were freed by the President's Emancipation Proclamation?"

"Yes, sir."

"And are you grateful to Mr. Lincoln?"

Butler was on his feet, objecting. An argument before the bench. Butler was livid. And loud. This was not relevant. Whether the man was grateful was of no moment. The trial was about what Lincoln did, not how people felt. Dennard's voice in response was pitched in his usual tones of low reasonableness, and Abigail could hardly hear.

Chase motioned for them to step back.

"The witness's feelings about respondent are not relevant. Counsel will confine himself to what the witness saw and heard. Continue."

Dennard smiled at the witness, his bulk making him seem clownish. Abigail trembled. She knew what was coming. The next few minutes were going to be bloody.

"So, Mr. Yardley," said Dennard. "You are now a free man. And, in freedom, you have been successful, I believe. You run a fair-sized feed business."

"Yes, sir."

"And you also have a political career, so I am given to understand. Is that true?"

"Yes, sir."

"Well. That is a great deal to accomplish in just four years. You are to be congratulated."

"Thank you, sir. I'm grateful, sir."

Dennard took a stroll back to the table. "Now, Mr. Yardley, you testified earlier that when the Ku Klux burned your warehouse, you went to the governor, and he wasn't any help."

"Yes, sir."

"The governor appointed by Mr. Lincoln."

"Yes, sir."

"If we brought the governor here to testify, would he support your account?"

The black man's gaze darted. "Sir, I believe he is a diplomat in Argentina or one of those places."

"Would he support your account, Mr. Yardley?"

"Sir, the governor told me that he would deny it ever happened."

Dennard let this remark, a useful one for the defense, linger in the room: just right. Then: "So, you met the governor where? At his office?"

"Yes, sir."

"And the governor said he was unable to be helpful because Mr. Lincoln thought it was time the Southerners took charge of their own destiny again."

No hesitation. "Yes, sir."

Dennard stood for a moment, staring. The tension froze Abigail in place. Kate noticed, and looked at her curiously, but said nothing.

"This was last September."

"Yes, sir."

Dennard put out a hand. Jonathan had the document ready. For a mad instant, Abigail hated him, even though it was she who had provided the knife.

"You are aware, Mr. Yardley, that your name does not appear anywhere on the governor's schedule."

"Yes, sir." He had plainly gone over this during preparation by the Managers. "We met after hours."

"You testified that it was the day of the hurricane, or maybe the day after. That's how you remember that it was September."

"Yes, sir."

Dennard opened the document before him. "Mr. Yardley, I hold in my hand two pages from the register of Burgess's, a colored hotel in Atlanta." He dropped it on the table with a snap that startled the whole chamber. "The hurricane was on September 7 and 8 of last year. According to the register, you were at Burgess's from September 6 through September 10 of last year."

Pandemonium in the chamber. Butler was on his feet again, furious. The provenance of the document had not been established—

Chase pounded the gavel. "Counsel will ask no further questions regarding this document," he intoned. "Not unless he is prepared to introduce testimony first as to its authenticity."

"We are so prepared, your honor," proclaimed Dennard, although in actual fact the owners of Burgess's had refused to come to Washington at all, once they learned that they would be called upon to testify against a man of what they called their own nation.

Butler sneered. "Let him bring the witnesses."

Chase adjusted his glasses. "Unless you produce the witnesses, Mr. Dennard, it is my inclination to set aside this testimony."

Dennard said, "I have no further questions on the matter."

"One moment," said Butler. "If I could please clarify. Is counsel saying that he has no more questions for the witness about the meeting with the governor, or that he has no more questions about the register? It is the position of the Managers"—thinking fast now—"that any further questions about the meeting will be designed to lead the Senators to contemplation of the register, and Your Honor has just excluded any further—"

Chase waved him silent. "Mr. Dennard?"

"Sir, I have no further questions about the meeting with the governor. I have further questions of the witness."

The Chief Justice told him to continue.

"Now, Mr. Yardley. You are one of the more prominent colored men in Columbia, are you not?"

"I don't know, sir. I wouldn't say that, sir."

"Still, for the past year you have sat on the city council in Columbia, is that correct?"

"Yes, sir."

"As a matter of fact, I do not believe any colored man before you has ever been elected to the council." Information gleaned from the newspaper articles stuffed in the package.

"No, sir. I mean, yes, sir. That is right, sir."

"So, you run a feed business in Columbia. You sit on the council. And you are also, I believe, a deacon of Reverend Johnson's church."

"Yes, sir."

"You are a man of influence. There are people who listen to what you have to say?"

"I suppose so, sir."

"Now, one of the big disputes in Columbia lately involves the Augusta Railroad and the South Carolina Railroad, isn't that so?"

Chase looked automatically toward Butler, who seemed about to object, but sank into his seat once more. By now even the Managers had guessed where the cross was headed.

"Yes, sir."

"Would you be so kind as to explain the dispute to the chamber."

Yardley scrunched up his face. "Well, sir, it's like this. The Augusta Railroad, they needs to connect to the Charlotte Railroad, but the

South Carolina Railroad tracks is in the way. So the Augusta Railroad wants to cross the South Carolina Railroad tracks, and the South Carolina Railroad says no. Matter of fact, some days the South Carolina just drives an engine right up to where the Augusta Railroad needs to cross and blocks the tracks so's they can't build nothing."

"And is the city council involved in the dispute at all?"

"Sir, it's in the court. White mens always suing other white mens."

Laughter in the chamber.

"Indeed." Dennard's smile was sympathetic. "Nevertheless, it is a fact, is it not, that there is a good deal of support in town for the Augusta Railroad? The Augusta Railroad employs many local people, isn't that so?"

"Yes, sir. They's real popular in Columbia."

"And the completion of the line all the way to Charlotte and back down into Georgia will be of benefit to Columbia, will it not?"

"Yes, sir."

"So the city council ought to be in favor of the new line." A statement.

For the first time, Yardley hesitated. "Sir, it's in the court."

"Isn't it a fact that, just five months ago, in October of 1866, the city council proposed to vote in favor of the new line?"

The black man seemed increasingly uncertain of his ground. He even glanced toward the Managers. "We didn't take no vote," he said finally.

"But there was a proposal to take a vote, was there not?"

"Not that I recalls."

"We have the minutes of the meeting," said Dennard. Again Jonathan rushed the papers into his palm. "There was a proposal to put the council on record in favor of the line, and several members of the council objected. No vote was taken." A pause. "You were among those who objected, were you not, Mr. Yardley?"

"Might have been. I can't say that I recollect clearly."

"You can't," said Dennard, in the tone of a disappointed schoolmaster. "Now, Mr. Yardley, you told us earlier that the Ku Klux burned your barn."

"Yes, sir."

"Has the barn been rebuilt?"

"Yes, sir."

"And when was the work begun?"

"In November."

"So, in September, you complained to the governor that the Ku Klux had burned your barn. In November, you had the money to rebuild. Was the barn insured?"

"No, sir."

"Then where did the money come from?"

Silence.

"I don't recollect."

"Let me understand, Councilman. You remember that the barn was burned by the Ku Klux. You remember to the day when the governor turned down your request for help. You remember that the governor told you that Mr. Lincoln had ordered him to cooperate with the white Southerners. You remember that conversation word for word. You remember that the barn was not insured. You run a successful business and you are a member of the city council. And yet you are telling this chamber that you do not know where the money came from to rebuild your own barn, completed just two months ago?"

Abigail could take no more. Drowning in guilt and confusion, she leaped to her feet and hurried up the aisle. The ladies of Washington exchanged knowing smiles. Poor thing, she imagined them thinking, she couldn't hold it any longer. Because of course she could not use the facilities here at the Capitol of her country. Any calls of nature would require her to walk, or run, four blocks to the nearest colored hotel, over on D Street. In truth, Abigail simply could not bear her complicity in the destruction of another human being: a person of her own color particularly.

She was in the Rotunda now, fists clenched as she marched back and forth under the wary eyes of guards who by now knew who she was and how much trouble she could cause them and liked her the less for it. She imagined the scene as it would unfold. Dennard had Yardley in a corner. He would squirm and lie and squirm some more, and the Managers would come up with one objection after another, but in the end, the truth would come out.

Poor Yardley had taken a bribe.

That was why he had been in Atlanta. He had gone to another state for safety's sake, and there had met officials of the South Carolina Railroad, and they had paid him to vote their way. They had paid white men, too—it was those very white members of the council who had told them Yardley could be bought—but it was the black man who would be forced to confess before all the world's press. Abigail harbored the secret theory that the Ku Klux had burned the barn to begin with on the rail-road's orders, first to intimidate Corbin Yardley and then, if necessary, to provide the means to bribe him. But he had taken the bribe neverthe-less, and had even boasted of it to friends. Chanticleer's notes quoted his words: "I've been sold four or five times in my life, sir. This is the first time I ever got the money."

Whoever Chanticleer was.

Before they left for Capitol Hill this morning, Dan Sickles had taken Abigail aside to applaud her magnificent work—meaning, her work of providing the means to destroy Corbin Yardley on the witness stand. Sensing her unease, Sickles had reminded her that the job of a lawyer was to do everything possible to defend the client. If she were to scruple at the truthful cross-examination of an untruthful witness, he said, her career would be short. Then he smiled and told her not to worry. It would be a great day for the defense, he said; and it was. But it seemed to Abigail that it was a wretched day for the race, and, at the moment, that mattered a lot more.

"Are you unwell?" said Fielding from behind. "Shall I drive you home?"

IV

She wiped away a tear. She had no idea that he had followed; or how long he had been observing her distress. "Thank you. I am quite well."

He tilted his head toward the massive, guarded doors to the Senate Chamber. "Is it like that every day? All that shouting and silliness and so forth?"

"I am afraid so."

"Then it is no place for a lady; or a gentleman." A laugh, not entirely self-deprecating. "I do not think I will be putting myself through that again. Say." Eyes aglow. "We should attend the theater again soon."

"The trial keeps me rather busy."

"I shall keep every night free for you," he said, and bowed.

As Fielding crossed the Rotunda, heading for the west lawn, Abigail felt watched. Swinging around, she saw Constance Yardley, the witness's sister, standing at the foot of the steps to the public gallery. In her eyes was the planation field hand's undiluted hatred of the house servant who treated her no better than the whites did.

CHAPTER 35

Interruption

I

AFTER COURT, THE lawyers went to the Mansion. Once more, they took Jonathan along; once more, they left Abigail to return, alone, to the office. She had hoped to join them in the corridor outside the conference room; when she reached the barrier, the guard told her where they had gone.

Annoyed, Abigail made her way out front, joining the line of those waiting for their carriages. A light snow had started to fall: almost certainly the last of the season. The rest of the afternoon had been occupied by battles over other documents the Managers wanted on the record, most of them letters telling tales similar to Yardley's. Chase had allowed some, disallowed others, marking the division according to no evidentiary theory that Abigail understood. She assumed that the constant stream of objections from the President's lawyers represented a holding action, that they wanted to make it to adjournment before any more testimony was admitted. That, in turn, meant that they were worried about what was coming tomorrow, and needed to consult their client.

Without Abigail, who seemed fated to remain a merely public face.

The line shuffled forward. Abigail tilted her head back, wanting the gently chilling prickle on her cheeks. As a child, she had believed that snowflakes on her face meant happiness. She shut her eyes and wished for a snickerdoodle. When she opened them again, Kate Sprague was standing beside her, a slight smile on her slim face. Now that Abigail thought back, she realized that Kate had been with her the whole time, not only in the carriage line, but earlier: Mrs. Sprague had even witnessed her humiliation when the guard told her everyone else had gone to the White House.

"Come to dinner," said Kate.

"It would be my pleasure to fix a date," stuttered Abigail, very surprised.

"I meant tonight."

Abigail had trouble taking in the words. Perhaps the snow was making her stupid. Or guilt over today's events. She stared at the woman beside her. She had taken both the invitation and her response as rote recitations, simply the way ladies behaved. "I . . . tonight?"

"Father is dining with Justice Clifford. My husband has a caucus. So it will be just the two of us."

"I . . . um . . ."

"I promise, we shall not speak of the trial." Kate, smiling, touched her arm with a gloved hand. "Well, not unless *you* bring it up."

Abigail said what had to be said: "Mrs. Sprague—"

"Kate."

"Kate. Please. There is no need to . . . to risk the opinion of others in order, uh, in order to prove . . . to prove to me . . ."

"I am inviting you for one reason, Abigail. Because I enjoy the company of intelligent, educated, fascinating people. Women in particular." She raised a slender hand to quell further objection. "As for the opinion of others, that has never concerned me before. I see no reason to allow it to deter me now. Shall we say eight?"

II

The dining room was too large for the two of them. The heavy, dark table was too long, the curtains were too red, the chinaware was too expensive, and the food was too plain. Given more time, Abigail was sure she could invent more reasons to explain the nervous flutter in her stomach as she sat alone with the most influential hostess in Washington, making social talk.

Casual conversation had never been among Abigail's talents—she did what she could to avoid situations in which she might be called upon to offer it—but Kate Sprague was sufficiently skillful that the conversation never flagged, and, indeed, became enjoyable. Despite her domination of the Washington social scene, Kate was only a few years older than Abigail herself; and told wonderful stories. She had a funny tale about a young woman whom Abigail had known at Oberlin and Kate had known at Miss Haines' School in New York; and another about one of Abigail's most terrifying professors, who turned out to have been a down-on-his-luck friend of the Chase family in their Cincinnati days.

Then, when Abigail was at her ease, Kate murmured, "Father has asked about you."

The black woman, raising her goblet, felt her hand freeze halfway to her mouth. She managed, with difficulty, to finish the sip.

"Has he?"

Kate laughed gently. "You needn't make that face. There is no impropriety. Simply, when this unpleasantness is over, he believes he can help you to find a more suitable place." Before the astonished Abigail could quite take this in, Kate had more: "If you seriously mean to be a lawyer, you should have the best tuition. Father would take you on himself. So would Senator Sumner." She leaned forward, blue eyes sparkling with mischief. "I believe that the two of them see you as a prize over which they might compete. There are, after all, only half a dozen colored lawyers practicing in American courts, and no women."

"I believe that Mrs. Bradwell out in Illinois means to sit for the bar next year," said Abigail, secretly hoping to impress.

But Kate was never topped. "Her husband is probate judge of Cook County," she said, stirring her soup. "He handed down the opinion holding that children born to slaves who are married to each other can inherit the property that their parents acquire once emancipated."

"I had not imagined that anyone would doubt it."

"I am afraid that, where the colored race is concerned, someone doubts nearly everything." She looked up, smiled. "I beg your pardon. I fear that I am now doing it."

"Doing what?" asked Abigail, tearing a dainty piece from the crusty roll, hoping she had the etiquette right.

"Telling you what it's like to be you. What those women did at the Eameses'. Forgive me?"

"There is nothing to forgive." She touched the water goblet to her lips. "Mrs. Sprague—"

"Kate. I keep telling you, Abigail. To my friends, I am Kate. Only Kate."

"Yes. Sorry. Kate." Still unaccustomed to addressing by Christian name one of the most prominent women in America. "May I have a turn now, and ask you a question?"

An amiable smile. "Please."

And Abigail, in turn, tried to put as much warmth as possible into her words. "You are a friend of Miss Lucy Hale. Known as Bessie."

The smile began to fade. "We are acquainted, as you know."

"Do you know why she has left the country?"

"Her father is minister to Spain."

"Yes." Another careful sip. A servant materialized and filled her glass, then vanished again. "But her departure was rather . . . precipitous."

"Was it?" Kate frowned. "I suppose it was. I understand that she canceled two dinner invitations she had already accepted. That is not done."

Abigail sensed the uneasiness her questions were provoking. She had to act delicately. Whatever Mrs. Sprague was concealing, she would surely divulge only to a friend.

"No," Abigail agreed. "That was quite rude of her." She hesitated. "Was Miss Hale often rude?"

"I am not sure what you mean."

Gambling. "It is my understanding that one of the dinners she canceled was with Mr. Grafton and his lovely wife."

Kate laughed nervously. "Oh, but that means nothing. Her family and Mr. Grafton's are very close. She saw them on many occasions. Missing one would make little difference." A glance at the door, as if to ascertain how closely the servants were listening on the other side. "To be sure, Mr. Grafton lives mostly in Philadelphia. His wife rarely joins him at Washington." She made a show of dabbing her lips with her napkin. "Mr. Grafton usually stays at Brown's Hotel. Bessie stays at the National. The two hotels are right across the street from each other. That is rather convenient, don't you think?"

So that was it. Kate had confirmed their theory without realizing it. It was indeed Bessie Hale who was in regular contact with David Grafton, the man at the heart of the conspiracy that she and Jonathan had come to believe in but were unable to prove. And what better way to conceal the true nature of their relationship than by pretending that they had another reason entirely to sneak about? A reason entirely consistent with the reputation Bessie had so assiduously cultivated?

"That is very interesting indeed," Abigail said. "Do you happen to know when Miss Hale will be returning to America?"

"It is my impression that Bessie plans an extended European tour."

"Extended?"

The two women locked eyes. The ticking of the grandfather clock was all at once the loudest sound in the world. "Indefinite," said Kate.

They understood each other: Katherine Sprague knew. Perhaps she had known for a very long time. Whatever Bessie's secrets, they had not been secrets from Kate. Abigail wondered, with a chill, whether there was anything of which this brilliant woman was unaware.

Kate's smile once more grew mischievous. "And now, dear, you must tell me what you think of Miss Margaret Felix."

Abigail put her glass down so hard she had to look to be sure she hadn't broken it. "I beg your pardon."

"Miss Felix. The young lady sitting on your right all day."

"Yes, yes, I know who she is—"

"So, then, what do you think of her?" Chewing thoughtfully. "You must have an opinion."

"She seems very . . . intelligent." Abigail felt cornered. "And very . . . lovely."

"Faint praise indeed," mused Kate. "I suppose I should not be surprised. She is, after all, your rival."

"She is in no sense my rival—" Abigail began hotly, but she got no further, because the door swung open, hard, and the butler hurried in to whisper in his mistress's ear; and Kate in turn went if anything paler still.

Kate Sprague rose shakily to her feet. "Something has happened," she said.

III

"This is a disaster," said James Speed, once more stating the obvious. "A disaster."

Dennard had his head in his hands. "By some mysterious magic," he said, "the blame for this outrage will indeed fall on the head of our client."

But Dan Sickles, the third lawyer in the common room, was serene. "I wouldn't call it magic," he said. "It's politics. In politics, whenever something bad happens—violent death most of all—the first thing you do is figure out how to blame your opponents. You don't need any facts. You just need friends." A wink at Abigail. "Reporters, say. Editors. That kind of friends."

It was Saturday morning, March 23, and Representative James Blaine was dead. Sliced up, just like Lincoln's lawyer. Unlike Arthur McShane, the congressman did not die in the company of a colored woman, but he did die near a brothel—in Hooker's Division, as a matter of fact—and the newspapers had already found two slants on the story, each rather clever. The pro-Lincoln press gave the tale plenty of space, making the point, often explicitly, that it was not Lincoln's supporters alone who were unusually decadent; it was the entire class of men who went to Washington City to run the country. The anti-Lincoln papers, on the other hand, had to tread more carefully, telling their side mainly by implication: Congressman James Blaine, longtime Lincoln supporter, changes his mind and, as a matter of principle, votes with the Radicals for impeachment. Weeks later, in the midst of trial, Blaine is murdered. The message to those wavering in their support for Lincoln could hardly be clearer.

Said his enemies.

"No matter whom we blame," said Dennard, "the sensationalism of the event will redound to the benefit of the prosecution."

"But there are arguments both ways," said Jonathan. He glanced uneasily at Abigail, who had been sitting silently all morning. Usually, she would be energetic, alive, full of probing questions, or wonderful advice for which others took the credit. Today she remained hunched into herself, as if guilt was eating at her from the inside. Her eyes were red, and he wondered whether she had been weeping; and why.

"True enough," said Sickles. Jonathan noticed that his eyes, too, kept straying toward the silent Abigail. "But when one side has a single public face and the other doesn't, it's the one with the public face that suffers more."

"Fine," said Speed, on his feet and striding. "Now, what are we going to do about it?"

"Nothing," said Dennard.

The former attorney general stopped. Spun. "I beg your pardon?"

"We do nothing. Our legal strategy remains the same. Neither the quality of the evidence nor the nature of our arguments will change."

"I agree," said Sickles, from the divan. "Why, I'll bet the trial doesn't even get postponed. Well, maybe one day for the funeral, but that'll be it."

"But a man is dead!" said Speed.

Sickles spoke crisply. "A man whose vote they no longer need. If he were a Senator, they would postpone for weeks if necessary, so that a replacement might be found to vote against Mr. Lincoln. But for a mere congressman? Not a chance." He subsided again. "The President has sent his condolences to the widow. Both Houses will adopt resolutions. And that will be the end of the matter."

Dennard nodded. "There is work to do, preparing for next week." His drawl was more pronounced than usual. He had known Blaine well. "Hilliman. You will come with Sickles and myself to see the President. Speed and Rellman will be on Capitol Hill, trying to work out a deal on these documents. Miss Canner . . ."

"I will hold the fort," she said, and even managed a smile, but Jonathan could tell that the mask was barely able to contain more painful emotions.

Sickles surprised them all. "I have work to do here," he said. To Dennard: "Tell the President, please, that I will be along shortly. He will understand."

IV

"The blame does not rest on you," said Sickles as she stomped around the common room hunting for something to break. "Put the responsibility on my shoulders if you like. I was the one who decided to approach Blaine. I was the one who kept pushing. If they were afraid that he might talk—afraid enough to kill a congressman—then I am the one who created the fear. Not you."

Abigail looked at him, resplendent, on a chair this morning rather than the settee, exuding confidence from every pore: a man who was never defeated. A man who took a perverse pride in having been the indirect cause of another man's death.

"Make your conscience free," she said, sourly. "I am not blaming you, Mr. Sickles."

"Do not blame yourself, either."

"And how should I not? The congressman would have disclosed the identity of the hand behind the conspiracy, but for whatever Inspector Varak told him about me."

"Actually, I think it was his fear of what his fellow conspirators might do to him that made up his mind. Turns out he was right to be afraid." Although the words were chilling, Sickles yawned. "But you're right that Blaine could have helped us a lot. Most of these fellow up on the Hill—

Wade, all that crowd—they don't need a conspiracy to make them hate Lincoln. Blaine might have been the only one in the whole Congress who knew who was behind the thing."

"You are saying that there are two conspiracies."

"Of course there are, Miss Canner. What the Radicals are doing is just politics. Lincoln could have handled them fine, if not for these other fellows. The real conspirators. The ones who killed Blaine."

Abigail was silent for a moment. "At least no one can deny the conspiracy now."

"Everyone will deny it, Miss Canner." Sickles made no comment on the mess. Or its cause. "Everyone will deny its existence, and everyone knows it is there."

"No. This time they have slain a congressman. Surely the House of Representatives will protect one of its own."

"What I said before is true. It will not even slow the Radicals down."

"The police will investigate—"

"And decide that it was the same madman or highwayman that killed McShane. Or a different one. But not a conspirator."

"Inspector Varak—"

"Has taken leave from his position. It is my understanding that he has gone to visit relatives in New York City, and his cases have been reassigned." She said nothing. Standing near the shelf, she could feel her body trying to fold up again. She made herself straighten.

"I am sure Varak is not afraid, Miss Canner. He is simply frustrated." She nodded, not looking up. She was working now to unclench her fists. "On the other hand, a reaction of this magnitude suggests how badly we have frightened them. Perhaps the conspiracy is smaller and weaker than we thought. To panic this way is not a sign of strength or organization. Remember that." Sickles stood. "Mention none of this to Speed, and certainly not to Dennard. It will only disturb him, and his only answer will be that we have a trial to win. He does not care for these flights of fancy, as he calls them."

"I understand."

"For now, better not tell Hilliman, either." He took up his cane. "I must get to the Mansion, Miss Canner. If you want to take the rest of the day—"

When she turned, her face was calm once more. It cost her blood, but she was, outwardly, her old self. "I, too, have my tasks to perform, Mr. Sickles." She waved a hand. "For one thing, cleaning this room."

Alone again, she took up the Chanticleer materials. There were four major witnesses to come, and Chanticleer had provided information about two of them. She did not know who he was, or why no more packages had arrived; but as she read through the folders, she took comfort in knowing, especially after Blaine, that somebody out there was still on their side.

V

A small epilogue was provided by Plum, from David Grafton's offices down on the first floor. He and Abigail passed each other on the stairway to the lobby: he was arriving as she was on her way out to pick up some books from a firm a few blocks away. He seemed more agitated than usual, and she asked whether all was well.

"Oh, no, well, yes. It's Mr. Grafton, miss. Not to speak ill of one's employer, naturally, but he has been increasingly anxious these last few days." The hands were making the familiar washing motion. "It's just, well, he hasn't been himself, you see. He's been ignoring urgent client matters, racing all over town for secret meetings and I don't know what else. It's getting so bad, it's even making *me* nervous. Me. And one prides oneself on one's calm in all circumstances. Oh dear." Turning his face bashfully away. "Only, if things continue this way, and one has to seek another position, it would be helpful, you see, were one to know whether there might be something available, say, at Dennard's firm. Hypothetically. Have I said too much?"

He hurried away up the stairs. When he was gone, Abigail leaned against the wall and, for the first time in what felt like years, laughed and laughed.

CHAPTER 36

Books

I

"I BELIEVE THAT I have solved your cipher," said Octavius Addison.

Abigail, beside him on the sofa, looked up sharply from the Shakespeare. "Truly?"

He flushed. "I do not mean that I can translate it. Not yet. But I do know now what kind of code it is. I also know what is needed in order to solve it."

She made no effort to conceal her delight, or her eagerness. Octavius felt the force of her passion; looked away. It was Sunday, March 24, the third consecutive Sunday on which the young man had come courting. Last weekend, as planned, they had gone riding together, and Octavius had impressed her with his knowledge of the minutiae of the city's history: he knew when the lockkeeper's house on Seventeenth Street had been constructed, and that Robert Mills, the designer of the still-unfinished monument to George Washington, had intended a structure that would be visible from miles around and thus would be the centerpiece of the young capital city.

Now Abigail said, gushingly but truthfully, "I knew you could do it." Added: "Tell me what else is needed."

Octavius smiled, his Adam's apple bobbing nervously. "What I need to know, Miss Abigail, is the context. What I mean is, I need to know something about where it was found."

She hesitated. "Let us say that it formerly was in the possession of a certain gentleman, now departed."

"Was the gentleman in question well read? Might he have had a library?"

Abigail was surprised; and freshly impressed.

"Why do you ask?"

From the inside pocket of his jacket, the young man drew a piece of fine paper, folded crisply along two axes. He flattened it on the table, beside the tea tray. "Because this"—he tapped the page—"is definitely a book code. And it contains within itself a clue to the book."

Abigail looked.

"I tried several different ways of dividing the message," Octavius was saying. "This seems to me by far the one most likely to be correct."

"Why?"

"Because all the others yield inapposite results," he said; not showing off, stating facts. "Symmetry is lost."

Abigail leaned over the paper, on which Octavius had written the same string of figures, but with slashes dividing them into groups.

13 / 163 / 222 / 232 / 121 / 244

Again he tapped the page. "I think this is the most likely division. I have tried it other ways, but this one is the most sensible. I believe that the '13' identifies the book. The other figures are either page numbers and line numbers, or, more likely, a page number, a line number, and a word number. So, for example, the '163' would mean page one, line six, word three. Understood this way, the message consists of five words. That's what the slashes are for." He frowned. "It is also possible, I should explain, that the first number is a line, the second a word, and the third a letter, so that '163' would mean line one, word six, third letter. In that instance, however, the cipher would represent only a single word, five letters long, which seems unlikely."

Abigail found his pedagogy delightful. "Which book is number thirteen?"

"I don't know."

Her face fell. "What?"

"I apologize, Miss Abigail. There is no way to tell from the cipher alone which book is number thirteen. It may be that the sender and the recipient have worked out a separate method of choosing books.

So—book number one might be the Bible, book number two a play by Shakespeare, and so forth."

"Then we'll never get it." From the heights of excitement, she felt herself cast into the pits of despair.

"Well, yes. If the sender and recipient worked out a sequence, we will never solve the cipher. That is what makes book codes so useful. But I am skeptical."

"Why?"

"Because thirteen is a fairly large number of books to remember in the proper sequence. The recipient can't write them down somewhere. That would defeat the purpose. So I suspect that book number thirteen is identifiable in some other way. Say, thirteenth from the end of a particular shelf. Or thirteenth on a list of books that exists for some other purpose and is easily accessible."

"A list," Abigail echoed, an idea forming.

"Yes. I think that is the most likely, because books on a shelf can be moved around by accident. The order can change. So I think it is probably a list. Of course"—tone suddenly bashful—"I could be wrong."

"Do you think you're wrong?"

An embarrassed smile, but at least he met her eyes. "No, Miss Abigail. I don't think I'm wrong."

"You know what? Neither do I."

Book number thirteen.

II

Abigail decided to begin at once, scandalizing Nanny Pork.

"On the Sabbath?"

"I'm sorry, Nanny."

"Goin out ridin with a young man is one thing. But you're goin to work. This is wrong, child."

"I have no choice."

"Child, there is always a choice. I hopes I raised you to make the right ones."

Along the way, Octavius continued trying to impress her with his knowledge of the city. He pointed out the house of the late Mrs. Rose Greenhow, a notorious Confederate spy, and told her how the South did little to disguise the identities of their secret agents, so that Mrs.

Greenhow was simply "Mrs. G"; whereas the North named their agents for birds—"Sparrow," "Eagle," and the like—making them harder for the enemy to track down. But Abigail, distracted, was hardly paying attention, and at last Octavius fell silent. Book number thirteen, she was thinking. A list of books. A pre-existing set of numbers.

A perfect cipher for a lawyer.

And a perfect distraction from the secret aching worry that somehow she had contributed to the death of Congressman Blaine.

At Fourteenth and G, she asked Octavius to drop her outside.

Now it was the turn of Octavius to be scandalized. "I can't leave you to enter the building alone, Miss Abigail. It is not gentlemanly."

She smiled. "Mr. Addison, it is sweet of you to be concerned, but I have been alone in this office at many different hours of the day, and I have yet to come to any harm."

He considered this. "But how will you get home?"

"Nanny will have Michael fetch me."

"Perhaps I should wait, just in case."

Abigail put a hand on his arm. "Any young lady would count herself lucky to have so fine a gentleman waiting on and protecting her. If ever I need protection, I shall call upon you. But, this afternoon, I shall be perfectly fine. I promise you."

III

Upstairs, she took a moment to orient herself. Don't think. Act. The cipher, not Blaine. Book number thirteen. The common room, of course, was lined with hundreds of books, and there were more in the partners' offices. But during the weeks of preparing for trial, volumes had been pulled free and shoved back, not always in the original order. Surely this volatility was a natural characteristic of any serious library. Books were shelved for the sole purpose of making them easy to store, locate, remove, and reshelve. It was the removing, not the shelving, that made them useful.

Not the thirteenth book on the shelf, then, or the book on the thirteenth shelf; these positional understandings would have no lasting meaning. A book could be thirteenth from the end of one shelf at breakfast, and second from the end of another by luncheon. Therefore, book number thirteen must refer to a book whose numbering was not dependent on its position.

She turned to the office's set of the reports of the decisions of the Supreme Court of the United States. Not every law office owned a full set, but Dennard & McShane possessed all the volumes.

She ran her fingers across their spines. The first four years of the Court were reported by Dallas; the next nine by Cranch; then twelve volumes of Wheaton, sixteen volumes of Peters, and twenty-four volumes of Howard. Black had produced only two volumes. Wallace, the current reporter, was somewhere in the vicinity of volume six. So two of the reporters, Peters and Howard, had each produced a thirteenth volume; or, if one counted from the beginning of the Court's existence, the thirteenth volume would be the ninth volume of Cranch.

She got to work.

13 / 163 / 222 / 232 / 121 / 244

She started with the ninth volume of Cranch, the thirteenth volume of the work of the Supreme Court. The first suggestion Octavius had made was that in the set "163," the first digit was a page, the second a line, the third a word. But there was nothing printed on page 1, so the numbers must mean something else. She tried page sixteen, which turned out to be the second page of a case called *Meigs v. McClung's Lessee.* The name meant nothing to her. She cared about the page. The third word was "Marshall." Then page twenty-two. No words. So already the idea was wrong.

What about page 163? No, that didn't work, because . . .

After two hours, Abigail had tried every permutation she could think of, in the Cranch volume and in the thirteenth volumes of both Peters and Howard. None returned a message that made any sense. Despairing, she slid the books back into place and searched for something else—anything else—that had a thirteenth volume. She found nothing. She pulled down a couple of the treatises—Chitty, Blackstone—but could not correlate to the cipher anybody's section thirteen or chapter thirteen or page thirteen. She tried such volumes as the office possessed of the *Statutes at Large,* and the reports of local courts in Maryland, Virginia, and Pennsylvania.

Nothing worked.

And, suddenly, it was dark. She had been at the office for five hours, pursuing the absurd theory that Octavius had concocted.

She curbed her irritation. The idea was *not* absurd. Every instinct

Abigail possessed told her that Octavius was right; not only that, but that between Rebecca Deveaux and Arthur McShane there had existed an understanding that would enable him to decipher the message: she would have hidden the treasure where McShane could find it.

The message told him where.

The thirteenth *something*. If not the thirteenth in a series of books, then what?

As she slipped into her coat and snuffed the gas lamp she did not remember lighting, Abigail Canner told herself that the answer, sooner or later, would suggest itself. Patience and determination had so far won every battle she had fought in her young life.

This one would, she told herself, be no different.

IV

Stepping out onto the landing, confident that Michael would be waiting, Abigail heard a familiar uneven clomping from below. Dan Sickles was making his painful way up.

Emerging from the stairwell, he mopped his brow with a handkerchief. She could read the agony on his face. Their eyes met, and she felt a flush of embarrassment at having caught so proud a man in a moment of weakness. Then he straightened, and flashed the familiar roguish grin. "Miss Canner. An unexpected pleasure."

"Mr. Sickles," she murmured.

He winked. "I would never have guessed that you were the sort to labor on the Sabbath."

She ignored his mockery, for she understood him better now: the world had taken his leg and left him in constant pain, and he responded by refusing to take anything seriously.

"I was looking for a book," she said.

"I see." He glanced at her empty hands, then back up at her face. Both waited. "You did well with the Chanticleer letters," he finally said, moving toward the offices. "Sometimes a lawyer's work is grubby."

Telling her he knew how her role in destroying poor Corbin Yardley had wounded her. She nodded, turned to go; turned back, remembering Octavius's lecture this afternoon in his carriage. Chanticleer—didn't the word—

"It is well that I ran into you, Mr. Sickles," she said. "I have an idea."

CHAPTER 37

Assignment

I

MONDAY BEGAN WITH a moment of prayer for "our fallen brother" James Blaine; but Sickles was right: the prosecution had momentum now, and the Managers were not about to postpone over so mundane a matter as the death of a congressman. After the prayer, the Senate adopted a resolution of condolence, and then the Chief Justice took the chair, and the trial resumed. After the clerk read the record of Friday's proceedings came a further tussle over documents.

"Mr. Chief Justice and Senators," said Benjamin Butler, "before we proceed with today's evidence, I would ask consent to say a word about Mr. Yardley's testimony of last week." He stood resplendent in an obviously new suit that did not completely disguise his not-quite-military physique. "Mr. Yardley gave us examples of the depredations suffered by his race at the hands of the white Southerners, who are attempting to build on the backs of the freedmen a version of the dominance that they exercised as slave owners. The Southern states, only two years after being defeated, have all enacted Black Codes, which, despite the legislation passed by this Congress, they have been loath to abandon. If you will indulge me a moment more, sirs, I should like to read aloud a short portion of the *Special Report of the Anti-Slavery Conference of 1867*, to review for this august body the life led at this time by the freedmen."

Dennard was on the verge of objecting, but Sickles tugged at his sleeve, and he subsided. The document might be formally objectionable, but it was also innocuous, and there was no point in angering either Chase or the Senators.

Butler shoved his pince-nez up his narrow nose and commenced reading: "'The idea of admitting the freedmen to an equal participation in civil and political rights was not entertained in any part of the South,'" he began.

"Or any part of the North," Abigail whispered, and both Kate and Meg gave her odd looks; they were well-bred Northern ladies, and understood the mistreatment of negroes as a purely Southern phenomenon.

"'In most of the States,'" Butler continued, "'they were not allowed to sit on juries, or even to testify in any case in which white men were parties. They were forbidden to own or bear fire-arms, and thus were rendered defenceless against assaults.'" He shut the book and resumed his proud stance. "Here, then, Senators, we see Mr. Yardley's dilemma. Even had he known the identities of the marauders who burned his barn, and even had he found a lawyer to press his suit, he would not have been able to give testimony, so his case would have been thrown out of court. If, on the other hand, he chose to defend himself against the criminals, his mere possession of the means of defense would have rendered him liable for arrest. And yet Mr. Lincoln would prefer, rather than protecting a man like Mr. Yardley, to treat with the very white Southerners—"

Dennard was bellowing, but only to be heard over the tumult. Senators were shouting. Chase slammed his gavel repeatedly onto its stand until the room calmed down. "The gentlemen will be in order," he commanded. He turned to Dennard. "Mr. Dennard, do you have an objection?"

"We do, Your Honor. Mr. Yardley's testimony was admitted only subject to the limitation that the purpose was to establish the state of mind of certain federal officials in the South. It was not admitted to show the truth of the claim of what Mr. Lincoln supposedly said, and therefore it is improper for the distinguished Manager to refer to Mr. Lincoln's supposed words as though they were established fact."

Butler half turned, so that his response was addressed less to the Chief Justice than to the Senators, his intended audience. "Your Honor, the Managers have adduced a superfluity of evidence of Mr. Lincoln's gentle dealings with the very white Southerners who previously so oppressed the black man."

Chase shook his head. "Counsel for the respondent is correct. The Manager will restrict his commentary to facts in evidence."

This time Abigail could not restrain herself. She leaned toward her companion. "His order applies only to the lawyers. He places no limits on what the Senators may say."

At this implied criticism of her father, Kate stiffened. "The Chief Justice is not empowered to do so. He has not the authority to limit the debate by the Senators."

Margaret Felix, once more sitting across Abigail from her rival, smirked. "I have noticed the Chief Justice gaveling Senators to order from time to time."

"Only when they are speaking out of order. The chair places no limit on what they are entitled to say."

"Suppose he were to try," said Meg.

"A meaningless supposition," answered Kate, and, fanning, leaned away.

Kate and Meg kept talking across Abigail, and their sniping distracted her from following the sharper sniping below. She had not realized until now that these two women, the former belle of Washington society and the current belle of Philadelphia society, detested each other. At the same time, their ability to remain warmly affectionate despite their inner seething was sufficiently impressive that Abigail almost wished she hated somebody enough to give it a try.

Down below, Butler had finished. Dennard, speaking even more ponderously than usual, reminded the body that the credibility of Mr. Yardley had been called severely into question. He suggested to the Senators that they rely on no part of his testimony. He added that the chamber was well rid of so unreliable a witness, and a man who had admitted to accepting a bribe.

Again Abigail cringed.

Kate Sprague, as usual, missed nothing. "If you are still feeling guilty," she said gently, "perhaps you are on the wrong side."

II

The Managers had moved back to the second count of the impeachment, and were trying to prove by documents alone, without any accompanying testimony, that the President had closed several opposition newspapers during the war, and in a few cases tossed the editors into prison. Because the charge was true, and everyone in the room knew it was true, the objections were mainly for show.

As the ladies fenced above, so did the lawyers down below.

"There is no more reason," said Benjamin Butler, "to challenge these documents than there was to challenge the documents admitted last week." He toyed with his golden locks. "The second count of the bill of impeachment alleges that the said Abraham Lincoln has violated the liberties of the people of the United States. To wit, he has thrown political opponents in prison and shut down their newspapers." A tiny smile, as if in acknowledgment of his own complicity: for Ben Butler, while running New Orleans, had also done a thing or two. "He has declared martial law even in cities of the North, and ordered the seizure of every telegram sent in the United States." Butler turned toward the ranked members. "Without exception."

Dennard rose to speak. Chase shook his head. "You will have your turn. Sit."

"There were no exceptions," Butler repeated. "Consider. Mr. Lincoln ordered the seizure of copies of every telegram sent in the United States. He said he was searching for spies, but he made no exceptions, say, for the correspondence of a member of this august body. Or the Chief Justice. Or anyone sitting today in the gallery." A nod toward the defense table. "Every person sitting in this room, if he had sent a telegram within the six months prior to the President's order, would have had his telegram seized."

Dennard objected. "I believe that copies of telegrams were seized. No messages were delayed in delivery."

A chuckle from the gallery. Chase was not amused. "Sit down, Mr. Dennard. I have told you to wait your turn."

A few minutes later, Butler was done. The Chief Justice decreed a fifteen-minute recess.

"I hope they admit all the documents," said Meg as they waited.

"Why?" asked Abigail.

"Because it will be fascinating to see the proof of Mr. Lincoln's misdeeds laid out for the country."

"Surely that is the question before this House," Abigail said. She had mastered, these past days, the playful conversational style of the finer Washington ladies. "Whether Mr. Lincoln's many good deeds are indeed also misdeeds."

"Oh, they are misdeeds," said Margaret, working hard to keep up. "They may have been meant as *good* deeds, but they missed their targets, and therefore are *mis*deeds."

"If they are misdeeds, it is because they *struck* their targets," said Kate, the clever smile stretching her small, prim mouth.

"Mainly rebel soldiers," said Abigail.

III

Dennard's turn arrived. He promised to be brief. The country was at war, he said. There were spies everywhere, the spies were sending messages by telegraph. If there was another way to get the messages without seizing the telegrams, the President and his advisers had not been able to come up with it in the heat of the moment. Nor had one been suggested since.

"And besides," he said, "telegraph messages aren't private."

The audience's attention tautened.

"Of course they are," said Butler, in his surprise speaking quite out of turn.

"A message sent by telegraph is read by the man who transcribes it at the telegraph office, the man who sends the code, the man who receives the code at the other end, and the man who writes out the words. The man who delivers the message might read it, too. So might the man to whom we give the assignment of carrying our message to the telegraph office in the first place." An elaborate shrug, as if to say that there were too many more potential readers to bother mentioning. "So the President's order did not violate anybody's privacy. Besides, there is no right to privacy in the Constitution. A right to property, surely. But the message forms—the actual papers seized—well, if they constitute the property of anybody at all, I suppose they would be the property of the telegraph company. Let the Western Union Company, if it chooses, come to the Capitol to seek damages. Let the company go into court. The company will lose. In wartime, the government has a call upon the property of the people if that property is necessary to the war effort. The President and his advisers judged that seizing the telegraph forms was necessary. I should think that would be the end of the debate." Dennard put his hands on his hips, no small matter for a man of his girth. "Now, you might disagree with the President's judgment of necessity. You might have made a different decision, sitting in his office.

But unless you are able to show the clear violation of a criminal statute, the proper forum for the expression of a disagreement over policy is the ballot box, not the court of impeachment."

Dennard's argument left a vast silence in the chamber. Once more he had aimed his delicate thrust at the heart of the prosecution's case. Maybe the President did everything alleged, he was saying. Maybe you think everything he has done is outrageously wrong. But so what? he was asking. These are at best political disagreements. This is why there are elections. True, the proposition would make no impact on the most adamant members of the anti-Lincoln faction; nor on those who, like Sumner, believed to a moral certainty in the principle of parliamentary supremacy. And the newspapers would miss the nuances entirely, and thus continue performing to perfection their task of misinforming the public. But a few wavering moderates might be swayed by the suggestion that there was nothing to this case but a political disagreement dressed in the language of high crimes and misdemeanors.

Or they might not.

Chase finally said, "It is nearly five o'clock. Unless there is objection, we shall adjourn for the day."

Customarily, a member of the Senate made the motion to end the day's proceedings. But the Chief Justice had more and more made the trial his own. Today nobody seemed to mind.

IV

Jonathan waited with Margaret in the carriage line. "It is a pity that you must return to the office," she said. "So many meetings."

"I have no—"

"No choice. I know. The pressure of work. You are much like Father." Her grip tightened on his arm. "No doubt that explains my affection."

"The trial will be over soon," he said loyally. "Then we will have more time for each other."

"A lifetime, my love." But Meg's words sounded as desperately stilted as his. Her rig drew up, and she pressed her head against his shoulder, then presented her cool cheek to be kissed. He handed her up into the carriage. About to signal the negro driver to depart, she had another thought, and leaned down, beckoning Jonathan close. "Father has to go up to Philadelphia for a few days. He leaves tomorrow." A pert nod, as if in agreement with herself. "He asked me to join him, but I told him

I would like to stay and watch the trial. Father says he is proud of you for trying, but Mr. Lincoln is bound to be removed in the end, and the country will never be the same."

Smarting from this casual statement of his own deepest fears, Jonathan felt honor-bound to protest. "I hardly think that is the likely conclusion," he said. "The prosecution has yet to adduce the slightest true evidence of—"

Margaret waved this away. "With Father away, it's just me and the servants and of course Aunt Clara." The green eyes held his. Something was shining there: decision, and perhaps invitation. Certainly the glow of competition. "The servants are very discreet, and Aunt Clara, after an evening glass of her favorite, is likely to sleep early." A suitable pause. "And soundly."

"I . . . I see," said Jonathan, warmth and confusion suffusing him once more. This was a very different Margaret from the one he had courted; her time in Washington City had changed her. Or perhaps it was he who had changed, and what he sensed in Meg was only a reflection. He could, of course, neither accept nor decline the implied invitation; indeed, as a matter of etiquette, although he could be as flirtatious as he liked, he dared not acknowledge the invitation at all. And so he said, "I trust that you will sleep soundly as well."

"I hope I shall be able." Meg had not released his hand. "That old house can be so drafty and creaky. Nothing like our house in Philadelphia. It is scary sometimes, down in that first-floor bedroom all alone."

V

Back at the office, Sickles once more met Abigail and Jonathan to give them orders.

"You will not be at trial tomorrow," he said. "Speed's clerk will sit at the table."

"Why?" asked Jonathan, his voice stricken. Plainly, he feared he had committed some error, and was being replaced by Rellman as punishment.

But Abigail had by now spent enough time with Sickles to understand the subtlety with which his mind worked. "Very well," she said. "Where will we be?"

"In Richmond."

She could not help herself. "Richmond, *Virginia*?" Because, to the colored race, everything across the Potomac River and southward remained enemy territory, where one did not, willingly, go. And Nanny's grotesquely embroidered tales of her own terrifying trek through Sheol scarcely made matters better.

Sickles yawned. He was sprawled, as usual, on the settee beside the coal stove. His eyes were in their accustomed position: all but completely shut. When he spoke, he seemed to have missed her point, perhaps intentionally. "Don't worry. You two won't miss much. We'll have a couple of aggrieved newspaper editors to cross-examine tomorrow, and the next day they'll find some widow who lost her house when Seward locked up her husband for sedition. Doesn't mean a thing legally, but it'll play to the masses of men, who don't exactly want to be reminded of what Lincoln had to do to win the war, mainly because they all went along with it." Another yawn. "Remind them that what he did, he had to do, or Mr. Jefferson Davis would now be in the White House, arguing with *his* Congress."

Abigail spoke gently. "About Richmond."

"Mmmm? Oh, right. Right. Remember your idea about the Chanticleer letters?"

"Yes," said Abigail, quite surprised.

"What idea?" asked Jonathan.

But Sickles preferred to take the long route around. "The package from Chanticleer arrived two weeks before the trial. With the mail at the South being what it is, he must have sent it at least a week or two before that. And God alone knows how long it took him to gather the information, including all the way from Atlanta. He might have been running around for months. Now do you see?"

"Not quite," Jonathan admitted.

Sickles shifted his gaze. "Miss Canner?"

She saw; and was furious at herself for not having seen sooner. "We did not know that Mr. Yardley was on the witness list until a few days before trial. But this Chanticleer knew a month or two earlier." Her excitement grew. "Chanticleer has connections to the Radicals, connections strong enough that he knows their trial strategy." A frown. "But why Richmond?"

"This is the interesting part." Sickles addressed himself to Jonathan. "Yesterday afternoon, Miss Canner had an excellent idea. She said she thought Chanticleer might have been a Union spy, because the code names of Union spies were mostly bird names, and 'chanticleer' is just another word for rooster."

Abigail could not restrain herself. "You mean I was right?"

"Yes, Miss Canner. You were right. Chanticleer was a Union spy." Sickles grinned. "Now, Stanton doesn't know about the Chanticleer letters, and I mean to keep it that way. But I have a source at the War Department. A source who's loyal to the President, not to Stanton. My source has access to the files, and, well, we're ahead of the Radicals for once. That is why the two of you are going to take the cars to Richmond tomorrow morning. By now, Chanticleer must know that McShane is dead. We need to find out what else he knows, and what else he is willing to tell."

"Are you saying you know who he is?" said Abigail.

"I do. The Reverend Dr. Hollis Chastain. Pastor of a big Presbyterian church down there. I don't think you'll have any trouble finding him."

"Why us?" asked Abigail.

"Because I trust you."

"There must be others you trust," she said, a bit desperate now.

"Not at the moment. Too many folks we thought were on our side have gone over to Mr. Wade."

"I appreciate that, Mr. Sickles, but I must confess that the idea of going down to southern Virginia—"

The roguish grin. "Don't worry, Miss Canner. We won the war." He sat up, eyelids at half-mast. "Mr. Dennard and I sort of came up with this ourselves. Mr. Lincoln is busy. We have not bothered him with any of this. Neither should you."

They could hardly mistake his meaning: If anything went wrong, the President would deny knowledge of what they were up to. The price would be on their heads, not Lincoln's.

VI

Nanny Pork was against the trip. Nanny was against everything these days. She sat Abigail down in the kitchen and told her stories, some of which Abigail had heard before, some of which she hadn't, and some of which she was certain Nanny was making up on the spot: stories of slavery, and of how black folk were treated at the South. And Virginia, said Nanny Pork, was the worst. Abigail objected that she had always heard that the slaves were treated better in Virginia than elsewhere, but Nanny was making a different point. All over the South, said Nanny, there was slaves to pick the cotton and slaves to do the laundry and slaves to raise the chilluns. The slaves did the work; the white folks counted the money. In Virginia, said Nanny, it was different. In Virginia, people made they's slaves have chilluns, and more chilluns, but not to do any work. To sell them. The rest of the South, said Nanny, bought slaves and made them work. In Virginia, they raised slaves like cattle, and sold them to the rest of the South.

"And Richmond was the worst. Richmond was where they sold us south. You didn't even get to say goodbye to your family. They took you down to the market in a cart. The market was right next to the train station. Once you was sold, they put you right on the train and took you to your new owner. The whole South was Hell, but Richmond was the capital of Hell."

Abigail believed every word. Yet she remained undeterred. After her initial reluctance, she had made up her mind. She had not found her sister only to lose her again. Judith had told her about Rebecca Deveaux, and then had promptly disappeared. Yes, it was possible that Judith had run away for her own protection. But the events of the past month cast a dire shadow. Whatever the truth of her sister's situation, Abigail had to know.

And she would walk into Hell itself to learn the truth.

CHAPTER 38

Spy

I

RICHMOND WAS RUBBLE.

Two years after the end of the war, the city was a long way from repairing the damage from Union shelling, and the even greater damage from the fires that had consumed half the city on the day the Confederate government loaded its treasury onto a train and fled before Grant's advancing army. Although residents blamed the North for the disaster, the truth was that Jefferson Davis, before abandoning his capital, had ordered the stores of food and tobacco and ammunition put to the torch, and the blaze had quickly roared out of control.

Jonathan took lodging for the night at the Lexington House. Abigail found a colored matron near the river who let rooms. Nor was this distinction their only reminder of the state of things. They had made the ride down in the third-class compartment, changing trains in Warrenton, all the while the objects of part-conjecturing, part-hostile scrutiny from fellow passengers. Actually, Jonathan had assumed that they would travel second class—the first-class car was full—but the clerk at the Baltimore and Potomac depot in Washington City had refused to sell Abigail a second-class ticket. It would be different, he said, if she were taking the cars for Philadelphia and parts north, although maybe not—he was unprepared to say for sure. Jonathan had tried to argue, on the ground that the railroads were common carriers, legally bound to sell space to all who were willing to pay. The clerk had shrugged. Railroad policy, he said. Jonathan was prepared to be angry, and a Hilliman in high dudgeon could be very angry indeed, but Abigail hissed that he must pick his battles, and must not embarrass Mr. Lincoln.

"He is the President," Abigail had reminded him as they dodged the beggars on the way to the platform. "And our client."

They sat side by side, Abigail in the window. The car was half empty. The other passengers were poor whites and a scattering of quiet negroes, who kept their eyes down. As Abigail watched the passing landscape, Jonathan told her how several Southern states were considering laws that would require separation of the races on the trains and other conveyances.

"And what will Mr. Lincoln do in that event?" she asked.

"He supports the Civil Rights Acts, which would hold such discrimination to be a violation of federal law."

"You say that he supports the Acts." They stopped somewhere, and the car began to fill. "Would he enforce them?"

Jonathan was uneasy. "You are beginning to sound like the Radicals."

The rest of the trip passed mostly in silence. Her eyes closed, and Jonathan wondered whether she was feigning, to avoid further argument. He wondered, too, how that peculiar head would feel on his shoulder. But Abigail, even in sleep, faced the window, the entirety of her self locked against his affection. Jonathan opened his newspaper and read for a bit. A report said Lincoln was going to call for repeal of the Morrill Tariff, but named no sources. Maybe. Maybe not. Jonathan turned the page, conscious of the stares all around. Maybe the other passengers thought him a carpetbagger, heading south to make his fortune. What, then, must they think of Abigail? His partner in corruption? His concubine? His wife? With speculations, not all of them proper, sloshing about his mind, Jonathan, too, very suddenly, escaped into sleep.

As for Abigail, she was wide awake. She regretted having spoken harshly. Alas, she could not control her growing tension as they progressed southward. Perhaps she was simply experiencing the understandable revulsion of her people at their treatment in the land of Dixie. But it was also possible that with every mile traveled toward Richmond, where her Aaron had been captured, she found herself closer to a simple reality: he was never coming home.

II

The coachman they hailed was black, and liveried, and polite in a silky way suggesting a shared experience of life. Jonathan supposed it was because Abigail was with him, although it was always possible that this projection of intimacy was simply one of the driver's gifts, for it would likely lead to frequent hires, and excellent gratuities. Although he was very skinny and very dark, he asked them to call him Big Red, and promised to wait on them exclusively, and take them anywhere they might choose to go, at any time of day or night, for what he called the "duritation" of their stay. As they rode in from the depot, he pointed to the few public buildings that had survived the devastation: the post office, the patent office, a handful of others. There were great piles of masonry everywhere, and sullen, defeated people who watched, empty-eyed, as mounted Union patrols passed by.

"In case we gets out of hand again," Big Red explained helpfully.

We: meaning, *the Confederacy.*

Big Red dropped Abigail first, then Jonathan, promising to be back in the morning to collect them, after they'd had the chance to "fresher" themselves. Jonathan gave him a couple of coins to be sure.

Inside the Lexington House, Jonathan wrote out a wire to inform Sickles that they had arrived, then went into the dining room, where nothing was left but overdone lamb. He slept poorly, haunted by memories of the terrible battles his regiment had fought on the outskirts of this city. In the morning, at the appointed time, Jonathan stepped outside the hotel, and, sure enough, there was Big Red. They drove over to the colored part of town to get Abigail, then headed for the hills on the outskirts of the city.

"Do you know Dr. Chastain?" asked Abigail.

"Everybody knows Dr. Chastain."

"What can you tell us about him?"

"Everybody likes Dr. Chastain."

Abigail frowned. "He was a supporter of slavery."

"Yes, ma'am."

"Doesn't that bother you?"

The coachman thought this over. "Ma'am, all the white folks was supporters of slavery. Am I spose to hate all the white folks?"

Abigail nibbled at her lip. She had no answer, and so she changed the subject. "It is just that Dr. Chastain was rather . . . ardent."

"Yes, ma'am," said Big Red.

After that, Abigail fell silent. She marveled that so fanatical a defender of slavery could have been a Union spy, but she had learned over these past weeks that few people were precisely as they appeared.

The carriage rolled through the streets of the shattered city. Twice they were stopped by soldiers, and twice the pass Sickles had obtained, signed by General Grant's adjutant, got them through without trouble. Abigail wondered what it would be like to live under occupation this way, no matter how great your crimes, and whether there might not be wisdom in Lincoln's rush to lift the Northern boot from the Southern neck. Memories lingered.

The carriage slowed, then stopped.

"Don't antagonize him, Abigail," Jonathan whispered. "Please. Don't argue with him."

"What are you saying?"

"That you do not suffer fools." He said it warmly. "We need his trust. We need to charm him."

"I can be charming," she huffed.

They alighted. The clapboard house was modest but somehow defiant: freshly painted, gleaming bright white in the early-spring sun. The flowers were tended, and the sense one had, mounting the steps, was of a prosperity that had miraculously survived the forces that had led to the dilapidated circumstances of the homes on either side.

The man who opened the door was tall—freakishly so, with a full head or more to brandish over Jonathan—and yet so thin that one felt from him a sense less of strength than of fragility. His expensive black suit hung loosely. Wispy white hair decorated his temples, but the bald pate shone. His eyes were small and disagreeable behind thick lenses, and his hand was clutching something just out of sight beyond the edge of the door frame: presumably a pistol.

"I have no need of clothing or food from your missionary society," he said, without preamble. His voice was thick and rolling, a preacher's voice. The accent suggested a provenance deeper in the South. "I have no need of an assistance from any Yankees. You have done enough damage to my country. Please leave."

All the while, his eyes were on the white man on the porch, as if he could not bear to look at a black woman. But all the same it was Abigail who spoke, before Jonathan could quite come up with an answer.

"We are not here, sir, to add to your burdens or your grief. We are not here to insult or offend your sense of honor. We are here only to ask you about this." She slipped a hand into her bag and pulled out the Chanticleer letter.

Chastain stared at her defiantly, but she continued to hold out the pages, and slowly, as if against his will, his gaze traveled to her hand. His mouth moved, but no words emerged.

"Arthur McShane is dead," she said. "We have come from Washington to find out what else you hoped to provide him, so that we can do whatever it is you wanted him to do."

III

It was unlikely that the Reverend Dr. Hollis Chastain had ever entertained a woman of color in the parlor, but he was evidently willing to try. A black woman who reminded Abigail in looks and manner but not age of Nanny Pork served them lemonade, despite the season, her narrow eyes flashing with resentment and disapproval every time they lit upon Abigail.

"So you worked for Mr. McShane," said Chastain, addressing himself so far entirely to Jonathan. "Tell me about his last days."

"He was preparing for the impeachment trial. He was busy."

"I should think so." Chastain sipped his lemonade. He sat, very still, in an ancient rocking chair. The furniture was comfortable without quite being plush. Ornate shelves held books. Magazines were stacked on the floor. "Defending that man."

"Yes, sir," said Jonathan, following his own advice never to disagree with their host, whose secrets they needed, and possessed no means to compel.

"A matter of professional obligation, I would think," the minister continued. "Or did he perhaps *agree* with that man?" Unable to say Lincoln's name.

"About what, sir?"

"Perhaps about that man's use of armed force to conquer independent states simply trying to depart in peace the compact they had voluntarily entered. Perhaps about the hundreds of thousands of deaths and the hundreds of millions of dollars of destruction caused by that man's policy." Chastain never raised his voice, but the eyes grew fierce. "And then there is the matter of that man's deciding for us, a free and independent nation, the particular matter of our social relations."

Abigail could no longer restrain herself. "You are referring to the freeing of my people from bondage."

Chastain turned her way at last, his gaze surprisingly gentle, even meek. "It pains me to hear you refer to the social relations formerly enjoyed by your people and mine as bondage. Zillah, whom you have met"—inclining his head toward the woman who had served them lemonade, and still lurked, disapproving, near the fireplace—"has always been a much-beloved member of this household. Much beloved," he repeated, and, for the briefest of instants, dropped his eyes. But when he spoke again his voice was forceful and clear. "There is a cruelty, surely, in tearing families forcibly apart, which is why the better men of the South always opposed the separation, through commerce, of negro women from their children, and fought against the restoration of the African slave trade. Here on these shores, the relations between blacks and whites were warm and friendly, at times even loving; and so they would have remained for a very long while, had not that man intervened." He pursed his lips, as if the next words carried a sour taste. "Naturally, in time, the social and economic system of the South would have become unsustainable. This has been true of every system ever developed by man. But, as I have argued in the *Southern Presbyterian Review,* it is one thing to let the forces of time and fate move the world, through the mysterious Providence of God. It is a different matter altogether to use force of arms in an effort to reorder the world according to the ideas of mortal and fallible men. Surely you see this point."

"I hardly think—"

For all the kindliness in his voice, Chastain did not take warmly to interruptions, least of all from a colored woman sipping lemonade in his parlor. "Perhaps, in the fullness of time, the dark race will be ready to take its place among the great peoples of the earth. I can imagine such an event. I do not believe that you are cursed. I do not believe that you are without the spark of God. I believe that you need, for a while longer, the guidance of those to whom the Lord has entrusted knowledge and wisdom, industry and pure manners. Miss Canner, it is obvious that you are an educated woman. Surely you do not imagine that those of your race who remain in the state of brutishness and immorality that we see so widespread at the South are prepared for a life without guidance, or, indeed, a life in which they are considered fit to rule their betters." Not waiting for a response, he turned back to Jonathan. "Consider the situation at the North. You are locked in a battle between two rising forces, labor and capital. Each one gains power from year to year. Soon they will be so powerful that they will determine the entire economy, and the entire social structure, at the North. Why would we not resist the impression of this precarious and ultimately violent system upon ourselves?" His voice rose. "You did not like our system. We did not like yours. But that man decided to inflame the North with the message that our system was the more evil of the two, in order that he might rouse a sufficient fervor to make war upon our system, for the benefit of yours." Chastain shut his eyes briefly. "Then, when the lunatic Booth shot him, Southern men of the cloth were ordered by our occupiers—ordered!—to preach Sunday sermons eulogizing that man and praying for his recovery. I told my flock that the shooting was wrong, but it would be a hypocrisy to turn that man into a hero on account of it. He is no hero. He is a conqueror and an oppressor."

Jonathan glanced quickly at Abigail, whose fingers had tightened on her untouched glass of lemonade. To his relief, she said, smoothly, "Despite our differences, Dr. Chastain, you did send the letter to Mr. McShane. You labored on behalf of the Union during the war." She gave him the opportunity to dispute this, but he did not. Instead, the pastor inclined his head, waiting. Abigail took a breath. "Sir, it is not our wish to impose upon you. But, as you know, time is now short. So, please, bear with me. You sent the letter to Mr. McShane because you hoped that he would come to you before the trial ended, and that he would use your information to the good. We were his employees. Both of us," she added, without emphasis. "The trial is nearing its end. We used the information about Mr. Yardley to good effect. But unless you tell us what else you planned to tell him, your secrets will be useless."

But Chastain had a pace of his own. "Miss Canner, I noted a moment ago that you are plainly an educated woman. And yet it is also plain to me, from the shade of your skin, that you have, intermixed in your line, the blood of the white race." He waved away her objection. "No, no. I make no criticism. Naturally, I do not approve of relations between our races, but it is well known that this occurs, and, indeed, if you examine the data collected by the census, you will discover that, as you move from the Lower South to the Upper South, the percentage of negroes with white blood rises. And of course among the free negroes, it is highest of all. I believe that in Maryland, more than forty percent of the free negroes have white blood. There is a reason, therefore, that you have succeeded so well in freedom."

"Perhaps, then," she said, "you should reconsider whether to approve of relations between the races, if white blood suits us so well."

Dead silence.

"You are a fascinating people," the pastor finally said. He licked his lips, nervous for some reason. "Absolutely fascinating. That man cares nothing for you. We loved your people, and you . . ." He could not find the words. Again the tongue snaked across his lips. He shook his head, and, shivering, turned the rocker slightly away, as if he could bear to look on them no more. "Say what you have come to say," he whispered, "and then go."

"Sir," said Jonathan, swiftly, "I apologize if we have given offense. That was never our intention."

No response. The pastor was hunching into himself, drawing the jacket more tightly across his withered shoulders.

Jonathan tried again. "Sir, we are not here to argue over the past. Our only concern is the trial, and why you sent—"

Chastain revived, although his voice was now less commanding than querulous. "You are mistaken. Both of you. I did not at any point labor on behalf of the Union. What I did, always, was for the benefit of my own beloved state of Virginia, now subject to conquest and oppression because of that man."

Abigail again: "But, sir, in the files of the War Department—"

"In the files of your War Department, I am doubtless listed as a turncoat, a traitor to my own nation who labored, as you say, on behalf of the Union." He took another sip of lemonade, let it slosh about in his mouth before swallowing, as if he sought to wash away the taste of his own words. "And I suspect that it is that wretched file, rather than any solicitude on the part of that man for teachers of the faith, that has left my home and my church unmolested, when so much has been taken from us." He lifted his chin, indicating the ruined city beyond the window. "But I was never a traitor. I wanted peace between our nations, rather than this pointless destruction. It was to that end that I was persuaded to labor."

"You were persuaded," Abigail echoed, gently.

A tight nod. Chastain had the rocker moving now, slowly, and in his worn suit looked suddenly old. "I am an imperfect man. A miserable sinner, as we all are, in need of our Lord's forgiveness. I have transgressions in my past." His eyes were cast, if anywhere, on the carpeting, and perhaps down to the smoldering depths of Hell below. "Naturally, one's associates . . . one's domestic staff . . . they are aware of more than one thinks. It is as I said, Miss Canner. Your race is not unintelligent, and . . . and fascinating, as I said. I suppose I did not imagine . . . Well, they knew. They knew what I had done, and they . . . they told, and she came to me and said unless I . . ."

Chastain ran down. He had nothing more to say.

"When you say 'she,'" Jonathan began, but Abigail put a hand on his wrist.

"You were coerced. Through the agency of your . . . domestic staff." She glanced around; Zillah stood beside the fireplace, heavy arms folded. She went out. "You were coerced into . . . into laboring for the Union."

"No," said the pastor, sharply. His gaze grew fiery, and he waggled an admonishing finger. "Never. I did not labor on their behalf. I did *not*. I was persuaded to labor for peace between our two nations, and *that was all*."

They gave him a moment to settle himself. "And these labors," said Jonathan. "What did they consist of?"

"I passed messages. That was all. I held messages, I passed them on, and I put packages in the post. Nothing else. Do you hear? *Nothing else!*"

"The Chanticleer messages."

"Yes. Yes. The messages from Chanticleer. I passed them on. That is all I ever did. All!"

In the ringing silence, Abigail caught the point an instant before Jonathan did: "You are not Chanticleer."

"I? I, Chanticleer? What? No! Is that what the files say? If they do, they are false!" He was half on his feet, voice breaking, as he shook a trembling fist. "You go back and tell them that!" Looking around wildly. "Zillah! Where is Zillah?" Raging at them once more. "I never betrayed my country! I only worked for peace!"

The black woman hurried back in, crouched beside the chair, took the sobbing figure in her arms. "You go on, now," she snarled.

"Wait," cried Abigail. "Please, sir. Who is Chanticleer?"

He shook his head, weeping. "I had my deposit," Chastain whispered. "My protection. Now it's gone. She took it. I have no protection. None."

"What does that mean?" said Jonathan. "What deposit?"

"I told you to go on," Zillah repeated. "Hurry up, now, before I get the law after you."

"We only have one or two more questions—"

"You done caused enough pain to Dr. Chastain. He's a fine gentleman. He don't never hurt nobody. Now, go on. Get out." She turned to Chastain, patted his shoulder. "There, there," she cooed. "There, there."

Startled, Abigail and Jonathan left them that way, found their own way out. In the brilliant March sunshine, the coachman was waiting, brushing his horse.

"Didn't I tell you?" he murmured happily. "Everybody likes Dr. Chastain."

IV

"He knew her name," said Jonathan as they rode back toward the depot. "Chanticleer is a woman, and he knew her name."

"Wait—" said Abigail.

"He was on verge of telling us." He rapped a hand against the side of the carriage. "I should have threatened him. One telegram to Sickles and I could have him arrested."

"To what end?" Abigail was thoughtful as they passed through the demolished city.

"To make him tell! He cannot hide behind that clerical nonsense." Big Red seemed to stiffen at this epithet, and Jonathan dropped his voice. "We should go back. We are leaving empty-handed."

"I do not think Dr. Chastain would tell us anything else," she said, staring at the coachman's back. "You saw them. Zillah will not let us in the house."

"I daresay Zillah will not withstand a company of Union soldiers!"

"Which we are not about to dispatch. Calm down, Jonathan." Whispering now, touching his hand. "Wait until we are on the train."

Again they sat in third class. The train back to Washington City was even emptier than the train down, as if the stream of commerce ran only in one direction. Or perhaps nobody at the South could get travel documents.

"I apologize," she said when they were settled. "Big Red was too interested in our conversation."

"Big Red? Ah, the coachman. Well, we are alone now. So tell me, please, Abigail. Why are we not going back to that house?"

"In the first place, Dr. Chastain never said that Chanticleer was a woman. He said that 'she' coerced him. But it is obvious, isn't it, who runs that household? I do not know what he did that allowed him to be coerced, or what Zillah knows, or whether what he did"—she blushed—"involved Zillah somehow. But it strikes me that it is Zillah, not Dr. Chastain, who is, or was, in contact with Chanticleer." The train was leaving the station. Abigail looked out upon the charred buildings. "It is my understanding," she said, "that the slaves themselves were a crucial part of the Union spy effort during the war, both gathering information and forming networks through which messages could be passed from hand to hand, or even from mouth to mouth."

"I had forgotten," said Jonathan. "But you are right. We used to call the messages from the slave network the 'black dispatches.'"

"Well, then, it is obvious what has happened, isn't it? Chanticleer, whoever he or she is, has revived the old network from the war—your black dispatches—and is using it to aid Mr. Lincoln, by providing damaging information about the witnesses called by the Radicals."

"So it is Zillah, not Chastain, who is part of the network."

"He gives Zillah cover. Perhaps she receives packages from Chanticleer, and Dr. Chastain posts them. And Zillah . . . well, she takes care of him."

Imagination briefly made them both uncomfortable.

"And the deposit?" Jonathan finally said. "What is that? What did he mean when he said he lost his protection?"

Abigail studied the wreck of a factory, then the remains of a fort. Pondering, she tapped her chin. He hid a smile. "I don't know, Jonathan," she said. "I'm not quite there yet. But we're closer. I can sense it. And I am quite certain that Dr. Chastain and Zillah, between them, have told us nearly everything that we need to work out what has been going on."

CHAPTER 39

Warning

I

THE PROSECUTION DECIDED to skip most of the widows and orphans. This, said Sickles, represented the sensible strategy. If the Managers brought to the witness box a parade of unfortunates whose husbands and fathers had been locked up by the execrable tyrant Abraham Lincoln, then Dennard, on cross-examination, would have the opportunity to explore exactly what those poor husbands and fathers were supposed to have done. "When they all turn out to be Southern sympathizers, Copperheads, and Knights of the Golden Circle," he said, "the country will swing back Lincoln's way." This, at least, was the way Sickles put it when, on Wednesday evening, he met Jonathan and Abigail at the office. Little had met them at the Washington depot, with instructions that Sickles wanted to see them at once.

Pudgy Rellman was there, too, and looked unhappy.

Speed and Dennard were at the Mansion.

"What that means," Sickles continued, "is that, no later than Monday, the real trial starts."

"Real how?" asked Abigail.

"The Radicals never expected to remove him from office with the first two counts. Those are just for show. The idea was to damage his standing with the public. It's a bit early to say how well it worked. The fact that they want to move on so swiftly suggests they think they've done enough damage already."

"Or that they're not doing enough," Jonathan suggested.

Sickles grimaced, put both hands on his stump, tried to find a more comfortable position. "Either way, they'll spend one more day making speeches about how Mr. Lincoln has violated the fundamental liberties of the American people, and then they'll move on."

"To Counts Three and Four," said Abigail.

"Precisely. Counts Three and Four. Ignoring congressional mandates on how to reconstruct the South. That's Count Three. Count Four, you will remember, says that Mr. Lincoln has been conspiring to make himself king of America. That's the way some of the Radical papers are putting it, anyway."

"The proposition is an absurdity."

Sickles lifted an eyebrow. "All that matters, Miss Canner, is whether the Managers can persuade people that it is true." He pointed to a sheaf of papers awaiting delivery to the copyist. "We can write as many arguments and motions as we like. The arguments don't really matter. This is politics, not law." He saw their faces. "Don't worry. We might be doing politics, but a trial is a trial, and if there's one thing I've learned over the years, it's that you can't tell midway through a trial how it's going to come out."

Jonathan said, "What would you like us to do?"

Sickles laughed. "Well, Rellman here has to go home and get a good night's sleep. I'm afraid that sitting in your place at the counsel table has worn him out. You, too." Addressing Jonathan. "Go on. Go home. Go get drunk. Go call on Miss Felix, or whoever it is you call on. Miss Canner and I have business to discuss."

"It will be better if I stay," said Jonathan at once. Rellman was already halfway to the door.

Abigail stared at Sickles. "I will be fine, Jonathan," she said. "Go."

II

"So it's 'Jonathan' now," said Sickles, once they were alone. "Even in public. Because, the way I remember, it is improper etiquette for a young lady to refer to a man by his first name in public."

"I do not consider a law office a public place," said Abigail. She was sitting at the conference table, its reassuring bulk between her and the reclining man. "Besides, Mr. Sickles, you are the one who keeps asking me to call you by your Christian name."

"Only when we are alone, Miss Canner."

"But that is not why you wished to see me."

"No." His face grew serious. As if on command, wind rattled the panes. "I want to know why you didn't follow Hilliman's advice. He wanted to wire me and have Chastain arrested. You talked him out of it."

Abigail's gaze was cool. "I do not believe that he knows who Chanticleer is."

"But Zillah probably does."

"Fine. Have them arrested tomorrow."

"Oh, well, I don't actually think that will be possible. I think, even if I can get the orders around Stanton's people and down to Richmond, we will find Chastain and Zillah long gone." He regarded her balefully. "And Chanticleer's identity with them."

Abigail said nothing.

"I think you've scared them off," said Sickles.

"Why would I do that?"

He swung his wooden leg up onto the adjoining chair, rubbed at his thigh. "Well, not by accident. You're too clever to make a mistake of that kind. No, Miss Canner. If you set them running, I am sure you had your reasons." He laughed. "I guess I have only myself to blame. I trusted you."

"And now you don't?"

"Well, let me put it this way. I don't think you've cast your lot with the Radicals. I don't think you've turned against Mr. Lincoln exactly. But I am starting to worry about exactly what you think you are doing." He used his right hand to count the fingers on his left. "One, you refuse to stop trying to figure out what happened the night Mr. McShane and the colored girl—I forget her name—Miss Deveaux—were killed, even though you are embarrassing our client, and even though you've been told to stop. Two"—he took another finger—"you don't say a word about your suspicion of Miss Bessie Hale until she's all set to flee to Europe." And another. "Three, you go to see Chastain, and by now I'm sure he's gone, too. Now, a lesser man than myself—or a more suspicious one, say—might guess that you are trying to sabotage the President's case. Me? I'm just guessing that you have a stake in this that you're not telling. A *personal* stake."

For a bad moment, Abigail's face almost betrayed her. She had spent years honing a confident yet inoffensive blankness to carry her through the higher levels of the white world, but the mask nearly slipped. Dan

Sickles might not have been the most brilliant of the President's men, but he was the one who saw most deeply into other people: their motives, their hopes, their fears. He was relentlessly seductive, and had drawn her out already over the past month on Judith, on her ambition, on her philosophy of life. If she tarried too long now, Heaven alone knew what secrets Sickles might winkle out of her.

"The hour is late," she said, rising. "My aunt will be worried."

"Those tricks might work with a young gentleman like Hilliman," barked Sickles. He, too, struggled to his feet. "But I'm not a gentleman, and I'm neither charmed nor fooled." Bad leg and all, he was moving around the common room. "Let's talk about Blaine for a minute."

"You told me that wasn't my fault!"

"And it wasn't." Leaning heavily on his cane, stroking his moustaches. "But I've been thinking, Miss Canner. Stanton is gone, but we still seem to be leaking information to the Radicals. And, meanwhile, the spigot from Chanticleer seems to have shut off."

"That has nothing to do with me."

"That is what I would like to believe." His face hardened. "Tell me, Miss Canner, have you heard anything lately from Mr. Yount?"

"*What?*"

"Your fiancé. Second Lieutenant Aaron Yount. Any news?"

"I'm sure I have no idea what you are talking about."

"Of course you do. My source has been through the records at the War Department, Miss Canner. Lieutenant Yount, of the Sixth Colored Troops, was declared missing after Petersburg. He was never officially identified as a prisoner of war. He also has not returned home. Most likely, he is lying in an unmarked grave—"

"He is *not*!" she cried.

Sickles was calm. "So you keep saying. And I am willing to believe that you believe it. But I marvel at your certainty. I wonder who might have given you the information on which you base your hopes that he is alive." He gave a sad little nod. "I wonder what you might not promise, or perform, in return for that hope."

Abigail looked at him for some while. The wind continued to whimper outside the windows.

"You accuse very easily, Mr. Sickles," she finally said. "But your own conduct in this matter has not been above reproach."

"In what way?"

"I am put in mind of our first encounter, when you removed a certain envelope from Mr. McShane's desk. Do you recall that occasion, Mr. Sickles?"

Sickles toyed with his moustaches. "Rings a faint bell."

"It occurs to me that the Managers are known to be searching for a certain letter, perhaps in the President's own hand, concerning his supposed plan to place Washington City under military government—"

"Let me put your mind at ease, Miss Canner. A man of the sort to conceal evidence in order to protect himself would hardly cavil at destroying it instead." A hard chuckle. "The letter you are describing would be too dangerous to preserve. It would have been burned in the grate at the first hint of trouble."

"Then you are telling me–"

"I am telling you nothing, Miss Canner. The same nothing you are telling me. Let us leave matters as they are."

He smiled. Feeling the tension lift, Abigail was emboldened to ask a question of her own. "What is a deposit?"

"I assume you do not mean bank deposit."

"I am not sure. Dr. Chastain spoke of a deposit."

Sickles looked interested. "What exactly did he say?"

"I do not recall his precise words."

"I am sure you recall his words very precisely." Shifting his weight, leaning on his cane. "Most of the better spies, if they'd been around for a while, would put aside what they called deposits. The deposit was a cache of papers hidden somewhere. Protection, in case the poor fellow met an untoward end." His eyes lit up. "So Chastain had a deposit. Means he was worried. Well, well."

Abigail was thoughtful. "I formed the impression that he had it no longer."

She would say no more.

III

The same night found Jonathan and Meg at the National Theatre, where a strange drama called *Brand*, by an unknown but clearly mad Norwegian named Ibsen, was being performed to great acclaim. The plot, which Jonathan followed only with difficulty, was somehow related to the mysteries of sacrifice and obedience, but he found concentration difficult, not because of the complexities of the trial or the exhausted state of his mind, but because Meg refused to keep her hands to herself.

She kept tickling his ribs. Margaret Felix, staid and prim daughter of the Lion, playing these games in the theater.

Most unlike her.

Most disturbing. Among those disturbed were nearby theatergoers, who were growing annoyed by the fidgeting couple.

The fidgeting couple left after the second act.

Back in the carriage, Jonathan asked Meg what exactly she thought she was doing.

Margaret Felix laughed. "Wasn't it fun? I want us to have more fun." She giggled, then hiccupped. "Where's dinner?" She slipped her arm through his, put her head against his shoulder. "You did say dinner."

"You've been drinking," he said, astonished. "I should take you home."

"Are you sure that's where you want to take me?" Jonathan turned to her, aghast. The golden eyes were clever, and moist. "I want you to take me wherever you took Miss Lucy Lambert Hale," she said. "That's where I want you to take me."

"Meg, I assure you—"

"I don't want you to assure me. I want you to take me where you took Miss Hale."

Jonathan was still objecting. "I never took Miss Hale anywhere."

"You dined with her, at the National Hotel."

"That was a friendly meal, Meg. Our families go way back."

"My understanding"—a saucy wink—"is that it was a *very* friendly meal."

"Someone has been spreading unsavory stories. You mustn't believe them."

Meg had begun to sniffle. Meg never sniffled; or drank; or was jealous. After that she wept for a little while. Jonathan turned the carriage toward her aunt Clara's, but decided to take his time. If the Lion heard about Meg's behavior there would be hell to pay.

"Then take me to Richmond," she said. "You took your colored girl to Richmond. Why not me?"

"Meg, please. Stop."

"Do you like her more than you like me? Is that it?"

"You know that isn't true."

"I don't like feeling this way," she said, suddenly. She shivered. He tucked the coach blanket more tightly around her shoulders. "I am not a miserable person. I am a happy person. I am marrying the man I love."

"Try to rest," he said awkwardly.

Meg put her head on his shoulder, linked her fingers around his arm. "I do not wish to tell you what to do, Jonathan. You are a man, after all. I told you in Philadelphia that I know, from living with my father, what men are." A tight nod. "It is just, those stories about you and Miss Hale, and you and Miss Canner—"

"Please, Meg. Put the stories out of your mind. I had to spend time with Miss Hale because her father is a powerful man. There was nothing more. And Miss Canner and I work together."

"A powerful man." She yawned. "My father is also a powerful man." Her voice was sleepy. "And he has powerful friends."

"Ssssh. Rest, Meg."

"His friends do not much care for your President."

"I know."

"They do not much care for Senator Wade, either." She sighed, pressed closer. "I believe they are searching for an alternative." Her eyes were closed. "Perhaps a military man."

CHAPTER 40

Supplicant

I

THE NEXT AFTERNOON, a sharp skirmish began. The third count claimed that the President had defied congressional statutes. The prosecution now sought to introduce further evidence on the theme. Dennard objected that all that had really occurred was a difference in interpretation, nothing rising to a level that would necessitate impeachment.

"Your Honor, we should here be absolutely clear. The defiance of which the Managers keep speaking is a matter of the appropriate disposition of military forces. Nothing more. The bill in question commanded the President to maintain military governments in the Southern states until such time as conditions set forth by Congress are realized."

Butler was on his feet. "Your Honor, counsel for the respondent is merely repeating what we have already established. This is not argument."

"These facts," said Dennard, "are crucial to our argument."

Chase waved an impatient hand. "Get to the point, counsel."

"Mr. Chief Justice, Senators, it is our contention, with all respect, that the Congress lacks authority to dictate to the President in matters regarding the disposition of military forces."

A murmur of dismay from the floor. Chase removed his glasses and pinched the bridge of his nose: a sure sign, as the whole room knew, of irritation.

"Continue, counsel."

"Sir," said Dennard, "under Article II of the Constitution, the

President is the commander-in-chief of the armed forces of the United States. Article I grants to the Congress the power to declare war and to make appropriations. But once a state of war exists—as it did during the late rebellion—and once the money to support the armed forces has been appropriated—which it was—it is up to the Executive, not the legislature, to decide how those forces are to be deployed." He mopped his forehead. "Members of this august body may have honest disagreements with the President's decisions on these matters. It may even be, in some circumstances, that the policy of the Senate would be a wiser one than the policy of the Executive. But the Framers of the Constitution did not place that authority in the Senate's hands. In their wisdom or their folly, they placed it in the Executive."

Dennard took his seat. The Chief Justice prepared to move on, but Thaddeus Stevens pounded a fist on the table, demanding to be heard. Although the two men were friends of long standing, Chase's eyes narrowed at the old man's discourtesy.

"Mr. Manager Stevens," said Chase, coldly.

"I consider counsel's contention an outrage," huffed Stevens, rising. "I cannot believe that counsel for the respondent seriously intend to come into this chamber and argue that an act of the Congress is unconstitutional. Plainly, the Senate has heard that case, and disagreed, for the bill passed this house overwhelmingly. Thus, the question of constitutionality is, in this chamber, a matter of *res judicata*." Stevens coughed, wiped his mouth, took a breath. He pointed to a sheaf of papers held by a colleague. "I would ask leave to file the argument."

Chase tapped his chin, then nodded. "So ordered."

A much more detailed version of the argument would be published in the *Congressional Globe*, creating on the printed page the impression that the entire chamber had sat rapt as counsel extemporized. In reality, as Sickles never tired of pointing out, hardly anybody even listened to the short versions of House and Senate speeches, so nobody was likely to read the long ones—although he supposed that scholars years hence might mistake them for arguments actually made on this bill or that one. "As for me," he liked to say, "when I was in Congress, I don't think I opened the *Globe* once."

Now, with Stevens silenced, Chase determined once more to move on. He glanced at Dennard.

"Does counsel for respondent wish to be heard?"

"Yes, Your Honor."

Chase puffed out a lot of air. Plainly, he had been hoping for a different answer. "Very well. Counsel for the respondent will be heard. But be brief."

"May it please the Court, I can state our position in two sentences. It is the Managers who have put the President's state of mind into issue. Surely, then, it matters that he believed the statute unconstitutional."

"So noted. He believed it. I am sure the Managers will accept that." Fully in charge once more, Chase did not wait for the prosecution to say whether he was right. "As to the rest, we will file the argument and we will move on. Now sit."

Stevens sought recognition. Chase ignored him. "Fifteen-minute recess," he declared, and left the bench in a temper.

II

"I have not had the opportunity to talk to you," whispered Kate, as Margaret, standing nearby, held court with several other Washington ladies. "About poor Mr. Blaine, I mean. That was horrible."

"Horrible," Abigail agreed, wondering why Mrs. Sprague chose this moment to bring it up.

"But, once again, the police seem to be making no progress."

"I am very sorry to hear that."

Kate leaned closer. "There is a rumor, dear, that *you* have been looking into what happened to poor Mr. McShane."

Abigail stiffened. "I was, briefly. I am no longer. I am busy with trial."

"So, you would have no interest in information about Blaine?"

"None whatever."

"Then there would be no point in my telling you," murmured Kate with that tiny smile, "that he was often in the company of a certain young lady about whom we spoke when you and I were last at table."

And she leaned away again, striking up a conversation with the woman sitting to her left.

III

Following the recess, the Managers called Eliza Caffey, the housekeeper for the Reverend Henry Ward Beecher, a popular Abolitionist preacher in New York and, when it suited him, one of the Lincoln's leading supporters. The President's lawyers had noticed her name on the witness list, but had been unable to ascertain precisely what the prosecution expected her to say.

"If I might," said Dennard, rising. "For what purpose is this witness offered?"

"Your Honor," said Bingham, "Miss Caffey's testimony will help to establish the President's state of mind at the time of the events in question."

"We object, Mr. Chief Justice. The President's state of mind is not relevant to any of the offenses charged."

Chase turned to Bingham.

"Mr. Chief Justice, Senators, counsel for the respondent has argued as recently as today that the offenses alleged in Counts Three and Four amount to differences in judgment. The Managers do not agree. But let us take counsel at their word. It is the position of the Managers that if indeed Mr. Lincoln did exercise poor judgment, the reason might have been his distress over the tragic death of Mrs. Lincoln. Perhaps, for a time, he lost his reason." He had to raise his voice to be heard over the rising tumult: gasps, cries, even curses. "We offer this witness, Your Honor, in order to establish this possibility."

Chase managed, with difficulty, to restore order. The fury was written on his round, soft face: although which upset him more, Bingham's proffer or the noisy affront to the dignity of the proceeding, was difficult to say. "Mr. Dennard," he said.

Dennard was sharp. "Your Honor, the distinguished Manager could no doubt conjure any number of impressive legal arguments for the admissibility of the testimony. Nevertheless, the true motive is clear. Having failed utterly in their effort to establish that the President has committed any high crimes or misdemeanors, they now seek to blacken his reputation, in the hope of damaging him politically, and perhaps swaying the public, which is hostile to this proceeding, in their direction."

Bingham flared. "I resent any implication that any of the Managers on the part of the House are motivated by any but the highest and—"

Chase waved him silent. "Counsel will have the opportunity for closing argument at the appropriate time. I am certain that the distinguished Manager does not intend what you have suggested, and I can assure you that the Court would never countenance such a thing. Unless there is objection from a Senator, it is the Court's intention to allow the testimony of this witness." He adjusted his glasses, glared down at Bingham. "Nevertheless, I must warn you, sir. The Court will require you to stay within the bounds of your own argument for the admissibility of the evidence."

"I understand, Your Honor."

Bingham quickly established who Miss Caffey was, and by whom she was employed. He then asked her whether she had ever met the President.

The room waited. Everybody knew something important was happening, but nobody was sure quite what.

"Yes, sir," she said, voice small and frightened. Her face was deathly pale. Her expression was that of a mouse toyed with by hunting cats.

"Please tell us how that came about."

"Yes, sir." Miss Caffey began to slump. She was so slight that if she slipped too far she might vanish from sight. "I met him when he came to the reverend. For counseling it was, sir, the way all of them do."

"All of who?"

"The ones who come at night, sir. They come at night so nobody will know they needs counseling."

"And when was this, that you met the President?"

October, she told them: this October just past. Late at night, after the master and the missus had retired. The bell rang, and Miss Caffey rose from her bed to answer. She opened the door, she said, and there was Mr. Lincoln, standing in the cold rain, wearing a black coat and a tall black hat.

"And there was a rig, like, sir, with a driver, waiting for him. Beautiful black horses they were, sir."

"And when was this again?"

"This past October."

Bingham consulted his note cards. "October of 1866."

"Yes, sir."

"Three months after Mr. Lincoln's wife died."

"After that. Yes, sir."

"And do you happen to remember, Miss Caffey, exactly how Mrs. Lincoln died?"

Dennard bellowed his objection, and Chase at once admonished Bingham to limit himself to relevant testimony. Abigail paled nevertheless; the damage had been done by the reminder to the chamber, so that everyone now recalled the rumors that Mary Todd Lincoln had been a suicide.

Bingham, meanwhile, continued in a gentle tone. "Very well, Miss Caffey. Let me be very sure that I am understanding you correctly. In October of 1866—this October just past—you saw the President at the door of Reverend Beecher's house in Brooklyn."

Again Dennard objected: the witness had testified only that she saw a man she thought was the President. Jonathan found the objection confusing. Chase was bound to overrule it, as he did: Dennard was free to challenge the identification on cross-examination.

But as the witness answered—yes, it was the President, she would know the face anywhere—Jonathan began to see the deeper wisdom of Dennard's interruption. The mood had been broken. No longer was the audience sitting in the dreary wet darkness of an autumn night in Brooklyn, peering over the shoulder of the nervous housemaid as she opened the door on an eerie late-night visitor. Now everyone was in the Senate Chamber once more, reminded that this was only testimony, a tale told by a witness who was every bit as mortal and fallible as the lawyers arguing over her words.

Bingham, meanwhile, was asking whether Lincoln had ever been to visit Reverend Beecher before.

"Oh, yes, sir. Twice that I know of."

"And of course he had attended Reverend Beecher's church before his speech at the Cooper Institute in 1860."

Dennard was on his feet. "Your Honor, may it please the court, counsel is testifying for the witness."

The silky smile again. "I was about to ask my question, Your Honor."

"Proceed, counsel." Chase was frosty. He hated affronts to his dignity, and he had taken pains to ensure that his dignity was entirely bound up in the conduct of this trial.

Bingham turned to Miss Caffey. "Were you aware of the President's visit to Reverend Beecher's church?"

The young woman looked down at her shapeless dress. "Sir, that was before my time. I have heard talk of it—"

"Objection. Hearsay."

"Sustained," snapped Chase, his anger growing.

Bingham strolled back to the table. Another Manager handed him a card. Looking out at the chamber rather than at the witness, he said, casually, "Would you please tell us once more the date of the President's visit to Reverend Beecher's residence?"

"In October."

"Do you happen to recall when in October?"

"No, sir."

"Perhaps we can sharpen your recollection." Not looking up from his card; voice casual. "Was the visit, say, before or after the incident involving Mrs. Tilton?"

For a moment, nobody reacted. An instant later came bedlam: shouts in the chamber, cries from the gallery. Chase banged his gavel, but in vain. Sickles, lurching around on his one good leg, looked every inch a man ready to pull out a derringer and slay his wife's lover. Senators were shaking their fists, several at each other.

Jonathan was astounded; and appalled.

The Managers, it turned out, had not invited Beecher's housekeeper for anything as mundane as attempting to imply that a distraught President might have lost his mind after the death of his wife. No. They were trying to suggest that somehow the President had been involved with sexual scandal.

They would never say so directly. They could not prove it, nobody would believe it, and, in any event, direct association was not necessary. The goal was to shock the public out of its Lincoln-worship. To accomplish that goal, the Managers needed only to create an atmosphere in which citizens across the country, when they thought of the man in the White House, would be reminded, if involuntarily, that he had somehow been "involved"—there was the word—"involved" in perhaps the most embarrassing ménage-à-trois of the age. Mrs. Tilton was a lady of means, a freethinker, and an advocate of intimate relations outside of marriage. She had gone to Beecher for counseling because of difficulties she was having with her husband. Her husband arranged for the publication of newspaper articles accusing Beecher of taking intimate advantage of his wife.

No wonder everyone was shouting at once, ignoring the repeated pounding of the Chief Justice's gavel.

Somehow Dennard managed to make his objection heard amidst the tumult. The sordid tale of Mrs. Tilton was irrelevant to these proceedings, and prejudicial as well—

Bingham insisted that he was only trying to fix the date more firmly in the witness's mind. He was fixing a good deal more than the date, and the mind of the witness was not the mind he sought to affect. Nevertheless, Chase said that the witness would be allowed to answer.

Again Bingham addressed the witness. "Was the President's visit before or after the Tilton business?"

"Before, sir. That terrible newspaper article was later. November."

Bingham turned toward the bench. "Your Honor, the Managers would like to introduce the article itself."

Dennard bounded to his feet. "Your Honor, the article in question is the subject of judicial proceedings in New York City, to determine whether it was obscene, and whether Mrs. Woodhull should be jailed for distributing it. Nothing so tawdry should be made a part of the record of these proceedings." He glanced at Bingham. "In addition, Your Honor, counsel for the respondent believe that the material is highly prejudicial, and would be admitted for no purpose other than to embarrass the respondent."

Bingham opened his mouth, but Chase shook his head. His round face seemed to have aged five years in the past hour. "Objection sustained. The article will not be admitted. Nor will any further testimony regarding it."

The witness seemed to think she was through, but before she could quite rise, Bingham turned her way once more. "Now, Miss Caffey. After you saw Mr. Lincoln at the door that night, what did you do?"

"Sir, I asked him his business. He said he was there to see the reverend."

"What happened next?"

"Sir, I invited him in. I would not ordinarily have done that in the middle of the night, but for the President . . ."

Bingham smiled. "We understand. Pray continue."

"Sir, I invited him to wait in the parlor. I went and woke Mrs. Beecher, and she went and woke the reverend. Mrs. Beecher told me to make our guest some tea, and that the reverend would be down in a moment."

"Did you tell Mrs. Beecher who the visitor was?"

"Yes, sir."

"Did the reverend come downstairs?"

"Yes, sir. He came downstairs, and he and Mr. Lincoln went into the reverend's study and closed the door."

"How long was Mr. Lincoln in the house?"

"Sir, I would say about two hours."

"Do you know what they talked about?"

"Objection. Hearsay."

"Sustained."

"Your Honor," said Bingham, "we tender the witness."

Chase declared a thirty-minute recess before the cross.

IV

Abigail was troubled. She enjoyed Kate's company, but was secretly a little frightened of her as well. The constant warnings about Mrs. Sprague's motives from Sickles and Jonathan had left her on edge. Now Kate had raised once more the specter of Bessie Hale. What was she trying to say? That Bessie, before fleeing to Europe, had been *involved* with the prim, disapproving, and very married Blaine? Or was she hinting at something else? Because, if Kate meant to imply that Bessie had carried messages to Blaine, then she had knowledge of the conspiracy; and assumed that Abigail had knowledge, too; or perhaps Kate was trying to impart knowledge, hoping that Abigail would look into the possibility of involvement and discover the conspiracy in its stead.

But if Kate knew about the conspiracy, why not take the knowledge to someone in authority? If she wanted to keep it all secret, then why tell Abigail?

It occurred to her that she would never be able to follow the convoluted paths of the experienced political mind of Katherine Sprague as she maneuvered to make her father President. She was the only person Abigail had met in Washington City she felt sure could outthink her.

"Let us dine together again soon, dear," said Kate. "We were so rudely interrupted last time."

"By all means."

"We have so much to discuss."

"Indeed," said Abigail, wondering.

V

Again it was the turn of Dennard. He stood at a distance from Miss Caffey, arms folded over his barrel chest, the look on his aged, plump face that of an affectionate but disapproving grandparent.

"Just a few questions," he said. "I want you to know how much all of us in Washington appreciate that you made the trip down."

"Oh, it wasn't no trouble," said Miss Caffey, fingers still twisting in her scarf.

"He's a very wise man, Reverend Beecher, isn't he?"

"Oh, yes, sir. Absolutely."

"I would suppose that lots of people come to him for counseling."

Miss Caffey's face darkened. "If this is about that Tilton woman and her mad husband—"

Dennard was already waving both hands for peace. "No, no, of course not. No sensible person believes a word they say."

Bingham objected at once, and Chase sustained it, as he had to, but Dennard had slipped in the main point of the cross: whether or not Lincoln was in New York seeking Beecher's counsel, the scandal made no difference if, as Beecher's admirers believed, the entire Tilton affair had been invented by an angry husband. A murmur passed through the chamber, quelled by the Chief Justice's gavel.

"Let me ask you this," said Dennard. "You said that many people come to Reverend Beecher for counsel. I assume they come because of his wisdom."

Chase glanced at the Managers, perhaps expecting an objection—Miss Caffey could not possibly know why the troubled sought out her employer—but Bingham remained in his seat.

"Yes, sir," she said.

"And his discretion."

"Sir?"

"They come to Reverend Beecher because he is discreet. He would never disclose a confidence."

"Oh, no, sir, absolutely not."

"Even during the scandal, when he could have told the world what happened during his meetings with Mrs. Tilton, he kept her confidences, did he not?"

"He did," said Miss Caffey, proudly.

"And, indeed, he is the sort of man who would not even admit to others that a particular person had been in for counseling. Isn't that true?"

Chase was growing irritated. He kept waiting for Bingham's objection. The fact that the prosecutor continued to listen calmly, Jonathan realized, could mean one of two things: either Bingham was a fool, or the Managers had laid a trap somewhere.

And Bingham was no fool.

Meanwhile, Miss Caffey, led gently by Dennard, was telling all the world that her employer would never disclose a confidence or betray a trust. He was known throughout the country, she said, for his discretion.

Dennard nodded, arms crossed once again. "So, when the man who resembled the President arrived at the door, you had no way of knowing, did you, exactly why he was there?"

For a moment Miss Caffey seemed confused. "He was there for counseling," she said after a moment.

"Did the visitor tell you that he sought counsel?"

"Well, no—"

"And Reverend Beecher didn't tell you, did he? He would never disclose a confidence, correct?"

"The reverend didn't tell me. No."

"Nobody told you that the visitor sought counseling, isn't that correct?"

"I assumed, when a man of that importance arrived so late at night in the middle of the rain—"

Again Dennard interrupted. His show of warmth had vanished. "So your earlier testimony that the visitor sought counseling was really just an assumption?"

Miss Caffey looked wounded. The friendly round-faced lawyer, her protector among all these great gentlemen, had abandoned her. "I guess it was," she whispered.

"Louder, please."

"Yes, sir. I guess it was. Just an assumption, I mean. Sorry, sir."

Dennard stepped closer still. "Now, this visitor. The one you took to be Mr. Lincoln. Was he alone?"

"He had two other men with him."

"Did you recognize them?"

"No, sir."

"Were they introduced to you?"

"No, sir."

"And the visitor himself. Did he tell you he was the President?"

A moment's hesitation. "No."

"Did anybody tell you that he was the President?"

"No, sir."

"I see." He turned toward the table. Jonathan had the note card ready and thrust it into his hand. Dennard adjusted his spectacles. "So, Miss Caffey, I take this to be your testimony. On the date mentioned, late at night, when it was dark, you arose sleepily from your bed to find at the door a man who resembled the President, accompanied by two other men, who wished to visit Reverend Beecher. Nobody told you who they were. Nobody told you why they were there. Is this a fair summary?"

Her voice had grown very small in a vast quiet. "Yes, sir," she said.

And Dennard found another smile for her, beaming as if she were after all his favorite daughter. "Thank you, Miss Caffey. Thank you so much for coming all this way and telling us the truth. You've been enormously helpful to us all in a very difficult time."

She could hardly conceal her pride as she stepped down. Dennard could hardly conceal his relief. He asked whether the Managers planned to call either of the two men the witness had seen outside the house with the man "who she thinks might or might not have been the respondent."

Bingham assured the body that the Managers had no such plans.

Dennard asked that the court strike the witness's entire testimony, as she had never clearly identified the respondent.

Chase said he would decide that motion at the close of the evidence.

Sweating from exertion but obviously happy with the outcome, Dennard returned to his seat. The Chanticleer letters had contained little information about Miss Caffey, and the coterie had been forced to guess at her testimony. But Dennard had done well. Even though Bingham had dragged a whiff of scandal into the chamber, the President's lawyer had carefully dissipated it. The strategy had failed completely. And yet the Managers still looked confident.

Too confident.

Something big was coming; and everybody knew it.

CHAPTER 41

Rescue

I

"THEY PLAN TO call Reverend Beecher as a witness," said the President. "That is their surprise."

"I would not have believed it," said Sickles, shaking his head as he sat none too straight on the sofa. There were moments when the constant pain he hid from the world threatened to overwhelm him. "But I think you must be right."

Lincoln stood near the fireplace, where a few coals smoldered. "There can be no other reason," he declared, voice heavy, "for the questions they asked of poor Miss Caffey yesterday. They were laying the foundation." He poked at the fire. He was so very tall that he had to lean a long way, even with the poker. His jacket rode up, producing a comic effect, although nobody laughed. "Beecher is by far the most famous and respected clergyman in the country. Whatever he pronounces, people will treat as Gospel truth."

Sickles squirmed into a more comfortable position. "They will ask Beecher to pronounce that you were . . . *distraught* . . . after Mrs. Lincoln's passing."

"They will not dare!" declared Speed.

But nobody paid attention any longer to his enthusiasms, and Sickles continued as though he had not spoken. "And they are betting that we do not dare cross-examine Beecher too closely, because of who he is."

Jonathan, taking notes, noticed that nobody asked their client what actually happened. Either they already knew whether Lincoln had indeed visited Beecher for counseling in the dead of night, or they wished not to know.

Dennard, more lawyer than politician, shifted his bulk on the straight chair beside the fireplace. Behind him the gaslights hissed and flickered. He glanced at them nervously, as if expecting any moment to be poisoned by the fumes. "I have never been involved in such a proceeding. If they call Beecher, they will look like knaves before the whole world."

"There has never been such a proceeding," said the President, his smile widening. "And I don't think the Managers are worried too much about looking like knaves. I think we passed that particular station a ways back, as the railroad conductor said to the—" He stopped. At first Jonathan thought he was weary of repeating the tale too often, for they had heard this one several times before. Then he realized that the President had heard something the rest of them had missed.

The door creaked open, and Noah Brooks stepped in. He excused himself, then handed Lincoln a telegram. He smiled his superior smile at Jonathan, then tiptoed out.

The President read, frowning. "I have here a dispatch from the commander of Fort Monroe," he said. "It seems that our friend Mr. Jefferson Davis has made bail."

"After two years!" Sickles exclaimed, fully awake again. "Wasn't the bail a hundred thousand dollars?"

Lincoln nodded. "I hear that Mr. Greeley has been raising the bail among his silk-stocking millionaire friends up there in New York."

"I don't understand," said Speed, who would much rather have been before a mob with tar and feathers than among politicians. "Why would they wish to bail the man who led the South in its rebellion? And why now?"

Jonathan was wondering whether August Belmont, rebuffed on the tariff, had been one of the silk-stocking millionaires who put up the money. Or *had* he been rebuffed?

Lincoln gestured impatiently. "They bailed him out so that they can tell the country that Mr. Davis was released on my watch." He sagged, and, for an instant, Jonathan saw the weight of ages in the deeply lined face. "The Radicals want the people to think I won the war but I've lost the peace. Well, maybe I have a little. It's true the peace hasn't been quite as peaceful as I hoped. Jefferson Davis." He shook his head in bewilderment, and then, as if against his will, smiled a bit. "You know, at the end of the war, General Grant asked me whether he should capture Jeff Davis or let him escape the country. I told him the story of an Irishman who took the pledge, and then got thirsty and wandered into a bar, where he ordered a lemonade. And while the lemonade was being prepared, the Irishman whispered to the bartender, 'And couldn't ye put a little brandy in it all unbeknown to meself?'"

Strained laughter all around. Everybody saw the point; everybody had heard the President tell the same story to defend the same policy; and everybody knew that the policy had failed in the end. For Davis had not escaped, but had been arrested in a raid by Union troops a few months after the end of the war. Newspaper accounts insisted that, when taken into custody, the onetime president of the Confederate States of America had been wearing women's clothes, although Davis's defenders down South called this hogwash.

The President's smile, meanwhile, had become wistful. "Well, never mind. I guess I can see what they're thinking. But I don't reckon we should worry too much about Jeff Davis being released. And I don't think we should worry about what Reverend Beecher might say if he does come down to testify. We still have a few surprises of our own on the way."

II

"They will send an emissary," said Jonathan. "Lincoln will send someone to visit Beecher, and Beecher will refuse to come to Washington."

"You seem to think Mr. Lincoln is a magician." They were side by side in the carriage once more. She was smiling her secret smile as the horses clopped along the broken cobbles of Pennsylvania Avenue. It was early evening, and this time she had asked Jonathan for a ride home, after first inquiring whether by any chance he had once more borrowed the Bannerman barouche. He had agreed, eagerly, but Abigail had diverted him, two minutes after leaving the firm, to a neighborhood near Capitol Hill.

He instantly knew why; thought she was crazy; said yes.

"I am only guessing," Jonathan admitted. "But he seems so confident. I know there are surprises in store for the Managers. I just don't know what they are."

"He will need to spring a large surprise indeed," she said, "if Stanton should testify that the President commanded him to establish the Department of the Atlantic." Then: "Good. We are here."

Here was Third Street, just above C Street, where even in the darkness it was possible to make out the charred remains of what had once been the bawdy house kept by Sophia Harbour, known to the trade as Madame Sophie.

III

"We should not be doing this," said Jonathan.

"I shall not detain you much longer," said Abigail.

"Why are we here?"

"I just want to see. That's all."

As Abigail studied the ruins, he craned his neck this way and that. Margaret Felix's aunt Clara lived four streets away, and although he could not quite imagine his Meg traveling four blocks in this particular direction, toward this neighborhood, at this time of night—well, in the modern world, anything was possible.

"You asked only for a ride home," said Jonathan nervously.

Abigail laughed. "Well, not *only*."

Jonathan could not quite work Abigail Canner out. One day she seemed prepared to forget her investigation of the death of poor Rebecca Deveaux and focus instead on the trial; the next she was dragging him halfway across the city to look at what was left of Madame Sophie's establishment. An hour ago, in the office, they had been discussing the day's events. Now she had drawn him once more into her . . . well, into whatever it was that she called herself doing.

The wind picked up. The horses whined. "Have you seen what you came to see?"

"Not quite." She was looking at the tenements across the way. "The fire was in the middle of the night. Still, the firehouse is less than a mile away. The building should not have burned to the ground."

Jonathan looked at her. "Very well. The fire brigade obviously dawdled. They, too, must be part of the conspiracy."

"I very much doubt that," she said, continuing to study the windows. "But I do wonder why the house burned so fast." She began to climb down.

"Abigail—"

"You may wait in the trap or you may come along."

He hastily tied the horses and followed her across the street. The firemen had thrown down some sandbags as a barrier in front of what

remained of the house, but the makeshift wall had not kept the neighborhood out. Peering through the windows, they saw signs of looting.
The smell of burnt wood permeated the rubble.

"What are you looking for?" he asked.

"I am not sure."

"Then how will you know when you find it?"

Abigail ignored this. She stepped through the front entrance—the
door had burned up, or been taken—and made her way to the stairs.

"You can't go up there," he said. He had seen a house in this condition at Petersburg; watched it collapse on the Confederate defenders;
been sent inside afterward to count the dead. "Half the risers are gone,
and there is very little flooring left."

"I am not going up." She crouched, and pointed at what had been a
closet beneath the stairs. Outside, the wind blew harder. "See here? All
the boards have burst outward."

"From which you conclude?"

"That this is where the fire started. Inside the closet." She stood.
The floor nearly gave, and she grabbed his hand for support. Did not
let go again. "Then it went along the carpet—see the burn marks? In a
straight line, more or less."

Something above them creaked heavily. Jonathan tugged her toward
the door. "We have to get out of here."

"One minute more."

"Abigail, the building is going to collapse."

"Look how the fire went up the walls." He followed her eye. "The
middle of the night," she continued, "so Madame Sophie and her girls
were asleep. I wonder which was her bedroom." She stopped once more,
peered into the shadowy closet. "Light," she announced. "The light
comes through. There is a room on the other side."

"Probably where clients were entertained." A loud crack, and a piece
of the stair rail crumpled before their eyes. "Come on. There is no more
time."

"I suspect that it was Madame Sophie's room. That is why the fire
began in the closet."

"You think the fire was set."

"Isn't it obvious that it was?" The closet floor had fallen into the
basement. She tried to find another path to the bedroom. "The fire
began in her closet to be sure that she would not survive it."

Jonathan gave her wrist another tug. "I am skeptical that we can reach that conclusion on so little evidence." An uneasy glance at what remained of the ceiling. "We are neither of us trained engineers."

"I agree. I could be wrong."

"I am glad to hear you say that."

"On the other hand, I could be right."

A fresh gust of wind shook the structure. Dust pelted down from charred rafters.

"We have to go now," said Jonathan, with vigor.

"I just need to see—"

"The whole place is swaying, Abigail. Look!"

She did; and it was. A window frame fell in.

"Almost done," she whispered, squatting on the floor of the closet, trying to work it out. Burnt tatters of clothing were on hooks. She sniffed the air. Embers, and now something else: kerosene. Someone had crouched where she was crouching, poured kerosene over Madame Sophie's dresses and robes, and set the fire.

Then she saw it, glittering in the corner: covered with soot, but very much out of place. She crawled over a broken beam to pick it up. The groaning above was sharper and faster.

"Jonathan."

"Yes?"

"I think you are right. We should go. Very fast."

They almost made the door. But a section of floor directly ahead fell into the basement, and would have carried them with it had they been running just a little faster. As they looked around for an escape, a weakened beam came down with a great crash, and bits of the second story with it. Abigail and Jonathan both fell hard and nearly slid into the hole, only to be yanked to their feet by a pair of strong arms. From what Jonathan could tell, a red-haired giant had pulled them from the rubble and was dragging them into the street.

Abigail turned to look, but the giant shouted at them to get down. Jonathan threw her to the ground, shielding her with his body as what remained of the building folded in on itself with a colossal roar. Burnt wood flew everywhere, the explosion possibly louder than the initial collapse. Windows were thrown open up and down the street. Lamps were lit.

They picked themselves up from the frozen mud. The giant had to be six foot six at least, probably more. Abigail made the introduction.

"Mr. Hilliman, this is Corporal Waverly, late of the Army of Northern Virginia."

The giant grinned shyly. "Just 'Mr. Waverly,' I guess. I mean, we did lose the war, I guess, didn't we?"

"You must be the gentleman Miss Canner was telling me about," said Jonathan, breathing hard, his hand vanishing in the huge fist as they shook. "The one who looks after Miss Berryhill."

"What I don't understand," said Abigail, "is what you are doing here."

Waverly blushed. "Ma'am, Miss Berryhill asked me to look in on you from time to time."

"Well, you certainly picked a good time to look in," she said.

Jonathan offered Corporal Waverly a ride to wherever he had to be, but the giant declined nervously, saying a man of his station should not be riding in so fine a carriage. When Jonathan tried to insist, the corporal shook his head, backed away, and, then, quite suddenly for a man of his size, vanished into the shadows.

Jonathan turned to Abigail, who was brushing off her coat. "Thank you for that little adventure," he said.

Abigail held out her hands. Her sleeves and skin were covered with soot.

"Nanny is not going to like this," she said.

"It was your idea."

"And well worth it." She was brushing dust from her find.

"What is that?" said Jonathan.

Abigail held the object up into the spill of a streetlamp, twisting and turning it as the metal glittered brightly. "A pipe tool, imported from Europe." She pronounced the next words with an air of finality. "It belongs to Mr. Grafton."

IV

This time they skipped Dennard and went straight to Dan Sickles. In the past, when visiting Washington City, Sickles had always stayed with his old friends the Stantons. Since his arrival to help with the impeachment trial, he had taken a suite of rooms at the Willard Hotel, the finest in the city. Now he sat at the dining table in his dressing gown, looking tired and drawn, the pain obvious in the lines of his face. Abigail and Jonathan were across from him. The pipe tool sat on the damask.

The double doors to the bedroom were closed, and Abigail, suspecting that they had disturbed Sickles at his revels, felt herself withdrawing just a bit.

"Let's think about this," said Sickles when they had told the story. "Let's assume that this contraption belongs to Grafton, although I'll bet there are fifty of them in the city. A hundred. But assume you're right. Do you have any way of knowing when Grafton lost it?" Looking from one exhausted face to the other. "Maybe he was a client of Madame Sophie's. Did you consider that? Or maybe he did the same thing you did, skulking around looking for clues. You have no way to know, do you?"

"Surely you will concede," Jonathan objected, "that Grafton is at the center of the conspiracy."

"Only in the sense that lawyers are at the heart of every truly terrible decision that truly powerful people make. Me, I prefer to judge the client rather than the lawyer—" He stopped suddenly, and laughed, as if embarrassed by his own thesis. It occurred to Abigail that he was probably drunk.

To their surprise, Sickles hopped rather nimbly to his feet. He was not wearing his wooden leg, but hobbled around instead on a crutch. The stump was hidden beneath the robe.

"Do you know where I was when Booth shot Lincoln?" he said. "I was in South America on a mission. If I had been in Washington that night, it probably would have been me in the box with Lincoln. Maybe I could have made a difference. He almost died." He was at the window. He plucked the curtain away, looked down at the city. "That's why I'm here. Oh, I might have said yes anyway, but once they killed McShane—" Again he stopped. Swinging back into the room, he settled himself on the couch, waving at them to remain where they were. "I suppose we should arrest him. Grafton. I wonder who we could have do it. Stanton? Baker?"

"Sherman and Grant are a train ride away," said Jonathan. "They would never betray Mr. Lincoln."

"True. They wouldn't." He seemed amused. "We could send a wire, they could march in and snatch Grafton and lock him up—I don't know—in Fort Lafayette or someplace. Far away from Washington, you see."

"But we won't," said Abigail, as usual a step ahead.

"No, Miss Canner. We won't. Know why?"

"Because, if Mr. Lincoln starts arresting people, claiming that they are part of a conspiracy, he will be convicted." She rubbed aching eyes. "Especially if he has the army do it for him."

"With this evidence—" Jonathan began.

Sickles snorted. "What evidence? A pipe tool that you and Miss Canner here found at the scene of the fire. That you *say* you found. We can't prove it belongs to Grafton, and we can't prove you found it where you say you did." Again he smiled. "Don't look so despondent. You did well."

"We were almost killed!"

"That is what happens in war."

Back in the carriage, Jonathan fulminated about Sickles's nonchalance. Abigail let him run for a bit, then drew him gently to heel.

"I have an idea."

V

At eight-fifteen the following morning, they met in the lobby of the building at Fourteenth and G. They were not due at the firm until nine-thirty. Together they trooped up the stairs, but only to the first floor, where, as expected, they found the lights on in Grafton's offices.

"Ready?" asked Jonathan.

Abigail nodded.

"Maybe I should do this alone."

"Open the door."

So they knocked, and walked in, and found Mr. Plum sitting at his desk, one hand washing the other atop the blotter.

"Oh dear," he was saying. He appeared to have been saying it for some time. He took in his visitors with a quick sweep of those huge eyes and then removed the thick glasses to look at them again. "Oh dear," he said again.

"We would like to see Mr. Grafton," said Jonathan, with the peremptory emphases of his class. "Immediately, please."

Plum was already shaking his head. "Oh, no, sir, that would not be possible. My apologies. It isn't possible."

"The matter is urgent. I am afraid we will have to insist."

"But he isn't here. He's gone."

"Gone where?"

"Away," said Plum. "He left a note. He said he had a wire last night. A crisis in his personal affairs. He did not say where he was going, only that he had no idea how long he would be away, and that I should see about assigning his cases to other counsel. This is most irregular, you see. Oh dear. Most irregular."

He was still muttering to himself as, stunned, they left.

CHAPTER 42

Hypothesis

I

THE MANAGERS DID not call Reverend Beecher. For two days, they brought in a parade of lesser witnesses. Two swore to erratic behavior on the part of the President, behavior that turned out to be not so erratic upon Sickles's ardent cross-examination; another was an employee of the Freedmen's Bureau, who testified that he had been told by his superior not to process certain reimbursement claims filed by colored families whose possessions had been destroyed by the night riders, but Dennard was able to show that the boss had been cashiered for diverting funds to his own use. The Managers did record a small success with a pair of witnesses who had heard the President make the most dreadful offhand remarks about the Congress, thereby—said the Managers—indicating his contempt for the body. But everybody was waiting for Henry Ward Beecher, and Henry Ward Beecher did not appear.

Rumors swirled. One story had it that the initial contact with the good reverend had been through Stanton, and that Beecher, outraged at Stanton's betrayal of Lincoln, had decided not to testify. Another, easier for many to credit, held that Beecher was not prepared to testify anywhere under oath until the litigation over the scandal with Mrs. Tilton was resolved. The anti-Lincoln papers insisted that the President was holding some sort of threat over Beecher's head, but nobody could come up with a plausible reason for the most famous preacher in America to fear a Chief Executive whose term looked about to end. The pro-Lincoln papers contended that Beecher had never intended to testify against the President, that the Managers had floated his name without consulting him, and that, upon discovering what he would actually say if called, had decided to dispense with him.

Whatever the true reason, Henry Ward Beecher never appeared. Certainly the Managers did not need Beecher's evidence, for they had presented a strong case so far but for two or three days at least, they nevertheless seemed confused and even incompetent in the eyes of the public.

The President's lawyers were jubilant; and thanked, in absentia, the still-unknown correspondent known as Chanticleer, for the damaging information about those witnesses who did appear.

Abigail had another theory; but, for the moment, she kept it to herself.

II

On Tuesday night, Abigail again allowed Jonathan to drive her home. On the way, she asked several questions about his family, and about Hilliman & Sons. Her tone was casual, but he sensed somehow that the questions were not.

"Tell me about your brother," she said. "I understand that he died in the war."

"Palmer? He was the heir apparent. He was supposed to run the business when my father died. Everyone understood that. I don't know how much you know about families like mine"—an uneasy glance, testing for offense—"but the idea is that you do not, under any circumstances, break up the fortune you have labored to build. You provide for all of your children, obviously, but you leave the bulk of the fortune, intact, to a single heir. That way the family power grows from generation to generation. The other way around, it declines. Not that there was much money left by the time the war began. Still, Palmer was supposed to inherit all the stock in Hilliman & Sons."

"But he died."

"He was a captain in the first detachment of the Rhode Island Volunteers, serving under Burnside. He died at Bull Run. The first hour of the first battle of the war."

They rolled on companionably through the chilly night mist. Now and then a tree or house would loom from the unbroken grayness. Jonathan kept the horses moving slowly, in the middle of the road.

"Your family must have been quite upset."

"My mother was despondent. She had lost her husband and a daughter to the influenza, and now her firstborn son to the war. When I joined up, she told me I was a fool." He shook his head. "The family was pro-Lincoln in 1860. Whigs from way back. But after Palmer died, Mother swore she would never support him again." He turned her way. "I know what you are thinking, Abigail. But when I said to you that if a conspiracy exists, my family must be involved, I was making a jest."

"I am not insisting that it is true." He heard her long sigh, like a surrender to the inevitable. "But, Jonathan, look at the facts. They hate Lincoln. They are doing everything to get you to quit Washington. And they are in textiles, so they are in favor of the high tariff to keep their profits up, and soft money to pay back the banks with."

"My mother has her moments of temper, and I would not trust my uncle with a nickel. But do not, for a moment, associate them with those vicious murderers."

They had crossed the canal, and now were waiting, as so often, for a freight train to pass on the Seventh Street tracks. It was steaming north, probably carrying cotton or tobacco, because the South had nothing else to sell.

"Mr. Sickles made an interesting point the other day," said Abigail. "He said that Blaine's murder suggested that the conspirators are panicking. But it occurs to me that there need not be one conspiracy only." She hesitated. "There could be silent supporters, Jonathan. Men—and women—who are prepared to provide resources but have no real idea how they are being used. They could think they are giving to a new political party, or that their funds will in some other way contribute to the removal of the President by legal means. They might well remain entirely unaware of Mr. Grafton's willingness to use violence—"

"I don't know where you are getting these ideas," he said. "But I will not discuss them further."

At the house, Abigail asked him to come in. Jonathan was astonished. "That would not be proper—"

"Nanny is always up." The pixie grin. "She will serve as chaperone if you are worried."

III

He sat with Nanny Pork at the kitchen table, sipping tea and nibbling on snickerdoodles. Abigail had disappeared upstairs. Not sure what to say, Jonathan asked after Nanny's health.

"A day closer to Glory," she said.

The cookies were far too sweet. Jonathan had noticed this with his own father, who was a good deal older than his mother: as age advances, the sense of taste begins to fade, and more robust flavorings are desired.

He tried again. "Abigail is doing excellent work at the firm."

"Did you think she wouldn't?"

"No, no, I—" He stopped. "Nanny, have I done or said something to offend you? Because, if I have, I apologize."

She twisted her mouth but did not quite smile. "Maybe you has a little fight in you after all."

Abigail returned. She had a folder under her arm. No words passed, but Nanny stood up and said good night. She tottered toward the stair.

When they were alone, Abigail slid the folder across the table.

"I want you to read that," she said, and set about tidying the dishes.

"What is it?"

But she offered no answer, and probably he did not expect her to, because he had already opened it. Badly handwritten pages, about ten of them, outlining the possibility of creating something called "The Columbia Unification Party" to oppose both Lincoln and the Democrats in the 1864 election. Dozens of these sects had cropped up, he remembered, and none had amounted to anything. Lincoln had won a landslide.

"So?"

"Read," she repeated.

The party was dedicated to a rapid peace . . . high tariffs to protect American industry . . . fiat currency, the polite term for soft money . . . and an end to the disastrous invasion of the liberties of the people by the perfidious Administration of Abraham Lincoln and his crony William Seward. . . .

And near the end was a list of people to approach for contributions, some with notations next to them.

Brighton Hilliman had promised five thousand dollars.

"It's just a political party," Jonathan protested, sinking fast. "So the family opposes Lincoln. What difference does that make? Lots of people are against him. Otherwise, he would not be facing this ridiculous trial."

"This was in one of Chanticleer's folders."

"I guessed that."

"Why did Chanticleer include it, if it isn't about the conspiracy?"

"Does the letter say that it is about the conspiracy?"

"No, but—"

"Is this the missing list of conspirators that Stanton is on about?"

"I don't believe so. My point is only that these are people willing to spend large sums of money—"

"Then I choose to make no assumptions as to Chanticleer's reason for including the list." He slapped the pages. "Most likely this is like everything else in the folder, included for purposes of impeaching potential witnesses. Should any of these people be called, we would show bias by asking whether they had ever given money to an anti-Lincoln party. Nothing more."

She was growing exasperated; so was he. "Please, Jonathan. Just bear in mind the possibility."

"I will," he said, and went out.

CHAPTER 43

Industrialist

I

"CALL THE NEXT witness," said Chase.

"Honorable James K. Moorhead," shouted Butler, taking the Chief Justice's instruction literally. "Honorable James K. Moorhead!" the clerk repeated, louder still.

Moorhead's name on the witness list had stunned the President's men. He was a Republican of little consequence, now in his fourth term as a member of the House, a quiet Pennsylvanian in his sixties, an entrepreneur, and the father of a noted financier. Early in the war, when the western end of the state was riven with strife, Moorhead had joined a committee of prominent citizens in petitioning the President to declare martial law in Pittsburgh. Although Thaddeus Stevens held enormous sway over the state's congressional delegation, Representative Moorhead was thought to be a Lincoln man through and through. Most important, he had voted against the impeachment resolution.

Why, then, had the Managers called him?

Once more, Abigail had found the answer by delving into the Chanticleer letters. She had discovered what they should have realized from the start: Moorhead's son Maxwell, the financier, was a heavy investor in the iron industry—indeed, the mighty McKeesport Iron Works had until a few years ago borne the Moorhead name. The iron-industry men were leaders of the soft-money crowd, a group whose chosen savior was of course Benjamin Wade.

So, by the time Moorhead was sworn on Wednesday afternoon, and

Butler rose to question him, the President's lawyers hoped they were ready.

Butler's first questions were innocuous: establishing Moorhead's membership in the House, and his friendships with several of the President's close advisers.

"Have you ever had occasion to meet the President?"

"Many times."

"Have you had any private conversations with him?"

For a moment Moorhead hesitated. He had a wide, stern face, his hair thin on top but gathered heavily near his ears. His eyes were set deep in their sockets, and it was easy to imagine him intimidating his inferiors. But, seated in the Senate, he was plainly ill at ease. His heavy, nervous gaze brushed upward over the gallery, then down across the ranks of legislators, and lingered, oddly, on Sickles, before finding its way back to Butler.

"Two," said Moorhead. "The President and I have had two private conversations."

"When?"

"The first was in January of 1861, when I traveled to Springfield to congratulate Mr. Lincoln on his election."

Sickles glanced at Jonathan, who understood. They had covered this ground. Moorhead had actually made the trip to urge the President-Elect to appoint to his cabinet Simon Cameron, the famously corrupt Senator from Pennsylvania. Lincoln had rebuffed him. Indeed, Lincoln had embarrassed Moorhead badly, albeit in private, pointing out that a man known as Honest Abe could not appoint a man "whose very name stinks in the nostrils of the people for his corruption."

Surely this testimony was not a long-delayed revenge for this slight? After all, despite Lincoln's resistance, Cameron had in the end been appointed.

"When was the second meeting?" Butler asked, skipping entirely the actual subject matter of the January 1861 encounter.

Again Jonathan sensed Moorhead's reluctance. "February of 1865." His darting eyes settled on the Managers' table. "I was one of several congressmen who went to the Mansion to urge the President to take a harder line against the rebel leaders. We did not agree with the President's soft line on the matter of punishment of those responsible for the war and all those hundreds of thousands of deaths."

"Did anything else happen at that meeting?" asked Butler.

"The meeting ended." Moorhead cast his eyes up toward the gallery, then the ceiling. "I remained behind with the President."

"And why was that?"

"I believe that Mr. Lincoln wanted to talk to me." His hands wrestled with each other in his lap. "I was one of the few men in Washington he could trust. That is what he said."

Butler nodded sympathetically. "Is that why it is so difficult for you to tell the story now? Because you are betraying a trust?"

"I do not like betraying a trust," said Moorhead. "But I love my country too much to keep the secret."

"And what is the secret?" asked Butler.

"Once we were alone, Mr. Lincoln told me that the nation faced a serious dilemma, and that few people in Washington City realized how serious."

"Did the President indicate what problem he had in mind?"

A slow nod. "He said that the Congress was getting to be a problem. He said that members were forgetting the limits of their constitutional function." He ran a manicured hand across his face. "He told me that he had many friends in the Congress, and that I, of course, had served with honor. But there were others, he said, who . . . who were seeking to usurp the proper functions of the executive. And I believe he said that something had to be done."

"And what did you say?"

"I believe I said that the Congress was only legislating as it always had, laying down the laws that the executive was bound to execute."

"And what did Mr. Lincoln say to that?"

"He told me a story. He said that when he was practicing law in Springfield, a man came to see him—a prominent man in those parts, the Old Squire, he called him—the Old Squire came to ask whether a justice of the peace could issue marriage licenses. Mr. Lincoln told the Old Squire no, the justice of the peace had no such power, at which point the Old Squire became very angry and said, 'You know nothing of the law. I'll have you know that I have been a justice of the peace for going on twenty years, and I issue marriage licenses all the time!'"

A titter in the chamber. Chase tapped the gavel.

"And what," said Butler, "did you take the story to mean?"

Dennard was up again. "Objection to offering the interpretation of the witness. He can say what he heard and saw."

"Overruled. The witness will answer."

Moorhead swallowed. "I believe that the President meant that his judgment on what was constitutional was superior to the judgment of the Congress."

Butler consulted his notes. "Did Mr. Lincoln say what should be done about the way the Congress was behaving?"

"He said that if the congressmen kept usurping his function, he might just have to find some way to usurp right back."

"Was that all?"

"No, sir, it wasn't. He said that I shouldn't worry, because, if worse came to worst, he knew who had been loyal and who hadn't. And then, I believe, he asked me to keep the conversation to myself."

II

Sickles began the cross-examination far from where Butler had ended. He went back to Moorhead's initial meeting with Lincoln, shortly after the 1860 election. After a bit of badgering, Moorhead conceded that one of his purposes had been to persuade Lincoln to appoint Simon Cameron to the Cabinet.

"You were for Cameron?" asked Sickles, feigning surprise.

"I thought he should be considered."

"And this is the same Mr. Cameron of whom Mr. Manager Stevens once said, 'I do not believe that he would steal a red-hot stove'?"

Laughter in the chamber, but anger, too, and Chase did not even wait for the objection before gaveling that line of inquiry to a halt. But the point had been made. This theatricality was what Sickles did best; no lawyer in the city was better.

"Stick to the direct examination, Mr. Sickles."

"Of course, Mr. Chief Justice."

"And no personal references to counsel on either side."

"Yes, sir. My apologies."

The room calmed a bit. Sickles faced the witness once more. "Now, as to the second meeting, the one in the President's office. Isn't it true that you went on so long that the President himself at last interrupted you?"

Laughter from the gallery, which Chase quelled with a quick rap of his gavel. But Moorhead was nothing if not self-possessed.

"As I am sure you are aware, Mr. Sickles, the President is in the habit of interrupting whenever he likes."

Sickles let this shot bounce off. "Do you happen to remember the content of his interruption?"

"No, sir."

"Didn't Mr. Lincoln ask you whether you had lived long enough to know that two men may honestly differ about a question and both be right?"

Moorhead colored, even though this thrust was not meant for him at all—it was a dagger aimed at the heart of the prosecution's case. The few wavering Senators would shortly decide whether it had hit home.

"I don't remember the President's words," said Moorhead. "I only remember his habit of interrupting."

"I see." Sickles reached into his jacket pocket—an act that always caused some tension, because his jacket pocket was where he had kept the gun with which he had killed Barton Key. But he withdrew only a handkerchief, and mopped at his brow. "Now, Mr. Moorhead. You said that, after you and several other members of Congress met with the President to discuss the treatment of the rebel leaders, you remained behind for a private conversation. Correct?"

"Yes."

"How did this come about?"

"Excuse me?"

"The private conversation." Sickles took a step to the right, placing himself between Moorhead and the Managers. "Had you arrived at the Mansion expecting to have a private conversation with the President, or were you summoned later?"

Sickles was playing to the pride of the great industrialist. He was not disappointed.

"I was not *summoned*, sir. I am a member of the House of Representatives. I am not at the President's beck and call."

"My apologies." Again he passed the cloth across his forehead. "Very well. How were you requested to remain behind to meet with the President? Did the President himself ask you, or was it one of his aides?"

Moorhead, on thinner ice, took his time. "I believe it was the President."

"I see. You were there in the office, with the other members of Congress, and perhaps a couple of the President's assistants, and Mr. Lincoln asked you to remain behind."

"I believe it was when we were shaking hands."

"Shaking hands?"

"When our public meeting ended. The President shook hands with each of us before we departed." Bolder, growing into the great confidence demanded by a great lie. "Yes. It was when we were shaking hands. The President put his hand on my arm and asked me to remain behind for a moment."

"Did anyone hear him invite you to remain?"

"Are you questioning my word, sir?"

Sickles played with his moustaches. "Just now, sir, I am only asking if anyone heard the President invite you to remain for a private conversation after the others left."

Moorhead drew himself up. The high, pale brow knitted. "I would hardly know who was listening, sir. Gentlemen do not listen to other gentlemen's private conversation, but I fear that Mr. Lincoln's White House is hardly a monument to discretion."

Sickles strolled back to the counsel table. He winked at Jonathan, then said, not turning back toward the witness, "So . . . you had a private conversation there in the President's office, and he joked about usurping the Congress. Is that your testimony?"

"He was not joking," said Moorhead heavily.

Sickles's tone remained casual. His back was still to the witness. "And how would you know that, exactly?"

"I know when a man is joking," said the industrialist, stubbornly.

"Very well. The President told you he wanted to usurp the Congress." A delicate pause, as he turned toward Moorhead once more. "By force?"

"Pardon me?"

"Did the President say he wanted to overthrow Congress by force? Or was he referring to an election?"

The industrialist glanced at the Managers, but their faces were stone. "I believe," he said, licking his lips, "that he was referring to force." By now everybody in the chamber understood, as Moorhead evidently did not, that when he began a sentence with the words "I believe," what followed was a fabrication. "Yes. He was referring to force."

"He said that?"

"He left me that impression."

Sickles moved closer. "Excuse me, Congressman, if I give offense. You are asking this chamber to believe that the President of the United States chose you—not a friend, not a close confidant, not an adviser, but you, a relatively minor member of the Pennsylvania delegation—you are asking us to believe that he chose you, and you alone, to confide so extraordinary a plan?"

Jonathan saw Moorhead's face, and knew that Sickles for once had allowed his natural theatricality to carry him over the edge. He had gone too far in making his point, and he was going to get slapped.

Hard.

"I have no reason to think," said Moorhead, heavily, "that he chose me alone. I believe he vouchsafed this desire widely."

Sickles made a nice recovery. "You know for a fact that he shared this desire, as you put it, with others?"

"I do."

"Did Mr. Lincoln tell you that he had told others?"

"Sir, others told me."

Again Sickles's hand went to his pocket. By now the whole chamber was enthralled by this aspect of his magic. He drew out a thick pencil and a diary. "Their names, please?"

Moorhead's frown of disapproval deepened. "I beg your pardon."

"I would like you, please, to tell the Court the names of those others who told you about Mr. Lincoln's plan to overthrow the Congress."

"I cannot."

"You don't remember?" The pencil was poised. "Surely you remember one name?"

"Sir, a gentleman does not disclose the confidences of other gentlemen."

"Except, evidently, to you." General laughter. "Your Honor, would you please instruct the witness to answer the question?"

Butler was on his feet. "Objection. Hearsay, twice over. The witness is being asked to say what others said the President said."

"Your Honor," said Sickles, "we are not asking the witness to testify to the words of others in order to determine their truth. We are asking the witness who else he believes"—a subtle emphasis on the verb—"to have been aware of the conspiracy to which he has testified. We will then, by way of subpoena, have them brought here and sworn."

The Chief Justice pondered—no doubt, thought Jonathan, weighing the politics as much as the law.

"Overruled," said Chase, at length. "The witness will answer."

Moorhead shook his head. "I apologize to the Court. I cannot answer."

Chase leaned forward, plainly irritated. "Sir, I have made my ruling. There is no ground on which you can refuse to answer."

"But I have already explained, Your Honor. A gentleman cannot disclose another gentleman's confidences."

"That is not a proper ground, sir, and, in any case, the witness is not permitted to object."

"Yes, but—"

Chase's patience was gone. "The witness will answer the question or the witness will be in contempt."

"Mr. President," came a voice from the back.

Heads craned. It was the fierce Zachariah Chandler of Michigan, one of the most devoted of Lincoln's opponents, addressing the Chief Justice according to the forms agreed upon.

Chase looked up, pink face full of wrath. "The Senator will be in order."

"Sir, I have a motion on the way to your desk at this moment." He nodded toward a running page. "I wish to poll the chamber on Your Honor's ruling on the admissibility of the question from counsel for the respondent."

Chase read the paper swiftly. He was struggling visibly to retain his judicial mien in the face of this slap at his authority. The whole point of the battle over who could appeal his rulings had been to avoid just this sort of public challenge. He mumbled something—perhaps a prayer—and nodded briskly. "Very well. There is a request to have the chamber polled."

A few voices called out to second the motion—quite unnecessarily, under the rules. Chandler said, "I have a further motion, on its way to the bench."

Again Chase glanced over the request. "There is a motion that the Senate retire to its conference room to consider the matter."

The motion passed swiftly.

"That was ill done," Jonathan whispered as counsel stood, watching the members file out. "All Chandler is trying to do is give them time to think up a better story for Moorhead to tell."

Sickles shook his head. "No. That's not it. This isn't about Moorhead. This is about Chase. He's showing surprising signs of independence."

"Good."

"Maybe." Sickles was thoughtful.

"Surely, if Chase refuses to lie down for his Radical friends, our chances of a fair trial are enhanced."

"You still don't understand the man, do you? He is driven by a single mania, remember. He wants to be President." Sickles waved toward the shuttered doorway. "Oh, they'll overrule him. They'll vote with Chandler, and then adjourn for the day, because the argument will take hours. The Radicals will see to it. They don't want us to have the opportunity to ask about Moorhead's son on cross. By tomorrow, Moorhead will come down with a case of Potomac fever, or be called out of town to tend to a dying relative, and we'll never get our questions answered." He closed his diary. "Not that he has any answers."

"And Chase—"

"Chase will have been instructed, by the vote to overrule him, that there are moments when he has to go along with his friends."

III

After court, Jonathan wanted to rush back to the office: to see Abigail, to find the right words to apologize for his behavior last night. She had come to him in good faith, genuinely worried, and he had been a boor. But Dennard detained him at the conference room down the hall from the Senate Chamber. He had become aware, Dennard said, of the various activities in which Jonathan and Abigail had been engaging. He knew that they were still searching for the conspiracy against Lincoln. He reminded Jonathan of his repeated warnings not to jeopardize the case by chasing some mythical—

And Jonathan, for once, interrupted his master. "Sir, please. At least let me tell you what we have discovered."

Dennard shrugged, as though there was nothing to be done, and told his clerk to go ahead. And so Jonathan offered a tightly edited summary of what they knew and what they guessed: Grafton, Blaine, Stanton, Judith, Rebecca, the bribes, and of course Chanticleer—

"I will grant you Chanticleer," said Dennard, grudgingly. "Whoever he is. The rest is supposition. Inadmissible and therefore irrelevant."

"A thing can be inadmissible in a court of law and nevertheless true."

"If it does not help our client," the lawyer rumbled, "I do not want my staff wasting their time on it. Bring me documentary evidence and we can proceed. Anything less, and your time is better spent on your assignments. Unless, of course, you feel that you are underworked, in which case I can add to your load."

For this and other reasons, Jonathan was in a sullen mood as he climbed the stairs to the second floor and let himself into the office. Little was there, stoking the fire. The partners' doors were shut. The room was otherwise empty.

"Where is Miss Abigail?" Jonathan said.

The old man, down on his arthritic knees, turned his head. "Ain't seen her tonight."

"She is supposed to be working!"

"Well, now, I know how it is with young people. Half the time, you uns don't do what you're spose to do."

Hiding a childlike disappointment, Jonathan sat down to his books.

I V

As for Abigail, she had indeed allowed herself to be persuaded to see Fielding again: even if she was now armed with an agenda. Once more, she had accompanied him to the late buffet at the National Hotel. Once more, he was beautiful.

"I was afraid you no longer wished my company," said Fielding.

"Don't be silly."

"Hills says—"

"I am not a woman who needs a man to speak for me."

Over those delightful crabs, they traded pleasantries for a good half-hour, and then she proceeded to the matter most on her mind.

"May I ask you a question, Fielding?"

"Anything."

"It's about Jonathan."

His face fell, but to show it was all in jest he folded hands over his heart. "I shall not survive it," he declaimed. "The course of true love never did run smooth!"

Abigail laughed along with him, hoping that he was serious about joking. Then she pressed on. "I would like to know about Jonathan's family."

"The Hillimans? There isn't much to tell."

"What are they like?"

"Are you asking if they would like you?"

She looked away. The conversation was going absurdly wrong. "No, no, I—I just want to know." She realized that there was no good way to put the question: *Would they conspire against the President?* She would have to seek information from some other source. And so she decided to have fun, and forced a smile. "Never mind. Tell me about your family instead."

"Mine? They like money. There's little else to say."

"I am sure there is a good deal more—"

"Well, well," said a voice at her shoulder. "I see you have found yourself another beau."

General Baker stood beside the table, with a man she did not recognize, although he looked every bit as cruel.

Abigail stood, but Fielding was faster. "Go away and leave us alone."

"This has nothing to do with you, son."

"I will have you know—"

The general ignored him. He turned toward Abigail. "Don't think I'm not still keeping an eye on you, miss. Because I am. Every minute of every day." He allowed this to sink in. Then he laughed. "Dinner with this one. Rides in the country with young Addison. Going down to Richmond for a couple of days with young Hilliman. And of course lunch with the scandalous Sickles. You don't half get around, do you?" To Fielding: "Please don't let me interrupt."

As Baker moved away, she heard the words "proper little hopper" drifting through the restaurant. Plainly she was meant to overhear. She had never come across the phrase before, not even in the pages of *Peterson's*, but had little trouble puzzling out its meaning.

"You care for him, don't you?" asked Fielding, a little sadly. "Hills, I mean. You really do care, don't you?"

Abigail drew herself up. "Don't be absurd."

"Shall I take you home?"

"I intend to enjoy my dinner. And the company."

But she was thinking about something else, something that had driven her questions about Jonathan's family right out of her mind. Twice now, Lafayette Baker had "happened" upon her when she was out on the town. As if he knew where she would be. Perhaps this was because of an effective system of surveillance. But another possibility worried her.

Both times General Baker had appeared, Abigail had been out with Fielding Bannerman.

CHAPTER 44

Department

I

"MAJOR CLANCY," SAID Benjamin Butler. "You are the President's military aide, are you not?"

"Yes, sir."

"Do you work in the Executive Mansion?"

"Sir, I have a desk on the first floor. I'm usually either there or over at the War Department. It's just a block away, sir."

It was Thursday afternoon, and the evidence for the Managers would shortly be concluded. They had entered upon consideration of the fourth count, and by far the most inflammatory: that the President had undertaken a design to overthrow the authority of the Congress. In all likelihood, Bingham had told the chamber, they would be calling only three more witnesses. Major Clancy was the first. He sat there in his blue uniform, trim and glistening, and sitting to attention. But his military bearing could not disguise either his nervousness or his reluctance to say a single word.

The President's lawyers had objected to Clancy's appearance, arguing that a presidential aide could not properly be questioned before the Congress about his conversations with the Chief Executive. The separation of powers, Speed had argued at some length, absolutely forbade such inquiry. Chase had sustained the objection—no man who hoped to serve as President could easily do otherwise—but the Senate had gone into caucus and, by an overwhelming margin, decided to hear the testimony. Even most of Lincoln's friends had voted to overrule the Chief

Justice: there were institutional prerogatives at stake, and they did not want to set a precedent holding the President's aides free of congressional inquiry.

"Tell us, Major," said Butler now. "When did you undertake your current assignment?"

"Sir, July of 1866."

"Eight months ago."

"Yes, sir."

Butler quickly established what was after all common ground: that the major's job was not to advise the President but to see that his orders were properly conveyed to the War Department, and also to keep track of any War Department correspondence coming into the President's office.

"So all communication with the War Department goes through you?"

"It is supposed to, sir. I'm afraid in this city things don't always work the way they are supposed to."

This was greeted with laughter. Even Butler smiled.

"Indeed. But is it fair to say that you see most of the correspondence?"

"I believe so, sir."

"And most of the President's orders? He would give them to you for transmission to the department?"

"Sir, like I said, the War Department is right near the Mansion. Most of the time, I'd just run the orders over to Mr. Stanton's office."

"Did you know the contents of the orders?"

"If the President dictated them, yes, sir. If he gave me a sealed envelope, then I wouldn't know, of course."

"Of course. Now, tell me, Major. Did any of the orders that he dictated to you—any correspondence known to you from the President—did any of it concern, in any way, a military department known as the Department of the Atlantic?"

Speed was back on his feet. Objection. Privileged communication with the President.

Chase was patient. "Counsel, your position is by now well understood. But the entire body has concurred in the admission of such testimony. There is no point to further argument."

For the briefest of instants, Speed seemed inclined to press his point. But he returned, restless, to his seat.

"The witness will answer," Chase said, kindly.

Clancy was growing noticeably more nervous. "Sir, I—I never transmitted to the War Department any orders regarding the Department of the Atlantic."

Butler smiled rigidly. "Did you ever discuss with the President a military department of that name?"

"Yes, sir. I did. Yes."

"What was the nature of that discussion?"

Speed looked about to rise. Everyone paused and glanced his way, expecting an objection just to break the flow, even if it would inevitably be overruled. But the lawyer remained in his chair.

"Sir, it was an afternoon in September or October of last year. I was in the President's office to collect some commissions he had signed, appointing, um, new officers, and he asked me to stay for a minute."

"Was that unusual?"

"No, sir. The President often asked me to stay, when he had an idea he wanted to discuss. He told me that several of his advisers had suggested that a new military department be created, with responsibility—"

Now Speed was on his feet, asking for permission to approach the bench. Chase waved him forward. Butler joined them. The argument was brief, but animated. Chase waved them back. He turned to the witness. "Let's leave the other advisers out. You may answer, but tell the story without them."

"Yes, sir," said Clancy. He looked confused. "Sir," he said, contriving to look at the Chief Justice and Butler at once. "The President said he had been considering the idea of creating a new military department, with responsibility for Washington City. He suggested that it might be called the Department of the Atlantic."

"And what is a military department?"

"Sir, when there is military government of an area, the military department is in charge of administration, keeping order, and so forth."

"So, when the President proposed creating this Department of the Atlantic—"

Speed was up at once. "Object to 'proposed.' That is not the testimony."

Chase turned to Butler.

"May it please the Court, it seems a fair interpretation."

"The witness has only testified," said Speed, "that the respondent said he was considering the idea."

"It's the same thing," said Butler.

Chase pondered. "Overruled," he said. "Continue, Mr. Manager."

"Thank you, sir. Major Clancy, just to clarify. A military department, you said, is responsible for administration and keeping order where there is military government."

"Yes, sir."

"So, when the President proposed"—tiny emphasis, just right—"the creation of a military department to be called the Department of the Atlantic in Washington City, what did you take him to be suggesting?"

Again Speed objected: it made no difference what the witness thought that the respondent was suggesting; he could testify only to what he had seen and heard.

"Overruled," said Chase. "The witness will answer."

Clancy swallowed. "Sir, I thought that he was suggesting a military government for Washington City."

A sigh ran through the chamber. The Managers had struck gold.

"A military government," Butler echoed. "With a headquarters here in Washington."

"Yes, sir."

"Are there other military departments in the country?"

"Yes, sir. There are departments in each of the Southern states, for instance—that is, except for the ones that have been readmitted—"

Chase did not wait for the objection. Lincoln held that the Southern states, although led astray by their leaders, had never actually left the Union, and should soon be allowed to send representatives to Congress; the Radicals sharply disagreed. "The witness will refrain from expressing a view on whether or not any states have been readmitted."

Clancy foundered a bit, but, with some prodding from Butler, at last found a phrasing that was acceptable: "Sir, there are military departments governing all the Southern states except the ones where the President has directed that the military government be phased out."

A helpful answer for the prosecution.

"Now, then, Major," said Butler, "would a military department typically be placed above the civilian government?"

"Objection. He is testifying for the witness."

"Overruled. The witness will answer."

Clancy was sweating now. Battle might not frighten him as much as sitting in this chamber, damaging a commander-in-chief he clearly admired. "Sir, yes, sir. A military government is placed above a civilian government. There would be no point, otherwise, would there?"

"So—just to be clear—when the President proposed the formation of the Department of the Atlantic, to be headquartered in Washington, you took him to be proposing a military government to be placed above the civilian government in Washington."

Clancy answered, albeit unwillingly. "Yes, sir. That is what I thought."

Butler half turned, waving his hand toward the ranks of Senators and, beyond them, congressmen. "When Mr. Lincoln offered this proposal, Major, were you aware of the law, passed by these gentlemen here, prohibiting general officers from entering Washington City without permission?"

Clancy sat, if anything, straighter. His voice trembled. "Yes, sir. I was."

"And were you also aware that the Congress had directed that there be no military department headquartered in Washington City?"

"Yes, sir."

"Was the President aware of these laws?"

Again Speed objected. Chase told Butler to rephrase the question.

"Major, did the President say anything to you to indicate an awareness of these laws?"

The look in Speed's eyes suggested that he was ready to complain again. But he kept his seat.

"Sir, not exactly," said the major.

"Explain that, if you please."

"Sir, the President didn't say anything about the congressional law—"

To everyone's surprise, the Chief Justice himself ventured a rare interruption. "Major, the statutes in question are statutes of the United States, not of the Congress."

The witness paled, his Adam's apple bobbing faster. "Yes, sir." He turned back to Butler. "Sir, the President didn't say anything about the, um, the law." He brightened. "But I did."

"What did you say?"

"I said that I wasn't sure that the Department of the Atlantic would be legal."

"An excellent point, Major." Butler nodded his approval. "And what did Mr. Lincoln say to that?"

"Sir, he laughed. He said something about how the world is full of highly legal illegalities and highly illegal legalities. I'm not trained in the law, sir. I wasn't really sure what he meant."

Butler smiled. "I am trained in the law, Major, and I'm not sure, either." Restrained laughter, but only from the gallery; the Senators were on edge. "And what else did the President say?"

"Sir, he said that he was the commander-in-chief, and if there was any legal trouble, that was his lookout, not mine." He hesitated. "That's what he said, sir. 'Lookout.' "

"Did the conversation return to the subject of Congress?"

"Yes, sir."

"And what else did the President say?"

"Sir, he told me a story. He said there was this farmer who bought himself a nice farm, and everything was fine until the storm came and knocked down a gigantic tree. The tree was in the middle of his biggest field. It was an old tree, too heavy to move and too big to run the plow through. Everybody figured the farmer would have to give up. But when the fall came, he had the biggest harvest of anybody. Turned out, he'd just left the tree where it was and plowed around it."

Butler paused for emphasis. In the chamber, not a sound. "He plowed around the tree?"

"Yes, sir."

"And you took the tree to refer to what?"

Speed objected: the witness could not possibly know what the President's story referred to, and in any event the President was obviously telling a joke.

Butler glared self-righteously. "Your Honor, the story about the plow immediately followed the discussion of the Congress and the discussion of the Department of the Atlantic. It is the position of the Managers that the subjects are obviously connected. What counsel for the respondent calls a joke might just as well have been an implicit order. He might have been telling Major Clancy that he wanted the military to plow around the Congress."

"On that point," rumbled Speed, "the witness's opinion is irrelevant."

Chase sustained the objection, but Butler had won the round. He had elicited the story from the unfortunate major, and, in the guise of responding to Speed's argument, he had put before the Senate the possibility that the President did indeed intend to plow around the Congress.

"The Managers have no further questions for this witness," said Butler.

The Chief Justice looked to his left. "Cross-examination?"

II

Speed sauntered toward the box. His posture was casual. He wanted it clear to everyone, from the start, that the defense would not be challenging this witness.

"Major, just a few questions."

"Yes, sir."

"For clarification." Speed leaned on the bar, as if he were in a circuit court back in Illinois, not the Senate Chamber. "Major Clancy, where exactly is the Department of the Atlantic located?"

The witness was puzzled. "Sir?"

"The Department of the Atlantic. You just testified about it. Where was it established? Where is it headquartered?"

"Sir, it was never established. It was just an idea."

"It doesn't exist?"

"No, sir."

"There is no Department of the Atlantic?"

"No, sir."

"There is no military government in Washington?"

"No, sir."

"I see." Speed was stern. "You testified that the President discussed with you the feasibility of creating a Department of the Atlantic."

"Yes, sir."

"And you told him that you thought the action would require the approval of the Congress, is that correct?"

"Yes, sir."

"And the President seemed not to care what the Congress thought."

"Yes, sir."

Speed nodded. "Can you recall his exact words? I'm not sure that the Managers asked you to quote him exactly."

Major Clancy squinted his eyes comically, as if a furrowed brow might aid his memory. "He said, 'Sometimes Congress gets a little too involved in military matters for its own good.' I think those were his words, sir. Or pretty close, anyway."

"Was that the end of the conversation?"

"Well, he told me that story."

"The story about the farmer?"

"Yes, sir."

"And did you take the President's story as anything other than a joke?"

Now it was Butler's turn to object, but Chase allowed the question.

"No, sir," said Clancy. "It was clear to me that the President was joking."

Speed nodded. His voice remained friendly. "And did the President say anything else about the Department of the Atlantic?"

"He told me he would give it some more thought."

"Did he tell you to give it more thought as well?"

"No, sir."

"Did he direct you to create the Department of the Atlantic?"

"No, sir."

"Not then and not later, either?"

Clancy seemed almost relieved as he answered. "He never brought it up with me again, sir."

"Did he ever tell you that creating the Department of the Atlantic would not require the consent of the Congress?"

"No, sir." He cocked his head to the side. "Now that I think of it, I believe he called it an interesting question."

"The question of whether Congress had to approve."

"Yes, sir."

"Did the President ever give you any orders regarding the Department of Atlantic? Say, to transmit to Mr. Stanton?"

"Sir, no, sir."

Speed consulted his notes. Then, rather showily, he sauntered back to the table. He was about to sit when he seemed to recall a point. "Oh, Major. One last thing. When you leave here today, where will you be headed?"

"Sir?"

"When you leave the Capitol building. Where will you go?"

"Oh, uh, I suppose, sir, back to the Mansion."

"The Executive Mansion?"

"Yes, sir."

"Where you are the President's military aide?"

"Yes, sir."

"So you haven't lost your assignment or anything like that as a result of your testimony here today?"

"No, sir."

"Thank you, Major Clancy."

Speed resumed his seat. The Managers had dragged a snarling cat of a story into the room. Speed had done his best to defang it. But the weighty silence in the chamber as the major stepped down from the stand suggested that the operation had enjoyed only limited success. Clancy's testimony had done exactly what it was supposed to do, leaving in the atmosphere a whiff of uncertainty over exactly how far the President might be willing to go. All through the war, he had insisted on using his "broader powers" as he saw fit for the benefit of the Union. He had defied courts and Congress alike. The Managers had searched and searched for a way to drive home the dangers of leaving such a man in office. In the unassuming person of Major Clancy, they had evidently found it.

III

"Jonathan, listen," said Abigail.

They were alone in the office. The temperature had dropped precipitously, and the common room was frigid. They were sitting side by side at the end of the table nearest the grate, where the remnants of the coal fire glowed weakly and provided little warmth. She had a shawl around her shoulders and had threatened to put on a coat. Helping prepare for closing arguments, she had spent the afternoon cataloguing the letters from military officers that the House Managers had introduced as evidence of the President's perfidy. Now she had open before her a heavy volume of the *Statutes at Large*, the official compilation of the laws of the United States. Her task of the moment was to copy out the citation and the text of each congressional enactment approving, after the fact, one of President Lincoln's more controversial wartime orders. Evidently, there were more statutes than she had expected, because the stack of notes piled on the blotter kept getting higher.

The coterie had spent two hours after court evaluating how the trial was going, and their conclusions had so depressed the company that nobody had bothered to wake Dan Sickles, who had fallen into what seemed to be a drunken slumber on the sofa in McShane's office. Major

Clancy's testimony had been particularly devastating, they all agreed, because his affection for the President was evident. True, the Mangers had misfired with Moorhead and Yardley, but the cumulative effect of the witnesses and the documents—said Dennard—did indeed put their client at serious hazard. In a disheartened spirit, the others had departed, save only Sickles, who slept on in the next room, snoring aggressively, as Abigail chafed under Jonathan's tender gaze; a gaze she felt even when he was not actually looking at her.

"Jonathan," she repeated. "About the other night—"

He covered her mouth: one of the few times he had ever touched her. Their eyes mutually widened in surprise, and he dropped his hand.

"I spoke too sharply," he said now. "You were trying to warn me."

"And you might be right. For all we know, the reason Chanticleer included the contributors to the Unification Party was in case any were called as witnesses."

"Yes. Yes. To show bias on cross-examination, should they claim to be loyal supports of Lincoln, testifying reluctantly." He brightened. "So the names need not be related to the conspiracy at all."

"But there is another problem."

She told him about Fielding, and Baker's talent for knowing when the two were together.

"Impossible. Fielding's family is for hard money, remember? And the hard-money people seem to be supporting Lincoln. Besides—I know this is old-fashioned of me—but Fielding is a gentleman. He is not underhanded. I have known him all of his life." He searched for the words. "And you must surely know that Fields is . . . is fond of you. Very fond."

She flushed, quite prettily. "Perhaps not Fielding but his family—"

"But his family could not possibly know where to send General Baker. And at the moment, he is the only Bannerman in the city."

"You are saying it is coincidence."

"I am saying that his fondness for you would not allow him to . . . to conspire against you." Jonathan, plainly having difficulties, was stumbling over the words. "And he is not alone in that . . . fondness."

I V

As there are precious moments between two people that can never be retrieved, there are also moments of tension that can never be avoided, no matter how they try. They had reached one; and neither quite knew how to advance; or retreat.

"Abigail."

"Yes, Jonathan?"

"I should like to talk to you."

Oh, no. "We are talking now."

He could not contain his anxiety, and so stood. After a moment, she followed his example. "No, no, I mean—well, about what has happened these past several weeks, and . . . and about other things."

"I am not sure which of the occurrences of the past weeks you mean," she said, hoping that her ornate circumlocutions would conceal her growing panic.

"This is difficult to say."

"Then perhaps you should not say it." His needful gaze was suddenly more than she could stand, and she swung away from him, took up a duster, began to brush the shelves. "We have much to do, Jonathan. Surely this matter, whatever it is, can wait until the trial is done."

He spoke slowly, as if his words surprised even himself. "I don't think it can wait, Abigail." A beat. "Please turn around."

She did, clutching the duster like a weapon. "What is it, then? What cannot wait a few weeks?"

Jonathan glanced at the door to McShane's office, but Sickles was snoring as loudly and disgustingly as ever.

"Abigail," Jonathan began, but those luminous gray eyes, as ever, distracted him from his purpose. Summoning such tatters of self-respect as remained to him, he made a second attempt. "When all of this is over," Jonathan declared, hand over his heart, "I intend to leave Washington. I shall be returning to Rhode Island, or possibly Massachusetts. My family has interests in both places. With my brother lost in the war, Mother wants me to take a more active role in the firm." This was the content of the letter that smirking Ellenborough had delivered last month, after no doubt contriving to read and reseal it. Abigail said nothing. Perhaps she did not know that it was her turn to speak. "Things are different at the North," Jonathan said. "Washington City might be the capital, but it is a Southern town, and we both know it. I do not see that your people will ever be fully happy here."

"Are you proposing, as Mr. Lincoln did before our leaders dissuaded him, that we accept colonization somewhere in Central Africa?"

"Oh, no, no." He hastened to correct her misimpression, before he noticed the ghostly smile dancing around her lips. "You are teasing me," he said.

"Perhaps," she allowed, wishing she had resisted the urge. "Pray continue."

Again Jonathan hesitated. It seemed to him that Sickles's snore had taken on a deeper timbre. Did that signify that he was waking, or sinking more deeply? Or was Jonathan's fevered imagination now inventing obstacles to what he meant to declare?

"The North," he resumed, "is a far better place for the negroes."

"Which no doubt explains why only a few dozen were lynched in the New York draft riots."

By now Jonathan Hilliman was of course well aware that this strange woman was smarter than he, and smarter than nearly all the young men he had known at Yale. But this was not mere wordplay. Abigail knew what he was leading up to, and sought to distract him. Emboldened by what he took to be her secret nervousness, Jonathan pressed on. "Abigail. I have never in my twenty-four years met anyone like you. That is the simple truth of the matter. You are a remarkable woman, and, in my experience, unique. I believe that my family would take to you, once they got to know you "

"Your family!" Her voice seemed faint, or perhaps his hearing was off, for every sound in the room, every creaking board and rattling window, swirled warmly about him. "Jonathan, please."

"The Hillimans are decent people. No matter what Chanticleer says. Not perfect, but decent. I would like you to meet them, and—"

"That is not possible."

"You yourself have spoken of your desire to move to the North, Abigail. I am simply suggesting that perhaps we might—"

"Stop, Jonathan. Just stop." Firmly. "Not another word."

At first he thought that she meant to reject his suit before it had fairly begun. But her hearing had detected what his had missed. Her eyes were fixed on a point behind his head.

On McShane's office; and the slouching figure filling the doorway.

"Mr. Sickles," she murmured. "So good of you to join us."

CHAPTER 45

Confidante

I

ON THE TRIAL'S second Friday sitting, the Managers called Mrs. Sally Orne to the stand. The President's lawyers had not been able to find out what Mrs. Orne was expected to say. Mrs. Orne, married to the Philadelphia industrialist, had been one of the late Mrs. Lincoln's closest friends and confidantes. Her name on the witness list had startled them all, and had shaken even Lincoln himself. But she had refused to meet his counsel to discuss her testimony, and the Managers, under the complex rules adopted by the Senate, had been required only to disclose the vaguest version of her testimony. "Re Count 4," was the only note the prosecution had turned over; no amount of investigation by the President's people had turned up any indication of what Mrs. Orne could possibly know about Lincoln's supposed plan to overthrow the authority of the Congress. The Chanticleer letters were silent. And so it was that Sickles rose, before she had even been sworn, to ask the purpose for which the witness was being called.

Bingham was silkily polite. "May it please the Court, this witness possesses firsthand knowledge about the President's plans concerning the Department of the Atlantic."

Consternation in the chamber. Chase slipped off his glasses, squeezed the bridge of his nose.

Sickles said, "May it please the Court, Mrs. Orne's knowledge cannot be firsthand unless she had it from the President's mouth. Else it is hearsay, and we would object on that ground."

"Your Honor, counsel is free to object to any particular question we might put to the witness. But we will not tell him in advance all that we expect Mrs. Orne to say."

Chase nodded. "I agree."

Sickles was not quite through. "Your Honor, we also wish to pursue another objection to Mrs. Orne's testimony. We believe that her presence in this chamber will itself be highly prejudicial, inevitably bringing to mind the unfortunate events regarding the death of Mrs. Lincoln."

"Mrs. Lincoln is not on trial," said Bingham.

"We agree," Sickles began. "And that is why—"

"If counsel will allow me to finish. We would much rather spare the nation, and Mr. Lincoln, any unnecessary pain. Unfortunately, it is the respondent himself who has created this situation, by refusing to appear and be sworn. In consequence, we are forced to reconstruct his words and actions through the testimony of others. No one was closer to Mrs. Lincoln than Mrs. Orne. She must be heard."

"Objections overruled," said Chase. To the clerk: "Swear the witness."

II

Bingham trod cautiously. Mrs. Orne's reluctance was obvious from the pious reserve of her face and the tension in her tiny body—and the fact that she, alone among all the witnesses, had brought her own lawyers, a whole squadron, seated at the back of the chamber in case needed. She conceded that she was the wife of the famous merchant, and a longtime friend and correspondent of the late First Lady.

"Would you describe yourself as her confidante?"

"If so, Mr. Bingham, the honor was entirely mine."

"Were you still close to Mrs. Lincoln at the time of her death?"

"Sir, we were lifelong friends."

"How often did you see her over the last two years of her life?"

"Every three or four months, Mr. Bingham." A faint smile of reminiscence split the aged, well-powdered face, and she flashed dimples that thirty years ago must have been spectacular. "Sometimes I would visit her in Springfield, sometimes she would visit me in Philadelphia. We also traveled to Europe together."

"And you corresponded regularly?"

"At least once a month. Occasionally more often."

"Could you describe for us the First Lady's mood during the last six months of her life?"

Sickles objected. Chase considered. "Overruled. The witness may answer, but must limit herself to her own impression based on observation."

"She seemed unhappy," said Mrs. Orne. She was looking down at her hands. "Very unhappy."

"What was she unhappy about?"

This time Chase sustained the objection.

"When was the last time you spoke to Mrs. Lincoln?"

"About a month before she died."

"And was she unhappy then, too?"

"She was, Mr. Bingham. Very much so."

Bingham asked for a moment, and returned to the table. He and Butler and Stevens engaged in brief and animated discussion. Jonathan, able to overhear snippets, had the impression that the others wanted Bingham to linger on Mrs. Lincoln's death, whereas Bingham preferred to move on to the substance.

Bingham evidently prevailed. And Jonathan thought his judgment correct. By eliciting testimony that Mrs. Lincoln was unhappy, he reminded the chamber of the rumors that she had taken her own life; to delve further, however, would make it appear that the Managers were dancing on her corpse.

"Mrs. Orne, have you ever heard of the Department of the Atlantic?"

Silence in the chamber.

"Yes," she finally said.

"Was the Department of the Atlantic at any time a subject of conversation between yourself and Mrs. Lincoln?"

Again Jonathan sensed the reluctance, the plea in the tired eyes that she not be forced to disclose her friend's confidences.

"Not conversation," said Mrs. Orne finally. "No."

"Did Mrs. Lincoln ever communicate with you by any means on the subject of the Department of the Atlantic?"

A whispered response.

"Please speak up, Mrs. Orne," said Chase.

She looked down at her hands. "She wrote me."

"Are you saying that you received a letter from Mrs. Lincoln that mentioned the Department of the Atlantic?"

Sickles was on his feet. The contents of a letter had to be proved by the letter itself—

"I fear counsel is mistaken," said Bingham. "The exceptions to that rule are as old as—"

Chase gaveled them both silent. He leaned toward the witness. "Mrs. Orne, do you have the letter in your possession?"

"No, sir."

"Has it been lost?"

"No, sir."

"Has it been destroyed?"

"No, sir."

"Then where is the letter?"

"Sir, I returned the letter to the President."

A murmur of surprise in the chamber, which Chase's gavel swiftly quelled. Butler spoke up, although Mrs. Orne was Bingham's witness. "Mr. Chief Justice, if the letter in question is in the possession of the individual against whom it is sought to be admitted, then the rule does not apply."

"No such exception exists," said Sickles. "The distinguished Manager is manufacturing new doctrines as needed."

"The doctrine is at least as well established," scoffed Butler, "as, say, the doctrine of temporary insanity."

A slow sigh rippled through the chamber, like air being squeezed from a bellows. Temporary insanity was the doctrine used successfully by Stanton when he represented Sickles in his trial for murder. Nobody other than the jury had believed a word of it. Butler had managed, once more, to remind the Senators of what sort of man the President had chosen to represent him.

Chase turned to Sickles, who was bright red but holding his temper. "Counsel, is the letter in question in the possession of your client?"

"No, Your Honor."

"If it were, and your client did not produce it upon demand, he would be in contempt. So would you."

"I am quite certain that my client possesses no such letter."

Chase turned to Butler. "Counsel?"

"May it please the Court, the witness has just testified that she returned the letter to Mr. Lincoln. The law presumes that it is still in his possession. If he does not produce it, she may testify to the contents."

"He is inventing another principle," groaned Sickles.

Chase nodded. "I am inclined to agree with respondent," he said. "Unless the Managers are prepared to present additional evidence that the letter is in the President's possession, the witness will be dismissed."

Senator Hickman, among the most fiery of the Radicals, demanded that the chamber be polled. The Senate divided evenly on whether to admit the testimony, so Chase's decision was upheld, and Mrs. Orne was excused.

The Managers conferred. Bingham rose. "Sir, on behalf of the People of the United States, the Managers rest."

Chase announced that counsel for the respondent would begin presenting their case on Monday at noon, then adjourned the proceeding for the weekend.

As the lawyers packed their bags, Jonathan touched Sickles on the arm. He pointed out that the Managers had rested because Mrs. Orne had not been allowed to testify, and Mrs. Orne's testimony had been excluded only because Sumner and the votes he controlled had been cast in favor of upholding Chase's ruling.

"I wouldn't weigh that too heavily," Sickles said. "Sumner was very close to Mrs. Lincoln, and he is not close to many women. I suspect that the Managers put on Mrs. Orne because they had some convoluted notion that they could remind him that the man on trial drove his friend Mrs. Lincoln out of her mind. They miscalculated. Sumner preferred not to have his friend's memory besmirched." He saw Jonathan's face. "No, no, it didn't happen that way. Mrs. Lincoln wasn't crazy. Or, if she was, it wasn't Mr. Lincoln's fault. She was what she was."

They headed for the side door, and the conference suite beyond. "I notice that Miss Canner left early today," said Dennard.

Jonathan looked up at the balcony, but it was already nearly empty. "I had not noticed."

"She departed immediately after the Senate voted not to hear what Mrs. Orne had to say." Dennard gave him a long look. "I wonder why."

Jonathan knew an order when he heard one.

III

But when he arrived at the house on Tenth Street, Louisa told him that her sister was out for the evening. Standing behind the screen door, she batted her eyelashes. "Aren't you going to ask me who she's out with, Mr. Hilliman?"

Sometimes we have no pride. "Very well. Who?"

"The other white gentleman. He brought her home, and she ran upstairs to get something and then ran right out again. Nanny was beside herself."

"The other—do you mean Fielding? Fielding Bannerman?" He recovered his aplomb. "Did they happen to mention where they were going?"

Louisa shook her head. "I heard them talking about some hotel."

"The National?"

She didn't remember, she didn't know. "He had a real fancy carriage," she said. "A whole lot fancier than yours."

Jonathan returned to Fourteenth and G feeling defeated and dejected. Last night he had tried to shape the words to let Abigail know how he felt about her, and although they were interrupted, she could hardly have mistaken his meaning. So her decision to go off this evening with Fielding had to be taken as her answer.

In the common room there was no sign of Abigail, but Dennard and Speed and Sickles were going over Mrs. Orne's testimony, as Rellman took notes. They were trying to work out a strategy in case the Managers were able somehow to call her as a rebuttal witness following the defense case. Jonathan joined them, and Dennard asked whether he had tracked down Miss Canner.

"No, sir."

"Peculiar, her running off like that."

"Yes, sir."

"Well, she isn't our problem just now. Mrs. Orne is."

The discussion went on for another hour. Speed argued that nothing in the respondent's case would justify allowing the testimony. Sickles, from his place on the settee, answered dryly that neither Chase nor the Senators seemed terribly worried about justification any longer. They continued in this vein. Jonathan, at Dennard's direction, pulled several volumes from the wall, leafing through to find precedents. He had just gone back to the shelf for a third time when Abigail walked in, quite breathless. All eyes turned her way, seeming to wait.

"I apologize for my tardiness," she said.

"There is no excuse for conduct of this kind," Dennard began. "If you hope to be a lawyer, or even to read law with reasonable success, you will have to learn to work in a hierarchy. One cannot go gallivanting about on a whim. Especially not at this point in a trial—"

For the first time, Abigail spoke over him. "I have been with Mrs. Orne," she said. "And I can assure you that under no circumstances will she testify against the President."

A general exhalation.

"Are you certain?" said Dennard.

"I am." She tilted her head toward McShane's vacant office. Jonathan she ignored entirely. "Mr. Sickles, may I see you alone for a moment?"

IV

"I think we should talk about what Mrs. Orne's testimony would have been," said Abigail when they were alone.

Dan Sickles's look was half smile, half grimace. There was nowhere to stretch out in McShane's office, so he perched on the narrow window seat, his foot on the floor, the bad leg up on the cushion, where he could massage it. As hard as he was rubbing, the pain tonight was obviously intense.

"So tell me," he said. "You're the one who talked to her. I imagine young Bannerman got you in. Old Philadelphia families, of course they'd have known each other for years. Sorry we didn't think of it before. Hilliman should have come up with this one."

Abigail refused to be distracted. "I don't know what she was going to say, Mr. Sickles. She never told me directly. She spent most of the time talking about Mrs. Lincoln. But she dropped enough hints for me to work it out." She could not remain still and so was striding back and forth on the narrow strip of available carpeting. "Mrs. Orne was one of Mrs. Lincoln's best friends. Mrs. Lincoln confided to her things she never shared with anyone else. In this case, by correspondence."

"So?"

"So, I am put in mind of that little speech you gave me the other day, all about how the envelope you took from Mr. McShane's desk could not possibly be relevant evidence. If it were, you said, a defendant inclined to hide it could just as well burn it. Since Mr. Lincoln hadn't burned it, it must not be relevant. Do you recall that conversation, Mr. Sickles?"

Sickles had closed his eyes. "Rings a faint bell."

"But what if he couldn't bring himself to burn it? What if the letter were from his own wife?" Hearing no response, she pressed on. "A letter Mrs. Lincoln wrote not to the President but to her friend Mrs. Orne. A letter describing certain plans that the President might be considering. Plans, say, to use the military to close down Congress."

For a moment, Sickles said nothing, and she wondered whether he might have fallen asleep: he had yet to open his eyes. She heard footsteps in the outer room and knew that Jonathan and the others were growing restless. If anyone walked in, she would never get the truth.

"Mr. Sickles—"

"I keep telling you to call me Dan," he finally said, eyes still shut. Then he sighed. "So I guess you're as smart as everyone says you are, aren't you, Miss Canner?"

"In truth, Mr. Sickles, I have been feeling rather dim of late. I should have realized—"

"There is nothing to realize." He propped himself on his elbows. "What you are suggesting, Miss Canner, is that Mrs. Lincoln—a lovely woman, devoted to her husband—would commit to paper information that could end his presidency and besmirch his good name for all time. Why would such a tale be even remotely plausible to a woman of your undoubted gifts?"

This point had indeed troubled Abigail; and she thought she had found the answer.

"Everyone says that Mrs. Lincoln was not well at the end. I refer not only to her body but to her mind. I have no idea whether the rumors that she was a suicide are true, and I am certain you will not enlighten me, but the fact that the rumors persist is testimony to a widespread impression that she was, as I said, not well. And some of the things Mrs. Orne said do suggest the possibility—well, it doesn't matter. The point is, if Mrs. Lincoln's husband had indeed vouchsafed his plans to her, and she found those plans to be frightening, it seems to me entirely plausible that she might, in a state of severe mental agitation, write to a friend. Later, she might regret having done so, but once words are on paper, they are difficult to retrieve."

Sickles was gazing at the ceiling, where the great lawgivers of history chased each other around in circles.

"I see." He nodded. "And her friend, recognizing the danger of this paper to the woman's husband, might then turn it over to him. Although I suppose she might also dispose of it."

"She, too, might have difficulty with the idea of destroying the letter. Especially once her friend had died."

"If you're right, Miss Canner—I'm not saying you're right, but, if you are—then it is apparent to me that the unfortunate husband would be faced with a difficult decision. If he destroys the correspondence, it is like killing his wife afresh. If he keeps it, it could destroy him." His pretense of working this through alongside Abigail was quite deft. "And perhaps, unable to destroy it, the husband might nevertheless realize that this letter, written by a woman in a distraught state, even perhaps out of control, would never be properly understood in the cold, hard light of politics. Or of—for example—the Senate Chamber. Nor would he want it said later that his wife had reached out from the grave and brought him down."

"Of course," said Abigail, gently, "that would depend a great deal on what the letter actually said." She hesitated. "And, of course, on whether what was described in the letter was not after all the product of a diseased imagination but the literal truth of her husband's words."

"It would indeed." Sickles was now sitting erect. "And I suppose one might also wonder whether, given all the great things that man had accomplished, this single careless but ambiguous conversation, even if recorded accurately by his wife, should be allowed to bring him down. I imagine Mrs. Orne has wondered exactly that." He yawned. "A long day, Miss Canner. A longer one tomorrow. We have to plan the presentation of our case. We both need our rest, and you—well, you have decisions to make."

"As do you, Mr. Sickles."

"Oh, no, Miss Canner. I made my decisions long ago. Other people fight for great principles, for political power, for the sheer thrill of victory. Me? I have one cause, and one cause only."

"And what cause is that, Mr. Sickles?"

"Abraham Lincoln." The pirate's grin. He actually patted her on the shoulder. "You did excellently well today, Miss Canner. But under no circumstances can you disclose, to anybody, what you and I have just talked about. I'm sure you see why."

Afterward, Jonathan of course wanted to know everything, and her polite refusals only wounded him further.

CHAPTER 46

Lantern

I

"NANNY SAYS YOU want to see me."

Abigail looked at her brother as the carriage rolled sedately along Pennsylvania Avenue. "Yes," she said. "Thank you for meeting me."

"Oh, well, I'm just glad you were able to find some time for us colored folk." Michael's laugh was hard and sharp, like the ricochet of a bullet. "What happened, Abby? All the young rich white gentlemen in town busy tonight? Although, from what I hear, you're always happy to meet them later in the evening."

She refused to be drawn. A lazy early-spring sun scudded toward the horizon. She shivered, and drew her wrap more tightly around her shoulders. It was a chilly Saturday, and the coterie had worked through the morning. She and Jonathan had been cordial to each other but no more. Abigail supposed that by now Fielding had told him that he had taken her to Brown's Hotel yesterday to meet Sally Orne, but he had absented himself for most of the conversation and had promised not to tell those snippets he happened to overhear. Abigail believed that he would keep his word: he was, as Jonathan said, a gentleman. The notion that Abigail and Fielding had shared an experience with each other that they would not share with him could hardly have improved Jonathan's mood.

Their labors stretched on into the midafternoon, at which point the men left for the Mansion to meet the President, and Abigail was dismissed. To her fury; but she soothed herself by reading Blackstone until well past full dark, when her brother finally knocked.

"That is an unspeakably vulgar suggestion," she said to Michael now. "And not worthy of response."

"Don't pretend to be one of the Washington ladies, Abby. They will tolerate you as long as you provide entertainment for them, but as soon as they grow bored, they will toss you back into the cage with the rest of us monkeys." He spoke over her sharp retort. "And, believe me, they bore easily."

Abigail felt the welling of panic. Michael had spoken to the most secret and most powerful of her fears—not of the police, or imprisonment, or even of death. No. The fear that drove her to accomplish what no one believed she could, but always lurked, ready to recapture and weaken her, was the desperate fear of *being found out*—the fear that, despite her best efforts, despite her uncommon intellect and her remarkable achievements, she would wind up as just another negro, utterly irrelevant to the course of history and, certainly, to the white people whose respect and even admiration, much as she hated to, she craved.

But she fought down her fears. She had requested this meeting. She knew what her brother was like; and how deeply his resentments ran. Everything he said was cruel, but none of it was unexpected.

"I wanted to know," she said, "whether you have heard from Judith."

"You mean, since your white friends ran her off?"

"If you wish to put it that way."

"I do." After a moment he added, "I haven't heard a word."

Abigail shut her eyes and drew the blanket up to her neck. They had reached George Town, the unincorporated village inhabited by freed slaves and poor whites, few people of either color possessing many prospects. No sensible person went into George Town at night. Michael was no sensible person.

"I suspected you hadn't," Abigail said. "Judith is very skillful at disappearing when she wants to, isn't she?"

"I suppose."

"Funny, isn't it? The whole of the federal Secret Service is looking for her, and she vanishes into thin air."

"I wouldn't call that funny. I'd call that lucky."

They passed small houses, some with lanterns hanging within, some with empty-eyed people sitting on the stoops, watching the night as though expecting the Second Coming. Here and there she spotted hard-faced men who looked as if they would steal a carriage for a nickel; but they took one glance at Michael and left the strangers alone.

"You're not worried," said Abigail. "She's disappeared, people are looking for her, you haven't heard a word, and yet you're not worried."

"Are you saying I should be?" But his voice was perfectly calm.

"No. I'm just thinking—all those years when we didn't hear from her. And then we'd get a letter. Somebody saw her at the South. In Richmond. In New Orleans. In Vicksburg. A cousin would come up from Georgia, and it turned out Judith had been staying with them for a week."

Michael turned the wagon around, heading back down the avenue. Tiny flakes of snow stung her face. "So Judith has a lot of friends," said Michael. "So what?"

"Even during the war, she kept going south. I know people said she was just following the troops—"

"That was a vicious lie."

"I agree. I just didn't realize it until now. She moved too easily, Michael. Far too easily." She twisted the blanket more tightly around her shoulders. "She moved too easily and she knew so much. She had so many friends. So many people willing to . . . to tell her things. To trust her with their secrets." She shivered. "Remember Rebecca Deveaux?"

A tight nod. "They killed her when they killed McShane."

"Exactly. Judith knew her. Rebecca was helping us. She was delivering certain . . . information . . . to Mr. McShane. Judith said she sent Rebecca to Mr. McShane because I worked there." Michael said nothing but Abigail sensed the rising glow of his attention. "But that could not possibly be true. Rebecca was meeting Mr. McShane long before I began working at the firm. I fear that Judith lied to me."

"From which you conclude what?" her brother asked.

"I think you know."

"I would rather hear it from you."

But Abigail was not prepared to say the words. Not aloud. Not yet. Not until she had the rest of the story.

Michael snapped the reins. The horse broke into a fast trot. The snow began to fall in earnest. He said nothing until they reached the White House. A pair of Bucktail sentries dozed at the gate. A light burned in the President's office: the rest of the coterie was planning trial strategy for the week to come.

"You should be up there with them," said Michael, following her gaze. His voice was surprisingly warm. "You're smarter than any two of them together, Abby, and they know it. But you know what? White folks don't like negroes who are smarter than they are. And the ones who claim to love equality the most seem to like it the least."

Now it was Abigail's turn to lapse into silence. She conceded the fundamental truth behind his incautious rhetoric. He had been right in his teasing since the first day of her employment. They would never accept her as an equal. A helper perhaps, a curiosity certainly, but never an equal. *I see you have a diary*, the late Arthur McShane had taunted her on that first day. *Every lawyer keeps one. But I doubt you shall be needing yours.*

Wait.

Her diary—

She turned to her brother. "I have changed my mind. I would like, please, to return to the office."

"Why?"

"That is not your affair."

Michael considered. "The cabs will not take you home," he finally said, "and it is not safe to walk."

"I am sure Mr. Hilliman will see me safely home."

"I am sure it would be his pleasure."

She wanted to slap him, but Michael was no gentleman, and one never knew where a confrontation might lead. "If you are so concerned for my welfare," she said, "you may wait for me."

I I

At Fourteenth and G, the faint yellow flicker of a lantern just visible through the corner window made her wonder whether Jonathan might have returned from the Mansion. Abigail alighted, unassisted by her furious brother, who had announced that he would wait, but not too long. He had added that he did not want that white man seeing her home again, so she would best hurry.

She ignored him.

At this hour there was no policeman. She let herself into the lobby with her key and climbed the stairs rather faster than a lady should. She was remembering how Professor Finney always used to say that the fireman is blameworthy who sleeps while the city burns. She had no intention of doing the same.

On the second floor, Abigail used her other key to open the door of the offices, and her unexpected arrival was what surprised the men inside, one of whom shouted a warning, the other of whom grabbed her by the wrists and tugged her further into the room. For a mad instant she relived that first meeting with Dan Sickles, and so guessed that the invaders' purpose must be innocuous. But they were masked, and when she slapped at the one holding her, his face was hard as granite. The blow as he hit her back was more painful than anything she had ever felt. She cried out, and the second punch made her thoughts turn to slush. She heard them arguing, but her wavery mind could make no sense of the words. Their hands, she saw, were white. She tried to rise and took another blow to the head. One of the intruders shoved her facedown on the conference table, scattering whatever papers they had not already tossed to the winds. The other protested, but the first man ignored him, and began to fumble with Abigail's skirts, and in her terror she was certain she had met the dreaded night riders of the Ku Klux Klan at last. She heard her frantic voice begging and weeping and moaning, doing all the things she had schooled herself never to. She felt what the man behind her was doing and she shrieked in horror. The other man, the one she had thought for a mad moment might be on her side, clapped his hand over her mouth and told her to shut up or they would really hurt her, and now the tears rolled helplessly as the man behind her delved in her skirts, poking and tugging and laughing, and then both intruders were standing very still, because that was what Michael had commanded, and a man pointing a gun at you, even a colored man, is, as a rule, to be obeyed.

III

Jonathan Hilliman was sweating and shivering, deep in a dream of war, when a firm hand on his shoulder shook him awake. Jonathan flailed, cried out, then sat up and slowly calmed. The familiar pilastered wall was in front of him. Ellenborough stood beside the bed—dressed impeccably, as always. Jonathan glanced out the window. The city was dark. Fielding, he recalled, had gone north for a few days, to the lake house.

"It is the middle of the night," he said, groggily.

"You have a caller," said the butler. "A young woman."

Jonathan sat up, damp blankets falling away. "Miss Felix?"

Once more he had offended Ellenborough's dignity. "I am sure that a lady as well raised as Miss Felix would never come calling on a gentleman at this time of night. Indeed, I do not believe that Miss Felix would come calling at all." He had thrown open the cupboard and was pulling out not a robe but a full suit of clothes. "The caller is a negress."

"What?"

"A negress," said Ellenborough, laying out the suit. "I warned her that the hour is late and you are not to be disturbed, but she insists that the matter is urgent. I have asked her to wait in the foyer."

Jonathan was on his feet, shucking off his pajamas. "Please, show her to the parlor."

"I beg your pardon." Waiting for him to correct his faux pas.

"I believe you heard me."

"I am sure Mrs. Bannerman would never—"

"The parlor, Ellenborough. The war is over."

IV

For Jonathan Hilliman, the rest of the night and the early hours of the morning passed in a not unpleasant blur. Rushing about the city in Abigail's company, he felt the way he sometimes did around Margaret, when he would take every action but follow entirely her direction, an experience that produced a not unpleasant hypnotic buzzing in his mind. The first thing Abigail told him as she led him from the house was that her brother had been arrested, and the second was that two men had broken into the offices of Dennard & McShane—having already read bits of Coke on the criminal law, she threw in the correct term of *burglar* for "he that by night breaketh and entereth"—and it took Jonathan some few minutes to understand that the two events were connected, and that the priority in her mind was arranging the release of her brother from custody. He argued briefly, then yielded. On the way to the police jail on Capitol Hill, Abigail explained that she had surprised the burglars on the premises, that they had attacked her—the details she kept determinedly vague—and that some bystander, passing in the night, had heard the tumult, and summoned the city policeman on duty at Willard's. The burglars, who were white, had easily persuaded the policeman that they were the wronged parties, especially because Michael had been holding a pistol—

"Why does your brother require a gun?"

"That is not the point of the story." But the pedant in her could not leave the query unanswered. "Many of the white men of this city go armed, especially at night. The ordinance forbidding black men to do the same was repealed before the war."

The horses' hooves were loud as they hurried along the frozen streets. They passed no one. The city was asleep. "I must inform Mr. Dennard of the burglary," Jonathan said, even as they continued toward the prison. "I should have sent Ellenborough. We need to know what is missing."

"We must see to my brother first," said Abigail grimly.

"Let's be quick."

"That will be up to you."

At the jail, Abigail waited outside, closely watched by a couple of policemen who evidently feared she might turn out to be a rebel saboteur, while Jonathan went inside to arrange matters. Which proved impossible. He was told that nothing could be done until morning, and no combination of entreaties and threats moved the guards an inch. But Abigail had no intention of leaving her brother in that horrid place until morning. She had heard the stories about the city's dank, lightless cells, ridden with rats and spiders and disease. Rumor had it that the prisoners murdered each other in the night, to pass the time; the guards laid bets on who would be alive in the morning.

"We must go to Stanton," said Jonathan.

"No."

"Abigail, there is no alternative."

"We dare not run the risk." Her voice steady as she gazed on the inky mist. "But there is another possibility."

Jonathan listened, then shook his head and said no, under no circumstances. What she proposed was unethical. It wasn't, she said. There was no conflict. He said absolutely not. Abigail pressed. He said no. Dennard would be outraged. And with reason.

"I have lost one sibling unjustly in this matter," said Abigail, head turned away from him as if emotion constituted an embarrassing motivation. "I shall not lose another."

Yielding, Jonathan turned the carriage west, running downhill toward the stolid brick mansion at the corner of Sixth and E Streets. This time she asked Jonathan to wait outside.

"If there are repercussions," Abigail said, "they shall fall on me alone."

"A gentleman can hardly allow a lady to—"

"Please, Jonathan." Despite the terrors of the endless night, she managed the pixie grin that so entranced him. "On this occasion, your duty as a gentleman is to let me have my way."

He handed her down. Jonathan watched her as she composed herself, then walked firmly to the door. She rang the bell. The door opened, and almost shut again as soon as the colored servant saw her, but Abigail whispered a few words, and the man seemed to nod. She stepped inside.

The door snicked shut.

Jonathan wondered how long she would be. He thought about tonight's strategy meeting, and the haunted look on the President's craggy face as he listened to Dennard, who narrated, without visible emotion, the progress of the trial so far. He saw again the coterie sitting around the Cabinet Room, arguing vehemently as Jonathan himself sat in the corner taking notes, until Sickles proposed the only good idea that any of them had come up with, an idea the President adamantly resisted until they could talk him around, and all the while, Abigail had been alone in the offices, fighting off attackers while the men who should have been there to protect her talked nonsense in the White House, and he tried not to imagine precisely what the burglars might have tried to do to her before her brother intervened, but sometimes his exhausted mind wandered paths the conscience would never—

"Jonathan?"

He sat up with a start, realizing that he had dozed. Abigail stood on the curb. He climbed down and handed her up.

"Did you get it?" he asked.

"Yes." She held up her bag, patted the side. "An order of habeas corpus for the release of one Michael Canner from the custody of the city police, signed by the Chief Justice of the United States."

CHAPTER 47

Sacrifice

I

"THE BURGLARY IS a clever touch," said Dan Sickles. He was lounging on the battered settee as the others, supervised by a weary Dennard, hunted through the debris. Sunday morning was dreary. Beyond the windows, a dull early April sun cast pallid gray illumination over the turbulent city.

"I fail to see," said Abigail, who had been cross all morning, "what is clever about it."

"I don't care if it was clever or not," Dennard griped. He seemed fatter than ever as he sat on a rickety wooden chair with his back to the grate. Little had laid a coal fire before joining the cleanup. Rellman was at the far end of the room, reshelving books. Dennard mopped his brow with a handkerchief. "I want to know what is missing. I shall need an inventory."

"So far," said Jonathan, sliding books back onto the shelf from which they had been ripped, "everything seems to be accounted for."

Speed frowned. "Maybe Miss Canner and her brother surprised them before they could depart with what they came for."

Abigail was carrying a small mountain of files toward the cabinet. The burglars had not even untied the green string. "You still have not told us why the burglary is clever."

"Not just the burglary," said Sickles, in the midst of adjusting his bad leg. "Taking nothing is even better for them."

"Why?"

"Because the anti-Lincoln folks can deny they had anything to do with it. It was just a third-rate burglary, foiled by our colored law clerk." He tipped his head in mock apology. "I am telling you what the papers will say, Miss Canner. The rest of us are grateful."

Abigail's anger was very near the surface. What had happened last night was bad enough. To be here this morning, surrounded by the very men who had continued to visit the Mansion without her, made the hot pounding in her ears that much more intense.

"Pray continue," she murmured, acidly.

Jonathan gave her a look but said nothing. Rellman drifted closer. Sickles folded his hands over his stomach and shut his eyes. "Think of it this way," he said. "The burglars had to be after the Chanticleer letters. How they found out about the letters I don't know, but we don't have anything else worth stealing. Well, they didn't find them, because they aren't on the premises. So they took nothing." He adjusted the bad leg. "Now, suppose we put a story in the newspaper. What are we going to say? That two men who we think might have been part of an anti-Lincoln conspiracy broke into our offices and took nothing? If the reporters go down to talk to the police, they will discover that the only man arrested was a negro, accused by two white men of assault. They will discover that the negro is the brother of Miss Canner. The next day, the stories will be about us, not about them. The *Times* might be with us, but the *World*, the *Tribune*, even the *Herald*—all of them will be writing about Miss Canner's brother."

Abigail felt the heat rise, and was unable to wrestle it down. "You are suggesting that they knew that I was returning to the office. That they planned Michael's arrest. That is absurd. Even I did not know I was returning until five minutes before I arrived."

"The arrest was a lucky chance for them," Dennard rumbled. "But I am afraid that Mr. Sickles is correct. Even had there been no arrest, even had you not arrived, the worst that we could have done would be to report the burglary. If the Chanticleer letters were taken, we would hardly admit to having possessed them. And if nothing was taken—the actual fact of the matter—any story the newspapers might print would give the impression that we, in our embarrassment over recent events, we were inventing fairy tales. Your arrival was, for the other side, simply the lagniappe."

Sickles was rougher. He lacked entirely the taste for Latinate English so much in vogue in the capital. "We look like fools now. We're scared, we're confused, we can't tell anybody what happened because it will look like we're trying to distract attention from how badly the trial is going." He rubbed his thigh. "And it is going badly for us. Very badly. Forget the burglary. We need to turn things around."

James Speed could not let the evaluation pass. "We have done our job. We have made the arguments. If the trial is going badly, it is only because Chase and his Radical friends have mangled the Constitution beyond recognition." He glanced around as if expecting contradiction. "Sickles is right. We need a fresh strategy."

"That was the purpose," said Dennard, "of last night's meeting."

"I do not believe," Jonathan said, "that Miss Canner has been apprised of the decisions we took last night." He looked at her. "She should have been there. Next time, we'll take her."

Sickles opened a single eye. "No," he said. "We won't."

Jonathan drew himself up. "Abigail is a clerk in this firm, Mr. Sickles. Just as I am. She should not be excluded from our meetings with our client."

"Maybe that was true before," said Sickles. He yawned. The eye shut again. "But it isn't true now."

"What are you talking about?" Jonathan demanded. He realized that he had balled his fists. He was looking wildly from Dennard to Sickles, and then over at Abigail, who sat in the armchair with a sad little smile on her face. "Why isn't it true?"

"You're a smart boy." Sickles's tone was mocking. "I am sure that you can figure it out."

"Tell him," said Dennard.

A hot red tension hung thick in the air. Even Little, who had gone to the anteroom to repair the broken door, sensed the nearness of battle, and drifted back into the common room, arms held loosely, as though he envisioned physical restraint of the younger and stronger white men.

"What is it?" Jonathan said, body trembling less with anger than with a growing fear.

"Mr. Sickles is correct," said Abigail. She was standing now, clutching her bag. Her voice was gentle and unhappy. "I shall resign my position." She actually put out a hand, and, quite contrary to etiquette, laid it on Jonathan's shoulder. "There is no choice."

Jonathan addressed Sickles. "You said this was a third-rate burglary. It cannot be that we must lose our most brilliant mind because of it!"

"There is no choice," Abigail repeated, not rising to the praise. "My brother was arrested for threatening two white men with a gun. It makes no difference that his arrest was without justification. If I remain an employee of this firm, the newspapers will destroy us. The trial will be a secondary story. The reporters will write that Mr. Lincoln's lawyers are scandal itself. One is murdered in the company of a negro call girl. They hire a negro whose sister is a friend of the murdered call girl, and whose brother—" Her voice broke. She dropped her hand. "It makes no difference what we say. There is no alternative." She looked around at the others. "I would like to thank you, Mr. Dennard, for the opportunity to apprentice here and study the law. I am grateful for the opportunity to assist in the defense of the President against these calumnious charges. But now I have my own calumny with which to deal. I cannot allow my situation to harm Mr. Lincoln's case." For an instant, the pixie smile was back. "I would, however, appreciate being allowed to keep my ticket to the gallery."

The grin faded. She shook hands all around, and went out.

And Jonathan's youth ended.

I I

That night was dinner with Meg and her aunt Clara, along with half a dozen of the great of Washington City. There might have been more, but many had declined their invitations, reasoning that, as Lincoln's sun was setting, the reflected light from his lawyers, once their glory, was growing that much dimmer: indeed, given the now obvious ascendancy of the Radicals, the ambitious might reasonably have worried that the rays, though fading, would actually prove harmful.

The conversation focused on trifles, although Jonathan could feel all eyes inching his way. His distraction was obvious, but few of the guests made a serious effort to draw him. Everyone knew the trial was going poorly. Everyone assumed that, once Lincoln had been removed from office and Benjamin Wade sworn in, Jonathan would marry Margaret and return to New England.

"You seem tired," said Meg, when Jonathan failed to crack the slightest smile at a series of ribald stories from a storied city wit. She was seated beside him: not precisely what protocol demanded, but Margaret had faced down her aunt's stony disapproval. "You seem dispirited."

Jonathan found a smile somewhere. "Work has been difficult."

"I know, my darling. I am so very sorry." She dabbed at her mouth with a napkin. "Father says Mr. Lincoln is going to be convicted."

"The matter is not yet settled."

"Father says that it is."

Jonathan took a bite of the overcooked fish. "There are witnesses yet to be heard," he said. "There are arguments yet to be presented." Ears as well as eyes began to turn. Jonathan found himself repeating what Dan Sickles had said a few days ago. "It is a mistake to assume midway in a trial that you know what the result will be."

One guest, who had imbibed more than the others, had a bright idea. "You fellows have some surprise waiting, don't you?" A near-giggle. "My question is, a *legal* surprise or some other kind?"

Aunt Clara told him to shush. "We should all be proud," she said, "of young Mr. Hilliman's commitment to his client." She raised a glass.

So did the others, not wanting to offend their hostess. Talk turned to other matters. But the impeachment trial remained, inevitably, the ghost at the feast, and the conversation was desultory.

After the guests had departed, Jonathan and Margaret sat together in the parlor. The maid had laid fresh logs on the fire before retiring.

"Spring is in the air," said Margaret, gaily. She squeezed his hand. "Can't you feel it?"

"I suppose." He forced a smile. "I'm sorry. Of course. Yes."

"You should be cheery. Soon this will all be over." She touched his cheek. "I know you had to speak bravely at table, but you and I both know that there is no serious possibility that Mr. Lincoln can prevail." A nod of acknowledgment of the tragic truth of matters. "He will be convicted, Jonathan. You must accept that."

"I told you—"

"That matters are not settled. I know. But they are. Father says so. And Father knows people." Her tone was one of affectionate correction. Flames leaped and crackled in the grate. "Father understands these things"—implying that her young man did not. Jonathan experienced a sudden vision of married life with this wonderful woman he had adored since they were young. *Yes, Jonathan, but Father says . . . No, Jonathan, because Father says . . . That's a bad idea, because Father says . . . We cannot move house, because Father says . . .* And always delivered with warm sincerity, a loving desire to make her beloved happy, because she knew, and would always know, that perfect happiness was identical to hewing to the wisdom of the Lion of Louisiana.

Before he could consider a reply, she kissed him, softly, then kissed him again. Her warm openness surprised him. "You are a good man," she said, holding his face, watching his eyes. "I love you very much, Jonathan."

"I love you, too," he said, after the barest hesitation.

Margaret seemed to consider. She stroked his hair. "Aunt Clara will be in bed soon," she murmured. Another kiss, and now he felt the desperation. "This time, I do not wish to hear of an urgent meeting."

"But—"

She stood, and took his hand. Her eyes were bright, full of joy and wonder, fixed on a magnificent future. "If we are to be husband and wife," she said, "we should practice our conjugal duties to one another."

III

As for Abigail, after leaving the office in the afternoon, she wandered vaguely eastward through an unexpected April snow, until the smoky rumble of a train on the Baltimore and Potomac tracks woke her from her reverie. Startled, she realized how near she was to the Chase mansion at Sixth and E. Embarrassed that habit had almost led her to fresh humiliation, she quickly boarded the horsecars of the Metropolitan Line and rode due south, alighting on the Island, less than a mile from her home. Marching through the city, Abigail was for once comforted rather than offended by the fetid breeze off the canal. She felt light-headed, yet her mind quested onward.

She was almost there. She could feel it. After last night's events, she was so close to the answer. Were the pain of her circumstance not clouding her judgment, she told herself angrily, she would have it. But it is difficult to think clearly through tears.

At home, she was railed at by Nanny Pork, who never let pass an opportunity to point out the horribles, as she called them, that happened whenever her advice was ignored. Nanny took pains to list all the many ways in which Abigail had ignored her guidance, not only in this matter of pursuing her foolish dream of becoming a lawyer, but all the way back to her childhood, including several incidents that Abigail did not remember, and in whose occurrence she entirely disbelieved. Yet she did not fight back. Not against Nanny Pork. All through the cruel years after Abigail's parents died, and then again in the crueler years after she returned from Oberlin to find her fiancé vanished, her great-aunt's unquestioning if disapproving love had been the only constant in her life.

Now, as Abigail sat sipping tea, and Nanny Pork limped around the kitchen listing her niece's deficiencies, the evening's mood began subtly to shift. Abigail found her thoughts drawn away from the mystery of the secret code, and even from the seemingly hopeless impeachment trial, and more and more toward the delicate matter of her own circumstances. Aaron. The collapse of her career, and of her hopes. And all at once she found herself telling Nanny what had really happened. Not Michael's arrest, a matter they had already discussed, and which Nanny had already dismissed; what had nearly happened to Abigail herself in the offices of Dennard & McShane in the late hours of the past night. Giving voice at last to her terror, Abigail was suddenly weeping, and in Nanny's strong arms, which, if the truth was told, was where she had longed to be ever since she walked into the office last night and confronted the two white men who, but for Michael, would certainly have raped her. Nanny said nothing, but tightened her embrace. Abigail was crying for all she was worth, crying hard for the first time since she learned two years ago that Aaron's regiment had returned from the war without him, crying because she had run out of reasons not to. And eventually, wrapped in those familiar arms, comforted by the massive chest, like the child every adult sometimes still is, Abigail cried herself to sleep.

Nanny Pork sat awake, stroking the child's curly hair, marveling that the good Lord allowed so much pain in this sinful world. She wondered why white folks, who had everything, spent so much time fighting over who got how much, while black folks, who had nothing, just sat around feeling sorry for they selves. And she wondered, too, whether it was God's work or Satan's that had caused her precious niece to fall so deeply and hopelessly in love.

IV

The light burned in the parlor window for another hour. When it finally was extinguished, the watcher across the street nodded in satisfaction. Soon, he told himself. Soon.

CHAPTER 48

Strategy

I

GENERAL WILLIAM TECUMSEH Sherman strode down the aisle. The Senators stirred, and many, although seated, very nearly came to attention. General Grant might have had charge of the Union armies and accepted Lee's surrender, and General Felix might have won the West, but it was this brilliant West Point graduate and former banker, tall and elegant, who had marched through the South, burning and blasting everything in his path, destroying the rebels' will to resist. If Grant was loved throughout the North, Sherman was revered—and, probably, feared.

He was also known to be a Lincoln man through and through.

It was Monday afternoon, and time was running out. Here, then, was the strategy on which the President and his lawyers had settled. The meeting had been contentious. Jonathan had sat in the corner, taking notes. From the beginning of the trial, Lincoln had insisted that no military officers be called to testify on his behalf. It was one thing, he said, for professional politicians to take their chances, but soldiers should not risk punishment for the sin of telling the truth. For as long as they could, the lawyers had indulged their client's preference. Now too much was at stake. It took some doing, but they finally wore Lincoln down, persuading him that there was no alternative. On Saturday night, the telegram had gone to Sherman, who was down in North Carolina, straightening out a dispute between two other generals. He had arrived in Washington this morning by train.

Standing before the Senators now, knowing the witness had their full attention, Dennard had Sherman state his name and his rank and his current assignment, took him crisply through his war record, and placed honestly before the Senate Sherman's warm affection for the President of the United States.

Then began the effort to pick apart the impression left by the testimony of poor Major Clancy.

"Now, General Sherman, in September of last year, were you summoned to the White House by the President?"

"I was, sir."

"And did you have a private meeting with him?"

"I did, sir." The general sat ramrod-straight, occasionally stroking his short brown beard, unanimously held to be the most neatly trimmed in Washington.

"What was the subject of this meeting?"

"The difficulties of Reconstruction," Sherman began.

"I have a concern with this line of questioning," said Butler, rising. "Just last week we established that the Managers would not be permitted to place into evidence the President's state of mind."

Dennard was firm. "That was for the limited purpose of deciding allegations of offenses where the state of mind is not in question."

"Such as the suspension of habeas corpus," Butler sneered.

"That is correct," said Dennard airily. "The only question, so the Senate decided by vote"—a small bow in the direction of the chamber—"was whether the President acted and whether his act was justified, not what his motive was."

Chase made a note. "Continue, counsel."

"Here we have an entirely different question," Dennard said. "We do not seek to delve into the President's state of mind. The Managers have made many claims about what the President ordered his generals to do. General Sherman himself is the best witness to the President's orders."

Butler remained unsatisfied. "The President's orders are still declarations, and are therefore outside the scope of what was decided on Friday."

"Your Honor," said Dennard, "the Senate did not vote to exclude all words or actions by the President, but only those intended to show his state of mind."

The Chief Justice nodded. "Objection overruled. You may proceed, Mr. Dennard."

Sherman resumed his testimony. Yes, the subject matter of the meetings had been the difficulties of Reconstruction. Sherman explained that he, among other commanders, had warned Lincoln repeatedly of the problems. There was not enough money. There were too many overlapping offices. The Freedmen's Bureau was understaffed, and unenthusiastic about its work. Where state governments had been reconstituted, there were still too many violations of the rights of the recently freed slaves, and up in the gallery Abigail winced, because their witness was in effect testifying for the prosecution. She noticed the satisfied look on Kate's pug face, and realized that the defense had been had. Butler had not really wanted to keep this part of the testimony out. When they got to the part that helped the President, however . . .

"Did the President agree with you?"

"Sir?"

"You said that you told the President about some of the problems in the Reconstruction of the South. I am asking if Mr. Lincoln made any response."

Butler was on his feet like a pistol shot. "Objection. Your Honor, they are still trying to elicit Mr. Lincoln's declaration for the purpose of showing his state of mind."

"No, Your Honor," said Dennard. "All we are trying to establish is the state of mind the President conveyed to his subordinates. Again, let me emphasize that it is the Managers who have put this matter in issue."

"Overruled. The witness will answer."

Sherman took his time. "Sir, the President at all times expressed great concern over the course of Reconstruction."

Chase leaned down. "The question, General, was whether the President agreed with your concerns, not whether he expressed any of his own."

"Sir, he agreed."

Dennard resumed. "Did you make suggestions for improving the situation?"

"I did."

"Did the President offer any?"

"Objection."

"Counsel," said Chase after a moment, "you may ask whether the President made any response. You may not elicit the content, if your intention is to show his state of mind."

Butler was unsatisfied. "Your Honor, we would ask that the presiding officer inquire of counsel what his intention is."

Dennard did not wait. "Your Honor, we are simply trying to meet the Managers' assertion that the President paid no attention to the complaints about some of the difficulties of Reconstruction."

Chase nodded. "Very well. The objection is overruled. The witness may answer."

The secretary read back the question.

"Yes," said Sherman. "Mr. Lincoln very kindly shared his ideas."

Dennard proceeded carefully. "Did his ideas meet your concerns?"

"Yes, sir."

"In what way?"

"Objection."

"Sustained."

Abigail realized that she was sweating. True, the gallery was stifling, as usual, and the great ladies of the capital were fanning away, but this was different; this was nervousness, bordering on panic. She understood the importance of Sherman's testimony. She did not understand how the Managers could allege a conspiracy, without any witnesses or documents, and then the Senate could refuse to hear any evidence intended to rebut the allegation.

Unless, of course, the Senators had already made up their minds.

Down in the well, Dennard was again circling toward his goal. Yes, the President answered each of my concerns. Yes, I thought his ideas were good ones. Yes, we talked about—a glance at Butler, but no objection came this time—the level of concern among members of Congress over the problems of Reconstruction. Yes, the President said he believed that he could settle with the congressional leaders and put this episode behind him. No, he did not tell me the terms of the deal. No, I never heard him say anything about ignoring any—

"Objection."

Perfectly timed. Dennard had just asked whether the President had ever, in the hearing of the witness, disparaged the Congress. Butler's plan was to leave standing the testimony that the President was concerned about Congress and planned to settle with congressional leaders, without allowing Sherman to explain just what the President meant.

Chase said, "Counsel, you may not use the respondent's out-of-court statements to establish his state of mind. The objection is sustained."

Dennard lumbered back to the counsel table and whispered briefly with the other lawyers. "Now, General Sherman," he said when he was standing before the witness once more, "when you had these conversations with the President, was anything said about the Department of the Atlantic?"

"Yes."

"Please tell us what was said."

Butler objected. "We have just argued the point. Counsel may not, through questions to witnesses, place into evidence declarations by the President, at least if those declarations are intended to show the President's state of mind. If Mr. Lincoln wishes to tell us of his state of mind during the events we are discussing, he is free at any time to come up to the chamber and be sworn."

Dennard was succinct. "A statement admitted to show state of mind is not hearsay. The principle is well settled."

Chase took off his glasses and rubbed the bridge of his nose, the sign that he was having trouble making up his mind. "I think the question is admissible," he finally said. "The Managers have charged the President with an intent to use the proposed Department of the Atlantic to overthrow the Congress. I do not see how else the respondent can answer the charge but by putting into evidence his contemporaneous statements."

"Mr. Lincoln can come to this chamber and be sworn," Butler persisted.

"I have made my ruling, Mr. Butler." Chase looked around the room, his fine sense of political judgment obviously at work. "Nevertheless, I consider it appropriate to put the question to the Senate."

Up in the gallery, it was Kate's turn to stiffen, and Abigail's to notice. The most prominent of Washington's ladies was worried. And, given that the only subject that ever worried Kate was her father's presidential chances, Abigail could only assume that she believed Chase had made an error.

She wondered what it was.

Down below, the secretary of the Senate was reading from the record Dennard's question to Sherman, and the ensuing argument. Then, the motion not being debatable, the secretary immediately called the roll. Sumner and the votes he controlled tipped the balance, and the tally ran twenty-three to twenty-nine against admitting the question, with Wade again abstaining, and Senator Sherman, the witness's brother, joining him.

The Chief Justice said, "The question will not be admitted."

All through the roll call, Dennard and Speed and Sickles had been whispering together, trying to come up with a plan. Now, with the matter settled, Dennard rose to try again.

"General Sherman," he said, "during these conversations with the President, did you yourself ever make any statements or any inquiries regarding the Department of the Atlantic?"

Butler was again on his feet, insisting that the previous ruling covered this form of the question, too.

"I am not asking for a declaration from the President," said Dennard. "I am only asking the witness what he himself said."

"He is asking the question," said Butler, "in order to elicit information on the state of mind of the President."

Chase hesitated. "Overruled. The witness will answer."

"I made no inquiries," said Sherman, the overprecise answer less helpful than the President's lawyers might have hoped.

Dennard checked his notes. Plainly, they had worked out several different permutations of the question. "General Sherman, during these conversations with the President, did you receive any written memoranda or orders regarding the Department of the Atlantic?"

Butler objected. Chase was succinct: "The witness may state whether he received memoranda but not what the memoranda said."

"I received no memoranda," said Sherman.

"And did you receive any spoken orders regarding the Department of the Atlantic?"

"I received no spoken orders."

"Did the President ever give you any order of any kind regarding the Department of the Atlantic?"

"He did not."

"What if anything did the President say to you regarding the Department of the Atlantic?"

"Objection. Same ground."

"Sustained."

Dennard kept trying to find a method of phrasing the question that would allow Sherman to say to the Senate what he had said to the President's lawyers: that at no point had the President said to him a single word about overthrowing the Congress, and that their conversation about the Department of the Atlantic and General Sherman's role was entirely innocuous, dealing with matters of reducing the cost of the occupation of the defeated South by reducing the number of separate commands.

Each time, Dennard failed. Either Chase refused to admit the question, or he admitted it and was overruled by the Senate. Finally, Dennard surrendered and moved on to less pressing questions, with no relation to the only matter Sherman had been called to explain. Abigail felt a growing despair. Tomorrow, she knew, the papers would imply that the entire matter of the Department of the Atlantic had been a desperate manipulation on the part of a vengeful madman trying to impose his will on the nation.

II

Butler's cross was brisk, and to the point.

"Now, General. Do you recall a newspaperman named Thomas Knox, a correspondent for the *New York Herald*?"

Sherman tilted his head away, as if Butler had uttered a vulgarity. "I recall Mr. Knox very well," he said.

"You ordered his arrest, didn't you?"

"I did."

"Would you please tell the Court why."

"Sir, Mr. Knox was authoring false dispatches, lying about the situation at the front, stirring up opposition to the war effort, and giving valuable military intelligence to the enemy."

"And you had him tried by a military court, did you not?"

"I did. The court-martial found Mr. Knox guilty, and expelled him from the front lines. Under the sentence, he would be imprisoned if found in the vicinity."

"And did Mr. Lincoln become involved in the case?"

"Yes, sir." For the first time Sherman seemed slightly uncomfortable. "Some other newspapermen appealed to the President. He commuted Mr. Knox's sentence."

Butler feigned astonishment. "Let me understand this, General. You warned Mr. Knox to cease his treasonous dispatches—as any of us would have—and when he did not, you turned him over to a court-martial, which convicted him and banned him from the front? And the President overruled you?"

"Sir, he overruled the sentence of the court-martial."

"Indeed." Butler made a show of consulting his notes. "And the *Herald* was at the time a pro-Lincoln paper, was it not?"

Chase sustained Dennard's objection, but everyone saw the point.

Butler, swaggering a bit, returned to the table and picked up a new card. "Now, General, do you recall the case of a certain Presbyterian pastor in Memphis who was turned out of the pulpit by his congregants?"

The entire chamber perked up. Nobody knew what this was about. At the defense table, the lawyers whispered frantically together.

"I do," said Sherman, unruffled. "The pastor, Dr. Grundy, was a loyal Union man. Most of his congregation were for secession. They expelled him. The new pastor preached treason, so when my army arrived, in 1864, we put the new pastor out and the old one back in."

Butler was no God man. "Grundy's theology was sounder?"

Laughter from the audience.

"I did my duty, sir," said Sherman.

"And did Mr. Lincoln become involved in that case?"

"Sir, he did. The congregants who had put Dr. Grundy out appealed to the President. He overruled me."

"Mr. Lincoln put the rebel pastor back in?"

"Sir, the President said that, absent military necessity regarding the building itself, we had no business interfering in the operation of the church, and that it was up to the congregation to choose its pastor."

"And this order had the effect of putting the rebel pastor back?"

"Yes, sir. However—"

"Thank you, General. Now, turning your attention to . . ."

Butler went on this way for another hour. Someone had plainly been through the War Department signal records quite thoroughly, and picked out half a dozen episodes in which Lincoln, or Sherman's superiors acting on Lincoln's behalf, had overruled military decisions made in the field. No doubt a similar search would have discovered similar orders issued to every high-ranking general. Nevertheless, with the President's men unprepared for rebuttal, the effect was devastating. Few would recall the bits of pro-Lincoln testimony that Dennard had managed to squeeze through the barriers raised by Chase's bizarre rulings. But everyone would remember that Lincoln had supported the rebels even over the great William Tecumseh Sherman, a general who revered him.

Battered by the combination of Chase's enmity and Butler's cleverness, the President's case was in ruins.

CHAPTER 49

Return

I

"I SUPPOSE THE Chief Justice has made up his mind," said Dinah Berryhill. "He thinks that your Mr. Lincoln is done for. Oh, look. What do you think?"

It was midday Wednesday, three days after Abigail's resignation. They were visiting a jeweler on the second floor of a building on Seventeenth Street, across from the Old Clubhouse, where William Seward was living, or perhaps dying, seeing nobody other than a few close friends, running the State Department through his son Frederick, the assistant secretary. There were many who thought that, had Seward not been so gravely wounded on the night two years ago, the impeachment would never have reached this point; for his skill at calming political storms was legendary.

"I fancy this one," said Dinah, fingering a diamond tiara priced in the thousands. Ordinary people, black or white, were not welcomed in the private suites of the city's finer jewelers; but Dinah was no ordinary person, and spent her father's money like water. "What do you think?"

"It's very nice," said Abigail, hardly looking.

"Pay attention. Tell me what you honestly think."

"Too showy."

"Nonsense. It is perfect." Dinah turned to the jeweler, who was all but rubbing his hands together in anticipation. "How much?"

"Two thousand," said the delighted man.

"Ridiculous. I will give you twelve hundred." She began writing out a draft without waiting to hear whether he agreed. She had been buying from him for some time, and they understood each other.

"Dinah."

"Wait."

"*Dinah.*"

"I want to look at earrings next. Something different this time. Emeralds, perhaps."

The jeweler went into the next room, where he kept his safes.

"What is it, dear?"

Abigail was at the window. "Come. I want you to see something."

They looked out across the street together, at Seward's grim granite prison. "Yes, dear?"

"See the soldier? The guard outside?"

"The one with the rifle?"

"The other one. By the carriage." She pointed. "Do you see him?"

"Yes, dear."

The jeweler was back, with several selections for her to look at.

"Wait. Dinah, look. Your eyes are better than mine."

"All that reading is ruining you, dear."

"Maybe so. Just tell me—from this distance—can you see his face? He seems to me to have long black moustaches."

"He does, dear. And a red band at his shoulder. Excuse me." Turning back toward the jeweler. "No, no, not like that. Those are *tiny*. Those are for *children*. Real emeralds. Big ones. Abigail, dear, come look. Aren't they hideous?"

But Abigail was staring at the Old Clubhouse, residence of Mr. Lincoln's closest friend and most trusted adviser, wondering why Edwin Stanton's personal bodyguard was skulking outside.

II

Abigail had not visited the trial since resigning her position. Jonathan had sought her out at home on Monday after court. He had started to describe the battle over Sherman's testimony, and she had asked him to stop. Then she had told him why she had returned to the office on Saturday evening: she wanted to see Mr. McShane's diary, hoping that the book so important to every lawyer might contain the key to Rebecca's cipher. Jonathan told her that the diary and any secrets it might have held had disappeared the night of the murders.

A few minutes later, Abigail asked him to leave the house.

But now, on the Thursday, she slipped back into the gallery, and there was the same seat, still empty, between Mrs. Sprague and Miss Felix.

"I was hoping you might return," said Kate as Abigail sat. "I gather everything turned out well for your brother?"

"It did. Thank you."

"You know, of course," said Margaret Felix, "that Fielding Bannerman has left the city."

Abigail was startled, and unable to hide her surprise.

Kate nodded toward the counsel table. "I believe that some sort of difficulty has arisen between Mr. Bannerman and Mr. Hilliman. I would not of course venture a guess as to what that might be."

"I had no idea," said Abigail.

"The two of you made a lovely couple," said Meg, venomously. "Perhaps you will choose to follow him."

Abigail looked at the malevolent eyes, then looked away. Margaret Felix was from Philadelphia. Mrs. Orne was from Philadelphia. Fielding Bannerman was from Philadelphia. The Belmont interests in Philadelphia were substantial. And of course David Grafton made his home in Philadelphia. Abigail was not ready to declare every prominent Philadelphian a part of the conspiracy. And yet, when she studied Margaret's mocking face—

Meanwhile, down below, the President's lawyers were foundering. There seemed little left for them to try. Sherman was the only military officer Lincoln had allowed them to call, and his testimony had been severely circumscribed. They put on several Southern negroes, from various walks of life, who testified to their gratitude toward and admiration for Mr. Lincoln, and assured the chamber that they had never had trouble getting assistance or protection from the Freedmen's Bureau or their local military commanders. They put on two War Department telegraphers who handled all communication with troops in the field, who testified that they had never heard of or transmitted any orders concerning the Department of the Atlantic. But Bingham embarrassed the second of the two very badly on cross-examination, naming several other subjects, and asking the man whether he had ever transmitted an order concerning it. Twice he said no, and Bingham had a copy of the telegraph message to prove him wrong. The next time, the witness guessed yes, and Bingham told the Senators that a search of War

Department records turned up no such message. Bingham then asked how many messages the telegrapher handled each day. At least twenty, the man said; sometimes fifty; and on especially busy days, a hundred or more.

Bingham than moved that the entire testimony of both telegraphers be stricken, because of the obvious difficulties of memory.

Dennard argued strenuously, but lost.

"Call your next witness," said Chase. He sounded quite exhausted.

Reduced to minutiae, the defense called several presidential staffers to prove that Mr. Lincoln had made no secret trip to New York to see Reverend Beecher. Sickles had argued adamantly against this strategy, suggesting that the evidence of Eliza Caffey was best forgotten: why bring the public attention back to it? But Dennard and Speed insisted that, whatever people outside the chamber might think, inside the chamber it was vital to meet the Managers' proof item by item.

Finally, Lincoln's lawyers were out of witnesses. The trial would be adjourned for the weekend. The Managers had planned beautifully. Next week, they would likely call Stanton as a rebuttal witness, and his testimony would bury the President.

Everyone in the room knew it.

As the lawyers prepared to depart, Dennard actually slipped an arm around Jonathan. "You did well, my boy," he said consolingly. The old man seemed to be ready to accept the inevitable. He lifted his paunchy chin toward the gallery. "I think Miss Canner is trying to get your attention."

She was leaning over the parapet, signaling him to meet her in the lobby. As Jonathan hurried up the aisle, he saw, in another corner of the balcony, his beloved Margaret, contriving somehow to stare at both him and Abigail at once. And he knew, as the bird knows when it takes to wing ahead of the approaching hurricane, that disaster was about to strike.

III

"Thank you for meeting me, Mr. Hilliman," said Abigail, with a crisp formality explained by the presence of Jonathan's fiancée on his arm. The three of them stood together at the barrier blocking the corridor to the lawyers' suites. "It's very kind of you, Miss Felix."

Margaret inclined her head and said nothing, but the baleful green eyes seemed to be taking notes. "I wonder," said Abigail, addressing Meg, "if I might borrow Mr. Hilliman for a brief moment."

Nobody moved.

"I have no secrets from Margaret," said Jonathan, after a noticeable pause.

"None," said Margaret, the intensity of her gaze rising. There were times, her face said, when one must engage the tools of diplomacy, and there are times when one must be prepared for war.

Abigail looked at Jonathan in appeal, then back at Margaret; seemed to reach a decision. She stood straighter, and gave a tight nod, fingers still clutching that purse.

"It's Michael. My brother. He's gone off somewhere."

"Gone off? What on earth does that mean?" Around Margaret, Jonathan often found himself slipping all too easily into the arch hauteur that Margaret and her father and for that matter his own family expected of him. He struggled to calm his voice, and to throw some warmth into it. "He's run away? Is that what you're saying?"

"This is not easy to say." Abigail bit her lip. She looked not at Jonathan but at Margaret. "You have an older brother, Miss Felix. You know what a bond that is."

Margaret might or might not have known; she was not saying, although her gaze suggested that the commonalities between the two of them were becoming less numerous by the minute.

"Michael's gone off," said Abigail again, this time addressing the dirty marble floor. She had to speak very loud to be heard above the storm of conversation echoing through the Rotunda. "He has a gun. I'm not sure what he's going to do. He was saying things, making wild threats and accusations."

"Against whom?" said Jonathan.

Abigail shook her head. "Just accusations," she whispered, voice as weak and hopeless as he had ever heard it.

Margaret finally spoke. "This is a matter for the police," she said, firmly.

"I can't go to the police. You know what they do to"—she searched for a neutral phrase—"to my people when they're thought to be dangerous."

"From what you're telling us," said Margaret, inexorably, "your brother *is* dangerous."

"He would never hurt anyone," Abigail said stubbornly. The crowd flowed around them, creating an island of calm; but she could feel eyes on her all the same.

"It is my understanding," said Margaret, "that he wanted to go off with John Brown to kill women and children in Virginia, but was not allowed because of his youth."

Abigail's head came back up. She stared at Jonathan in surprise.

"As my fiancé told you," continued Margaret, coolly, "we have no secrets from one another."

"My brother"—Abigail struggled visibly for control—"would never harm anyone. Whatever Michael's desires, Miss Felix, he did not actually *go* on Mr. Brown's raid." Her voice was flat. In the lobby she was backing away, but Jonathan felt the sudden distance as enormously greater. "I am sorry to have troubled you both. Do enjoy your evening."

She left them.

IV

They stood together in the crowd at the carriage block outside the West Portico. Several grand city personages waited ahead of them. Margaret's rig was fourth or fifth in line.

"There was no need to be so hard on her," said Jonathan, having battled his demons to a draw, and now seeking only compromise.

Margaret seemed not to hear. Her cheeks were rosy from the cold. "I suppose you will be going back to the office."

"I have responsibilities."

"It's simply that the Jay Cookes are only in Washington two or three times a year. How can we miss their soirée?" When Jonathan only shrugged, she leaned into him once more. "Ah, well. I suppose one of Cousin Fielding's Harvard friends can always escort me." A thought struck her. "And Miss Canner? Will she be at the office, too?"

"You know she is no longer employed at Dennard & McShane."

"She retains her ticket to the trial."

Jonathan managed a smile. "You have nothing to fear, my darling."

"Fear?" the Lion's daughter repeated, playing with the word as if he had uttered a charming vulgarity. "Goodness me. Whatever would make you imagine that I am afraid of something?" Before he could answer, she punched him lightly in the side. "Whereas you, my dear, would seem to have much to fear."

"I do?"

"Miss Canner seemed very . . . distraught. And guilty. Very guilty." It was the turn of Margaret Felix to play detective. "From the way she was behaving, my love, I rather believe that those mad threats her brother was making must have been against you!"

"Me?"

"Why else go to all of this trouble to warn you? Oh, Jonathan! Do you suppose this mad brother of hers would try to shoot you?" A shiver of delight. "That would be so exciting."

"Only if he missed."

"*I* should find it exciting either way. I do see how your experience of the matter might be limited." Her pale brow furrowed. "This is the same brother who was arrested for assaulting those two white men, is it not?"

"That isn't what happened—"

"But he was arrested." Firmly. "Father says that Mr. Lincoln can afford no more scandals. I accept that Miss Canner is quite talented, but scandal does seem to attach to her, does it not?"

He handed her up into the carriage.

And reached a decision. "Meg, look—"

But the Lion's daughter was ahead of him. "I believe that I shall follow Cousin Fielding north," she said. "It is time, Jonathan. The trial is coming to its end, and you will not profit from the distraction of my presence in these final days. I have written to Father, and he agrees. A period apart will doubtless benefit us both." She slipped off a glove and touched his face with her fingers. Her green eyes were wondering but without doubt. "After the verdict is rendered, and you have had the opportunity to rest, and to reflect on the future you prefer to pursue, you will know where to find me."

"Meg, I—"

"Farewell, Jonathan, dearest."

She signaled to the coachman and clattered off. Jonathan stood watching.

Neither waved.

CHAPTER 50

Conversation

I

THE MOOD AT Dennard & McShane was dispirited. On Monday, the respondent would rest its case. There were no other witnesses; there was no more evidence. Nevertheless, the President's lawyers refused to concede the defeat that even the pro-Lincoln newspapers called inevitable, now that Salmon P. Chase seemed to have chosen sides.

"A trial is war" is the way Dennard put it; he had fought in the Mexican War and knew what he was taking about. It was Saturday afternoon, April 13. Closing arguments would be held on Tuesday. Then each member of the Senate would have his say, a process that would take all of Wednesday and most of Thursday. The vote would be taken no later than Thursday afternoon, so as to finish the trial before Good Friday.

"This isn't a battle," said Sickles. Perhaps marking the seriousness of the occasion, he was sitting at the table, not lying on the divan. "It's a slaughter."

"A slaughter for which side?" asked Speed, charmingly unwilling to waver in his steadfast belief in his friend the President.

Sickles chuckled. Not happily. "In this particular battle, the Managers had all the big guns. Moorhead, Yardley, that Caffey woman. The kind of witnesses people read about in the newspaper next day and are still talking about next month. We put on a swarm of gnats. Irritating, sure, but nobody remembers them later."

"We put on General Sherman," said Rellman, who, since Abigail's departure, seemed to have shed most of his shyness. "He's as big a gun as there is."

"And we were not allowed to ask him anything important," said Jonathan, who had made it his task, for reasons he was able to perceive but dimly, to disagree, rudely, with every word out of Rellman's mouth. "And the cross hurt us. None of it was important, but all of it hurt us."

Rellman's pink face twisted. He was not done. "Also, the Managers never called Mr. Stanton." He struggled to keep the analogy going. "So that's one gun they haven't fired."

"Do you really think—" Jonathan began.

"Stop it, you two," said Sickles, too tired to play. "They will put on Stanton this week."

"But they have rested their evidence!" cried Speed.

Dennard spoke heavily. He, too, was exhausted. "They will call him as a rebuttal witness. We put on evidence of what the President did *not* say. They will want the last impression of the trial the public gets to be the face of the Secretary of War, giving evidence of what the President *did* say. And then the Senators will convict, at least on Count Three, and quite possibly on Count Four as well."

The grim words sobered even Speed. They all understood that conviction on even one count was sufficient to remove Mr. Lincoln from office. By Good Friday, if not earlier, Benjamin F. Wade would be President of the United States.

II

Jonathan returned to the Bannerman mansion. Ellenborough had a cold supper waiting. Sitting alone at the long dining table, Jonathan hardly noticed what he ate. Meg was gone. Abigail was gone. And three days ago, he had risen in the morning to find Fielding's bags in the front hall, waiting to be loaded for the ride to the depot.

"It's like this, old man," said his friend when Jonathan tracked him to the library. "There's two of us and one of her. We can fight a duel or we can go our separate ways."

"I'm engaged to your cousin," said Jonathan—who, at that time, still was.

"And yet I doubt that you shall marry her." Clapping him on the back. "Well, maybe if your man is convicted."

Jonathan stood silent, wondering whether Abigail was the true reason for his friend's departure from Washington City. Fielding paused in the open doorway. Down by the carriage block the horses snorted and shied in the freezing rain.

"Oh, say," he continued. "Heard the glad news about General Baker?"

Jonathan, now pressed on all sides by the prospect of solitude, shook a weary head. "Who's he arrested now?"

"Nobody. He's sick in bed. Might not live. I was down at the club tonight, and Tubby Longchamps was saying that everyone on the Hill thinks Baker's been poisoned. But you know Tubby and his stories."

Watching the carriage clatter off through the freezing rain, Jonathan found himself wondering whether the conspiracy was finally beginning to show cracks.

III

And, sitting up late in the kitchen of the house on Tenth Street, munching on one of Nanny Pork's snickerdoodles, her notebook open in front of her, Abigail Canner smiled in triumph.

She had figured it out.

CHAPTER 51

Confrontation

I

ON TUESDAY MORNING at half past eight, Abigail Canner boarded the horsecars on Seventh Street, just as she had every morning of her now ended employment at Dennard & McShane. She sat in the middle, as usual. High wispy clouds drifted across a distant slate sky. The weather had not yet realized that it was spring. At Pennsylvania Avenue, she changed to the Washington & Georgetown Line. Watching the hotels and office buildings slip past, she had the sensation that once she left each vista behind she would never see it again, as if this was a day for endings, not beginnings. Rather than alighting from the car where the tracks crossed Fourteenth Street, as she would if heading for the office, Abigail remained aboard until Lafayette Park. Here the carriage block was broad and flat and meticulously maintained. And no wonder. Lafayette Park was directly across the street from the White House.

She hesitated a moment, glancing at Secretary Seward's grim castle to the west, going over the logic in her mind, then proceeded boldly across Pennsylvania Avenue. A uniformed soldier stopped her at the gate of the Executive Mansion, and she asked to see one of the doorkeepers. Once the guard realized that she was not undertaking some sort of elaborate joke, he passed her on to the front entrance. She knocked, then handed the startled doorkeeper a sealed envelope, addressed to Noah Brooks, the President's private secretary.

"Put it directly in his hand," she said, trying for the easy imperiousness that Dinah Berryhill would have mustered at such a moment. "Make sure the note goes to Mr. Brooks and no one else."

Her attitude evidently made an impression, because the doorkeeper, an ancient and toothless Irishman, invited her into the lobby to wait. He hurried up the marble stairs. Under the watchful eye of a Bucktail, Abigail stood very still, continuing to disguise her nervousness in a show of hauteur.

The anger helped.

She had required three nights to make up her mind and prepare a plan. She had spent the past two months reacting to events, as, in a sense, she had done her whole life, working out what was expected of her—whether at the Quaker school, at Oberlin Collegiate Institute, or at Dennard & McShane—and then performing those tasks with an excellence so implausible that those around her—the white people around her—had no choice but to acknowledge the superiority of her brain. Yet all of that success was only reactive. The time she had spent with Kate Chase Sprague—and, although she hated to admit it, with Margaret Felix as well—had taught her the value of the life spent not responding to the demands of others, but making demands of your own. The path she had followed up until now guaranteed a form of success; but the path of acting rather than reacting, although riskier, led not to mere success but to triumph.

More now than at any moment in her young life, Abigail Canner was determined to triumph.

The doorkeeper was back, astonishment in his aged eyes. "Mr. Brooks instructs me to bring you right up."

I I

"May it please the court," said Bingham, "the Managers have one rebuttal witness."

Chase squinted down at him. "Call your witness," he said.

"The Managers call Edwin Stanton."

The secretary of the Senate echoed the call, the far door swung open, and the most feared man in Washington stepped into the chamber. His beard for once was dry, but his twisted sneer told the world that nobody had better notice.

Dennard was already on his feet. "Your Honor, we object to this witness."

Bingham said, "Counsel for the respondent have built their case around the assertion that Mr. Lincoln neither knowingly flouted the will of this Congress nor acted at any time in a way that might lead to the overthrow of its authority. We have the right to rebut their evidence."

Chase turned back to Dennard.

"Sir, the Managers will attempt to elicit privileged testimony—"

"This body has already ruled on the claim of privilege, Mr. Dennard. Step back." To the clerk: "Swear the witness."

Bingham stepped to the lectern.

"Mr. Stanton, what is your position?"

"I am the Secretary of War."

"And you are therefore in constant contact with the President of the United States?"

Stanton never faltered. "Sir, it is my privilege to serve as one of Mr. Lincoln's closest advisers."

"Indeed, since the incapacitation of Secretary Seward, have you not been his closest adviser?"

Dennard objected. Chase told him to sit.

"That assessment is correct," said Stanton smoothly. He began to comb the luxurious beard with his fingers.

"Mr. Stanton, I am going to ask you a series of questions regarding conversations you have had with the President of the United States. If at any time you feel that honor dictates leaving some matter aside, please feel free to specify."

"I understand, Mr. Bingham."

"Good. Now, then, Mr. Stanton, did you have any conversations with Mr. Lincoln regarding the implementation of the Reconstruction Acts?"

"Of course. We spoke of it frequently."

"And did you bring to his attention the complaints of various general officers and military governors about the level of protection being afforded the freedmen?"

Again Dennard's objection was overruled.

"I did."

"What was the President's response?"

III

"They tell me that you have been rather busy," said Abraham Lincoln. "They tell me that you have been all over Washington City, and down in Richmond, too, gathering information."

This time, only the two of them were in the office. Abigail, a bit overwhelmed to be alone in the presence of the President, managed to keep her voice relatively steady.

"Yes, sir," she said.

"You have just refused to leave this alone, haven't you? You have had plenty of warnings—from Baker, from Stanton, even from that police inspector—but you will not stop, will you?" He was sitting behind his desk, chair leaning back against the wall. "Even when you don't know where you're going, you won't stop. You're like the man who says he can't get his boots on until he's worn them for a day or two to stretch the leather." No smile. "Well, you've stretched the leather about as far as it will go, haven't you? And Seward says you have about everything you need to work out what's been going on."

"Not everything, sir." Don't react. Press forward. "But I have figured out enough to know that the House Managers are in for a surprise."

The President's sleepy eyelid drooped into a wink. "I suppose they are, aren't they?"

IV

"Mr. Lincoln was angry," said Stanton. "He told me that the treatment of the freedmen was an outrage. He ordered me to use whatever force was available to protect them."

Bingham frowned, and consulted his notes. The play was not unfolding precisely according to script. "And was much force available?"

"No, sir."

"And why was that?"

Dennard was about to object, but Sickles put a hand on his arm. Jonathan heard the men whispering together, and Dennard subsided.

"Sir, after the war, the President and this Congress worked out a reduction in the troop levels, as a means of saving money. Most of the conscripts were sent home. Our forces at the South were therefore spread more thinly than during the war."

"Was the lack of money the only reason that there were few troops?" asked Bingham, obviously trying to signal the witness.

"Sir?" said Stanton.

"Hadn't decisions been made by the President to withdraw most of the troops from certain states?"

Again the question, as phrased, was objectionable, and Chase glanced at the defense table. But Dennard didn't budge.

"Sir, there are three states where a sufficient number of the white males of voting age have taken the oath of allegiance. They have formed governments in which no one who served in the rebel government is allowed to serve. They have also ratified the Thirteenth Amendment, abolishing slavery. Those states have met the terms set out by the Commander-in-Chief and are therefore no longer under military government. We nevertheless have forces in those states, but the forces are relatively small."

"So it would be fair to say that in three states, at least, the reason there are few troops is because of Mr. Lincoln's decision?"

"Sir, we are no longer at war with those particular states."

An uproar in the chamber. Stanton had hit on precisely the issue dividing the President and the Congress. When the tumult subsided, Bingham, back where he had hoped to be, asked the question he had been waiting to spring:

"So the freedmen received less protection in the states that the President has allowed to form governments?"

"No, sir," said Stanton. Bingham, who had been swaggering a bit, stopped. He was stunned. "Mr. Lincoln ordered me to transfer such troops as were necessary to combat the night riders."

"But—"

"We were moving troops constantly, sir. There were not enough to cover the entire South, but that was not because of Mr. Lincoln's decision. That was because of the decision, concurred in by this Congress, to reduce the amount of the budget allotted to the Department of War. If there is fault, sir, it lies on both sides."

V

"Tell me how you worked it out," said the President. "I would like to see where we went wrong."

"If I may, sir," said Abigail, still refusing to react, "I will tell you what I think occurred, and allow you to correct me when I err in my analysis."

Lincoln looked at her with fresh respect. "By all means."

"About a year ago—maybe a bit more, maybe a bit less—you and Mr. Seward and Mr. Stanton decided that the threat of an impeachment trial was serious. Your divisions with the Congress had grown so great, and your humiliations of the Radicals had grown so frequent, that there was serious doubt whether the situation could be salvaged. You differed with the Congress over Reconstruction, but that was only one of many issues. And there were personal animosities as well. Your wife had recently died—excuse me—and, somehow—I don't know—that increased the difficulties."

The President had steepled his hands. "It was the worst time of my life," he conceded. "Even worse than when we lost our boys. I considered leaving this horrible place, returning home. I seem to recall that a few of our friends on the Hill even suggested such a course of action." He laughed. "Why, I do believe that Mr. Sumner might have been among the most . . . sympathetic." The humor faded. "But I had not yet completed the task laid before me. The task of binding up the wounds of war."

"Yes, sir."

"The Radicals want to punish the South. And, Heaven knows, I understand the impulse. But we will never re-create ourselves a mighty country"—a wink. "Never mind, Miss Canner. Tell me the rest of what I did, and why."

And so she did. She told him what she knew or guessed. He had known that the Radicals were plotting against him, and he had known that there was another, separate plot, by powerful interests opposed to him on other grounds—"principally the tariff"—and had suspected, but could not prove, that the two sets of opponents, knowingly or unknowingly, had joined forces. At the same time, as Wade's influence advanced in the capital, Lincoln had been less and less sure whom he could trust.

"And so you sent Secretary Stanton. He was to join the Radical faction, and to pretend that he was working secretly against you, when, in fact, he was searching for that connection. I don't know how much he found out about the plot, but I am quite sure that he learned a lot about the impeachment case. In particular, he learned the names of those likely to testify long before the Managers turned them over to your lawyers. This enabled him to arrange for the gathering of information that might be turned against potential witnesses."

"And how would he gather that information, Miss Canner? If, as you say, we did not know whom we could trust?"

"He used the Secret Service. The network of spies run by Mr. Seward during the war, and the network of federal police run by General Baker now."

"Surely even the Secret Service could be corrupted."

"No doubt. Except for one highly trusted agent. Chanticleer."

VI

Bingham had moved on hastily from Count Three to Count Four, as the consternation in the chamber grew. It was obvious to everyone that the witness was not responding as expected, and that the Managers had made a mistake by calling him. The wily Stanton, it seemed, had changed sides again.

"Now, Mr. Stanton, let us discuss the Department of the Atlantic."

"Please."

"You have heard of it?"

"Yes, sir."

"In what context?"

The eyes were growing watery again. "Sir, the President and I several times discussed the possible establishment of a military district in Washington. The district was to be called the Department of the Atlantic."

Bingham was visibly relieved. "What was the nature of these discussions?"

"The President was worried about the security of the capital. You will recall that after the war there were rumors of a Confederate regiment hiding out in the Smoky Mountains, living off the land. If that regiment existed, and we drew down our troop strength as planned, then that regiment would have a straight line of march through North Carolina and Virginia to this city. They could cross the Potomac River up high during low tide, as General Lee did during the war, and come down through Maryland. That was the President's concern, and I shared it."

"And the Department of the Atlantic was the solution?"

"It might have been, sir, but we never went beyond the talking stage."

"Why not?"

"Sir, the President was of the opinion that establishing the Department of the Atlantic would require the consent of the Congress, and that consent would not be forthcoming."

A flurry at the prosecution table. Someone handed Bingham a note.

"Mr. Stanton, did not you tell Mr. Manager Stevens in private conversation that Mr. Lincoln wanted to establish the Department of the Atlantic, and that it was only your own adamant opposition that prevented this?"

"Sir, if I said those words, I was mistaken."

Bingham groped for control. "Did not you tell Mr. Manager Stevens in private conversation that the President stated that he saw the establishment of the Department of the Atlantic as the only way to rein in the Congress?"

"Sir, if I said those words, I was mistaken."

"Did you not tell Mr. Manager Stevens in private conversation that Mr. Lincoln, on frequent occasion, referred to this august body as obstreperous and obstructionist, and that he expressed the wish that he could shut the Congress down and send it home?"

"Yes, sir. And, might I add, that anyone who serves in the executive branch will at times yield to that view. I have had the honor of being acquainted with a number of Presidents, sir, and I daresay Mr. Lincoln yielded to that temptation a good deal less than others I have known."

VII

"You faced two difficulties," said Abigail. "One was concealing Mr. Stanton's dual role. The other was finding a plausible way to route the information that he obtained out of his hands and into yours, and the hands of your counsel. Needless to say, this had to be done in such a way that it would never reflect on you, or on your Administration. If the plan went sour, it would be Mr. Stanton, and he alone, who would be punished. Beyond that, nobody from this White House could have any official role."

The President was amused at the casual description of his convolutions. "So, how did we accomplish those tasks?"

"Through the agent Chanticleer. Chanticleer had been a highly reliable agent during the war, traveling frequently through the South, collecting information from a wide variety of sources, and returning to Washington to deliver the information to Mr. Seward. Chanticleer was never suspected, by either side, of playing this key role during the war. Therefore, when Mr. Seward reactivated Chanticleer after the war, nobody was the wiser. Two flows of information were established. One of the flows, the identities of the prosecution witnesses and the nature of their testimony, went from Mr. Stanton to Chanticleer, who would then contact sources around the country to gather damaging facts to be used in cross-examination. These were delivered to Mr. McShane's office quite openly, as they would be on the surface entirely innocuous, and nobody would guess that they involved the impeachment trial. The other flow—the trickier one—was information more closely related to the conspiracy. This was the more valuable information, and so a more elaborate system was devised. This information flowed from Stanton, to Chanticleer, through Rebecca Deveaux, to Mr. McShane."

"Why would Chanticleer be necessary? I was under the impression that Miss Deveaux had worked for the Stantons."

"I believe that to be the fulcrum, Mr. President. I suspect that the arrangement began with Rebecca, not Chanticleer. They knew each other already, you see. Rebecca had worked for at least one of the conspirators, and possibly more. She removed notes from their houses and shared them with Chanticleer. Rebecca was likely unaware of Chanticleer's involvement in the Secret Service. Probably she was simply frightened by what she had discovered, and wanted advice. I suspect that Chanticleer went to Mr. Seward, who had previously run the Secret Service, and who, from his sickbed, devised the system under which Rebecca would continue to provide information on the conspiracy and Chanticleer would revive the slave network to investigate the backgrounds of the witnesses against you." She was watching the President closely now, but the wise, experienced face gave not a flicker.

"But the plan went wrong. The friendship between Chanticleer and Rebecca Deveaux led to two unexpected consequences. First, Chanticleer, who knew how the world worked, was worried that something might happen to Rebecca, who was after all little more than a child. And so Chanticleer advised her to hide a document that would protect her, just in case. Chanticleer called this the deposit. This led to the second problem. The deposit could obviously not be one of the documents that Chanticleer obtained from Mr. Stanton."

"Why not?"

"Because the conspirators would not be the only ones with a motive to harm Rebecca. Mr. Stanton, or General Baker, might also decide that her usefulness was at an end. Rebecca needed protection against both sides." Abigail paused for response, but none came. "And so," she resumed, "Chanticleer gave Rebecca a precious gift. Chanticleer required protection, too, and had, back at the beginning, discovered, then hidden away, the most valuable document of all—the list of the conspirators, rumored for some time to be missing. This is what everyone has been looking for, and I believe Chanticleer had it almost from the moment it went lost in Virginia. The document first found its way into the hands of Dr. Chastain in Richmond, who kept it for his own protection. Chanticleer learned of the list through Zillah, and instructed her to obtain it. Chanticleer's network of friends and sources was, frankly, amazing."

The President nodded. "So Mr. Seward tells me."

"Chanticleer told Rebecca to hide the list and tell no one, even Chanticleer, where it was, but to leave behind a clue that only Mr. McShane would understand. I believe that Rebecca and Mr. McShane worked together to develop the cipher, but I don't know. In any case, Rebecca and her connection to Mr. McShane were discovered by the conspirators, and they were killed. Both of them. That was the point. The location of the list died with them."

"I would imagine," drawled the President, "that poor Chanticleer at that point was in a bit of a quandary."

"Yes, sir. I think it was desperation that caused Chanticleer to contact me. And, just in case there was a slip—in case Chanticleer died, say, instead of Rebecca—arrangements were made to place my name alongside Rebecca's in the ledger of a local hotel. Sooner or later, someone would ask if I knew her, and we would get in contact."

"But why contact you?" Lincoln asked, not unreasonably. "You are undoubtedly a talented woman, Miss Canner, but why, of all the tens of millions in America, all the tens of thousands in Washington City, would the great Chanticleer choose to trust you?"

"Because she is my sister. Chanticleer is Judith Canner."

VIII

"May it please the Court," said Bingham, "we would seek to strike the testimony of this witness, in its entirety."

Dennard stood at once, but Chase was faster. "Mr. Manager, may I point out that Mr. Stanton is your own witness."

"Yes, Your Honor. But we have been misled. There is perfidy here somehow, although I cannot work out exactly how—"

"It is the despot Lincoln!" cried Stevens, lurching to his feet. "It is all a scheme of Lincoln's, to embarrass us! First he intimidates Beecher, and now Sherman! Senators, sirs, we have seen today perjury as well as perfidy, and somebody will pay!"

He began to cough, and his clerk helped him back to his place.

Dennard said, "Sir, we would waive cross-examination of this witness, if his testimony is allowed to remain on the record."

"So ordered," said the Chief Justice, banging his gavel. A Senator or two rose, but Chase was faster. "The evidence is closed. We will resume tomorrow. This session is adjourned."

He hurried from the bench.

IX

"My sister had amazing mobility," said Abigail. "She went all over the South. She knew people everywhere. At the same time, she was able to keep out of harm's way. And she knew things. She knew that I had been your emissary to Fessenden. I doubt, sir, that the knowledge was available casually in Hooker's Division. She said she sent Rebecca to see Mr. McShane because I worked there, but Rebecca was passing him information long before I was hired. And of course the indication we had from Dr. Chastain was that Chanticleer was a woman."

The President nodded, that slight smile on his face. "Please, go on, Miss Canner."

"Sir, you asked where you erred. Only twice that I can see. First, if you will excuse me, you erred because you are a man. Men think of great ideas first, and of friends and family after. With respect, Mr. President, you yourself voiced that very sentiment just moments ago, when you said you could not leave this office, no matter what tragedies struck your family, because your work is unfinished. It is in the nature of men, sir, especially great men, to see themselves as indispensable. Whereas it is in the nature of women to see their friends and families as indispensable. You were a man, relying on other men for advice, and so you overlooked the possibility that my sister's love for Rebecca would be greater than her love of her own duty, and so she might give Rebecca what she had denied her employers: the list of conspirators."

"And my other error?"

"A minor one, sir, but it started me thinking. Why would Noah Brooks, your private secretary, be sent to warn Judith to flee when the links in the chain were being hunted down? At first I thought I might have been mistaken in associating the description of the man who took Judith with Mr. Brooks. Then I thought that perhaps Mr. Brooks, too, had joined Mr. Wade's side in this thing. But he was too close to you, you trusted him too implicitly, and you are said, Mr. President, to be an outstanding judge of character. And so I said to myself, suppose the President did not misjudge Mr. Brooks? Suppose he did not misjudge Mr. Stanton? Then, when I saw Mr. Stanton's bodyguard outside Mr. Seward's house, I knew."

The President pondered. The early-spring sun had burned its way through the late-morning haze, and the window cast a pattern of crosses on the worn blue carpet. "You have told me what you think," Lincoln finally said. "Now tell me what it is that you want."

"You don't believe I could simply be curious to see whether I am right?"

"Miss Canner, from all that I have heard of you, I have no doubt that you are highly curious, and also that you are usually right. But, no. In this particular case, I do not believe that would be enough to bring you to this office." Steel slipped into his voice, reminding Abigail that she might be clever but he was cleverer—and President besides. "Now, answer my question, please."

"Sir, I ask three things. First, that my sister be protected. Second, that the murderer of Rebecca Deveaux be punished. Third, that no one with any official standing ever again refer to Rebecca as a prostitute. I understand entirely why you could not allow the police inquiries to continue, but I do not believe that it is necessary, in order to keep your secrets, to drag her name through the mud. And, besides, sir. If matters have gone as you expected them on Capitol Hill, I do not believe anyone imagines any longer that Mr. Stanton is with the Radicals."

"No." Another wink. "Still, they might imagine that he has simply had a change of heart. My hand in this thing must remain invisible." He stood. The meeting was over. "As to your requests, Miss Canner. Without in any way confirming any of your suppositions, I can assure you that, according to my most recent information, your sister is perfectly safe. And I believe there are those who will take my advice about how we might, in future, refer to the unfortunate Miss Deveaux. But as to punishing her killer, there we run into a small difficulty."

"Because you are going to make a deal!"

"No, Miss Canner. Because we do not know who killed her." He was escorting her to the door. "We don't have the list of conspirators, Miss Canner. We have no idea where it is." He paused, measuring her. "You've heard about poor Baker, I suppose? They tell me he has the catarrh. The doctors say they have not seen a case so serious in years. He is stronger, but he may not survive. A couple of days ago I had word that he had told Stanton he was close to finding the list of conspirators. A mighty peculiar coincidence."

Noah Brooks showed her out.

CHAPTER 52

Summation

I

ON WEDNESDAY, ABIGAIL was back in her seat.

Jonathan was delighted, if also worried; Kate Sprague was concerned; so concerned, in fact, that, shortly after her father gaveled the session to order and announced that the Managers would now present closing argument, Kate leaned toward Abigail and asked in a murmur whether there was any truth to the story that she had been seen at the White House yesterday.

"I cannot say," Abigail whispered back, "whether there is truth to the story that I was seen, as I do not know whether the witness was there." A smile of inspiration. "And if I was seen there, I should expect your witness to bear a better witness than words."

The blue eyes widened. Kate was stumped, Abigail knew at once; and knew, also, that she must return grace for grace, and never hint that she had won the round.

"I was there," Abigail said. "Briefly."

"To see Mr. Lincoln?"

"I had business in the Mansion."

"Was this related to your decision not to attend the Cookes' dinner with me on Monday evening?" When Abigail did not answer, Kate tried another tack. "Did you know that Miss Margaret Felix has left the city? I gather that she and Mr. Hilliman had a disagreement of some sort. Another woman perhaps." Still Abigail did not rise to the bait. Kate sat back. "In any event, Miss Felix has returned to Philadelphia, and her cousin Mr. Bannerman has gone off to upstate New York. A fascinating coincidence, don't you think?"

But Abigail was watching the scene below. She had not planned to attend today's session, and was not entirely sure what had drawn her, except that she was unable to stay away, drawn to the Hill the way we are drawn to objects of exquisite beauty, and moments of horrific disaster. So many tiny twists and turns, seemingly unimportant, had brought her to this moment.

She realized that Benjamin Butler was speaking, that he had been on his feet for some while, as she sat brooding, Kate uneasy beside her.

Butler was discussing Lincoln's supposed jokes about the Congress: "Counsel for respondent contends that the President can never be held answerable for what comes out of his mouth, no matter how outrageous. They point to his freedom of speech. By doing so, they concede the words themselves, and thereby strengthen our case. Read the speeches. There they stand in history as monuments to Mr. Lincoln's disgraceful conduct. The defense insists that the President is free to say what he will. I should like them to address just how far a public official may go in threatening and embarrassing the other branches of the government before the only power that can, will step in and correct the wrong. I submit that we have reached that point, unless we are to say, with the Bard, that judgment has fled to brutish beasts, and men have lost their reason."

Soon after, he sat. Bingham had summarized the evidence on Counts One and Two, Butler on Counts Three and Four. It was left to Thaddeus Stevens, the mightiest orator in the House of Representatives, to complete the argument. By now he could barely stand; everyone understood that the presentation he was about to make would likely be the final feat of an illustrious life. He had already picked out the plot where he wished to be laid to rest, insisting on one of the few cemeteries in Pennsylvania that permitted black and white to be buried side by side.

But the voice was as powerful as ever. Stevens had a simple argument. Lincoln was a tyrant, no more and no less. Say what you want about this count or that, but the words of the impeachment resolution were but faint reflections of the reality that the nation lived, in effect, under military government, answerable to the will of one man only. Even the laws were constitutional only if the President said they were.

"You will remember, of course, that Abraham Lincoln has twice taken the oath of office as President of the United States. This means

that he has twice promised to take care that the laws be faithfully executed. Now imagine the scene that counsel for respondent would have
us accept, that Mr. Lincoln, having been sworn on the Holy Evangels
to obey the Constitution, and being about to depart, turns to the person administering the oath and says, 'Wait. I have a further oath. I do
solemnly swear that I will not allow certain statutes, even if passed by
Congress over the presidential veto, to be executed. I will prevent their
execution by virtue of my own constitutional power.'"

Stevens's eyes smoldered as they passed over the ranked Senators.
"How shocked this Congress would have been," he said. "How shocked
the thirty millions or more who live in this country would have been.
Surely the United States would not have permitted the man's inaugura-
tion as President. And yet that is the man Mr. Lincoln has become, by
both his words and his conduct of the office."

At that point, Stevens fell to coughing. He begged the Court's indul-
gence, and explained that he could no longer stand. By unanimous consent, he was permitted to continue his remarks while sitting. Soon even
that was impossible. His voice had grown too weak. He could not continue. As Thaddeus Stevens handed to Benjamin Butler the last pages
of the final speech of his career, the ladies of Washington dabbed their
eyes. Abigail dabbed hers. She greatly admired the little man, even
though they had never met.

Kate sat stoically, watching her father, who was showing signs of restlessness, perhaps because he was no longer the focus of the proceeding.

"I should like to conclude," said Butler, still reading for Stevens,
"with a memorable and powerful quotation from an American political figure whom even counsel for the respondent, I suspect, will revere.
We have heard a great deal these last few days on the necessity or pru-
dence or even the inevitability of the breaking of the laws of the land in
order to accomplish a great task. In response to which, let me read the
following:

Let every American, every lover of liberty, every well-wisher to his
posterity, swear by the blood of the Revolution, never to violate in
the least particular, the laws of the country; and never to tolerate
their violation by others. As the patriots of seventy-six did to the
support of the Declaration of Independence, so to the support of
the Constitution and Laws, let every American pledge his life, his
property, and his sacred honor;—let every man remember that to

violate the law, is to trample on the blood of his father, and to tear the character of his own, and his children's liberty. Let reverence for the laws, be breathed by every American mother, to the lisping babe, that prattles on her lap—let it be taught in schools, in seminaries, and in colleges;—let it be written in Primers, spelling books, and in Almanacs;—let it be preached from the pulpit, proclaimed in legislative halls, and enforced in courts of justice. And, in short, let it become the political religion of the nation; and let the old and the young, the rich and the poor, the grave and the gay, of all sexes and tongues, and colors and conditions, sacrifice unceasingly upon its altars."

Butler looked around the room. "Those mighty words were spoken on January 27, 1838, in an address to the Young Men's Lyceum of Springfield, Illinois." The whispers in the audience and on the floor were quite loud now. "Their message of absolute reverence for the laws of the nation, their dismissal of all explanation or excuse, is one that we here today must take to heart. And the speaker on that occasion," Butler continued, inexorably, "was Abraham Lincoln."

He sat. The Managers had completed their case.

In the ensuing silence, Chase declared the court of impeachment adjourned for the day. Trial would resume tomorrow at noon, he said, with closing arguments offered by counsel for the respondent.

Abigail found herself wreathed in gloom once more. The cause was lost, but that was not, perhaps, the reason for her mourning. Her genuine sadness was for what she herself had lost, and what she would now be required to do. Listening to Mr. Lincoln's bold words, quoted by Thaddeus Stevens and read aloud by Benjamin Butler, Abigail had realized that she knew now the key to the cipher; and she knew, without so much as looking at the text, exactly what the message was.

I I

Jonathan Hilliman returned to the office to put the folders and exhibits away. He summoned Plum, who was sitting on his hands downstairs, to come help. Dennard had insisted that everyone take the night off, and the lawyers had gone straight home from the trial to change for the evening's receptions. Jonathan, much against his better judgment, had accepted a dinner invitation from Jay Cooke, of the great banking family, who was in town, most likely to see Salmon Chase, whom he was backing for President. What Cooke wanted, Jonathan could not imagine: even if the great banker, too, wanted to argue about the tariff or hard money, there was nothing whatever at this point that Jonathan could do about it. There were no deals left to be made, least of all with Lincoln. Senator Fessenden had told the group last night that although the embarrassment the Managers had suffered over Stanton had played well in the newspapers, it had at best swung two or three votes back into the undecided column. Not a single Senator had switched to Lincoln's side. Worse, Senator Sprague—Kate's husband—who had been counted on as a likely vote for acquittal, might be swaying toward conviction. His father-in-law's position as both presiding officer and likely candidate next year had been thought to make it unlikely that Sprague would dare vote against Lincoln, lest he appear entirely calculating and cynical; but his business interests also demanded a high tariff, and by now the entire capital suspected that Lincoln had made a secret deal to lower it. There were even whispers that an anti-Lincoln vote or two, under the influence of the bankers, had made closet commitments to switch on the final tally. True, the rumor had almost certainly come from Wade's supporters, but in politics all rumors tend to be believed as long as they are harmful to the other side.

And so, after Jonathan shut up the last of the exhibits in the cabinets and allowed Plum to depart, he let his gaze linger with real sadness on the long, drafty room he would soon be leaving for good. He was thinking of Meg. He supposed that he would write to her, and she would write back, and they would patch things up, and marry as planned in October, and he would join New England society, just as his family wanted. He did not know yet how he would wiggle free of Belmont's effort to take over Hilliman & Sons, but he would do it; he would liberate the family company, and rebuild the family fortune, and never again, for any reason, have the slightest involvement in politics.

And the only other thing he needed was—

"Woolgathering?"

Abigail.

III

"I was not woolgathering," he said, hiding his delight. "I was trying to be sure that I had completed all my tasks before going to dinner."

Abigail shut the door behind her. "Dinner," she repeated, as if she had discovered a new vice. "I see."

"I am dining with the Jay Cookes."

"Very impressive. At what time?"

"Eight." He glanced at the grandfather clock. "It is half past six. I must be going, or I shall be late." An expression crinkled her face, an emotion Jonathan was afraid to identify. An instant later it was gone. His next words were blurted, unthinking; and it was some while before he could explain the impulse, even to himself. "I am not escorting Miss Felix. She has left the city and returned to Philadelphia."

The gray eyes widened slightly. "So I am given to understand."

"She had urgent family matters to attend to," he gabbled.

"I am sorry to hear that. But let me tell you why I am here—"

"Wait. That was a lie." His face burned; he felt a fool; yet could not stop. "The reason Margaret left is that we had a disagreement. It became obvious to both of us that another—"

Abigail held up a palm. "Please, Jonathan," she said, voice a little faint. "Not now."

"We have to talk about this."

"I said, not now. I, too, am here on urgent matters."

"Not Mr. McShane's diary again. I told you, it is missing."

"I was mistaken about the diary." She opened the door to McShane's office. "The diary could not in any case have contained the key to the cipher, because Rebecca Deveaux would have had no means of consulting its pages."

Abigail tugged a slim volume from the shelf. As Jonathan watched, she turned a page, then another, then a third, until she evidently found what she wanted. She ran her finger down the text, nodded to herself, replaced the book.

"What are you doing?" he asked.

"Come with me, please. I need you to drive me in your carriage."

"Where are we going?" He pointed to the clock. "I really do have to meet the Jay Cookes." Those gray eyes, as always, weakened his resolve. "Everyone is taking the night off," he muttered in exasperation.

"Not everyone."

CHAPTER 53

Possibility

I

"WHY ARE WE here?" asked Jonathan, not for the first time. "Surely it would represent a conflict of interest for me to go inside."

Abigail sat grimly, no whisper of fun on her smooth countenance. Bits of paper and brush swirled in the gentle night wind. They were on Sixth Street, very near the train depot. "You may wait in the carriage if you like," she said.

Bewildered, Jonathan stared at the three-story brick mansion of the Chief Justice. It was well lit, yet forbidding rather than welcoming in its stolidity. To arrive at such a place, at such an hour, was of a piece with the entire mad course of this maddening relationship. Dennard had instructed all of them, but Jonathan in particular, to have no more contact with Abigail Canner until the trial reached its end. But here he was again, charging around the city with her.

"Please tell me what we are doing," he said.

"Only what I told you. Solving the murders of Rebecca Deveaux and Arthur McShane."

"My priority is the impeachment trial—"

"The solution is inside, Jonathan." She glanced at him, eyes cool. "To your dilemma and mine."

II

They were admitted without difficulty: this was Abigail's third or fourth visit to the house, and Jonathan knew, whether he approved or not, that she had become close to Mrs. Sprague. The butler bade them wait in the library rather than the parlor: a mark, under the rules governing such matters, of a business rather than a social visit.

Somehow the domestic staff always knew.

"Are we here to see Mr. Chase?" Jonathan whispered. "I thought your friend was Mrs. Sprague."

"We are here to see whoever will see us, Jonathan. Rebecca's deposit is in this house. We are known to be searching for it. Let us therefore wait patiently to see who greets us."

"Are you suggesting that the Chief Justice might—"

"Let us wait."

The room was redolent of cigar smoke: Salmon P. Chase did not use tobacco, but most of his associates who came calling did. Bookshelves reached to the ceiling. The silver-blue carpet was new, and absurdly expensive: they could sense its quality by merely standing on it. The heavy damask curtains and furniture belonged to a larger house. Chase was building a second home on his estate, Edgewood, a few miles away. In that great expanse, the furnishings no doubt would seem less overwhelming.

"I understand that General Baker has recovered from his illness," said Jonathan.

"Indeed."

"Do you credit the rumor that he was poisoned?"

Abigail's voice was bleak. "In this dreary city, there is little that I would not credit."

The doors opened, and Kate Sprague stepped inside.

"I knew you would be back here sooner or later," she said, her eyes more on Abigail than on Jonathan.

"Then you know why we are here." When Kate said nothing, she continued, softly. "I think it is time to tell the truth. You have the missing list, don't you? A hundred different people searching, and you've had it all along."

Kate licked her lips: a most unladylike gesture. She was dressed, radiantly, in an evening gown and tiara, but whether she was on her way out or had just returned was unclear. Jonathan wondered where the family was: her father, her husband, her two children.

"Yes," Kate finally said.

"The list is here?" Jonathan began, still not believing any of this, but Abigail shushed him.

"May I ask how long you have had the names?" she asked.

"Almost a year."

Abigail now looked less angry than sorrowful. "And yet you never told me. All those days sitting in the gallery, and you never told me."

Kate lifted her narrow chin. "I was sworn to secrecy. I was in a dilemma. It is not that I wanted to hide them, it was that I had no choice. And so I decided that if you worked it out for yourself I would give them to you. Not otherwise." She read the disbelief in the eyes of her guests. "Please, Abigail. I was quite certain that you would, in time, correctly interpret Rebecca's clues."

The two women watched each other, and Jonathan caught some, not all, of the facets of their visual duel: intelligence, admiration, ambition, envy, and much more. He sensed, even now, that the two of them were privy to a secret knowledge that he lacked; a knowledge not only of the documents themselves, but of the significance of their existence, all this time, under this roof.

"That is why you befriended me," said Abigail, and Jonathan sensed the anguish beneath the surface chill. "You wanted to see how close I was to uncovering the secret."

"But you are wrong, Abigail. I genuinely like you." Kate seemed to expect a response in kind; hearing none, she pressed awkwardly on. "I never asked you about what progress you were making in your search. The reason I spent time with you is that you are the most fascinating woman in Washington City."

But Abigail refused to be diverted. "How did you come into possession of the missing papers?"

Kate sighed, hesitated, glanced uneasily at Jonathan as if to say that this was a matter only a woman would understand. "Rebecca Deveaux gave them to me," she finally said.

"To hold for her."

"Yes. In case something happened. She called them her deposit. I was to hold the papers until . . . until I was asked. Until someone broke the code, she said. She had left a coded message for Mr. McShane, who was a signals officer and understood ciphers."

Abigail skipped what seemed to Jonathan the next logical question—indeed, the next logical series of questions—and instead asked, with no warmth in her tone: "Will you give me the deposit?"

"You must promise to keep Father and me out of it. You must tell no one how you obtained them."

Jonathan, perhaps unwisely, spoke up. "But that is not possible, Mrs. Sprague. You have been conspiring against the—"

Abigail's hand over his mouth surprised him into silence. "We will tell no one," she said. When Kate still seemed reluctant, she added, gently, "We will use the papers as Rebecca would have wanted."

Kate hesitated. "Father knows nothing of this matter. And he is not to learn anything of this matter."

"Of course," said Abigail.

"Wait here, please," said Kate, and left.

"I don't understand," said Jonathan when they were once more alone in the library. "Mrs. Sprague is obviously a conspirator. Why are you being so kind? No, I will not shush. Why is she turning over the deposit so readily? What do the two of you know that I don't?"

Abigail rounded on him, and for the first time tonight, he understood that her anger, whatever its source, did not exempt him. "Please be so good as to let me handle this my own way," she hissed. "I suggested that you wait in the carriage. You did not. But you are not going to ruin this, Jonathan. You are not. I know what I am doing, and I am asking you to trust me. Now, hush."

So intense was her fury that Jonathan actually stepped back two paces, thereby nearly colliding with Kate as she marched back into the room.

"Excuse me," she said, and actually smiled, if weakly. She had removed the tiara, and most of her jewelry. She was holding two envelopes, both battered. "I have your word," said Kate.

"You do," said Abigail solemnly.

"Everything that I did, I did for Rebecca." She hesitated. "And for Father, of course."

"I understand."

"And I . . . I truly do like you, Abigail. You have been a good friend."

"As have you."

"But I suppose that is over now," said Kate sadly, handing over the letters.

For an instant, Abigail wrestled with an unexpected emotion: despite her anger, she was unable to hide the clouds of sorrow and pain. It occurred to Jonathan that she really did like Kate; and that their time together had been, for Abigail Canner, a taste of what might have been . . . if only . . .

"I suppose," Abigail finally said.

Although etiquette demanded that the butler see guests to the door, Mrs. Sprague conducted them herself. In the front hall, Abigail had a last question. "Why didn't you destroy the papers?"

Kate seemed surprised. "Goodness, dear. Why on earth would I do that?"

"To protect yourself."

"But I am unimportant. I care little for my own future. If I destroyed those pages, I could never put them to use."

III

"Where are we headed now?" asked Jonathan when they were in the carriage once more. He had started north because the horses happened to be pointing north. "Shall I take you home?" A thought. "And how did you know?"

Abigail spoke from an exhaustion so deep she could barely form words. "Oh. Rebecca told us. She'd been trying to tell us. That code. It was so simple. So simple."

"So Octavius was right?"

"Octavius is a genius. Of course he was right." A brittle laugh, immediately swallowed in the frosty, foggy April night. "It was number thirteen, just as he worked out. It's just that it wasn't Mr. McShane's favorite book. It was his favorite document."

"Document?" Jonathan saw. "You don't mean it was the Constitution?"

"Of course it was, and I am a dunderhead not to have guessed earlier. You remember his eloquence on the perfection of the Constitution. And his words, as you quoted them to me: the mightiest achievement in the history of the Republic."

"He was referring to the Thirteenth Amendment."

"Precisely. The Thirteenth Amendment, abolishing slavery." She leaned into the pitted leather, closed her eyes. Jonathan turned west, through the railroad yard. "It all works out. The number groups. The first was 1-6-3. The first section of the amendment, the sixth word, the third letter. That's a 'C.' Take the others, one at a time, and the letters spell 'C-H-A-S-E.'"

Jonathan actually slapped his forehead. "It seems so obvious."

"Octavius says that every great idea is obvious, once someone has thought of it."

He slowed to cross a line of track. Although no trains were moving at this hour, some of the boilers had steam up, and would simmer all night. "But why are there two envelopes?" he asked. "Surely the list of conspirators cannot be that long."

"I am not certain."

"We should open the envelopes."

"No."

"Abigail—"

She shook her head. "Jonathan, no. We have to think this through. We need a plan. We need to know what we are going to do before we look at the names." She saw his face. "Oh, yes. We know what's inside. Kate as good as told us. It's a list of the names of the men—women, too, maybe—who participated in the conspiracy."

"Then we need to turn it over to—to—" He groped for the rest.

"To whom, Jonathan? Mr. Stanton? General Baker?"

"We can't just keep it to ourselves! We know who the conspirators are! We know that Mrs. Sprague is the young woman who was carrying messages for them!"

"I promised to keep her out of this, and I will keep my word." Her tone brooked no disagreement. "And, besides, Jonathan. I am quite certain that Kate Sprague is *not* the young woman in question."

Jonathan's head snapped around. "What?"

"Mrs. Sprague has no need to join a conspiracy against Lincoln. He will be leaving office within a year in any case. Her only goal is to make her father President. She might have been on the track of the deposit, as others were. She simply tracked them better. I suspect, however, that her only intention was to use those names to garner support for her father. Kate might have used the list for blackmail, but that is the worst she would have done."

"You cannot be serious."

"I am quite serious." She turned the envelopes over and over. "I do not believe that Kate would take such a chance. The risk to her father would be too great." A shake of her head. "Besides, she is too fine a lady. She would never stoop to conspiracy."

"But a little blackmail isn't beneath her?" He laughed, surprised at how, in his relief that the search was over, he felt almost inebriated. "I think you are allowing your friendship to run away with you." He snapped the reins. "And, look here. If the young woman who carried messages for the conspirators was not Mrs. Sprague, then who is it? You have established that it cannot be Bessie Hale." Jonathan had another thought. "And if Mrs. Sprague is not the young lady of the conspiracy, then how was Rebecca Deveaux able to know that she possessed the missing notes?"

"Because Kate's story was true. Rebecca gave them to her." Abigail was sunk in thought. "Think, Jonathan. It all hangs together. Rebecca was frightened for her life. The only person in Washington City she trusted was my sister Judith. And Judith said to hide the letters where not even Judith would know where they were, so that if she were . . . taken . . . and asked where they were hidden, she would have nothing to confess."

"But why Kate Sprague?"

"Because Rebecca knew her, from having worked in the household. Remember what Judith said? Rebecca worked in several of the great houses. She must have worked for the Chases before she worked for the Stantons. It hangs together. She would have needed a reference to work in the household of the Secretary of War, and what better reference than the Chief Justice, his friend?"

Jonathan considered. "But if Rebecca worked for Mrs. Sprague, whom you insist was not a conspirator, and then for Mr. Stanton, who merely pretended to be one, then where did she come across the documents that sent her to your sister and set all of these dreadful events in motion?"

They emerged from the train yard, turned south on Eighth Street. "I am not all the way there yet, Jonathan. I am overlooking something. But the rest of it hangs together. Consider. Dr. Chastain said that Chanticleer took his deposit from him, remember? The list of conspirators was lost in Virginia. Is it too much to assume that it made its way into Dr. Chastain's hands? And that he put it aside for his own protection, until my sister stole it or coerced it from him? After that, no doubt it was meant to be Judith's deposit. But Judith saw Rebecca—young, frightened, and very much in danger—and gave it to her instead, then told her to hide them as security, not only against the conspirators, but even against Stanton himself."

"But why would the list of conspirators provide security against Stanton? He was only feigning membership in the conspiracy."

"I believe," said Abigail, "that we now know why there are two envelopes." She smiled at Jonathan's mystification. "There is the list of conspirators, taken from Dr. Chastain. That was Rebecca's deposit against the conspirators. The other envelope, I suspect, holds papers that she took, under my sister's advice, during her time in service at Mr. Stanton's house. That was her deposit against Mr. Stanton and General Baker."

"Surely you do not mean to suggest"—he stopped, then started again, as a look of painful comprehension crossed his face—"Abigail, we have to know what is in that second envelope!"

"Not yet. Not until we have decided how to—"

Both of them looked up at the same sound. Rushing out of the gray, misty darkness was a wagon, huge and massive, designed more for battle than for these grimy streets. It flew across the frozen meadow, the steeds pulling it directly toward their own carriage. Jonathan automatically snapped the reins and called to his own horses, but it was too late.

The battlewagon struck the carriage midships, and then they were tumbling, Abigail and Jonathan, flying through the air and onto the verge of the railroad track, where they lay, dizzy and bruised.

A figure marched toward them, nearly as massive as his wagon.

"I'll take that list now," said Dinah Berryhill's protector, Corporal Alexander Waverly.

CHAPTER 54

Contest

I

THERE WERE TWO of them and one of him, but he had a knife in each hand, and that made up the numbers. Jonathan sat up slowly; Abigail, still stunned from the impact, lay still.

"Don't get up," the red-haired giant said. "Stay on the ground."

"I thought you were her bodyguard." Jonathan rubbed grime from his face. "I thought you worked for the Berryhills."

Waverly's grin was fierce. "Work for those nigras? I pretend to work for them. Took the oath, too. No better cover in this city." He pounded his chest. "I'm with the Confederate secret service."

"What secret service? Your side lost!"

"Turns out, we're not done just yet."

"What are you saying?" Jonathan had trouble taking in the swift change of circumstance. "Are you the . . . the conspirators?"

Waverly ignored this. "Where is the list?"

"What list do you mean?"

"The one that if I don't have in my hand in half a minute I am going to slice out Miss Canner's intestines and make you watch me strangle her with them." He saw Jonathan tensing, shook his head. "I'm faster than you, I'm stronger than you, and I can throw a knife very straight." He opened his coat, showing a large Colt revolver. "And if the knife misses, there is always this."

Abigail was stirring. Her eyelids fluttered, and she moaned.

"Intestines," said Waverly, his voice itself somehow sharp and slithery in the night. He took a step toward her, carefully keeping out of Jonathan's reach. "Such a juicy word."

"You're insane," Jonathan breathed.

The corporal seemed unbothered. He stooped beside Abigail. "Maybe so. But you are going to tell me where that letter is." He held one of the knives up, turned the blade this way and that, catching the dull reflection of the fog-shrouded moon. "With enough time, I can make the strongest man in the world tell me what I want to know. And you are not the strongest man in the world."

"The letter was in the carriage."

"You're not much of a liar."

"It was—"

"Fine. Go get the letter, and bring it back. I'll wait here with Miss Canner. If you're not back in a minute and a half . . ."

He tossed the knife in the air. It flipped, and when he snatched it from the air, the point of the blade was an inch above Abigail's stomach.

"Well," said the corporal, "I guess you know what happens next, right?"

Her eyes fluttered open.

"Don't move," said Waverly and Jonathan at once: Jonathan's voice by far the louder.

She obeyed, the gray eyes wide, and terrified. The blade flicked the front of her coat, and she stiffened.

"The list," said Waverly.

"I have it," said Jonathan.

"I think Miss Canner probably has it." The knife flicked.

"Wait!" Abigail cried, breath coiling whitely. "You're a Confederate! Why do you want the list of conspirators? What difference can it make now?"

"What difference?" Waverly thumped his chest. "What difference? These are the men who will decide when to remove the Northern boot from the Southern neck, and we'll have the evidence that they conspired against their own ape of a President! They'll be dancing to our tune soon enough!" He smiled coldly. "Now, come on. Tell me where the list is, so you can go home to your aunt."

"You're going to kill us anyway," said Jonathan.

"I'm going to kill you a lot more slowly if you don't give me the list." Without warning, he stabbed Abigail in the hand.

She shrieked, rolled over, grabbed her wrist.

He turned to Jonathan again. Flipped the knife again; caught it; pointed one blade at him, the other at her. "And that was just a pin-prick. I can make her dance and sing for us—"

Abigail was on her back. One of her hands was injured. The other came up, very fast, and crashed an iron spike against the side of Waverly's head.

He did not go down; he was stunned, but did not so much as drop the knives.

Jonathan was already pulling Abigail to her feet. He struck Waverly now, with the board he had been cradling, and this time the giant went over, but only onto his hands. He dropped one of the knives, shook his head, began to recover.

Abigail scooped up the fallen knife, and they ran for the carriage; they could unhook the horse and—

A shot rang out, then another, missing them but felling the steed.

They ran deeper into the railyard.

II

They crouched behind a freight car. Abigail wanted to climb in and hide, but Jonathan vetoed the idea: surely that was the first place the giant would look.

"What do you suggest, then?"

"That we separate."

"Why would we do that?"

"Because you have the letters. If I can get him to chase me, you can escape."

Abigail looked at him. "You don't have to try to impress me—"

"It's the only sensible course. Wait while I divert him, then go."

"But—"

"You know I'm right," he said.

She put a hand on his arm. "Jonathan, I—I want to tell you—"

"Later," he said, and, shoving at her, ran noisily in the other direction. Abigail continued crouching as Jonathan kicked up gravel, bumped into a pile of crates, and noisily cried out as if hurt.

Too noisily.

She heard footsteps approaching from the darkness, precisely where he had run, and they were too heavy to be Jonathan's. Still holding the knife, she slid beneath the freight car; and saw Jonathan sprawled in the snow twenty yards away.

"Come on out," said Waverly, directly beside the car.

She went very still. Her wounded hand throbbed.

"You know I'll find you. Make it easy on yourself. Come out."

Abigail rolled out the other side, raced over the next track, where a line of open coal cars sat, waiting to be unloaded. Nanny had taught them that the railyards were dangerous places, full of various criminals and drunkards who slept beneath the trains. But the night mist was cold and silent.

"Come on, girlie. Just give me the letter and you can go home."

She ducked behind the open coal car, peering into the darkness, but could see nothing except the lights of the stock house up the hill and the station beyond. In this frozen, swirling rain, no shout would carry. Even the gunshots were unlikely to have been overheard. And although she still had the envelopes tucked in an unmentionable place, she was quite certain that the mysterious inviolability of her sex would cause the former Confederate spy not a moment's hesitation. He would strip her naked if that was what it took to find the letters.

Worse, he might not kill her first.

She spotted an empty bottle, wondered whether it would do as a second weapon. She was not really sure how one swung a bottle to do damage. In *Peterson's Magazine*, scoundrels did it with ease, because at least one story per number was bound to feature a bar fight. Men were always breaking bottles over each other's heads. But Abigail, shivering with cold and terror, could not work out a way to do it. Corporal Waverly was, after all, a foot and a half taller than she. To bring the bottle down on his head, she would have to be higher than he; but if, say, she climbed aboard one of the cars, even if she were able to mask her presence, and even were the corporal so foolish as to stand beneath her, she would be too busy hanging on for dear life to get any leverage.

The knife then.

The crunch of ice under a man's foot sent her scurrying farther along the train. She was almost at the engine. She could smell the smoke. Staying low, she moved forward, feeling her way with fingers on the frigid steel. If there was smoke, the boiler was stoked, and if the boiler was stoked, someone would surely come to check on it. She remembered

Octavius Addison telling her once that they ran them at low pressure on nights like this, to keep the machinery from freezing.

Low *pressure*.

High pressure.

One of the useless facts Octavius had shared as they rode around the city: On cold nights, the engineers ran the boilers on low so that they would stay warm but not begin to build up too much steam. There was a small relief valve open at night: use a larger one and the fire would go out. The relief valve was adequate for low pressure. At higher pressures, however, a larger valve was needed.

Otherwise, the boiler would explode.

Abigail found the ladder, climbed up into the cab. The noise of the boiler drowned the clatter of her shoes. Her hand was shrieking. She peered at the controls in the darkness. She recognized almost nothing. Octavius had said something about the throttle. . . .

She located the throttle lever; pushed, then pulled. The lever resisted. She found a flange blocking the way and shoved it aside. Another pull. Suddenly the hiss was louder. She pulled harder. She was not sure what all the dials meant, but when she felt the steel begin to shudder, she knew the pressure was building. She did not know how swiftly. She only knew that she had to get very far away, very fast.

She jumped down, and there was Corporal Waverly, his ear partly severed, blood pouring down the fiery-red beard.

"The letter," he said. "Now."

Abigail backed away, along the engine. She still held his knife.

"Last chance."

She shook her head. Waverly came at her. She led with the knife, the way Michael had taught her, but she was slow and clumsy, and he hopped aside without difficulty. Even had she made contact, she suspected it would have been like trying to stab a rhinoceros.

"Don't do that again," he said.

He grabbed for her, and this time Abigail sliced downward, catching his wrist, which spurted blood. Waverly looked at the cut. He seemed impressed, but not frightened: he had been stabbed before.

"I warned you," he said, and, with a sigh, swiped at her with his huge hand. The almost casual blow knocked Abigail to the ground. She could not catch her breath.

Waverly leaned over her, and that was when the boiler exploded.

The sound deafened her.

The corporal crouched and spun, and a piece of metal caught him in the face; and Abigail, with what strength she had left, drove the knife into his thigh. As he began to turn, Jonathan, a trickle of blood on his own forehead, smashed a plank against Waverly's ear.

The giant went down.

But, again, only to his knees.

He shook his head, blood flying, and punched Jonathan in the groin. The young man folded to the ground. Waverly kicked him in the chest, then turned to Abigail. He grabbed her leg, dragging her toward him. Jonathan managed to get a hand on the giant's neck, and bent his head back. Waverly stood with a roar, and threw him off.

"Enough," he wheezed, and drew the Colt.

The crack of a gunshot seemed to surprise him, for he spun around and clawed at his back. A second shot missed him and nearly hit Abigail, but the third put the corporal down on the frozen mud.

Looming from the darkness were several figures in dark uniforms. Two of them held rifles.

A scrawny, familiar figure emerged from the shadows between two freight cars. He was carrying a large pistol, and looked straight and confident and not the least bit nervous.

"The boiler was an excellent idea," said Mr. Plum. "Otherwise I might not have found you in time."

Jonathan stooped for the Colt that had fallen from the giant's twitching hand.

"Please don't do that," said Plum.

"Who are you working for? Grafton? Belmont? Who?"

Plum ignored the question. He was crouching beside Waverly, checking for signs of life, and finding none.

Abigail had managed to sit up. "I think he's on our side," she said, shakily.

"Why?"

"Because unless I am mistaken, those are Union soldiers approaching. And General Baker is with them."

CHAPTER 55

Conspirators

I

THERE WAS EVEN an ambulance wagon, where they patched up Jonathan's forehead and Abigail's hand. There were soldiers and police and quiet men not in uniform who were evidently federal detectives. And the part that worried Abigail most was that she had no clear picture of how long they had been watching before they intervened; she wondered whether, had Waverly managed to kill them both before being stopped, Baker would have been entirely disappointed.

"So Plum works for you," said Jonathan, as a surgeon cleaned the gash on his head. "He used to be at the War Department. I suppose Grafton thought Plum was giving him information from the files, but it was the other way around, wasn't it? Plum has been working for you all along. Keeping an eye on Grafton." A grimace of pain from a stitch. "And maybe on Dennard & McShane as well."

"Mr. Plum is a valued member of the Service," said Baker, primly.

The subject of their conversation was several yards away, conferring in hushed tones with the detectives, and it was plain from their deference that Plum was the one giving orders.

"I suppose that Plum arrested Mr. Grafton for you," said Jonathan. "Everyone thinks he's missing, but you have him locked up somewhere, don't you? Undergoing interrogation? Or was he just shot?"

But Baker preferred not to answer questions. His illness had left him pale, and a good deal thinner, but his contempt was undiminished. "When we reached Mrs. Sprague's, we were told that you had just left.

We searched the area, but it took us some time to imagine that you might have gone into the railroad yard."

"You must have heard the explosion," said Jonathan.

"That's what brought us running."

"But I don't understand," said Abigail. "Why were you looking for us to begin with? And why on earth did you think we had been to see Mrs. Sprague?"

Baker smiled blandly. "I have my sources."

Someone was watching. That was the only answer. One of Baker's detectives had followed them from the office to Kate's house, then gone to summon the general, only to return and find them gone.

"I believe you have something for me," said Baker.

"Something like what?" asked Abigail, innocent.

"I am quite sure that Mrs. Sprague gave you Chanticleer's deposit."

"I beg your pardon."

"The letters she was holding. She gave them to you."

Abigail knew her friend. "Did Mrs. Sprague tell you that?"

"Yes."

"Actually, General Baker, I don't believe you."

He wanted to hit her; that was plain. He wanted to grab her, shake her, place her under arrest, drag her off for interrogation. But he dared not touch her, and they all knew it. Not only because she had just made a deal with the President of the United States; but also because Jonathan Hilliman was there to watch, and there were families whose wrath one did not risk.

General Lafayette Baker believed, albeit mistakenly, that the Hillimans were still of that ilk. Furious, he strode away.

Mr. Plum joined them. "Now would be an excellent time for the two of you to depart," he said softly. "I fear that the general's recent illness has left him highly irascible."

They had questions, of course, but Plum offered no answers.

"If we are not going to give the list to General Baker," said Jonathan as he drove a freshly borrowed carriage across the Island, "what exactly are we going to do with it?"

"Use it as evidence."

"The Chief Justice will never admit the letters into evidence."

Abigail's eyes were shut. "We are not going to ask him." Her voice was crisp. "Don't you see, Jonathan? Corporal Waverly kept asking about the *list*. Singular. General Baker mentioned the *letters*. Plural.

The corporal didn't know there was a second envelope. Baker did." Her bandaged hand waved away his questions. "We have been making a false assumption, Jonathan. Perhaps when we have examined the list of names, we will know where we went wrong."

II

They sat in the kitchen of the house Abigail's father had built, the list of conspirators—"potential conspirators," Abigail kept warning him—on the table. The list ran to four pages, in an aggressively slanted copperplate that she did not recognize. The two of them sat side by side so that they could read the names together by the light of a single sputtery lamp, the candle within almost down to the nub. Jonathan had argued that they would be safer at the Bannerman manse, or even the office, but Abigail said she wanted to go home. And she had run upstairs to check on Nanny and Louisa before allowing him to slit the envelopes. When she returned, she placed a derringer on the table and leaned a shotgun against the wall.

Jonathan said nothing.

The thinner envelope contained what appeared to be two pages from Stanton's private diary. The first entry, dated a year and a half ago, began with the observation that the writer was beginning to harbor reservations concerning "certain policies pursued by the President whom I loyally serve." Jonathan was about to comment, when Abigail slipped the pages from his hand and put them away.

"The other is more important," she said.

They turned to the list of conspirators: "Potential conspirators," she cautioned again. "People they considered approaching."

There were about forty names, and over half were unfamiliar to her. Jonathan pointed out a few industrialists whom he knew by reputation.

"I would like to know whose handwriting this is," she said.

Some were politicians. James Blaine was on the list, along with five other members of the House. No Senators.

But . . .

"Oh, Jonathan."

He had found it already. Was staring. Trembling. The name was sixth down on page three, in that same beautiful hand: "Elise Hilliman."

Not Brighton after all. His mother, not his uncle.

There was nothing to say, but she slipped an arm around his shoulders, and drew him by instinct against her own: a gesture she had never performed for any man but Aaron.

"I should have known," he whispered through gritted teeth. "Oh, Mother."

"You had no way to know."

"I had many ways to know." Turning the page. "We have to finish."

So they did, sitting very straight now, finishing the page—a reporter here, a lawyer there, the owner of a steel mill—and then, page four—

"Oh, Jonathan," she said again.

"Abigail, I—I don't know what to say."

Not possible.

"*Potential* conspirators," she breathed, as they stared together at the name. "Some of them must have said no."

"We have to find out."

III

They headed north, then watched the houses thin and the forests gather as the borrowed rig proceeded northwest along Massachusetts Avenue. There were boulders in the road, and the going was slow. There were fewer lamps the farther one moved from the center of things. Night shadows crowded the road. No other carriages were in evidence; no horses.

They were not being followed.

"Maybe your mother turned them down," said Abigail. The shotgun was under the seat. The derringer was lying between them. "The list is potential conspirators. Your mother might never have been contacted. Or she might have said no."

"Never. She hated Lincoln after my brother died."

"But the risk—"

"Mother has never been one to worry about risk. She worries about revenge." He was silent for a moment, watching the trees. Here and there, a wavery brightness was the lighted window of a distant house. The coach lamps along both sides of the carriage provided a choking, sooty illumination. "Let me tell you a story. You know that my older brother died in the war. I also have a younger brother. Calloway. Mother calls him her miracle child, because he was born when she forty-three. What nobody in the family ever mentions is that my father died when Mother was forty. About eight years ago, a Providence newspaper published a tiny item in the gossip column—two sentences, no more—about the 'miraculous birth' of the youngest son of a prominent but unnamed Newport widow. Mother bought the paper, fired the staff, and flattened the building. She left the lot empty. She still owns the lot, and it's still empty." His eyes were very red. "Turn them down? Mother would join them because her toast was buttered wrong way up the day they asked."

Abigail squeezed his hand; said nothing; reminded herself that, just as there were people in the world who had grown up loved, there were people who had grown up the other way around. Jonathan, despite his insistence that his family was merely "decently off," had grown up with everything money could buy. But Abigail would not trade an hour of her childhood for a year of his.

"We are very near my school," she said when she could no longer bear the silence.

"The Quaker school?"

She nodded, nervous excitement making the color rise girlishly in her cheeks. "On the original plan of the city, that bluff up ahead is supposed to hold the national cathedral. But nobody expects it to be built. Look how long it took them to put the new dome on the Capitol, and of course poor General Washington's monument looks as if it will never be finished." She laughed, lightly. "Anyway, my school is right down there, a little bit south of here. My sister attends now."

They were turning right. The road flattened, and the land opened out. Tennally Town was farm country, with the occasional factory or warehouse sprinkled in.

"Why don't you want to look in Stanton's envelope?" he asked suddenly.

Abigail stiffened. "The pages are from a private diary, Jonathan. Surely you as a fellow gentleman—"

"You're afraid of what you'll find there, aren't you? You're afraid that the pages Rebecca stole may prove that Mr. Lincoln did indeed give serious consideration to establishing the Department of the Atlantic." She looked away; said nothing. "Or is it the other fear? Are you worried that Stanton might have been a conspirator after all? Perhaps the rumors are even true, and Baker was poisoned. For investigating Stanton!"

"You are being very silly," Abigail said.

"And you are being very secretive. Most of the time you're bursting to tell me what you suspect." Jonathan's hands trembled as he drew in the rein. He nodded toward the frozen lane. "We have arrived," he said.

The house was small and sedate, set back from the road, screened by trees. Another carriage stood in the driveway.

Jonathan slipped the derringer into his coat.

"Is that really necessary?" said Abigail.

"He may have a visitor." Jonathan was scrutinizing windows and trees with an intensity she had not seen in him before: soldier's eyes, she realized. "You should wait here."

"No."

"Abigail—"

"I am not staying out here by myself."

"Very well." He helped her down. They walked slowly up the path. Lights were burning in two lower windows. Jonathan pulled the bell rope, but kept his right hand near his jacket pocket.

The door opened.

"I heard about what happened," said Rufus Dennard. "I am so glad to see that you are both well."

IV

Two hours later.

They sat in the carriage up on the bluff, waiting for the sun. Down below, the nation's capital city was swaddled in gray predawn mist. Behind them was the low wooden Quaker school where Abigail's long road had begun. At this moment, Jonathan wanted more than anything to feel her head on his shoulder. But they sat straight, close together yet worlds apart, each hoping the other might produce a suggestion.

"We have to stop the trial," said Jonathan for perhaps the fifth time. "They are proceeding under taint. It cannot be allowed to go forward."

"Events have their own momentum," said Abigail. "I am not at all sure that we can deflect them."

"We have to try."

"There is no one left to tell," she said.

A thin red glisten on Washington's monument hinted that morning was very near. Abigail could not remember the last time she had stayed up all night.

The meeting with Dennard had been painful. The old man, usually so dignified, had been almost in tears.

No, he insisted, he was not a conspirator, and never had been. Yes, they had approached him, as he assumed they had approached everyone on that blasted list—a list that should never have been set down in writing, and the loss of which had caused so much trouble. Yes, that was what had led to the split from Grafton—Grafton had been one of the prime movers, and Dennard had refused to join.

Wasn't that the time to alert General Baker? Abigail had asked.

He could not, he said. He owed Grafton for favors he would not discuss, in much the same way that he owed Dr. Finney. Grafton had saved his life in the Mexican War and, later, had helped Dennard and his wife through a terrible time. He would not turn on them. But he refused to help.

Jonathan suggested that was the reason Dennard wanted the firm to stay out of the impeachment battle.

Dennard nodded. He tried to keep the firm out, and then, when McShane died, and Grafton organized the telegrams from clients, he tried again. But then Lincoln asked him personally, and a true patriot did not refuse his President. Still, Dennard had tried his best to steer Abigail and Jonathan away from the investigation, not from a desire for self-protection, but to keep them out of harm's way. . . .

Eventually, they had to leave. The séance of self-justification had become too eerie.

"Do you think Dennard was giving information to Grafton?" said Abigail—too exhausted to maintain the formalities. The sun was peeking over the horizon. She answered her own question. "No. I cannot believe that Dennard's representation of the President was at any time other than energetic and honorable. He did his best." Another thought struck her. "But why would Grafton tell me all those terrible things about Dennard? Why would he try to draw me away?"

"Maybe he didn't want Chanticleer's sister so close to the impeachment."

"But how could he have known about Judith?"

Jonathan shook his head. If Abigail could not get her capacious mind around the whole story, he knew that there was little point in his trying.

"I suppose we might consider Mr. Grafton the spider," she mused. "The others were in his web. The men of wealth who wanted Mr. Lincoln out of the way. The Radicals. Grafton saw to it that their interests coincided."

"And Waverly?"

"The corporal as much as told us. What remains of the Confederacy would obviously be interested in blackmailing the powerful of the North. Grafton played on that, using their people to do what violence might have been necessary to protect the conspiracy. No doubt the rebels thought they were using him, too. But I very much doubt that most of the conspirators were aware of the Confederate role. Or of the violence."

"And Baker? He knew that there were two envelopes."

"Surely General Baker's motive is simplest of all. Mr. Stanton knew what Rebecca had stolen. He wanted his papers back, before harm could be done to the President's cause."

Jonathan wondered at Abigail's smooth assurance, and her determination to absolve their client; but chose to mention neither. "I just wish I knew whom we could tell," he said. "I think we've been over everyone. Baker was too excited at the thought of getting his hands on the material. No Baker means no Stanton, even now. You don't trust Noah Brooks. I don't trust Fielding. Varak is gone. Chase is obviously impossible. So, again, I ask you: who's left?"

"Sickles?" she said. "When he says his only cause is Abraham Lincoln, I believe him."

"But that 'only cause' is the reason he has been visiting generals and stirring up the army. In a way, telling Sickles is as bad as telling Stanton. He would not be particularly sorry to see everyone on that list hang." He paused, remembering Abigail's words at Tenth Street. "Whether or not they rejected the approach."

Abigail touched his arm. "We have one consolation. Fielding's name is not on the list. No Fielding. No Bannerman."

"Then why did he leave town so suddenly?"

But they both knew the answer to that: he was a gentleman to the end. There was only one Abigail, and Fields and Hills were . . . two.

"There's something else you should know," Jonathan said as they waited. He was trembling. "The handwriting. The list." He had trouble forming the words. "The handwriting is Margaret's."

"I'm sorry, Jonathan," she said. "I suppose we know who the young lady who ran messages is, don't we?" She laughed. "I hope you will not be offended if I say that, in this case, you are definitely better off without her." When Jonathan said nothing, she added, "At least poor Bessie is off the hook."

They sat for a while, watching the sun, out of ideas.

"I just don't understand," said Jonathan after a bit. "How can so many of those elected to office abuse that trust so badly? They don't care about truth. They don't care about argument. They only care about winning elections and holding on to their power."

Abigail smiled wistfully. "Professor Finney always says that the right to govern belongs to those whose moral attributes best qualify them."

"Moral attributes. We live in a world of . . . of moral pygmies. Not like the days of the Founders. They could see beyond the needs of party. Beyond the needs of interest. Beyond the needs of the next election. There are few men like that today."

"I doubt," she said dryly, "that the generation that wrote the Constitution was so much wiser than ours." Then: "Jonathan. I have an idea."

CHAPTER 56

Moralist

I

"THIS IS QUITE manifestly irregular," said Charles Sumner. A servant poured lemonade. "Rather *ex parte*, don't you think?" He toyed with his gray-blond locks. "The Democratic newspapers would make quite a meal of this meeting. I suppose the Republican papers would, too, if they thought they might earn a few more pennies."

Yet, for all his complaint, Sumner seemed curiously at ease. He was in no hurry to be rid of them. They were all seated in his long study, its high shelves piled with thousands of books. His admirers claimed that he had memorized every word; certainly he could recite, accurately, long passages of history from Pliny the Elder, or Descartes, or the Bible.

It was Thursday morning; Jonathan should have been at the firm. Instead, he had gone home to change before rejoining Abigail, who had concluded that the only option was the one they were now pursuing. To see Sumner, the man who, as he proclaimed repeatedly to all the world, was in the business not of politics, but of morals; Sumner, who had met all the crowned heads of Europe, and who corresponded with half the prime ministers on the planet; Sumner, who spoke as many languages and knew as many capitals as anyone could ask; Sumner, who had forced Lincoln to take on Abigail, and who still controlled the three votes the President would need to prevail.

"We would not be here," said Abigail now, "were the matter anything less than the most urgent." She smiled, as best she could after the depredations of the night before; it was her name and not Jonathan's that had opened the most private door in the city.

"I did hear, of course, of your eventful evening." He sounded less sympathetic than amused. "I am pleased to see that you emerged unscathed." He glanced at Jonathan. "Both of you, naturally."

Dinah, who had dined with Sumner at her father's table, insisted that he was the only white man in Washington who seemed genuinely to believe in equality of the races: a legacy of his education in France, where the young Sumner had sat in lecture halls alongside students from Africa and the West Indies.

Abigail, conscious of her role, continued to hold the stage. "We have something we should like to show you," she said. "And then we have something we should like to tell you."

"If it involves the impeachment, I fear I may not properly listen. The Senate, as you know, will vote this afternoon on the Articles."

"Not directly," said Jonathan.

Sumner shook his heavy head. "I will not compromise," he said. "I am interested in no deals. There is nothing the President may offer that I would take. My vote shall be based, entirely, on what I think right. It is for my moral judgment, and that alone, that the legislature of the Commonwealth of Massachusetts sent me to the Senate." He made to rise. "I am sorry if you have wasted your time; or mine."

"I assure you," said Jonathan hastily, "that we are not proposing a deal of any sort—"

Abigail interrupted. "All we ask is that you hear us out. You may decide for yourself what to do about what we tell you."

And so they told him.

Abigail did most of the talking, because they both sensed that Senator Sumner preferred it that way. She started with the murders, went over their own investigations, explained how Stanton played both sides at once. Finally, she reached the events of last night, and could not go on. And so Jonathan, his own voice a bit clotted, told him what had happened with Waverly.

"We did not know whom we could trust," said Abigail, in conclusion. "And so we came to you."

Jonathan expected that the great moralist would next ask to see the list of conspirators; but he did not.

Sumner sipped his sherry. "You have omitted two details." He waited, but neither contradicted him. "You have not told me who had custody of the list for the past year or so. And you have not told me how you persuaded this individual to give it to you."

"We gave our word," said Abigail.

Plainly, Sumner liked that answer; he even smiled. "And Dennard? Why have you not brought your tale to your employer?" He saw their faces. "Ah. I see. Like that, is it?"

"I am afraid so," said Jonathan.

"Here is your difficulty," said the great moralist. "You are adhering to the classic argument *ad hominem*. You are suggesting that a proposition should be rejected not on its own merits but due to the merits of those who happen to be in favor of it. The Greeks disproved this nonsense long ago." Sumner tilted his head toward one of the shelves. "You're a Yale man, Hilliman. So—tell me. Have you ever read the *Characteristics*, by the Right Honorable Anthony Cooper, third Earl of Shaftesbury? No? Well, perhaps you know the volume by its formal title? *Characteristics of Men, Manners, Opinions, Times*? No? Sad. And you, Miss Canner? Are you familiar with the volume?"

"I fear not, Mr. Sumner."

"Pity." He stretched out a long arm, pulled the volume free, flipped through the pages. "Cooper, in his excellent discussion of goodness, demonstrates that men act out of a multiplicity of motives. Thus, in the process of achieving that which morality dictates, one must invariably accept as allies some who lack the same moral sense. There will always be those who will seek the right result for the wrong reason. If the moral man dismisses all allies because he disdains their motives, then he will never be able to move toward a more moral world. Thus, in the struggle against slavery, the moral man accepted as allies those who wanted war for selfish reasons of commercial or political success. And in the struggle against the tyranny of Lincoln, one might accept as allies those who are, again, motivated by dreams of commercial or political success."

Abigail blanched. "But we are speaking of a great conspiracy—"

"Indeed. And if the conspirators are caught, and found guilty, then they should be sent to the scaffold. I shall applaud their executions, even if they prove to be my closest friends. But, as we await that event, it cannot be the case that their improper motivation discredits the end toward which they are working. The evidence you have brought me is disturbing indeed. Nevertheless, the question of impeachment must be judged on its own merits."

She tried again. "You have the list! It is right there before your eyes!"

Sumner was gentle. "Miss Canner, what I see before me is a list of names. I have no idea of its provenance. Neither do you. The writer of the list tells us that those whose names appear are committed to the great cause of undoing Lincoln's tyranny, or may be persuaded to join. He further tells us that some among them will require further consideration. You are taking this to mean that bribes have changed hands. Perhaps you are correct." He stacked the papers neatly, handed them back. "Now, suppose that everything you say is true. Look at the list. Yes, some members of the House of Representatives appear. As many as a dozen. But the bill to impeach Mr. Lincoln passed by far more than a dozen votes. And there are no names of any Senators. Therefore, by your own hypothesis, the actions of the Senate are beyond reproach." He tapped the pages. "There are merchants here, a few men of commerce, a lawyer or two, some newspaper editors. A relative of Mr. Hilliman's—your mother, I gather?—and, of course, Mr. Lincoln's own lawyer. Perhaps they were all conspirators. Perhaps they were all bribed. None of that tells us whether or not Mr. Lincoln deserves the office he has so dishonored."

"What are you saying?" cried Jonathan, in a voice too loud for this cozy, bookish room. "You will still vote to convict? Even in the face of this evidence?"

Sumner was gentle. "I have not yet decided my vote, Mr. Hilliman. I will, however, say this much. The fact that some wicked men want Mr. Lincoln out of office has no bearing on the question of his guilt or innocence. The argument *ad hominem* has no proper place in the consideration of moral questions." This time he stood all the way up, and his bodyguard, who had remained in the shadowy corner throughout the conversation, eased closer. "I am grateful to you for bringing all of this to my attention," he said. "But I fear that there is nothing I can do."

Two minutes later, they were on the sidewalk in front of Sumner's modest house.

Jonathan said, "Maybe Sumner is part of the conspiracy."

"He isn't."

"Why? Is this the Kate Sprague business all over again? He cannot be a conspirator because you admire him?"

"No. It is because he let us keep the list." Abigail sighed: a sound she rarely uttered. But much had changed over the past few days. "Senator Sumner does not think as others do. Others always ask who is helped or hurt by a proposal; or who is for it or against it. Only armed with this information can they make up their minds about whether to support or oppose it. They do not care about the proposal. They care whether it helps or hurts their side. Senator Sumner is different. He cares for what is right, and nothing more." Jonathan was helping her up into the carriage. "And that," she said, "is why we failed." She shook her head. "Remember what Mr. Sickles said? That, no matter what we found, it would not change a single vote, because the trial is politics, not law? He was right."

Jonathan was sardonic. "He also said that if we ever did find such a list we should just give it to Stanton, and General Baker would see to it that they did not survive their arrests."

Abigail sighed. "Do you know what Mr. Lincoln said to me? He said, even if he had the list of conspirators, there was nothing he could do about it. If he ordered their arrests on the eve of the impeachment vote, the entire country would believe that he was locking up his opponents in order to stay in office."

"What you are saying is, we have the list and there is nothing we can do with it?"

"Not until after the trial." She held the envelope in her hands. "It is over, Jonathan. We are done."

I I

And so they went up to the Capitol, to watch the Senators give their speeches, explaining which way they would vote. If all who wished to speak could be heard today, the Senate would vote. Otherwise the trial would adjourn for Easter weekend, resuming on Tuesday. Closing arguments were over. Counsel were no longer seated in front of the body, although the Chief Justice still presided. There was a special section set aside for the lawyers in the back of the chamber, just behind the rows of members of the House. Jonathan joined Sickles and Speed and Rellman there.

Dennard was absent. He had sent word that he was ill.

Nobody criticized Jonathan for his tardiness; after the events of last night, they were surprised that he had come at all. To be sure, the lawyers knew only that the two young people had been attacked by a madman in the railroad yards; they knew nothing of any list of conspirators; and if they had, nothing would likely be changed.

Senators were speaking in alphabetical order, but, according to the notes Jonathan read over Rellman's shoulder, several had passed, preferring to make their remarks after they had heard more argument. This did not necessarily betoken any potential uncertainty about their votes; more likely, they wanted time to hone the speeches that historians would study for generations to come.

Senator James Rood Doolittle of Wisconsin was speaking, an opponent of both slavery and negro suffrage, who had strongly supported the war and just as strongly supported Lincoln in the impeachment fight. Jonathan was embarrassed to have the man on the President's side; but, with the outcome yet in doubt, they could hardly afford to reject any votes for acquittal on grounds of politics.

"The true basis of the present trouble," Doolittle proclaimed, "is the constant agitation of those for whom no change is ever enough, those for whom the contrary opinion of their fellow man is to be dismissed as the vicious or unintelligent maunderings of—"

A flurry at the door.

Kate Sprague was absent from the trial for the first time, so Abigail was sitting alone. She perked up, watched as the messenger hurried down the aisle.

A *military* messenger—in full uniform.

Doolittle droned on, but nobody was listening. Everybody was watching the runner as he handed a note to the clerk, who handed it up to the Chief Justice. A rising tumult outside caused heads to turn. Chase adjusted his spectacles. He read. He blinked. His soft pink face went pale. Outside, the furore rose. Chase gestured to counsel, then waved them back and gestured instead to Wade, who rose from his desk and marched down the aisle. Chase leaned down. The two men conferred. Wade staggered, and seemed to clutch at his heart. Abigail heard a murmur running along the Senate floor. Chase rapped his gavel.

"Gentlemen," he began, voice barely audible. He glanced up at the gallery, swallowed, lifted a trembling hand, began again. "Ladies and gentlemen. It is my—my sad duty—my tragic duty to report that Mr. Lincoln has been shot." Cries of horror. "We do not yet know whether he will survive." The gavel came down. Now Chase was shouting to be heard above the tumult. "These proceedings are adjourned, to be resumed upon notice."

Pandemonium.

CHAPTER 57

Cacophony

I

THE HORSECARS HAD vanished. Everywhere, people were running, crying, shouting at no one and everyone, rushing about madly without any thought to destination. Struggling away from Capitol Hill, Abigail heard a military trumpet in the distance, and, closer in, voices raised in vicious argument as three or four men came to blows. Jonathan had firm hold of her hand, and she was grateful for it. She saw no soldiers. She saw no police. She saw no sign that authority existed, or ever had. It was as though the nation's passions, having spilled over into a horrible war, had been but briefly bridled, and were now running once more at full steam.

They tried to ask if anyone knew how badly the President was injured, or even where or how the shooting had taken place, but there existed no reliable means of conveying information swiftly, and for every six screaming, rampaging people, there were as many versions of what had happened.

Abigail had been among the last to leave the turmoil of the Senate Chamber, because the great ladies of Washington had all but climbed over each other in their rush up the aisle and down to their carriages, no doubt hoping to reach their homes before—well, before what was now occurring. The Senators and congressmen, too, had streamed disorderly toward the door, but when Abigail had looked down, there was Jonathan, looking up at her, cupping his hands, trying to signal, trying to point: *Meet me out there,* he was saying. Unfortunately, by the time she reached the stairs, the sergeant-at-arms and his men were forcing the crowd out through the west exits.

Moments later, she was outside the Capitol in the midst of the jostling, struggling throng, not sure where she should be going. Home? The office? Sixth and E? But even as she stood indecisively, Jonathan had materialized beside her. They had to shout to hear each other. He had come straight through the Rotunda when he had realized that she would not be allowed in. He took her hand and dragged her in the direction of the carriages, but the crowd was too thick, and he was certain that the other lawyers had already left.

"We'll have to walk!" he yelled.

"Walk where?"

"I don't know, but we should go."

They did, finally reaching the corner of Second and B. The throng was thinner here, and a streetcar came clattering up, part of the Anacostia & Potomac Line, the driver shouting and cursing and sounding his horn to clear a lane. The entire crowd converged as one, and Abigail and Jonathan found themselves pushed to the front. Jonathan stepped on and tried to tug her aboard, but she lost her grip because she was being pummeled. She wound up lying in the mud. An egg struck her shoulder. She heard epithets. Somehow she was on her feet. Angry hands snatched at her. She broke free. Jonathan was beside her again. A bottle shattered on the cobbles. The streetcar started off. A voice said to get the nigger. Then Abigail was moving, skirts billowing, as, running beside Jonathan, she fled the growling mob. From the frenzied shouts, she was able to distill one fact:

This time, the man who shot Abraham Lincoln was black.

II

Their pursuers thinned, then vanished. Abigail and Jonathan walked along C Street, remaining south of Pennsylvania Avenue but north of the canal, in the sliver of Washington City where respectable people never went. The newspapers had their late editions out. Lincoln had been shot as he left Mr. Seward's Old Clubhouse to walk back to the Mansion. The stories did not say where he was now, or whether he was alive. By the time they reached Seventh Street, they could see that the mobs now had direction. They were heading west, toward the White House.

"Where do you want to go?" said Jonathan.

Abigail considered. But briefly; for the ambitions of former days had been drained. "Home," she said.

"I shall walk you."

They crossed the canal on the Seventh Street Bridge, and continued south, then southwest, striding along in near-silence, each alone with the painful thoughts. They passed carriages and streetcars, houses and farms, and barely spoke. They were no longer touching; but their presence together was a message of its own.

"I should have known," Abigail said, at least twice, through her tears. "From the night we saw Mr. Lincoln outside the Mansion, my brother has been plotting. His talk of violence, his hatred of Mr. Lincoln, his threats before he vanished—"

"You don't know that it was Michael."

"I do know, and so do you."

On the Island, lights were burning in every house. She thought she heard dancing on the air the sound of keening, but imagination might have been playing her false. She remembered how Wilkes Booth's entire family had been arrested, interrogated, imprisoned, except for a brother who escaped to Canada. But Nanny was not physically capable of flight, and Abigail would never abandon her.

"Suppose it was the rebels," Jonathan finally said. "John Wilkes Booth was a rebel sympathizer. Colonel Waverly was with the Confederate secret service. Why not whoever shot Lincoln today?"

"I would very much like to believe that. It would make things"—a grim smile—"ever so tidy." The humor faded. The crunch of the odd spring snow underfoot had grown quite loud. "But the South is better off with Mr. Lincoln in the Mansion than if he should be succeeded by Mr. Wade. Nor are the Radicals likely to be guilty. They are, after all, on the verge of removing Mr. Lincoln through entirely legal means."

"Unless the rumors are true that Lincoln has done a deal to repeal the Morrill Tariff. That would likely switch a vote or two."

"It no longer seems probable," said Abigail, heavily, "that the votes in the Senate shall matter."

To this there was no reply to be made, and they trudged on in silence, until at last they reached Tenth Street.

"I can make it from here."

"No doubt," he said, and stayed beside her.

But as they approached the house, a good forty-five minutes after starting out, it was clear that something was wrong.

Standing outside were several soldiers, commanded by a lieutenant. Two military carriages blocked the road.

Already!

Abigail broke into a run. Jonathan followed.

The soldiers stopped them at the gate. "Are you Miss Abigail Canner?"

"Yes."

"You are to come with us."

Jonathan got between her and the soldiers. On the porch, Nanny was being physically restrained by Louisa and Octavius and a couple of neighbors: she would do battle with the Devil himself to protect her niece, and a squad of infantry frightened her not at all.

"What is the meaning of this?" Jonathan demanded.

"Who are you?" snapped the lieutenant.

"My name is Jonathan Hilliman, and I will have you know—"

"Good. Then we have both of you."

The soldiers put them in the back of one of the carriages. An armed sergeant climbed inside and sat across from them. Two others grabbed onto bars on the outside. As they rolled off, Abigail turned to look at Nanny.

They had not even given her a chance to say goodbye.

III

"Where are you taking us?" demanded Jonathan, in his best Hilliman.

"Mr. Stanton's orders, sir."

The guard sitting across from them had drawn the curtains over the windows, and although he was scrawny, he looked battle-hard; not a man to argue with. By this time, most of the conscripts were out of the army. Those who remained were the ones who wanted to.

Abigail, sitting silent, was struggling against her own restlessness, fed by her fear of small spaces and her fear of failure and her fear of . . . well, of *this*. Of what was happening right now. This was how Michael had always said it would be. Some night, when you least expected it, they would scoop you off the street and spirit you off to some hidden place, where they would do to you the things they did to colored people who failed to smile fast enough, or grovel deep enough: that was Michael's phrase. And what kept her from drowning in fear was only the knowledge that whatever they did to colored people they would not dare do to a Hilliman.

"Are we under arrest?" said Jonathan.

The guard, stony-faced, did not respond.

"Because you know we had nothing to do with what happened today." He banged a hand against the side of the coach. Abigail had never seen him so unnerved. "You can't just arrest people without warrants."

But of course they could. Abigail almost smiled. Just the other day, on the floor of the Senate, James Speed had laid out an elaborate argument for the proposition that during times of national emergency the military could indeed "sequester" those who threatened efforts to bring order. And, certainly, tonight qualified as an emergency.

"Is the President even alive?" Jonathan demanded.

The guard stared.

The carriage shuddered to a halt, bumped forward, stopped again. They heard a gate open. The rig moved slowly up an incline, and then the door was flung open from the outside. There were soldiers everywhere.

They were at the White House.

CHAPTER 58

Elegy

I

THE PRESIDENT'S BREATHING was raspy and, even to Abigail's untutored ear, far too slow. His skin had taken on the gray waxiness that she remembered from her mother's final battle with the varioloid. They had laid Lincoln on his modest bed in the cramped confines of the presidential apartments on the second floor. The tiny room was crowded, and Abigail was still not entirely sure why she and Jonathan were present, but Dan Sickles had told them downstairs that Stanton had insisted.

The President would have wanted it this way, Sickles had whispered. *That's what Stanton says, and, right now, what he says is all that matters.*

The Mansion was full of soldiers; as, evidently, was the city. So swiftly had the military glided in that a half-hysterical part of her wondered whether what had happened might have been less an assassination attempt than the signal for a coup d'état.

"Robert is on his way from Philadelphia," said Noah Brooks, standing by the door, looking less shaken than keen to observe. "Tad and his aunt are in Springfield. It will take them two days to get here."

"He won't last that long," said Stanton harshly.

Abigail was standing no more than three feet from the bed. She had been reluctant to move so close, but the throng had jostled and shoved, and here she was. Nobody paid her any mind. Perhaps they thought she was a nurse, or a domestic. It occurred to her that there were times when the near-invisibility of the colored servant class to their white masters could constitute an advantage. She gazed down at the wrecked, fading figure of the man by whose direction the war to liberate her people had been fought, and all at once the future that had always seemed to her so bright and rosy was pale and dim, and very far off. Her eyes grew misty. She heard sobbing, womanly and aching, then noticed that she was the only woman in the room. She wiped her eyes.

"Maybe we should go," said Jonathan kindly. He was beside her, quite close, but he was a stranger, a man she had never known and never would.

"No."

"There is no earthly reason to put yourself through this," he said, and took her elbow.

"Leave me be." She shook him off. She felt half asleep, caught in a nightmare yet dangerously calm. It was not possible that she was in this room, watching the life force ebb from the sixteenth President. She would wake soon, to find herself in her room at the back of the house in the Island, listening to the gurgle of water in her father's pipes. Or she would not. She wondered if her brother had really done it; and, if so, when it became known who the killer was, what those here present would say or do at the realization that Michael Canner's sister had stood in their midst and watched Abraham Lincoln die. And she wondered, too, in a distant, dreamy way, why Stanton had brought her here, when surely his career and reputation were the things most keenly at stake; and whether they would hang Michael or shoot him on sight; and whether she herself might, through the inexorable logic of political necessity, be hanged beside him as a conspirator.

There was a bustle. Somebody said that the Chief Justice was downstairs. Stanton was on his feet. "By no means let that man in this room."

Speed, who had been weeping in the corner, stood. "You cannot keep the Chief Justice out, Mr. Stanton. You cannot command the judicial branch."

"I will command what needs commanding." Stanton turned to a brigadier who stood in the doorway. "I want you to prepare orders to place the city under martial law. I want arrest warrants prepared for"— his yellowy eyes roamed over the gathered faces, seemed to pause at Abigail's, then moved on—"for unnamed conspirators."

"Yes, sir."

"Some of them may be on the Hill."

The general swallowed. "Yes, sir."

In the corner, Fessenden had been whispering with Speed. Lincoln's old law partner was shaking his head. Fessenden turned to Stanton. "This is difficult to say, Mr. Secretary. But I believe someone should fetch the president pro tempore of the Senate."

"No," said Stanton.

"Senator Wade is next in the line of succession—"

"He may be first in line at the gallows after this day's work."

In the chilly silence, the only sound was the labored struggle of the scrawny figure on the bed. The doctors had cleared away most of the blood, but it was plain to everyone that the clever eyes would never again open. The bed was too short for him, so they had laid him sideways.

Dan Sickles spoke up. He, too, had been weeping quietly. "Senator Fessenden is right, Mr. Stanton. At least send someone to guard Mr. Wade."

The Secretary of War for a moment seemed ready to erupt. Certainly his eyes narrowed, and the familiar dangerous flush rose from his neck. Then he turned and snapped a series of angry orders at the general, who fled.

"Mr. Wade will be perfectly safe," Stanton told the room. "One way or the other." He laughed, mirthlessly.

Lafayette Baker entered. He beckoned to Stanton, and the two stepped out into the hall. Abigail watched them go.

"They have arrested my brother," she said.

Jonathan looked at her.

"We always know what happens to each other, the people in my family. We can sniff disaster." She closed her eyes briefly. "That's what Nanny says, anyway."

II

Stanton and Baker had not returned. Another doctor had arrived, and now three were poking and prodding the dying man. Sumner had somehow slipped in, and sat on the far side of the bed, face drawn and pale, holding Lincoln's hand. His own trembled. Abigail wondered how the great orator had planned to cast his vote, then decided it made no difference.

A black woman came in, head down, with fresh linen and a basin of warm water. The surgeons relieved her of these burdens and placed bloody towels in her cradling arms, and Abigail understood how she herself had been so thoroughly overlooked.

"You know why the two of you are here, don't you?"

Abigail looked up. "No, Mr. Sickles. I do not."

"Part of it is political theater: the end of the world as staged by Edwin Stanton. When they do the famous paintings of this moment, he would not want the Great Emancipator to have nobody of your race at his bedside." Sickles wiped his eyes, and, for once, made no effort to hide the physical pain that was his constant plague. "But there is something more. Stanton feels that he owes you."

"Owes me for what?"

"For Judith."

Abigail shook her head. "I don't understand," she said, although she thought perhaps she would have, but for the overwhelming grief that made it difficult just now to take in anything at all. She shook her head again, and then realized that she was up next to the bed once more, and Sickles was in the corner talking to Jonathan.

"A tragic day," said Charles Sumner, close beside her. In the half-light of the late afternoon, the blond-white hair was like a halo around that highly moral head. "To survive the ordeal of the past month, only to fall to the assassin's blow."

Evidently, he had decided to vote for acquittal; or so he said, now that it no longer mattered. Yet Abigail longed to believe him, to believe that there might be a second great Washingtonian, after Mr. Lincoln himself, whom she could, unreservedly, admire.

"Mr. Lincoln and I had our disagreements," said Sumner. "But in the end, I could not be a part of this extra-constitutional revolution." He blinked, and, to her surprise, tears began to run down the high-boned cheeks. "He did not destroy slavery as I would have destroyed it, but he did destroy it. He did not fight the war as I would have fought it, but he did fight it. And"—wavering on his feet, as if overcome—"and history, I suspect, will judge that he did better than anyone else would have."

Behind her the surgeon said, "He is gone."

Abigail spun. So busy had she been staring in surprise at Sumner that she missed the moment of Lincoln's passing. Now the weeping was general: all these powerful men, and most of them were crying. Stanton placed his hat on his head, then removed it in silent salute. The room blurred, faded, steadied again. Somehow her face was against Jonathan's chest, and his arms were around her, as, helplessly, she sobbed.

She heard a couple of voices suggesting, timidly, that the new President be sworn in; and louder voices echoing Stanton's suggestion that the gallows might be a more fitting fate.

"You must not say such a thing," said a stern voice, which, to her surprise, she recognized as Jonathan's. "We dare not challenge the line of succession."

"*They* challenged it," said Speed, who had known Lincoln longer than anyone in the room. He looked hard at Sumner.

"No," said Sickles, tone surprisingly gentle. "That is the one thing they did not challenge." He actually smiled. "They believed their version of the Constitution, and Mr. Lincoln believed his. There is a kind of honor on both sides."

Speed would not compromise. "Their side acted out of financial interest—"

"As did some on our side," said Jonathan, scarcely milder than before. It struck Abigail that he had, in the past few days, grown up. "It is time to let him go."

"Hilliman is right," said Sickles, and put his arm around Speed's shoulders, as the old lawyer wept unashamedly.

The ensuing silence was less prickly than elegiac; the group was mourning, separately and collectively.

"It is a strange thing," Stanton finally said, watery gaze on the middle distance. He was seated once more on the bed, beside the body. "Had Lincoln lived, he would have been removed, and history would have counted him as yet another in the line of unsuccessful Presidents who have occupied the Mansion since Mr. Jackson's day. But now he will be celebrated. In centuries to come, America will sing his praises. The man who ended slavery." A sour look, the words curdling. "The man who saved the Union." He gestured vaguely toward the window. "One day, a monument to the great Lincoln will stand out there, beside Washington's."

Abigail stirred herself. "Are you saying Mr. Lincoln won't deserve it?"

Stanton's rheumy eyes swiveled her way, and one had the impression that here was a man who never forgot an enemy. Or forgave one. "That verdict is for history, Miss Canner. Not for us." Again he turned toward the figure on the bed. Abigail caught something in the Secretary's expression, an oddly heated look that she first mistook for contempt. Only much later did she identify the emotion as jealousy. Stanton shook his head. "As for Mr. Lincoln, now he belongs to the ages."

Epilogue

June 10, 1867

FOR ABIGAIL CANNER and Jonathan Hilliman, the ensuing weeks passed swiftly, yet, when they turned their memories back, the days possessed all the bleary slowness of our nightmares. There was, first, the larger story: Lincoln's funeral, his sudden and majestic elevation from feared dictator to adored martyr. There were the arrests of a nest of conspirators, including the one girl who had survived the bombing at Madame Sophie's. Many of those arrested by General Baker managed to be shot and killed in the process; therefore, the outlines of the plot that had led to the death of the beloved President were never quite clear.

The rumor that the actual assassin had been a colored man was dismissed as just that: a rumor. The newspapers announced that it was a disgruntled Confederate corporal named Waverly who had done the deed, wearing blackface, hoping to stir up a race war. Secretary Stanton said so, and all the dozens of witnesses agreed, even those who had previously said something else. As for Waverly himself, although it had been thought at first that he had made his escape, his body was found a day or two later, crushed to death in the train yards beyond the Seventh Street depot.

Poetic justice, the leader-writers agreed—although some of the pro-Lincoln papers insisted that he had been killed by his own employers, and wanted Stanton (who was obviously running things) to determine exactly who those employers had been.

Then there was the mysterious disappearance of the prominent Washington attorney David Grafton. A warrant was issued for his arrest, but nothing came of it. As it happened, Grafton's clerk, a man named Plum, vanished, too; but nobody noticed. The lawyer was obviously the more important mystery. Some stories placed him in the West Indies, others in Canada or Mexico. A handful of papers reported that Grafton had been murdered by "his own people"—like Corporal Waverly—and the body disposed of in secret, in order to prevent disclosure of the names of the wealthy men at the very top of the conspiracy. But the wealthy were always being accused of everything in America, and nobody took the stories at all seriously.

Less noticed were the announcements by eight separate congressmen and two Senators that they had decided not to seek re-election. Several disclosed plans for extended travel abroad. In this they were joined by a handful of industrialists and their sycophants, who moved to second or third houses in France or England until matters calmed a bit at home. August Belmont was not among them. Belmont issued a public statement decrying the vicious murder of Lincoln, and demanding a further investigation. In this he was joined by several other great men whose firms would profit from a lower tariff.

In a less public action, Belmont & Co. sold its warrants in Hilliman & Sons back to the issuer, at considerably less than par.

Benjamin Wade, seventeenth President of the United States, made clear that he would not, as had been his intention, raise tariffs and soften the money. On the contrary: he would govern, to the best of his ability, as his great predecessor would have, had he survived. Indeed, President Wade himself was ill; there was some question whether he would survive the year and a half left to the term.

Certainly nobody expected him to run in 1868. The smart money was still on Chase, but the violence and conspiracy in the nation's capital, along with the continuing unrest at the South and the continued looming threat of the dying but still-dangerous powers of Old Europe, were leading already to calls for a stronger hand at the helm, the hand of a warrior. A successful Civil War general, say. Sherman, maybe. Or, best of all, Grant, who continued to disclaim any interest in the White House, but with an increasingly decreasing fervor.

As for Hiram Felix, another military leader who had once been spoken of as presidential timber, he had taken ship with his daughter Margaret, and his widowed sister, Clara, to Central America, hired by one of the banking combines to manage their affairs in that region of the world.

All of which brought Jonathan and Abigail, on this fine June Monday morning, to the Seventh Street railroad depot, a short stroll from the Bannerman house. She had allowed him, this one last time, to drive her. The porters had loaded the bags onto luggage carts and wheeled them away. Now Jonathan stood with her beside the gleaming cars that would carry her south. Abigail was wearing a blue ladies' traveling suit, ordered from a Boston dressmaker under the guidance of Dinah Berryhill. She looked fresh and smart and beautiful.

"What will you do?" she asked. The gray eyes glistened. "Sit for the bar as planned?"

"I suppose I might." Jonathan looked away. "Only the firm is shut."

"You suppose." She pouted in mock disapproval. "It is my understanding that President Wade has also offered you a position."

"As a deputy in the Treasury Department."

"It is said to be lucrative."

He colored. "I suppose I shall consider it. I shall need a source of income, as I have declined to enter the family business."

"Once more, you 'suppose.'" Her tone was stern. "If I may say so, Mr. Hilliman, you seem to possess an insufficiency of information about your own life."

He tried for a jolly tone. "And what about you? Will you once more take up your quest to read law? Sumner said he would take you on. Chase. Any one of the Radicals would be delighted."

"I will decide when I return from the South." Jonathan was about to speak, but Abigail covered his mouth with a gloved hand. "I know. Probably my Aaron is dead. But I have to see for myself. I have to *know* that he is dead. I am sure you understand that. President Wade has made Mr. Baker give me all of the information his people have gathered on where the rebels kept colored prisoners from the war. If Aaron is alive, I will find him. If he is not, I will prove it. Either way, the uncertainty will end."

"And then?"

The pixie grin, first time in a long while. "Why, I shall return north, I *suppose*, finish my studies, and obtain admission to the bar. After that, perhaps I shall allow some clever young man to marry me." *Allow.*

But the grin faded. Judith fell like a shadow between them, as, most likely, she always would. For Lincoln had been wrong. Judith had not stayed safe. She had been warned by Noah Brooks that the conspirators had come to suspect her role. They wanted the list; they might reasonably guess that Judith knew its hiding place. And so she had fled, relying on her own resources as always. But down in Virginia, the great Chanticleer, already suspected as a link in the chain, had walked into some kind of trap—not even Baker had all the details—and was not seen again. That was what Stanton had felt the need to make up for.

Of Lydia, the baby, there was no word.

Nor was there word of Michael. But Jonathan had a theory. Abigail obviously believed that her brother knew or suspected that their sister was a Union spy. It was not clear exactly when Judith was captured; but suppose that Michael had heard, perhaps through his own contacts in Virginia, of what happened to her; and, in a fury, had stalked Lincoln and shot him?

Obviously, Waverly could not have done the deed: he was shot the night before. Let future historians make of that detail what they might.

What Jonathan could not see clearly was why Stanton had let Michael escape. The answer, he suspected, was that he hadn't. Michael had been cornered in some abandoned barn and shot dead, as those Baker tracked were almost always shot dead, and then Waverly had been substituted as a more publicly acceptable assassin.

Maybe.

But another question tickled at the back of his mind. Abigail had never told him precisely what became of the list of "potential conspirators," or of the pages from Stanton's journal. Jonathan had never asked—

He realized that he had missed what Abigail was saying. She had asked him about next year's presidential election: an event he cared about not in the slightest. He was, indeed, done with politics. But Abigail, as so often, was raising a question only in order to answer it.

"I suppose it makes no difference," she murmured, finger on her chin in that gesture that so fascinated him. She spoke with the confidence now of the experienced political observer. "Mr. Chase can run. Mr. Butler can run. They can all run. Whichever party nominates General Grant is going to win."

"You are sure, then, that Grant wants to be President?"

"If there is one thing I have learned over the past two months, Mr. Hilliman, it is that every man in this city wants to be President."

"Not I."

"Not yet."

Two porters passed them, trundling a cart laden with baggage. A sharp whistle announced a train's departure, although not Abigail's.

They looked at each other, reminiscing without speaking. They had come a long way from that silly day they met, when the first words out of Jonathan's mouth had been an unintended insult. Now, as they walked toward the second-class car, there was much he wanted to say to this remarkable woman: That he would be here waiting when she returned. That she would love New England. That he would not trade an instant of their time together for any prize available in this life. That he would wrap Hilliman & Sons in a ribbon and hand it over to Belmont for half a penny if it meant that they could be together.

But he understood Abigail too well by now, and knew that such proclamations would only embarrass her. She was no longer interested in promises. The only way to prove his willingness to wait would be to wait. From what he had seen of that Octavius fellow, he would be waiting, too; and even Fielding might return; but Jonathan resolved to wait better.

They were at the foot of the steps now, searching for the words with which to say goodbye.

"What do you think would have been different?" he asked finally. "If Lincoln had lived, I mean."

"You might as well ask what would have been different had Mr. Booth succeeded back in 1865." Abigail smiled. "The answer, I suspect, is very little. History is larger than any one man, even when that man is Abraham Lincoln. And, certainly, history is larger than any one bullet. Either way, America would roll on toward empire."

"You seem to believe that our destinies are fixed."

"At the moment," she murmured, "it would seem so."

"And you're satisfied with that answer?"

Abigail dimpled prettily. "Oh, no, Mr. Hilliman. Not at all. I am never satisfied. But I am content. And so must you be." She looked him up and down. "I wish you well in the days ahead."

"Thank you," he said.

"You are welcome," she answered, eyes measuring him.

Jonathan gave a final try. "Don't you ever wonder if—"

"Constantly," she said, and left him.

Author's Note

I often shove around historical events in my novels. Here, by keeping the sixteenth President on his feet after Booth, I have committed more mayhem than usual. In the next few pages, I offer a sampling of the ways in which I have played with history. Before we reach that point, however, let me be crystal clear: this is a work of fiction. It is not intended as a brief in support of Lincoln's impeachment. Historians rank Lincoln as America's greatest President, and I wholeheartedly agree.

Whether Lincoln committed any impeachable offenses is another matter. Nowadays, the more politically engaged among our citizenry tend to cry "impeachment" whenever a President they happen to dislike does anything remotely controversial. Our sense of history has grown dangerously thin, and our sense of proportion with it. We have forgotten that there was an era in our history—almost an entire century—when members of the Congress talked constantly about impeachment, and on more than one occasion attempted it.

When I told people I was writing a novel about a hypothetical impeachment trial of Abraham Lincoln, they tended to have one of two reactions. Some assumed that I must believe that Lincoln *should* have been impeached and removed from office. Others were skeptical that Lincoln *could* possibly have done anything even colorably impeachable; or assumed that the most likely political attacks would be from the forces favoring slavery. Lincoln has become so large in our imaginations that we might easily forget how envied, mistrusted, and occasionally despised he was by the prominent Abolitionists and intellectuals of his day, including leaders of his own party.

Great people can sometimes do terrible things, and Presidents of the United States are no exceptions. Perhaps Franklin Roosevelt should have been removed from office for herding Japanese-Americans into internment camps, or Harry Truman for incinerating, by design, tens of thousands of innocent people. Then there is Woodrow Wilson, whose contempt for the First Amendment was so complete that he argued, fervently, for the incarceration of critics of American entry into World War I, on the ground that they were disloyal—and partly accomplished his unconstitutional goal. As for Lincoln, the accusations set forth in my novel are nearly all matters of historical record. Lincoln *did* shut down newspapers he believed were impeding the war effort. He *did* arrest opposition spokesmen. He *did* suspend habeas corpus, and ignore court orders demanding the release of prisoners. He *did* place Northern cities under martial law. He *did* shut down the Maryland legislature by force. Are these impeachable offenses? That question I leave for the reader to decide; bearing in mind that no recent Chief Executive, no matter how controversial, has any similar litany to his credit.

Those are the facts. What about the fiction?

Fiction revolves not around "What *would* have happened" but "What *could* have happened." The possibility that Lincoln *could* have been impeached is the fictional premise that tantalized me for many years before I started work on this novel. Let me be clear: I do not believe Lincoln, had he survived Booth's bullet, *should* have been impeached. Do I believe he *would* have been impeached? The question whether Lincoln, had he survived, would have suffered Andrew Johnson's fate and faced an impeachment trial is of little interest to contemporary historians. But scholars avidly debated this proposition a hundred years ago and more—that is, closer in time to the titanic battles between Radical Republicans and Andrew Johnson, Lincoln's successor. Some writers, many of them apologists for the Southern cause, thought a Lincoln impeachment likely. They pointed out that the Radicals largely despised Lincoln, whom they thought unfit to be President in the first place. They argued that Johnson faced impeachment precisely for carrying out Lincoln's own "let 'em up easy" policy toward the defeated South.

More recent scholars scoff at the notion that so canny a politician as Lincoln would have seen his presidency wrecked on the treacherous shoals that nearly doomed Johnson, who entirely lacked the talent for persuasion or compromise. And while it is true that Johnson in many instances followed his predecessor's policies toward the defeated South, and that Congress hated those policies, it is also true that he went a good deal further, committing a series of political blunders that would have been unimaginable from Lincoln. Furthermore, the mercurial, hard-drinking Johnson often seemed to go out of his way to antagonize his congressional adversaries. I quite agree with the consensus: I consider it highly unlikely that the Radicals in Congress would have challenged Lincoln so directly. But it is the "what-ifs" that make fiction such fun.

What about the other facts in the novel? What is real, what is invented?

Let us begin at the beginning. On the night of April 14, 1865, John Wilkes Booth entered the Presidential Box at Ford's Theatre and shot Abraham Lincoln, who died the following morning. That same night, Secretary of State William Seward was stabbed in the face and neck by Lewis Powell, one of Booth's coconspirators. Vice President Andrew Johnson was also supposed to be assassinated that night, but George Atzerodt, assigned to do the job, lost his nerve and got drunk instead. In my fiction, it is Booth who failed, and a braver Atzerodt who succeeded. Seward, in real life, recovered from his injuries, although this took some weeks. In my fiction, he went into a steep decline, lingering for years, but as a disfigured invalid who refused to go to the office or receive callers.

In real life, Mary Todd Lincoln survived her husband by many years. But even while her husband was alive, she struggled with what was likely depression, although some historians believe that she suffered from bipolar disorder. Much of Mrs. Lincoln's life after the assassination was spent in penurious circumstances, and she spent time in a mental institution.

My foreground characters—in particular, the Canners, the Hillimans, and the Bannermans—are all invented. But most of the background characters, including all of the named political figures and journalists, are real. In the White House, the only invention is Major Clancy. Among Abigail's circle, although the Mellisons, the Berryhills, and the sisters Quillen are all invented, George Vashon, Charles Finney, and Kate Sprague are real. So are the other great women of Washington whom Abigail encounters, including Fanny Eames, Crete Garfield, and Mary Henry. Among Jonathan's paramours, Margaret Felix, like her father, is fictional. Lucy Lambert "Bessie" Hale is real, and likely did have a romantic relationship of some sort with Booth, although most serious historians doubt that they were engaged.

I have necessarily invented a great deal of dialogue, but I have tried, when the record supports it, to have my characters speak words they actually spoke, even if, in real life, they spoke the words on a different occasion and on a different subject than the one I might have assigned. The anecdotes I attribute to Lincoln all appear in various Lincoln sources, most of them in a form very close to the form they take on the pages of my novel. (This includes the story in chapter 10 that mentions Lincoln's brother. The story is almost certainly untrue, as his brother died when Lincoln was still very young. But that is the way he told the tale.) Many of the phrases I place in August Belmont's mouth during his meeting with Jonathan Hilliman are adapted, albeit freely, from Belmont's speeches and correspondence, as compiled in *Letters, Speeches and Addresses of August Belmont*, privately published in 1890. The pro-slavery argument presented by Hollis Chastain in chapter 38 is certainly drawn from an article in the *Southern Presbyterian Review*, just as he says—but, being a fictional character, Dr. Chastain was not the author. In addition, the sermon Dr. Chastain describes giving on the occasion of Lincoln's shooting was actually delivered by the Reverend John Lansing Burrows of the First Baptist Church of Richmond. Most important, several of the speeches at my fictional impeachment trial are borrowed in pertinent part from speeches at the trial of Andrew Johnson. For example, Speed's defense of Lincoln's suspension of habeas corpus is drawn from a similar speech by one of Johnson's lawyers, who asked during the trial whether the Senate would have been prepared to impeach Lincoln for that act—and then proceeded to explain its necessity, much as Speed does here.

What about the black community at this time? Our shared notion that the entire darker nation in the middle years of the nineteenth century was just out of slavery and grindingly poor is the sort of racist nonsense that continues nowadays to provide a peculiar comfort to black and white alike. Although history has little to say about them, there were indeed a handful of wealthy black families in America at this time, and the Berryhills in particular are something of a composite. Moreover, there were at that time many black families in what we might now think of as the middle class. Business ownership was not unusual, and not a few held college degrees and were trained professionals. And so an ambitious and well-educated young woman like Abigail Canner could indeed have traveled in the circles she does in my story, and dreamed of involvement in great events.

AS TO THE games I have played with history, I have no doubt that the astute reader will have spotted many. For example, Major General Dan Sickles did not actually retire from the army until 1869, but that would be too late for him to ride to Lincoln's aid as in my story. Howard University was not actually founded until March of 1867, just about the time my hypothetical impeachment trial begins. Also, in 1861, George Vashon was living in Pennsylvania, and therefore, unless he visited Washington, is unlikely to have advised Abigail Canner's parents to send her to the Oberlin Collegiate Institute in 1861.

As far as I have been able to determine, Ibsen's play *Brand* was not performed in the United States in 1867. My invented Columbia Unification Party should not be confused with the Unification Party formed in 1873 by former Confederate officers in an effort to harness the black vote in the South. (It failed.) For dramatic reasons, I have changed the date of Nevada's admission to the Union from 1864 to 1866, and moved Nebraska's admission in 1867 ahead by a few days. In real life, the price of Nebraska's admission was indeed the promise to send to Washington two Senators who would support the impeachment—albeit of Johnson, not Lincoln.

Port Hudson, Louisiana, was actually captured by General Nathaniel P. Banks, not, as in my story, by General Hiram Felix; and the siege took place simultaneously with, not subsequent to, the siege of Vicksburg. Senator William Pitt Fessenden, at the time of these events, was likely living in a boarding house near the Capitol, not in the cottage I built for Abigail to visit. And although it is entirely plausible that an upwardly mobile middle-class household such as the Canners presented would have subscribed to *Peterson's Magazine*, the article about the fashions of the previous century and the short story about the lovers in the snow were actually published some years prior to the events in my novel.

At Yale, Third Society (now known as Wolf's Head) was not founded until 1884, and therefore Whit Pesky could not possibly have been a member. The Anti-Slavery Conference, from whose report Benjamin Butler reads during the trial, would likely not have ended in time for him to have the report available. His quotation, however, is accurate. The Beecher-Tilton scandal did not take place until the early 1870s, and therefore could not have been debated during a trial occurring in 1867. (As in my novel, the Managers of the impeachment case against President Andrew Johnson also sought to imply the respondent's involvement in sexual scandal.)

The men of Company K of the 150th Pennsylvania Volunteer Infantry, known as the Bucktails, were assigned to guard the Executive Mansion (as well as the Soldiers Home, where the President had use of a cottage) in 1862. But the Bucktails were disbanded at the end of the war, and so could not have provided continuing security, as in my story. The episodes Mr. Manager Butler raises in cross-examining General Sherman in chapter 48 are told just as history says they occurred. The closing arguments of Managers Butler and Stevens in the novel are adapted somewhat freely from closing arguments offered by the Managers in Johnson's trial.

Lafayette Baker's term as head of the federal intelligence service was more checkered than my tale suggests, but I have tried to incorporate parts of the truth into my central mystery. So, for example, the real-life Baker was indeed accused of spying on Secretary of War Edwin Stanton, an accusation that ended the general's career. But it is unlikely that Baker's motives were anything other than either self-aggrandizement or paranoia. Incidentally, Baker died in 1868, a year after my story takes place. Although a few writers do indeed believe Baker was poisoned, I am skeptical. Still, the possibility works wonderfully well in a novel.

I also redated certain real documents, to fill the gap between the date of the real Lincoln's death and the years of my fictional Lincoln's presidency. For example, the letter from the Reverend Ezra Kinney requesting the President's autograph was actually sent in December 1864, not, as in the novel, December 1866.

The speech by Curran de Bruler quoted by Abigail in her initial encounter with Dan Sickles was not actually delivered until 1898. The Soldiers and Sailors National Convention did indeed adopt the resolutions mentioned by General Felix in Chapter 19, demanding more money for veterans, but in January 1866, more than a year before the novel begins.

I have altered the order of mortality, and not only by allowing Lincoln to live and causing Johnson to die. So, for example, Congressman James Blaine—whom some historians believe to have been as corrupt as in my tale and others do not—was not murdered in the spring of 1867. He actually died of a heart attack a quarter of a century later. Thaddeus

Stevens was indeed a dying man at the trial of Andrew Johnson in 1868. In 1867, he was failing, but not nearly as rapidly as in my story. History has little to say about the life of Sophia Harbour, but she also did not die in 1867. For the record, Madame Sophie, as she was known, did indeed run a brothel of two prostitutes. It is listed in the report of the Provost General, who, just as in my novel, kept detailed records of the city's bawdy houses. However, the record-keeping function lapsed with the end of the war, and the office of Provost Marshal General was actually abolished in 1866, its functions handed over to other agencies. I needed it to last a bit longer because, without its existence, I could not have made a plausible case for an official registry of prostitutes in the capital.

I have altered several aspects of the Senate rules for impeachment trials, as adopted at the trial of Andrew Johnson. Perhaps the one most noticeable is that at Johnson's trial, only one lawyer from each side was permitted to present opening argument; and only one was allowed to present closing argument. (Incidentally, Dennard is right and Butler wrong in their colloquy about the hearsay rule. The Senate should have heard Sherman's testimony.)

On the other hand, many aspects of the era that the reader might believe to have been invented were not. Thus, although I have no reason to think that chess champion Paul Morphy visited Washington, D.C., in 1867, he did indeed serve on General Beauregard's staff at the Battle of Bull Run, and his family fortune did indeed come from the importation and trading of slaves. The corrupt reselling of military discharge papers, in which Whit Pesky may have had a hand, was a considerable business both during and after the war. The word "progressive," which I put in Senator Sumner's mouth, actually did not appear as an adjective until some years later, but already by the end of the Civil War had popped up in public speeches as a noun. The tale of the dispute between the Augusta Railroad and the South Carolina Railroad is true—including the part about the engine being moved to block the tracks—but I have played with the timing just a bit.

For those wondering what became of B Street, the address of the Smithsonian Institution in the novel, the name was later changed to Independence Avenue along the southern border of the Mall, just as B Street north of what is now the Mall became known as Constitution Avenue. (B Street remains in both Northeast and Southeast Washington.)

I have kept most of the terminology of the day, and of the Senate, with some important exceptions. For example, during an impeachment trial, as during any other session of the Senate, the presiding officer of the body is always addressed as "Mr. President"—even when the President of the United States is on trial, and the Chief Justice of the United States presides. I decided that this might cause too much confusion. Therefore, in my story, the Chief Justice is addressed as "Your Honor," as he would have been in a regular courtroom.

Although I have tried to be cautious in my language, I have not been entirely fair to the linguistic style of the nineteenth century, especially in the upper classes, where contractions, for example, were frowned upon, and the language of formal occasions was even more elaborate and Latinate than the novel suggests. Except for the formal presentations on the floor of the Senate, I have rendered much of the public speech in slightly less flowery form than that effected by public figures of the time. I have spelled the word "negro" throughout with a small "n," in keeping with the practice of the day. Similarly, I have spelled "moustache" with the "o" that is no longer a part of the American usage. I have also used a handful of words anachronistically. For example, to say that someone has flown the coop is probably an early twentieth-century coinage, and certainly did not occur earlier than the late nineteenth; but the phrase just fit too well into the scene at the end of chapter 28. There are others, too.

AS ALWAYS, I am grateful for the commitment and perseverance of my literary agent, Lynn Nesbit, and my editor, Phyllis Grann. I have had the benefit of conversations with historians and legal scholars about the subject matter of the story, but I will not embarrass them by mentioning their names, lest they be held vicariously responsible for my historical distortions.

Finally, I must echo what has been true of every one of my books: the writing that I do would be impossible without the love and support of my children, Andrew and Leah, and of my wonderful wife, Enola Aird, whose patient and painstaking readings of draft after draft once more enabled me, in the end, to tell a coherent tale. I am grateful to God for my family, the greatest blessing in my life.

Cheshire, Connecticut
March 2012

A NOTE ABOUT THE AUTHOR

Stephen L. Carter is the William Nelson Cromwell Professor of Law at Yale University. His debut novel, *The Emperor of Ocean Park*, spent eleven weeks on the *New York Times* best-seller list, and was followed by the nationwide best sellers *New England White*, *Palace Council*, and *Jericho's Fall*. *The Impeachment of Abraham Lincoln* is his fifth novel. His acclaimed nonfiction books include *God's Name in Vain: The Wrongs and Rights of Religion in Politics*; *Civility: Manners, Morals, and the Etiquette of Democracy*; and *The Violence of Peace: America's Wars in the Age of Obama*. He lives with his family in Connecticut.

A NOTE ON THE TYPE

This book was set in Janson, a typeface long thought to have been made by the Dutchman Anton Janson, who was a practicing type-founder in Leipzig during the years 1668–1687. However, it has been conclusively demonstrated that these types are actually the work of Nicholas Kis (1650–1702), a Hungarian, who most probably learned his trade from the master Dutch typefounder Dirk Voskens. The type is an excellent example of the influential and sturdy Dutch types that prevailed in England up to the time William Caslon (1692–1766) developed his own incomparable designs from them.

Typeset by Scribe,
Philadelphia, Pennsylvania

Printed and bound by Berryville Graphics,
Berryville, Virginia

Designed by Cassandra J. Pappas